BLACKBI
THE BIRTH O1

TO THE READER

This is the story of Edward Thache—former British Navy officer and notorious Jamaican privateer-turned-pirate, who lorded over the Atlantic seaboard and Caribbean during the Golden Age of Piracy and has captivated the minds of children and adults alike for three centuries now. This story of Blackbeard is told through the eyes of not only the Robin-Hood-like American patriot and master of the sweet trade himself, but his primary nemesis Alexander Spotswood, the Lieutenant Governor of Virginia and British Crown's man in Williamsburg who illegally hunted him down; the African slave Caesar who sailed with Thache as a free man during his short three-year stint as a sea rover; and Stede Bonnet, the wealthy "Gentleman Pirate" from Barbados who also sailed with the capable Blackbeard. The history you will find in these pages is most likely not one you have heard before as it relies little upon Captain Charles Johnson's (Nathanial Mist's) oft-cited but largely discredited, propagandist tome *A General History of the Robberies and Murders of the Most Notorious Pirates*, completed six years after Blackbeard's death. Instead, the story of Edward Thache presented herein is based principally upon reliable historical records and the research findings from the last two decades from eminently qualified Blackbeard and pirate experts David Moore of the Queen Anne's Revenge project, Arne Bialuschewski, Kevin Duffus, Angus Konstam, Colin Woodard, Baylus Brooks, David Cordingly, Marcus Rediker, Mark Hanna, Benerson Little, David Fictum, and others. It has been reconstructed not only from deed, marriage, and death records, court transcripts, and first- and second-hand accounts in British, French, Jamaican, and North and South American archives, but from a synthesis of the *most* plausible arguments put forward regarding the character and motivations of the man by this new generation of historical experts.

My interest in the Golden Age of Piracy stems from my direct descendance from Captain William Kidd. In 1701, the British privateer was convicted of murder and five counts of piracy, hanged at Execution Dock in Wapping, London, and gibbeted over the River Thames—as a warning to future would-be pirates—for three gruesome years. A crowd of thousands gawked and jeered as the privateer captain, who was wrongfully thrown to the wolves by his political Whig backers, kicked and breathed his last in a macabre "dance of death." Though the iconic Kidd is my ninth great-grandfather on the Marquis side of the family, I must confess that he is only the third most famous sea robber of all time to Blackbeard and Sir Henry Morgan. In fact, it is Blackbeard's name that has resonated more than any other "Pyrate" for three centuries now—and yet he is perhaps the most misunderstood and historically misrepresented of all the sea captains who went on the account in the seventeenth and eighteenth centuries.

Fortunately, since the three-hundredth anniversary of my ancestor Captain Kidd swinging from the gallows at Wapping, the pendulum has swung in the other direction for Edward Thache of Spanish Town, Jamaica. As Colin Woodard, author of *The Republic of Pirates*, states, "In recent years, researchers have dug up new evidence, buried in the archives of England, France and the Americas, or beneath the sands of the American coast, allowing them to piece together a fuller and extremely compelling picture of Blackbeard and his cohorts, one that shows him to have been a canny strategist, a master of improvisation, a showman, a natural leader and an extraordinary risk taker." *This* book is the story of *that* Blackbeard, a story that has been lost to us in a "fog of legend, myth and propaganda" for three hundred years. It is also the story of the birth of America and one of the first American revolutionaries in the War of Independence against the British Crown.

Praise for Samuel Marquis

#1 *Denver Post* Bestselling Author
Foreword Reviews' Book of the Year Winner
Beverly Hills Books Awards Winner & Award-Winning Finalist
Next Generation Indie Book Awards Winner
& Award-Winning Finalist
American Book Fest-USA Best Book Award-Winning Finalist
Colorado Book Awards Award-Winning Finalist

"*The Coalition* has a lot of good action and suspense, an unusual female assassin, and the potential to be another *The Day After Tomorrow* [the runaway bestseller by Allan Folsom]."
—James Patterson, #1 *New York Times* Bestselling Author

"*Altar of Resistance* is a gripping and densely packed thriller dramatizing the Allied Italian campaign...reminiscent of Herman Wouk's *The Winds of War.*"
—Kirkus Reviews

"Marquis is a student of history, always creative, [and] never boring....A good comparison might be Tom Clancy."
—Military.com

"In his novels *Blind Thrust* and *Cluster of Lies*, Samuel Marquis vividly combines the excitement of the best modern techno-thrillers, an education in geology, and a clarifying reminder that the choices each of us make have a profound impact on our precious planet."
—Ambassador Marc Grossman, Former U.S. Under Secretary of State

"Marquis grabs my attention right from the beginning and never lets go."
—Governor Roy R. Romer, 39th Governor of Colorado

"*The Coalition* starts with a bang, revs up its engines, and never stops until the explosive ending....Perfect for fans of James Patterson, David Baldacci, and Vince Flynn."
—Foreword Reviews

"Old-time spy buffs will appreciate the tradecraft and attention to detail, while adventure enthusiasts will enjoy the unique perspective and setting for a WWII story....[A] combination of *The Great Escape, Public Enemies*, a genuine old-time Western, and a John Le Carré novel."
—BlueInk Review (for *Bodyguard of Deception*, Book 1 of WWII Series)

By Samuel Marquis

BLACKBEARD: THE BIRTH OF AMERICA

WORLD WAR TWO SERIES

BODYGUARD OF DECEPTION
ALTAR OF RESISTANCE
SPIES OF THE MIDNIGHT SUN (JUNE 2018)

**NICK LASSITER-SKYLER INTERNATIONAL
ESPIONAGE SERIES**

THE DEVIL'S BRIGADE
THE COALITION
THE FOURTH PULARCHEK

JOE HIGHEAGLE ENVIRONMENTAL SLEUTH SERIES

BLIND THRUST
CLUSTER OF LIES

BLACKBEARD

THE BIRTH OF AMERICA

SAMUEL MARQUIS

MOUNT SOPRIS PUBLISHING

BLACKBEARD
THE BIRTH OF AMERICA

Copyright © 2018 by Samuel Marquis

MOUNT SOPRIS PUBLISHING
Trade paper: ISBN 978-1-943593-21-7
Kindle: ISBN 978-1-943593-22-4

First Mount Sopris Publishing Premium Printing: January 2018
Cover Design: Christian Fuenfhausen (http://cefdesign.com)
Formatting: Rik Hall (www.WildSeasFormatting.com)
Printed in the United States of America

To Order Samuel Marquis Books and Contact Samuel:

Visit Samuel Marquis's website, join his mailing list, learn about his forthcoming novels and book events, and order his books at www.samuelmarquisbooks.com. Please send fan mail to samuelmarquisbooks@gmail.com. Thank you for your support!

ATTENTION: ORGANIZATIONS AND CORPORATIONS
Mount Sopris Publishing books may be purchased for educational, business, or sales promotional use. For information, please email the Special Markets Department at samuelmarquisbooks@gmail.com.

Dedication

For the real Blackbeard—who has been maligned, co-opted, exploited, and misrepresented as a ruthless villain and sociopathic cutthroat in the name of propaganda and profit for three centuries now. May ye rest in peace.

Blackbeard: The Birth of America

So our Heroe, Captain Teach, assumed the Cognomen of Black-beard, from that large Quantity of Hair, which, like a frightful Meteor, covered his whole Face, and frightened America more than any Comet that has appeared there a long Time...In time of Action, he wore a Sling over his Shoulders, with three brace of Pistols, hanging from Holsters like Bandoliers; he wore a Fur-Cap, and stuck a lighted Match on each Side, under it, which appearing on each side of his Face, his Eyes naturally looking Fierce and Wild, made him altogether such a Figure, that Imagination cannot form an idea of a Fury, from hell, to look more frightful.
    —Captain Charles Johnson (Nathanial Mist), 1724, from the sensationalist *A General History of the Robberies and Murders of the Most Notorious Pirates*

As surely as Alexander Hamilton, John Hancock, and the terrorist Samuel Adams, the pirate "criminal" Edward Thache might have been one of our earliest founding fathers, long before Washington, Madison, Jefferson, or Franklin. Thache, however, lost his revolution and certain British factions murdered him as certainly as King George III would have hung or shot Washington, Madison, Jefferson, and Franklin if these Founding Fathers had lost their revolution.
    —Baylus Brooks, 2016, *Quest for Blackbeard: The True Story of Edward Thache and his World*

The reputation, at least in literature, of Blackbeard as a roving, ruthless barbarian hardly withstands historical scrutiny. There is strong evidence that his fearsome image is a fabrication that emerged in the course of his short, lawless career. The real Edward Thache was...a skilled sailor who tried to make the best of difficult circumstances in the early eighteenth-century seafaring world.
    —Arne Bialuschewski, 2010, *Blackbeard: The Making of a Legend*

I have come to know Black Beard the man as he truly was. He was a son and a brother...He was not the bloodthirsty murderer, despicable slitter of throats or strangler of women as he has been so often described. [He] was no more immoral or corrupt than many who lived during his time, from the lowliest thieves to governors, ministers and lords. He was a paradox in a paradoxical age.
    —Kevin Duffus, 2014, *The Last Days of Black Beard the Pirate*

[P]iratical institutions reflected the brilliance of Madison's arguments for democratically divided power more than half a century before Madison wrote them down. In this sense pirates were harbingers of our most sacred ideas about social organization. America's Founding Fathers, to borrow the slogan of a popular pirate-inspired rum, "had a little Captain in them." In these ways pirates were truly pioneers.
    —Peter T. Leeson, 2009, *The Invisible Hook: The Hidden Economics of Pirates*

Cast of Historical Figures

CAPTAIN EDWARD THACHE AND HIS CREW

Edward Thache, Jr.: Former British Royal Navy seaman in Queen Anne's War (1705-1713) and merchant-privateer who sailed as mate out of Philadelphia and Jamaica (1713-1715); independent pirate raiding British, French, and Spanish ships from 1716-1718; known as "Blackbeard" by 1717; born approximately 1687.

Caesar: African-American slave owned by Tobias Knight of Bath Town, North Carolina, and pirate with equal rights and shares aboard Thache's various piratical vessels between 1716-1718; twenty-three years old in 1718; one of Thache's many Bath County pirates, released prior to trial in 1719 and returned to Bath Town.

William Howard: Quartermaster with Thache from September 1717 to June 1718; son of Hyde Precinct, North Carolina, landowner Philip Howard; quartermaster under pirate Captain Benjamin Hornigold prior to Sept. 1717; one of Thache's many Bath County pirates.

Israel Hands: Navigator and second-in-command to Thache; captain of the *Adventure*.

John Martin: Quartermaster with Thache in 1716-1717 prior to Howard; seaman with Thache from April through late June 1718; one of Thache's many Bath County pirates.

William Cunningham: Gunner aboard *Queen Anne's Revenge* until spring 1718.

Garret Gibbons: Bosun and one of Thache's many Bath County pirates.

Thomas Miller: Quartermaster of *Adventure*.

Philip Morton: Gunner aboard *Adventure*.

THACHE'S PIRATICAL CONSORTS AND ACQUAINTANCES

Captain Stede Bonnet: Wealthy Barbadian planter-turned-pirate; former major in the Barbados militia and father of three children; called the "Gentleman Pirate"; sailed with Blackbeard on board or in consort from September 2017 to June 1718.

Captain Benjamin Hornigold: Bermudan-Bahamian pirate who sailed in consort with Thache on at least four occasions between 1716-1718; elder leader of Nassau's Republic of Pirates, the "Flying Gang."

Captain Sam Bellamy: Former common British Navy seaman who rose to pirate captain of former slave ship *Whydah*; friend of Thache's and admired by him for his anti-elite, Jacobite, egalitarian political philosophy; nicknamed "Black" Sam.

Captain Charles Vane: Truculent English pirate captain and member of the Flying Gang; friend of Edward Thache; torturer of captured prisoners.

Captain Paulsgrave Williams: Middle-aged silversmith from a wealthy Rhode Island family who turned into pirate sea captain, working in consort with Bellamy and French corsair Oliver La Buse; friend and piratical cohort of Edward Thache.

Captain Henry Jennings: Wealthy, bombastic Jamaican privateer and later pirate from Bermuda; commissioned by Governor Hamilton of Jamaica in November 1715 to plunder Spanish wrecks off Sebastian Inlet, Florida; enemy of Hornigold.

Ishmael Hanks (fictional): Quartermaster with Stede Bonnet to June 1718.

Ignatius Pell: Bosun with Bonnet; likely acquitted and released in November 1718 for testifying against Bonnet's crew.

Robert Tucker: Jamaican merchant seaman who voluntarily joined Bonnet's crew after capture by *Queen Anne's Revenge*; quartermaster with Bonnet from June through September 1718.

ROYAL AND PROPRIETARY COLONY GOVERNMENT OFFICIALS AND CITIZENS

Alexander Spotswood: Lieutenant Governor of Royal Colony of Virginia; fervently loyal to British Crown; took aggressive stance against colonial piracy.

Charles Eden: British Governor of impoverished Proprietary Colony of North Carolina; acquaintance of Edward Thache; target of Spotswood and Moseley.

Tobias Knight: North Carolina Council Secretary, Collector of Customs, and Interim Chief Justice; acquaintance of Edward Thache; owner of black slave and pirate named Caesar.

Philip Ludwell the Younger: Speaker of the House of Burgesses, prominent plantation owner, and head of the Ludwell-Blair faction opposed to Spotswood.

Robert Beverley: Historian, former member of Virginia House of Burgesses, and chief clerk of the Governor's Council; author of *The History and Present State of Virginia* (1705), the first published history of a British colony by a native of North America; close friend and mentor of Spotswood.

Reverend James Blair: President of William and Mary College, commissary of the Bishop of London, and supervisor of the church in Virginia; along with Ludwell, one of Spotswood's biggest opponents.

King George I: Hanoverian-born king of Great Britain and Ireland beginning in 1714; loathed by Thache and other Jacobite members of the Caribbean-Atlantic pirate fraternity, who saw Queen's Anne's Catholic half-brother, James III, as the rightful heir to the British throne.

Governor Lord Archibald Hamilton: Governor of Jamaica in 1715 and 1716; officially commissioned Henry Jennings and other privateers to fish the Spanish wrecks off the Florida Coast, giving birth to the Golden Age of Piracy and Hornigold's "Flying Gang" on New Providence, Bahamas.

Edward Moseley: North Carolina landholder and lawyer; formerly served as speaker of the House and surveyor general; opponent of Tobias Knight and Governor Eden.

BRITISH ROYAL NAVY OFFICERS

Lieutenant Robert Maynard: First lieutenant aboard Royal Navy fourth-rate warship HMS *Pearl* stationed in Virginia; subordinate of Captain Gordon.

Captain George Gordon: Commander of the *Pearl*.

Captain Ellis Brand: Commander of the Royal Navy sixth-rate warship *Lyme* stationed in Virginia.

Rear Admiral William Whetstone: Commander of flagship HMS *Windsor* stationed at Port Royal during *Queen Anne's War*; Thache's commanding officer when he served as naval officer aboard *Windsor*; Stede Bonnet's grand-uncle.

THACHE LOVE INTEREST AND FAMILY MEMBERS

Margaret: Thache's documented lover of Swedish ancestry who lived in Marcus Hook outside Philadelphia, Pennsylvania; he is reported to have spent considerable time with her when he wasn't at sea; last name unknown.

Edward Thache, Sr.: Mariner captain, plantation owner, and father of Thache; born in England but settled in St. Jago de la Vega (Spanish Town), Jamaica, by at least 1699; died in 1706.

Lucretia Poquet Maverly Axtell Thache: Step-mother of Thache to whom he deeded his deceased father's Spanish Town plantation and slaves in 1706 so that she and her three children from an earlier marriage could survive.

Elizabeth Thache (2): One Elizabeth was his biological mother who died in Spanish Town in 1699, the other was his younger sister from his father's first marriage.

Cox, Rachel, and Thomas Thache: Edward Thache's younger step-siblings from his father's second marriage to Lucretia.

PART 1

THE SPANISH WRECKS

CHAPTER 1

MARCUS HOOK, PENNSYLVANIA

SEPTEMBER 22, 1715

ON SUMMER'S LAST DAY IN THE YEAR OF OUR LORD 1715, Edward Thache took his first step towards a short-lived but legendary career as a pirate when he set sail from Philadelphia for Port Royal to go a-wrecking. It was on that same fine morning that he found himself in the arms of a beautiful young Swedish woman he had fallen in love with named Margaret of Marcus Hook. The couple were enjoying their last intimacy together before he journeyed to Jamaica. Though born in Great Britain, he had grown up on the Caribbean island under privileged circumstances and been posted in Port Royal during his stint with the British Royal Navy aboard the HMS *Windsor* during the late Queen Anne's War, or the 1702-1713 War of the Spanish Succession as it was formally known. They lay in bed in her small plank house along the Delaware River, softly kissing and caressing one another after having made love a second time during the night. As was typical of their final evenings together before he returned to the sea, they had gotten little rest.

A part of him always dreaded having to leave his beloved Margaret of Marcus Hook behind when he set sail for another port as a first-mate merchant mariner and occasional privateer. But another part of him, his more adventurous and mischievous side, couldn't wait to smell the tangy scent of the sea, to taste the saltwater on his lips, and to hear the brisk snap of sheets in the wind and the husky voices of seamen about the decks. After all, the first love of the man who would one day become the notorious Blackbeard the Pirate was the deep blue sea.

"I wish you didn't have to go," said Margaret with a trace of sadness in her voice, running a hand through the luxurious growth of hair on his head, hair as black as night. "It seems as though you only returned a few days ago."

"It's been a fortnight, my love," replied Thache, feeling the usual melancholy inside but not letting it show on his moonlit face. "But I agree it has gone by too fast."

"How long will you be gone this time?"

"That's just it—I don't know."

"Well, you're still sailing to Jamaica, aren't you?"

"Aye, it appears so."

"Normally, that would entail a month's journey to Port Royal followed by a week of debauchery and then a fortnight's return sail. If that were the case, I should expect to see you shortly after Thanksgiving. But that isn't the case, is it now, Edward?"

Ye are one clever girl, he thought admiringly. *Beautiful and clever, in equal measure.* "I'm afraid it's a tad complicated."

"No, I don't believe it's complicated at all. What are you not telling me? Out with it before I give you a sound whipping."

Now he couldn't help a devilish smile in the moonlight peeking through the intricate lace curtains, but still he offered no reply.

"Come now—I've been keeping your bed warm and your belly full of ale and my fine Swedish cooking these past two weeks. The least you can do is tell me what you are up to."

"Alas, I can only say that this time it is different."

"Different? Different how?"

"As I intimated, I'm not at liberty to discuss it."

"Not at liberty to tell *me*? What is it a secret mission on behalf of King George?"

"That schnitzel-eater from Hanover is not my bloody king. Besides, I happen to be an American."

"A what?"

"An American. I am part of the New World—the 'Americas' or simply 'America' is what they are calling it on the docks. It's something new in the air. We are breaking free of Mother England by taking the matters of the colonies into our own hands and carving out something new and unprecedented."

"My, my, aren't you the revolutionary? But what exactly is this 'America' of which you speak?"

"It is what seamen around the globe are calling the New World here. They call it 'America,' and the people born and raised here, or like me who have grown up here since an early age, are 'Americans.' We are set apart from the British. Some like to call themselves 'Indians' to differentiate themselves from the British and demonstrate their colonial pride. But foreign seamen call us 'Americans' or 'American colonists,' both of which I happen to like better."

"I am an *American*, too, then."

"Aye, that you be my fair maiden. And our numbers are growing every day, so much so that one day we will be stronger than Great Britain itself. I would wager that in the not too distant future we will break free and govern ourselves."

"It sounds to me, Edward Thache, like you have given this considerable thought. Are you sure you are planning on going to sea because it seems as if you're fixing to incite a rebellion?"

"I just don't like the excesses of the Crown. Britain may be our sovereign, but the King and his henchmen needn't lord over everything we do. They certainly shouldn't be asserting the rule of England in her distant dominions in an authoritarian fashion that breaks our backs and leaves no room for local decision-making. Britain's empire reaches into distant lands, but its decisions are made in the smoky, dark-paneled back rooms of White Hall. For practical reasons, that can no longer be. We need stronger self-rule here in the Americas."

"Well, I can tell you have thought this through. But back to the subject at hand. You need to tell me what you are up to with this new venture of yours. So I would appreciate it if you would dispense with the theatricals and just tell me. You know perfectly well that if anyone can keep a secret, it is I."

He had to admit that was true: his beloved Margaret was certainly no gossip. But did he dare tell her when it was critical to keep it a secret? After all, this was the golden opportunity of a lifetime and he didn't want to run the risk of buggering up the entire business with a loose tongue.

"Out with it, Edward. You set sail in less than three hours, and I want to know what you're up to before you make for the open sea. What is so important that you have to be secretive like this? You're up to mischief, I know ye."

He couldn't help but grin at the sassy look on her face, while simultaneously marveling at the incandescent beauty of her aquamarine eyes, the color of the Caribbean.

"All right, I'll tell you. But you have to promise me you will breathe not a whisper to anyone."

"My lips are sealed. Now what is this all about?"

"It's about a hurricane and a treasure fleet."

"I'm afraid I don't follow."

"In July, the worst hurricane in fifty years struck in the Florida Straits. An entire Spanish treasure fleet was sunk off the coast in shallow water. The wrecks are said to be located a day's sail south of St. Augustine."

"Aye, mister first mate, you have my ear. But what does this have to do with you?"

"Millions of pieces of eight were spilled onto the sea floor from ten galleons that went down in the flotilla. When I reach Jamaica, my plan is to obtain a commission from Governor Hamilton to salvage the remaining silver, gold, and jewels that have yet to be found from the wrecks. The Spanish have set up a camp and are reported to be fishing the wrecks with dozens of native divers daily, but there is still a vast treasure remaining to be salvaged."

Sitting up in the bed, she looked at him wryly. "I believe I understand the situation now. You're going a-wrecking and you aim to get your greedy little mitts on those sunken treasures before anyone else."

"Unfortunately, it's already too late for that. The Spanish are there, and reportedly also some Bostonians, Bermudans, and Bahamians. I just want to get in early so I don't come away empty handed. I told you that I gave away my inheritance to my step-mother Lucretia who lives in Spanish Town with her three young children."

"Yes, young Cox, Rachel, and Thomas. You did it for the family so they could make ends meet and continue to live in Jamaica."

"Well, this is my chance to make my own fortune and perhaps captain a ship of my own."

"That was a most generous thing you did for Lucretia and the children, and I can see why you would want to strike out and make a name for yourself. But won't it be dangerous?"

"The sea is always dangerous."

"You know what I mean. The Spanish aren't going to just let you sail in and steal their treasure."

"It's not their treasure anymore. It belongs to those that pull it from the littoral sands."

"So my lover is going a-wrecking—that's what all this is about. Mother Mary, it's going to be a feeding frenzy amongst a school of sharks."

"Which is why I'm sailing for Jamaica today. The news of the wrecks is just beginning to filter in and I want to have a proper piece of parchment in hand that allows me to fish those wrecks legally."

"A piece of paper won't make it legal, Edward, and you bloody well know it."

She was right, of course, but he said nothing. They fell into a thoughtful silence, the moonlight trickling in through the fluttering curtains lending her face a gentle glow. In 1702, when Queen Anne's War had first begun, the Spanish plate fleets that shipped the treasures of the New World to the Iberian Peninsula were temporarily discontinued so they wouldn't fall prey to English attacks. The end result was that during the war huge amounts of treasure remained locked away in Vera Cruz, Mexico. It had been more than a decade since Spain had dispatched her last treasure fleet and she had accumulated a plethora of riches in the New World. But now with hostilities terminated, the fleet had embarked for Spain only to promptly sink from an early and unexpectedly catastrophic hurricane in the Florida Straits. The ten sunken galleons were reported to have been carrying an extraordinary haul: coins, silks, porcelain, ingots, and jewels worth an estimated seven million pieces of eight. With such a priceless cargo just sitting there on the shallow sea bottom, Thache was determined to get his fair share of the spoils, preferably with official government backing through a letter of marque and reprisal. Given that Spain, France, and England were no longer at war, the legal commission that would hopefully be signed by Lord Hamilton might very well be disputed by one or more nations, but he would still be on more solid footing if he had the official backing of the governor of Jamaica than if he ventured to the wrecks of his own accord. Given the stagnant wages for seamen since the war's end, it was an opportunity that no experienced New World mariner in his right mind could ignore.

"I'm sorry, I should have been honest with you and told you I intended to go a-wrecking from the start," he said after a moment of introspection. "But the truth is, I felt a tad guilty."

"I'm more worried that it will be dangerous." She reached out and touched his black beard; he was just beginning to grow out his facial hair, and to date, it amounted to little more than a horseshoe-shaped archipelago of stubble framing his handsome, sunburnished face. "I don't want anything to happen to you."

"Don't worry about me. I can acquit myself quite nicely with both pistol and cutlass, thank you very much."

"Of that I have no doubt. But it is still going to be dangerous down there with greed and anarchy ruling the day. The Spanish will no doubt maintain that the riches are theirs and all other parties are to give the wrecks a wide berth. There's bound to be fighting. How long did it take for the Spanish to notify their superiors in Havana of the loss of their vessels?"

"The survivors reached Cuba by mid-August, and the salvors have been busy for more than three weeks now. So the word is out, passing from ship to ship and one harbor to the next. I've also been told that in Jamaica, the reports of the sunken treasure are being received with what can only be described as jubilation. They're calling it a fair and just reprisal for Spanish aggression. I have to agree. During the war, I saw how the Spaniards operated."

"I know, you've told me—they were brutal."

"I saw their cruel work when I was aboard the HMS *Windsor*, and I heard the tales of the attacks and tortures they made on our brethren on the privateering vessels. Even after 1713 when the treaty was signed, the Spaniards still seized legitimate privateering vessels from Jamaica and sent them to their ports as legal prizes. Salvaging the plate fleet gives merchants and ship owners in Port Royal an opportunity to retaliate for previous losses and grievances. But that's not the only reason. The truth is earnings from these types of raids have long boosted the prosperity of Jamaica, providing an important source of capital for the island. At the same time, they continue to keep the Spanish in check here in the New World."

"So you see it as not just an excursion of profit but of revenge, is that it?"

"I don't particularly like the Spanish. Or the French either, for that matter."

"Why if I didn't know better, I'd say you talk like a freebooter, Edward Thache of Jamaica. Are you sure this is a wise decision to go a-wrecking?"

He chuckled. "Come now, I'm no pirate. I'm but a simple seaman."

"Well, just keep it that way. The only thing going on the account will bring you is a rope around your neck. Come now, do you really want to end up a seagull-picked carcass in a gibbet like poor Captain Kidd?"

No, he didn't, of course. But he had read Alexandre Olivier Exquemelin's engrossing *History of the Buccaneers of America* and William Dampier's *A New Voyage Round the World*, and he had heard the tales of the privateers Henry Morgan, William Kidd, and Henry Avery as a boy and had always been inspired by them. In fact, he firmly believed the ex-Royal Navy man Kidd had gotten a raw deal from his financial backers, who had turned their backs on him during his trial and sealed his grim fate.

"What makes you so sure Hamilton will issue you a privateering commission to be a treasure hunter?"

"The word on the docks is that he will be willing to do it—for a *select few*. I want to be one of those gentlemen of fortune."

"You are a bold and enterprising young man, Edward Thache. I knew there was another reason I am going to miss you."

He nuzzled up close to her. "Remind me again, what was the first reason?"

She smiled a winsome smile and slipped her shapely leg over his upper thigh so that she was astride him. "I think you know the answer to that one, Mister Soon-to-be-Sea-Captain."

"The third time's a charm," he said with a mischievous grin, and he took her in his arms again, feeling the visceral power of his love for her along with the thrill of returning once again to his truest love.

The wild blue Sea.

CHAPTER 2

SPANISH TREASURE SALVAGE CAMP
PALMAR DE AYZ, LA FLORIDA, SPANISH TERRITORY

DECEMBER 27, 1715

AS THE THREE ATTACK BOATS crept towards shore, Edward Thache studied the enemy position. Palmar de Ayz was as the Spanish mail boat captain, Pedro de la Vega, captured near Key Biscayne just off the Atlantic coast, had said. The campfires of the main salvage camp, located six miles north of the secondary camp, flickered a dampened yellow against the pitch-black shoreline. It was here, on a sandy beach fringed by rustling palm trees, that the Spaniards had secured the coin and valuables they had thus far managed to salvage from the ten vessels lost in the July hurricane. Offshore, in the shallow waters of the Oculina Banks, was the final resting place of the late General Ubilla's flagship and the treasure-laden fighting galleon *San Cristo de San Roman*.

Commanded by privateer captain Henry Jennings, the British-American attack force carried official orders from Jamaican Governor Hamilton to "execute all manner of acts of hostility" against pirates—and private, unwritten orders to make haste to the Spanish wrecks and "bring back whatever treasure they could." With fifty men in each of the three attack boats, they were armed to the teeth. Most carried a cutlass of some kind, many the latest official British Navy variations used for slashing and stabbing during boarding and ground-based military actions. Many carried short-barreled, flared, shoulder-fired British Sea Service musketoons, while others wielded flintlock trade pistols, muzzle-loading blunderbusses, or dragons. Still other carried pikes and cudgels. With a flair for the dramatic, Thache himself carried a sling over his shoulders bearing a triumvirate of Queen Anne breech-loading screw-barrel pistols, manufactured by Thomas Annely, gunsmith, of Bristol, England. They hung from holsters like bandoliers. He also wielded a brass-hilted cutlass called a "dog's head hanger." He had never killed anyone with the weapons in the handful of instances he had boarded enemy vessels while in the service of the British Navy during the war, or as a merchant seaman and sometimes privateer in the last two years of peace since the signing of the Treaty of Utrecht; but he had been amply trained in how to use them. He was a good shot with a pistol and musket and an expert in offensive and defensive maneuvers with a cutlass.

To the sound of the oars dipping and stroking through the water and the gentle roar of waves crashing to the west, Thache continued to study the salvage camp. It was illuminated not only by a bonfire but a crescent moon overhead. He wondered how many defenders the Spaniards fielded? A hundred men? Two hundred? Or perhaps as many as three hundred? He hoped it was closer to one hundred—then his side would have the weight of superior numbers. But perhaps it wouldn't even come to that. They might be able to catch the Spanish by surprise and force them to surrender without a fight. Somehow, that prospect seemed unlikely. The Spaniards were known to be fierce fighters in close combat and stubborn when it came to surrender. They generally neither gave nor expected quarter when it came to a scrap.

Soon the three boats reached shore, just north of the midpoint between the two Spanish salvage camps. Jennings gave the order for the three companies to hide out among the palm groves and rest for a few hours. The attack would come at dawn.

Taking a half dozen palm fronds, Thache fashioned a crude bed and laid down to rest. After two weeks of sailing, he was exhausted. In mid-December, he had sailed out of Bluefields, Jamaica, as captain of a sloop purchased from privateer ship owner and family friend Daniel Axtell—along with Jennings and his eight-gun *Barsheba*, John Wills and his twelve-gun *Eagle*, and two other privateer vessels. Thache owned a two-thirds share of the vessel, Axtell one-third, and he had christened the six-gun sloop *Margaret* after his Marcus Hook love. As commander of the more than two hundred men in the five-vessel flotilla, Jennings brought along with him fourteen skilled divers and a variety of "warlike stores" in addition to muskets and pistols, including fuse-lit hand *grenadoes*, consisting of gunpowder, bits of metal, and fuse stuffed into glass bottles, and stinkpots, teargas-like grenades packed with rancid meat, fish, and other putrid items found aboard a ship. With such an assortment of lethal weaponry, Thache was confident they would be able to hold their own against the Spanish *guardas costas* and easily overwhelm the enemy's lightly manned trading vessels.

After departing from Jamaica, the flotilla had skirted the mountainous shores of Cuba, pausing to take on fresh water and other necessities in the wild harbors of Honda and Mariel until, sometime after Christmas, they entered the Florida Straits in search of signs of the sunken treasure fleet. When they stopped the Spanish mailboat to inquire the location of the wrecks, they took Captain de la Vega and his crew captive and forced them to lead them north to the salvage camps. They were not the first to inquire. De la Vega's mailboat had been looted the day before by a pair of English sloops near one of the ruined treasure galleons. Like Jennings's invaders, the Englishmen had wanted to ascertain the strength of the Spanish camp, the nature of its defenses, and the quantity of recovered treasure stored there.

Throughout the day and following night, the five sloops-of-war comprising the well-armed flotilla made their way up the deserted Florida coast, flying stolen Spanish flags to present the appropriate "colors" and thereby disguise their advance. The next morning, they stared out mesmerically at the first signs of the wrecked treasure fleet broad off their port bow. Storm-disgorged fragments of the patrol ship, *Nuestra Senora de las Nieves*, were scattered all along a barrier island beach. The hull projected above the surface in the shallow water a few hundred yards offshore, and Thache could see that the battered ship had already been picked clean by the Spaniards. On the beach were signs of the Spanish operations: remains of campfires and crude crosses marking the graves of the many that had died from drowning, diving the wrecks, and disease. The flotilla continued northward, passing the remains of the grounded *Urca de Lima*, which had also been thoroughly salvaged by her surviving crew, and then burned to the waterline to discourage freelancers. Finally, a hundred miles to the north along the east coast of La Florida from where they had captured de la Vega, they located the two Spanish salvage camps.

Thache awoke to the smell of gunpowder. Smears of predawn light assaulted his tired eyes, and he realized that he must have slept for two or three hours. He looked up to see several of his comrades loading and priming their firearms.

Jennings appeared at his side with his lieutenant, the feisty privateer Charles Vane. An outspoken Jacobite, Vane looked upon James Francis Edward Stuart—the Catholic Prince of Wales, who had lived in exile in France and Rome following the failed Jacobite Rising of 1715—as the legitimate heir to the British throne. He often spoke vociferously of wanting to string up the fat Hanoverian imposter who had stolen James III's rightful place and didn't speak a lick of English, King George I. Like Thache and Jennings, the irrepressible Vane was an educated property owner, and also like Thache, he hailed from Jamaica by route of Mother England.

"We go now, Thache," whispered Jennings, in an upper-middle-class Bermudan accent. "Pass the word along."

"Aye, Captain."

Charles Vane stepped up to him and grinned like a dervish. He reeked of strong rum. "Are you ready to kill some Spanishers, Thache?"

"If need be," he said, without much conviction.

Vane slapped him on the back with bibulous bonhomie. "Keep a sharp eye out and a steady hand with those breech-loaders of yours. The men look up to you and will follow you anywhere."

"They will?"

"Aye, I've seen it with my own eyes. So that's why you will be up front with me and Captain Jennings. Be sure to keep the men moving forward. You're a natural leader, my Jamaican friend."

"I'll be right beside you. You can count on me."

"I'd better be able to, ye scupperlout—otherwise, I'll have to cut off your bloody fucking head and stick it on a pike!" He cackled with inebriated laughter and was gone.

Five minutes later, the two-hundred-odd men had formed up into three separate companies, one commanded by Jennings, another by Wills, and a third by the wild-looking Vane. To the sound of banging drums, they began marching up the flat, featureless beach towards the fortified northern treasure salvage camp. As they marched forward, Thache couldn't help but feel like the heroic Sir Francis Drake at Cadiz or Morgan at Panama—even though he knew he and the others were actually invaders marching illegally into the Spanish sovereign territory of La Florida. After all, Palmar de Ayz was far south of the twenty-ninth parallel, the boundary claimed by the Carolina Charter of 1665, which meant there was not the slightest legal justification for what they were doing. But at the moment, with the steady roll of the drumbeat and the marching footsteps on the sandy beach, none of that mattered.

Like Drake and Morgan, they would one day be hailed as conquering heroes. Or so twenty-eight-year-old Edward Thache hoped.

As Vane had instructed him to do, he marched out in front of the three companies with Jennings, Wills, Vane, and the British flag-bearers. Up ahead, he saw that the enemy soldiers were withdrawing from their fortifications and a general agitation was spreading within the camp. The Spaniards had constructed a sand embankment to defend against attacks, but it was obvious that they lacked adequate numbers and proper arms for a defense against two hundred muskets and pistols. The militant drumbeat rolled across the sandy beach, like a warning shot fired across a bow.

Now he could see a dozen of the Spaniards break away from defending the sand wall and run to the rear.

"Aye, we've got the cowardly pups on the run now!" shouted Jennings.

The invaders gave a hearty huzzah, and several more defenders threw down their arms and retreated from the embankment. Thache could see now that the Spanish were badly outnumbered. Maybe they would give up without a fight after all. *No,* he thought, *that's not the Spanish way. The officers will force them at the point of a muzzle to regroup and fight.*

The invaders marched forward implacably, the drumbeat now rising to a fever pitch.

"Forward, men! At the quick step now!" commanded Jennings.

The three columns picked up their pace and high-stepped towards the Spanish position as the drumbeat rose to a martial crescendo.

Suddenly, a Spanish officer wearing a sunbleached, tattered naval uniform stepped over the wall with an orderly carrying a white flag. They walked towards Thache, Jennings, and the others out front. Jennings held up a hand, silencing the drummers as the mustachioed Spanish officer stepped up to them cautiously with his terrified-looking flag-bearer.

He bowed formally. "I am Admiral Francisco Salmon, commander of this camp," he said in surprisingly fluent English, his posture erect and demeanor courtly. "As this territory of La Florida belongs to His Catholic Majesty King Philip the Fifth, I must ask why you have come here. Is it to make war with Spain when our countries are now at peace?"

"No, this is not war," replied Jennings, squinting disapprovingly at his Spanish counterpart, for whom Thache could tell he felt only a muted hatred. "We came to fish the wrecks, to claim the mountain of wealth that belongs rightfully to England and her colonies."

Admiral Salmon shook his head. "There is nothing for you here. To whom am I speaking, by the way? Are you and your men pirates?"

"I am Captain Henry Jennings of Bermuda and lately Jamaica, and I, sir, am no lowly pirate. We come by the order of the Governor of Jamaica to protect against piracy. Me and my men have valid commissions to perform our duty as protectors of the realm."

"Your commissions are worthless. You are nothing but pirates."

Thache saw Jennings's face redden, and the privateer commodore took a step forward as if to strike a blow. "Damn your impudence, Spanisher—ye don't talk to me that way!"

"I apologize for my forthrightness. But these wrecks belong to His Majesty King Philip and you have no right to be here. Me and my men are securing the King's treasures. If you and your men don't turn around right now and return to your boats, you risk instigating a war."

"You know we cannot do that. The treasure is here and we outnumber you three to one."

"My country and the Pope himself will vehemently protest this invasion of our sovereign territory."

"Protest all you want—we're taking the damned silver and gold. Now where is it? I'm growing impatient."

"I cannot just hand over the treasure to you or my King would be angry with me. But in the interest of keeping our two countries out of war, I might be able to offer you a substantial amount. Let's say twenty-five thousand pieces of eight. That is, if you agree to leave peacefully at once."

"No, that's not enough," snorted Charles Vane. "Why ye are but a small bantam cock crowing on his own dunghill. If we want the treasure, we're going to bloody damn take it. And that means every single peso, by thunder!"

"He's right," agreed Jennings. "We're going to have to have it all. My men greatly outnumber you and will have it no other way. I mean, just look at them."

He turned and gestured towards his well-armed company of young adventurers, experienced privateers and merchant seamen, freebooters, wreckers, divers, and social misfits. They raised their muskets, blunderbusses, pistols, and cutlasses and gave a martial cry that was as menacing as a pack of howling wolves surrounding a quivering lamb. It was a terror tactic, Thache saw at once, and it worked to startling effect, as Salmon's face turned a shade paler and his flag-bearer began to noticeably tremble at the sight of the motley crew of seafaring warriors, none of whom were wearing military uniforms.

Jennings turned back to face the Spaniard, bearing the confident smile of one who knows he holds a winning hand. "I command you to stand down now, Admiral, or I will kill you and all of your men where you stand. We're taking the treasure— all of it—so ye have only one choice to make here today: to live or die. Which is it to be, sir? As I've intimated, I'm running out of patience."

Thache watched as the admiral looked back dejectedly towards his men behind the wall, weighing his options. There were only twenty or thirty left guarding the front line, and though they had a pair of cannon, they looked hungry, tired, and defeated. The mailboat captain de la Vega had told them Salmon was a proud man who would likely not give up without a fight, even though he and his men had endured substantial hardship since the storm and were barely hanging on. Though supplies had recently arrived from St. Augustine and Havana, during much of their stay on the beach since washing ashore they had been forced to subsist on dogs, cats, horses, the bitter berries of palmetto trees, and the occasional fish or seabird. Salmon himself had taken gravely ill, but he still refused to leave the wreck site. "I will stay on this island in bad health and half-dressed even if it means sacrificing my life," he had told de la Vega. He had posted his strongest men as sentries near the hulk of the *Regia* in an attempt to prevent looting and then set about trying to recover as much of the fleet's cargo as possible. His men were not eager to enter the shark-infested waters, and those that did sickened within a few weeks under the strain of the heavy work, so he had sent a man to Havana with orders to round up African and Indian divers. But according to de la Vega, more than a third of the enslaved divers at Palmar de Ayz had died and more were dying every day. Still, the ever-loyal Salmon was determined to recover the treasure on behalf of His Majesty the King and he had already salvaged over four million pesos in coins and cargo. A substantial portion of the treasure was reportedly already in Havana under heavy guard.

Salmon's eyes met those of Jennings. He was still looking for a compromise solution, and Thache couldn't help but admire him for his resolve and sense of duty.

"I assure ye, your men will be treated well, Admiral," said Jennings. "We'll even give you some of our food and drink."

Still, the proud admiral hesitated. Thache continued to study the faces of the two commanders, trying to gauge who would give in first.

"Very well, I accept your terms," said Salmon finally, his jaw trembling. "But I implore you to treat my men honorably. They have been through a most terrible ordeal, and it is a miracle that any of us has survived."

"I am a man of honor, sir, and would have it no other way," said Jennings, and he withdrew a silver flask. "Let's toast to peace then."

"My apologies, Captain Jennings, but I do not feel like drinking a toast to your victory and my defeat."

"Very well, sir. Then lead us to the treasure."

"As you wish, Captain."

Two hours later, under the direction of Vane and Thache, a large contingent of men loaded what would prove to be nearly ninety-thousand pounds sterling worth of Spanish silver and gold into a launch, along with some silver plate, four bronze swivel guns, fifty copper ingots the size of bread loaves, and dozens of personal valuables seized from Salmon's staff. They had also sabotaged three cannons that were too bulky to transfer to the flotilla. After releasing the Spanish mail boat, the five vessels comprising the attack force sailed off to the southeast, in the direction of the closest safe harbor where they could divide their plunder.

The island of New Providence, Bahamas—on the fringes of colonial America where scores of out-of-work seamen from across the English-speaking world were forming a governmentless Republic of Pirates.

CHAPTER 3

COLLEGE OF WILLIAM AND MARY
WILLIAMSBURG, ROYAL COLONY OF VIRGINIA

DECEMBER 28, 1715

VIRGINIA LIEUTENANT GOVERNOR ALEXANDER SPOTSWOOD—a former lieutenant-colonel in the British Army born into a Scottish royalist family in Tangier, Morocco, in 1676—peered up with satisfaction at his latest architectural achievement. The Wren Building was the signature building of the College of William and Mary. Since his posting five years earlier as the seventeenth Crown-appointed administrator of Virginia, Spotswood had spent considerable time refurbishing, and where necessary rebuilding, the edifice from the ashes of a 1705 fire, faithfully adhering to the original design of Sir Christopher Wren, the architect of St. Paul's Cathedral in London. The brick building stood three stories tall and contained a great banquet hall, handsome dormer-windowed roof, and massive chimneys. It was topped by a well-proportioned cupola and slender clock tower with a wind-seeking weathervane. To Spotswood, it projected the grace and power of the British Empire and His Majesty King George I, who he believed benevolently watched over his colonial stewards like a stern but judicious patriarch.

Adept at geometry and mathematics, the thirty-nine-year-old bachelor Spotswood had taken an active role in the architecture of his adopted town on behalf of the Crown since his arrival to Williamsburg. He had overseen the design and construction of not only the Wren Building but a brick powder magazine on the south side of Market Square, a public prison or gaol, the airy Bruton Parish Church, and the governor's lavish official residence. His unfinished residence was disparagingly called the "Governor's Palace" by his many enemies in the House of Burgesses, the lower legislative assembly of elected representatives that governed Colonial Virginia. The colonists resented what they regarded as his exorbitant spending on the building project. But that wasn't the main reason Spotswood was unpopular in his colony. The House of Burgesses and the American colonists they represented considered him to be too loyal to the Crown and not devoted enough to the concerns of the people he governed.

The discord between him and the lower chamber had disintegrated to the point where three months earlier, on September 7, 1715, he had dissolved the House after only a five-week session, publicly excoriating its members as a set of representatives "whom heaven has not endowed with the ordinary qualifications requisite to legislators." The two warring factions had yet to reconcile, which was one of the reasons he had called upon the man standing next to him. Robert Beverley was a former member of the House of Burgesses and chief clerk of the Governor's Council, as well as the venerated author of *The History and Present State of Virginia*, the first published history of a British colony by a native of North America, written in 1705. Beverley served as both mentor and advisor to the governor in matters of state, and Spotswood made a point of seeking his valuable counsel whenever he was confronted with a thorny issue.

"Don't fret, Alexander," said Beverley in an assuaging tone. "Things will get better with the Burgesses and Council. They certainly can't get any worse."

"I wouldn't be so sure about that," sniffed Spotswood. "These men are a recalcitrant lot—and most of them are scoundrels to boot."

He was speaking specifically of the eight disaffected men on his Governor's Council that were firmly opposed to him. Known as the Ludwell-Blair faction, they were led by Philip Ludwell the Younger, prominent plantation owner and speaker of the House of Burgesses, and Reverend James Blair, the most powerful religious figure in Virginia. In the last six months, he and his colonial adversaries had not seen eye to eye on anything and tempers had flared repeatedly. Ludwell in particular often lectured him on the proper limits of British authority, taking particular exception to Spotswood's authoritarian manner and open contempt for the colony's lower house of elected representatives and the colonial democratic process. The governor's many critics claimed he employed heavy-handed tactics to control tobacco exports through his 1713 Tobacco Inspection Act, rewarded his loyal friends with patronage positions, and acquired large tracts of valuable land through shady practices.

Most recently, Spotswood had incensed Virginians with his Indian Trade Act. The legislation granted the Virginia Indian Company a twenty-year monopoly over American Indian trade, and charged the company with maintaining Fort Christanna, a settlement in the southern tidewater region for smaller Indian tribes. Establishing the company was Spotswood's attempt to circumvent political opposition by shifting the financial burden of defense against Indians from the colonial government to private enterprise, but in doing so, he angered those who had invested in private trade, such as William Byrd of the Governor's Council who was combating Spotswood from London. All in all, his policies were unpopular with Virginia tobacco planters, landholders, and commoners alike since all sought to maintain their independence from the British Crown.

The fatherly Beverley resumed their exchange as they walked. "I'm afraid, my friend," he said to Spotswood, "ye shall simply have to ride out the storm."

"Yes, but I am growing weary of the constant bickering."

"Have you tried compromise?"

"Why should I? I represent the Crown—not a rag-tag of tobacco merchants and backwards farmers."

"You can't look at it that way, Alexander, and you know it. I was speaker in the House once and know these men. In fact, that was one of the reasons I believed you sought my counsel today."

"Yes, I know I shouldn't be so stubborn. But these rascals do vex me so."

They came to a halt before one of the Wren Building's newly installed first-floor windows. Spotswood peered at his own reflection. Gazing back at him was a middle-aged man with a slight paunch and receding hairline beneath a long gray periwig. His clothing was sartorially splendid: a red velvet coat, ruffled cuffs, and gold-embroidered waistcoat. Though it was late December, the temperature was in the mid-fifties and he and Beverley had no need for bulky greatcoats. After pausing a moment before the window, they took off to the east, heading down the pothole-riddled, wagon-tracked Duke of Gloucester Street in the direction of the Governor's Palace.

Suddenly, Beverley tensed up. "Oh dear," he said. "It looks as though two of those very rascals are headed this way."

Spotswood looked up to see his two fiercest adversaries: Philip Ludwell the Younger and Reverend James Blair. A direct, blunt, close-mouthed man, Ludwell came from a powerful Virginia landholding family and was ten years Spotswood's senior. Blair—the commissary of the Bishop of London—was also older and served as the supervisor of the church in Virginia and president of the College of William and Mary. With a firm mouth and watchful eyes, he was known as a man of action who had broken two past governors: Andros and Nicholson. Despite the animosity Spotswood felt towards his two adversaries, he proffered a friendly smile.

"Good day to ye, gentlemen," he said, giving a formal bow.

Ludwell tipped his tricorn hat and gave a cool smile. "Good day to you too, Alexander. But it would be a far better one if you repealed your ill-conceived Tobacco Act."

Spotswood felt his whole body tense up. "Now look here—"

"Come now, Alexander—it's an abomination to our colonial economy," cut in Blair before he could finish. "You know perfectly well we speak the truth. The act needs to be swiftly repealed. That will be best for all concerned parties."

Spotswood shook his head. "As you well know, that is impossible. The Assembly is not in session."

"Because you dissolved in September," pointed out Ludwell. "The point is our tobacco crops have not been strong in recent years and we need help. We have to be able to export all of our tobacco, regardless of quality, to account for the dry years. There's no way around it for plantation owners, small farmers, and merchant shippers if they are to make a fair living."

"You have strenuous opposition from the people on this, Alexander," said the barrel-chested reverend. "As you know, nineteen counties sent grievances. Everyone is losing money on this—except the Crown. But you can reverse it all by doing the right thing. You can with a stroke of your pen repeal the act. I dare say, you might very well be the most popular man in America if you did that."

Spotswood frowned. "*America?* What are you talking about *America?*"

"That is the new name that is being bandied about," said the reverend. "It started with seamen in the ports around the world. They call the New World colonies here 'America' and the people who inhabit them the 'Americans.' Surely you must have heard the terms?"

Spotswood scowled. "No, I have not. And truth be told, they carry a whiff of sedition. I don't like them."

"Well, you'd better get used to them," said Ludwell. "Americans are who we are. Not you, of course, but the reverend and me. And your friend Mr. Beverley here, who has been known to fancy himself an 'Indian.'"

"America. Why the name is laughable. There is no such united force of colonists as the 'Americans,' I can assure you."

18

"Oh, but there is such a force," pointed out Beverley, taking Spotswood by surprise. "And it is growing every day. These men and their adherents are part of a growing cadre of independent-minded thinkers They see themselves as patriots fighting against the excesses of the Crown. They have taken to calling themselves 'Americans' to distinguish themselves from Britain and from the individual colonies of New England, Virginia, and the like. It's quite real, Alexander, I can assure you."

"You'd better listen to him," said Ludwell with a subversive smile. "Your friend knows of what he speaks."

Spotswood just shook his head. He was disappointed at his mentor, but was not surprised. Though loyal to the Crown and to the lieutenant governor personally, Robert Beverley had never been shy about expressing his own political views, which on occasion were opposed to the King.

"This is not provocation," pointed out Ludwell. "We are simply letting you know that we advocate for the rights of the American people we represent rather than serving the will of you, acting governor of the colony, or the Crown."

"Yes, you shouldn't take it personally," added Reverend Blair, who at fifty-nine still looking feisty and commanding in his long white wig and black gown with prim white neckbands. "It's the same old British feud betwixt the King and Parliament being waged on a new battleground. But if you want to come out on the right end of history, you'll need to rethink your position on tobacco."

"So what you're telling me is that colonial policies should be decided in Virginia coffee houses—such as St. Michael's Alley off Threadneedle Street— rather than from experienced representatives of the Crown?"

"There are no practical benefits to overregulating our tobacco trade solely to benefit the King," said Ludwell.

"Is that so? And do you recall what I said in my final address to the Assembly in September?"

"How could we forget? You admonished the burgesses for disregarding their King and governor while they followed the giddy resolves of the illiterate vulgar in their drunken conventions. Oh yes, I remember your ugly tirade quite vividly."

"I stand by what I said. Your spending time on bills which you know very well can never pass is surely done more with regard to your own position and profits than the country's advantage. And yet you want me to defend this colony against Indian attacks when you reject a claim of nine shillings for the forage of three horses which I sent to draw cannon to the frontiers?"

Ludwell grinned with challenge. "We don't approve of your profligate spending habits. It's as simple as that."

"Yes, well gentlemen, since you seem to have it out for me in the midst of the Christmas season, I have some strong words for you."

"Is this really necessary?" asked Beverley, trying to avoid further unpleasantness.

But Spotswood, whose face had reddened in the heated atmosphere despite the cool temperature, was too worked up to stop now. "Indeed it is," he said. "To be perfectly plain with you, Mr. Ludwell and Reverend Blair, the true interests of your country—this so-called *America* of yours—is not what you trouble your heads about. All your proceedings have been calculated to answer the notions of the ignorant populace. Which is precisely why I am glad I dissolved the Assembly this September past when I did. To keep such an Assembly on foot would be a discredit to a country that has many able and worthy gentlemen in it, including Mr. Beverley here. Now, gentlemen, I bid ye good afternoon."

Ludwell laughed disdainfully. "Now I know why William Byrd calls you *Arroganti.* Your arrogance, sir, truly knows no bounds." He was referring to William Byrd, who had a seat on the Governor's Council and was living in London. Byrd was every bit as much Spotswood's enemy as Ludwell and Blair, and the lieutenant governor knew the man was working tirelessly across the Atlantic to have him removed from office.

"Before we take our leave, I'd like to point out one thing," said the reverend. "It seems odd that a man who seldom raises his voice or swears before his numerous Indian charges and African slaves should speak so harshly to his political colleagues. Apparently, you save your anger only for your Council and the House of Burgesses. Good day to you, sir." He then turned to Beverley. "For heaven's sake, Robert, please try and talk some sense into him."

With curt bows, Ludwell and Blair left, heading west towards William and Mary College. Boiling over with anger, Spotswood walked on with Beverley towards his governor's residence. After several minutes of venting, Spotswood got to the reason he had sought his esteemed friend Robert Beverley's counsel in the first place.

"I assume you've heard about this Spanish treasure fleet wrecked off the coast of Florida."

"Yes, I've heard the stories, but I don't know much about it. I know nothing as to the value of the Spanish losses. What's your interest in the matter?"

"I believe there may be an opportunity."

"An opportunity?"

"The news of the wrecks is spreading like wildfire. It has attracted the attention of not only those inclined towards piracy, but gentlemen investors and merchants all the way north to Maine."

"So I have heard. It is no longer a local affair of South Carolina, the Bahamas, and Bermuda. The word I have from Virginia's merchant seamen is that the whole Atlantic community has learned of these wrecks and plans to fish the waters for the rich cargo of spilled gold, silver, and precious gemstones. So you want in, is that what I'm hearing?"

"Even upstanding gentlemen can hardly be expected to avoid the call of the treasure gleaming from Florida's shores. Wouldn't you agree?"

"Absolutely. But the Spanish will not see it that way. From what I've heard, they have already pulled perhaps half the treasure from the offshore sand."

"Which means that half still remains."

"That is true. And it is also true that the legalities of fishing treasure-filled shipwrecks are not well-defined. It depends so much on one's definition of ownership during salvage operations. From a legal standpoint, it is a gray area. Which is precisely why there is an opportunity."

"Are you suggesting that the fine royal colony of Virginia send an expedition down to fish those wrecks?"

"Why shouldn't we get in on the excitement?"

"That's precisely what I thought. Which is why I wrote a letter to Mr. Stanley Stanhope of the Board of Trade last month." He came to a stop, withdrew from his leather satchel a copy of the three-page letter he had sent to London in November, and handed the third and final sheet of foolscap to Beverley. "It's in the postscript there," he said as his friend began reading.

P.S.–Here is advice of a considerable event in these parts that ye Spanish plate fleet, richly laden, consisting of eleven sail, are, (except one,) cast away in the Gulf of Florida to ye southward of St. Augustine, and y't a Barcalongo, sent from the Havana to fetch off from the cont't some passengers of distinction 133 who were in y't fleet, having recovered from ye wrecks a considerable quantity of plate, is likewise cast away about 40 miles to ye northward of St. Augustine. I think it my duty to inform His Majesty of this accident, which may be improved to the advantage of His Majesty's subjects if encouragement be given to attempt ye recovery of some of that Immense Treasury.

When Beverley was finished, he looked up. "Are you planning on waiting until you receive royal authority, or are you going to send in your own company of salvors to complete the job?"

"That's what I wanted to talk to you about. I don't want to fall into His Majesty's disfavor by overstepping my authority. At the same time, though, if we don't strike while the iron is hot, we have no chance of reaping the benefits of this vast treasure."

"Yes, I can see your conundrum."

They started walking again. A pair of squawking chickens scratched across the muddy street, and three cows mooed from the shaded corners of a pasture lot.

"So what do you think?" asked Spotswood. "Do you think it would be a mistake if Virginia were to send down her own crew on behalf of the Crown?"

"We're at peace," replied Beverley. "'Tis my belief that such an act might stir the pot with our newfound Spanish friends by violating the Treaty of Utrecht."

"I understand your position, Robert. And that is why I sought your counsel."

"Yet you're disappointed in my answer. I can see it on your face."

"You are a good judge of men. I must confess that while I hold strong views against piracy and unsanctioned looting, I have been, shall we say, bitten by the treasure-hunting bug."

"That is understandable. It is a tantalizing prospect. But I would refrain from sending down a sloop to recover Spanish treasure until you have been authorized by the Board of Trade, or at the very least your Council."

"Oh, I have no intention of telling my Council."

"But they will no doubt find out and then where will you be?"

Spotswood scratched his double chin, thinking. Across the road, a young woman in a linsey woolsey and shawl and a man wearing a feathered tricorn hat, waistcoat, and cravat passed by them. He didn't recognize them and realized they must be visitors. They appeared to be heading in the direction of Market Square. He waved politely to them before resuming his conversation with the elderly Beverley, who had recently retired to his estate, Beverley Park, in King and Queen County.

21

"I see your point, Robert," he said to the patriarch. "But no matter who I tell, I will have to dress it all up as a way of protecting Spanish property. For it would no doubt be interpreted by my many detractors here in Virginia as plain looting."

"Which is what it would be."

"Yes, but I am told that Governor Hamilton of Jamaica is planning on sponsoring privateers to seize some of the treasure before the illegal salvors pick the wrecks clean. In fact, he may very well have done so already, which means that we are already late to the party."

"It's a tricky business, though. If the men you commission plunder under the pretext of clearing the coasts of pirates by diving for silver and gold, you could be held accountable. In my view, what is happening down there in the Straits of Florida is about to lead to a full-scale epidemic of piracy."

"How do you figure that?"

"There are already more than a dozen ships fishing those wrecks. Once most of the readily recoverable treasure has been collected, those men will be out of work and have nowhere to go. Many of them will sign on as pirates."

"I see your point. When the wrecks no longer pay out, even the professional privateers who fought against Spain and France will turn pirate and raid ships that have already scooped up the spoils from the seabed."

"Indeed. My prediction is that soon, very soon, it will be out of control and even veteran merchants and gentlemen privateers from Barbados, Bermuda, and Jamaica will turn from fishing the wrecks to outright piracy. They'll start by taking only Spanish ships and plundering the salvaged riches under guard ashore. Then when that is no longer profitable, they'll raid all the vessels carrying away the treasure regardless of nationality."

"*Hostis Humani Generi*," intoned Spotswood, picturing a band of foul-smelling, snarling, drunken, cutlass-wielding sea marauders.

"Yes, that's what the Admiralty calls them: the enemy of all mankind," said Beverley, and a ghost of a smile appeared on his lips. "But I'm a romantic at heart, so I have to confess that if I were but twenty years younger, I would be right there alongside those lads headed for La Florida."

Spotswood was intrigued by his friend's admission. "Ye would?"

"Aye verily. The sheer thrill of being a freebooter even for just one day would be worth the risk. I have always dreamed of what it would be like to have the wind in my hair and blunderbuss in hand, like old Captain Morgan himself."

"Come now, Robert, you mustn't romanticize them. They are but lowly outlaws and brigands who prey upon the high seas. They have no honor."

"Perhaps not," replied the elder man. "But they still spark the imagination."

And with that, they continued to the British lieutenant governor's unfinished "Palace" and ate a fine meal of roasted venison, hot breads, and savories prepared by an army of Spotswood's slaves and indentured servants, washing it down with Irish usquebaugh and Canary wine.

22

CHAPTER 4

NASSAU, NEW PROVIDENCE ISLAND
PROPRIETARY COLONY OF THE BAHAMAS

DECEMBER 31, 1715

TAKING ADVANTAGE OF THE BRISK NORTHERLY BREEZE, Edward Thache sailed his six-gun Jamaican sloop south of the outer Bahamian island of Eleuthera and several patch reefs towards Nassau on New Providence Island. When he reached the harbor entrance, a pilot guided the *Margaret* through the channel to the harbor along a long, narrow stretch of water. With Hog Island to the north and the Nassau waterfront to the south, he dropped anchor in three fathoms of water directly across from the island's most prominent landmark: old British Fort Nassau. Standing next to the larboard shroud, Thache reached for his spyglass and peered south, first at the fort then at the fledgling pirate enclave. The former British Navy seaman who had grown up in Jamaica, sailed up and down the Atlantic coast, and circumnavigated the Caribbean wasn't particularly impressed with what he saw. But the outlaw town did capture his attention.

Years earlier during the war, the Spanish had landed on New Providence, burned down the houses, and plundered the inhabitants so that they fled to the surrounding woods for shelter—and Nassau had never recovered. The fort peering out over the harbor was in ruins, with crumbling walls and half-beveled bastions. Further east, he could see a dozen or so dilapidated houses, a handful of buildings, and a derelict waterfront with a smattering of taverns and ordinaries. On the white sandy beach stretched spare masts, rigging, bowsprits, coiled rope, fishing nets, planking, and piles of conch shells along with dozens of makeshift lean-tos and canvas sail tents for the lowly wreckers, fishermen, and scroungers who couldn't afford the luxury of even a shanty. The paths to and from the beach appeared to be overgrown with tropical undergrowth. Gazing at the little town, Thache thought to himself that this was most certainly not Philadelphia, Charles Town, or Boston. Hell, it wasn't even Port Royal.

But at the same time, he couldn't help but feel a sense of fellowship and adventure finally witnessing this strange new Republic of Pirates that he had heard so much about the past six months. And he could tell at once that the new Bahamian stronghold was the perfect hideaway for those that had chosen to go on the account. In addition to lacking any enforceable government or naval policing authority, it lay tantalizingly close to the Florida wrecks as well as to the shipping lanes between the Caribbean and American colonies. The harbor was huge and could accommodate many vessels. Among those at anchor he could already count Jennings's eight-gun *Barsheba*; John Wills twelve-gun *Eagle*; five other unfamiliar sloops, powerful-looking vessels in good order and well-armed with carriage- and swivel-guns; three good-sized periaugers; and a half dozen small canoes. And sweeping into the channel in his wake were a pair of large Bermudan sloops. All in all, the harbor looked like it could anchor a hundred vessels.

The Bahamas had first begun to be used as a base for pirate operations shortly after the War of Spanish Succession ended. That was in 1713, though the attacks by many privateers had not ceased until 1714 when the Treaty of Utrecht was finally recognized by the majority of New World seamen. Now New Providence and the surrounding islands were gaining a reputation as a lawless refuge for the "enemies of all nations," as the Admiralty had been fond of calling pirates since Kidd had swung from the gallows at Wapping in 1701. This growing international fraternity of sea rovers had no British government to prevent them from raiding, and Thache had heard that Benjamin Hornigold and other formerly legitimate privateers were taking advantage of the favorable situation. The Bahamas were a tenuously held dependency of the Lords Proprietors of Carolina, and the proprietors had not appointed a new governor to the Bahamas since 1704.

He focused his brass spyglass on the men onshore. The inebriated, wild-looking rabble on the docks and beaches he spied through the optical instrument didn't look as though they would be very receptive to governmental authority. He began counting numbers. After a couple of minutes, he estimated that the current number of seamen on the island had to be at least five hundred individuals, probably double the size of the town the previous Christmas and dwarfing the civilian population inhabiting the island year-round.

Upon setting anchor, he posted a watch and headed to shore while his crew received their shares of the Spanish spoils from Jennings's quartermaster on the deck of the *Barsheba*. Thache had already received his captain's shares, and he would soon be sailing with Jennings and his men to Jamaica to present their prizes to the Vice-Admiralty Court, which was presided over by Governor Hamilton. Once onshore, he went to the White Gull Tavern, where he spotted Charles Vane sitting at a table. He purchased a tankard of ale and bottle of rum and went over to him. Seated at the table talking to Vane was an older man with an air of command about him whom Thache had never laid eyes on before.

"Charles Vane, ye old sea dog," he said to his newfound friend and one of Jennings's right-hand men. "Do you mind if I pull up a chair?"

Vane's drunken eyes lit up. "Edward Thache," he said in a slurred voice. "You don't know how pleased I am to see you. You be just in time for a toast."

"And what might we be toasting?"

"Why to the damnation of King George, of course!"

"Well, holding James III the 'Pretender' in high regard as I do, I have to drink to that."

The three men clinked their pewter tankards, tossed back a hearty portion of their ales, and smacked their lips with satisfaction.

Thache looked at Vane and grinned. "And who, Charles, might I inquire is your friend here that I be toasting with?"

"Oh, how neglectful of me. Edward Thache meet Benjamin Hornigold, leader of the Flying Gang."

Hornigold held out his hand.

So this be Ben Hornigold, thought Thache, taking measure of the Bahamian sea rover he had heard so much about as they shook hands. His face was deeply fissured from sun, rum, and age, his wide-brimmed black Spanish hat was set at a jaunty angle, and he carried a slight paunch about his midriff. He and Jennings were the two elder statesmen amongst the new interlopers that had taken over New Providence, and there was reported to be bad blood between them. The upper-middle-class, landholding Bermudan Jennings apparently viewed himself as a legitimate privateer sailing on behalf of the Crown—and Hornigold as a common robber and lowly wrecker without scruples and beneath his station. But Charles Vane didn't seem to mind Hornigold's company; though he sailed with Jennings, he seemed quite comfortable with the man and they appeared to be deep into their cups together.

"The Flying Gang, you say? And who might that gang be?" asked Thache.

"It's all of us, lad," replied Hornigold. "We run the Bahamas now. This pirate republic is our military base of operations, and there not be a soul in the British, French, or Spanish Navy powerful enough to dislodge us. This is *our* home and *our* time. We be the new sea dogs, ye see—the masters of the sweet trade from Newfoundland to Portobello. And we live by our own rules."

"And what rules would those be?"

"We share the plunder equally amongst ourselves instead of serving under privateering contracts that give the bulk of the earnings to owners and captains."

"A democracy indeed."

"Aye and it works, my good fellow—or I be a lubberly Dutchman. Apart from a few forced men, service aboard a Flying Gang vessel is purely voluntary. A man can serve for as long as he likes as long as he but follow the code, and he can quit at any time. Furthermore, we elect our own captains, quartermasters, sailing masters, and bosuns. If we don't approve of their performance, we can vote them out just the same."

"So what authority does the captain have then?"

"In the Flying Gang, the captain has absolute authority while involved in a chase or in combat, or during a storm. All the other decisions are made equally in a council of the crew. That includes where to go, which vessels to attack, which prisoners to retain or set free, and how to mete out punishment for infractions while at sea within the companies. Like I said, it's a code—and it works because it makes no man the servant of another."

Thache nodded in understanding. From his experience in the Royal Navy during the war and merchant service after the war, he knew that many pirates were mariners who had long suffered abuse and exploitation at the hands of brutal and greedy captains and ship owners, and only later turned to piracy. Obviously, Hornigold had no intention of replicating that system, but rather turning it on its head. It was a system in which everyone profited or suffered equally, and Thache understood implicitly that that's what made it so dangerous in the eyes of the British authorities and the ruling elites that dominated maritime trade. Pirate criminality bred a sense of democracy that exposed the world's inequality.

"A captain and quartermaster eat the same victuals as their own men and have to share their cabins. And a captain is only paid two times more than his seaman, a quartermaster one and a half times. If the men trust their leaders and are satisfied with their performance, they'll follow them to the bitter end. If not, they'll depose them in the blink of an eye. Most of all, they have to show results and keep their men well fed and well stocked with rum. So, what do you say Mr. Thache?"

"It's Captain Thache. From Jamaica."

"Yes, I can see ye be a gentleman—and yet you don't have airs about you. Not like Master Vane's cohort, Mr. Jennings, captain of the *Barsheba*. Now there's a pompous ass for you. He thinks that just because he received a commission from Governor Hamilton that he's better than the rest of us."

"I have a commission from the governor too," Thache reminded him. "But you won't see me looking down my nose at anyone."

Vane raised his tankard. "As long as I get my fair share of the prizes we take, I don't pick sides. I say drink up and live and let live."

"Good words to live by, Mr. Vane," agreed Hornigold. "Now what say ye, Captain Thache, about what I've just told you?"

"I say this is all happening awfully fast and I am struggling to catch up. Like I said, I'm but a humble privateer with an official commission from Governor Hamilton. For the time being, I'd like to keep it that way."

"You've never been a-pirating?"

"No sir, not me. What I've taken has been from the Spanish and French under commission. It has been aboveboard and legal."

"Well, lad, I suspect that's about to change. You see, there's something brewing in the air."

"Something brewing?"

"Yes, a big change is upon us on account of those Spanish wrecks, and I'm afraid there's no way to put the genie back in the bottle."

"Aye, I must confess I feel it too, Captain Hornigold. There is indeed something going on that I am only dimly beginning to fathom."

"You can call me Benjamin, or Ben."

"Aye, and you can call me Edward."

"Very well, Edward it is. And I want you to know that I only plunder Spanish and French vessels. I never agreed to the terms of that damned Treaty of Utrecht, so I continue to take what is rightfully mine just as long as it be Spanish or French. Or Portuguese. I'll rob them, too, if I have half a chance."

"Me, I'm not too particular about who I plunder," said Vane. "It's the riches I care about. Now let's hoist our glasses, mates, and make it a double toast. To the damnation of King George and to the Flying Gang!"

"To the damnation of King George and to the Flying Gang!" the three men roared in unison.

A crowd of drunken seamen at three of the nearby tables echoed the cheer and suddenly the whole tavern was up and on its feet, lively ho and drinking the same toast.

It was then Edward Thache—still a legally-sanctioned Jamaican privateer— knew a true revolution had begun. Hornigold and his Bahamian Flying Gang were going to change everything.

CHAPTER 5

KINGSTON, JAMAICA

JANUARY 30, 1716

WHEN THACHE STEPPED OUT OF THE CARRIAGE and stared across the bay at Port Royal, he remembered back to the terrible earth tremor that had destroyed the town when he was five years old. The year was 1692. He had just returned from sailing with his father and was heading for Spanish Town when the first of three devastating cataclysms struck. More than two thousand people had died as a result of the ground shaking and subsequent giant wave of seawater and mudslides that followed. Three-thousand more would perish in the days following the catastrophe due to injuries and disease. The clergy claimed that the tremor was the result of a judgement of God upon the town, which had acquired a reputation for debauchery and wickedness as the British possession became the home port for pirates operating within the Caribbean. Even before the destruction was complete, some of the survivors began looting, breaking into homes and warehouses to plunder just like buccaneers. In a macabre display, many of the dead were robbed and stripped, and, in some cases, had fingers cut off to remove the rings they wore.

Fortunately, Thache and his father had managed to get to high ground south of St. Jago de la Vega, and no one in his family had died that morning or in the diseased days that followed. But he still remembered the violent ground shaking, the roar of the mudslides, the devastating power of the earth's forces at work. The next morning he watched the surviving sugar plantation slaves pulling the battered corpses from the rubble and pools of evaporating seawater. He remembered staring out at the death and devastation all around the harbor: the floating bodies fed on by sharks, the gaping fissures in the roads, the collapsed homes and shanties, the aprons of muddy debris on the hillsides, and the stench of death and rot as the stranded seawater from the tidal wave dried up. But what had terrified him most was the sight of the broken, lifeless bodies being pulled from the wreckage. He saw dozens of boys and girls scarcely older than he, and at the time, he remembered how poignantly unfair it seemed to him that children his own age should perish.

He looked at his step-mother Lucretia and his younger sister Elizabeth, then at Lucretia's three children: fifteen-year-old Cox, eleven-year-old Rachel, and his favorite, ten-year-old Thomas. Cox, Rachel, and Thomas were his step-siblings from his father's marriage to Lucretia Poquet Maverly Axtell following his mother Elizabeth's death in 1699 in Jamaica. Upon his father's death seven years later, the then-nineteen-year-old Edward, Jr. had, as the eldest son, settled his father's ailing affairs by deeding his inheritance, including his father's Jamaican plantation and their slaves, to Lucretia and her family so they could survive. At the time, Thache had been serving aboard Admiral William Whetstone's flagship, the *HMS Windsor*, stationed at Port Royal. He had joined the Royal Navy as an officer only a year earlier to fight in Queen Anne's War, and the ship had returned from a two-month patrol in enemy French territory when his father died.

"What are ye thinking about, Brother?" asked his sister Elizabeth, staring down at Port Royal and the more than fifty ships anchored in the harbor.

"My mind was harkening back to the earth tremor of ninety-two. I was but a wee lad, but I remember it like it was yesterday."

"That's funny, I don't remember it at all," said Elizabeth, two years his junior at the age of twenty-six.

"You were too young to remember. You couldn't have been more than three at the time."

"I remember it only too well," said his step-mother Lucretia, as the servants set out a pair of blankets, picnic baskets, and bottles of ale on the ground on the hillside overlooking the bay. "It is a miracle that any of us survived. Of course, I had not met your father yet."

"Then we had the fire in 1703," said Elizabeth. "Now that I remember."

"And father died three years later," said Thache, picturing the old gentleman who had taught him how to sail at a young age and who had enjoyed being a mariner far more than a sugar plantation owner. He looked over at Cox, Rachel, and Thomas throwing pebbles down into the ocean, smiles on their luminous faces. His father Edward, Sr.—their grandfather—had died so young that they had barely known the man. Probably only Cox would remember him.

"Your father would be proud of you, Edward," said Lucretia. "Receiving a commission to hunt pirates from Governor Hamilton. Now that is truly something."

Thache smiled. "Aye, except for the fact that we haven't been hunting pirates at all. We just marched right up to Admiral Salmon at the Spanish salvage camp on the beach and demanded he surrender his treasure. So much for an honest privateering commission. It was more like taking candy from a baby."

"Oh dear, I wasn't aware of that," sniffed his step-mother.

"Nor was I," said his sister, also with a note of disapproval.

They fell into an uncomfortable silence as the servants began spreading out china plates, pewter mugs, silverware, and the picnic lunch on the blankets. The lunch would consist of ackee and saltfish, Johnny cakes, fish-and-meat pie, plantains, freshly baked sweet potato bread, and salt crackers.

"Did you meet with the governor?" asked his sister Elizabeth after a quiet moment had passed.

"Yesterday morning," he replied. "Captains Jennings, myself, and the other ship captains brought in our *claimed salvage* in accordance with our commissions."

"Did you and your cohorts tell the governor that you seized the treasure from the salvage camp, as opposed to the offshore wrecks themselves?" asked Lucretia.

His sister shot both them a worried look. "We should keep our voices down. We don't want the children to overhear."

Thache looked over at them as the oldest Cox gave a rousing cheer. Thirty feet away, the children were ensconced in tossing pebbles over the edge and into the bay and didn't appear to be listening to them.

"They're busy playing their game," he said. "But to answer your question, no we did not tell Governor Hamilton. But it didn't matter because he knew the truth. There were too many pieces of eight for us to have recovered it from the seafloor in so brief a time. In fact, I believe he had already received word about the raid on the salvage camp."

"And during the meeting, the governor didn't even bother to ask?"

"He just wants his share of the plunder and to even the score with the Spanish. Just like the rest of us."

"Can't he still arrest you?"

"I very much doubt it."

"But what you did…was it legal?"

"For me and my men it was because we had a signed commission, but it might not be for Hamilton. I have been told that the Spanish have made a formal protest and that the governor's enemies will likely pursue his removal."

"Oh my, this is turning into quite an incident."

"All I know is the King's men have made no move to arrest us. We're free to enjoy the pleasures of the island and our ill-gotten gains, if that's what they in fact are. So are all the crews of the other privateers the governor commissioned. He gave out ten commissions in all, I am told."

At that moment, the children shrieked in delight, startling the two women. His step-mother's hand flew to her chest.

"Good heavens, they scared the wits out of me," she said.

"Me too," agreed his sister. "But I think it is all this talk of piracy that has put the scare into us."

"Piracy? We're not talking about piracy—we're talking about a reprisal against the Spanish for their ill treatment of us all these years."

"Somehow, it doesn't sound that simple, Brother."

"Well, maybe this will change your mind." He reached into his pocket and retrieved a leather coin-filled bag. "This is half of my share of the treasure and I'm giving it to you two. It will help ends meet for you as well as the children."

His sister frowned. "I don't need money. My husband does quite well as a surgeon, thank you very much. And I know he will not accept money from questionable sources."

"Questionable sources? I have a legal commission from the governor, and what me and my men did was a service on behalf of the Crown. If the King's men haven't questioned what we did, why should ye?"

"We just don't want to get into trouble, or for you to tarnish your father's good name," said Lucretia. "God bless his Christian soul."

Thache felt the sting of their disapproval. "Come now, no one's tarnishing the family name. The Spanish have been hard on us and taking from them is our God-given right. So please take the silver. I've already settled up with Axtell and own the *Margaret* free and clear now," he added, referring to Daniel Axtell, the privateer ship owner and his fence in Port Royal with whom he had in the past sold cargoes as a merchant mariner and occasional privateer.

His step-mother looked at her three children. "Are you sure about this?" she asked, taking the leather purse.

"Yes, I'm sure. You need to take care of yourself and the children. There's no war on now, but there could be soon enough. If that happens, times will be hard again. The Spanish might even invade and take back the island."

His sister took him by the hand. "This is very generous of you," she said with emotion in her voice and sincerity in her eyes. "You gave up the estate when father died and now you're doing this. You are a good man, Brother, of that there is no doubt. But you must be careful. The last thing either of us wants is to see a rope around your neck and your carcass rotting in a gibbet. We tell you this because we love you and don't want anything to happen to you."

He took both women in his arms. "You don't need to worry about me, my bonnies. I'm quite sure I can take care of myself. I'm not going to be here long anyway—I'm due to set sail the first of next week."

"Next Monday?" gasped his younger sister. "But you've only been here three days!"

"I know, but I'm afraid those Spanish wrecks can't wait."

His step-mother was stunned. "You're going back to La Florida?"

"I have to," he said laconically. "I'm afraid I've caught Spanish fever and plan on working those wrecks until they're tapped out like a mine. As part of my extended family, you stand to profit greatly from the silver and gold they produce."

"Oh, Edward, I just hope it's the right thing to do and ye won't get into trouble," said Elizabeth.

"Don't worry about me. I know how to stay one step ahead of the law. Now let's eat this fine picnic lunch of yours—I'm starved."

CHAPTER 6

OCULINA BANKS
LA FLORIDA, SPANISH TERRITORY

MARCH 12, 1716

AT THE SIGHT OF THE SECOND TIGER SHARK, Caesar began to worry. He wasn't afraid of the big hammerheads or the smaller reef sharks that were everywhere among the Spanish wrecks—it was the big, striped Tigers that put the fear of God into him and the other salvage divers. Feeling his heart rate click up a notch, he wanted desperately to climb out from beneath the diving bell suspended above the sea bottom and swim to the surface and safety of his boat, the *Flying Horse*. But he didn't dare move out of the bell, not yet anyway.

A twenty-one-year-old West African slave originally auctioned in Charles Town, Caesar had grown up in the South Carolina capital before moving at age ten with his owner, Colonel Robert Daniel, to Bath Town, North Carolina. Sold there, he was now the property of Tobias Knight of Bath, the North Carolina council secretary, collector of customs, and interim chief justice. As slave owners went, the government official and his wife could only be described as enlightened. They had never once whipped him, encouraged him to learn to read and write, and insisted on his being Christianized. Two months earlier, to bring much-needed capital into the poor proprietary colony of North Carolina, Knight had commissioned a dozen Bath County adventurers, most with seafaring experience, to fish the Spanish wrecks. Caesar was his hand-picked representative and labor investment in the enterprise.

Knight had done so on behalf of Charles Eden, governor of North Carolina. Governors Hamilton and Spotswood weren't the only colonial officials obsessed with outfitting expeditions to the Florida coast to salvage Spanish silver and gold. Royal and proprietary governors, legitimate merchants, and beady-eyed profiteers all up and down the Atlantic seaboard were outfitting ships to salvage as much as possible of the treasure gleaming from Florida's shores—before the Spanish and competing wreckers retrieved it all.

Caesar and his Bath County cohorts had been fishing the wrecks for three straight weeks now. They had signed on with the *Flying Horse* in Charles Town. The vessel was captained by a merchantman who had proved to be not only incompetent but a drunken lout and tyrant, and William Howard, John Martin, and the other Bath County men were close to mutiny. Caesar and several of the other black and native West Indian divers had already been whipped more than once for refusing to go back down to the bottom when they were exhausted or afraid due to the large sharks prowling the area; and two of the divers had already died, and another was badly disabled, from ruptured lungs under the martinet captain.

The company only had one diving bell, so most of the divers were sent out over the wreck sites on simple rafts. The procedure involved taking a large rock and a deep breath before jumping overboard and sinking to the ocean floor ten to twenty feet down. There they scoured the sea floor for a minute or two, searching for treasure and scooping up coins and other small objects when they located them, marking the locations of chests, boxes, cannon, and other large valuable objects. On the surface they were searched and sent back to the bottom with ropes or chains to attach to the larger objects, so they could be raised with ship-mounted windlasses.

In three weeks' time, Caesar had established himself as the most productive diver and was, therefore, given priority using the company's one and only diving bell. He much preferred using the bell. When he ran out of breath, he could stick his head beneath it and inhale a deep breath from the air pocket at the top. He had to be careful though. If he didn't take care to exhale completely before heading to the surface, his lungs could rupture, resulting in the agonizing death that had claimed the lives of two divers thus far.

The morale aboard the *Flying Horse* was low, not only from the deaths and ill health of the divers but from the overall lack of success. The diving work at Palmar de Ayz was taxing, dangerous, and competitive. During their time thus far on the wrecks, there were more than two dozen English vessels anchored at the sunken galleon they were currently working—the *Santo Cristo de San Roman*—and at four of the other scattered wrecks. These included the flagship, *Nuestra Senora del Rosario*, which had had her bottom torn off by a reef and sank in thirty feet of water, and the treasure galleon *Urca de Lima*. Having difficulty locating the main hull sections of the great ships, they had to settle for salvaging scattered cargo and coins. Since their arrival, they had managed to scrounge up only twelve hundred pieces of eight, ten feet of gold chain, a pair of cannons, fourteen pounds of broken silver plate, a dozen leather hides, and several chests of Chinese porcelain, indigo, and vanilla beans to share between more than fifty men—and only after the merchant captain and his backers had taken their designated two-thirds share. It was simply not enough, and they were already beginning to run low on food and water and didn't want to have to give up what they had salvaged thus far to obtain both.

He took a deep breath of air and stepped from beneath the bell. One of the Tiger sharks had swum off, but the other still remained, circling above. The wind was moderate and the visibility of the water more than a hundred feet. He studied the shark. It had to be at least thirteen feet long. He watched as the creature swam above him, its dorsal fin cutting the surface like a knife, gills flaring, and tiger-like stripes glinting in the sunlight refracting through the water. The free divers to the south of him were keeping a wary eye on the big shark too. It was terrifying, moving so swiftly yet effortlessly that it seemed like death itself.

Something about this particular shark gave him the chills and he decided that it would be best to return to the surface. He had collected several pieces of eight and a gold medallion in his leather pouch and might as well hand the valuables over now and wait for the sharks to leave. Ducking beneath the diving bell to take another breath, he waited for it to swim further away from him so he could make a move for the boat. It took several minutes and repeated breaths beneath the bell before the shark swam off to the north.

It was then he made his move.

Expelling all of his air to evacuate his lungs, he undid his weight belt, quickly fastened it to the hook on the rope attached to the diving bell, and then swam for the surface. He was gripped with the urge to go fast—an overwhelming, primal urge to flat out fly up to the surface and swiftly climb the boat ladder—but he knew he needed to move slowly and methodically so as not to rupture his lungs and kill himself.

Though his heart was racing wildly, he calmly kicked his way upward with his legs and breaststroked with his arms. He told himself not to be afraid, but after three kicks and strokes instinct told him he was being hunted.

He began to swim faster.

To his infinite horror, he heard a noise below him. The source was unmistakable: a squirt of bubbles from something slicing through the water.

He looked down, but nothing was there.

In panic, he looked to his left and right.

Still nothing.

Then he saw one of the other divers below a raft motioning at something behind him.

He turned abruptly, but there was nothing. Continuing to search the water, he still saw no sign of the shark despite feeling a tickling sensation on the back of his neck, as if he was being stalked. He wanted desperately to swim to safety, but at the same time he wanted to know where the shark had gone. Or both for that matter. He could feel a vague presence nearby that was disconcerting—and yet he couldn't see anything.

And then he felt a powerful blow.

It was one of the Tigers and it caught him in the stomach, nearly knocking the wind out of him.

He spun crazily and struggled to breathe, but still he swam on towards the boat. At least the shark had only rammed him and not sunk its dagger-like teeth into him.

Then he was attacked again, this time from the other direction. He felt a sharp pain along his midriff and realized that he had been bit. For an instant, he was completely disoriented, unable to tell up from down. Blood leaked out from the wound in a thin spray that was diluted by the sea water. It was a nip, not a deep bite, but it still stung.

But had he been attacked twice by one shark, or once by two different sharks? He realized it didn't matter; he was in deep trouble.

Feeling a wave of desperation, he broke for the surface and began to swim madly in the opposite direction from where he had been bitten, unaware that he was heading away from the *Flying Horse*.

A Tiger came at him again.

Seeing his life flash before his eyes, he punched the shark in the snout and swam on, churning through the water desperately. It was only then that he realized that he was swimming away from his own boat towards another, now-closer salvage vessel. He had to make a choice: turn back and try and swim to the *Flying Horse*, or haul ass to the nearer sloop with the British flag snapping in the wind.

Suddenly, the seamen on the sloop made the decision for him. They began cheering him on from the deck and a pair of divers in a longboat tethered to the sloop, both white men, began paddling hard towards him.

"Come on, mate! Come on!" they yelled encouragingly.

He swam hard towards them.

But a Tiger shark came at him again. And now, to his dismay, he could see that there were in fact two Tigers hunting him. This time the shark that came at him aggressively bumped him without biting him, while the other one circled around him, stalking him.

Terrified out of his mind, Caesar shit himself and continued swimming towards the skiff.

Twenty feet, that's all you have to go is twenty damned feet!

The second Tiger came at him, but at the last second it darted towards the reef as bullets began tearing into its dorsal fin and splashing the water around it. The men on the spar deck of the sloop were now shooting at the pair of aggressive creatures with pistols, muskets, and blunderbusses to drive them off.

He swam on, fueled by the raw animal fear of the hunted. With three powerful strokes, he closed the gap between himself and the longboat. Two pairs of strong arms reached down and pulled him aboard as a great cheer rose up from the starboard railing of the sloop. The sharks raced off to a smattering of gunshots, their bleeding dorsal fins slicing through the water.

A moment later he was hoisted on board the ship. A passel of darkly-tanned seamen with sun-bleached hair took him by the legs, held him up triumphantly, and patted him on top of his glossy, hairless, single-ear-ringed head and muscly back before setting him back down. He beamed at all the attention, feeling like some sort of hero.

It was then he saw him.

Smiling down upon him from the quarterdeck was a tall, spare man with a short, raven-black beard wearing a crimson brocaded cotton jacket, tricorn hat, and three brace of pistols suspended in a kind of bandolier. The man had an unmistakable air of command about him and was obviously the captain, but it wasn't clear to Caesar if he was in fact some sort of pirate or a British officer.

The captain stepped down onto the spar deck and walked up to him, briefly examined his shark bite—which Caesar was thankful was only a superficial wound though it still stung like hell—and smiled through his deep ebony beard. "Looks like you'll live, lad," he said. "It is but a flesh wound and I would have to say that you got the better of those sharks than they of you. Well done!"

At this, the seamen gave a rowdy cheer. Someone stepped forward with a bottle of rum, splashed some on his wound, and shoved the bottle into his hands. Wincing in pain at the stinging sensation of the alcohol, he took the bottle and drank a huge swig, feeling suddenly more alive than he had ever felt in his entire life.

When the cheering died down, the captain with the black beard said, "Seeing as you swam to the *Margaret* instead of your own ship, I think it only fair that ye sail with us now. What say you to that? Do ye speak English?"

"Aye. And I can read and write as well."

The tall man nodded approvingly and turned to his crew. "What do you think of that, lads! Not only can he outfight a pair of sharks, but he's an educated man! Well then, I say he's going to have to join our crew!"

The men agreed. With their heads bobbing up and down, they laughed and cheered uproariously in support of him joining the company. The captain turned back towards him. "What say ye? Are you willing to leave behind your mates over there and sail with us? I could use a good diver and another deck hand, especially a man who knows his letters for my record-keeping." He motioned towards the *Flying Horse*. "But I must point out that your captain looks like he wants you back. Is he your master?"

"No."

"Well, do you belong to anyone else that I should be aware of?"

He shook his head, not wanting to tell the truth.

"What is your name, lad?"

"They call me Caesar."

"After the emperor of Rome himself. My, my, you are quite the high and mighty one, aren't you? But you are a poor liar, son. Now who do you belong to? Is it someone aboard that sloop yonder or not? Because I like to know who might not take kindly for my taking his property aboard my ship as a full crewman."

He realized he had no choice but to come clean. "It is true I am a poor liar. But it is also true that I belong to no one aboard the *Flying Horse*. The truth is I belong to Thomas Knight of Bath Town, collector of customs of North Carolina."

"North Carolina, you say?"

"Aye. It was Knight who sent me down here to fish these wrecks with a dozen men from Bath County where we all live. We've been here three weeks and have not much to show for it."

"I've seen you and your crew at work. Your captain is a mean fellow—I've observed him in action through me spyglass and don't much like the way he treats you fellows. Is he a former Royal Navy man by chance?"

"No, I don't think so. He's a merchantman from Charles Town. I don't much care for him, but I wonder if it would be right for me to leave my shipmates. Mr. Howard and Mr. Martin brought me down here as they were the one's commissioned by my proper owner Tobias Knight."

"I understand your predicament. But know this: if you sail with me, you sail as a free man."

"A free man?"

"Aye, a free man, free as the wind in our sails. Any soul that can outfight a Tiger shark and read and write is no ordinary being and I want him aboard my ship. I don't care the color of your skin. What do you say, Caesar? You'd better make up your mind quick because your captain is calling you."

He peered over the deck railing. The captain was standing on the poop deck next to several of the Bath County men, including Howard and Martin. He had pulled out a speaking trumpet and was shouting out that he was sending over a boat to collect *his* slave, which made Caesar angry.

I'm not your slave, you bastard; I belong to Thomas Knight, who at least treats me fairly and lets me read books even though I be in bondage.

"He seems convinced that you belong to him. So what is it to be, Caesar?"

"First, can I ask your name?"

"Thache—Edward Thache. As you may have surmised, I'm the captain of the *Margaret* here."

"There's no better captain than Thache, mate!" said one of the seamen.

"Aye, Captain Thache always treats us square, all right!" gushed another. "Don't make no difference if you're a darky or not."

There were cheerful mutters of agreement all around, including from two bare-chested black men armed with pistols and wearing shell and bead necklaces and golden earrings. He noticed them standing off to the right along with a bronze-skinned West Indian with a dark-blue ink "gunpowder spot"—or tattoo as the Caribbean natives called them—of a crescent moon perched above a brigantine on his chest. None of them appeared to be slaves, rather free men aboard Thache's ship. Caesar decided then and there that this was indeed the kind of captain that he wanted to serve under.

Studying him closely, Thache gave a knowing smile. "Quite frankly, my good man Caesar, I didn't know I was so popular," he said with a shrug. "What say you after that unexpected endorsement?"

He nodded his head vigorously. "Count me among your crew members, Captain—that's what I say!"

The crew gave a loud cheer that echoed all the way to the white sandy beach.

Thache nodded. "Good, it's settled then. Now let's make it official, shall—?"

But his words were cut off by the demonic whistle of a cannon ball, followed by a loud splash off the starboard bow. Crouching down to protect himself from a second projectile, Caesar saw Thache raise his spyglass and point it to the southeast.

"Spanish man-o-war!" he cried. "Hands, battle stations! Cut the anchor cable and raise the jib!"

The crew scrambled into immediate action and orders were shouted, only to be smothered by the deafening roar of a second round of cannon fire. Dropping to the deck, Caesar scuttled to the shelter of the larboard bulwark, took cover behind a pair of water-filled barrels and coils of rope, and covered his head with his hands.

"Looks like Captain Ayala Escobar has returned from Havana with reinforcements!" shouted Thache, peering through his glass on the quarterdeck behind the helmsman. "Make headway, Mr. Hands, due east and out of range of those devilish Spanish guns! We make for Nassau!"

A moment later the seventy-foot Jamaican sloop *Margaret*, an eighty tonner with fine lines, was on her way and the sweeps were deployed for added propulsion. Though terrified, Caesar couldn't help but feel he was in capable hands now with Thache in charge; he was glad he had abandoned his previous ship and cruel sea captain for this new vessel and particularly its leader.

Another cannon ball whistled overhead. But this time it wasn't intended for them, but the British wrecker sloop to the east. The ball struck the ship's stern, shattering the glass windows of the great cabin, blowing away a railing, and splintering the fragile wooden structure that surrounded the cabin just as the sloop came about. Caesar could smell the acrid sulfuric stench of gun powder and hear the screams of death and anguish from the sailors aboard the stricken vessel. It was his first time in battle and he found it terrifying yet utterly exhilarating.

He inched his way closer to Thache at the stern of the sloop, feeling that he would be safer nearer the captain, who already appeared to be a man who knew what he was doing.

He heard the long, drawn-out moaning sound of another lobbed Spanish shell and, again, he felt the blood curdle in his veins. It sounded to him like the cannon ball was headed straight for them, but it ended up splashing innocently into the water just short of a fourth boat trying to make its escape.

"Faster, Master Hands! This is not the time to spill the wind!"

"I'm on it, Captain! She'll be in New Providence before you know it!"

Another Spanish shell explosion rocked the previously hit ship. Peering over the gunwale, Caesar saw a pulverized foredeck with nine men down, five of them lying very still and the other four wriggling and moaning in agony. Were they just unlucky or was it destiny that they should take the brunt of the attack? he wondered as he watched Thache barking out orders from the raised quarterdeck.

And then, before he knew it, they were all alone at sea with no ships in sight and the smell of gunpowder was gone altogether. Cautiously, he stepped towards the quarterdeck.

"Thank you, Captain," he said. "Thank you for this chance to sail with you. I will be there for you when you need me and won't let you down, I can promise you that."

Thache smiled down at him, the dying orangish sunlight forming a kind of halo around his bearded head. "You'll have your work cut out for you, Caesar," he said. "Mark my words, you'll have your work cut out for you. But we'll make a seaman out of you yet."

"Aye, Captain," he said.

"Now go see the surgeon belowdecks and have that shark bite looked after. I wouldn't want anything to happen to you before I've made an old salt out of you, now would I?"

And with that he gave a wink and shouted out more instructions to his crew in a commanding yet mellifluous voice, looking to Caesar like Poseidon himself with the last rays of Floridian sunlight bleeding from the sky behind him.

PART 2

THE FLYING GANG

CHAPTER 7

NASSAU

MARCH 16, 1716

WITH BENJAMIN HORNIGOLD MATCHING HIM DRINK FOR DRINK, Thache sat outside on a splintery wooden bench at the Blue Parrot. The two sea captains—one well into his thirties, short and squatty, clean-shaven, and prone to violent outbursts, the other almost a decade younger, tall and sinewy, heavily bearded, and calm under fire—had taken a shine to one another and were enjoying their tankards of ale beneath a canvas awning while staring out at Nassau Harbor. The elongate stretch of shimmering blue water lay between Bay Street and the wharves lining the town's waterfront, and the low offshore spit of sandy beaches and palm trees of Hog Island. Though Thache had been gone only two and a half months, the nascent sea rover community had close to doubled in size in that short time. More than a dozen single-masted sailing vessels were anchored in the middle of the channel along with twenty or more small trading sloops, periaguas, canoes, and woodcutter launches. The streets, taverns, and beaches were packed with people of a mix of origins: British, West Indian, African, Portuguese, Danish, French, Irish, Dutch, with more arriving every day.

The biggest change he noticed was the increase in the number of women, woodcutters, wreckers, runaway slaves, and Indians on the island as word of the Florida treasures continued to spread. Where before females had been in the extreme minority, there were now a large number of wives and unattached women taking up residence on the island: serving at taverns, mending sails and clothing, laundering, cooking meals, and keeping the seamen company at night. Augmenting the growing female population were woodcutters driven from the Bay of Campeche in Central America; black and West Indian slaves on the run from their masters in the Windward and Leeward Islands, Cuba, Hispaniola, and Jamaica; and young adventurers without sea experience bent on going a-wrecking.

With the limited housing, a class system had developed with regard to living arrangements on the island. The new pirate republic's leading figures took up residence in the best homes: simple wood-framed houses looking out onto the bay. These notables included the most successful pirate captains and the merchant-smugglers who provided critical logistical support by buying the pirates' plunder with cheap rum, tobacco, and ammunition. Once these homes had belonged to New Providence's most reputable law-abiding colonists, but in the last few months most of these citizens had been forced to flee from the horde of surly and unruly gentlemen of fortune that had overtaken their island. Hornigold, as leader of the Flying Gang, and Thomas Barrow, chief of the wreckers, had harassed the law-abiding locals without mercy, shaking them down for drinking money and threatening or whipping anyone who refused them until only a few stubborn holdouts remained. The next best homes were the thatch-roofed huts of the second tier of wealthy pirates, usually former mariners, and those wreckers who had been smart enough to get in early on the action, before the Spanish began aggressively patrolling the waters around the shipwrecks. The humblest shelters were the tents, lean-tos, and hovels fashioned of driftwood, worm-eaten hulls, old spars, and palmetto thatch occupied by the logcutters, runaway slaves, West Indians, and unsuccessful wreckers.

All in all, Nassau now resembled an encampment of castaways, with bacchanalian sailors singing, dancing, drinking, and fornicating amid the cooking fires of a hundred huts, tents, and hovels. The air along the gently lapping beach was infused with fragrant smells of sea salt, tar, wood smoke, tobacco, gunpowder, smoldering meats, savory fish stews, and ale, wine, and rum punch to go along with the musky odor of the seamen. For most of the mariners it was a dream come true: ample food, drink, wenches, and leisure time. And when the loot ran out, there was always another merchant vessel to pillage or treasure wreck to dive upon.

"Where to next, Edward?" asked Hornigold, who though older and more seasoned as a privateer was not a mentor to Thache, but rather an equal on account of Thache's upper-middle-class background, experience as a Royal Navy officer, and ownership of his own vessel. "Are ye but finished with the wrecks?"

Thache lit his long-stem white clay pipe, which he had packed with fine Virginian tobacco. "The pickings are getting slimmer, but they're not tapped out yet. I was losing too many divers to sickness is the problem. It's a hard business taking gulps of air and poking along that sea bottom with sharks all around."

"Aye. That's why you were smart to go in with Jennings and plunder the camp. Though I hate to give that pompous Bermudan any credit after he stole me bonny Spanish sloop and claimed I was a lowly, thieving pirate. He thinks he's better than the rest of us."

"No, Benjamin, he's tricked himself into thinking that he's still a privateer fighting for Queen Anne when he, too, is little more than a common pirate. But it's just a game in his head that doesn't mean a bloody thing."

"He doesn't want no dance of death. Truth is, I don't either. That's why I'll stick to plundering the Spanish and French and won't lay a hand on an English or Dutch prize."

He took a hearty gulp of ale and puffed thoughtfully on his pipe. "Easier said than done when you have a demanding crew to contend with."

"Aye, but for the time being that's how I plan to operate. There ain't no use in making it easy for the King's Navy to hang you. Isn't that why ye obtained your commission from Governor Hamilton, so that you would be legal?"

"Upon my honor, but I'm beginning to think it doesn't mean much. The whispers out of Jamaica are that the governor may be recalled and the latest commissions he's awarded to Jennings, Leigh Ashworth, and the others may be revoked. The Spanish are up in arms and want Jennings hanged."

"When you were in Jamaica, you didn't arrange it with the governor to sign new departure papers?"

"Honestly, I didn't see the point."

"But you had a privateering commission, Edward. You had protection. At the time, didn't you think it was worth something?"

"By my reckoning, 'tis all a sham. But for the time being, I, too, plan on sticking to only Spanish and French prizes. As you say, there's no sense making it easy for the hangman."

"So you're definitely going on the account? Yesterday you weren't so sure."

"I'm still not. But I plan to seize prizes. They're far richer plunder than those wrecks, and I'm tired of the merchant trade."

"By the blood of Henry Morgan, you're going on the account, just like this old fart."

"You're not that old, Ben."

"Like hell I'm not. I'm nearly a decade older than ye, whippersnapper." Hornigold downed his ale, gave a satisfied sigh, and belched loudly. "We should sail in consort, Edward."

"I was thinking the same thing. The Straits and Hispaniola are ripe for the plucking, and with two sloops working in tandem we can take bigger prizes."

"And we can fence our plundered goods right here in Nassau. There's no government to stop us from doing as we please."

"I agree. But mark my words, they'll clean this place up and come for us eventually. The Crown always does when its commerce is at risk."

"That may be, but I wager that day is a long ways off. For now, we've found our lair for raiding prizes coming in and out of the Caribbean—and for trading on the black market. And its right here in the Bahamas."

It's true, Thache thought. Not only New Providence, but Eleuthera was being increasingly used as a remote outpost beyond the reach of the British Admiralty for fencing pirated goods. The freebooters were supported by the patronage of a growing network of resourceful Bahamian merchant-smugglers. Two of those were Hornigold's old pirate mate John Cockram and Cockram's influential father-in-law, Richard Thompson, the owners of the *Richard & John,* a fourteen-ton sloop with a shallow draught used to smuggle piratically-plundered goods. Cockram and his brothers, Joseph and Philip, were running a successful trading operation out of Harbor Island, shipping illicit cargoes to Charles Town and sugar and provisions back to Nassau. They competed with Benjamin Sims, a forty-year veteran of New Providence, and Neal Walker, owner of the sloop *Dolphin* which had been used to sell Henry Jennings's plunder. Through these savvy merchant-smugglers, the Bahamian pirates were able to sell their plunder and acquire in return much-needed ammunition and hard-to-get provisions to outfit their pirate fleets—all taking place along the margins of an overextended British Empire.

A bar maid with a hideous wart on her nose but a friendly smile came by their table and they ordered two more ales, which were promptly delivered. A moment later, the black sailor Caesar whom Thache had recently taken aboard his ship came by his table with a passel of white seamen. He recognized several of them as Caesar's old shipmates from the *Flying Horse,* which had limped into Nassau Harbor only this morning. His fingers inched towards his sling over his shoulders that held his holstered Queen Anne pistols. But from the men's earnest and friendly looking faces, he realized that they weren't here to cause him trouble for making their black friend part of his crew.

"Captain Thache," said Caesar. "These North Carolina men would like to have a word with you, if we not be interrupting. In fact, they would like to sign on with you. Or at least that's what they tell me."

He looked the men over, puffing on his pipe. "Is that so, gentlemen? I may have some openings, if you are indeed skilled mariners. What are your names?"

The tall one with the lantern jaw stepped forward. "I'm William Howard, quartermaster of the *Flying Horse*. We've left the company and want to sail with you, Captain Thache. Like Caesar, we were sent down to Florida to fish the wrecks by the order of Governor Eden of North Carolina and his customs inspector Tobias Knight. As you know, Master Knight is…or perhaps *was* the proper owner of our friend Caesar here. But now we want to sail with you, Captain. We've talked it over with Caesar and we want to join your crew."

"And just what kind of sea captain do you think I be?"

"Why you're a pirate captain, sir—a master of the sweet trade. Or that's what our mate Caesar led us to believe."

"Caesar told you that, eh?"

"Aye, Captain, he did."

"Well then, Caesar here is a sound judge of character. It is plain beyond disputing that you have come to the right place at the right time. I do happen to captain a vessel that proudly hoists the black flag, or will soon enough anyway, and am looking for able-bodied seamen to sign on as I will be going on the account soon, very soon."

Benjamin Hornigold, who had been watching the exchange with amusement, now spoke up. "Now wait just a minute, Edward," he protested. "I get at least one of these scallywags." He frowned at them. "Do you know who I am?"

"No, sir, not a clue," said Howard.

"Why I'm Ben Hornigold himself, the chief of the Flying Gang. Gut me for a preacher if ye haven't heard the name bandied about."

Howard removed his weather-beaten tricorn, stiffened ramrod straight, and looked at him deferentially. "Begging your pardon, Captain. Indeed, we all know of ye and your exploits," he said. The other men nodded vigorously.

Hornigold gave a curmudgeonly smile. "Thank the Lord up high for that. Now I want you to know that while you're in Nassau, you're under my personal protection. Were you also aware of that?"

Thache couldn't suppress a grin. "He's just putting on airs with you fellows. Now tell us who the rest of ye be?"

A second man stepped forward. "I'm John Martin, bosun."

"Garret Gibbons, helmsman," said the next man.

"John Giles, seaman," said a fourth.

"Richard Greensail, seaman," said a skinny black African, who made friendly eye contact with Caesar, which told Thache that they were mates.

Six more men stepped forward and gave their names and positions aboard the *Flying Horse*. When they were finished, Hornigold said, "William Howard, I want you aboard my ship as my new quartermaster. But of course it will have to be voted on by my crew."

"Might I inquire, Captain, what happened to your previous quartermaster?"

"He got so drunk last night that he cracked his skull and is in a very bad way. He won't be able to sail with us, I'm afraid. Now the rest of you can sign on with Captain Thache as you like, but I want Mr. Howard here." He looked back at him. "You look to me to be a man who brooks no opposition and can lead a boarding party. Would I be right in assuming that, Mr. Howard?"

"Curse me for a lubber, Captain Hornigold, if I'm not your man. And if I am to serve as your quartermaster, providing the crew accepts me once we set sail, would it be for that fine eight-gun sloop in the middle of the channel called the *Benjamin*?"

"That would be correct, Mr. Howard. What do you think of the name?"

"The name?"

"The name *Benjamin*. I named the ship after myself. You don't find issue with that, do you?"

"Why should I? All it means is you take pride in your skill as a sea captain."

"No, he's in love with himself just like Narcissus—and that's God's truth," quipped Thache. "But he can take a prize as good as anyone. Which is why we'll be sailing together, gentlemen, in the coming days. Mr. Martin, Mr. Gibbons, Mr. Greensail, and the rest of you—welcome aboard the *Margaret*. But first you have to agree to the articles."

"Yes, yes, the articles," said John Martin. "I've heard it's the way of the sweet trade, but I haven't seen it for meself. How does it work for your ship?"

"They're the rules we live by. Every man gets a fair share of plunder, has a vote in councils, and gets taken care of when he's disabled from sickness or battle. It's an oath we swear by, and I'll expect you to sign your name or make your mark to prove that you've agreed to follow the articles, as your mate Caesar here did three days ago in the Straits. You can sign once you're on board, and when you do, it'll be for yourselves and not no king, parliament, merchant man, or cruel navy captain. Mr. Howard will do the same for Captain Hornigold here. What do you say, men? Shall we drink on it?"

The men let out a hearty rumble of concurrence and John Martin smiled and raised his tankard. "We'll drink with you and Captain Hornigold, all right! We'll curse all Spanishers and King George too, and we'll drink to the health of the rightful heir to the throne, King James, who ain't no pretender! But first can you tell us where we're headed?"

Thache stroked his growing black beard, which now ran a full hand below his chin. "The Windward Passage and Hispaniola—to take Spanish and French prizes."

"Aye, Captain, we're your men," said Martin with a gleam in his eyes. "I suppose then that we be the Bath County pirates."

"Oh no you're not, lads," cried Hornigold. "We are—all of us—part of something much grander than that. We're the bloody Flying Gang—and don't you ever forget it!"

CHAPTER 8

BAHIA HONDA, NORTHWEST CUBA

APRIL 9, 1716

SINCE THEY HAD SET COURSE from New Providence and began their campaign of plunder along the northern edge of the Spanish Main, what Caesar had enjoyed most of all was the feeling of freedom. By getting an equal vote and an equal share of the prizes with the other sailors in the Flying Gang, he inhabited a new world where ability, not color, determined his status. It made him feel somehow whole again. He was a real person in control of his own life, someone of value in the world instead of a slave to another man's dreams, a determiner of his own fate.

Every day was a new and exciting adventure, and he was grateful to Thache for giving him the opportunity to be free again, something he had not been since his capture from his West African village as a small boy. Caesar was born of the Ibo people in the northeastern corner of the slave-trading province of Benin, and his father had been an important tribal sub-chief. Unbeknownst to him, his fellow Ibo tribesmen had predominated among those enslaved in the Chesapeake region during the past thirty years, specifically those in Virginia and the Low Country plantations of colonial South Carolina. Though as an equal-wage-earning seaman he was not truly one-hundred-percent equal—the quartermaster tended to assign him and the other Africans, West Indians, and mulattoes more than their fair share of the strenuous labor like moving cannons and cleaning the scuppers—he knew he was as free as any black man outside of Africa. Given his harsh treatment during his transport from Africa to Barbados, and during his enslavement in South Carolina prior to being sold to the kindly Tobias Knight in Bath Town, that was freedom enough.

Sailing in consort with Hornigold, Thache had piloted the *Margaret* from Nassau to the sporadically settled coast of northwestern Cuba, which straddled the shipping lanes connecting Havana and the Spanish Main, New Orleans, and France. Passing through the Straits of Florida and giving Havana a wide berth, they scoured the scantily patrolled coastal waters ringing the island's northern shore until they found a prize. Making landfall on April 8, they found the *Mary of Rochelle*, a large merchant sloop flying French colors, near the secluded harbor of Mariel. Undercrewed and lightly armed, the French vessel was no match for Hornigold in his *Benjamin* or Thache in his *Margaret* and the captain surrendered without a fight. In his first boarding action, Caesar joined the rowdy prize crew and helped transfer half the cargo to the *Benjamin*, while Thache kept the rest aboard the *Mary of Rochelle*, had the *Margaret's* stores moved onboard, and converted the captured vessel into an eight-gun sloop-of-war with a total crew size of more than eighty men. The nearly empty *Margaret* was then handed over to the vanquished French captain along with food, water, and navigational instruments.

With the new prize *Mary* rigged for piratical action, the two sloops continued west along the coast. They were making fourteen knots now, and Caesar liked the feel of the wind on his face, watching the flocks of seabirds and schools of dolphins racing the boat, and the warmth of the tropical sun on his bare chest. Under questioning, the captured French captain had told them that they would find a large French merchant sloop called the *Marianne of Santo Domingo* further west at *Bahia Hondo*—the Bay of Hounds. The secluded bay in Northwestern Cuba was a favorite rendezvous for English forces to obtain fresh fish and careen their vessels between Jamaica and points northward. The merchant ship was said to be en route from Hispaniola to the swampy French port of New Orleans under the command of a French naval officer, Ensign Le Gardew. It was also said to possess a very rich cargo consisting of European goods for the Spanish trade.

Two hours later Thache and Hornigold reached the Bay of Hounds.

"Four sail!" Caesar heard Garret Gibbons, the masthead lookout, shout down to the captain when they reached the bay entrance outside the fringing reef. Since they had taken the new ship, Caesar had been acting as the captain's steward on the quarterdeck.

Squinting into the sun, Thache called up to him. "How stand they, Mr. Gibbons?"

"To the southward, two points upon the larboard bow."

"Colors?"

Now that Gibbons had identified the number of the ships with the naked eye, he proceeded to peer through his brass telescope. "Three British, one French."

"What class?"

The lookout spied for several seconds through his glass. "Frenchie's a merchantman. The King's vessels…I cannot tell. Two appear to be sloops-of-war, though they fly no black flag. The other, to the east of the French vessel and privateers, is a small merchantman with British colors."

"Are the sloops plundering the Frenchie?"

"Looks that way, Captain. There also appears to be a periagua tied up with the fleet. Aye, they've joined, too, in plundering the merchantman."

"Is the French vessel the *Marianne*, Mr. Gibbons? Can you make out her stern through the glass?"

From the quarterdeck, Caesar watched with eager anticipation as the lookout studied the ship closely. "Can't tell, Captain. No clear view. But she be big enough and well-armed."

Thache nodded. "All right, stand by." He turned to Israel Hands, the ship's navigator and first mate. "I need you to climb aloft to be certain, Master Hands. You have the best eyes of all of us and we need to be sure what the bloody hell we've got here before we sail into that bay. Take me glass, man."

"Aye, Captain."

While Hands quickly scaled the rigging to the maintop, Thache was hailed by Hornigold from the quarterdeck of the Benjamin. Caesar handed Thache his speaking trumpet and the two sea captains conversed for several minutes as Israel Hands and Hornigold's masthead lookout closely scrutinized the flotilla anchored inside the Bay of Hounds. The anxious seconds ticked off. As the drama built up with still no resolution, Caesar felt a ripple of nervous excitement. Who were these interlopers taking the French prize in the bay? Were they pirates? But then why would they fly British colors if they were common freebooters?

And then suddenly, the voice of Hornigold's lookout cut through the thick tropical air. "By thunder, it's Jennings and the *Barsheba!* She and her consort have weighed anchor and are coming for us!"

"They're giving chase?" demanded Hornigold.

"Aye, Captain! And the French vessel, it's definitely the *Marianne* all right! I can make her out clearly now!"

"He's right!" confirmed Israel Hands from aloft to Thache and the *Mary's* crew. "They're hard on our bow! And they've got twenty guns betwixt them!"

That's a lot of firepower, thought Caesar. All the same, the *Benjamin* and *Mary* could match Jennings's cannons pound for pound. A part of him wanted desperately to fight a pitched battle; the other, more pragmatic side of him, said that the best thing to do would be to unlimber the jib and make a run for it. But which one would Thache and Hornigold, the only ones with actual authority during an engagement, choose?

Suddenly, Thache sounded the general alarm through his speaking trumpet as Hornigold did the same aboard the *Benjamin.*

"Hands to quarters! Hands to quarters!"

As the crew scurried about, Thache yelled up again to Israel Hands in the maintop. "What about the other vessels? What the devil are they doing?"

"The *Marianne* is staying put with the periagua and British merchantman."

Now Thache looked at Hornigold and spoke again through his brass trumpet. "What do you want to do, Ben? It appears your nemesis is heading our way with the intention of taking your ship from you again. Tell me now, do you intend to hand it over to him like you did your Spanish sloop in Nassau, or put up a fight?"

"Damn that foppish prig Jennings to hell—of course I'd like to fight him!" shouted back Hornigold. "But you know as well as I that a man who shows too much of the lion and not enough of the fox does not last long at sea. Unless my crew chooses to fight, I'm afraid I will have to hold back from an engagement."

"If you're taking a vote, I wouldn't be laggardly about it. As for me, I have no intention of crossing swords with Jennings and risk losing my ship. I'm taking my crew and continuing towards the setting sun in search of prizes."

"Godspeed then, Edward! We'll rendezvous near *Cayo Buenavista!*"

"Good luck to you too, my friend! And keep a weather-eye over your shoulder! There's worse scupperlouts out there than Jennings!"

As the *Mary* dashed off with the wind hard on her starboard beam, Caesar noticed that the hour glass had turned. He flipped it over and the fine white sand began to filter down again, signifying the beginning of another hour. But to him, it was far more than that. It was another hour of excitement among a flotilla of pirates. Another hour of freedom from the drudgery of slavery as a gentleman of fortune in search of rich plunder. Another hour of sticking it to greedy ship owners, slavers, and merchant captains who thought they ruled the world and could order others about like chattel with no repercussions. He felt a powerful sense of subversive pride knowing he was bringing such men down, even if only a peg or two and for a brief moment in history.

He looked at Thache standing next to his helmsman, whom he towered over by at least six inches. The man was indeed a wise captain with the best interests of his men at heart, which Caesar realized was why the crew stood steadfast by him. He would not risk their lives in a fight they were not guaranteed to win, or that might result in significant death or injuries. It was a code of honor for him, an unspoken pact between him and his men.

And having seen Thache do it on two separate occasions—once in the Florida Straits and now here off the northern coast of Cuba—Caesar knew he had just learned an important lesson he would never forget.

Don't engage an enemy unless you can win at no cost to yourself—or are backed into a corner and have no choice.

CHAPTER 9

WESTERN CUBA AND ISLA DE LOS PIÑOS

APRIL 12-MAY 26, 1716

EDWARD THACHE FIRST MET "BLACK" SAM BELLAMY—the young, dark-haired Massachusetts mariner who would one day go on to command the *Whydah*, one of the most powerful pirate men-of-war ever—three days later on the west coast of Cuba. The two struck an instant chord of friendship. Both had served in the Royal Navy and knew firsthand the brutality and hypocrisy of that service, and they were equally suspicious of avaricious merchant men. Though Thache had grown up in relative wealth as the son of a Jamaica planter-mariner while Bellamy was born into a poor family in Devon, England, Thache never adopted the sneering contempt for the lower classes of his well-born contemporaries. That was one of the reasons, along with his inherent love of the sea, that he had never followed in his father's footsteps and taken to being a sugar plantation owner.

Since he was a boy, a part of him had looked down with disgust upon the forced labor of black African men and women. His father had been considered one of Spanish Town's "enlightened" slave owners and had treated those indentured to him far above average, but Thache was still disgusted by the whole enterprise of enslavement. Not only that, but the young future Blackbeard looked suspiciously upon the increasingly rigid discipline and authoritarian approach of both the Crown and Jamaica's plantation elite. Unlike most of his peers, he believed in the equality of men and that a person should be judged for his individual merits rather than his royal blood or the economic station held by his father and mother. Which was why he and Bellamy were instant brethren. It was a bond that would not be broken until one of them died.

The story behind "Black" Sam Bellamy's induction into the Flying Gang with Thache and Hornigold was an amusing one, and Thache had insisted that the young sea captain, two years his junior, tell it to him more than once while deep into their cups of rum. At *Bahia Honda*, it was Bellamy and his crew of New Englanders in the periauger that had helped Jennings and his Jamaican cohorts take the French *Marianne* and then subsequently plunder her. From the bay's entrance, Thache had observed Bellamy's small, fast boats tied astern, but at the time he hadn't known to whom they belonged. When Jennings had spotted Hornigold and his consort outside the entrance—who unbeknownst to the pompous Bermudan happened to be Thache in the recently taken *Mary of Rochelle*—he had immediately given the order for his flotilla to weigh anchor and give chase. In the meantime, Bellamy and his second-in-command, Paulsgrave Williams, were still aboard the *Marianne* with their periagua tied astern. They helped the prize crew raise the French ship's anchors and watched as Jennings and his two sloops raced off. By the time the plundered *Marianne* was underway, the fleet had passed out of sight. It was at that moment Bellamy saw an opportunity.

As the *Marianne* pulled out of the harbor, he gave a signal and his men rose up in unison, surprising Jennings's prize crew and the French prisoners, and took possession of the ship and nearly thirty thousand pieces of eight, worth over seven thousand British pounds. While a portion of Bellamy's men held their captives at gunpoint, the others quickly hauled their periauger alongside and loaded sacks and chests of coins aboard. Keeping an eye on Jennings and his two ships in pursuit of Hornigold and Thache, more than six miles off, Bellamy got his men aboard the small vessels and rowed off into the wind. Meanwhile, Jennings, realizing that he was never going to catch up to Hornigold's two boats and wondering why the *Marianne* had fallen so far behind, decided to turn around and return to the bay. But Jennings was too late. Bellamy had run off with his entire haul, leaving nothing behind but a furious crew close to mutiny. Three days later, Bellamy and Williams caught up with Hornigold and Thache off the western coast of Cuba and the pirates agreed to join forces.

Thache had never seen a bigger smile on Ben Hornigold's face than when Bellamy told him how he had stolen Jennings's treasure from right under the pompous son of a rum puncheon's nose. Then and there Hornigold decided to add Bellamy and his crew to that of the *Benjamin*. After the pirate articles were read, they joined the crew, and when the Flying Gang took its next prize, the ship was awarded to Bellamy. Thache knew that the twenty-seven-year-old Bellamy did not have the experience he or Hornigold possessed, but he liked the young upstart's spunk and he had earned the respect of his crew by daringly outwitting the veteran privateer Jennings. Bellamy now had a well-built ocean-going sloop at his disposal, a chest of treasure in his hold, and two of the most experienced sea rovers of the day as his consort—Hornigold and Thache. All the impetuous "Black" Sam needed was a few three- or four-pounders to arm his new bellicose pirate-of-war.

During the next two weeks, the Flying Gang continued to prowl the western end of Cuba, hoping to intercept Spanish and French vessels navigating through the busy sea lanes of the Yucatan Channel. But instead of a fat prize, they came across yet another pirate: a Frenchman named Olivier La Buse, captain of the armed sloop *Postillion*. Although Hornigold clung to the notion that he was merely a British patriot carrying on a righteous war against England's two biggest enemies, Spain and France, he was convinced by Thache and Bellamy to form an alliance with La Buse and his French corsairs, who were bona fide buccaneers with no reservations about plundering any country for profit. After all, Thache and Bellamy reminded the older, stodgy Hornigold, they were "enemies of all mankind" now that they had clearly chosen to go on the account and there was no turning back. But even more importantly, they weren't fighting for Britain, they were fighting against the system: European navies, royals, captains, shipowners, slave traders, the whole bloody lot of them, and many of Hornigold's crew members agreed, especially his highly influential North Carolinian quartermaster, William Howard.

Soon, the powerful new pirate consortium—with Hornigold as the flotilla's overall commodore and Thache, Bellamy, and La Buse as captains—had taken several English and Spanish ships and they decided to make anchorage at *Isla de los Piños* to careen their vessels. In only three weeks' time, they had accumulated solid stores of drink, coins, provisions, spare rigging, gunpowder, needles and twine, and cocoa as well as some much-needed skilled crewmen pressed into service. As they put into a sandy bay on the Southern Cuban island for fresh water and repairs, they came across four English sloops topping off water and firewood supplies. The pirate captains promptly announced to the British seamen that their vessels were to be commandeered to assist with the careening process: removing the sea debris that had accumulated on the hulls of the flotilla's vessels and patching up any holes.

It was a grueling ten days in the sweltering mid-May heat, but Thache knew it was a necessary duty to perform at least twice a year, and preferably three times. Below the waterline, wooden vessels were vulnerable to the destructive, hole-boring powers of the shipworm or teredo, a warm-water mollusk that, unchecked, could perforate the hull of a ship in just a few months. The first step was to lighten the load of each of the ships before they could be hauled-over. All the ships' guns, stores of food, water and spirits, the topmast, and most of the ballast stones were removed temporarily to the shore. The English sloops were then used to heel the *Mary*, *Benjamin*, and other vessels over onto their beam ends using a line running from the English ships' capstans to the masts of the pirate vessels. Using the English support vessels during the careening process made the job significantly easier, allowing the vessels to be heeled over onto both sides for cleaning and refitting. The main drawback of the process was that when exposed in this state, pirates made for vulnerable targets to prowling Royal Navy ships and Spanish or French pirate hunters.

Once the ships were ready and in position to be properly cleaned and repaired, the bottom planking was inspected by Thache and the other captains personally, as well as by their respective master carpenters. Where the wood planks were weak, rotting, or penetrated by boring shipworms, they were replaced. The hull was then scraped clean of encrusted seaweed, barnacles, and other bottom-clinging organisms that drastically slowed a vessel down. Speed was a pirate ship's most cherished attribute and every possible obstruction was scraped off the hulls to make the ships sail faster. The final step was to restuff all the narrow seams between the planking with oakum, a mixture of individual strands of hempen rope and tar, and seal each seam with heated pitch. Meanwhile, while all of this was going on, Thache had the crew repair all the worn and tired rigging, patch and replace the sails, and clean, oil, and prime his six guns and repair their carriages to make sure they were ready for use at a moment's notice. When he was finished, he removed the name *Mary* from the escutcheon and painted on the name *Margaret* for his true love, making her look like a brand-new ship.

It was a tough job to repair and refit all four of the ships, but the English boats made it much easier and the Flying Gang was sailing east again by mid-May. The diverse rogue fleet continued along the southern shore of Cuba and then eastward to the western shores and coves of Hispaniola. The island was well positioned for raiding merchantmen coming in and out of the Caribbean, and its western shores were an ideal place from which to launch lightning strikes against shipping passing through the frequently-used Windward Passage. La Buse knew of some good hideouts along the shores of sparsely populated island, and directed the fleet in that direction. A lair was located and the members of the roving flotilla resolved to work in tandem to take as much treasure and necessary provisions as possible.

Though the multifarious company made for an unusual team, Thache truly enjoyed the company of Hornigold, Bellamy, La Buse, Paulsgrave Williams, and their opinionated and occasionally unruly crews. He took a particular liking to Bellamy—indeed the lad was like a feisty younger brother to him. Together, they hoisted cups of wine and rum in honor of the James Stuart living in exile in Rome and to the damnation of the schnitzel-eating, Hanoverian imposter King George. Unlike Hornigold and Jennings, Thache and Bellamy no longer had any illusions about being privateers. They were pirates, pure and simple, with no sympathy for the shipowners, merchant and navy captains, and royals who dominated commerce at the expense of the working people of colonial America. Eventually, Bellamy was able to convince him that they were, in fact, really no different that Robin Hood and his Merry Men, taking from the wealthy merchants and enriching poor and mistreated colonial sailors. Although Thache and Williams came from well-to-do backgrounds, that didn't make one iota of difference in their outlook. More than Bellamy and Hornigold who had risen from humble roots, they knew how rigged the system was against the common, hardworking seaman and those indentured to a world of servitude to rich men. They were both swept up by "Black" Sam's powerful revolutionary words, but they were also motivated by their desire for adventure and riches of their own coupled with their Jacobite aversion towards King George and sympathy for the Scots and their deposed Stuart king.

While Thache and Bellamy got along famously, Hornigold would eventually butt heads with Bellamy and La Buse regarding the prizes the group took. Hornigold remained steadfast in his insistence that the Flying Gang restrict their attacks to the vessels of England's former enemies—France and Spain. La Buse was, of course, one of those former enemies, and Bellamy had no misgivings about seizing the property of all nations and desired to openly wage war against the rich, as a Robin Hood of the sea. By the end of May, with the friction amongst the pirate leaders increasing daily, Hornigold decided to leave his new partners and return to Nassau to cash in his share of loot, with the intention of regrouping with Thache, Bellamy, and La Buse later that summer.

It was then Thache decided to sail home to Jamaica to fence his own goods and visit his family. But there was just one problem: Like his new hero Robin Hood, he was now a wanted man.

CHAPTER 10

GOVERNOR'S PALACE
WILLIAMSBURG, VIRGINIA

JUNE 15, 1716

"THANK YE FOR COMING, HARRY," said Lieutenant Governor Alexander Spotswood to his guest, Captain Harry Beverley, seated across from his expansive mahogany desk. "You know why you are here. I have a mission for you that will render great service to His Majesty King George. Here are the official orders."

Picking up two pages of foolscap from his desk, he handed the orders with an air of officiality to Beverley and then waited in formal silence while his guest read over the directive. Spotswood took unabashed pleasure in his lordly station, even though he was merely a deputy governor for the absentee earl of Orkney, George Hamilton, the older brother of Jamaica's governor, Archibald Hamilton. He wanted to build up the suspense of the moment and underscore the importance of the enterprise to both the Crown and the King's immediate representative in Virginia. In fact, every aspect of the scheduled meeting between the governor and captain of the armed merchant sloop *Virgin* of Virginia was arranged to emphasize both Spotswood's and the Crown's authority.

En route to the governor's *sanctum sanctorum* and chamber of power, Captain Harry Beverley—the older brother of Spotswood's friend Robert Beverley of the notable Virginia Beverley family—had been politely shuttled by a small army of butlers, secretaries, and servants through a carefully orchestrated procession of spaces moving toward and culminating in Spotswood's elegantly appointed, second-floor office. Down Palace Green, through the ornamental iron gates, across the forecourt, up the stone steps, into the great hall with its display of bayonet-tipped muskets and the royal coat of arms, up the stairs, down another resplendent hallway, into the governor's upper middle room, and finally into the upholstered silk chair in front of Spotswood's spacious desk where the captain now sat reading his maritime orders.

But despite the glamor of the governor's new residence, it was still unfinished and he, his family, and staff had yet to move in since many rooms had yet to be finished. Spotswood was unmarried and had no wife and children of his own. But he did have a niece, a secretary, and several other non-Negro servants that lived with him in his current temporary home and would share the Governor's Palace with him once it was complete. The loud whacking of hammers and grinding of sawblades echoed down the hallway throughout the work week and showed no signs of letting up.

When Beverley turned to the second page, Spotswood said, "As you and I have discussed, a nest of pirates has taken over New Providence. Their presence will prove dangerous to British commerce if not timely suppressed. These men are mostly English wreckers salvaging the remains of the Spanish treasure fleet. But I am told their numbers are augmented daily by logwood cutters from the Bays of Campeche and Honduras being expelled by the Spanish. It is both events that have led a considerable number of rough and dangerous characters to head for the Bahamas. The sheltered harbor at Nassau has become the meeting place for this motley gang of treasure hunters, logwood cutters, privateers, and unemployed seamen. That is why I am officially commanding you to provision a crew and take your sloop *Virgin* to visit the sites of the Florida shipwrecks. Once there, you are to recover what you can of the Spanish silver and gold, and from thence you will sail to New Providence and take an inventory of these pirates."

Captain Beverley continued to read. "Yes, I see. It's all spelled out here."

"In your investigation of the current situation on New Providence, the scope of your inquiries and observations will include but not be limited to the following: assessing the total number of inhabitants, the number of pirate vessels and pirates among the population, the nature of their armament, and the state of old Fort Nassau. You shall, of course, carry the King's arms for your own protection."

"Of course, Governor."

"If we're going to stop these malicious scoundrels, we're going to need to know everything about them: how they operate, their leadership structure, number of ships in their consort, and number of men and guns each vessel carries."

"We'll have to be armed to the teeth just to get close to the wrecks."

"No doubt. I leave the details to you. Your orders also call for you to determine whether any of the wrecked treasure ships are near any coasts or islands belonging to His Majesty."

Beverley looked up from reading, eyebrow raised. "And if they are?"

"Then you are to recover as much treasure as you can. And by doing thus, you will be asserting the claim of His Majesty to ye said wrecks by the Law of Nations as being within the jurisdiction of the Admiralty of Great Britain."

"How am I to be financed?"

"You will receive the Crown's backing to cover all of your expenses, as well as financial aid from individuals who hope to share in any recovered treasure."

"And if something happens to me and my crew? How will their families be looked after?"

"The shares from any money or other returns from the wrecks will be disbursed to wives, children, and grandchildren, as appropriate. But nothing's going to happen, Captain. It's going to be a stroll through the park."

Beverley's skeptical expression showed he didn't believe him. "It will be a lot more dangerous than that, Governor, and you know it."

Spotswood feigned a look of casual disregard. "Perhaps, but I know you're up to the task. You are up to it, aren't you, Harry?"

"Yes, Governor, of course I am. I just want to make sure I have the latest intelligence and the government's full support. From what I've heard, there are some five hundred of these pirates down there, and more arriving every day. They've been salvaging from the Spanish wrecks and engaging in robberies, mostly on the Spanish."

"Quite right. So you know the likely consequences of allowing such a motley crew of robbers to establish themselves on the island. Why I am told that they've captured a ship of thirty-two guns. What a vessel of that force, manned by a company of such wicked desperadoes, may be able to attempt is easy to imagine."

"Is His Majesty the King aware of the extent of the problem?"

"I have notified the King, the Board of Trade, and the Admiralty concerning this scourge in our hemisphere, and will be sending them another detailed report in the coming weeks, at which time I shall inform them of your enterprise. I consider it of the utmost importance that the full extent of the problem be brought to the attention of His Majesty and his ministers. It goes without saying that it is in the interest of Great Britain that some government be speedily established upon Providence Island and the place made defensible against the sudden attempt of pirates or the neighboring Spaniards, who have so often obstructed the settlement thereof. But that, of course, is going to take some time. So in the interim we have you, Captain Beverley. You are the eyes and ears of His Majesty in assessing the strength, whereabouts, and disposition of these seafaring rogues."

"It will take three weeks to outfit my boat. I can set sail in early July."

Spotswood shifted his itchy powdered wig on his head, gently rubbed his bald pate, and smiled officially as the knock of hammers and scraping of saw blades reverberated down the hallway. "Splendid," he said.

"Before I take my leave, Governor, I should like to point out one thing."

"And what would that be, Captain?"

"Many merchants here in Virginia and in the Carolinas believe that the men fishing those Florida wrecks are not pirates at all. It's been said that Governor Hamilton of Jamaica and other governors have issued letters of marque to lawfully salvage the Spanish treasures."

"You're referring to Henry Jennings and his gang of marauders who invaded the Spanish camp under Admiral Salmon."

"Yes, sir, him and others."

"Jennings and his ilk are nothing but pirates. They are the villains of all nations for their predations."

"But the laws of salvage are not clear."

"They are clear enough that Hamilton's so-called 'privateers' are but simple thieves. They plundered Spanish gold, from Spanish property, while still in possession of Spain's citizens, and in a time of peace no less. And they did this from a part of Florida further south from the Spanish territory lawfully claimed by Carolina at the twenty-ninth parallel. Furthermore, they also illegally disguised themselves with Spanish colors."

"So you consider my commission authorized by you as somehow different than the commission issued by Governor Hamilton?"

"Yes. For the simple reason that it *is* different."

"With all due respect, the two enterprises sound awfully similar. If I take Spanish silver and gold, whether from the sea bottom or not, how am I any different from Jennings and his crew?"

"Ye just let me worry about that, Captain Beverley. I am your guarantee."

"Yes, but why then did you imprison Captain Forbes?"

"Oh, you've heard I had him locked up?"

"Aye, Governor."

"The reason is not because he was one of the original salvors and drove the Spaniards from their batteries on the coast of Florida, but because he was involved in the illegal capture of a French merchantman. Unfortunately, Captain Forbes escaped from confinement."

"If you're sending me to visit the sites of the shipwrecks and recover what I can of the Spanish treasure, is it not really just plain looting dressed up in the guise of protecting Spanish property?"

"I believe you're overthinking this, Captain. You and me, we are on the side of the righteous—we are not the evil, lawless ones here. What we do, we do on behalf of His Majesty—not to line our own pockets. That, sir, is the difference."

"I must confess that I am surprised at this explosion of piracy resulting from the wrecking of the Spanish treasure fleet. It seems to have inspired something approaching madness."

"The Spanish blame the British government for their losses, so diplomacy is essential at this juncture to the preservation of our overseas trade. Mark my words, this nest of pirates—which has been established on New Providence and is being built up by the addition of loose, disorderly people from the Bay of Campeche, Jamaica, Bermuda, and elsewhere—is going to prove disastrous to British commerce, if not timely suppressed. With this new thirty-gun vessel of force they have captured, they are already formidable compared to the number of merchantmen passing through these seas from Jamaica. That is why I am commissioning you to make inquiries as to their strength and designs."

"I am told that the residents of Carolina, as with residents in the Caribbean, have begged the King for some resolution to the lack of government in their colony. In my view, the sooner His Majesty clears out the pirates and establishes a legitimate government in the Bahamas, the better."

"The Bahamas hold the key to the Gulf of Florida. That's why I've asked the Admiralty for an additional guardship. We certainly cannot rely on that gang of cutthroats in New Providence to police the area. The bandits claim that they will only seize French and Spanish ships, but as we both know they have already plundered some trading vessels belonging to these parts. They must be stopped."

Beverley stood up and gave a formal bow as he took his leave. "And they will be, Governor," he said, firmly clutching his orders. "Together with the Admiralty, we shall drive these vipers from their viper nest."

"I am told they call themselves the 'Flying Gang.' As if they are some sort of sporting club. Well, I don't believe that rabble will be feeling very sporting when we are finished with them."

"No, sir, I should think not."

"Godspeed, Captain, and for heaven's sake don't get caught by the Spanish."

"Upon my honor I'll do me best, Governor."

"No, ye will have to do better than that, Harry. Don't get caught—savvy?" And with that Spotswood—the former British Army officer wounded from an exploding cannonball at Blenheim—sent him off with a crisp military salute.

CHAPTER 11

THACHE PLANTATION
SPANISH TOWN, JAMAICA

JULY 27, 1716

WITH HIS BODY ON HIGH ALERT and eyes searching the woods for signs of the King's men, Thache put his booted heels to his horse. The fleet-footed Arabian lurched forward, quickly gaining him much-needed distance between himself and his pursuers who wanted to shackle him in chains. His father had given him the horse for his sixteenth birthday, and he had named him "Henry" after the legendary British privateer Sir Henry Morgan, whose romantic swashbuckling exploits he had listened to with starry-eyed reverence at his father's side growing up in Jamaica. As he reined Henry and pointed the equine north again, his lengthy black beard fluttered gracefully in the wind beneath his tricorn hat. He had long been an excellent rider from his years in the fields on his father's Spanish Town plantation, and he knew how to get as much out of a horse as a ship at sea.

The eastern sky showed the first streaks of pre-dawn, and the air was fragrant with wet tropical dew and the sweet smell of cane sugar. The deeply rutted dirt road was rough and uneven but Thache paid it little mind as he galloped at full tilt, Henry's neck stretching parallel to the ground and legs churning in a perfect rhythm. At one point, he came upon a British foot patrol and was forced to dash through the woods, ducking under low boughs and leaping over fallen trunks until he was able to return to the road. Soon, he reached his family's plantation and coaxed Henry up the final dirt lane that led to the main house. Tying the horse to a wooden rail, he slipped quietly into the house, tip-toed to his room, stuffed his clothes and valuables in a pair of satchels, and woke up his step-mother Lucretia and sister Elizabeth to tell them the unfortunate news of his impending arrest and to say goodbye.

With a pair of lit candles, they went into the parlor so they wouldn't wake his step-siblings: young Cox, Rachel, and Thomas. "I am sorry to have awoken ye," he said to them as they stood there startled in their bed gowns. "But I wanted to come and say goodbye because...because I know it may be the last time I see you for some time."

"What are you talking about? What has happened?" asked his step-mother.

"You know how I told you that Lord Hamilton had put out orders that Jennings and the other privateer captains were not allowed to leave the island. Well, since he issued that order, the situation has gotten much worse. The governor himself has been arrested for complicity with pirates, and all commissioned and non-commissioned sea captains who have taken Spanish or French prizes are to be arrested as well. That's me, my fair ladies."

"Good heavens," gasped his sister Elizabeth. "So you think the King's men are coming here to arrest you?"

"Aye, they'll be here soon enough. They almost got me at the Yellowfin Tavern."

"But how do they know it was you?"

"A traitor there recognized me and pointed me out to the King's men."

"Good heavens," exclaimed his step-mother. "That is bad luck."

"The man's a drunken lout named Forrester. He has an axe to grind against me for turning him away as a crewman before I sailed off with my commission for the Florida wrecks. I instructed my quartermaster, John Martin, to make ready the ship while I said my goodbyes to my family. I didn't want to leave without bidding you both farewell, and I also needed to fetch some valuables that are dear to me. One of them being an engraved silver pocket watch from my Margaret, the young woman from Philadelphia I have told you about."

"If Governor Hamilton has been removed, who has taken his place?" asked Lucretia.

"Peter Heywood, the leader of the opposition on the governing Council."

"So he's been officially appointed governor then?" asked Elizabeth.

"Aye, since yesterday when the HMS *Adventure* arrived from Britain. The Assembly of Jamaica and a former commodore submitted damning evidence against him to the King. As his first act as governor, Heywood has launched a full investigation of anyone issued a commission by Hamilton. The former governor is to be loaded onto the *Adventure* and delivered to England in chains."

Lucretia shook her head. "I've heard the Spanish were making waves, but I had no idea it was going to come to this."

"The Spanish and French are both out for blood. A flurry of hostile letters has been sent by the governors of Cuba and French Hispaniola. They name names. Jennings, Willis, Fernando, Ashworth, and several other commissioned privateers are on the list. Governor Ayala of Havana claimed that Hamilton was part owner of the vessels sent to raid the Spanish salvage camp at Palmar de Ayz. He demanded that all the treasure be returned and Jennings and the perpetrators seized and punished. Supposedly, the Cuban governor's ambassador in Jamaica has traced some of the stolen money to Hamilton's own house."

"What about you? Are you on the list?"

He shook his head. "Nay, I'm not on there. But that traitor Forrester apparently told the authorities about my taking the *Mary of Rochelle*. The French are complaining, too, and that's one of the vessels they named. Not only that but a little Bahamian sloop named the *Dolphin* recently showed up in Port Royal packed to the gills with goods Henry Jennings and his consorts had recently plundered from a French ship. Then some days later Jennings himself sailed into port with the *Marianne* in tow. Of course, she be much lighter now without all the coins and valuables she once carried that the good captain has fenced in Nassau."

"The French and the Spanish have no right to complain," said Elizabeth. "Why they plunder ships just as often as we English."

"The French apparently sent an official delegation here some time ago and they carried with them a letter from the governor of Hispaniola."

"What did it say?" asked Lucretia.

"The French demanded the return of the *Marianne* and another French sloop supposedly captured by Jennings. But the second ship wasn't captured by Jennings. It was captured by Hornigold and myself and she be my current sloop, the *Mary of Rochelle*. She's sea-worthy, trim, and answers sharp, which is why I swapped her out for the *Margaret*. But for some reason, the French think it was Jennings that done it because he captained a big flotilla along the north shores of Cuba and no one seems to remember me or Hornigold. Then when I was in Hispaniola, I careened and repainted the *Mary* and renamed her *Margaret*. It is she that is anchored in Port Royal Harbor now. I didn't want to alarm you, which is why I didn't tell you until this moment. I didn't want you to know that I had gone over to the other side and become a full-fledged..." He left the words hanging.

They looked at him in dismay, making him feel all twisted and shameful inside.

"Please don't look at me like that," he said.

"How are we supposed to look at you?" said his sister, whose face had reddened. "You're a freebooter, a buccaneer."

"'Tis true, I am such as that."

"Father would be ashamed, you know. He gave us everything—and this is how you repay him? You could have been a comfortable planter living out your days in—"

"I never wanted to be a bloody plantation owner! I am a seaman, by thunder!"

"No, you're not—you're nothing but a lowly pirate!"

"Stop this," interjected their step-mother. "This is not the time to have an argument between blood brother and sister. It's time to say our goodbyes because we all love one another and there's no denying it. The King's men will be here any minute and wasting time arguing amongst yourselves isn't going to save your beloved brother's neck."

"Unfortunately, I think they're already here," said Thache, pricking his ear alertly towards the front door. "Do you hear that?"

The three of them stopped right there and paused to listen. Slowly, the faint sound of snorting horses, clomping hooves, and groaning wagon wheels drifted up through the warm Jamaican night.

"He's right, they're close and getting closer by the minute" said his sister. "And they have a wagon, probably filled with troops."

He went to the window and the two women followed him. They couldn't see anyone yet, but dawn was just breaking and it was still a misty and gloomy gray outside with poor visibility. Thache quickly checked the top pair of his three brace of pistols bandoliered about his chest. They were primed and ready to fire.

When he looked up, he saw that they were staring at him.

"It's all right," he said to mollify them. "I know what I'm doing."

"Clearly, you don't," said his sister. "Otherwise, you wouldn't have the King's men coming after you."

"You can poke fun of me as much as you like when I'm gone, but for now just give your roguish brother a hug. And you too, Mother."

They stepped forward and leaned into him, tears in their eyes now, and he embraced them, drew them close and tight, feeling the great lonesomeness that he knew he was increasingly going to feel now that he had set out on a path of piracy. There really was no longer any turning back—and they all knew it.

"Please don't cry, my bonnies," he whispered reassuringly. "I love ye like I love the heavenly father himself, and my love will never die. And say goodbye for me to the little ones. I shall miss Cox, Rachel, and Thomas more than you know."

"We will. We will," they said in unison, openly sobbing now. The sounds of the horses and wagon were growing stronger.

Damnit, he thought, *they must already be at the main entrance off the road.*

He hugged them tighter. "Aye, saying goodbye is the hardest part of this bitter life. But I will see you again, if not here then in the afterlife. Assuming that I can one day mend my evil ways."

"Don't say that," sobbed Elizabeth, clutching him fiercely. "We *will* see you again!"

"Indeed we will, my son," said Lucretia lovingly. "It is God's will."

"Tell the King's men I have gone to Kingston. Act surprised and ignorant of everything else, and shed plenty of tears because it will garner you sympathy and distance yourself from me. They know you belong to a good landholding family and will treat you accordingly. I love you both and the children dearly. Be sure to tell them that. Thomas is bound to be especially disappointed."

"We will, Brother. Goodbye."

"Goodbye." He picked up his two satchels and rushed out the door to Henry. Down the driveway, he could see through the mist a pair of redcoated officers and an open-topped wagon clattering towards the main house. His horse raised his ear alertly and stomped his hooves then turned his head and looked right at him. He went up to Henry and whispered in a soothing tone to calm the animal before quickly fastening his satchels to the English saddle. Then he led the horse on foot through the trees along a footpath oriented at a ninety-degree angle to the driveway; it led to the main road down into Spanish Town and beyond to Kingston and Port Royal harbor. Once he reached the path, he climbed up in the saddle just as the King's men came clomping up to his house.

As the officers and wagon rolled up, he took one last look at the home of his youth. This was the place he had come of age, an emotionally treasured place where he had collected frogs, painted tin soldiers, played hide-and-seek and leap frog, shot arrows with a cedar bow, learned to ride a horse, and read the adventurous tales of Drake and Morgan, Kidd and Avery. Deep down, he had the dreadful feeling he was seeing it all for the last time and would never return.

He let his eyes linger for a moment as the redcoats armed with bayonetted muskets poured from the wagon, swarmed towards the house, outbuildings, and servant quarters, and began setting up a perimeter to cover all possible escape routes. He shook his head in dismay, praying that no harm would come to his family. And then, with the stealth of a wolf, he and his trusty horse he had named after his childhood hero Sir Henry Morgan disappeared into the night.

CHAPTER 12

WINDWARD PASSAGE, WESTERN HISPANIOLA

AUGUST 15, 1716

WATCHING THE SECOND BRITISH MERCHANT SHIP OF THE DAY sail past without Hornigold's black flag raised to signal pursuit, Thache felt his heart sink. He knew that his friend "Black" Sam Bellamy, his crew, and two-thirds of Hornigold's own men were close to insurrection, and this latest show of cowardice on the part of the Flying Gang's leader, at least in their eyes, might very well push them over the edge. Ever since Hornigold had returned to Hispaniola with his newly acquired sloop *Adventure* and the separate pirate companies had reformed, there had been an air of tension amongst the men. Bellamy and La Buse were insistent that the consortium plunder English ships, in addition to those of other nations. Lookouts on the four sloops comprising the pirate fleet had spotted several British merchant vessels loaded with goods, but the flotilla's commodore Hornigold, elected by the pirate articles all the voluntary seamen had signed, refused to give chase.

The Bahamian sea captain thought himself a vigilante, settling old scores with the French and Spanish. His policy was to board friendly vessels only as a last resort to acquire wine and spirits, ammunition, powder, navigational instruments, medicine, and other vital supplies, or to take on skilled crewmen. Bellamy and his second-in-command, Paulsgrave Williams, disagreed with such a narrow view, and La Buse and his mostly French crew also saw no reason to spare English vessels. In fact, while Hornigold had been away in Nassau and Thache in Jamaica, Bellamy and La Buse had plundered several British merchant ships loaded with treasure off the southern coast of Cuba. Hornigold was incensed to learn of their exploits upon his return to Hispaniola and that marked the beginning of the impasse.

In the past two days alone, four fat prizes had been spotted but still Hornigold had steadfastly refused to hoist the black flag, insisting that the consortium limit their attacks to the vessels of England's former enemies, France and Spain. Now he had become openly defiant against the majority of men in the companies, and many saw him as behaving like a tyrant. Proud of his English roots, he continued to stick stubbornly to his policy of not robbing British ships, no matter how valuable a cargo they might carry. The arguments between the two camps were growing more heated every day, especially between Hornigold and his protégé Bellamy, and Thache knew something had to give.

An hour after the two ships had passed, with the ball of sun sinking fast on the horizon, the flotilla anchored in a protected bay on the western tip of Hispaniola to take fresh water. It was then Thache realized just how prescient he had been. With seething expressions on their faces, Bellamy and several of his key crew members were rowing over to his ship along with Hornigold's quartermaster, William Howard. They obviously wanted to hold a council and vent their frustration. Gathering his chief lieutenants, Thache invited the group into his cabin, where he had two bottles of fine Jamaican rum waiting. While many pirate captains had to share their quarters with their officers and other seamen, Thache's crew members insisted he take the expansive stern cabin beneath the quarterdeck, where he kept his navigational instruments and dozens of rolled-up cartographic maps of the Caribbean, Atlantic, and Gulf of Mexico. He also had a modest collection of books that included the complete collections of Thomas Aquinas, Geoffrey Chaucer, William Shakespeare, and Daniel Defoe, as well as Alexandre Olivier Exquemelin's *History of the Buccaneers of America*, Woodes Roger's *A Cruising Voyage Round the World*, and William Dampier's *A New Voyage Round the World, Voyages and Descriptions*, and *A Voyage to New Holland*. Thache had received a first-rate education growing up in Jamaica and had long been an avid reader, particularly of maritime history and its colorful cast of characters.

As the men shuffled into his private cabin, Thache had the slightly younger Bellamy stand next to him so that the two of them could lead the discussion as equals. Like Thache, the twenty-seven-year-old Bellamy cut a tall, dashing figure. He wore a long deep-cuffed velvet coat, knee breeches, silk stockings, and silver-buckled shoes. For weaponry, he carried a sheathed cutlass on his left hip and a pair of pistols on his sash. In keeping with his egalitarian Robin-Hood's-Men philosophy, he never wore a fashionable powdered wig, but grew his dark hair long and tied it back with a black satin bow. But what distinguished him most of all was the very same thing that set his host apart: he bore an unmistakable aura of command.

Once all eight men were packed into his quarters with a glass or tankard of rum in hand, Thache opened the proceedings to the thorny issue at hand. Since they were aboard his ship, he would be the one to run the meeting.

"Welcome aboard the *Margaret*, and I can only say I wish it were under better circumstances," he said to begin the conference. "We all know what this is about because there's been quite a bit of simmering this past week. And we also know that we have to come to an accord that is agreeable to the majority of the men in each company. So that is what this council is about. Now every man will get his chance to speak and every man will have an equal vote on how we proceed from here. But I think we should start with Master Howard since he is the quartermaster of the *Adventure* and is in the best position to tell us the current state of mind of Captain Hornigold and the crew. Any objections?"

There were none.

"All right, Mr. Howard, please begin."

Howard gave a nod and took a half-step forward to address his audience. Like Henry Jennings, Thache, and Paulsgrave Williams, William Howard came from a well-to-do colonial family and was an educated man. As the son of a prominent North Carolina landholder, he ran in the same circles as the colony's top two officials, Governor Charles Eden and Tobias Knight. This made him the opposite of Hornigold and Bellamy, who had been born penniless and had to scrape and scrounge their way up from the bottom to attain their pirate captaincies.

"I'm just going to lay it out for ye like a plate of supper, lads," said Howard. "Tensions amongst the crew aboard our ship have reached a breaking point. The majority of the men agree with you, Sam, and with La Buse that we should be plundering English vessels just the same as the Spanish, Portuguese, and French. They believe the commodore is overlooking valuable prizes, and they're not happy about losing the *Benjamin* and having to be crammed up in the smaller *Adventure*. The men want to put it to a vote and are considering breaking up the companies."

"So that's where matters stand?" asked Thache.

"Aye, but there's more to it than that, Captain. They want to know which side *you'll* take if it comes to a vote."

"I'm afraid I can't tell you that, Mr. Howard. But I will say that I've got nothing personal against taking ships of all nations. I know I haven't been as outspoken on this matter as some of ye, but that don't mean I agree with Hornigold's way."

"Fair enough, Captain. Then I suppose all I need to add is that I plan to put this to a vote to see who stands with Hornigold and who don't. It may end up that he is deposed as commodore of the combined companies. He's lost the confidence of most of our crew, and if I had to wager, I would say that many of them will vote for no limits on what ships we take and will want to join up with you, Captain Bellamy, or La Buse. But even though I stand before you now asking for a vote, I want you to know that doesn't mean I will surrender my post as quartermaster and sign on with another ship." He looked at all the faces. "I don't know what the future holds— I have come here only to tell you the disposition of the crew and to see where Captain Thache stands."

Thache nodded. "It will have to come down to a vote then." He looked at Bellamy. "Sam, what are your thoughts on this matter?"

The young pirate captain took a moment to study his audience and clear his throat before speaking. "The first thing I have to say is that Hornigold's way no longer works. Not only for me and my crew, but for the vast majority of seamen aboard each and every ship in this bay. I know the mind of La Buse and can speak for him as well. But it's more than just Hornigold's way don't work no more. It's that it be the wrong way, plain and simple. We're freebooters and it's our God-given right to plunder whatever we can store below our decks. Whether that plunder belong to an Englishmen, a Spaniard, or a Frenchie. An English ship's as good a prize as any by my reckoning, and me and my crew won't be holding back from giving chase no longer."

"Aye, there's no way around it any longer, mates," agreed his second-in-command Paulsgrave Williams. "The time has come for a change."

Bellamy nodded vigorously. "We're rovers of the sea, and we live for plunder and the excitement of the chase," he continued, his dark brown eyes suffused with raw passion. "But many of us also do all this for something bigger. That is what I want to talk to you about tonight. In my view, a man has got to sign the articles and go on the account for the right reasons. That's what makes him a good man in the eyes of God even as he takes away from other men. I want you all to understand why I am willing to engage in piracy on the high seas, because it is the crux of the matter."

Here he paused, building up the moment, and Thache could feel the full power, conviction, and allure of the young man—and why his crew was so devoted to him and inspired by him.

"I didn't go on the account to bring harm to men," Bellamy went on, gesturing with his hands now, "for I scorn to do anyone a mischief who has led a fair and just life. But I do scorn all those who willingly submit to be governed by laws which rich men have made for their own security, for the cowardly whelps have not the courage otherwise to defend what they get by knavery."

"Hear, hear!" rumbled several men. Thache couldn't help but notice that Israel Hands and John Martin under his command were two of the loudest voices along with Hornigold's own quartermaster, William Howard. They, too, were taken in by the charismatic young leader.

"Damn the crafty royal politicians, slaveholders, and greedy merchants—damn these men who take most everything in this world and leave only the crumbs for the rest of us. And equally damn those who serve them for they are but a parcel of hen-hearted numbskulls. They vilify us, the scoundrels do, when there is only this difference: they rob the poor under the cover of law, and we plunder the rich under the protection of our own courage. That is why we are freebooters, mates: to shake up this bloody hypocrisy and make the world right for all men!"

"Aye, we are Robin Hood's men!" roared Paulsgrave Williams. "And damn proud of it, I say!"

"Huzzah, huzzah!"

"Aye, mates!"

"Damn King George and his scoundrels! Damn them for villains!"

The room swelled and rumbled for a full minute with wild cursing, cheering, and clanging cups, and Thache couldn't help but smile. He found Black Sam Bellamy a flat-out inspiration, a voice that captured his sentiments precisely, and those of his own men aboard the *Margaret*. But at the same time, he knew that this situation had to be handled delicately. Hornigold was a fine sea captain and a brilliant leader, but most importantly the man had stood by them both. In the case of Bellamy, it could be argued that without the fulsome praise and support of Hornigold, who had given him his first prize sloop for outwitting his nemesis Jennings, he might very well still be paddling about in a tiny periauger, plundering fisherman and logcutters instead of one-hundred-ton sloops so packed with treasure that the water nearly reached the gunwales.

"Avast, you scurvy dogs!" he shouted over the din. "We need order!"

The men continued to roar like rebellious schoolboys. To quiet them down, he banged his pewter tankard on his map table.

"I call for order, damn you!"

This time, the men snapped obediently silent. He stood in front of them, pausing a moment to gather his thoughts, quietly inhaling and exhaling. "Well-spoken, Sam. Well-spoken indeed," he said finally to the assembled group to break the silence. "Now who else would like to say some words?"

Paulsgrave Williams stepped forward. "William and Sam have spoken for all of us, it would seem. I don't know if there are any words that can top what each man said. The main thing is that we're all in agreement something has to be done. Which means we have to put this matter to a vote of all the companies."

More head nods and murmurs of assent from the group.

Taking control as moderator once again, Thache said, "Aye, gentlemen, that is what must be done. In the Flying Gang, each man has a vote and every vote counts the same. It's all spelled out in the articles each of us men here signed, and all of our crewmen as well. It doesn't matter what country he once called home, the color of his skin, or what god he believes in. One man, one vote. And that is what we must now do."

"Aye," agreed Bellamy, and several others voiced their agreement. "The articles are our guide. That is given."

"And when we vote, we have to make sure that we handle it right and fair. There can be no injustice done to the captain." He looked sharply at Bellamy. "He's been good to you and me, Sam." He then waved expansively at Howard and the others. "In fact, he's done right fair by all of us. Which is why we can in no way do him wrong if we take this to a vote and the majority wants him relieved of command. There has to be no doubt that it was fairly done."

"Aye, by the blood of Henry Morgan we will make it so," said Bellamy.

Thache surveyed the room. "Does every man here agree?"

Again, there were nods and murmurs of agreement all around.

"All right then, it's time to call a meeting of all the companies and put this matter to a fair vote."

Israel Hands looked at him. "When are we going to do it?"

"There be call to do it tonight for we can wait no longer. We'll hold the meeting onshore around the fire, with plenty of rum to go around for everyone."

"Then it will be settled," said Bellamy. "Once and for all."

Thache nodded. "Aye, Sam, then it will be settled. And whichever way it goes, we're all going to have to abide by it. After all, that's what the articles be for."

CHAPTER 13

WINDWARD PASSAGE, WESTERN HISPANIOLA

AUGUST 15, 1716

CAESAR STARED INTO THE SNAPPING FIRE, feeling the pleasant effects of the rum while taking in the lingering aroma of boiled sea turtle. Bonfires lit up the beach and the companies had made soup from several tortoises that Thache's and La Buse's crews had managed to catch. A few minutes earlier, criers had come by each bonfire to announce there would a general meeting of the companies at the south end of the beach at the top of the hour. Caesar was well aware of the rancor amongst many of the crew members regarding Hornigold's stubborn refusal to take British prizes. The commodore's quartermaster, William Howard, Caesar's Bath County cohort and associate of his owner Tobias Knight, was holding a council where a vote in accordance with the articles would be cast. Caesar only hoped there wouldn't be fighting and bloodshed when the verdict was announced.

Five minutes later, he made his way along with his fellow black friend Richard Greensail and several other crewmen from the *Margaret* to the south end of the beach. Driftwood logs, thatches of palm, wooden stools, and a few canvas sheets had been laid out for the council. He and Greensail took a seat on a piece of gnarly driftwood near the front. The captains of each of the four ships stood quietly before the still-gathering group of two-hundred seamen, along with Howard, John Martin, and the other quartermasters. The men were quietly chatting, passing around bottles of wine and rum, and smoking red and white clay pipes.

They wore an eclectic mix of clothing, much of it literally taken off the backs of their captives. Perpetually on the move with little time to shop, pirates had fewer resources and greater needs than their counterparts on land and had to take what they could get when they could get it. For headgear, they wore black wool felt or cow-leather tricorn hats, knit "Monmouth" caps, and broad-brimmed Spanish hats cropped short on the sides and left long at the front. The remainder of their attire consisted of plain white gentleman's shirts or checked seaman's shirts, most of coarse linen and some encased by waistcoats; colored kerchiefs and cravats about necks; and narrow or wide seaman's breeches, open or closed at the knee. In colder climes, they would wear short tarred seaman's jackets called osnabrigs, medium-length coats, and a sprinkling of long coats, some of rich fabric with silver and gold lace and others consisting of cheap sackcloth. But today not one among them wore a jacket in the tropical heat and humidity of August. All carried more than one pistol, cartridge boxes, and cutlasses. Many had gold chains, strings of pearls, or other pillaged jewelry fastened about their necks. A few dozen bore "gunpowder spot" tattoos on hands and arms, created by pricking the skin with a needle and rubbing in crushed gunpowder or antimony for ink. For the most part, only the Africans and West Indians in the company wore a single silver or gold earring in their ears and cloth head wraps, but a few of the white sailors donned them as well.

Caesar waited for the council to begin. Next to a pair of glowing bonfires was a barrel of water, a crate of untapped liquor, and boxes of crackers. Someone, he could tell, was trying hard to pass this event off as a pleasant social gathering instead of the pirate power struggle that it truly was. But the men weren't fooled: a somber mood filled the star-lit Hispaniola night. It was obvious they wanted to get on with the meeting so they could move on from the festering discord.

William Howard opened the proceedings.

"Mates," he began in a booming voice that carried over the gentle lapping of the waves on the beach and the crackle of the bonfires. "We all know why we are here. Many of you aboard the *Adventure*, and others from the rest of the fleet, are sore. You're sore because Captain Hornigold won't let us take English prizes. You have asked me to put it to a vote, in accordance with the signed articles, whether we want to change this rule. If we vote to change it, then we're also going to have to vote on how to handle the companies. Meaning who is in charge as commodore." Here he looked at Hornigold. "I promised the captain that before we voted he would get to say his piece. Then after that we'll hear what each man has to say. We're going to conduct our affairs civilly, like grown men not children throwing a tantrum, and each quartermaster is responsible for the conduct of his crew. And whatever decision is made in the end, we abide by it, per the articles."

As Howard stepped back, Hornigold stepped forward into the illumination of the bonfire. To Caesar, he clearly looked uncomfortable and irritated at being called before his own men, as if he was on trial by a jury of his peers. But he swallowed his pride and did it nonetheless. Caesar was reminded yet again what a great equalizer the articles were, for they held the captain to the same standards as ordinary crewman, making sure they were supported in their decision-making by the vast majority of their crew.

"Here I stand humbly before you, mates," Hornigold began, his tone more contrite than Caesar had expected. "We have taken many prizes together and shared much plunder. Now times have changed and we've had a falling out. There are many of you who don't agree with me. I can understand that. But I want you to hear me out before you set to voting. Because many of you don't know exactly why I have chosen the path I have chosen. And because once you vote and things get set in motion, you can't take them back. Their effect will be permanent."

He paused a moment, allowing the words to resonate.

"Now I want you all to know, if you don't already, that I have good reasons for doing things the way I do. First off, I'm an Englishman and I don't believe in plundering my own country. I don't much support the Crown or insolent government officials, but I also don't want to bring harm to my countrymen. But that's not the most important reason. No, the most important reason is that I don't want to give the Admiralty, or any other party for that matter, a good reason to take a strong interest in what I do. For in addition to being the leader of the Flying Gang, I am a Christian man, believe it or not, and I don't much want to hang from bloody Execution Dock."

At this the crowd laughed and many nodded their heads in agreement. Looking around at the faces, Caesar saw that the men were listening closely and that many still seemed to be in Hornigold's camp. In his own way, he was inspiring them through their fraternal bond as members of the Flying Gang.

But then his tone sharpened. "Unlike young and inexperienced Captain Bellamy here"—he turned his balding head and delivered a hard stare—"I am no idealist. I have no desire to be a martyr to my fellow brethren of the coast. I have no desire to soil my breeches during a dance of death in Port Royal or Boston and have dismal songs sung about me. By taking only French and Spanish prizes, I hope to keep the executioner at bay, or at least stall him until I can make a clean escape. That, lads, is my motivation."

Here he paused a moment, and Caesar could see the men hanging on his words. He had expected Hornigold to put up a fight, but he had not expected such convincing oratory.

Now Hornigold wagged a bony finger in warning. "You keep raiding them British ships, lads, and I tell you all you're going to accomplish is to bring a British man-of-war or two and an official Bahamas government down upon the rest of us. If you want to seal your own fate and end up with a rope around your neck, then be my guest. But what gives you the right to spoil things for the rest of us?" Again, he glared pointedly at Bellamy. "What gives you the right to make the high seas unsafe for your fellow brothers by increased patrols, harsher sentences, and the Crown's presence on New Providence? Can you tell me, Black Sam, what gives you the right to imperil the rest of us? Can you? Because that's what you'll be doing if you vigorously be raising the black flag against King George. Mark my words, that's what you'll be doing. That's all I have to say. Now you best think properly on my words before you vote, men."

He tipped his head in a kind of bow and stepped back with the other captains. Some of the men hissed and booed, but to Caesar the response was surprisingly restrained. Looking around at the faces, he could tell that some men had been moved by Hornigold's argument, and a few appeared to have been genuinely frightened. The members of the combined companies had never thought about the impact their actions might have on other seamen. By linking the plundering of British vessels to an increased Admiralty presence in the Caribbean and the possibility of a formal British government in Nassau backed by the military, Hornigold had made the men think twice about how their actions might affect their freebooting brothers-in-arms.

But what Hornigold had done most masterfully, Caesar saw at once, was raise the specter of punishment and death. Most of the men were raised as Christians and believed in God, heaven, and a fiery hell. That they would likely be hunted down like animals, caught, and convicted as criminals in a court of law was a prospect that terrified them. But what they feared most of all was that their unconsecrated mortal remains might be tarred, gibbeted, and left to the elements to rot as an example to the world, or their bodies tossed into unmarked graves between the low- and high-tide marks where their souls would roam restlessly for all eternity. To avoid the fate of hanging and an unchristianly end, some pirates would choose to blow themselves up rather than be captured or plead for the King's forgiveness if they were ever offered a pardon.

Quartermaster Howard now turned the floor over to the other captains. It was then Caesar saw Black Sam Bellamy step forward to speak.

"Captain Hornigold's words were chosen well," began the young pirate captain diplomatically. "At first glance, they seem to make sense. That is until one begins to look at the larger picture here. We don't serve no king or country, and we don't live in fear of the law—on land or the high seas. What we stand for is fairness in the face of an unfair world. A world dominated by the high and mighty. We're not the bandits here. The real thieves are the royal pigs in their powdered wigs, the titled landowners, the wealthy merchants, and the cruel captains that lash a seaman for taking a simple ladle of water from a barrel in the heat of a summer sun. Make no mistake, they are the real thieves. They are the ones who should answer before the courts and God Almighty, not us."

Vigorous nods and murmurs of assent circulated through the companies, and already Caesar could feel a change in the air.

"I have said all along that we are but Robin Hood's men and the rest of the world is the Sheriff of Nottingham. We have no country but each other. For us, there is no flag except the Jolly Roger, and until the rest of the world changes, that's the way it's going to be. But wretches though the sheriff's men think we be, the truth is we have a system of legal government that is fairer than anything else from Norfolk to Glasgow, from Port Royal to Calcutta. For we choose a captain from amongst ourselves, who in effect holds little more than a title, excepting in an engagement. It is then and only then that he commands absolutely and without interference from the rest of the company. Many of us have suffered from the ill-treatment of the ruling classes, the merchants, and Royal Navy and merchant sea captains that fill their troughs. The articles we have created protect against such tyrants. We have chosen a more democratic way by putting the power in the hands of the many rather than into the hands of any one man. We provide for our sick with an equal share and the color of a man's skin don't matter aboard our ships. We have provided carefully against the evils of tyrants. By our code, we provide for quarrels such as is happening among the companies at the present to be settled by a simple vote. We and our world, mates, is the way things ought to be. With an eye towards fairness for all and a little sliver of the pie, a sliver so small that it harms no one but those who have stolen too much for themselves and don't even have the eyes to see it!"

Caesar watched as dozens of men jumped suddenly to their feet and began shouting out their support, including his good mate Richard Greensail.

"Aye, Black Sam! Aye!"

"The black flag is the flag we fly—and there ain't no other!"

"Huzzah! Huzzah!"

Caesar quickly found himself up on his feet with the rest of them, yelling and cheering and pumping his fist. Several pirates yanked out their pistols and began firing them in the air. For several minutes the rowdy crowd roared its approval and the men shot off their weapons. Finally, Howard and Bellamy raised their hands and waved to quiet the crowd. It took a full minute before the men went silent again. Caesar looked at Hornigold; even he seemed surprised by the outpouring of support. But he also looked dejected. Clearly, he saw the writing on the wall.

"I have to wonder, mates, if Captain Hornigold don't want to take British ships, then why don't he join the Royal Navy or work for the Crown as a privateer? We all know the answer: because he wants his fair share of the pie just like the rest of us. He don't want his hard labors and all the risks he took to go towards nothing but filling another man's pockets. He don't want to share his plunder with King George and his supplicants. He has no more sympathy for the merchants, shipowners, and sea captains who have made our lives miserable than you or me. So why does he do it? I'll tell you why. He does it out of fear. He does it because he is still cowed by the authority of King George. He thinks that by not taking them English ships, he will somehow be safe from the long reach of the Admiralty. But that is nonsense, mates. The King has already declared Jennings, Wills, and several other of them Jamaican privateers as pirates. They are the same as us. They can no longer hide behind a governor's commission and are freebooters just like the rest of us. They are wanted outlaws by all nations!"

Again, the crowd exploded with a cheer, but this time it was near a frenzy as dozens of men discharged their pistols and rattled their cutlasses. It took several minutes for Howard and the other quartermasters to bring the men under control.

"I have only one last thing to say, and it's something I've said before and will no doubt say again. We are truly Robin Hood's men, and we need to continue to act like it. We take from the wealthy merchants and give to ourselves as poor sailors not because we are heartless bandits, but because that is what is fair. Because that is what is just in a world where only a minority of men take the most, and the rest of us get only what trickles down through their fat, greedy fingers. They vilify us, these scoundrels they do, but there is but a single difference between them and us. They rob the poor under the cover of law, forsooth, and we plunder the rich under the protection of our own bravery. And that is why we are free princes, and have as much authority to make war on the whole world as those who own or command a hundred sail of ships at sea or an army of one-hundred-thousand strong in the field. My conscience—and the laws of men and Christian charity—tell me this, men! And I swear by it or I be not Black Sam Bellamy!"

For several seconds the crowd was simply awestruck and not a word was whispered. The inspiring young sea captain stood with his head and shoulders in a dignified, resolute pose, gazing out at two-hundred dirty, half-drunk seamen with determination. For a moment, Caesar thought, Bellamy and his audience seemed to be united as one. He had read about an ancient slave, gladiator, and powerful orator named Spartacus who had defied the Roman Empire by leading a two-year revolt, and Black Sam reminded him of that legendary figure who had fought for the equal rights of men. In his eyes, the dashing young pirate commander was a modern-day Spartacus.

He couldn't help but feel here was history in the making. Even Hornigold seemed deeply moved.

And then, like a sloop-of-war firing across a merchantman's bow, the mesmerized crowd suddenly awoke and roared its approval. The sound was so loud that Caesar could feel the beach sand shake beneath his feet. Cutlasses and cups were hoisted in Bellamy's honor and pistols again exploded into the warm Caribbean night.

Five minutes later, the vote in accordance with the articles was taken. By majority vote, Hornigold was out as commodore of the combined fleet, the consortium would be led by Bellamy, and they would no longer spare English prizes.

Adding further insult, two-thirds of his crew made it clear that they were going to join Bellamy, La Buse, or Thache aboard their gunships rather than continue to avoid raising the black flag against the Crown. The deposed Flying Gang leader, they decreed, could keep the *Adventure*, but he and the twenty-six men who remained loyal to him, including his formidable quartermaster William Howard, were to leave the rendezvous immediately and not show their faces there again. When the votes were cast, some of the men gloated, some even going so far as to wave their pistols and cutlasses at Hornigold menacingly and spit in his direction, as if purging a foul taste from their mouths.

It was then Edward Thache fired his pistol into the air to gain control over the crowd and stepped forward to issue a cautionary warning. Looking into his eyes, Caesar could see that rubbing it into the deposed pirate commodore's face had raised his ire. As he came forward, the firelight danced off his heavily-bearded face in little flickers and the crowd instantly hushed, as if a king had entered a room. Above his towering figure hung a three-quarters moon and a marine-blue sky filled with glimmering stars.

"I want to remind you all that although we've followed the articles, taken a vote, and found resolution, no one has won here today," he said to the assembled men, his voice forceful but tinged with sadness and regret above the thin crackle of the fire. "Like most of you, I am of the mind that English ships should be ours for the taking, and I don't serve no king. And also like you, I believe there isn't any flag for us but the black one, our beloved Jolly Roger. But that doesn't mean that I'll abide people kicking a man when he's down. Ben Hornigold's been good to us. He's been good to me"—he turned and looked sharply at Bellamy—"and he's been especially good to you, Sam. There's no denying it. If it weren't for him in fact, you, Paulsgrave, and the rest of your sea dogs might very well still be paddling about in your glorified canoes." He turned back again and stared at the rest of the men, who stood mesmerized by his forceful presence. "All I'm asking of the lot of you is to show Ben and his remaining crew the respect they deserve and say goodbye to them like men—like men, by thunder—and don't be walking around boasting and spitting at them like vengeful schoolboys. Sam's right about our fight. It's about something bigger than simply taking plunder. Which means that we must be better than the tyrants we take from. The articles are about humility, too, mates. Which means that we must show the proper respect to those to whom the vote hasn't been too kindly. You hear me, men? Tread softly and with humility—otherwise, we're just like them, just like the very fat royals and bloated merchants we wage this war of ours upon."

The crowd remained silent, soberly taking in the words. Caesar could see that they had had an impact, as scores of men were quietly nodding.

"As for me and my crew, I would humbly suggest that we set about on our own for a spell and let the other companies go their separate ways. I have nothing against any of you—Ben, Sam, and Oliver. I would sail with any of you again in a heartbeat, but I think we need some time apart to heal." He looked now to his quartermaster. "Mr. Martin, if you would please take a vote."

John Martin stepped forward and did just that. The crew of the *Margaret* voted to proceed on their own, without either Hornigold or the Bellamy-La Buse contingent who would continue to sail in consort.

"That's it then," said Thache to conclude the council. "Remember, men, the articles aren't just about taking power away from one man and giving it to another. And they're not only about making things right. They're also about humility and fairness before God and one another. That's all I have to say."

He stood there in silence, staring out at the men. There was a tense moment as no one seemed to know what to do, and then someone clapped their hands. One clap turned to two, then two swelled to a dozen, and then there were a hundred clapping men, and then more than two hundred—until every single one was clapping his hands together in praise. Deeply moved, Caesar and his African mate Richard Greensail were up and on their feet and clapping thunderously along with the others as the applause slowly picked up in intensity before building to a crescendo and then quieting down again. Thache continued to stand there gazing out at the men, and the world seemed to unfold in slow motion and the night had a strange quality about it, the kind of strangeness that happened only in a dream.

In that moment, Caesar thought Edward Thache—the experienced seaman who had plied his trade in the ports of Jamaica, Philadelphia, Barbados, the Carolinas, the Bahamas, and many points in between—looked like a larger-than-life statue. By any standard, he was no ordinary man. His prominent cheekbones, jutting jaw, robust shoulders, lean sinewy frame—all appeared to have been chiseled from pure granite. The flickering light of the fire brought out the deep stormy-gray of his eyes, which, when combined with his thick owlish brows, gave him a quiet, focused intensity to go along with an acute intelligence. But his sublime gifts were his titanic height and his long, jet-black beard: it gave him an aura of almost mythical power, as if he had been unleashed upon mankind from the submarine lair of Poseidon himself.

And yet, Caesar knew, he was really just an ordinary man. A man who had confided in him just last night on the quarterdeck that all he had ever wanted was one simple thing: to be a great sea captain.

After tonight, it was readily apparent he was a lot more than that.

Thache was about something bigger in this world, the black man knew. He and Bellamy were not misguided youthful rebels, common thieves, or petty disrupters of oceanic commerce, they were leading a revolution against the injustice of the Old World, a war against the British Crown and all other crowns, a war against oppression and the unearned right of one man to rule over or exploit another—and Caesar the former slave saw it as clear as day. He knew he was witnessing something new and unprecedented, and it made him feel an electric tingle down his spine.

Because he knew—absolutely knew—he was a part of something important here in America, something patriotic and rebellious in which the ground was shifting beneath his very feet.

CHAPTER 14

BLUE RIDGE MOUNTAINS AND SHENANDOAH VALLEY, WESTERN VIRGINIA

SEPTEMBER 6, 1716

WHEN HE REACHED THE CREST OF THE RIDGE, Alexander Spotswood truly felt on top of the world and all of his problems seemed to disappear. The threats of Indian attacks to his royal colony, his ongoing battles with the House of Burgesses and Governor's Council, and the growing menace of the new Bahamian Republic of Pirates—all these instantly vanished from his mind at the sight of the lush green valley and breathtaking meandering river below that would one day be called by the Native American name of *Shenandoah*—the River of the Stars.

"It's utterly magnificent. There's no other way to describe it," he exclaimed with feeling.

"I believe this calls for another toast," said his friend Robert Beverley, brother of Captain Harry Beverley, who had sailed off two months ago for La Florida.

"Hear, hear," agreed Lieutenant John Fontaine, a Huguenot who had served in the British army and become a friend to the governor in the past year.

Staring out at the pristine frontier scenery, they quickly lightened the burden of a pack horse by drinking rye whiskey and champagne, making toast after toast to King George and each member of the royal family. They had reached Swift Run Gap, a notched gateway through the Blue Ridge, and while drinking their toasts they officially christened the two promontories framing the gap "Mount George" for the King and "Mount Alexander" for the governor. The expedition had departed Germanna eight days earlier on August 29 to explore the mountainous region west of the royal colony. The party included Spotswood and a dozen of his gentlemen friends, fourteen rangers, four Meherrin Indians, more than seventy riding and pack horses, and a bevy of slaves to ensure they experienced not a single privation. Spotswood wanted to survey the Blue Ridge in an effort to open up settlement on the western side of the mountain range and into the valley beyond for white settlers, particularly groups of Protestant immigrants who were arriving in the colony as indentured labor, and also to keep the French to the southwest at bay.

"What a wonderful day," said Robert Beverley after a hearty pull from a whiskey flask. "I wish my dear brother Harry could see this view. By the way, have you heard from him?"

Spotswood felt a sudden jolt, though he said nothing. He nor anyone else had heard a peep from Captain Harry or his crew since Beverley had sailed off in July in his armed sloop *Virgin* of Virginia "in quest of pirates, Spanish wrecks, etc." The lieutenant governor was feeling guilty about it as the captain was supposed to have reported in two or three weeks ago.

"No, I'm sorry," he said to Robert Beverley. "Before we left on our mountain journey, I hadn't heard anything."

"I hope he's all right. It's been two months now."

"I'm sure nothing's happened. Florida and Nassau are a long way off."

"Yes, but two months? I know there was a storm the day after he left, but he still should have been back by now. It doesn't take but a fortnight from here to the Bahamas and back even in foul weather."

"His mission called for him to survey the wrecks and size up the pirates' strength. I'm sure he's just been delayed obtaining supplies and outfitting his ship for the return voyage."

"I hope so," said Beverley. "But I have a bad feeling about it."

"Perhaps another toast to the King would make you feel better?"

"Hear, hear. A good spirit always does the trick," agreed the dashing young Huguenot John Fontaine.

They proceeded to drain two bottles of burgundy and one of claret. Again, they gave toasts to King George and his extended royal family while the slaves fed grain to the horses, checked the cinches and packs, and fanned the group to keep them cool. Following the toasts, several in the company were tipsy and wanted to turn back, but the governor and Fontaine persuaded them to continue.

Following an Indian trail, the explorers descended into the majestic valley, walking a full seven miles through woods and meadows, marked with the paths of elk and buffalo, until they came to the river, which in their exalted mood they called Euphrates. Crossing the river at a fording place, the party fished and hunted to provide a celebration feast. John Fontaine carved his name on a tree trunk and Spotswood buried a wine bottle with a proclamation of possession of the valley in the name of the King.

That evening the woods resounded. After a festive dinner of perch, venison, and turkey, the men loaded all their guns. They drank the King's health in champagne, and fired a volley; the princess's health in burgundy, and fired a volley; and all the rest of the royal family in claret, and a volley. At the end, they drank the governor's health and fired a final volley. They then proceeded to get obscenely drunk, partaking in Virginia red wine and white wine, Irish usquebaugh, brandy, shrub, two sorts of rum, champagne, Canary wine, and potent cider.

Spotswood vomited twice, drank more, and had a wonderful time. And yet, in the back of his mind, he couldn't help but wonder what had become of his friend Captain Beverley and his crew aboard the *Virgin*. Had the storm claimed them? Had they been taken by pirates and killed? Did the Spanish manage to capture them? Or even worse, had the devilish Spaniards executed them?

Staring into the dying embers of the fire just before going to bed, he thought: *I'll bet it's the damned pirates. And if it is, there's going to be hell to pay.*

I will crush them.

CHAPTER 15

OFF CAPE DONNA MARIA
WINDWARD PASSAGE, WESTERN HISPANIOLA

DECEMBER 13, 1716

FROM THE *MARGARET'S* LARBOARD RAILING, Thache stared out at a school of dolphins racing through the azure blue water, swimming with astonishing speed. A dozen miracles of nature with bottle-nosed beaks and gray dorsal fins glinting in the fading Windward Passage sunlight. They moved alongside the vessel with disarming ease, leaping out of the water every so often, carefree smiles clinging to their snouts as if there was nothing they'd rather be doing than racing against a ninety-ton pirate sloop-of-war.

What Thache liked most about them was their sense of freedom: they made the ongoing battle over control of commerce on the high seas and independence from Britain seem remote and distant.

A familiar voice from behind pulled him from his reverie.

"Just look at them. Now aren't they the lucky ones, with no scurvy dog Royal Navy to chase them down and blow them out of the water."

He turned to see his quartermaster, John Martin. With an unassuming manner, Thache slipped his hands over the railing, peered down at the dolphins, and grinned. "They are wonderful creatures," he said, smiling at his friend and comrade-in-arms. "I think they're on our side."

"Why is that, Captain?"

"Because they value their freedom just as we do. They don't have anyone telling them what to do. Why even the sharks don't tamper with them."

"Aye, Captain. I didn't know you were a philosopher."

"I'm not. I'm just a crusty old sea captain."

"Pardon me, but you ain't old. Not yet on the wrong side of thirty by my reckoning."

"You would be right about that, John. Lucky guess, I suppose."

He winked and they both laughed. Five minutes later, still gazing out from the quarterdeck, they saw a pair of giant sea turtles paddling next to a thin trail of sargassum. Hawksbills. Their heads poked out of the water like little islands, their flippers turned lazily, and their shells were a rugged, yellowish brown and splotched with algae. Thache didn't find them as amazing as the streamlined dolphins but they were intriguing just the same. A naturalist he had met in London had told him that turtles, like sharks, had been around long before the advent of man. He wondered if it was true or if the man had been pulling his leg.

He took a deep breath of the salty air and smiled inwardly. The life of a pirate commander had its challenges, but he was in a good frame of mind right now with the coming of Christmas. His most difficult task was making sure he took enough prizes and seized enough quality food and liquor to keep the men happy and preoccupied. His crew was fiercely loyal to him, but they still had to be placated constantly with barrels of rum and casks of wine, heaping bags of silver and gold, and, when in the rough-and-tumble ports, ample dark-eyed native lasses who knew how to pleasure a man.

He had taken several prizes in the Florida Straits and Windward Passage in the past two months and was sailing again in consort with Benjamin Hornigold. Following his removal as commodore of the joint fleet, Hornigold had limped back to Nassau with his twenty-six crewmen, sold the *Adventure*, obtained a new eight-gun, ninety-ton sloop named the *Delight*, signed on sixty-five new crew members in accordance with the articles, and was now patrolling the western coast of Hispaniola as an equal partner with Thache, who still remained loyal to his old deposed and humiliated cohort. For reasons that were readily apparent to Thache and everyone else, Hornigold was no longer reluctant to attack English and Dutch vessels, though he continued to proclaim his fealty to Great Britain and prefer Spanish and French prizes.

Thache's men were calling their captain Blackbeard now. It was Caesar who had come up with the nickname in the early fall when they were refitting in Nassau, and Thache liked the *nom de guerre* from the moment he heard it. But it was his crew that enjoyed it the most: the name gave them a leader they could rally around and that set them apart, like Sir Francis Drake and his "Sea Dogs." He had been growing his beard for a year and a half now and it was so long that he looked somewhat wild and unkempt. To hold it together, he twisted it into many little braids, each tied off with a small ribbon, some of which he tucked behind his ears. To his crewmen who had served in the military, the plaited beard resembled a British infantryman's powdered Ramillies wig. Judging from the reactions of the captains and crews of the merchant ships he captured, he quickly learned just how effective a tool of terror his physical appearance could be. They were utterly terrified of the giant of a man with the wild-looking beard and crimson jacket who wielded a huge cutlass and three brace of pistols slung in holsters about his chest in the manner of a bandolier.

Having been a rover now for over a year, he had learned that the two most important things were to constantly take prizes and to make his maritime targets surrender quickly and efficiently without a fight, both of which had the positive effect of maximizing profits, ensuring the safety of his men, and protecting his victims. To strengthen his targets' incentive to peacefully submit, he had developed his own version of the Jolly Roger. The purpose of the black pirate flag was not to chill the blood of his victims—but rather to "signal" that as long as the merchant captain surrendered without a fight no harm would come to him or his men, thus ensuring a peaceful theft instead of resistance and the possibility of a bloody battle. Most pirate flags were black and white, or black, white, and red with clear ominous markings that were associated with death: devils, skeletons, skulls, and bones; spears, swords, and daggers; and hearts and blood. For his pirate flag, Thache chose a special design: a black background with a superimposed white skeleton clutching an hourglass in one hand, signifying that time was running out and capture was imminent, and a spear piercing a bleeding heart in the other hand. Both the spear and the hourglass signaled death and destruction—but only if the captain resisted.

To get within cornering distance of a merchant ship, Thache typically had to fool the vessel into thinking he was harmless or friendly by flying false flags and feigning innocuous approaches. Thus, in a pursuit, he kept his pirate flag hidden until he had closed on his prize and there was no chance of escape. This enabled the *Margaret* to be mistaken for an innocent merchant sloop until he had effectively cornered his prey, at which time the pirate flag was hoisted and the merchantman was made aware of the solemn choice he faced: swift surrender or total annihilation.

When the sun set in a brilliant burst of orange, Thache gave the order for the topman to trim the sails and went below. A half-hour later, Caesar scrambled up the rigging for nighttime lookout duty as a waning crescent moon appeared along with a smattering of stars. An hour after that, Thache returned to the quarterdeck and heard the call from the maintop high above the deck.

"A sail, I believe!" cried Caesar.

"You believe?" snorted Thache incredulously from the quarterdeck. "What do you mean? Is there a sail or not, man?"

"I'm…I'm not sure."

"Not sure!" He tossed away the ashes from his clay pipe and stuffed the pipe in his captain's jacket. "Well, is it Hornigold and the *Delight* or not?"

"I don't know if it is the *Delight*, Captain. All I know is I thought I heard something. I can't see anything—it's just the sound."

"Where?"

"Broad on the starboard bow. It sounded like…like voices."

Thache looked at Israel Hands at the helm. "Voices? Rot my bones how can he make out voices?"

"He's got a sharp ear," said Hands. "Got to be Hornigold."

"Aye, or it could be the bloody HMS *Scarborough* ready to blast us to perdition," he fired back, referring to the British Navy's man-of-war patrolling the shipping lanes from Honduras to Barbados, a thirty-two-gun fifth-rate greatly feared by the pirates.

"I don't think so, Cap—"

His words were cut off as the sky lit up as if from a sudden flash of lightning. This was followed by a giant concussive blast that echoed through the night. When the dark sky was illuminated, Thache was able to make out a pair of vessels several leagues off his starboard gunwale, in the direction of Jamaica.

"It's the *Delight*, Captain!" yelled down Caesar. "She just fired a shot across the bow of a frigate!"

"Aye, I saw it, lad!" he shouted back, feeling a surge of energy now that they were back in the game. "Set a new course, Mr. Hands, on that flash of light. I believe we're about to share a prize with old Ben and his crew."

"Aye, Captain."

"Caesar!" he then called up to the maintop. "You get first dibs in the boarding party for identifying the fresh sail. Will it be a new pistol for you, lad!"

"Aye, Captain. That's what I want!"

There was another bright flash of light followed by an explosion. Once again,

Hornigold's *Delight* and the brigantine were as clear as day in the sudden burst of illumination.

"Damnit man," cursed John Martin as he stepped up onto the quarterdeck. "Why doesn't she turn into the wind and surrender?"

"Maybe she's going to put up a fight," said Thache. "But we both know that would be a very bad choice." Now to his navigator. "You saw those flashes, Mr. Hands. Hard to starboard and steady as she goes."

"Aye, Captain. Sou' by sou'west."

When no more warning shots were fired, Thache knew the brigantine had quickly surrendered after Hornigold had fired his second round. But even though the wind had died down and the sea was only mildly choppy, it took them nearly an hour to locate and then weigh anchor beside the two ships. Thache came up alongside the captured vessel and went over in a longboat with John Martin, Caesar, and the other members of the twelve-man boarding party. After politely introducing himself to the captain, Henry Timberlake, in the presence of Hornigold, he quickly learned that the forty-ton *Lamb* had sailed out of Boston less than a month earlier and was bound for Port Royal. At the mention of Timberlake's destination, Thache felt a wave of homesickness for his family in Spanish Town, but he suppressed his emotions in front of Hornigold and Timberlake.

Over the next six hours, he and Hornigold's boarding parties relieved Captain Timberlake and the *Lamb* of three barrels of pork, one of beef, two of peas, three of salted Atlantic mackerel, five barrels of onions, seven dozen kegs of oysters, fresh sail cloth, and all the ship's stores except forty biscuits and ten pounds of meat to ensure that the captain and crew would make it to Jamaica without going hungry. By order of both Thache and Hornigold, not a single hand was laid upon Timberlake or anyone in his crew. However, Hornigold's pirates threw some forty pounds sterling worth of Timberlake's wooden staves overboard because he had made them fire two warning shots instead of turning his vessel into the wind after the first cannon ball was fired.

At three in the morning, Hornigold and Thache sent Timberlake on his way on his much-lightened *Lamb*. As the brigantine slipped away into the night, Thache tipped his tricorn hat from the railing and bid him a safe journey.

But Captain Henry Timberlake did not tip his hat in return. No doubt he was not pleased with having been plundered a mere two day's sail from Port Royal.

However, Caesar was very pleased. By being the first crew member to spot the prize, he had gotten himself a new Queen Anne breech-loading screw-barrel pistol, manufactured by gunsmith Thomas Annely of Bristol.

The same pistol wielded by his captain.

CHAPTER 16

CARLISLE BAY, BARBADOS

APRIL 30, 1717

AS THE *REVENGE* CAST OFF and slipped quietly out of the Careenage, Bridgetown's narrow harbor, Major Stede Bonnet had second thoughts about his recent decision to become a pirate. The wealthy Barbadian planter had outfitted his own sixty-ton sloop, armed her with ten guns, and hired on more than seventy experienced seamen to operate her. Now he was sailing past old Fort James, into gently curving Carlisle Bay, and out into the open sea where he would be free to lead a life of freedom and adventure without the shackles of domestic life—and yet he felt miserable and ashamed. He was more than happy to leave behind a lonely island, a world of slavery and eternal boredom, and an unsupportive and nagging wife, but he felt miserable and ashamed because he was abandoning his three young children: Edward, Stede Jr., and his sweet little baby girl, Mary.

How have I let it come to this? he asked himself, as the *Revenge* picked up speed in the light offshore breeze and began to roll in the swells. *How can I leave behind three young ones, sad and fatherless?*

He didn't know the answer, and deep down wondered if he ever would. Staring out at his four-hundred-acre plantation southeast of Bridgetown, bequeathed to him upon his father's death in 1694, he pictured his three small children asleep in the nursery. Although he had told his family and friends he was embarking on a short trading voyage, he knew he would never return. He had decided to give up his life as an aristocrat, major in the militia, husband, and father to become a freebooter— and now that he had set out to sea there was no turning back. He had imagined this very moment since he was a little boy, reading the swashbuckling yarns of Drake and Morgan, Avery and Kidd. But he had never imagined himself as a twenty-eight-year-old father abandoning a four-year old, a three-year old, and an infant, nor had he ever anticipated the crushing guilt he would feel as he stole away in the night on the ebbing tide, like an escaping criminal. Why he hadn't even bid his wife or children a final farewell.

In a sudden pique of shame-induced anger, he turned away from his birthplace and the family he was leaving behind and stared out into the darkness of the sea. Despite the guilt he felt inside, he loved his new ship. The single-masted Bermuda sloop was fast and nimble with fine lines and a shallow draught that would allow her to slip into small coves and inlets not accessible to British men-of-war or the powerful, well-armed privateers that might pursue her. Although light at sixty tons, she was big enough to carry ten heavy guns, and would be able to field more if necessary. But what made her most unique was her library. An avid reader of not only military history and piracy, but philosophy, theology, the natural world, and the history of conquest of Europe, Asia, and the New World, Bonnet had had the shipwrights install a commodious great cabin lined with enough shelving to serve as a personal library for his plethora of books.

He watched as his bosun Ignatius Pell directed the helmsman to steer a course out of Carlisle Bay northwestward into the swiftly moving waters of the Atlantic Ocean. He knew he had not been right in the head for quite some time now. There had simply been too much death around him. The passing of his father and mother before he had lived to see his tenth birthday had been the first crushing blow. Then there was sweet Mrs. Whetstone, the guardian that he and his older brother and two sisters had dearly loved who had died when he was twenty. And finally, five years ago, his first-born child Allamby had passed away in early childhood from the fever. The boy's death had made him so distraught that he had seriously considered taking his own life. So much loss in the family, but it was the passing of his beloved Allamby when Bonnet was twenty-three that had pushed him over the edge.

Death tore him up inside and brought on terrible demons at night. He knew he was unable to cope well with loss—it was just the way he was mentally put together. Which was why he hated his wife so: she could never understand his bouts of melancholy and called him a coward, an unmanly disgrace for drinking away his misery and dwelling on the death of the boy. Since his childhood, death had been an ever-present reality in his life and he regularly fell into a depressed state. Even he was surprised that when his wife bore him three more children, his spirits still did not rise.

Behind his back, his planter friends whispered he suffered from a disorder of the mind. He knew it was true, but he also knew he could do nothing about it. There was certainly no one he could talk to, for even his own wife called him a coward for his bouts of sadness and inability to move beyond the death of their son. Desperate to find something that could distract him from his troubled mind, he had stumbled one day in the late fall on the idea of becoming a sea rover. Somehow, he thought that would be the cure for his affliction.

But what he needed most of all was to be separated from his wife, whom he genuinely detested. She nagged him constantly and was always telling him what a weak man and insufferable fool he was and how he should be expanding the size of their Barbados estate and obtain more Negroes to work the land, tend the crops, and top off the sweltering tubs of cane syrup in the sugarhouses. He had one of the most prosperous estates on the island: four hundred acres of sugarcane fields, two windmills, a cattle-operated mill to grind the syrup from the cane, three servants, and ninety-four slaves. But it still wasn't enough for her. Mary Bonnet wanted more, and nothing he did was ever good enough. He could hardly blame her for growing increasingly annoyed with his bouts of depression and his admission that he was bored with his all-too comfortable life of a sugar planter on Barbados. But he still wanted to be free of her, enough that he was willing to give up his three young children that he genuinely adored.

Taking a deep breath of crisp sea air, he tried to clear his head. His mind was definitely not right, and he couldn't help but wonder if it ever would be. Probably not, he decided. But at least he was making a fresh start by wiping the slate clean aboard his new sloop, amply stocked with provisions, powder, shot and, of course, his prodigious library of leatherbound books. He had christened his new pirate man-of-war *Revenge* in honor of James III, his Scottish ancestry, and his Jacobite proclivities, but the name was appropriate for another reason as well. He was also seeking vengeance against his cruel and nagging wife and the demons that had tormented him most of his life, and most especially since baby Allamby's death. For the wealthy planter of aristocratic upbringing who knew nothing of the sea was waging a war against the misery of the world.

He lit his long-stem white clay pipe and began pacing the quarterdeck as a pair of clouds scudded past a pregnant moon. The new pirate captain wore a powdered wig, rakish black felt hat, neatly pressed blue militia jacket, ruffled full-sleeved shirt with lace at the wrists, knee britches, silk stockings, polished buckled shoes, a cape, silver hilted sword, and a brace of pistols. Compared to his barefoot, salty, and sunburnished crew, he looked like a dandy. And he was, at least when it came to the sea. As the nimble Bermudan sloop transitioned from the calm waters of Carlisle Bay into the rolling swells of the open ocean, he began to feel queasy. A seaman he was not and the new sensation put him into a cold sweat. Five minutes later, he gripped the stern railing and vomited over the side.

He retched once, twice, and then a third time. When he turned back around, his quartermaster, Ishmael Hanks, bosun Ignatius Pell, and the other officers on the quarterdeck were looking at him funny. Several of them exchanged knowing glances at one another and seemed to be suppressing laughter at this most improbable of pirates, this landlubber entirely unversed in the arts of seamanship and navigation. For the first time, he realized that he was going to have problems with his officers, despite the fact that he owned the ship and they were his subordinates since he was paying them a cash salary instead of shares based on prizes and booty taken, which was the traditional pirate custom. To ensure the loyalty of his officers, he had chosen to pay Hanks and the others well, since he was entirely reliant on them to operate the *Revenge* and needed to be able to count on them.

Assisted by a pair of crewmen, he retreated to his great cabin packed with books, collapsed in his bunk, and went to sleep. The next morning, he arose bleary-eyed and held a meeting with Hanks, Pell, and the other officers to determine the *Revenge's* course. He made it clear that he wanted to put as many miles as possible between the ship and his previous life on Barbados. A course was promptly set northwest towards the Virginia and Delaware capes and the nearby crowded sea lanes of the North American mainland, more than two thousand miles away. He then dismissed them. But as his new pirate lieutenants were about to leave, he remembered one last thing.

"Oh, before you go, gentlemen," he said from his commodious bed, "I have one last request."

The men turned around and stared at him, already with noticeable disrespect on several of the faces. "And what would that be, Major?" asked Hanks.

"Captain, please call me captain."

"Aye, captain it is. And what is your request, Captain Bonnet, sir?"

"I am issuing orders that I am no longer to be called by my last name."

The men exchanged looks. "What shall we call you then, Captain?" asked his bosun Ignatius Pell.

"You are to address me as Captain Edwards."

"Captain Edwards? That's what you prefer?" asked Hanks, looking confused by the request.

"Yes, Captain Edwards. That is what you officers and the crew shall call me henceforth at all times."

"Very well. Captain Edwards it is then. I must needs say what might be the reason for the name change?"

"It is quite simple, Mr. Hanks. I don't want the captains of any of the prizes we take to know my real name. You see, gentlemen, in case we are captured, I want to spare my children."

"Spare your children, sir?"

"Yes, I want to spare them the shame of being the son or daughter of an outlaw pirate."

CHAPTER 17

NASSAU

AUGUST 24, 1717

WITH HORNIGOLD AT HIS SIDE, Thache spotted a pair of sails on the horizon from the north battlement of Fort Nassau. Taking out his spyglass, he studied the vessels closely. They were too far away to make out their flags or identify, but something about the sloop to leeward seemed familiar. He passed the glass to the gray-whiskered Hornigold, but he didn't recognize the vessels either. But the ships definitely appeared to be making for the harbor so they would know soon enough.

They returned to their survey of the fortifications and surrounding harbor. Since Hornigold had launched the fledgling pirate republic two years earlier, Nassau had grown into a bustling yet still governmentless little city. To defend against incursions by English, French, or Spanish men-of-war, the Flying Gang had gathered up cannon, pulleys, shot, and powder, and began rearming the old fortress as well as re-strengthening her ramparts, caissons, and buildings so she could withstand an all-out attack and keep meddlesome authority at bay.

The Flying Gang leader had also taken a large Spanish ship from Cadiz captured by a pirate company, anchored her at the harbor entrance, and armed her with thirty-two cannon scavenged from various prizes. The stationary man-of-war at the harbor entrance acted as a floating gun platform capable of fending off unwanted visitors. The pirates swiftly discovered what a strong deterrent the new improvements to the growing pirate enclave were. When a group of concerned British merchants sent a pair of ships over from London to investigate how the pirates might best be dislodged, Hornigold and his Flying Gang captured one of the vessels and sent the second packing back across the Atlantic.

The pirates had succeeded in driving out most of the law-abiding citizens that had taken up residence on the island prior to their takeover. Thomas Walker, who had assumed the role of acting deputy governor of the Bahamas in the absence of the lords proprietors, had been driven out months earlier along with his family, and most others followed soon thereafter. Though Walker and others had pleaded with the outside world to stamp out the pirates before they grew too strong, the Crown had done nothing. Some gathered their families and fled to the nearby islands of Abaca, Harbor Island, or Eleuthera; others wanted to put more distance between themselves and the outlaws, fleeing as far away as Port Royal, Charles Town, or Boston. The end result was the surrender of Nassau to the Flying Gang.

Hornigold and Jennings were now the undisputed leaders of the pirate republic. The crusty leader of the Flying Gang and pompous captain of the *Barsheba* maintained an uneasy alliance, but Jennings no longer harbored the delusion that he was a British patriot and licensed privateer who was better than his piratical cohorts. After all, he was a wanted fugitive himself who had escaped Port Royal just in the nick of time. Humbled by his change in status, he found that there was enough room for both himself and the rough-and-tumble Hornigold in the motley pirate enclave of Nassau. Unlike the Flying Gang leader though, he still refused to take British prizes and kept his lodgings far from town, lest he be forced to mingle too frequently with his low-brow peers.

New Providence was continuing to attract rogues, adventurers, and unemployed seamen from across the English-speaking world. But there was a new class of immigrant to whom the absence of government in the Bahamas held great appeal. Disaffected people willing to look the other way when it came to the law were now streaming into the pirate republic from the colonies. With ample affordable land, New Providence attracted small farmers, former indentured servants, and other poor people. Many blacks and native West Indians sought refuge in the new governmentless island. Even before the pirates took control, blacks, mulattoes, and West Indians had enjoyed considerable freedom in the Bahamas, intermarrying extensively with the white settlers. With the pirates now in control of the island, New Providence became a sanctuary for runaway slaves and free mulattoes alike, as many moved in to join the pirate crews or the merchants, tradesmen, and farmers who supported them.

The presence of the outlaw state was disrupting the slave societies of the Caribbean, and Thache and Hornigold delighted in the reversal of fortune. If a man was willing to sign the articles, join a crew, and work hard as a crew member, it didn't matter to them if he was black, brown, yellow, or white in their eyes. Regardless of the color of his skin, he drew an equal share of the spoils and had equal voting rights, pure and simple, as long as he remained a consistently competent seaman who pulled his fair load on deck.

Thache stared out at the harbor's clear pristine water. Nassau Harbor was littered with dozens of merchant vessels of various nationalities, most taken as prizes in the Florida Straits or Windward Passage between Cuba and Hispaniola. Many of the prize vessels had been stripped of masts, riggings, and fittings and were piled up like whale bones on the white sandy beaches of the harbor. The bigger and more cumbersome vessels had been beached and burned on the shores of Hog Island. Several lay half-submerged, their exposed timbers still smoldering from having been set aflame. The harbor was a veritable junk yard of prizes taken by the pirates of New Providence. But to Edward Thache it was home, a safe haven, and most importantly, a place where one man didn't rule over another by virtue of his birthright, the amount of property he owned, or the weight of the coin in his pocket. In his eyes, Nassau may have been uncouth and lawless, but here men were for the most part free and equal.

Though he had been born into wealth in Jamaica, he had never identified with the planter's lifestyle or held the unshakable sense of entitlement of the upper-middle and ruling classes. For Edward Thache of St. Jago de la Vega had always identified with the common man, and his brief but illuminating experiences with Sam Bellamy and his band of Merry Men who had adopted the Robin Hood philosophy of taking from the rich and helping the poor had made a lasting impression on him. Now a successful and influential pirate captain, he was a "gentleman of fortune," as freebooters of all nations enjoyed calling themselves, but he did it because he wanted to make a handsome living, loved adventure, was a natural leader of men, and had deep and pervasive feelings of egalitarianism. He truly believed in the equality of all men based on a system of merit and competence that was at odds with the landed gentry and merchant class of his day.

That was why he had decided to grow his beard so long: to symbolically defy authority, represented most prominently by the non-English-speaking, Hanoverian imposter King George. It was unfashionable to wear beards of any length in England or the colonies and shaven faces on men represented enlightenment, propriety, and Europeanism. So he did the opposite. True, his beard represented a certain identification with rugged masculinity and he enjoyed standing out from a crowd and intimidating the merchant captains of the vessels he took, but the beard was much more than that. He did it to show his discordance with mainstream society and his affinity for a world of justified piracy as a member of Robin Hood's Merry Men transplanted to the high seas, a physical demonstration in support of the philosophy of his friend Black Sam Bellamy. On the one hand, the prominent dark beard set him apart from the civilized world; but more importantly it set him apart from the unfair world of the wig-wearing royals, merchant tycoons, and slave-holding plantation owners that dominated world affairs at the expense of the common man. He was at war with the Crown and the ruling classes and commercial leaders of all nations. He was a patriot for this new fledgling thing called 'America' and the ideas of democracy and equality. He felt its world-changing power deep in his bones.

"Can you make them out now?" Hornigold asked him.

From the battlement, Thache looked again through his spyglass at the vessels on the horizon. Now the leeward vessel looked familiar, though her sails were ragged, her mast jury-rigged, and she appeared to be limping into port.

"By God, I think it's Paulsgrave and the *Mary Anne*. Here take a look."

He handed Hornigold the brass telescope.

"Aye, it be Williams all right, the bastard," observed Hornigold as he brought the ships into focus. "He and that impetuous brigand Bellamy stole my command from me, the rascals."

"Oh shut up, Ben. You know you deserved it by refusing to attack English vessels. Your own crew wanted to string you up from the mainyard, not just Sam and Paul."

"Aye, but I'm still sore about it."

"I know you are. But you've got to get over it."

The weathered old sea captain mumbled some curse that Thache couldn't quite make out. He was less than a decade older than Thache, but the creaky-kneed, deeply-lined pirate looked much older. "I see Williams on the quarterdeck, but where's your brother Black Sam?"

Taking the spyglass from him, he scrutinized the incoming sloops. Hornigold was right: Paulsgrave Williams stood at the quarterdeck, but his inseparable companion Bellamy was nowhere to be seen. The last he had heard of Bellamy, he and Williams had captured a massive slaver called the *Whydah*, converted her into a thirty-gun ship-of-force, and sailed her north to the Atlantic coast along with Williams in the *Mary Anne* and Richard Noland in the *Anne Galley*. Their goal had been to intercept vessels sailing to the colonies from Europe and the Caribbean. Thache had even heard that the French pirate Olivier La Buse had acquired a powerful twenty-gun ship of his own that he had intended to cruise to New England, reconnoiter with Bellamy, and continue on as far as Nova Scotia and Newfoundland. But he had heard no word of the pirates in more than a month.

"We'd better get down there to welcome them," said Thache.

"I'm not going down there," snorted Hornigold. "That bastard stole my men from me and sent me back here in humiliation."

"Aye, and look at you now, you lummox. You're the bloody King of Nassau. A little more humility like that and you'll replace that scupperlout King George."

Hornigold smiled, which was a rarity. "Okay, that was funny. You can fill me in later. I'm going to take a fucking nap."

They parted company. Thache headed down Bay Street towards the harbor. By the time he got there, the *Mary Anne* and the *Anne Galley* captained by Bellamy's former quartermaster, Richard Noland, limped into the harbor and dropped anchor. Both vessels were battered and he wondered if they had been in a battle or perhaps suffered through a bad storm. He also noted that they were drastically undermanned.

He studied the two ship crews as they lowered a pair of longboats into the water. A crowd of onlookers had gathered along the beach at the water's edge and they watched in silence along with him as the two boats rowed to shore. In the lead boat, Williams brought the small craft up to where Thache stood as a mob of sailors waded into the water and crowded around the longboat. Many of the pirates knew Williams and his crewmen by name and they instantly plied the group with questions. "From whence had they come, what had happened to their vessels, and where in the world was the notorious Black Sam Bellamy?"

"Leave them be, you bilge-sucking swabs!" snapped Thache, stepping into the fray. "Can't you see they've been to hell and back! At least let them enjoy an ale at the tavern before you bombard them with questions!"

To his surprise, the swarthy pirates obeyed his command and moved in to help the men from the boats. Ten minutes later, Thache was seated at a table at the Blue Parrot drinking an ale with Williams, Richard Noland, and Charles Vane, who had awoken from an afternoon nap and staggered onto the scene.

"What the hell happened, Paul?" asked Thache when the four of them were seated at a corner table with a crowd of curious, lubricated seamen gathered around them, hanging on every word.

It took Williams and Noland a full half hour to relate the tragic news. Black Sam Bellamy was no more, they said in a somber voice. The *Whydah* had been split apart by a terrible gale offshore of Cape Cod and Bellamy and most of the crew had drowned. He recited the names of two dozen of the most noteworthy that had been lost to the storm, several of whom Thache had known personally from their time together last spring and summer in Cuba and Hispaniola. The nine survivors were said to be awaiting trial in Boston with little chance of acquittal. Following the disaster, the governors of Massachusetts and Rhode Island had responded to the invasion of pirates in their colonies by outfitting several privateers to hunt Williams down, forcing the pirates out of New England waters. Williams had continued plundering vessels as he worked his way down the coasts of New Jersey, Delaware, and the Carolinas, pilfering enough wine and provisions to keep his men alive—but he had been harried by constant pursuit. Through death and desertion, his company was down to just over thirty men. Noland, with whom he had reunited along the way, had some twenty men aboard. Of the nearly one hundred and thirty sea rovers who had shipped north from the Bahamas with Bellamy early last spring, only slightly over fifty remained.

"Damn them for villains!" cursed Blackbeard, his voice a low growl like a wild animal despite the unabashedly human tears in his eyes. "Damn them for hunting us down like dogs and taking our friends away from us!"

"We should kill them—kill them all—goddamnit!" snarled Charles Vane, his face crimsoning and veins in his neck bulging with anger.

"Aye, Black Sam was a good mate!" said one of the men gathered around the battered wooden table. "The Prince of Pirates, he was!"

"Aye!" agreed Williams and he was echoed by a dozen angry pirate throats. "But I wish we hadn't gone so far north. We should have waited until May."

"Avast, Paul, avast," said Thache in an assuaging voice. "You can't blame yourself. It's Mother Nature and the pious fools in Boston that are to blame for the disastrous state of affairs. I promise you one thing, they're going to pay for this. Damn them for the villains they be!"

Vane tossed back his ale and nodded vigorously. "I can't believe they're going to execute the survivors! This can't be allowed to happen! We should sail a fleet up north, attack Boston, and break them out of fucking prison! We could do it, you know!"

Cries for vengeance went up from the assembled crowd around the table. Thache knew it was nothing but a pipe dream. He shook his head in anger and disgust at the injustice of it all. In his eyes, there were few men in the world like Black Sam. The man was a true hero, and so were his crewmen. Muskets should be fired in the air for all of them.

Feeling a sudden fit of fury, he stood up from his chair, his dark eyes blazing. The men crowded around the table backed up fractionally.

"If those Boston men see fit to hang them," he roared with the ferocity of a Puritan minister at a pulpit, "I will exact a terrible revenge upon the people of New England. Their ships will be plundered and burned such as the world has never seen, and their captains will live in mortal fear whenever they take to the sea. That is my promise to all ye here today. Aye verily, when I get through with them, they are going to wish they had never been born!"

With that, he stormed out of the Blue Parrot Tavern, walked a mile down the beach, and kneeled down in the soft sand beneath the refurbished fort. There he said a short prayer for his friend and comrade-in-arms—whose Robin-Hood-like vision of the world he had adopted as his own—and then he wept as he had not wept since he was a little boy.

For despite their short time together, Black Sam Bellamy had truly been like a brother to him.

CHAPTER 18

STRAITS OF FLORIDA

SEPTEMBER 2, 1717

"THAT'S A SPANISH MAN-OF-WAR. She's out of our class—there's no way we can take her," warned Ishmael Hanks. "If you do, you'll kill us all, and that's the Lord's truth."

Captain Stede Bonnet—who had ludicrously insisted his crew call him Captain Edwards to conceal his identity only to be discovered by a Barbados merchantman off the Carolina coast—peered through his telescope. For the past four months at sea, he and his crew had taken countless prizes and not shied away from anything, and now his quartermaster, gunner, bosun, and sailing master were all arguing with him and instructing him to cower before the enemy. Why the ship calmly parting through the waters before them looked like nothing but a plump Spanish merchant vessel ready to be plundered of silver and gold.

"I disagree, Mr. Hanks," he retorted. "I think she's nothing but an overstuffed merchantman and we can take her without a fight. Indeed, that is precisely what we're going to do."

His officers just stared at him incomprehensibly, which made him even angrier. He had been at loggerheads with them for two straight months now and was growing increasingly irritated by their snide and mutinous mutterings when his back was turned. But the situation had grown even more dire during the last fortnight. Now his officers and even some of the crewmen were openly challenging him and expressing their contempt for his lack of experience as a seaman. His quartermaster, Ishmael Hanks, was the only officer who did not show him flagrant disrespect or openly challenge him, but Bonnet could tell that even he was close to crossing the line and joining the dissenters. Though the *Revenge* had met with success on the Virginia capes and up north along the New York coast— taking the *Anne* and *Young* of Scotland, the *Endeavor* of Bristol, the *Turbet* of Barbados, and a pair of prizes off Charles Town—the crew whispered that it had been in spite of, not because of, his leadership.

He despised himself for allowing the situation to verge on the cusp of mutiny. But at least he knew the source of the problem. The truth was that he still had not mastered the art of being a sea captain and was, therefore, unable to win the men's trust and loyalty. Time and again during the course of their piratical journey northward, he had been obliged to yield the decision-making to others due to his lack of knowledge in maritime affairs, and consequently, his hold on the captaincy of his sloop-of-war was growing tenuous.

The only reason his officers and crew hadn't marooned him was because he owned the *Revenge* and was paying the wages of the officers and crew. On most pirate ships, the position of captain was voted on by the volunteer members of the crew not pressed into service, and his authority was only absolute during a pursuit, in time of boarding or battle, or during a storm. The captain and key officers could be stripped of their command at any time through a simple majority vote. But the unprecedented nature of the arrangement onboard the *Revenge* of the salaried crew and Bonnet's sole ownership of the ship blurred the line between sea rover and worker-for-hire, which was the only thing at the moment that was saving him.

"Captain, you must listen to me," implored Hanks. "That ship off our starboard beam is no merchant vessel. I know she hasn't shown us her guns yet, but she doesn't need to. She's a Spanish man-of-war all right, most likely sent here from Cuba to patrol the nearby wrecks and run off English marauders."

Bonnet continued to peer through his spyglass. "You don't know that, Mr. Hanks. So I suggest you run the black flag and bring the *Revenge* in closer so we can discern their intentions."

"And if she opens fire on us?"

"Then we'll sink her to the bottom of the sea."

"Captain, please don't do this!" pleaded the bosun Ignatius Pell. "We already know she flies Spanish colors. If she be a man-of-war bristling with cannon, we'll never get out of these straits alive."

"Oh avast, you cowardly whelps—we're taking this ship. Now throw up the black flag and that's a direct order from your captain!"

"Now just hold on," said Hanks, his face purpling with barely suppressed indignation. "You need to listen to me, damn you. I've stood by you when no one else has so you hear me out. What you're doing here is a bad decision, and once you've made it, there's no turning back. Do you understand that?"

"Of course I do. I'm the one giving the bloody orders, not you Mr. Hanks."

"Aye, that be the way she be. All I can say then is may the Lord have mercy on your soul if any of these good men should die here today."

"Duly noted, Mr. Hanks. Now throw up the damned flag, make all sail, and close on that blasted ship before she gets away." He picked up the speaking trumpet and lifted it to his mouth. "Hands to quarters! Hands to quarters!"

With the decision made, the officers and crew shuffled about the deck to battle stations. For a moment, the spirits on board seemed to rise as the Jolly Roger was hoisted to the top of the mast and the guns were run out. High above the deck of the *Revenge*, the new black flag caught the wind. A white skull above a horizontal long bone between a heart and a dagger, set against a black field, had been Bonnet's choice, and after four months of piracy the merchant ship captains of the Atlantic seaboard had become painfully familiar with it. He also had a dark blood-red flag to signify that no quarter would be given, but he had yet to fly it. All the same, he liked the Jolly Roger the best.

Bonnet was shocked when the Spanish vessel also ran out her guns. He had hoped that the sight of his black flag and bristling cannons at his gunwales would once again prove intimidating enough for his prey to surrender without a fight. But today that would not be the case. Now that they were closing on the vessel, he could see that that she was indeed a man-of-war. He gulped as he took in the dark, swarthy faces of the Spaniards and began to count the number of cannons. Suddenly, the vessel didn't look like a fat merchant ship waiting to be plundered like a lamb before the slaughter.

"Damn you, Bonnet! She be nearly thirty guns!" shouted his master gunner.

"What the hell? We have no business with her!" shouted another.

"Clap on the wind and get the *Revenge* out of here! The guns of the enemy be too strong!" rejoindered a third.

Taking the counsel of the officers and crew, the helmsman began to turn the wheel hard to port and steer away from the Spanish vessel.

"Damnit man, what are you doing?" cried Bonnet, jerking the wheel hard to starboard and correcting the course so that they were once again heading directly towards the Spanish man-of-war. He drew his cutlass and raised it above his head.

"Make clear and ready for engagement!"

But Hanks and Ignatius Pell just stood there shaking their heads, their faces composed in expressions of disbelief. He turned his gaze to the master gunner and his gun crew loading the four- and six-pounders. The gunner's mate and a loader scowled at him. It was plain that everyone but him believed that engaging the Spaniard would prove a foolish and most likely suicidal mission. There was another shout of protest from the helmsman, but Bonnet overruled him too.

The *Revenge* closed in on the man-of-war. Bonnet waited to give the order to fire. He wanted to wait until the last second so they could come alongside her, do severe damage to her masts and rigging, and thereby cripple her into submission.

But before he gave the order, the Spanish cannons erupted with a broadside into the *Revenge*. The impact rocked every timber of the ship and instantly sent men belowdecks and diving for cover. With his vessel strafed with grape shot and suddenly enveloped in smoke and splinters of wood, Bonnet was forced to duck down low on the deck and make himself small. Squinting through the smoke and flying timber, he saw Hanks shouting in his direction, but the deafening roar of cannon fire on both sides swallowed his words. The air was suddenly hot like a bonfire and carried the acrid stench of gunpowder. The breath of flame and burning ashes stung his eyes.

Again the cannons thundered, the explosive discharges pounding inside his skull and forcing him to curl up on the quarterdeck and cover his ears. The gun crew placed the cannon fire so the big guns went off in succession, raking the Spanish ship's three vulnerable mastheads and her larboard gunrail as they passed. But the Spaniards delivered as good as they got, and the deck of the *Revenge* sustained massive damage from a second volley. Suddenly, he realized he had been hit as he felt a painful burning sensation in his head and upper chest.

He felt along his head. Blood seeped from a projectile wound.

The *Revenge's* four- and six-pounders unloaded again, the big guns shaking from the recoil. Shuddering from the tremors and ear-splitting roar of the cannons on both sides, he rolled onto his side and looked out across the deck, taking in the gruesome scene. Already as many as two dozen corpses littered the bloodied and battered fore and aft decks. Some were slumped over cannons at their gun stations, others lay peacefully amid a tangle of rigging and dislodged detritus, still others were nothing more than limbless torsos or decapitated heads pierced by cannon balls, grape shot, and huge splinters of wood. A score of wounded lay twitching and crawling for cover, like worms wriggling through the grass. There was no escaping it: he had blundered badly by engaging a far more powerful ship.

Those that had survived the broadside fired again at the Spanish, but the enemy vessel had turned onto the stern of the *Revenge*. The sloop was most vulnerable when fired upon her aft or stern, as gunpowder was stored in a compartment in her belly. A well-placed shot from stern to bow could easily ignite the gunpowder stores, blowing the ship to kingdom come in a fiery conflagration.

Still lying on quarterdeck, Bonnet saw the flash of the Spanish guns as they fired again, and he heard the crash of glass as his aft cabin windows shattered. He crab-scuttled his way to the protective cover of the larboard bulwark as bar shot and chain shot, musket balls, and scraps of metal from the man-of-war's two stern chasers rained down upon them. As the pirates moved from under cover, another, louder report broke the air. A powerful hail of debris and small shot tore through rigging and canvas, bringing down part of the topsail yard and crushing a pair of seamen when it toppled onto the deck.

"We're not making another pass! Take us out of range and get us the hell out of here!" he heard Hanks shout to the helmsman, who had ducked down and was steering the ship on his knees.

Crushed and defeated, disgusted with his own hubris and stupidity, Bonnet offered no objection.

"We'd better pray the wind stays with us and they don't rake us again, or we'll lose our canvas and we're done for!" shouted Ignatius Pell.

"What…what's the damage?" mumbled Bonnet.

Hanks, Pell, and the other two remaining officers ignored him. He heard a shuffle of feet, the shouting of the gun crew.

"Damnit, they're comin' about!" cried Hanks.

"We're fish in a barrel!" lamented Pell. "I need to get someone topside! The mainsail's tore up but holding, but we've got to get more canvas on that jib!"

As he dashed off, the deck came under fire again. Bonnet felt the wood beneath him seem to pulse and swell like a living thing as the hot shot passed between him and the keel. The *Revenge's* decks were awash with blood; the pitiful screams of the wounded and dying filled the air. Thankfully, the ship's gunpowder magazine didn't ignite, but the shot tore through not only the main deck and quarterdeck but belowdecks, tearing through bodies and bulkheads. Blood streamed into his eyes, and he again felt the splinter of wood that was lodged into his head. His chest and right arm throbbed with agony, too, and he realized that he had sustained three separate wounds. He rubbed his head again, looked at the deep red blood covering his hand, and collapsed unconscious.

ψψψ

When he awoke, he found himself lying in bed in his battle-scarred great cabin. The floor was littered with shards of glass, splinters of wood, and shredded books. Blood-soaked bandages covered his head and chest, and his right arm was in a sling. His bony fingers touched the stitches freshly sewn into his scalp. He wondered how the *Revenge* had escaped and how long he had been unconscious. He tried to sit upright in the bed but lacked the strength.

It was then he heard a voice: Hanks.

The quartermaster laid it out plainly for him. By going forward with the ill-advised battle with the Spaniard, he had deeply wronged his crew and no longer had any standing whatsoever with them as captain until they reached port. A commander worth his weight in salt, Hanks patiently explained, knew better than to engage a ship far more powerful than his own, and could tell a lumbering merchant ship from a deadly man-of-war. Bonnet, the quartermaster said pointedly, completely lacked these skills. Through his own pride, weakness, and incompetence, he had allowed the *Revenge* to engage in a full-fledged fight with a superior Spanish warship. As a result, more than half his crew—over forty men—were dead or wounded, and Bonnet himself had suffered a severe injury that might ultimately cost him his life.

"How did we get away?" he asked when Hanks was finished, his voice a mere croak.

"Because the *Revenge* be lightly built and quick as a cat, and Mr. Pell was able to quickly replace the jib topsail to get us out of the Spaniards' range."

"So you're telling me that we could have outsailed her and avoided the encounter altogether?"

"Aye, and we wouldn't have no forty dead 'n wounded."

He licked his lips, for a moment feeling the pain of his humiliation far worse than the physical suffering from his wounds.

"For what it's worth, I'm sorry. I had no idea it would turn out this way."

"You can hold onto your words because they don't mean spit to me or anyone else aboard this ship. We'll get you to port, but I can't guarantee what will happen after that. I suspect you may have to *buy* yourself a new crew."

Though he wasn't surprised by Hanks's harsh words, they still stung. "And the *Revenge*?"

"She's been gutted like a pig. But with proper refitting, she may just be herself again, the poor wretch. Upon my honor she deserves a better captain than the likes of you, *Major* Bonnet."

He bit his lip. For a moment, he wished he had been killed in the battle; then at least he wouldn't have to suffer the indignity of being despised and disrespected by his officers and crew.

"I'm sorry, Mr. Hanks," he said with genuine feeling. "I'm sorry for…for everything."

"Aye, 'tis beyond doubt you mean well, lubberly though you be. But it won't bring those men back."

"I know it won't and I'm sorry for that." He felt an excruciating pain in his head and upper chest and groaned heavily. But he saw little sympathy on his quartermaster's face. "By the way, where are we headed?"

"We've set a course for New Providence."

He couldn't help an involuntary wrinkle of his nose. "New Providence? You mean the…the…"

"Aye, *Captain Edwards*. We're headed for an island governed by a gang of cutthroats. So you'd better rest up, for I know not what's going to happen to you when they learn of the devilment you've brought to your poor, hapless crew."

PART 3

BLACKBEARD AND THE GENTLEMAN PIRATE

CHAPTER 19

NASSAU

SEPTEMBER 4, 1717

FEELING A TOUCH OF MELANCHOLY, Thache stared out at the gently bobbing vessels in Nassau Harbor and the azure-blue sea beyond. For some reason, today he missed his beloved Margaret of Marcus Hook terribly. He pictured her nubile young body lying beside him in their warm bed overlooking the Delaware River. He remembered back to the countless times he sat stroking the curve of her back when they lay naked; to the way she smiled when they strolled holding hands through the streets of Philadelphia; to how she kept her lodgings neat and clean and tastefully furnished; to her long flowing blonde hair when she combed it out to its full length; and to the savory Swedish meatball dinners she used to cook for him on Sunday nights, smothered in brown cream sauce and accompanied with lingonberries, pickled cucumber, and mashed potatoes. God, did he miss her and her wonderful cooking!

He knew he should never have left such a fine woman to become a privateer. Now he was a full-fledged pirate, a wanted criminal, and he could not turn back the clock to the way things once had been. True, he and his sea roving brethren seemed virtually unstoppable despite the recent setback with Bellamy and his crew, but that was bound to change. However, at present their control of the Atlantic sea lanes remained uncontested and the British Royal Navy was powerless to stop them. Based on recent intelligence from skilled seamen pressed into pirate service and captured merchant captains and their crews, the HMS *Shoreham* had only recently returned to Virginia and was said to require such extensive refitting that she was not allowed to leave the safety of Chesapeake Bay. Freebooters had so terrorized the British Leeward Islands that the mere whisper of their return had compelled the colonial governor to cancel a tour aboard HMS *Seaford* for fear of capture. In Barbados, the crew of the HMS *Scarborough* was gripped with tropical disease and unfit for service. Outside of Jamaica, that left only two or three of His Majesty's warships to patrol thousands of miles of coastline from Barbados to Maine. Reinforcements were reportedly en route from Great Britain, but for the present, it appeared, the Americas were solidly in the hands of the masters of the sweet trade. But Thache knew that would soon change as he and his fellow freebooters continued to take a bigger and bigger slice of the pie away from the wealthy merchants who controlled Atlantic commerce.

A part of him couldn't help but feel that his friend Black Sam Bellamy's death was the beginning of the end for outlaws like himself. He had said as much to Charles Vane, who had laughed uproariously and insisted they drink again to the damnation of King George rather than entertain such morbid thoughts. The hard-drinking and incorrigible Vane thought he was being overly pessimistic. He predicted that the Flying Gang and other pirate squadrons menacing the New World sea lanes would remain uncontested, free-spirited "gentlemen of fortune" for at least another decade before the authorities could muster the strength to stop them. Thache didn't believe that for a minute. A change was coming, and it was coming sooner than his Bahamian brothers-in-arms believed, he felt certain.

The truth was the Crown and Admiralty protecting its colonial interests would eventually terminate its hands-off policy of benign neglect by flexing its muscles, shutting down the pirate republic in the Bahamas, and installing a legitimate government. When that fateful day come, Nassau would turn overnight from a protected base of operations to a heavily regulated extension of Great Britain. The only reason that piracy was thriving and that day had not yet come was due to His Majesty's lack of international naval strength and the mobility and dispersion of pirates across the Atlantic seaboard and Caribbean. The combination made it difficult to track pirates down. But Thache knew one day that would change and that would be the beginning of the end for himself and his fellow sea rovers.

As he stared sadly out at the sea, pining for his love Margaret, he spotted a sail on the horizon. He watched it for several minutes through his spyglass, which he carried with him at all times these days. The sloop tacked its way towards the island, negotiated the turn into the harbor, and fell off the wind under the protection of Hog Island and the half-submerged, burnt-out ships wrecked off her shallow blue waters. Next to him, a growing crowd of seamen gathered along the beach, stumbling out of the taverns and crawling out of their canvas awnings and lean-tos to have a look at the new arrival. From the Jolly Roger flying from her mast, it was readily apparent that she was a pirate sloop and not a privateer or merchant vessel.

As she drew near, Thache could see that she had fine lines and trim sails. All in all, she was a bonnie sloop, better than the *Margaret*. But there was a problem: she was badly damaged. Her sails and rigging were in tatters and appeared to have been jury-rigged to allow her to sail. The hull and railing were battered and pockmarked from cannon and grape shot. Parts of the gunwales, mast, rigging, and deck appeared to be splintered and actually stained with iron-red blood. At the captain's great cabin at the stern of the vessel the glass had been shattered. He noted that the vessel was even more badly damaged than Paulsgrave Williams's *Mary Anne* or Richard Nolan's *Anne Galley* that had limped into the harbor last week. Her captain and crew must have fought in a pitched battle and come out on the losing end.

He studied the crew. They were a sullen and defeated-looking bunch. More importantly, the size of the crew visible on deck was not even half that which would be necessary to handle a sloop-of-war of her size. The men appeared tense and drawn, devoid of the usual bonhomie of the Flying Gang members and other pirate crews sailing into Nassau. Looking around at the sailors on the beach, Thache couldn't help but sense a trace of disdain in the way they looked at the battered newcomers. How could they have allowed themselves to be manhandled like this, their eyes said, especially when even an average pirate sloop could outrun anything on the high seas?

When the ship set anchor, Thache could make out her name: *Revenge*. He liked the name—an obvious tip of the hat to the Jacobite rebellion and Stuart dynasty of Queen Anne and James III—and he liked the sleek cut of the vessel. But who the hell did she belong to and what in heaven's name had she been through?

A longboat dropped beside the vessel and quickly filled up with members of the crew coming ashore. With four men manning the oars, the boat made its way towards the beach. But even the longboat had been damaged in the *Revenge's* recent action, and a pair of crewmembers were embarrassingly forced to bail buckets of water over the side as they made their way towards the crowded beach.

"Scupper, sink, and burn me if another of our brethren hasn't ventured to hell and back!" exclaimed a boisterous voice. "What the devil is going on here?"

Thache turned to see Charles Vane. He had just saddled out of the Blue Parrot with a tankard of ale. "Can't you see? We're at war," he said to his opinionated Jacobite friend, who as usual was drunk as a skunk.

"Aye verily, I can see that. But this one looks like she's been through a meat grinder. Take a gander at her starboard railing."

"She must have taken a half dozen broadsides. Too bad because she be a bonnie ship."

A dozen pirates waded into the water and began barraging the exhausted seamen with questions.

"Who are you and from whence have you come?"

"We be the *Revenge* out of Barbados," answered a grizzled veteran of a seaman whom Thache took to be a senior officer. "We were returning from the Carolina coast when we came across a Spanish man-of-war. We've been on the account for the past four months. Sailing up and down the coast and taking prizes from New York to Charles Town."

"So you were attacked? Where?"

The weary and battered seamen began to offload from the longboat, and the pirates in the water began to help them from the vessel. "Florida Straits, south of ye wrecks. Two days ago, it was. Had the misfortune of making our acquaintance with a Spanish warship. She fired many a ball through our brisket and nearly sent us to Davy Jones' Locker. Lost over half our original crew of seventy men as casualties, we did. Those that be too poorly to be moved are belowdecks, recovering from their wounds."

Thache and Vane stepped to the edge of the water and Thache posed a question to the man. "How did you manage to get away?"

"'Twas only through the spryness of our ship *Revenge* that we were able to evade the much larger Spanisher and avoid being put to the bottom."

Thache nodded. Looking into their faces up close, he could now see that they were bleary-eyed from exhaustion. Many of them must have been standing nonstop watches for the past two days as they made their way to Nassau.

"What's your name?" he then asked him.

"Ignatius Pell, bosun."

"Now why in the world would a ten-gun sloop engage a Spanish man-of-war in the first place?" asked Charles Vane after taking a hefty gulp of ale.

"Because we were ordered to by our captain. We tried to talk him out of it, but he wouldn't listen."

Thache shook his head in disbelief. The foremost priority of any sea captain worth his salt was to protect his ship and crew at all costs—and yet, whoever the bastard was in command of the *Revenge* had done neither. One thing was clear: the man was finished as a pirate captain. No one would dare sail with such a bad-luck commander ever again.

"What kind of fool captain gave that order?" demanded Vane. "That not be making sense."

"Aye, that's what we told the man," answered another experienced-looking seaman. "But as Mr. Pell said, the captain's blood was up and he wouldn't listen to no reason. He almost got himself killed. He suffered several wounds and is all bandaged up. Looks like an Egyptian mummy, he does."

"And who might you be, sir?" asked Vane.

"Ishmael Hanks, quartermaster. Now if you'll excuse me and my mates here, we're in dire need of a good stiff drink and a bow-legged woman. One who knows how to show particular kindness and enthusiasm to bedraggled gentlemen of fortune such as ourselves."

The crowd in the water and on the beach rumbled its approval, and Thache smiled. He liked the cut of Hanks and Pell. But he still had a few more questions.

He stepped forward, partially blocking their path. "Just a couple more inquiries, lads, if you don't mind. I'm Captain Thache of the *Margaret* and I must say I find your story of great interest. Could you tell me please, who by chance is the name of your captain as I might want to pay him a courtesy call, seeing as he has met with some misfortune?"

Hanks's eyes narrowed suspiciously on the unusually tall man blocking his path, but he came to a halt on the gently sloping beach. "His name is Captain Stede Bonnet, but he insists we call him Captain Edwards. But he ain't no sea captain at all. He's a wealthy planter and a major in the Barbados militia, though he ain't never fought none but an unruly slave."

Thache felt his body become suddenly alert. "Major Stede Bonnet of Barbados, you say?"

"Aye," said Hanks. "What, you know of whom I speak?"

"I sailed with the HMS *Windsor* under Admiral Whetstone during the war and spent some time on Barbados. There was a young man there by the name of Bonnet. But that was over a decade ago."

"Well, Bonnet's have been gentleman sugar planters on Barbados for three generations, or so I have been told. So you sailed with Whetstone, eh, out of Port Royal?"

He nodded, stroking his beard thoughtfully. "He had just been knighted and appointed commander-in-chief of the West Indies fleet. There were terrible storms that summer. I believe this Bonnet may be the grandson of the admiral's first cousin, or something like that. It appears that the world is smaller than I thought."

"That be Bonnet all right. His mother was a Whetstone. All I know is the major should have stuck to soldiering on land because he doesn't know spit about the sea."

"He got forty men kilt or wounded, he did!" shouted one of the sailors as they hauled the longboat up onto the beach. "The no-good squab!"

Thache filed away what Hanks had just told him. So the clumsy Stede Bonnet was the son of a sugar plantation owner just like himself. And here they had both given up a life of wealth, privilege, and a liberal education to go off a-pirating. Then again, it wasn't so surprising. After all, living and working on a tropical plantation in the sweltering heat every day, even if you were an owner and not a working slave, wasn't very enjoyable. In fact, Thache had found the life tediously boring. Since a young age, he had always dreamed of escaping to the sea, and this Bonnet fellow must have felt much the same way and wanted to give up his lubberly life as a plantation owner for the promise of adventure upon the high seas.

"If you want to set eyes on the lubber, there he is now," said Pell, pointing north.

All eyes turned to the deck of the *Revenge*, anchored in the bay between a pair of recently careened pirate sloops. A plump figure had materialized from the stern great cabin and stepped forward onto the deck. Walking slowly like an old man, he wore only a silken dressing gown. His head and upper chest were wrapped in bandages and his right arm was bound in a sling. The figure hobbled to the starboard railing and peered at the crowd gathered on the beach and along the waterfront staring back at him. To Thache, he looked pale as a ghost, and in his hand he clutched a leatherbound book that he had been reading.

Peering through his spyglass at the man, Thache could tell, despite the heavy bandages, that it was indeed the young planter he had met on Barbados during the war: the Scotsman Stede Bonnet. Back then, he had been a thin young man with his whole life before him, brimming with hope and confidence, instead of a plump gentleman with a broken look and general weariness about him, but it was still the same man.

Thache felt sorry for him.

"Aye, that be our Major Bonnet," said Quartermaster Ishmael Hanks in a mocking tone. "As miserable wretch of a seamen as God ever saw fit to put aboard a ship."

The *Revenge's* crew echoed that sentiment with disdainful laughter and headed off for the taverns and brothels. Thache kept his glass trained on the inexperienced sea captain.

"What the hell are you looking at, Edward?" Vane needled him. "The man is an utter miscreant and scupperlout."

"That may be," said Blackbeard without taking his gaze off the portly, bandaged pirate captain hobbling across the deck in his dressing gown. "But sometimes even miscreants and scupperlouts have something to offer."

CHAPTER 20

WILLIAMSBURG, VIRGINIA

SEPTEMBER 4, 1717

"THROUGHOUT MY TENURE AS LIEUTENANT GOVERNOR, I have endeavored to be an honest man and faithful subject—and yet these backwards burgesses and their anonymous cronies continue to assail my character. As sure as day, the seditious scoundrels will not stop until they have removed me from my appointed post."

Here Spotswood stopped and adjusted his powdered wig, as it had nearly fallen off his bald pate due to his vigorous head shaking. His two companions, Robert Beverley and his older brother Captain Harry Beverley, stood there staring at him, unsure what to say at his unexpected outburst. The three men had taken lunch at a tavern and were walking along Duke of Gloucester Street towards the Capitol when Spotswood had taken his two companions by surprise and abruptly vented his frustration.

Captain Harry Beverley had only returned to Virginia two weeks earlier. After setting sail under Spotswood's directive in early July of the year before, he and his crew had met with disaster just as his brother Robert and Spotswood had feared. The day after setting out, the *Virgin* was surprised by a violent hurricane that forced Beverley to sail as far east as Bermuda. On the fifth day of the rerouted voyage, a Spanish man-of-war seized the sloop as it approached the Florida wrecks, even though Spain and England were not at war. As the captain had conveyed to Spotswood in his deposition for his August 29 transmittal to the Board of Trade in London, the ship was then "rifled, and the men stripped, abused, and made prisoners." Following his capture, Harry and his crew had been sent to St. Domingo, Hispaniola, where he had petitioned for a trial but had been refused. At that point, he had expected that he and his crew would be "sent to the mines." Instead, they were shipped to Vera Cruz, Mexico, where conditions worsened. Their captors provided them "no subsistence" and again refused them a trial. Because of provisions in the 1713 Assiento Treaty between Britain and Spain, there were Englishmen in Vera Cruz, and they donated what food they could to the prisoners. Even so, several of Harry's men died for lack of food and other necessities. After seven months of captivity, the captain managed to escape and make his way back to Virginia. He didn't know what had become of his crew and he had never managed to find any pirates.

Looking at the returned sea captain and his retired brother, Spotswood hadn't meant to work himself once again into a frenzy over his colonial rivals, but that is precisely what he had done. Though he hated to admit it, they were truly beginning to wear him down.

"I'm terribly sorry, Alexander. I know what a difficult bunch they can be," said Robert Beverley, who, having served four terms in the Virginia House of Burgesses understood well what Spotswood was up against.

The lieutenant governor shook his head in dismay. "They sent a letter to the Board of Trade in London. In it, they made accusations against me in the form of fifteen queries. I responded in detail to each allegation, but my greatest enemy is in London and I am not there to defend myself."

He was referring to William Byrd, who had a seat on the Governor's Council and was reported to be jockeying for the post of the House of Burgesses' General Assembly's London agent on behalf of Governor George Hamilton, earl of Orkney, the British Crown's top representative of Virginia who governed in absentia from his palatial offices in London. Byrd and Spotswood had had a troubled history. Years earlier, the lieutenant governor had, over Byrd's opposition, reorganized the collection of quitrents in order to enlarge the royal revenue. At the time, Byrd regarded the receiver's office as his own property and Spotswood's actions as a personal affront and the two had clashed repeatedly. In 1715, Byrd sailed for England and since then had sought to undercut Spotswood's agenda, lobbying to have him removed from office based on damaging information provided by disgruntled members of the House of Burgesses and powerful merchants like Micajah Perry. The colonists were opposed to Spotswood's Tobacco Inspection Act of 1713 and Indian Trade Act of 1714, which they felt were favorable to Spotswood and the British Crown but not Virginia or its colonists. The first regulated the quality and distribution of tobacco exports, and the second established a monopoly over commerce with the natives—with Spotswood as a prime beneficiary.

"My accusers even failed to sign their names," he went on, his voice high-pitched and nasally. "Why they made me out to be as corrupt and dictatorial as a Roman proconsul."

"What did they say exactly?" asked Captain Harry Beverley.

"They said I held no regard for the law, forcing customs officials to extort illegal fees and placing foreigners in courts of judicature. They proclaimed I was a mercenary seeking my own ends at public expense and building forts upon the frontier to further my private interests. And they said that I refused to permit the King's subjects to take up land while accumulating great tracts for myself."

"Oh my," said Robert Beverley. "I can see that our friend William Byrd has been busy."

"Yes, but it is Ludwell and the powerful merchants like Micajah Perry that are carrying the torch for him."

"What else are they saying?"

"That under me there is little justice in Virginia. Not only Englishmen, they claim, but Indians and slaves suffer from my tyranny."

"Why that is most unfair," bristled Captain Harry. "After everything you have done for this colony."

"They claimed that I have aroused sedition and rebellion by fostering disregard for the existing forms of government. They said I am greedy for power, driving from office those who oppose my will and seeking to establish a military dictatorship by the creation of a standing militia."

"And how did you respond to these charges?" asked Robert Beverley.

"I firmly declared most of them to be false, justifying the course I pursued, and maintained that the remainder of the accusations were too vague to warrant a formal response. To show that Virginia was not disaffected by my administration, I sent the Board of Trade a request presented to me by the grand jury at the October general court begging me to resume my place upon the general court bench."

Captain Harry nodded. "What do you think the outcome will be? Do you think you will be removed?"

"I don't know. But I wouldn't worry if I were you. I still command the respect of God-fearing gentlemen like yourselves and have a few tricks up my sleeve."

The two brothers nodded and the group fell into silence. But Spotswood could tell that his friend Robert Beverley still had something to say.

"What is it, Robert?" he asked him. "You know I appreciate your wise counsel."

"You know that I consider myself an 'Indian,'" said Beverley, referring to the moniker colonial Virginians liked to call themselves to demonstrate that they were first and foremost Americans and not merely pawns of Great Britain.

"A rather quixotic term, I must say," sniffed Spotswood. "So what is your point?"

"That perhaps a softer touch on your part might be what is needed to salve the wounds and usher in an era of cooperation betwixt you and your detractors."

"Nonsense!" snapped Spotswood. "How can I submit to them when I am wholly in the right!"

Beverley wagged a disapproving finger at him like a schoolmaster. "Now that is just the type of stubborn certitude that draws the ire of Ludwell, Byrd, Reverend Blair, and the others. These men just don't like being told what to do by the Crown at every turn. They want to be in charge of their own destiny."

"But they call themselves loyal subjects of the Crown."

"Aye," said Captain Harry, "but they still want their independence. That is why they resist you so."

Thinking for a moment, Spotswood realized they were right. His opponents considered him an obstacle in their path of gaining control of Virginia's affairs, and they were now so emboldened that they openly challenged him in virtually all matters of state. To accomplish their agenda of maintaining colonial independence, the Ludwell-Blair faction had cleverly installed William Byrd as their London agent to have him recalled. Though Byrd had claimed his mission in England was on behalf of "private business," Spotswood had learned from his own sources that he spent the majority of his time trying to undermine Spotswood's influence and support. Clearly, Byrd's long-term goal was to unseat him and win the appointment for himself as governor. Spotswood couldn't help but feel a major showdown was coming.

He was already facing increasingly stiff opposition in his day to day operations and ability to govern. For two straight years now, he had been at odds not only with the House of Burgesses, but his own Council and in particular Ludwell and Blair. He was currently embroiled with the deputy auditor over the collection of quitrents, and with the reverend he continued to battle over the control of assignment of clergymen to Virginia parishes. In addition, his quarrel with his own Council concerning the judiciary had not abated. While his colleagues insisted that only Council members should be given authority in the new criminal courts, Spotswood still clung to his prerogative of unilaterally naming judges of his own choice.

"We can't allow sedition to take root in our royal colony," he said to the two brothers to break the silence. "That would be anathema to His Majesty."

"We're not saying you have to capitulate to them," said Robert. "We're just saying you should be more diplomatic and show a willingness to compromise."

"Compromise? But I am the governor!"

"You are the lieutenant governor," pointed out Captain Harry. "The earl of Orkney getting fat and rich in London is the official royal governor of Virginia."

"I'm tired of Ludwell, Byrd, and their henchmen. Why they're as uppity as my Negro slaves."

"Which makes them only half as intransigent as mine," said Robert Beverley. "Now see here, Alexander. The fractious relationship that exists between yourself and the representatives of the Royal Crown, and the elected representatives of the colony's various counties, can only end one way." His silver eyebrows flexed upwards. "The same way it has for our King."

"You're saying that Parliament controls the King?"

"Precisely, just as the House of Burgesses and the Governor's Council control you. Do you understand now? If you can't learn to get along with these planters and merchants, as well as the commoners that support them, you are going to be out of a job."

"I shall never submit!" snorted Spotswood, his jaw set in an intractable pose.

"You may not have a choice," pointed out Captain Harry. "Just like me with the bloody Spanish."

"It was bad, wasn't it?" said his brother sympathetically, and all of a sudden the conversation shifted to the perilous journey that had ended in disaster for Captain Harry and his crew aboard the *Virgin*.

"Aye, and I still have the scars to prove it. As for my crewmen, I have no idea what's happened to them."

"I'm sorry, Harry," said Spotswood, feeling guilty for sending him on the dangerous mission in the first place. "I'm sorry for how it all turned out."

"I am too," he said. "But the worst part about it is we didn't even make it to the Florida wrecks and never even saw one damned pirate."

"I hear now that they have completely taken over New Providence and the other nearby islands, and that there are several black market traders that are moving their goods to Charles Town, Philadelphia, and Boston," said his brother Robert.

"Pirates are good for business," affirmed Captain Harry. "That's why the colonists protect them. They bring in cheap and abundant goods and even help offload them."

Spotswood was aghast. "Harry Beverley, what in the world has gotten into you? These men are villains—and those that fence their illicit goods are too!"

"Aye, but the point is the pirates have an underground network of traders that support them. You take away that network, you take away the pirate."

He had not thought of that before and found that he liked it. It was the opposite of the carrot and stick approach that the British government had long attempted to thwart piracy, by simultaneously offering pardons to those who gave up the account and severely punishing those who refused to quit the game and go on to live honest, law-abiding lives. He whispered under his breath the pet theory, making a mental note of it.

Take away the trading network, you take away the pirate.

"Yes, but it's easier said than done," said Robert Beverley to his older brother. Spotswood was intrigued. "Why is that?"

"People don't want to turn them in. As Harry has pointed out, pirates are very good for American business."

CHAPTER 21

NASSAU HARBOR

SEPTEMBER 4, 1717

STEDE BONNET smelled flame-broiled grouper and the smoky smell of charred mesquite. It came to him like a dream, but he knew he wasn't dreaming. The smells were too real and could mean only one thing.

He was still alive.

It was too bad because all he wanted to do was die. Overwhelmed with depression, heavily bandaged, still clad in his flimsy dressing gown, he had been sulking in his cabin since his arrival in Nassau several hours ago. Meanwhile, all but a handful of his crewmen had deserted the *Revenge* for the town's taverns and brothels. It pained him that his piratical career was over so shortly after it had begun—and yet he couldn't return home. He was an outlaw now and could no more reunite with his family that he had abandoned than he could restore the Stuart dynasty to the throne of England. So where did that leave him? Any remaining faith and respect that his crew had held for him had been lost after the disastrous engagement with the Spanish man-of-war.

He tried to open his eyes, but could manage only one. The world came to him in a blur, like the first streaks of predawn. Slivers of dying, late-afternoon sunlight slanted through his drawn shutters. He followed one of them with his good eye, laddering up to the little crack. The faint light bleeding through the little opening cast a bluish tint on everything around him, giving his great cabin an airy, ghostly quality. He took a sniff of air. Now he realized what he was smelling: pirates were cooking freshly caught fish over their beach fires on the shore.

Damnit, why can't I be dead? he lamented.

He felt dreamy and lightheaded. Nearby, he heard the sound of muffled voices—two voices he dimly realized, one deeper and richer than the other. The only other noise was the sound of the *Revenge* bobbing and creaking at her mooring as the tide rolled in on her Barbadian-cedar underbelly. Turning towards the sound, he felt a sharp pain shoot through his face. He recoiled, drawing his head down into his shoulders, and let out a groan.

My face—the splinters hit my face. He remembered his men screaming and his gunners unleashing their cannons and the swarthy faces of the Spaniards and the hot, burning sensation when the splinters struck him. Or was it a volley of swan- or grape-shot? He remembered falling to the quarterdeck and then the all-consuming blackness. But that was all he remembered.

Slowly, he brought his fingertips to his cheek, curious to know by what strange alchemy God Almighty had allowed a miserable wretch like him to live. He touched carefully, as he would caress the soft skin under the chin of his sleeping children: Edward, Stede Jr., and Mary. Instead of flesh he felt a poultice, covering his face like paste beneath a layer of heavy bandages.

He heard something bump against the hull followed by an exchange of voices. *Who is it?* he wondered nervously. *Was he being raided while he lay maimed and defenseless in his bed?* A moment later, he heard a knock on the door to his great cabin. He wanted desperately to hide under the covers like when he was scared as a little boy, but he coaxed himself not to do so and be strong.

"Yes, come in," he said crisply, hoping through the loudness of his voice to come across forcefully. He sat up in his bed. As he did so, the book he had been reading slipped off his chest and onto the floor. It was a copy of Woodes Roger's *A Cruising Voyage Round the World: The Adventures of an English Privateer.* One of his favorite books, it had just come out only a few years ago.

He looked up as a towering figure filled the doorway for a moment, blotting out the sun, and then the door closed behind him.

"Captain Bonnet? Hello, I'm Edward Thache, captain of the *Margaret.*"

It was the voice of a supremely confident yet humble and polite man—and Stede Bonnet found himself wishing that he had just such a voice. Despite the burning pain he still felt on his face, he smiled cordially at his visitor. But no introductions were necessary as he was well aware of who the man was.

He studied him in the dim light. His eyes were a piercing brown, the color of an El Greco painting. His thick, bushy beard was as black as a moonless night and braided into six plaits that were tied at the ends with ribbons. For armaments, he carried a long steel cutlass and a silken bandolier from which were suspended three brace of pistols, no doubt loaded and primed. All in all, a formidable looking man who was clearly not someone to cross swords with. And yet, there was an intelligence, grace, culture, and gentleness about him that suggested an affluent upbringing and liberal education.

"You're the one they call Blackbeard," he said. "My crew has been talking about you."

The man smiled with amusement. "I suppose I should be honored."

"It appears your reputation has preceded you. And unfortunately, so has mine. No doubt my men are drinking toasts this very minute to the bungling stupidity of the wealthy gentleman from Barbados who gave up his family to play pirate. Why I'll bet I'm the toast of the town."

"Aye, their words are none too kindly. But I happen to be a man that believes in second chances."

He hadn't expected that and took a moment to gather his thoughts. "So I take it this is a business proposition, not a courtesy call."

"Aye, I have a proposition for you. That is, once we get to know one another a bit better." He stepped to the shutter, opened it part way so that the sun streamed into the cabin, and then strode towards the bed to pick up the book on the floor. "Old Woodes Rogers, *A Cruising Voyage Round the World.* A favorite of mine."

"It's a first edition."

Thache opened it. "Indeed, it is." He waved his big hand expansively around the room. "You have quite a library here."

"I had it specially built and now it's half blown apart." He motioned towards the east wall where cannon shot had torn through the floor-to-ceiling bookcase and knocked down the leatherbound books, leaving behind a small pile of them next to splintered wood and broken glass. "You've heard all about it, I'm sure. How I insisted on attacking a Spanish ship-of-force when my officers and crew were yelling at me not to do it—and how I murdered half my crew and ruined my sloop. Look at her now"—his eyes darted around the room—"and tell me I haven't destroyed her through my bravado."

"She can be repaired and refit," said Thache laconically. "And so can you and your crew, *Captain* Bonnet. I can help you and you can help me. *We* can help each other."

"What sort of arrangement did you have in mind?"

"I will provide you with new crew members for the *Revenge*. I will send over my carpenter to repair your damaged sloop and my able surgeon to tend to your wounded. After handing over command of the *Margaret* to my first mate, Richards, I would assume command of the *Revenge* as a flagship—but only as long as it takes for you to recover from your appreciable wounds and earn back the trust of your crew. You would still occupy this great stern cabin with all your fine books."

Now that he had definitely not expected. "That is quite a proposition, Captain Thache. But what makes you think I trust you at all?"

"Because I know you."

"You know me? We've met before?"

"Aye, years ago on Barbados. But that's not what I mean when I say I *know* ye."

"Then what do you mean? I'm afraid you have me confused."

"It means that I come from a similar background as you and we have a connection."

"A connection? Well, now you have me intrigued."

"I grew up the son of a sugarcane planter the same as you. Only I was in Spanish Town, Jamaica, not Bridgetown on Barbados. I know precisely why you left your family behind and went on the account as a pirate captain." Here he paused, a gleam in his eye. "The sea called out to you, my friend, the same as it called out to me. You could no more stay put on that island than I could on Jamaica. It just took you longer to decide is all."

Mother Mary, it's as if he's peering into my very soul. "You presume a great deal, Captain Thache."

"But I am right, aren't I? I see a lust for adventure in your eyes. Your boredom with the life of a landlubber and thirst for bold action on the high seas are what made you do it. Surely, it wasn't just about your nagging wife and the loss you have endured. My parents are both dead so I, too, know a thing or two about loss, Captain Bonnet."

"So my crew told you about my wife and my son that died?"

"Aye, they told me. And from the look in your eyes I can tell you loved that boy dearly, the same as I love my young step-siblings: Cox, Rachel, and young Thomas. The King's men were coming for me and I had to sneak out without saying goodbye to them just last summer. Verily, I fear I will never see them again."

"Why not?"

"Because of the life I have chosen. It has changed my situation appreciably."

He stared off at the battered wall and bookcase. "It has changed mine as well," he said with a note of sadness, like a crestfallen prince.

"What was your son's name? The boy that died."

"Allamby. His name was Allamby. He was our first child. He died in his first year."

"I'm sorry. I know it must have been hard on you. And what about your wife? How do you think she's getting along now that you've gone a-pirating?"

"I have no idea. I just know that I could no longer stand living with her. But you're right, that wasn't the main reason I left. It was just as you said."

"The sense of adventure."

"Yes."

"The freedom of the wind in your hair and your sails."

"Truly. But I must confess it's not quite what I expected. In my mind, I romanticized it—all of it. And now there's no going back."

"I'm sorry. I didn't mean to make the mood glum."

"There's no way around it. We may be gentlemen, you and I, but we have chosen a career with a short life expectancy and little hope of redemption."

"Aye, but we're free and we're judged by our skill and resourcefulness, not the wealth or title of our forebears—and there's no bones about it. If you didn't believe in that, as I do, you surely would have never become a master of the sweet trade, now would you? You would be sitting in the comfort of your fine plantation home dreaming of being on a ship sailing to Jamaica or Charles Town with the damp salt on your face and wind in your hair."

"Yes, I suppose you're right."

They fell into silence. When he had first seen this Blackbeard fellow step into his cabin, he had feared that he would be dealing with some lower-class ruffian or cutthroat that had come here to shake him down or threaten him. But already the notorious pirate captain had put him at ease with his folksy charm. The man was an able listener with a sympathetic ear, had a sense of fairness about him, and appeared to be a good judge of character. Bonnet found himself quite taken by the pirate commander. At the same time, he knew he was suffering from mental and physical pain and was hardly in a position to refuse Blackbeard's generous offer.

He felt the man's powerful gaze upon him. "Do we have an accord, Captain Bonnet?"

"Yes, we have an accord, Captain Thache. But first you have to answer me one question. When did you and I first meet?"

"It was over a decade ago. I was an officer aboard the HMS *Windsor*, the flagship of Rear Admiral Sir William Whetstone, and we met in Bridgetown."

"The admiral is my grand-uncle. My mother's side is Whetstone."

"Aye, so I have been informed by your crew. You said as much when I met you as well. You came on board the ship to visit with your grand-uncle. That's when we met."

"Now I remember." He studied him more closely and gestured towards his lengthy ebony beard. "With the beard and all, I didn't recognize you."

"That's all right. 'Tis a bit different, isn't it?"

"I must confess that I like it. It must terribly frighten the ship captains of the prizes you take."

"Aye, I'll admit it has a tendency to make them quake at the knees and cry out for their mothers. But that's part of the magic of a long tangle of hair and its dressing up for show, isn't it now?" He grinned with mock nefariousness and stepped to the door, turning around when he reached it. "I'll send my carpenter and surgeon over straight away. We'll have your *Revenge* up and sailing in no more than a week. How does that suit you, *Captain* Bonnet?"

He couldn't help but feel excitement at his sudden reversal of fortune. When he had first sailed into Nassau, he was certain that his pirate career was over—and now he would be sailing with a legend.

Blackbeard.

"It suits me just fine, Captain Thache," he said with the composed smile of a gentleman. "It suits me just fine indeed."

CHAPTER 22

CAPE CHARLES, VIRGINIA COAST

SEPTEMBER 29, 1717

WITH FLYING FISH SCATTERING BEFORE HER BOW and seagulls wheeling and shrieking around his head, Caesar gazed out from the maintop at the escaping merchant vessel. The *Revenge* sliced through the white-tipped waves off the Virginia capes towards the fleeing prey, which had tacked into the wind and passed hard to starboard in an effort to evade the pirates' two-vessel flotilla. The captain had given the "Hands to quarters!" call minutes earlier when Caesar had first spotted the merchant vessel, and now every crewman was on high alert and every gun primed to deliver a warning shot or deadly payload—depending on whether the opposing captain chose to resist or not.

"Crowd that canvas and let her run before the wind, Master Hands!" Caesar heard Thache yell down below from the quarterdeck. "To lay alongside her, we'll need the weather, so get to it, man!"

Caesar smiled. For him, this was the best part of being a pirate: the chase. From his lofty perch at the top of the mainmast, he looked down at the crew. Nearly one hundred seamen were busy manning the sails, rigging, and cannon. Still more lined the starboard rail ready to deliver a musket volley and board their quarry. They stared intently, like wolves, at the fleeing merchant sloop.

Caesar shifted his gaze to Blackbeard, the name that the crew was openly calling their venerated captain now. He presented a tall, imposing figure even from a bird's-eye view with his crimson rover's jacket, bandoliered pistols, and thick black beard tied in plaits and ribbons, fluttering in the brisk wind like a hoisted Jolly Roger. Standing next to him was the "gentleman pirate" Stede Bonnet, who had joined up with the company in Nassau. During the past week as they had navigated their way north up the Atlantic seaboard, the former Barbadian planter had spent most of his time in his cabin reading his books and healing from his wounds. Caesar had spoken to him only once when he had brought him supper and found him a curious fellow, since he appeared to be uncomfortable on a ship and more interested in his books. But the captain seemed to like him and treated him with respect, allowing Bonnet to quarter in the great cabin though he carried no apparent command aboard the ship.

Caesar had seen the captain teaching the Barbadian gentleman pirate about seamanship. In Bonnet's quarters and once upon the deck, he had observed Thache showing him how to navigate by the sun and stars using a strange device the captain called an "English quadrant." The only crew members Caesar had seen using the instrument were Israel Hands, Richard Richards who was now captaining the *Margaret*, and now Bonnet, so he knew it was a difficult and important instrument to master to navigate a ship. He made it a point to listen in whenever Thache was on deck and in command of a vessel, usually during and after a chase, so he could learn what it took to be a sea captain.

It was clear from what Caesar had seen that Thache had mastered a wide variety of maritime skills. These included the ability to navigate, read charts and piloting instructions, recognize tidal changes, evaluate currents, and understand varying weather systems. Not only could he read, write, and make quick decisions about seamanship, he was able to make complicated mathematical computations. But his greatest gift was the simplest: he knew which way to point a ship to get to where he wanted to go, and he went ahead and did it time and again without hesitation. Caesar knew that very few others aboard the *Revenge* and *Margaret*— including Major Bonnet who spent most of his time in his cabin—could do that. Which was why he wanted to learn how to captain a ship so badly; if he could learn to command and navigate a boat, he would truly be someone to contend with in a world where most black men like him were worked to death and died at an early age as impoverished slaves.

It took them an hour before they had the weather gage on their target and hoisted the black flag from the *Revenge's* topmast. The sloop flew British colors and was named *Betty*. As they drew closer, Caesar estimated her size at forty tons and saw that she was armed with six carriage guns that looked to be two pounders. He wondered why the *Betty* hadn't struck her colors. Why wasn't the captain surrendering and instructing his helmsman to turn his sails into the wind? Was the man stupid enough to actually dare to put up a fight?

"Helm quarter to starboard, Mr. Hands!" commanded Thache down below.

"Aye, Captain!"

"Mr. Cunningham, you may prepare your guns and fire a single shot across her bow when ready!"

"It would be my pleasure!"

As the *Revenge* angled nearly alongside the merchant ship, twelve cannon muzzles rolled out from her gunports, primed and ready to fire. Caesar waited with tense anticipation. It was always a thrill to hear the boom of the cannons and the whistling sound of the cannon balls as they arced in front of their prey. He especially enjoyed it when he was lucky enough to be up high on lookout with a good view. Below William Howard—the *Revenge's* new quartermaster who had left Hornigold to sign on with Thache, replacing John Martin—stood along the starboard railing with the boarding party he would lead. The men were armed to the teeth with not only muskets and pistols, but blunderbusses, cutlasses, boarding knives, fuse-lit *grenadoes*, and ammunition pouches secured with leather straps about shoulders and belts. It was a determined, motley group of mostly white men with perhaps twenty percent African, West Indian, and mulatto—democratically united as one—that would brook no opposition and take what they wanted. Among them was Caesar's fellow black friend, Richard Greensail, who had streaked white, black, and red war paint on his cheeks along with several of the other Africans and smattering of West Indians to terrify their prey. The boarding party brandished and waved their weapons menacingly to strike fear into the captain and crew of the *Betty* to compel him to surrender without a fight—for if there was one thing a savvy pirate didn't want to do it was fight. Fighting, and the injuries and destruction it resulted in, posed a serious risk to profits and was to be avoided like the plague.

It was then something happened that stunned and incensed everyone. Caesar was the first to see it and couldn't believe his eyes.

"She's rolling out her guns, Captain!" he yelled down to the quarterdeck.

"Aye, I can see! Fore and aft, all hands!"

"She's coming into the wind!" cried Israel Hands. "They're going to heave to!"

"Bring us about, damnit!" Then to the master gunner. "When you have her in your sights, open fire, Mr. Cunningham!"

"Across her bow?"

"Aye verily. Two shots, Mr. Cunningham—we'll give her two shots. Though she's made the mistake of rolling out her cannon, we'll give her captain a fair chance to acknowledge who is master and turn into the wind!"

Cunningham nodded and waved his arm forward in a dramatic gesture. "Fire a double across her forefoot!"

Before Caesar had taken another breath, the first cannon erupted along the starboard gun port, followed quickly by another blast that again rocked the *Revenge*. The shots screamed across the bow of the merchant sloop, and he saw at least a dozen seamen dive for cover. Shifting his gaze to the quarterdeck, he saw Thache, Bonnet, and Israel Hands nodding their heads in approval at the show of force. The warning shot sent a clear message: yield and strike the colors immediately, without a fight, or no quarter would be given. Clearly, they were confident that the stubborn captain of the *Betty* would finally be cowed into submission and lay by to be boarded with no further resistance.

But again, Caesar and everyone else on board was stunned by the *Betty's* next move. Instead of striking her colors, the captain proceeded to set more sail and try to escape, his British Union Jack flapping defiantly astern in the stiff breeze.

"I dare swear I've never seen the likes of such a thing before!" roared Thache in disbelief, so loud that to Caesar he sounded like he was standing next to him and yelling into his ear. "Whoever be that stubborn squab who calls himself a sea captain, he needs to be taught a lesson!"

Caesar agreed. What could her captain be thinking? There was no escape: he would be caught sooner or later and would have to submit. And then his punishment would be far more severe on account of his resistance. Below, Thache was livid with anger at this stunning lack of respect for him and the force at his command. Caesar wondered if perhaps the notorious Blackbeard would have the captain flogged in front of his men or tortured in some way for his ill-advised defiance. Or would he even go so far as to kill him and his crew as a warning to other merchantmen?

"Mr. Cunningham, please take down her mast and sails with a round of carefully placed shot! Mr. Howard, a volley from your muskets would do nicely as well! Make her surrender, gentlemen, and do it quickly! I'm fast running out of patience with this deviltry!"

All along the starboard gunwale, Caesar now saw an eruption of cannon and musket fire. The *Revenge* hummed and vibrated from the concussive blasts and the *Betty* was quickly enveloped abovedecks in bar and chain shot. The tide of battle swiftly turned. With her mast and spars severely damaged, her mainmast shredded and jib ripped apart, her forward lines snarled, and her crew driven belowdecks, the captain of the *Betty* had no choice but surrender. Caesar saw the colors struck. The helmsman turned the sloop into the wind and the captain relinquished his command as the vessel drifted to a halt and bobbed up and down in the rolling swells. The crew aboard the *Revenge* raised their weapons and gave a raucous cheer that echoed across the water, reverberating all the way to the trembling crewmen aboard the *Betty*. They knew they would pay a heavy price for their captain's defiance, even as feeble as it was.

Caesar scrambled down the rigging to claim first prize with the boarding party for spotting the vessel. He still had his sights set on another pistol like the captain's, which would give him four total to be slung about his midriff. When his bare feet touched down on deck, he saw Thache standing with Bonnet at the quarterdeck. He appeared to be explaining something to the portly gentleman pirate, but overall he seemed angry over the ill-advised defiance of the *Betty* and her captain. As the boarding party threw grapnel irons over the side and lashed the two ships together, Thache stepped away from the Barbadian and came over to the starboard rail to join the boarding party. Given the *Betty's* open defiance, it would be a strong show of force and most of the crew would take part to send a message.

"You'll be joining us then, Captain?" Caesar said to him as the two men withdrew their primed pistols.

"Aye, I'll be joining you," he said. "I want a word with the captain."

And with that, an angry horde of yelling and taunting pirates swarmed aboard the *Betty* with pistols and blunderbusses, knives and cutlasses, ready to bring severe harm to any soul that offered the least bit of further resistance.

CHAPTER 23

MARCUS HOOK, PENNSYLVANIA

OCTOBER 9, 1717

THACHE WAS IN THE THROES OF RAPTURE. He had waited nearly two years for this. The world spun in a pleasant way, as if he were swimming the aquamarine waters off the stately granitic Baths of Virgin Gorda, one of his favorite places on earth. He arched his back and kissed his love Margaret's lips as she slid back and forth on top of him. A churning euphoric sensation took hold of his lower stomach, and he suckled on her hard, slippery nipple as they continued to thrust in unison. Her womanly scent was sweet and thick, like the dense tropical air of his father's Spanish Town plantation when he was a boy. His arms reached out, clasping her smooth bottom, and he pulled her to him, penetrating upward, deeper. She let out a moan and he could feel himself about to let go.

He had waited almost two years for this. Two long years.

This was the way it was supposed to be.

As their naked bodies rubbed together and worked in unison, he knew he should have married her and never left Marcus Hook to go a-pirating. To his chagrin, his life had changed irrevocably. There was no turning back the clock and starting all over again. He couldn't help but feel a sense of regret at the path he had chosen, despite the thrill of the chase and commanding men at arms, and the pure fun of being independent and rebelling against authority.

But what he felt most of all right now was love and passion amid a feeling of desperation that his time was running out. Despite their being apart for so long, he still felt a powerful connection, a sense of profound intimacy with her, and he knew that she felt it too. It was almost as if he had never left. But even more viscerally, it was like when he was a young first-mate sailing out of the port of Philadelphia and they frequently spent time together. He felt that same youthful passion, as if he were a young adolescent experimenting with sexuality for the first time, swept up in the adventure of pure discovery.

He dearly loved his Margaret of Marcus Hook.

Outside, along the banks of the Delaware, a light rain fell. Puffy gray cumulus clouds shrouded the river basin. The rainfall coming off the moisture-laden nebula was slowly picking up in intensity.

He pushed upward and their lips touched softly. He had wrapped his heavy beard in ribbons to keep it under control for their love-making. He felt desire flowing through his veins, but it was different than the last time they had made love before he had set out for the Florida wrecks. His head swam with euphoria, but also a sense of danger, knowing that he was an outlaw wanted by the authorities and this might be their very last moment on earth together.

"Oh, Edward," she whispered in his ear.

He rolled her over so that he was on top. His tongue reached inside her mouth, softly, and she kissed him back. He felt a delightful shudder of excitement take hold of his body, but it was the emotional connection that truly gripped him. He knew he was tapping into something sacrosanct, something only true lovers felt. But he also knew that he didn't deserve her. She could have had any number of promising men in Philadelphia and yet she chose to love and stand by him.

He kissed her mouth, nibbling her lips gently. They slowed down for a moment to a softer and gentler rhythm, and it felt like a perfect dream. Everything about it felt right, natural.

Then they again picked up the pace. As they began to move together in sync, he took more and more pleasure in her body, in her sweet kisses and caresses and thrusts. And her body was responding with a passion that resurrected glorious emotions from their younger years together when he was a simple merchant seaman and privateer—and not a wanted pirate.

I want you to feel what I'm feeling, Margaret my love.

She thrust back and forth knowingly, in a gentle rhythm. His hands squeezed her swelling nipples, and she gasped with delight.

For a moment, he wondered if it were possible to go insane with pleasure.

He kissed her on the lips tenderly and she slid her tongue deep into his mouth, clasping his tight buttocks and pulling him deeper inside her. She moaned softly between kisses and the sound of her voice excited him all the more.

As the pace quickened, the air filled with desperation. He felt himself about to let loose with his seed. He sensed that she, too, was about to let go.

"Look into my eyes," she gasped, pulling him still deeper.

His eyes locked onto hers. "I'm looking, I'm looking!"

She stared at him mesmerically, her eyes as wide as pebbles as the climax came. They held each other's gaze as their bodies shook fitfully and he felt his warmth flow inside her. Then suddenly tears streamed from her eyes.

"I dare say are you all right?" he asked worriedly. "Did I hurt you?"

"No," she cried.

"Are you upset? What...what happened?"

"I'm overwhelmed, Edward. I'm overwhelmed with joy."

ψψψ

Afterwards, they lay in bed—idly hugging, kissing, stroking—before she asked him what he had done with the *Betty* after seizing her off the Virginia capes. She had posed the question to him a half dozen times since he had made port late last night, but he had not yet answered it to her satisfaction. He had told her only brief snippets about his privateering and piratical adventures since sailing off for the Spanish wrecks almost two years ago. She was fully aware that he was an outlaw of the high seas now, and though she didn't approve, she was interested to know the details, especially since he had named his ship after her. But he was determined to limit the flow of information, for fear that she would come to despise him for his villainy and end their relationship altogether. For he loved her dearly and didn't want to lose her.

So instead of answering the question, he proceeded to tell her about his friend

Sam Bellamy and his unusual philosophy of pirates as not "villains of all nations" as they were made out to be by the Crown and America's foremost newspaper, the *Boston News-Letter* controlled by the British government, but rather as Robin Hood's Merry Men of the high seas. He told her how he had sailed with Bellamy and that his friend was now regrettably deceased, killed in a shipwreck when a catastrophic storm drove him and his pirate ship onto the banks of Cape Cod. He told her how the "Prince of Pirates" had been attempting to return home to show off his newly acquired flagship, the formidable three-hundred-ton armed merchant galley *Whydah*, to his love Maria Hallett. He told her how nine of Bellamy's shipmates had somehow survived, but had been captured and jailed in Boston, where they were about to be tried and would likely be convicted of piracy and hanged. And finally, he told her how the news had so outraged him and his crew that they vowed to wage a war of retribution against ships of New England. That was why he had returned to the Atlantic seaboard: to avenge Bellamy and take on the new mantle of Robin Hood and his Merry Men.

"But the *Betty* wasn't a New England vessel," she pointed out. "So what did you do with her? Don't tell me you killed anyone or sunk her to the bottom."

"We didn't harm anyone, that I promise you. That is not how I operate."

"But you did sink her?"

"Aye. She continued to sail away when we called for her to yield. We put the captain and his crew in a longboat and made sure they were well-stocked with water and victuals. That's better than they deserved after the fight they put up."

"Did you fire upon them?"

"We fired two warning shots and tore up her mast and rigging, but we took the life of not a single man—and that's all there is of it."

"Oh, how generous of you. I suppose those poor seamen should have thanked you that they had the honor of meeting the big, bad Blackbeard himself."

"That's not funny. Are you trying to start a quarrel when I haven't seen you in two nearly years?"

"As a matter of a fact, I am. Look at what you've become, Edward. You're nothing but a common thief. I should have known it would come to this when you took off for those wrecks to seek your fortune."

He sat up in bed, irked by her lecturing tone. "I don't have to take this from you. I may be a low-down pirate, as you intimate so incisively, but some would call me but a true cock of the game and an old sportsman. Most importantly, I am a man that deserves a fair and honorable wage. And to do that, I will not bow to the likes of King George and allow thieving merchant tycoons to take all the pie, leave me with nothing, and drink toasts with their peers that they are better men than me when they have not a quarter of the smarts or courage of I."

"Oh, aren't you the high and mighty one."

"I told you we are the same as Robin Hood's men. Nothing more or less."

"Oh, you fancy yourself Robin Hood, do you? Well then, in that case you are even more naïve than I thought. Your dead pirate friend Black Sam Bellamy has filled your head with childish nonsense."

"There's nothing childish about such thoughts. We freebooters are no more lawless than the royals, slavers, and merchant men who steal from the common man every day. They press down upon him with their thumbs to keep him in line and sap him of everything until there's nothing left of him but his grounded-down bones. We are after what is fair and that is all."

"So you're a rebel now, is that it? You—born of landed Jamaican gentry."

"The devil himself may doubt it, but it takes a true devil to know one. I've seen the plantation world up close because I lived it in Spanish Town for more than a decade, and I've sailed with the Royal Navy and merchant service and seen those bastards in close action as well. I know what they take from and leave a hard-working man—and I don't much think it's fair. I understand that enslaved and indentured men and much-abused sailors are what have built up these colonies and made the Thache family of St. Jago de la Vega a wealthy one. But I don't think one man owning another, or telling him what to do, on account of his father's name or station in life is right by the laws of man. I have known that since I was a young pup, but it was Bellamy that brought it to the fore. The lad made me think upon what is right and wrong in this here world. Do we look at it from the top down, or the bottom up? Like Sam, I believe we are obligated as men to do both. And that's the honest truth. Me and those that sail under me just want fairness, our own little sliver of the pie, Margaret. We're not that complicated or greedy. We are, in fact, simple men with a simple purpose. We want but what is fair and right, damnit!"

The room fell silent. He hadn't meant to sound so passionate, but he felt strongly about the subject, more strongly than he had ever felt before. Thankfully, he could tell by the expression on her face that his words had had an effect upon her. Her eyes were sincere and watery, and he suddenly wanted to take her in his arms and marry her. Was there any way he could be forgiven for his crimes of piracy and go on to live a normal life? Was it truly too late to start anew? Or was there a chance?

"Once again, you have surprised me, Edward, with the strength of your convictions. You are a good man—the truth of that could not be more obvious from the words you just spoke—but you're still a bloody pirate. You're still a wanted man, an outlaw, a villain of all nations as the newspapers have taken to calling you of late. And that is what worries me so because I love you very much."

He touched her cheek. "I love you too," he said.

"Yes, but it's quite clear you love the sea more. Now what became of the *Betty* when you were through with her?"

"I told you we sunk her."

"Put her down to Davy Jones' Locker. Just like that."

"Aye, just like that. We plundered her of her pipes of Madeira wine and other goods, merchandize, and personal valuables—and then we sank her and her remaining cargo."

"You just wasted a perfectly good ship?"

"We didn't waste anything. The captain resisted and that was his mistake. I ordered the destruction of the *Betty* and its unplundered cargo in retribution for the captain's stubbornness. Sinking the ship sends a message to other vessels to the futility of resistance."

She was eyeing him disapprovingly. "How did you sink her? Did you blow her up?"

"Nay, I had my quartermaster William Howard drill holes in the *Betty's* hull and then sink her once I had secured the captain and crew aboard my flagship, the *Revenge*. We didn't want to allow her to alert all of Virginia and Maryland to our presence in these coastal waters. That way I could come here to see you."

"Oh, how generous of you."

"It's just the way I've chosen to make a living, Margaret. I'm no better or worse than Governor Keith or Governor Hunter," he said of the governors of Pennsylvania and New York-New Jersey. "I just want a fair slice of the pie, and so do my men. That's all."

"How did your quartermaster get off the boat?"

"As the *Betty* sank, Mr. Howard and his men climbed aboard a longboat and returned aboard the *Revenge*."

"So the *Betty* was a wine ship?"

"Lucky for us, eh? Her captain said she sailed regularly from Virginia to Madeira. That be an archipelago in the North Atlantic southwest of Portugal. But she won't be sailing there anymore. The captain shouldn't have resisted."

She sat up in bed. "You know perfectly well, Edward Thache, that one day you'll be doing a fine dance at the end of a rope if you keep up this line of work. Surely, I can't be the first person to tell you that."

"You're right, you're not. And I'm sure you won't be the last one either."

"I don't approve of what you're doing."

"I believe you've made that abundantly clear."

"You may share my bed and I may cook you up fine Swedish meals because we've shared some memorable times together, but I don't like this new world of yours. It scares me and eventually it's going to get you a date with the hangman. Just like poor Captain Kidd."

"That will never happen. Me and my crew will blow up our ship with our powder stores before we let them take us alive."

"How can you even talk like that? Do realize how you sound at this moment?"

He felt his blood about to boil over, but told himself to remain calm. "Upon my honor, I do. But this is the path I have chosen, Margaret. I will not let them capture me. If they corner me, I plan to go out with a loud bang not a whimper."

She drew closer to him, draping her leg over his thigh. "That's not funny, you know. I don't like you talking like that. It's so dark."

"I'm just telling you the truth. You deserve that much. That's why I can only promise you one more thing."

"And what would that be?"

"If my time comes, I promise I won't go out like Kidd. That's no way for even an outlaw to meet his Maker. No way at all."

CHAPTER 24

PHILADELPHIA, PENNSYLVANIA

OCTOBER 10, 1717

THE NEXT MORNING, the two young lovers strolled down High Street arm in arm, enjoying the pleasant fall weather before he and the other crew members had to return to the *Revenge* and *Margaret*. The sky was an untrammeled blue and the two- and three-story brick buildings lining the cobblestone street were bathed in luxurious sunlight creeping over the Delaware River to the east. There wasn't much breeze, but what little there was blew refreshingly on their faces as they made their way down the central east-west thoroughfare of the city to the tolling of Sunday church bells.

Philadelphia. When Thache had sailed as a first-mate out of the Quaker port city beginning shortly after the war and for two years afterwards, he had divided his time as a merchant officer between the town founded by William Penn and Port Royal. He was at ease in the burgeoning colonial city, and its townspeople were equally comfortable with him. The bustling streets and docks of Philadelphia were an awe-inspiring sight for young sailors, and Edward Thache of Jamaica had quickly come under the city's magnetic spell.

It was a big town, one of the New World's biggest. He enjoyed seeing the endless masts sprouting up from the river and the clouds of luffing sails and standards drying in the light air as dozens of ships lay at anchor, bobbing up and down along with periaugers, barges, and canoes. He enjoyed hearing the staccato of clomping horse hooves and clatter of drays, carriages, and carts grinding up the cobblestone and dirt streets. He enjoyed standing at the wharves and watching the cargo ships loading and unloading merchandise from all around the world: stacks of animal skins, lumber, carpentry tools, and munitions; kegs of gunpowder, grain, and seed; rounds of cheese, cases of books, and other sundries; casks of salted beef, fish, and pork and wet goods of wine, beer, and spirits, rolling this way and that. And he enjoyed smoking his pipe, drinking an ale, and sharing the latest news with the arriving and departing sailors loitering about the wharves, taverns, and ordinaries.

He liked this City of Brotherly Love. It was a part of him—and so was his beloved Margaret.

He gently squeezed her hand, smiled at her, and gave her a warm kiss on the lips. She looked up at him with surprise.

"What was that for?"

"Because I am quite fond of you. You didn't have to wait for me, though."

"I didn't wait for you. I just haven't found anyone that can hold a candle to you yet."

"And I haven't met anyone that can hold a quarter of a candle to you, my dear."

"None of those dark-eyed West Indian girls struck your fancy?"

"Not above the waistline, they didn't."

She shoved him hard in the chest. "You bastard!"

"Avast!" he shrieked with laughter. "Curse me with everlasting torments, I was just pulling your leg!"

"I don't believe you, Edward Thache."

"Well, you'd better because I speak the truth."

"If you truly loved me you wouldn't leave me to go off a-pirating."

"I humbly disagree. The love a seamen possesses for his woman ashore is the strongest love of all. It never dies, because whenever he returns it's just like falling in love all over again. Landlubbers don't understand that, but that be the truth of it."

"Distance is just a matter of space, but hearts are connected by love, is that it?"

"Now you're getting the gist of it, m'lady"

She leaned into him, her flowing blonde hair fluttering in the gentle wind. "You make it sound so romantic."

"It is romantic—and I am a romantic myself, as you well know. The bond betwixt a sea captain and his true love, even when they are apart, is greater than any love a pair of landlubbers feel. It is the power of the sea and the distance between the pair that sets them apart from most mortals."

"You sound like a philosopher."

"Aye, a pirate philosopher I be on occasion. But what I say is true for all men."

He took her by the hand and they kept walking, passing row after row of simple and unadorned Quaker houses. There was also a smattering of Swedish- and English-style designs in the neighborhood, but the architecture was dominated by Quaker lodgings. One of Thache's favorite buildings in the city was the elegant Old Swede's Church beyond the southern outskirts of the city, near the banks of the Delaware. Several of Margaret's Swedish family members lived near the church, so she had attended mass there before and he had accompanied her on two prior occasions.

They came upon a furrier and jewelry shop and went inside. Thache bought her a little silver locket necklace and clasped it around her neck. She thought it too expensive, but he convinced her that he would not take no for an answer from such an attractive woman, which made the proprietor and Margaret both smile.

When they were walking again arm in arm down the street, he said, "The locket and necklace are fine, but not half as fine as the woman wearing them."

"Do you really mean that, Edward Thache?"

"Verily I do."

She ran her fingers along the silver necklace, appreciatively. "I still can't believe you bought it for me. Three pounds is quite a lot of money."

"Not for a notorious pirate," he said with a grin.

She rolled her eyes and laughed. He drew her close and gave her a kiss. Though they were both a touch sad over his impending departure, he couldn't help but feel a great warmth inside seeing her toss her head back and laugh. He knew how to make her giggle and cheer her up when she was blue. He knew that was his special gift: he had a knack for reading people and lifting their spirits when they were down, even while he felt his own sadness inside and kept his feelings to himself. But then he saw the tears in her eyes.

"Come now, my beauty, what are those for?" he asked her.

She sniffled. "I don't want you to leave. And I'm scared of what might happen to you."

"Don't be frightened, my dear. Nothing is going to happen to me."

"But I had a dream and in it you—" She stopped right there, covering her hand with her mouth. "I'm sorry, I didn't mean to say that."

"In your dream, I died."

She nodded.

"Whatever happens, it is God's will. So you shouldn't worry yourself over it."

"I am going to miss you terribly," she said. She struggled mightily, but could not hold back a torrent of tears. He held her in his arms, consoling her. He ached to think that he was going to leave her again and wouldn't be able to hold her like this for a long time, how long he didn't even know.

"What if I promised to come back for you, one day, as a wealthy gentleman and we were to be married? Would you wait for me?"

"Aye, I would wait for you for an eternity. I have never loved anyone as I love you, Edward Thache."

He leaned down and kissed her again.

"I'd have my own shipping company, but I would be a fair and kindly merchant, and we'd live in a fine house right here on bustling High Street with our five children."

"Five children?"

"Aye, three sons and two daughters, who would all grow up to be big and strong and smart as foxes."

Her eyes lit up. "It sounds wonderful. I can picture it in my mind."

He smiled at her as she rested her head gently upon his shoulder. "Our house will be a fine Swedish house—not one of those drab Quaker shanties—and the boys and girls would have their own separate rooms. It would have a fancy parlor and a big kitchen table for when your family came to visit on Sunday evenings for your fine Swedish dishes."

"It sounds so romantic."

"It is going to be romantic. In addition to living in our fine house, we would visit all the cities from New York to Charles Town for social functions. And of course, you would wear only the latest French fashions."

"Oh, stop it. You're so silly."

"We can have it, Margaret—we can have it all. I'm going to take me a big ship as a prize, a ship so big that not even British fifth-rates will dare to challenge me. And then I'm going to get rich with plunder and retire with you here in Philadelphia."

He felt her body tense and the contented and dreamy expression had evaporated from her face, replaced again with a look of worry.

"Don't go," she said. "Just stay here with me and don't go off on the account. Please, I don't want you to die."

He gently rubbed her head. "I am not going to die. I am too clever for that."

"But they'll catch up to you eventually. You know they will."

"I will have quit by then—and you and I will be living the life that we always dreamed."

119

"But that's just a fairy tale. It won't happen like that and you know it. You'll end up like Black Sam Bellamy and his crew—taken by the sea or the gallows. It doesn't matter which, it will be a cruel end for you."

"Hush, now you're scaring even the notorious Blackbeard himself."

"That's not funny. You need to quit the pirating life, and you need to do it now before it's too late. It may be merry, but it is altogether too short."

A gang of wild young boys raced past them. He watched them for a moment, remembering back to his boyhood in Jamaica long before he had become a pirate. Suddenly, he felt the oppressive burden of the life he had chosen. It was going to be intolerably lonely again without his dear Margaret. It was then she took him by surprise. Tears burst from her eyes and she began to cry uncontrollably, her usual stoicism withering before him. He felt for her, knowing that he felt the same desperate feelings as did she. But he also knew that she was right. The law would close in on him eventually, and he had the dreaded feeling that sooner rather than later he would face more danger than he had ever faced before.

"I don't want you to leave!" she cried, gripping his sturdy shoulder fiercely.

"I don't want to go either," he said to her, feeling miserable. "But I have to. I have a hundred and fifty men counting on me. But everything's going to be fine."

"Will you at least promise to come back for me?"

"Aye, I promise I will return for you. I have never loved anyone like I love you, Margaret my dear."

She wiped away the tears. "Truly you promise? You're not just saying that to make me stop crying?"

"I'm coming back for you, I promise. And when I do, you and I are going to be properly wed and live together to a ripe old age."

She put her lips to his and they kissed with unbridled passion, his tricorn hat falling from his head in all the excitement and tears pouring from her eyes, and then he picked up his hat, dusted it off, and they were walking hand in hand once again along High Street. He felt the power of his love for her, and wondered by what strange alchemy he had managed to win over such an amazing woman.

Forever, he thought. *When I come back, we're going to be together forever— with our fine Swedish house and our five wonderful children.*

In his mind, he could picture it perfectly. But he knew, deep down, it was most likely never going to happen.

CHAPTER 25

MOUTH OF DELAWARE BAY

OCTOBER 12, 1717

THACHE STUDIED THE FACE OF CAPTAIN CODD. In his last year and a half as a pirate, he had seen the look more than two dozen times before. Codd was typical: having surrendered his vessel to a gang of wild-looking, heavily armed pirates, the merchant ship captain's face and body language showed a combination of abject fear and morbid curiosity. He had been sailing from Liverpool and Dublin with one hundred fifty passengers, most of whom were indentured servants, and a substantial cargo of supplies, when the *Revenge* and *Margaret* took him along the high sandy capes of the Delaware. Thache promptly sent his longboat over to the surrendered vessel to secure him, his officers, and his official mariner's logbook, bills of lading, passes, navigational charts, and other documents. He was now asking the prisoner questions regarding the nature of his cargo while reviewing his official documentation and charts—all following standard protocols used by both privateers and pirates. Meanwhile, Quartermaster William Howard and his raucous boarding party were taking inventory and plundering the vessel. Captain Codd and his officers would be held onboard until all their valuable plunder was located and subsequently secured in the holds of the two pirate vessels.

The merchant captain appeared unusually anxious sitting in the wooden chair of the *Revenge's* refurbished great cabin. Despite how deliberately cordial and accommodating Thache was being to his guest, Codd's mannerisms were halting and nervous. To put his mind at ease, Thache poured his guest a glass of Madeira and shared a drink with him. But Codd was still tense. He had expected his opposite number to be a drunken cutthroat and appeared unsure of what to make of the uncannily calm and polite gentleman whose rowdy crew was making clamorous sounds pillaging his vessel. It was as if Codd thought his host was merely feigning common courtesy and would at any second transform into some sort of monster bent on having him and his crew tortured and killed.

Blackbeard found the whole situation ironic. After all, it wasn't he, but Captain Codd, who was acting unconscionably—by transporting nearly one hundred fifty indentured servants in his cramped hold. True, they weren't actually slaves, but if you had asked them how happy they were to be on the hook for seven years of backbreaking labor and serfdom to answer for their unfortunate choice of politics, escaping a press or labor gang, stealing a loaf of bed so their children wouldn't starve, being born a Scot, or merely to secure passage to the New World, they would have said not at all. It always amazed Thache how merchant captains like Codd believed that they themselves weren't profiteering rascals, that they were superior to morally corrupt pirates even though they made vast sums of money as mariners by treating people like chattel. It didn't make any sense. Merchant seamen like Codd were as big as thieves as any sea bandit, but they would never own up to it. It made Thache angry at the unfairness of the world. He aimed to set things right.

Early on in his piratical career, working the sweet trade in consort with Hornigold, he had shown a measure of restraint, taking mostly French and Spanish prizes and then only the goods he needed from those he captured. But now in the wake of Bellamy's death and with his crew soon to swing from the gallows in Boston, Thache had proposed his own personal agenda to his shipmates. The American pirate was declaring war on the whole British Empire, and he would use piracy and terror to bring the Crown, and particularly its greedy ruling and merchant class, to its knees. While Hornigold had limited his operations to maritime theft, the ambitious Thache was now prepared to raise the stakes of the contest to embrace the philosophy of his good mate Bellamy. His goal was to bring as much damage to British commerce as possible, short of the unnecessary taking of human life. From now on, he and his crewmates would indeed be Robin Hood's men and seize, destroy, or liberate all cargo taken from the prizes of all nations they boarded.

After taking a moment to examine one of Codd's bills of lading, Thache looked up at the captain. "What will happen to the indentured men and women in your cargo hold when you get to Philadelphia?" he asked him.

"They will work as farm laborers or domestic servants. A handful will be apprenticed to skilled craftsmen."

"What's your percentage of the merchant profits?"

"I don't know what you mean."

"You know perfectly well what I mean. You hold the indenture on at least a portion of these slaves, do you not?"

Codd frowned at the choice of words. "But they're not *slaves*."

"They will be for the next half-decade or more. And some will be for life, and you damn well know it. So don't lie to me. It makes me angry when people—especially holier-than-thou scupperlouts like you—take me for a fool and lie to my face. It's not a very gentlemanly way of going about one's business, now is it?"

Codd bowed his head meekly. "If I have angered ye, I offer me apologies."

"No need to apologize, just don't lie to me. Now what is your take in this?"

"I get seven pounds per head."

"How many head?"

"One hundred forty. The ten others are paying passengers."

"So your take is just shy of a thousand pounds. That's quite a lot of money for a merchant captain. But not one, I suppose, involved in the slave trade."

The man started to argue but then thought the better of it and said no more. But then he seemed to have second thoughts and couldn't resist defending himself and his actions. "I told ye, Captain Thache, they be not *slaves*."

"Tell that to the seventy of them that will die after a year or two in the fields, or who will be whipped to death by their masters."

This time, Codd knew better than to challenge him and snapped silent, not wanting to push his luck. Thache stared at him in disgust. Dealing in human cargo—whether it was slaves or indentured servants—was no way to make a living in his view. Unless, of course, it was pirated cargo that could be offered a better life by exchanging one master for a better one. In that case, slave or indentured cargo could be used to tip the scales more favorably for the dispossessed.

"I do believe I'll have a look at your cargo," he then said to the captain, who tried, unsuccessfully, to talk him out of it. Fifteen minutes later, they had rowed back to Codd's vessel and all the indentured servants stowed belowdecks were brought up to the main deck so they could be inventoried.

Nothing could have prepared Thache for the sight he saw. Having spent most of the ten-week oceanic journey from Dublin stuffed into cramped quarters belowdecks, the indentured passengers were in a miserable state. Disease had run rampant in the immigrants' overly crowded, poorly ventilated quarters. Many of the men, women, and children were rail thin, had unhealthy complexions, coughed uncontrollably, and had black circles around their eyes and open sores on their faces and lips. Thache saw at once that Codd had treated them no better than rats. They were hungry and thirsty and had been subjected to extremes of confined space, frost, heat, dampness, and the illness of their co-passengers. Many of them were covered with lice. Thache felt an overwhelming pity for them and knew that all they wanted to do was make land. Instead, they had the added misfortune of now being the prisoners of pirates, which would delay their long-awaited arrival to the New World.

He couldn't do much for them, but he could at least feed and water them and make Codd and his men pay for their ill treatment. Thache did precisely that as his men continued to plunder the ship. When it was all over, they had taken whatever cargo and valuables they fancied: silver coin, jewelry, rum, foodstuffs, ammunition, and navigational instruments. But unlike in the past, Thache did not leave anything behind for the captain and his officers and crew. This time they dumped the remaining cargo into the sea. When one of the merchant passengers on board the ship saw his commercial cargo worth more than one thousand pounds sterling being tossed overboard, he begged to be allowed to keep enough cloth to make just one suit of clothes, but the pirates refused, throwing the last bolt of textiles overboard. By the time they released the ship, nothing remained of its cargo and Codd and the other merchants stood there in open-mouthed disbelief. Never in their lives had they witnessed such wanton destruction.

But in Blackbeard's view, there was nothing about it that was wanton. He knew exactly what he was doing.

He was waging a war not only against the British Empire but versus all empires. A war against the strong on behalf of the weak. And he was doing it for his friend Black Sam Bellamy and their brotherhood of pirates all around the world. The British authorities and newspapers would, of course, now brand him and those who sailed with him under the black flag as *hostis humani generi*—the enemy of the human race. But he knew they were nothing of the kind. For they were not waging a war against all humanity, only against the rich and powerful political and commercial interests and slaveholders that dominated an increasingly interconnected world. In his view, *they* were the true enemies of mankind.

And he was going to make them bloody pay.

CHAPTER 26

GOVERNOR'S PALACE
WILLIAMSBURG, VIRGINIA

NOVEMBER 12, 1717

"GREETINGS, GOVERNOR. I wanted to be the first to congratulate you on your recent failure."

Sitting at his palatial desk, Lieutenant Governor Alexander Spotswood stared with stupefaction at Philip Ludwell the Younger, seated haughtily before him. On the governor's desk was a miniature golden horseshoe inscribed *Sic Juvat Transcendere Montes*—Thus It Is A Pleasure To Cross The Mountains. Caught off guard by Ludwell, Spotswood glanced at the souvenir ceremoniously given to himself, Harry Beverley, John Fontaine, and each of the gentlemen adventurers who had participated in the 1716 expedition to the Blue Ridge Mountains, thus forming the immortal order of the *Knights of the Golden Horseshoe*. With Ludwell before him once again to make his life miserable, the relaxing and bibulous mountain journey seemed like a lifetime ago, and for a fleeting moment he found himself wishing he could return to those halcyon days of chivalry.

He looked back at Ludwell, snapping back to reality. He had thought his longtime nemesis and leader of the insurrection against him had come to his office to offer an olive branch—but instead his sole purpose here was to gloat in Spotswood's most recent political defeat. Earlier this morning, he had received news that the Crown had repealed his 1713 Tobacco Act and 1714 Indian Act. During the past seven years, he had grown accustomed to criticism from his enemies on the Governor's Council and in the House of Burgesses, but seldom had they attacked him with such blatant vitriol. Looking into Ludwell's icy-blue eyes, he realized that the man and his tobacco-plantation-owner cronies didn't simply desire to have him removed from office—they sought to have him shipped back to England in chains.

"The people have spoken, Governor, and King George has disallowed both acts," Ludwell added. "The repeal is to be announced by proclamation this afternoon. If you would like to attend the formal announcement, your lordship, you would be more than welcome. It should be a celebratory crowd indeed."

Spotswood knew what that meant: he would be heckled by the disaffected members of his Governor's Council and House of Burgesses as well as their tobacco merchant backers. "You mean you and your fellow colonial elite have spoken, Mr. Ludwell. These acts were designed to protect the King's subjects, your so-called *people*, as well as the Indians who are taken advantage of by unscrupulous men such as yourself."

Ludwell gave a disdainful snort. "You are one to talk of unscrupulousness. You have set aside thousands of acres of land for yourself and made enormous profits directly from your policies. But now the people and the Crown have had their say. By royal veto, your two reforms have been crushed and you will now have to proclaim their repeal."

"Does it give you satisfaction to gloat like a vindictive schoolboy?"

"As a matter of fact it does."

"I am sure that your fellow Cassius, Mr. Byrd in London, played no small part in this outcome."

"You have pushed us too far. This is not England—this is America."

"America? I have heard of no such nation and to talk of one is treason against the Crown."

"What is going on here in Virginia and in the other colonies is not treason—it is simple justice. The times are changing—and you and your draconian policies cannot stop it."

"Come now, Mr. Ludwell. You, William Byrd, and Reverend Blair don't care a lick about my policies. In fact, the sole reason Mr. Byrd sits in opposition to me in London is because he covets my post. For years now, he has been trying to steal the governorship for himself. As a matter of fact, I am quite aware that he was the principal traitor and a key signer in the statement you and the others made against me to the Board of Trade."

"He was but one of fourteen."

"Along with yourself, Micajah and Richard Perry, William Hunt, William Dawkins, Thomas Sandford, John Maynard, Humphrey Bell, and several other traitorous miscreants whose names shall go unmentioned."

"Have you learned nothing in all of this? Your misguided Tobacco and Indian Acts have been great grievances to British subjects trading in Virginia and a discouragement to the navigation of Great Britain."

Spotswood felt his indignation rising, and though he wanted to throw Ludwell out of his office, he was naturally pugnacious and enjoyed a good verbal brawl with a worthy opponent. "You know as well as I that that is absolute poppycock, Philip. You just want to be rid of me."

"I would never deny that, but in your pomposity, sir, you miss the point. The truth is that instead of removing trash tobacco through improved inspections, the corrupt agents that you personally appointed have increased its currency."

"You stretch credulity with the rancor of your argument."

"No, you just don't listen. Poor-grade tobacco is routinely approved by one agent or other to their own personal advantage through a tax of eight thousand pounds per annum on the tobacco traders. This is in addition to what charge it is to the shipping. And this without any benefit to the trade, which was the pretense of the law in the first place. But now thankfully, His Majesty has stricken this pernicious Tobacco Act so that it will no longer remain a load and clog to the trade."

"And the Indian Act too. What an accomplishment, Philip, you have succeeded in making sure the peaceful natives of Virginia and the Carolinas will be openly hostile to us for a generation to come. Not only that, they will be thoroughly taken advantage of by the hostile tribes and white men like yourself."

"Your Indian Company is a monopoly."

"No, it protects the Indians from predators like yourself. You and Mr. Byrd are only angry because the company buys stores directly from local suppliers and you and the other merchants have lost out on lucrative business."

Ludwell grinned condescendingly. "Not anymore."

"With no Assembly in session, all you will be accomplishing is to endanger the lives of the peaceful Siouan tribes at Fort Christanna in the name of profit. Iroquois bands are roving the borderlands as we speak. Dismantling the Indian Company post at Fort Christanna will leave the tributary Indians helpless. At the same time, the hostility of the Iroquois and Carolina Indians will be provoked by an abrupt ending of the trading at Christanna."

"You don't know that."

"But I do. That's why I'm going to request that the Council allows the company to maintain the garrison and trading post until we are back in session in the spring."

"That might be achievable, provided you pay the schoolmaster's salary out of your own pocket. The Burgesses are tired of your prodigal spending habits."

"No, you just don't want me in power."

"You have brought this upon yourself, Governor. Even Byrd tried to work with you, but you drove him across the sea."

"Yes, and even from afar, he's as dangerous as a viper."

"We tried to work with you, but you had to go and play the tyrant. Until the past year, me and the other merchants were undecided whether to support the Tobacco Act or to demand its repeal. So great was the depression in the trade that we were ready to welcome any measure which promised relief. Many of us were willing to wait and see if the act would rise the quality of Virginia tobacco. But poor-grade tobacco continued to be shipped by your hand-picked inspectors, and it cannot be used to pay customs in Britain. That was the decisive factor in turning the merchants against your act."

"I will offer an alternative theory. I believe your chief objection against the act is that it was authored by me."

"No, the chief objection is that it's a restraint on trade."

"In that case, we might as well hand over all commerce to the smugglers and pirates."

"Maybe we should. At least they bring in high-quality products for sale at cheap prices without the Crown and its appointees taking an unfair cut."

"Surely, you don't mean that. Why smugglers and pirates pose not only a threat to trade and foreign policy, but to the foundations of our colonial system."

"It's time it was shaken up in my view. The pirates have a governance system based on their own self-interest—and that's precisely why it works. Consequently, their ships are more orderly, peaceful, and well-organized than most merchant ships, vessels of the Royal Navy, or indeed, those of our British colonies. They take a great deal of pride in doing things right and will not answer to martinet captains who beat them senseless with as cat-o'-nine tails, imprison them, and dock their pay for the slightest infractions. Maybe we should have this Blackbeard fellow I've been hearing so much about take your job. He certainly couldn't do any worse than you. Why you've made enemies of half this colony."

"Damn your impudence, Philip Ludwell! Pirates—and this Blackbeard in particular—are a menace to society and the villains of mankind. Why over the past month alone, this monster has brought a tide of terror and destruction from Virginia to New York such as had never been seen before. He has captured vessels bound for Philadelphia from London, Liverpool, and Madeira; sloops traveling between New York and the West Indies; and Pennsylvania merchantmen outbound to England and beyond. It is my understanding that he has seized nearly twenty ships and picked them clean, throwing overboard whatever fails to suit his fancy. Surely, you cannot compare a reprobate such as this man to *me!*"

Ludwell held up his hands, palms out. "Now just calm down, Alexander. I want to hear what you know of this Blackbeard."

He took a deep breath to compose himself, glad that they didn't have to argue, at least for a moment. "His real name is Edward Thache. It's my understanding he did a stint in the Royal Navy."

With his curiosity concerning the pirate now piqued, Ludwell assumed a more conciliatory expression. "Quite embarrassing for the Admiralty, I would imagine. Especially since overnight Blackbeard has become the most feared pirate in the Atlantic—and a folk hero to the people."

"Certainly not to those loyal to the Crown. The man is nothing but a brutal thug and showboater. Did you hear what he did to Captain Spofford?"

"As a matter of fact, I did. Not a day out of Philadelphia and he was forced to watch as Blackbeard's men dumped a thousand barrel staves into the sea. Then he filled his cargo hold with the terrified crewmen of the *Sea Nymph*, a snow from Bristol the pirate captain had captured as it started its journey to Portugal."

"Not only that, but one of the *Sea Nymph's* men, a merchant by the name of Joseph Richardson was very barbarously used by the pirates. They threw his cargo of wheat into the sea."

"That's what the *Boston News-Letter* said. But I wouldn't be surprised if the newspapers exaggerate." The *Boston News-Letter* was controlled by the British Crown and noted for its pro-British sympathies, with the words "Published by Authority" appearing on its front page. Consequently, although it was the most authoritative publication in the New World, it was viewed with suspicion by many colonials.

"Exaggerate? Oh, I highly doubt that," sniffed Spotswood. "With drunken animals like these, no words could exaggerate their terrible deeds. Captain Peter Peters told how the pirates seized his sloop, stole twenty-seven barrels of Madeira wine, hacked away his mast, and left him to run aground. And then, apparently not satisfied with their debauchery, the pirates left the sloop of another captain, a man named Griggs, at anchor at the mouth of the bay with his masts chopped off and his cargo of thirty indentured servants whisked away. The pirates then took all the wine from a Virginia-bound sloop before sinking her. Captain Farmer's sloop had already been looted by other pirates on its way from Jamaica, but Blackbeard's men insisted on unrigging it and removing her mast and anchors to serve as spares for their ship, before they put the thirty captives aboard and let them sail *free* near Sandy Hook, New Jersey.

"He set the indentured servants free?"

127

"Yes, can you believe the audacity of the man? *Free* indentured servants, can you imagine? And then Captain Sipkins was relieved of his command of a great sloop from New York, which Blackbeard's men kept as a consort after mounting her with thirteen guns."

"This Blackbeard is definitely a man to be feared. They say that he makes it a special point of terrorizing captives from New England on behalf of the surviving members of Samuel Bellamy's crew."

"Yes, I heard that too."

"They are this minute rotting in a Boston Prison. Apparently, Blackbeard has said that if any of his fellow pirates suffer in Boston, he will revenge it on them."

"The word is that they are to be hung in less than a weeks' time."

"Once they swing from the gallows, Blackbeard is going to show no mercy whatsoever and no one can do a bloody thing to stop him. Right now, he's a king beholden to no one."

"His state of good fortune is only temporary. Help is most assuredly on the way. The King has apparently ordered a proper force to suppress piracy in our waters. Two frigates are said to be at Boston, the HMS *Rose* and *Squirrel*. HMS *Phoenix* has arrived at New York, and in Virginia the sixth-rate *Lyme* is now backing up the decrepit *Shoreham*. Two Royal Navy frigates have also recently come into the harbor, one en route to New York, the other to Virginia."

"So where is Blackbeard now?"

"I'm not sure. He was last seen not far from Long Island. Perhaps Gardiner's or Block Island. They may have been going to one or the other to pick items left behind by the crew, or perhaps to bury some of their ill-gotten treasure. They say that he was due to sail south back down to the Caribbean where he and his men hope to take a special prize."

"A special prize? And what might that be?"

"A ship-of-force that will allow him and his gang of thieves to take on our Royal Navy fifth-rates without blinking."

"A ship-of-force, you say?"

"Yes, Philip. And when Blackbeard finds one and refits her into his own personal flagship, he'll be unstoppable. And you can quote me to the Council on that. Unstoppable!"

PART 4

QUEEN ANNE'S REVENGE

CHAPTER 27

ONE HUNDRED MILES SOUTHEAST OF MARTINIQUE

NOVEMBER 17, 1717

STARING OUT OVER THE STARBOARD RAILING in the direction of his former home of Barbados, disgraced sea captain Stede Bonnet pictured an image of his first-born child. Though little Allamby had died five and a half years earlier, seldom a day went by that the Barbadian mariner-planter didn't picture him in his mind. He had loved the boy with all his heart, but God had mysteriously taken the child from him after only a year of life. Why? he had often wondered. Why poor Allamby? It seemed pointedly unfair to take the life of something so beautifully young and innocent, and Bonnet had long ago decided that only a very cruel and wicked Heavenly Father could allow such a terrible thing to happen. One who regarded his earthly creations as nothing more than meaningless pawns undeserving of kindness and mercy.

As he continued to picture the boy in the swells and troughs of the sea, he felt tears coming to his eyes. There wasn't a damned thing he could do to stop them so he closed his eyes, stuck his face in the wind, and let the breeze flow over him like a mighty river. He remembered holding Allamby's limp body in his arms and how feather-light and peaceful he had seemed once he had succumbed to the fever. That was the day Bonnet's heart had been utterly broken and his relationship with his wife had started to deteriorate. She had somehow managed to blame him for the boy's death and, over the next few years, she had turned into a pitiless wretch and a tiresome nag. His troubles of the mind may have started with the death of his mother and father and Mrs. Whetstone, the family's beloved guardian after his parents had passed, but the event that had pushed him over the edge was the death of his pride and joy Allamby. That's when the first cracks in their marriage began to show. God, how he had loved the boy, so much so that his three subsequent children could never quite measure up, though he loved them, too, with all his heart and missed them now terribly. But Allamby had been his first-born son so he was special. Something had broken inside him the day the boy had died and he knew he would never be whole again.

He continued staring out at waves rolling by like fields of wheat. After having left the Atlantic seaboard for sunnier southern climes, Blackbeard's flotilla was a mere day's sail from Bonnet's Barbadian home in the Windward Islands. There were three ships in the pirate fleet now trolling for prizes: Bonnet's twelve-gun *Revenge*, still captained by Thache with Bonnet occupying the captain's quarters; a great twelve-gun sloop taken from one Captain Sipkins before they had left the capes of Virginia for the Caribbean; and a forty-ton, eight-gun sloop from Curacao taken recently as a prize from one Captain Goelet, who had been given the *Margaret* as compensation. For the past two weeks, Thache and his growing gang of over two hundred seamen had been on the lookout for a massive ship that would make them the most powerful pirate flotilla in the New World. They had brashly declared their intentions to every sea captain and crew they had captured in the past month.

Bonnet still couldn't quite believe that he had stolen away at night from his wife and three children to become a pirate. Nine months ago when the *Revenge* was being built, the life of a buccaneer had seemed such a romantic undertaking to him. The high adventure of the open sea and sharing the merry comradery of fellow gentleman of fortune had seemed exotically appealing, and a part of him thought his family would be better off without him and his morose moods. But now he knew the reality of the pirate world: endless days of boredom punctuated by bursts of raw violence, orgies of drunkenness, and the constant threat of rebellion on the part of the crewmen opposed to his leadership.

After more than six months at sea, he was a social outcast who commanded virtually no respect among the crew. Banished from captaining his own ship that he had purchased with his own funds, he couldn't help but feel old and tired though he was not yet thirty. He felt especially useless when he compared himself to Thache, who had won over the respect of his crew through his skilled seamanship and leadership and was commodore of three sloops-of-war and over two hundred men. A part of him was envious of the man for being so well-respected and well-liked by his crew, but the other, more pragmatic side of him couldn't help but admire the man. Unlike many of the crew members, Thache treated him respectfully and deferentially at all times and was the consummate gentleman.

The truth was they had much in common. They both came from wealthy colonial planter backgrounds, had received a liberal education grounded in reading and writing, mathematics, lessons in Latin, and a mastery of the French and Spanish languages. With a shared class and history, they were both well-acquainted with the customs of the elite of their respective islands of Jamaica and Barbados, as well as the human suffering of the black Africans held in bondage in the sugarcane fields. But with their privileged backgrounds, they had other things in common and Bonnet could tell that was why Thache gave him the benefit of the doubt and regarded him more substantially than the other crew members drawn mostly from the working class. Bonnet's mother was a Whetstone and piracy had long been in his blood. Thache formerly served on HMS *Windsor* in 1706, flagship of Rear Admiral Sir William Whetstone, a kinsman of Bonnet. They also both shared Jacobite sympathies. They were firmly opposed to King George, the foreign ruler of Hanover, occupying the British throne over the "Pretender" James III, feeling that the Stuart line represented the rightful heirs to the throne. Bonnet knew it was for all these reasons that Thache was exceedingly tolerant of and generous towards him despite his lack of maritime experience.

All the same, Bonnet often felt inferior in Thache's presence. At times, he couldn't help but feel like a *de facto* prisoner aboard his own sloop. In the past week, he had lobbied Thache several times to return the command of the *Revenge* back to him, but the pirate commodore had told him that the timing wasn't right. He claimed that the men wouldn't stand for it and maintained that only once they had taken a ship-of-force as a prize would the crew be amenable to a restructuring of the command. Bonnet knew he was right, but that didn't take away the sting of still being looked upon as a pariah. Thache recommended he be patient and said that he would stand firmly behind him when the time was right. But Bonnet wasn't sure he trusted him to stay true to his word despite his hospitable treatment to date. He felt a growing sense of agitation at being demoted and playing second fiddle, which was exacerbated by Bonnet's feelings of impotence and self-loathing.

Feeling glum, he gazed off at the ocean and the edge of the horizon beyond. It was an expanse so vast that he lost himself staring off into it, the sensation of smallness magnified by the endless pale blue sky and his own feelings of impotence. *Damnit,* he thought miserably. *How have I let myself come to ruin like this, a captive on my own bloody ship? Is this God's cruel doing, just as he took Allamby and Father and Mother from me at a young age? Can I ever go back to my old life, or am I consigned to die at the end of a rope? Would my family even take me back after what I have put them through?*

A cry from the lookout pulled him from his reverie. A sail had been spotted to the east on the horizon, and it was heading in their direction.

"Lively it is, mates!" shouted Thache from the quarterdeck. "This may be the one!"

Feeling a jolt of excitement, Bonnet strode quickly over to him and Israel Hands at the helm. While Thache issued further commands to the sailing master and his bosun and the crew shaked out the main and crowded on sail, Bonnet took a moment to peer through his glass at the approaching ship. During the course of the next hour, as the *Revenge* maneuvered eastward along its intercepting path, the vessel grew bigger and bigger through his glass until he could make out many of her details. The ship was a massive brigantine—over two hundred tons, he estimated—with more than a dozen cannon and flying French colors. She looked formidable and yet...and yet something about her wasn't quite right. Somehow she seemed defenseless. And then he saw what it was: with only perhaps twenty-five crewmen visible on deck, the vessel contained only half the number of hands needed to sail such a large vessel while at the same time operating her guns. Which meant that she was totally vulnerable. He looked at Thache and could see the same dawning realization going through his mind. So where was the rest of the crew? Had something happened to them? Or were they hiding down below waiting to make a fight?

"Helm quarter to larboard, Mr. Hands! Let's take a closer look at her!"

"Aye, Captain!"

Soon the *Revenge* closed within cannon range of the French vessel with the eight-gun Curacoan sloop taken from Captain Goelet to leeward. The twelve-gun sloop seized from Captain Sipkins was further to the north and out of view and would not take part in the chase or boarding if it came to that.

They drew within two hundred yards, the sheets snapping in the wind and more than a hundred armed pirates crowding the starboard rail.

"She's an undermanned slaver, gents—just ripe for the plucking though she be heavily armed," declared Blackbeard to his eager crew. "All hands, hoist the black flag and crowd the rails! Mr. Cunningham and Mr. Howard, guns and muskets when you are ready! Let's see if she intends to put up a fight!"

"Aye, Captain! Prepare to fire, men!"

Peering through his spyglass at the massive French slave ship, Bonnet felt the excitement of imminent battle coursing through his veins as the guns ran out of their ports, the decks jammed with musketeers, and the Jolly Roger flew up the mainmast. The flag was not his personal pirate emblem—a skull flanked by a heart, a dagger, and surmounting a single bone—but rather Blackbeard's standard displaying a skeleton holding an hourglass with a blood-tipped spear and a bleeding heart next to it. For some reason this bothered him, and he couldn't help but wonder when he would get his ship and his personal flag back.

In the next instant, puffs of smoke arose along the length of the *Revenge* as she unleashed a full volley of cannon at the French vessel, which Bonnet would later learn was named *La Concorde*. He watched as the cannonballs splashed in the water and flew over the deck, followed swiftly by a salvo of musket balls. The French captain tenaciously stayed his course and tried to rally his crewmen, but they were heavily outgunned and appeared to be in no condition to fight the pirates. The second volley of cannon and musketry sapped the last modicum of resistance from the Frenchmen and Bonnet saw the captain order his ship's colors struck. The *La Concorde's* helmsman swung the brigantine into the wind and she drifted slowly to a halt in surrender. The pirate crews aboard the *Revenge* and eight-gun sloop captained by Richards raised their weapons and let out a raucous cheer.

Bonnet stepped up to Thache and held out his hand. "Well done, Captain. It appears you've acquired your new flagship. She's quite a beauty."

"Aye, Major, she is at that, and with twenty new guns she will be as formidable as any man-of-war in the Atlantic," came the hearty reply as they shook hands. "But this day does not auger well only for me, my good man, it is a triumphant day for us all. Especially the new captain of the *Revenge*."

"The new captain of the *Revenge*?"

"You, Major Bonnet. Like a phoenix you have arisen from the ashes and are once again in command of your fine ship. Or at least once we've refitted this French slaver and turned her into a proper pirate-of-war. I believe this is cause for celebration, is it not?"

Bonnet felt his whole body seize up with the exhilaration of redemption. "Thank you, Captain! Sweet merciful heaven, thank you!" he gushed, clasping the towering Blackbeard with both of his plump hands with the giddiness of a schoolboy. "You don't know what this means to me!"

"Every man in God's creation deserves a second chance, *Captain* Bonnet— every man. I wish you the best of luck. Now if you don't mind, I'm going to have a word with our French guests. I do believe they have quite a story to tell."

CHAPTER 28

ONE HUNDRED MILES SOUTHEAST OF MARTINIQUE

NOVEMBER 17, 1717

AS HE AND CAPTAIN PIERRE DOSSET OF *LA CONCORDE* took their seats in his great cabin with a trifle of sherry in hand, Thache knew he had finally found the perfect flagship. *La Concorde* was a massive, swift, powerful vessel of well over two hundred tons, with a strong oaken hull and enough gun ports to accommodate up to forty cannon. With such a potent ship-of-force, he and his flotilla could cause more mayhem than the rest of the old Flying Gang put together. All the French brigantine required was a bit of refitting and a good pirate name. Once she was properly outfitted, not even the Royal Navy frigate HMS *Scarborough* or sixth-rate *Lyme* said to have arrived recently in Virginia would dare challenge her upon the high seas.

"You did well to surrender without a fight," said Thache graciously to begin the conference, speaking in rusty but adequate French. "Because of this, I offer my full assurance that you will be treated fairly."

The Frenchman looked skeptical, but dipped his head in acknowledgment. Thache felt badly for him: the man had dark rings around his eyes, his cheeks were gaunt, and he looked like he hadn't slept and had eaten very little in the past week. From the looks of him and his men, it was obvious that Dosset, his officers, and crew had been through quite an ordeal in crossing the Atlantic. He was curious to know the details and could only imagine the miserable state of the poor human cargo shackled belowdecks.

"Who is the owner of ye ship?" was his first question.

"It does not belong to me and I own no interest in it. It is owned by *Monsieur* Rene Montaudoin, based in Nantes and one of the most prominent merchants in all of France. He is going to be very angry at me for being captured."

"What port did you sail out of and what happened to your crew?" he then asked Dosset. "I can tell you have had a most difficult journey."

"I sailed from Nantes in late March, carrying seventy-five officers and crewmen, to the port of Whydah on Africa's Bight of Benin. I arrived there in early July. En route we were crippled by a pair of storms and lost a crewman and our anchor. In Africa, we traded our goods of cotton prints and took on a cargo of more than five hundred captive Africans. We set sail again in mid-September with Martinique as our destination. We have been at sea the past eight weeks, but the hardships of the Middle Passage have taken a toll on everyone: the Africans and my French crew. I have thus far lost sixty-one slaves and sixteen crewmen to the diseases we picked up in Africa, and more are dying daily. Thirty-six of my men are presently sick with scurvy and the bloody flux, and unfortunately my doctors have been unable to do much for them. It has been such a miserable journey that I believed it couldn't get any worse. Then I saw your two pirate sloops approaching from the west and I realized I was wrong."

"*Mauvaise rencontre.*"

Dosset smiled wearily. "*Oui,* it has been a most *bad encounter.*"

Thache nodded sympathetically and they fell into silence. From growing up on a West Indian plantation, he knew the trials and tribulations of the slave trade from both the perspective of the slaveholders and the slaves. The system revolted him, but he knew that it was part of the very fabric of life in an ever-expanding colonial New World. The leading merchants in Britain, France, Denmark, and other nations involved in the triangular slave trade would sail from European ports loaded with trade goods and make their way to the west coast of Africa. There, the captain and his officers would purchase a cargo of enslaved Africans rounded up from nearby and distant villages to be transported to the Americas. The subsequent trans-Atlantic voyage, known as the Middle Passage, would take up to two months to complete and typically ten to twenty percent of the slaves would perish en route from disease, starvation, or suicide. The surviving African prisoners were most often sold at the British West Indian islands of Barbados and Jamaica or the French islands of Guadeloupe, Martinique, and Saint Domingue, where they served as laborers in the sugarcane fields. Emptied of their human cargo, the slavers would then take on new freight, usually sugar and cocoa, and return to European ports, thereby renewing the brutal and highly profitable cycle of enslavement and overseas commerce.

Thache posed another question. "If you had had a full crew, would you have put up a fight?"

Dosset nodded in the affirmative. "Unfortunately, we could not run out our guns and man our sails at the same time."

"For a moment, you thought about bluffing your way out, didn't you?"

"No, I knew I could never get away with it. Because I increased my cargo capacity for this journey to account for one hundred extra slaves, I was only able to mount sixteen guns. Even with three-quarters of my regular crew, I would have had to go up against your twenty guns with no more than three or four of my cannon. All you would have had to do then was board me and it would have been over in a matter of minutes."

"Ye made the right choice."

"*J'espere*—I hope so. What are your plans for me, my ship, and my cargo?"

"I'm going to be on the level with you. I'm taking your ship and probably a half dozen of your most useful crewmen, plus the handful that will be only too glad to join me to get away from this diseased vessel. I'm also going to seize most, but not all, of your provisions as well as some portion of the Africans. But I'm afraid I haven't made my final decision with regard to the number of slaves yet. You see, so much depends on you."

"On me?"

"Yes, on you. For instance, whether you and your officers tell us where you have hidden all of your gold dust, silver coin, and other valuables. You see, my crewmen are a very determined lot. They become, quite literally, enraged like wild animals if they think a prisoner is keeping items of a precious nature from them. So of course, that always puts me in a quandary."

"A quandary?"

"A quandary on whether or not to stop them from becoming violent if you and your crew do not tell them the truth. They'll know if you're lying or not, and I'm afraid I can't stop them from taking out their vengeance upon you if they believe you haven't been fully forthcoming. Does that answer your question, Captain?"

Dosset's face had visibly paled and he said nothing.

Thache stroked one of the braids of his long black beard and smiled reassuringly. He had indeed gotten his message across, but he decided to make it even clearer.

"As long as you are completely honest with us and willingly hand over everything of value, you have nothing to worry about. Me and my crew will treat you like absolute gentlemen, I can assure you."

"And if I don't?"

"Believe me, you don't want to do that, Captain Dosset. As I've warned you in good faith, I cannot control my men. My authority ended when I seized your vessel."

The Frenchman's lips trembled ever so slightly. "Where are you going to take us?"

"I was thinking of the remote island of Bequia."

"Bequia?"

He smiled graciously again. "Aye, the Island of the Clouds as the Arawak Indians call it."

"*Mais oui*, I know of Bequia. I can see why you would choose that island to refit your pirate fleet. It is a quiet place and out of the way."

Thache nodded. In fact, the hilly forested island with a large protected anchorage located nine miles southeast of St. Vincent was the perfect pirate hideaway. He and his men were unlikely to be pursued by the authorities there, for unlike most of the surrounding islands, St. Vincent and Bequia were not controlled by Europeans, but by the mixed-race descendants of Carib Indians and the African survivors of the 1635 wreck of two slave ships. These people, the Garifuna, had tenaciously defended their land from European invaders in their Carib-style war canoes, but they had no problem with pirates and smugglers who resisted the authority of the ruling powers. In fact, Thache was counting on them being quite pleased to see that he and his burgeoning pirate navy had stopped a French slave ship from reaching its final destination.

"I am glad you approve of my choice, Captain Dosset. Because you and your crew are going to be our humble guests for the next week or so."

The Frenchman's face fell. "Your guests?"

"Our most humble guests. You see, you and those poor slaves you have cooped up in your hold are going to help me and my crew outfit my new flagship. When we're done with her, she's going to be quite bonnie. Quite bonnie indeed."

And with that, he gave the defeated Frenchman a devilish wink.

CHAPTER 29

NEVIS ISLAND, LEEWARD ISLANDS

NOVEMBER 29, 1717

"HOW IS HE?" asked Quartermaster William Howard.

"The captain is still very sick," replied Caesar, who had been acting as Thache's personal steward since the captain had refitted *La Concorde* into his new flagship, which he had rebelliously named *Queen Anne's Revenge* after the last monarch of the Stuart line. "The doctors have confined him to his cabin."

"When can I see him?"

"They said to wait for two hours," replied Caesar. "That's when I'll make him eat some breakfast if he can hold it down. But for now he needs to rest."

"Aye, we'll let him sleep until then, but not a moment longer," said Howard. "We need to make a decision as to whether to enter Nevis Harbor. The men want to know his mind."

"Don't worry, ye can see him then. He just needs a couple more hours rest. He is very sick, sicker than we all thought."

"Aye, I'll be back in a couple of hours then," said Howard, and he stepped down from the quarterdeck and disappeared down the companionway.

With dawn having just broken, Caesar went to the starboard railing of the new massive ship-of-war and stared at the luxuriantly verdant island of Nevis, the second most important island in Great Britain's' Leeward Islands colony. He was worried about his captain. Thache was a tough one all right, but whatever disease had decimated the captured French slaver had now afflicted Blackbeard and was running rampant through the crew. More than a dozen men had come down with a bad case of the fever passed on from the African slaves chained belowdecks and the sick Frenchmen aboard *La Concorde*. After seizing the French slaver twelve days earlier and sailing to the remote island of Bequia, the pirates spent a solid week converting the brigantine into a powerful pirate-of-war. Securing the French prize inside the quiet confines of Admiralty Bay on the west side of the island, they released the French crew and most of the slaves onshore and proceeded to refit the brigantine with bristling cannon, turning her into a menacing twenty-eight-gun pirate flagship. It was during the refitting that the pirate crew had come into close contact with the sickly Africans and Frenchmen, and now Thache and a number of the men had come down with the fever.

During the refitting, Blackbeard directly oversaw the transfer of his personal effects from the *Revenge* to *La Concorde*, along with the cannon and supplies from Richards' forty-ton sloop, and much of the pirate company. Though many of his officers and crewmen were opposed to it, Thache had Stede Bonnet reinstated as captain of the *Revenge* as he had promised he would. The Barbadian gentleman pirate had finally recovered fully from his battle wounds and, despite his continuing lack of maritime expertise, he was given a crew of over fifty men.

The three-vessel fleet—with Thache as overall commodore and captain of the *Queen Anne's Revenge*, Bonnet reinstated as captain of the *Revenge*, and Richards in command of the twelve-gun sloop seized from Captain Sipkins off the Delaware Capes—had sailed northward though the night from Montserrat after several days of taking prizes in the Windward Islands to the south. Thache had ordered a course for Nevis Harbor, the main anchorage on the island's western shore. But Howard and the other officers in the growing pirate fleet wanted to know the plan once they reached Nevis. As for the long-term objective of the piratical voyage, Thache had proposed to the company that they sweep the 1,400-mile island chain from end to end, raiding ships and harbors alike until they reached the northernmost islands of the Windward Passage, where they might snare a Spanish galleon carrying the payroll to Cuba. His officers and crew had readily agreed. The expanding pirate flotilla would hop from island to island, stripping prizes of valuables as if they were walking through a store and taking what they wanted from the shelves.

Blackbeard's pirate gang now numbered more than three hundred men, including a pilot, three surgeons, two carpenters, two cooks, a gunsmith, and a musician pressed into service from *La Concorde*. Augmenting these numbers were four other crewman and two cabin boys who voluntarily joined the company and one hundred fifty-seven black Africans retained by the pirates. While dozens of the blacks were inducted into the crews of the three vessels and would draw equal shares and voting rights, more than sixty were retained unshackled in the hold of the *Queen Anne's Revenge* to serve as laborers and perhaps be available for future sale as commodities from which all the crew—black, white, mulatto, and West Indian— would benefit. Though Blackbeard had several crewmen in addition to Caesar that were of African descent, they had been born in or had lived most of their lives in the West Indies or Carolinas, conversed in English, and were familiar with European customs and technology. Only those "straight off the boat" Africans with useful maritime skills, or that appeared to have the qualities necessary to make good warriors for boarding parties, were treated as equal seamen instead of as cargo or creatures from an alien culture who were ineligible to join the pirates' ranks. While Blackbeard was philosophically opposed to the institution of slavery from his childhood experiences on Jamaica, he and his pirates were driven by the motive of profit first and foremost, and only those African slaves who could serve right away as valuable crew members were accepted into their democratic floating society, and thus allowed to vote and draw an equal share of the profits.

From the French slaver the pirates also plundered all the cannons and the usual haul of alcohol, medical supplies, sail cloth, close-combat weapons, navigational instruments, foodstores, and linen they could get their hands on. They also took most of the Frenchmen's clothing and togs, literally stripping the shirts off their victims' backs.

In addition to taking these items and a large number of slaves, the pirates took a valuable haul of gold dust from Dosset and his officers. One of *La Concorde's* cabin boys, fifteen-year-old Louis Arot, had informed the pirates that the officers had a secret stash of gold dust hidden somewhere on the ship or their persons. From Howard, Caesar had learned that Arot had had an axe to grind against Dosset and his lieutenants. As one the worst-paid members of the slaver's crew, he went out of his way to cause them harm and then offered to join the pirates. Howard and other members of Blackbeard's crew proceeded to interrogate Dosset and his officers, threatening to cut their throats if they failed to turn over the gold. The Frenchmen complied, and were subsequently rewarded by Blackbeard with the small, forty-ton sloop since the pirates were keeping *La Concorde* for themselves. Thache also had Howard give them three tons of beans to feed the remaining slaves and ensure that they did not starve. Dosset promptly rechristened the eight-gun sloop *Mauvaise Recontre*—Bad Encounter—and would use it to transport his crew and remaining slaves to Martinique.

Since leaving Bequia, Blackbeard's armada had taken several vessels and accumulated even more plunder. The biggest prize was the *Great Allen* of Boston. The massive merchantman was en route from Barbados to Jamaica and they took her in the deepwater passage north of St. Vincent. Blackbeard, still furious with Massachusetts authorities over their treatment of Bellamy's crew, allowed the crew to threaten the *Great Allen's* captain, Christopher Taylor, to get him to reveal the whereabouts of his valuables and then burned his huge New Englander to the waterline. Upon making his political statement, Blackbeard the next day politely put the uninjured but thoroughly terrorized Taylor and his crew aboard a longboat and had him rowed to a sparsely inhabited shore on Martinique.

As the British island of Nevis came into close view, Caesar went amidships to the water barrel and ladled himself a cupful. It tasted coppery but was refreshing. Off the starboard beam, the central volcanic peak of Nevis soared more than three thousand feet above the shimmering ocean, its top shrouded in a bank of gray-rimmed clouds. At the base of the volcano, he saw several fumaroles slowly releasing volcanic gas and steam, and stretching towards the ocean in all directions were endless sugarcane fields. He felt badly for his black brothers who would be forced to toil under a tropical sun day in and day out under threat of a whip from their slave masters. Once again, he was glad that he was no longer a slave and that Blackbeard had granted him the opportunity to become a full crewman aboard his growing flotilla.

He remembered back to the dreadful Atlantic crossing after he had been kidnapped from his Ibo village in the West African slave-trading province of Benin. Like the trans-Atlantic journey of *La Concorde*, the voyage had been a disaster, killing a quarter of the people on board. No one was spared as slaves, convicts, indentured servants, and even the captain and many among the crew all suffered through the diseases brought on board and the lethally unhealthy conditions belowdecks. Slave traders were driven by greed and crammed as many people into the holds as possible, packing them onto wooden racks like codfish on a fishmonger's tray. He remembered the oppressive stench of the overcrowded humanity and the airless gloom of the main ship hold. He remembered the aching in his legs and the biting cold of the heavy leg irons shackled about his ankles. He remembered shoveling the slop of horse-beans and rice down his famished throat and being whipped by the slavers when he and the others refused to dance on deck, so they would retain their physical stature and fetch a good price when sold. For seven weeks, he was chained to another slave like an animal, and he was only allowed on deck for fresh air once or twice a day during the course of the horrible journey. He had been lucky to survive.

They soon came to the approach to Nevis Harbor. He and Howard went to check on the captain, but he was still too ill to leave his quarters. Stepping back on deck, Howard summoned Israel Hands and the other officers and they inspected, through a spyglass, the vessels anchored against the sugarcane-fringed shores. A general excitement spread amongst the crew. Caesar quickly learned what all the commotion was about. There anchored in the harbor were a variety of merchant vessels for the taking: sloops, sailing canoes, a few large brigantines, and one frigate that was almost as big as the *Queen Anne's Revenge.*

"I swear by God that be the HMS *Seaford* herself!" exclaimed Howard, referring to the sixth-rate warship assigned to the Leeward Islands.

"No, that can't be her!" Caesar heard William Cunningham the master gunner reply.

"It doesn't matter if it's her or not," proclaimed Israel Hands. "She's just sitting there for the taking."

"Aye! Aye!" roared a crowd of crewmen that had gathered at the edge of the quarterdeck and along the larboard gunwale. "We should strike now while the iron is hot!" cried one among them.

Howard agreed: "We'll pounce on her where she lies, storm her decks, and cut her anchor line! Then, before the King's men ashore have time to react, we'll sail her out to sea as our own prize ship!"

"Aye, this be our chance to humiliate the Royal Navy!" said Cunningham. "If we can quickly board that frigate, we can outman her right smartly!"

"It will be easy to take her if we surprise her at anchor!" said Israel Hands.

A rumble of agreement navigated across the deck. Caesar could tell that the men were not only unafraid but excited at the prospect of taking on the Royal Navy vessel. It would be an extremely bold action, he knew, but even he couldn't help but be swept up in the enthusiasm of the moment.

"We should talk to the captain!" announced Howard. "Once he hears about this, he's going to want to attack!"

"Aye! Aye!" the crew roared back.

It was then Caesar noticed Blackbeard had arisen from his bed and stepped from his great cabin. He looked terrible: a gaunt, wraith-like figure and mere ghost of the legendary sea captain whose name was now being uttered in children's bedtime stories throughout the maritime world. He had lost so much weight in the past few days that he appeared diminutive and exceedingly fragile despite his towering height. His skin was sallow and chalky as if he had jaundice. His eyes were puffy and bloodshot from lack of sleep. Whatever the terrible disease carried from Africa aboard *La Concorde* was exactly, it was taking a heavy toll on him. A blanket was draped loosely across his bony shoulders, like a woman's shawl.

"What's this I hear about us taking on the *Seaford?*" he demanded hoarsely.

Caesar watched with great anticipation as Howard stepped forward and recounted his bold plan to Blackbeard. Once again, he proposed to race into the harbor and take the frigate at her anchorage, storm her decks, cut her anchor line, and before anyone ashore could resist, sail her out to sea, thereby adding another man-of-war to the growing pirate armada. As he made his case, Thache calmly withdrew his spyglass and studied His Majesty's warship bobbing gently up and down in the harbor.

When Howard was finished with his flowery and quite convincing oratory, the crew roared its approval, fully expecting their captain to raise the war cry and turn them loose. But Thache just stood there with a knowing smile on his haggard face, the kind of wistful smile that Caesar suspected King Arthur would have worn. When the noise failed to die down, he signaled his men to quiet down so he could speak and, in a grand paternal-like gesture, he made a big show of shaking his head.

"I admire your spirit, lads, surely I do, but I'd drink a bowl of brimstone and fire with the devil himself before I would recommend such a course of action."

The faces of the men instantly dropped, as if they had been reprimanded by their fathers. "But why, Captain?" asked Caesar.

"Aye, why sir indeed?" echoed Israel Hands.

Thache nodded to indicate it was a good question. "Two reasons, gentlemen. First off, whether the man-of-war we see before us is in fact the HMS *Seaford* or not, I consider it to be too risky an enterprise at this juncture," he said.

"And the second reason?" asked William Howard.

"Because my ill health will not allow me to lead you into battle. Which I believe adds to the risk and makes it even altogether more dangerous and inclined to fail. I don't want to be sounding overly apt with my tongue, gentlemen, and confess that this be just my point of view, but I see danger afoot and am not willing to risk ye lives for booty. You can heed my captainly words or spit on them altogether—it be your choice. The articles give each man aboard this ship a proper vote in all matters."

For a moment, the men just stood there in silence. Though Caesar thought he saw a few expressions of disagreement, not a single man offered a word of protest.

"There will be other opportunities—opportunities in which I will not be laid up in my bed stricken with illness and will be able to lead you decisively. In fact, I would venture that once we are more familiar with our newly christened flagship, we will be as formidable as the mightiest man-of-war in all the Atlantic. But until then, methinks we should concentrate on easy targets. What say you men?"

The officers and crew looked around at one another. After a moment, Howard stepped forward. "I agree with the captain and say we sail for Antigua," he said, referring to the capital of the British Leeward Islands. "It is supposed to be without naval protection."

Howard then put it to a vote. It was unanimous. The crew of more than one hundred fifty men voted for pulling out of Nevis and sailing directly for Antigua.

"By all accounts, that settles it then," said Thache. "Make all sail, Mr. Hands. And Caesar, my friend, if you would be kind enough to fetch me some breakfast, I believe my stomach is feeling better now that we have a plan of action in place."

"Straight away, Captain," snapped Caesar, feeling a new spring in his step. But he was still a little stunned. He had never heard or seen anything like what just happened before: a pirate captain calling off an attack because he was too sick to fight. It showed how powerful Blackbeard truly was, underscoring the impressive authority he wielded over his large, unwieldy crew. True, pirate captains were only in command during pursuit and engagement of an enemy ship or prize, or during a storm, but with three vessels bristling with cannon and hundreds of pirates under his command, it was amazing that one man not feeling well caused the entire company to call off the attack on the *Seaford* or whatever Royal Navy vessel lay anchored in Nevis Harbor, especially when it appeared that's precisely what the majority wanted to do. Most pirate commodores would have been deposed for such weakness—but not Blackbeard. His competent seamanship, charismatic personality, and gentlemanly nature endeared him to his men as if he was some sort of god. He pushed his men hard, Caesar knew, but they would go to hell and back for him if he asked them to because he knew when to back off and not put their lives at risk— unless he was guaranteed of success. It was true a pirate captain best served his own interest by serving his crew's interest, but this was much more than that. In Caesar's view, this was the very essence of leadership.

He realized he had absorbed yet another important lesson from the master. It was a lesson he would never forget.

CHAPTER 30

CRAB ISLAND, EASTERN TIP OF PUERTO RICO
LEEWARD ISLANDS

DECEMBER 5, 1717

FROM THE LARBOARD RAIL, Edward Thache watched intently as the captain of the *Margaret* of St. Christopher clambered down into his sloop's tender and rowed over with five of his crew members to the now thirty-six-gun *Queen Anne's Revenge*. Wisps of smoke drifted menacingly from the flagship's open gunports, announcing to the prisoners that his gunners were ready with lengths of burning slow-match held in their fists, while his terrifying-looking boarding party stood leering at the railing. They were armed to the teeth, and several of the Africans and West Indians and three of the Scotsmen brandished colorful war paint. Thache's fever had broken the day before, and though he had lost several pounds and was not fully recovered from the Africa-borne illness that had plagued him for the past week, he was well enough to leave his cabin and resume his responsibilities as captain. He closely studied the approaching captain of the *Margaret*, whose name he did not yet know, as the man cast an experienced eye over the massive pirate ship looming above him.

As always, Thache made sure to present his signature frightening appearance to cow his victims into submission. His pirate's beard was long, unkempt, and plaited, hanging wildly down over his chest. The same wild hair seemed to surround his face, and more plaits stuck out on either side of his cheeks. The ends of these rat-tailed black plaits were tied with twists of ribbon, which made his appearance all the more unique yet disconcerting. For attire, he wore his trademark long sea captain's coat, crossed by two belts—a sword belt and a bandolier—while three brace of pistols hung from improvised holsters over his chest, making him look like a walking armory. Despite the winter sun of the Caribbean, he wore a small brown bear-fur cap, of the kind commonly worn by seamen in cold weather. The fur cap gave him an aura of animal-like power, like an Indian warrior.

Once the captured captain and his officers climbed on board, though, he dispensed with the stage theater and was the very picture of civility. This, too, tended to throw his prisoners off-balance and add to their disorientation, thereby increasing his chances of seizing every bit of their valuable plunder. He politely introduced himself and shook the hand of the captain, who reluctantly gave his name as Harry Bostock, and then Caesar led the group into the great cabin so they could talk. While Bostock's officers seemed nervous and frightened, the righteous Bostock appeared morally outraged that anyone had the gall to violate him. Once they settled into the cabin, Caesar opened a bottle of Madeira wine, poured glasses for each man present, and took his leave. As he stepped from the cabin, Thache thanked him kindly for his services then turned back to face Bostock.

Grateful that the man had shown the good sense to surrender his vessel after only a single shot fired across his bow, he began the conference by thanking his prisoner for not trying to play the hero and jeopardizing the fate of his men. But Bostock just grunted, refusing to even acknowledge the compliment, and looked at him disdainfully. Thache could see he was a prideful man, loathe to admit that his ship was about to be plundered by sea bandits who would most likely leave him with almost nothing.

"I like the name of your sloop," said Thache ingratiatingly to try to break his stubborn prisoner's icy demeanor. "My true love's name is *Margaret*. Lord knows I should be snuggling up with her next to a warm winter hearth in Philadelphia rather than sitting here in the Leeward Islands talking to you."

"Why bother talking? You're just going to take whatever you fancy anyway," Bostock blurted rudely, not even bothering to disguise his displeasure as most of Thache's victims tended to do to ensure their safety and that of their crew.

He smiled graciously, ignoring the affront. "I have a few questions I'd like to ask you, Captain Bostock."

"What kind of questions?"

"Ones like this: What other merchantmen are trading off the Puerto Rican coast?"

Bostock looked at him defiantly. "I'll be damned if I tell you that, you rascal. You'll have to find that out on your own."

"I admire your resolve, but it is to no avail. For no doubt members of your crew will be more forthcoming than their beloved captain. You *do* treat your men right and are beloved by your men, aren't you Captain? They *do* enjoy sailing under you, correct?"

Bostock's eyes narrowed. "Like you, I have my detractors."

"But that's just it, I don't have any detractors. So I would actually have to say that we don't have that in common. But I suppose that could change. Crews are sometimes so fickle."

"No doubt lowly pirate crews like yours are just so."

"Oh, now I see. You think that because you're a merchantman that you're better than us, is that it? You truly believe that you make an honest living and are a good man and that we are but roguish thieves?"

"You said it, I didn't, Mr. Blackbeard the pirate."

"You're but a pawn of King George and the bloated carcasses that promote his empire and steal from the common man whose labors have built up his colonies. I'm talking about hardworking men like your underpaid sailors. My crew and I are going to enjoy talking to them and hearing what they have to say about your treatment of them. You *do* treat them right, don't you Captain?"

Now Bostock looked worried. "I'll not sit here and argue with ye. If you're going to plunder me ship, you best get on with it and let me be on my way."

"We're already up to our gunwales in provisions. My quartermaster will probably only relieve you of your wine and spirits, live cattle, hogs, cutlasses, and firearms. But I'll be wanting your navigational instruments. You know how it is— one can never get enough."

Bostock nodded around the cabin. "I can see you have taken a goodly amount of silver plate in recent days, including that fine cup there."

"Courtesy of Captain Taylor, commander of the *Great Allen*. He had the misfortune of sailing a merchantman from Boston. Burned her to the waterline."

"You truly are a scoundrel. Why did you have to do that?"

"And you've the tongue of some fouled scupper rather than a gentleman, but I shall answer your question. We burn all ships from Boston. We don't appreciate the way New Englanders treat our sea roving friends."

"You're talking about Bellamy's crew. Last I heard they were very near to being hanged."

He jolted upright in his captain's chair. "But they haven't been hung yet? Is that what you're saying?"

"They hadn't swung when I left port. That's all I know."

"If they do swing, there's going to be hell to pay for Boston merchantmen. Now that I promise you."

"Aye, and you have the means to do it. When did you acquire this guineaman and her thirty-six guns?"

"A fortnight ago. She's quite a beauty, eh?"

"A beast from hell and fast to boot. Now I have a question for you. Are you a real gentleman, or do you intend to abuse me and my crew?"

"I don't abuse captains or their crews. It's not my way. And as I said before, we are so rich in plunder we may very well burst amidships, so I would wager that my quartermaster will be rather selective in the matter of plunder."

There was a knock on the door. William Howard entered with a man Thache didn't recognize but Bostock did. He nearly jumped up from his seat.

"What are you doing here, Mr. Biddy?" he demanded to the man, who, unbeknownst to Thache, was an ordinary seaman and a Liverpudlian.

"Why I'm joining Captain Blackbeard's crew here and leaving ye behind, you lump of deviltry!"

Bostock's eyes narrowed. "You'll swing from the gallows by Christmas. That be what you want, Robert?"

"A man's got to make a living. You certainly don't pay enough, you greedy bastard. You get a hundred times the share I get and I'm done with ye. I'm signing these men's articles. At least they be fair and honest."

"Dying ain't much of a way to make a living, Robert. Signing these pirates' articles is nothing but a ticket to your own funeral. Remember, son, me and every officer in this room be a witness."

Thache smiled. "Maybe, but at least he'll die rich and merry among men who treat him as equals." He held out a big bony hand. "So it is to be a short life but a merry one for you, is it, Mr. Biddy? Welcome aboard the *Queen Anne's Revenge*. Your niggardly captain here has told us precious little information about the merchant vessels sailing in these waters. To draw your equal share of the prize of the *Margaret*, would you care to enlighten us?"

"Aye, what do you want to know, sir?"

"No need to be calling me sir now. Just tell me, if you would please, who might be trading currently along the Puerto Rico coast?"

"Don't tell him, Robert. There's no reason to make it easy for him to steal from hard working men like yourself."

Seaman Biddy stepped forward and punched his former captain hard in the chest with his first, eliciting a howl of pain. "No, there's every reason to do it, you pug-faced squab! You and merchant captains like you are nothing but thieves! The lowliest pirate scraping by robbing turtle fishermen has got ten times the honor of devils like you!"

He delivered a fierce scowl and then proceeded to rattle off a half-dozen French and Danish sloops that the *Margaret* had passed en route from St. Christopher. As Thache quietly listened, he decided that he would send Bonnet ahead in the *Revenge* to chase them down, while he would have Howard and his boarding detail continue transferring squealing hogs and unhappy cattle onto the *Queen Anne's Revenge*. Then the three-vessel pirate fleet would make sail for Samana Bay, Hispaniola, where they would careen and lie in wait for the Spanish Armada they expected would sail from Havana with money to pay the garrisons on Puerto Rico. The Spanish would think he and his men had vanished, but he would soon be at their backs unawares. With his new flotilla, he would strike the fear of God into the Spanishers.

He looked at Bostock; he had heard enough from the insolent merchant captain, even though he had managed to extract virtually no useful information from him and certainly nothing to compare to what Biddy had told him. "Is there any information you would like to tell me, Captain, before I turn you over to my officers for general questioning. They always like to have a go as well, you know, and to give you fair warning they are seldom as cordial as me."

Bostock gulped at the mild threat, but then quickly recovered. "As a matter of fact there is one thing."

"And what would that be?"

"It appears that King George has offered you and your *Queen Anne's Revenge* cohorts and all the other pirates of the Atlantic a most gracious pardon."

"A pardon?"

"An Act of Grace pardoning all pirates for their crimes, provided they surrender to the proper authorities."

Thache looked at his quartermaster and then at his new pirate volunteer. "Is he telling the truth, Mr. Biddy?"

"Aye, I heard it meself. The proclamation has not reached the authorities in the Leeward Islands, but we've spoken with seamen who have seen the decree back in England. It be published in the *London Gazette* three months ago."

"A copy of the decree will arrive to these waters any day," declared Bostock. "King George issued the royal proclamation on September 5 decreeing that any pirate that surrenders to a British governor within one year would be pardoned for all piracies committed before January 5 of next year. They are calling it a *Proclamation for Suppressing of Pirates* and it should be arriving any day now on merchant ships bound for Boston, Charles Town, and Barbados. When the ships reach their destinations, even currently jailed pirates will be set free. The pardons were conceived of and promoted by Woodes Rogers, a former privateer—"

"Woodes Rogers, the author of *A Cruising Voyage Round the World?*"

"Aye, one and the same. The word is that he will be taking over as governor of the Bahamas and will reestablish control of the proprietary colony. Looks like you and your ilk will have to find a new safe haven to skulk away to."

"Watch your mouth, or we may have to set you adrift in your own longboat and make pirates out of *all* of your crew members, not just Mr. Biddy here. Once they get used to the comforts of the *Queen Anne's Revenge* and realize that they can obtain a lifetime's worth of wages in six months' time, I would wager they won't be too eager to go back to the greedy likes of you and *your ilk*."

For once, that seemed to shut him up and the cabin went silent.

Howard said, "Maybe that German pig who calls himself king isn't as dumb as we thought. He's trying to reduce the number of pirates prior to sending over Woodes Rogers. And then, once Rogers takes over as governor, he will attempt to sweep the colonies clean of piracy by taking away our one and only refuge."

Bostock nodded. 'Tis hoped those pirates who take advantage of the Act of Grace will return to being law-abiding subjects. Personally, I think that unlikely."

"We don't need to hear your opinions, Captain," Thache scolded him, "just whatever news you have to deliver. Now tell us more about this pardon."

"Holdouts are to be hunted down without mercy. King George has ordered the Admiralty to seize such dead-enders, providing a reward of one hundred pounds for every pirate captain captured, fifty pounds for senior pirate officers, and twenty to thirty pounds for other crew members. The Crown is wagering that, between captures and pardons, you and your fellow sea rovers will be too weak to resist Rogers when he arrives to reestablish control of the Bahamas."

Blackbeard felt a fluttery feeling in his stomach. "When is he due to arrive in New Providence?"

"Some time next summer."

"Who knows, maybe it's all a bluff," said Howard.

He shook his head. "No, the offer is real. They did it in Kidd's time too. It's the classic carrot and stick approach—and it usually works."

"It still be a pirate's life for me," said Biddy. "The prospect of Davy Jones' Locker or a Kidd-like dance of death is better than what I got now."

"Bad decision, Robert," warned Bostock. "Bad decision indeed."

"Avast with your threats on the lad, or I'll string you up from my mainyard," snarled Thache, and he pondered the situation for a moment. The King's most gracious pardon was going to have a huge impact on him and his crew. Once they had plundered Bostock's vessel, he would have to hold a council and discuss the shocking development with the entire fleet. More than one meeting would have to be held, votes would have to be taken and retaken, and arguments would surely ensue. He and every single one of the nearly four hundred men in his growing flotilla believed they had taken an irrevocable step into criminality and rebellion, but now it seemed they had a second chance. How many times had he thought about quitting piracy and retiring with his ill-gotten gains to a simple life with his beloved Margaret? Now, if he played his cards right, he had his opportunity.

But now that he was in command of nearly four hundred men, it was not so easy a choice. *What the devil am I going to do?* he wondered. *What the devil am I going to do?*

CHAPTER 31

ROATÁN, BAY OF HONDURAS

MARCH 28, 1718

AS STEDE BONNET STUDIED the four-hundred-ton British merchantman with twenty-six cannon protruding from her gunports, his mind flashed back to last year's ill-advised attack on the Spanish man-of-war that had very nearly ended his piratical career. That disaster had cost him his command of the *Revenge*, and he certainly didn't want a repeat performance. At the same time, he couldn't just sail away and avoid a fight, not when his company was desperate for a prize. It had been more than a week since he and his crew had seized a vessel and they were in dire need of a victory to boost morale. Somehow, he would have to use stealth and cunning and shift the odds in his favor.

For much of the winter, Blackbeard's flotilla had lurked west of the Campeche Bank, prowling the waters in the hopes of intercepting one of the silver-laden galleons departing from New Spain. The Spanish referred to the *Queen Anne's Revenge*—which was now armed with thirty-eight cannons including swivel guns—as "the Great Devil" and kept a watchful eye out for her and her two consorts. But instead of Spanish treasure, the fleet had to content itself with taking mostly modest prizes. By late winter, the three vessels had split up and were hunting on their own on the other side of the Yucatan Peninsula, heading south for the busy shipping lanes of the Gulf of Honduras.

With mixed results, Bonnet had continued to fight off bouts of depression. Despite the many prizes he and his crew had taken since his reinstatement as captain, his personality weaknesses and poor seamanship continued to lead to a state of turmoil aboard the *Revenge*. Even the handful of crew members that he got along with were growing tired of his melancholy states and overwhelming feelings of shame at leaving his wife and family behind. And despite the fact that he was once again commander of his own ship, he still felt like a prisoner and was dominated by the charismatic Blackbeard in all maritime matters. To the pirate commodore, he had admitted that he was ready to forsake his criminal life if he could find exile in Spain or Portugal and never see another Englishman who might recognize him by sight.

Through his spyglass, he watched as the armed merchantman turned a point to larboard. Despite the odds and a sick feeling of déjà vu, he and the majority of the crew were anxious to prove their mettle and had already decided to launch an assault despite the objections of his quartermaster Ishmael Hanks, bosun Ignatius Pell, and a dozen crewmen, thus risking a reenactment of the disastrous engagement with the Spanish warship from the September before. They had caught up to the vessel—the *Protestant Caesar* of Boston captained by William Wyer, they would soon learn—just a few minutes earlier at nine o'clock, cleverly maneuvering the *Revenge* onto the massive ship's vulnerable stern.

Who knows, thought Bonnet, *maybe my luck has changed?*
He gave the signal to his master gunner to open fire with the starboard-side guns. The *Revenge* let loose with five cannon and a stiff volley of musket shot. To Bonnet's surprise, the merchant vessel returned fire from a pair of stern chasers and also answered with a hailstorm of bullets.

"Damn them!" snapped Bonnet. "I'm only going to give them one chance to surrender!"

"I don't think the captain gives a damn!" fired back Ignatius Pell. "With nearly thirty guns to our ten, he be not afraid of us!"

As the smoke cleared, Bonnet grabbed his speaking trumpet. "If you fire another gun, we shall give no quarter! This is your only chance to stand down! It's your choice: stand down or everyone on board dies!"

A long pause followed. Bonnet knew his bluff was a weak one, but it was all he had, and in the oceanic darkness his adversary didn't know how strong or weak he truly was. Could he be lucky this time and someone actually back down from him, like they always seemed to do for the great Blackbeard? He began feeling a note of optimism.

And then the *Protestant Caesar's* veteran captain let him know precisely what he thought of his bluff and opened fire with another salvo from his booming cannons.

"Fire! Fire!" cried Bonnet, gripped with outrage and anger.

A staccato of cannon and small arms' explosions rocked the *Revenge* and hot white streaks filled the night sky. Regarding his adversary as nothing more than a pesky insect, Wyer continued to return a brisk fire at the smaller vessel. The running battle continued for three full hours, cannons flashing in the night, until Bonnet finally gave up and skulked away into the darkness, like a dog with its tail between his legs.

"Damn your impudence man!" snarled Ishmael Hanks. He crowded in aggressively with Pell and the vocal minority of other crew members who had objected to the ill-conceived attack. "You have committed the same stupidity as before believing you would come out with a different result! Have you learned nothing after your year-long apprenticeship under Blackbeard?"

Now the seamen who had opposed the assault quickly chimed in as well.

"Aye, you're finished, Bonnet!"

"What the hell are we doing following you when we should be in Turneffe with Commodore Thache! He knows what to do!"

"You bastard! We've just lost a dozen good men and fine sail and rigging to boot!"

"Why we ought to throw you overboard to the sharks! That's what you deserve, you squab!"

With slumped shoulders, Stede Bonnet returned in silence to his great cabin. There he picked up his battered but precious books from the floor one by one and dusted them off, wanting nothing else in the world except to die like his poor son Allamby.

CHAPTER 32

TURNEFFE LAGOON, HONDURAS

APRIL 2, 1718

BLACKBEARD STARED OUT at the Turneffe Atoll's endless coral fringing reef, then at the expansive backreef flats, large lagoon, seagrass beds, and mangrove forests behind it—taking it all in as if he was a boy again out sailing with his father at Port Royal. He liked this little hideout in the Spanish Main; it was his special place. To his right, he saw a school of permit fish, their thin dorsal fins slicing like scythes through the lapping blue-green Caribbean waters. Their broad bodies, large round eyes, and blunt faces were unmistakable and they were tasty eating indeed. The pirate company had cooked up a dozen twenty pounders yesterday obtained from local fishermen, holding a feast on the beach over mesquite coals. To his left, a pair of bonefish navigated through the clear waters above a cluster of starfish, and on the little sand bar in front of him scurried a small army of Turneffe and Rag Head crabs—the crustaceans the permit fish fed upon. He inhaled the pleasant sea breeze and closed his eyes.

Blackbeard enjoyed his days of leisure off the beaten path; they offered him a chance to take a deep breath and regroup. This was one of those times. In the past few weeks, the enormous burden of managing and feeding the combined pirate flotilla—the ranks of which had recently swelled to over six hundred souls aboard four vessels—and supplying the vast quantity of food and spirits consumed by the men on a daily basis was becoming an oppressive burden. The four vessels had split up and fanned-out in the Gulf of Honduras to cast a wide net for prizes. But they were still sailing in consort and sharing their plunder. Every single healthy, sick, or wounded seamen drew at least one full share—except the forced skilled men who refused to sign the articles and the sixty African slaves from *La Concorde* kept unshackled in the hold of the *Queen Anne's Revenge*, whom the crew had decided would be sold for profit when a favorable opportunity presented itself. But it was the crushing weight of having to oversee and control so many wild, disorderly, and inherently rebellious men that was taking a toll on the captain, and his quartermaster William Howard as well.

In the past month, a group of around fifty men had emerged to become a particular thorn in Thache's side, and it was the members of this fractious group that vexed him now. Many of them were well-liked, experienced, and charismatic seamen, and two weeks ago, they had come close to mutiny when the rum supply had briefly run out. "Our company somewhat sober," Blackbeard had written of the incident in the journal he kept by his bedside and wrote in religiously. "Damned confusion amongst us! Rogues a plotting and great talk of separation. Fortunately, the fleet's next prize had a great deal of liquor onboard that kept the company hot, damned hot, and then all things went well again." But he never forgave the plotters, and had no intention of allowing them to ever again undermine his authority. He decided that he would have to have a plan going forward to deal with the men, a plan that he would share with only his most trusted officers and crew members.

In the past week alone, he had held two secret meetings with this inner circle—which included William Howard, Caesar, and several other of his trusted Bath County pirates as well as men he trusted such as Israel Hands—and explored options on how they might go about a breakup of the companies and seizure of the company's arms and powder, accumulated prize-money, and provisions if it became necessary. It was becoming painfully apparent that the outfit was growing too large and unwieldy, with too many independent voices, and that there was a portion of the crew in a constant state of quarrelsome rebellion, ready to mutiny the next time the rum supply ran out. It wasn't the first time he had joined forces with the Bath County men. He found that, having come from North Carolina, they had a good grasp of the situation in the colonies with regard to commerce with pirates and he often sought their counsel on these important matters.

Howard and his associates had long held that Bath Town was the ideal port to sell piratically-taken goods and slaves, since the place was becoming increasingly important as the seat of the North Carolinian government, even though it was still something of a backwater. Thache had been assured by the Bath Country pirates that he would receive favorable treatment from Governor Eden and his customs collector and interim chief justice, Tobias Knight, the owner of Caesar, especially since he had met both men on two prior occasions during his merchant sailing day's out of the port of Philadelphia. With the recent offer of King George's official Act of Grace, Thache had explored the various options that Governor Eden and Bath Town might represent for his bloated pirate fleet. Unfortunately, the terms of the King's pardon required that pirates turn themselves in by September 5 of the current year, 1718, and only acts of piracy committed prior to the 5th of January of the year would be forgiven—any after that date would not be eligible. This meant that he and his men were already in violation of the terms of the pardon.

The news of the King's *Proclamation for Suppressing Pirates* had sparked a lively debate amongst his men for the past three months, but he already knew what the outcome of the debate would be. Roughly a third of his men would take the offered pardon and surrender to the new British-appointed governor of the Bahamas, Woodes Rogers, when the pirate flotilla returned to Nassau next month, giving up their life on the account for good. Another third would staunchly resist and flatly call for the rejection of King George's terms. And another third would try to delay the process or come out somewhere in between, by signing the pardon but actually refusing to adhere to it, or at least restricting prizes to Spanish and French vessels. At a minimum, this would buy them time and follow the precedent of hoping that the Crown would simply turn a blind eye to the plundering of Britain's usual enemies, Spain and France, as they had done so often in the past.

Staring into his crystal ball, Blackbeard saw what lay ahead for him and his men as brigands of the sea. Once Woodes Rogers gained a toehold in the New World, it would be only a matter of time before the pirate enclave of New Providence would be broken up and dispersed. The days of lawless anarchy would be over and Nassau and the other pirate safe havens in the Bahamas would no longer be a refuge for those who were increasingly unwelcome elsewhere. Once Rogers authority took hold in the proprietary colony, it would be copied elsewhere throughout the Atlantic world as a new generation of governors and their leading commercial backers no longer tolerated or encouraged pirates in their colonies. But Thache was counting on that not happening with Governor Eden of North Carolina and his second-in-command Tobias Knight.

All the same, he still hadn't decided where he might fall out. For the time being, he was keeping his options open. But he liked what the Bath County men had to say about North Carolina as a new pirate hub, or at least a place to lay low. It appeared that the officials there were not corrupt; rather Eden and Knight had been so decimated by Indian wars, Virginia Governor Spotswood's' draconian tobacco laws, and political infighting amongst various factions that they had no choice but to find suitable financiers to bolster their decimated economy. On the two occasions he had met the two men in Bath Town as first-mate aboard a Philadelphia merchant vessel, he had found them to be intelligent men who clearly had the best interests of their colony at heart. With so many problems to deal with and a moribund economy, they had to be open-minded when it came to commercial ties to rogues of the sea—otherwise they soon might not have a proprietary colony to govern. To respond to the needs of their people, they had to promote the interests of their colony, even if that included turning an occasional blind eye to pirates, smugglers, and the like. North Carolina was in a battle for its survival, and its leaders recognized this, or at least that's what Howard and the other Bath County men maintained. In his brief but telling interactions with the two colonial officials, Blackbeard had seen nothing to dissuade him from that perspective, and he decided that he would keep his options open with regard to pursuing a relationship of mutual benefit with these men if and when the time came.

The fate of Bellamy's crew factored heavily into his decision to prepare for the future. A couple of weeks ago, he had learned from one of his captives that six of the crew members had been hanged from the gallows at Boston. Based on this information, he vowed that going forward he would renew the vigor with which he would punish New England ships and their owners, and he would simultaneously have a plan in place for his retirement from piracy to avoid the same fate as Bellamy's men. If there was one thing he and his fellow brethren of the coast fretted over, it was the prospect of dangling by their necks from a hempen rope, fouling their breeches, and doing the macabre dance of death that so entertained the common masses in cities such as Boston, Charles Town, Port Royal, and London. He would never give the swabs the satisfaction of seeing him hang.

"Sail! A sail!" came the sudden cry from Richard Greensail, who was acting as lookout.

"English?" inquired Thache.

"No, she be not a prize," said Israel Hands. "It's Bonnet returning from Roatán."

He smiled. "Well, well, the prodigal son returns."

"Aye, but you're not going to like the look of the *Revenge*," said Hands. "She's taken a pounding."

Having an uneasy feeling of déjà vu, Thache reached for his spyglass. It was the *Revenge* all right and she had indeed taken a terrible beating: sails tattered;

shrouds, halyards, and braces torn up; gunwales and decks splintered from cannon fire. The damage was not as extensive as after the bout with the Spanish man-of-war last September, but it was devastating nonetheless.

As Bonnet and his crew set anchor, pirates crowded the decks of the *Queen Anne's Revenge* to see what all the ruckus was about. Patters of gossipy conversation filled the vessel until finally the pirates were rendered silent as a group of Bonnet's officers rowed over in a longboat. Thache received them on the quarterdeck of the great ship.

Still smarting from their recent defeat, Bonnet's men quickly informed him of the encounter with the *Protestant Caesar*, which they had since learned from local logcutters was from Boston and captained by William Wyer. Out-classed and out-gunned, the bungling Bonnet, they declared, had attempted to wage a running gun battle with a heavily-armed, four-hundred-ton merchant vessel captained by the stubborn New Englander—and he had failed. Clearly, their commander had learned little from his yearlong apprenticeship under Thache, and he now needed to pay the price. Ignatius Pell and several of the others begged Thache to use his influence to terminate Bonnet's command altogether, which was a messy situation to begin with since he owned the ship and his crew worked for him on a wage basis rather than based on shares per the articles. And now here he was skulking back to his commodore like a worthless puppy with his tail between his legs.

With Bonnet not there to defend himself, Thache diplomatically called a meeting of the entire company. He wanted to ensure that Bonnet had the opportunity to tell his side of the story, and that the men would adhere to the articles and cast their votes for a new course of action for the *Revenge* and her captain. A half hour later, all parties had arrived for the meeting, including Bonnet dressed in a satin shirt with ruffles, a hunter-green velvet vest, a powdered wig, and buckled shoes. Thache patiently listened as Bonnet recounted the details of the stern-attack on the *Protestant Caesar* and subsequent battle. He then proceeded to pose several questions, which, out of a sense of fairness, were for the most part favorable to the gentleman pirate from Barbados. When he had heard out both sides and refereed the accusation-filled debate that followed, Thache stood up and asked for the floor to speak.

"I believe there is a simple solution," he said. "I propose that Captain Bonnet be replaced for the time being by Captain Richards, who will now command the *Revenge*."

"And what of Bonnet?" asked Ishmael Hanks, glowering at the major. "Where will he go?"

"As my wayward colleague has not been used to the fatigues and care of such a post as ship captain, it would be better for him to stay with me aboard the *Queen Anne's Revenge*. Here he can live easy, at his pleasure, where he will not be obliged to perform the necessary duties of a sea voyage."

"So you're placing me under house arrest," snapped Bonnet, who at first had seemed supportive of the outcome but now bore a stubborn look on his face.

"I wouldn't call it that, Major Bonnet. I would call it by another name: a second chance. Or really a third chance as it appears that you have two strikes against you. Mind you, this is only a temporary relief from command. Just while we recuperate here in Turneffe—gorging on permit, bonefish, and sea turtle, and capturing wayward vessels. The time will go by fast."

Bonnet rolled his eyes. "One can only hope."

"You brought this upon yourself, damn you," hissed Ishmael Hanks. "And yet now you're ungrateful to the very man who spared you, our commodore Blackbeard?"

Thache and Bonnet looked at one another. "I didn't mean to appear ungrateful," said the Barbadian apologetically.

Thache gave an understanding nod. "We all have our good days and our bad on the open sea, lads. It's how you rebound when you've been knocked to the deck that counts most. We need to put this behind us and move forward. Be that plain enough, gentlemen?"

There were nods and words of agreement. He looked again at Bonnet and couldn't help but feel sorry for him. But what took him by surprise was the simmering anger and hatred he saw just beneath the surface of the eccentric planter's face. Showing kindness and impartiality towards him appeared to have only made him feel more ashamed and spiteful. From here on out, he decided, Bonnet would be his worst enemy, and he would have to watch him like a hawk. But at least the man had virtually no influence with the men and would remain something of a pariah. It would take some time before he would become a viable threat.

"Is it settled then, men?" he asked.

"Aye, it's settled," said Bonnet, more forcefully than Thache would have thought possible for such a weak and compromised man. "I'll be moving my books and clothing into this ship's more spacious quarters."

"Of course."

"And might I also ask, where are we going now, Captain?"

Blackbeard smiled bloodlessly. "Why we're going after the *Protestant Caesar*, of course. I'll be damned if I let her captain brag, when he returns to New England, that he has beaten a pirate. No one who sails with me shall be bettered by a Boston ship—and that's all there is of it."

A rowdy cheer rose up from the men. "May the Lord have mercy on her and Captain Wyer both when we get through with them!" shouted Howard.

"Aye verily," agreed Blackbeard. "Damnation to him who ever lived to wear a halter. We're men not animals, by thunder, and we will take our vengeance upon all those high powers who want to keep us harnessed in yokes. Amen!"

"Amen! Amen!" shouted the company—their rebellious, democratic sentiments in the name of both profit and common fairness echoing all across Turneffe Lagoon.

CHAPTER 33

COAST OF HONDURAS

APRIL 8-11, 1718

THE SEA BREEZE chased up and over the fringing reef, bringing with it the salty scent of the Spanish Main. Caesar inhaled the salt air deeply. He stood on the quarterdeck of the *Queen Anne's Revenge* with William Howard, Stede Bonnet, and Thache, watching a flock of seagulls wheeling against silvery-gray clouds. They had plundered several ships during the past few days, bringing the size of the burgeoning pirate fleet up to seven hundred seamen spread amongst five cannon-studded vessels: the "Great Devil, as the Spanish and British logcutters called Thache's flagship; Captain David Herriot's *Adventure*, seized in Turneffe Lagoon and now captained by Israel Hands; two pirated supply sloops carrying "bloody" red flags to indicate that they were also serving as privateers; and the refitted *Revenge* captained by Richards, which also bore crimson colors.

"There she be!" cried the lookout from the maintop, high above the deck. "The *Protestant Caesar* in all her high and mighty glory!"

Caesar removed Thache's brass spyglass from its leather case and handed it to the captain, who had it against his eye and scanning the bay and mangrove-infested land beyond within a fraction of a second.

"She has nowhere to go, Master Howard," said Thache, his voice calm and composed but carrying an unmistakable trace of excitement. "We'll close on her with full sail and prepare to stand to her forefoot if she shows her heels."

"Aye, Captain. I've been looking forward to this moment."

"As have we all, Mr. Howard. But none have been looking forward to it as much as Major Bonnet here. He has graced us with his company on deck to watch the spectacle."

He gestured deferentially to the Barbadian planter, who gave a polite bow. Though Bonnet's expression remained courtly and impassive, Caesar could see how badly he wanted to take out his revenge on Captain Wyer of the *Protestant Caesar*. The merchant captain had thoroughly embarrassed him by outfighting him, which had in turn led to his once again being stripped of his captaincy.

The man wants revenge so badly he can taste it, thought Caesar. *Well now, Major Bonnet, it looks like you are about to get your chance.*

"Fore and aft, all hands!" shouted Thache.

The crew mobilized swiftly and precisely, the sailors, gun crews, and armed boarding party forming up into their designated positions.

"She hasn't struck her colors or turned out her cannon. What do you think her play is, Captain?" asked Garret Gibbons.

"I don't know, but our fine Captain Wyer only has three choices: to flee, to stand and fight, or to run his vessel ashore with the hope that he can later return and save his ship once we have left the scene."

Caesar looked at him. "Which one do you think he will try?"

"I don't know. But being as he is from Boston, he and his men are truly in for it now. Mark my words, they will feel my wrath upon them."

ψψψ

Captain William Wyer couldn't believe his bad luck as he stared at the five-vessel pirate flotilla sailing directly towards him with the weather, numbers, and armament in their favor. His four-hundred-ton *Protestant Caesar* carried twenty-six guns and a fifty-man crew—but she was no match for the thirty-eight-gun behemoth racing towards her like a hound unleashed from hell itself, or the group of sleek-bodied consorts that together brought the grand total of cannon to more than eighty pieces. It would be suicide for him to resist at all, but of course that would be for his men to decide.

He quickly called them on deck for a conference.

"Take a look there," he said, looking through his glass. "We've got quite a large ship and a big sloop with black flags and deaths' heads, and we have three more armed sloops with bloody flags, and they are coming straight for us. If they don't have us trapped already, they will in the next five minutes. Now I'm asking what ye want to do? Are you willing to defend the ship from these pirates?"

His crew nervously studied the armada of approaching vessels, which were slowly growing bigger on the eastern horizon.

"There's no way to outrun them?" the quartermaster asked the first-mate.

"Not likely. Our holds are more than half filled up with logwood and it's more than likely every one of their vessels can outrun us."

"Look at that big monster," said the bosun. "Why she must carry thirty guns."

"Closer to forty," said the first-mate.

"She carries a lot of sail and looks to me to be Dutch-built with a hull sleeker than most," observed the captain. "I would wager that she can overhaul any vessel she encounters short of a small sloop."

"What should we do then, Captain?" asked the bosun.

"Why it's up to you men. That's why I called you up on deck."

"I think we should stay and fight," said the first-mate.

"No, that's crazy," countered the quartermaster. "If we fight them, they'll destroy us. There's five ships in that flotilla."

"You've got to make a decision, men," said Wyer. "Needless to say, our backers won't be happy if we surrender without a fight, but they're not the ones whose lives are at stake. I'll stand by whatever judgement you make."

"Well, will we get our full wages or not?" demanded one of the sailors.

"It's complicated. On the one hand, they may decide to—"

"What the hell are you talking about?" another seaman cut in, his face red with anger. "What does our standing and fighting or not have to do with us getting paid? They don't have anything to do with one another!"

"Shut up and listen, all of you," the bosun broke in. "There is no way in hell we are going to resist a pirate force of five hundred or more men with only fifty. And they're English too—they're not even Spanish."

That was enough for the first-mate and he changed his position. "If they were Spaniards, Captain, we would stand by you as long as we could take a breath. But these are pirates, and Englishmen to boot."

"Not only are these men pirates," pointed out a seaman, "they are the same men we fought the other night."

Wyer squinted. "What? Ye be certain of it?"

"Aye, they be the same freebooters who came upon our stern. And now they've returned with that big monster with her forty guns. That's got to be the Great Devil the logcutters spoke of. They say it's captained by Blackbeard himself."

"Blackbeard!"

"By the blood of Henry Morgan we're all dead men," lamented the quartermaster, whose legs were now visibly shaking. "That be the *Queen Anne's Revenge* right there coming at us like a giant black whale!"

At the mention of the notorious Blackbeard, the crew flew into a panic that Captain Wyer was unable to control, with men running and stumbling in all directions and yelling and screaming in pandemonium like a terrified pack of children. While longboats were hastily unfastened, the deck rang out with voices making the wild accusations of desperate seamen who were convinced they were about to meet a gruesome end from bloodthirsty pirates.

"Blackbeard is the devil incarnate! Upon my honor we have all drawn our last breath!"

"They say he puts lit cannon fuses beneath his cap and his face smokes like the devil himself when he goes into battle!"

"They say he cuts off the heads of all his prisoners except one, leaving a single seaman alive to tell the terrible tale!"

"They say he's had fourteen wives and has given them to his crew to brutally rape before slitting their throats!"

"We be doomed! We be doomed!"

"Now stop this at once and get a grip on yourselves!" admonished Wyer. "Blackbeard is but a man, by thunder! He does not have supernatural powers, so avast all of ye!"

The quartermaster shook his head. "He may not be a vengeful god or Lucifer himself, Captain, but he is a monster and vicious killer! We need to get out of here! There's no time to waste!"

"He's right!" said the bosun. "If we stay here, we'll all be murdered! We need to load provisions, abandon ship, and make for the coast in the longboats! If we hide in the jungle, maybe he'll take what he wants and leave us alone!"

"All right, that be not a half bad idea. But everyone needs to calm down," said Wyer, knowing if he didn't control his men quickly it would be every man for himself. "Let's go, lads. To the shore it is then."

After throwing in basic supplies, including food, water, small arms, spare ropes and canvas, and a medicine chest, they lowered their longboats into the water and beat a hasty retreat towards the jungles ashore. South of the mouth of the muddy-watered Rio Balis, Wyer and his men found shelter amid the dense tropical foliage, piles of logwood, and mangrove swamps. From there, they watched the pirates plunder their massive merchantman. Day passed into night and the next day and night into another until on the third day, the pirates had picked the vessel clean and a huge bare-chested black man wearing a weather-beaten, wide-brimmed Spanish hat close-cropped on the sides and a huge golden earring in his left ear was sent to parley with them. The dark African rowed straight up to Wyer and his crew members along the edge of the mangroves.

The seaman didn't bother to step from the boat. "My name is Caesar and I am here to deliver a message from Captain Thache. It is the only message you are going to get so you must listen closely."

Wyer pushed aside the thick foliage and inched closer so he could hear and see better. Patters of excited conversation and rumbles of fear filtered up from his huddled merchant sailors along the edge of the jungle.

"Thache be the pirate known as Blackbeard, correct?" asked Wyer, wanting to make sure who he was dealing with.

"Aye, and here is his message for you," said Caesar. "He says if you and your men surrender peacefully, no harm will come to you and you will be free to go. The captain is waiting for your answer in his great cabin."

Wyer looked at the African then at his men then back at the black man. "That's it? I surrender and we all go free?"

"Aye, Captain Blackbeard does not like to settle disputes with violence. It is against his nature—unless of course you refuse to accept his most generous offer."

Several men stepped forward and began talking all at once. "Don't do it, Captain! He'll kill you! He'll kill us all! You can't trust him!"

Caesar raised his hand, silencing them. "That is not true," he said. "Captain Thache is a man of his word. You can trust him just as sure as I sit in this boat before you."

Wyer thought a moment before coming to the conclusion that he had little choice but to surrender himself and his men and hope for mercy. "I'm inclined to agree," he said, drawing unflattering curses from several of his crew members. "Now just hold on," he pleaded. "Blackbeard does indeed have a fearsome reputation. But he has never been known to go back on his word."

More protests erupted from his men, but he cut off the resistance with an abrupt hand-chopping motion. "Plague on your scurvy heads, keep quiet!" he bristled. "I am the one taking the risk here, so if you'll be kind enough to let me dispose of the present situation in my own way, I would appreciate it. The truth is, men, we have no choice. We're out here in the bloody middle of the Spanish Main and can't survive even another week on our provisions. We have to surrender—and that's all there is of it!"

"If that's the case then the decision is an easy one for you," said Caesar. "Come with me to speak with the captain. He has brandy, wine, and food waiting for you. He also has a surprise."

"A surprise?"

"Aye, and I think you're going to like it."

CHAPTER 34

OFF COAST OF HONDURAS

APRIL 11, 1718

"I'VE BEEN REVIEWING your bill of lading and crew payment records," said Thache to commence the much-anticipated conference with Captain Wyer. "And you know what I've discovered? Commerce is a funny thing." He pointed at the signed paperwork on his map table. "Oftentimes, ye have one country produce something, while another exploits it for gain or improves upon it, making it into something bigger and better. Take this champagne we're drinking, for instance." He leaned across his map table and topped off his guest's crystal flute. "A Frenchman named Dom Pérignon, from the Abbey of Saint-Hilaire in Limoux, first developed this wonderful sparkling wine we are drinking. But it be the English who took it and put it in a bottle, experimented with different glasses, temperatures, and corks, thereby mastering the art of making sparkling wine by fermenting it using suitably robust glass bottles. If the English had not done this and thereby learned to properly add bubbles to the local white wines of the region, we would not now be graced with champagne in Port Royal."

He raised his glass and the two men took a sip, both of them grimacing slightly as the making of sparkly wine was still in a process of experimentation and refinement.

"We pirates are like England," Thache then went on. "We take a sliver of the pie from some nation's commerce, but in the process we transform that sliver into something else entirely."

Wyer appeared skeptical. "And what would that be?"

"Hope. We give the average sailor hope for a better future. At least in the short term."

"When those around James the Pretender talked like that, they called it treason and hung them. Why you almost make piracy sound respectable."

"That's because it is respectable, which is why gentleman pirates from fine Atlantic families have been going on the account for more than a century now. In truth, a pirate's life not be any different or worse than what you do to exploit your crewmen or the logcutters of Campeche, who are paid mere pennies on the pound for the wood they cut."

Wyer's grizzled face scrunched up. "I make an honest living, I do."

"So do I then. In fact, we are no different. We just go about it differently. That's the only thing that separates us: our methods."

"I might be inclined to take offense to such kind of talk."

"That's because you're ignorant and don't know who the real winners and losers are in international commerce."

The captain's face had reddened and he now stood up from his chair. "I'm not going to sit here and suffer this kind of humiliation. Not by the likes of you."

"Oh, get off your high horse and sit down. I'm not trying to badger you—I'm just trying to make a point about maritime commerce. And the point I was about to make is my men earn more than you do. Black, white, brown, yellow—it doesn't matter, they earn better than a captain's wages. That is the value they bring to the commercial marketplace."

Wyer just stared at him as if he was staring at the face of the devil. It appeared he was too speechless to summon actual words.

"Your average underpaid seaman has to work a decade just to earn what my men take in a month's time. That's a significant restructuring of the colonial wage structure, wouldn't you say? It also happens to be the dirty little secret that ship owners, capital investors, sea captains, and the like don't want them to know. And it also illuminates, in a very stark way, your true value as a sea captain. In a world of commerce with the lines drawn by us, you earn far less than what my seamen earn. Mind you, they drink and fuck it away within a fortnight every time we hit port, but it's good to know they bring a greater commercial value to the colonial economy than you do." Here he gave a conspiratorial smile and waved his hand expansively towards the paperwork resting on his map table. "Remember, William, I snuck a peek at your records. That's how I know of what I speak."

Wyer shook his head in disgust. This egalitarian world of Blackbeard—driven and sustained by the pure pirate motive of profit—was a world he and the powerful merchants and government that backed them wanted no part of.

"What the hell do you want from me? Are you trying to rub it in my face, is that it?"

"No, William, that's not what I be doing at all. My goal was actually to enlighten you, in the hopes that you might actually have a modicum of common sense and empathy betwixt your ears. But perhaps I was wrong. I actually called you here because I wanted to thank you for making the right decision."

"The right decision?"

"By standing down and surrendering your vessel."

"To be perfectly honest, I don't feel very good about any of this."

"And who could blame you? But you did the right thing and were smart not to burn or sabotage the *Protestant Caesar*."

"And if I hadn't, what would have happened to me?"

"We would have done you and your men irreparable damage. Irreparable damage."

"Is that so?"

"Aye, I would not like to be listed in the survive of the devil by describing it, so let's just say it crosses what I would call the bounds of good taste. But I also don't want to focus inordinately upon the past because I feel that, at this moment, you need to brace yourself for the future. I have some unsettling news."

Wyer shook his head disparagingly, as if he were talking to a common street thug and not a maritime expert who had outsmarted him on three occasions thus far in their short relationship: the first by taking him by surprise and cutting him off before he could escape, the second in seizing his ship without any opposition whatsoever, and the third by getting him to stop hiding out in the jungle and meet with him—after his ship had been completely ransacked and plundered.

"I'm afraid I have some bad news, William my friend," he said in the tone of a consoling family patriarch. "Unfortunately, I have to burn the *Protestant Caesar*."

"But why?"

"Because she hails from Boston, and my little gang of gentlemen of fortune is committed firmly to destroying all Massachusetts vessels in revenge for the six pirates that were executed."

"You're referring to the survivors of the Cape Cod shipwrecks?"

"Aye, Captain Bellamy's men. They were our mates and we loved them like brothers."

"The ones that fancied themselves Robin Hoods' men."

"One and the same."

"But they not be Robin Hoods' men—they be nothing but sea monsters and hell hounds who would sell their own mother for quick and easy plunder." His voice turned to a low hiss. "As are you, you devil incarnate."

Despite the anger he felt inside, Thache forced himself to control his emotions. "William, William, William—what are we going to do with you? I suspected you might resort to losing your temper, but this...this vile language you bring into my cabin as my guest, well let's just say I had expected more from a supposed gentleman like yourself."

"But there's no reason to take me ship."

"As I just told ye, there quite plainly is. New England—and the city of Boston in particular—has declared war on us. What kind of shepherd would I be to my flock if, like the great Puritan spokesperson Cotton Mather, I refused to fulfill the wishes of my men in this great crusade of maritime equality and self-government of ours. No, Captain Wyer, the *Protestant Caesar* shall burn and, in one hour, you and your men are going to watch her burn. In return, I'm going to give you my smallest sloop, minus the cannon of course, along with plenty of food and water. No longboats for you, William. Only the best from Captain Blackbeard."

Wyer gritted his teeth, like an enraged dog. "Why you devil you. You take everything from me and then make me watch while you burn me own ship. What kind of man are ye? Who does a thing like that? Why I'll tell you just who: a violator of all laws, humane and divine!"

"No, William, 'tis a just and fair man who does such things, to impart an important lesson just like your Reverend Mather," he replied calmly and without rancor. "In fact, I would have to say that this is far better than a greedy merchant captain like you—who pays his men a slave's wages—deserves. Far better indeed."

CHAPTER 35

WILLIAMSBURG, VIRGINIA

MAY 1, 1718

AS SPOTSWOOD watched a dozen of his black slaves hard at work tending to his grounds and keeping his Governor's Palace in fine working order, he wondered if they would ever have the temerity to rise up against him. Slave revolts were a great fear for Virginians, and he had pleaded for a strengthened law to prevent and deter slave insurrections in 1710 shortly after taking office. In his speech, he reminded the Virginia Assembly that constant vigilance was the price of continued subjugation: "the trials of last April's court may show that we are not to depend on either their stupidity, or that babel of languages among them; freedom wears a cap which can without a tongue call together all those who long to shake off the fetters of slavery." In his view, freedom wore the red cap of bloody rebellion, and he and his fellow slaveholders never doubted for a moment that their human chattel might one day suddenly rise up, clap it to their heads, and win their revenge.

With his slaves drawing a visible sweat despite the pleasantly cool spring weather, he turned his gaze to his beloved "Palace" that his Council and the House of Burgesses thought was costing too much to build. The five-bay Georgian-style home was done up in Flemish bond with glazed headers and rubbed brick window jambs and lintels. Three stories in height, the residence sported elaborate exterior ornamentation, a cellar with eleven wine bins, a row of dormers on the roof, and a wrought-iron balcony at the central upper window. Just inside the gate, guarded by a stone unicorn on one side and a stone lion on the other, stood two brick advance buildings with gabled roofs that ran perpendicular to the main structure. Beyond the house was a formal garden, and a stable, carriage house, kitchen, scullery, laundry, and an octagonal bathhouse were arranged in service yards beside the advance buildings.

The palatial residence formed the architectural centerpiece of Williamsburg while serving as the political nerve center of the second most important colony following New England. It had taken a continuous army of slave labor to build the mansion during the past eight years—yet it was still unfinished. All the same it was a masterpiece. Virginia planters were already beginning to build their own great houses to emulate and exceed it, even as they heckled the governor over its exorbitant cost to date.

Spotswood required a total of twenty-five indentured servants and slaves to tend to the overall estate, in addition to the African slaves he owned and directed at his powder magazine. Depending upon their duties, some of these servants and slaves lived and worked in the outbuildings, while a portion lived and worked in the main house. There were stewards, personal servants, butlers, footmen, cooks, laundresses, gardeners, maids, grooms, and laborers. None of them received payment of any kind for their toils and services. Spotswood also hired tradesmen and laborers on an as-needed basis, and physicians from town attended to the governor's family, indentured servants, and slaves—although for his servants and slaves Spotswood only rarely approved medical expenses to keep costs down, usually for significant injuries such as broken bones.

He took a breath of the morning air and sighed contentedly. Spring had come to Virginia and with it the pleasant perfume of irises, peonies, and other perennials, Carolina sweet shrub, flowering dogwood, oak-leaved hydrangea, and red buckeye. The sun shone down resplendently and a periwinkle-blue sky loomed overhead. He was comfortable in his red velvet tail jacket, knee breeches, and buckled black leather shoes as he started for the front entrance.

"You've nearly bankrupted the colony to build the damned thing, but I have to admit it is a beauty."

He turned to see his principal adversary, Philip Ludwell the Younger, staring at him pugnaciously beneath his brand-new tricorn hat. He looked at his watch: 09:08 hours. He had hoped to avoid getting into an argument with Ludwell or his belligerent cronies until this afternoon's Assembly session, when he knew it couldn't be avoided.

"Yes, it is wonderful. I am so glad you approve, Philip."

"I *don't* approve and you shouldn't have built it in the first place. Not at the taxpayers' expense."

"Well, it's almost finished now and I'm paying for much of the landscaping and perimeter walls from my own pocket. Even that should be satisfactory to the great Philip the Younger."

"Don't call me that. I don't like that name."

"And I don't like being called a proverbial skunk. Now what is your business here today, Mr. Ludwell. I trust that we can carry on in a civil fashion from this point forward."

"Further complaints have been made to His Majesty regarding your many abuses of power. I came by to see if there was anything I should add to the list before this afternoon's plenary session."

"That is ridiculous. You're just trying to lure me into a trap on the off chance I might say something compromising that you can later use against me."

Ludwell grinned with grudging approval at the observation. "At least you're a clever adversary, I'll give ye that. I don't know how you and I could possibly go on like this if you were a complete dullard. But mark my words, you will not remain in your post for long if you do not stand down on this issue of erecting courts of oyer and terminer. You, sir, are a tyrant, and we will stand no more of it."

"Is that so? I think you're forgetting one thing: the power to erect courts rests with the Crown—which here in Virginia is me, Mr. Ludwell—and the governor can appoint commissions to investigate any matter with or exclusive of the Council."

"The issue here is whether you have grossly exceeded your authority—on behalf of selfish motives."

"No, the issue here is whether the governor or his Council should be paramount in the public affairs of Virginia. And on that score, Mr. Ludwell, the Board of Trade backed by the Crown has made its position well known to all here in the colonies.

You may have defeated me and forced me to repeal the Indian and Tobacco Acts, but you do not control me as you would a puppet. Much to your consternation."

"You need to come down off your high and mighty perch and listen to the voice of the people."

"You, the voice of the people? Your only reason for existence—and that of the Council and Burgesses as well—is to line your own pockets, to acquire as many Negroes and sell as much low-quality tobacco as possible, and to exploit the poor Indians. All you care about is profit so don't blather on all holier-than-thou to me like Reverend Blair."

"A man needs to know when to stand down."

"Like a slave, is that it?"

Ludwell scanned the area, casting his gaze in the direction of the more than a dozen slaves tending to the gardens, performing construction and carpentry activities, tilling soil, hauling supplies, and clearing brush and objects at the Palace Green and immediately surrounding areas. "You should know," he said. "You seem to have more slaves than anyone else in Williamsburg."

"And I treat them well."

"They're still slaves, Lieutenant Governor. Ye couldn't possibly treat them that well."

Feeling his anger building up, he began walking for the ornamental iron gates. "I believe we're done here, Philip. If you can't be civil, there is really no reason to continue this discussion."

"I'm afraid I'm just getting started. There is a common theme here, Mr. Lieutenant Governor, that me and my colleagues want to make sure you understand. We want you *less*—not *more*—involved in colonial affairs. And yet, I have recently learned that you have been busy laying the groundwork for an offensive against pirates in Virginia waters—and apparently anywhere else you see fit."

"What of it? As colonial governor, I am the commander of local militia and all naval forces in this colony. As a matter of fact, my commission specifically gives me the right to execute everything which doth and of right ought to belong to the governor."

"I'm afraid me and my associates don't view piracy with the same jaundiced eye you do."

"What are you saying?"

"Mr. Perry, myself, and the other members of the gentry do not mind English pirates, so long as they prey only on vessels of other nations or simply take provisions as needed. Indeed, privateers are often good for our business and help bring in low-priced goods to diversify our assets."

"That is seditious talk, especially coming from someone who represents one of Virginia's finest families."

"Seditious or not, one man's so-called pirate is another man's much-needed smuggler."

"Is that so? I was of the impression that piracy was uniformly bad for trade and, therefore, only hurt your pocket."

"It is true that of late there have been far too many British victims of English pirates, especially on the Virginia coast where my good friend Mr. Perry and I conduct our business. But not all sea rovers need be lumped into the category of murderous cutthroats and barbarians in order to fulfill the greedy prerogatives of ye governorship."

"What's that supposed to mean?"

"Pirate incursions make you appear weak and incapable of protecting the colony's merchants. That is one reason why you want to rein in the pirates. But your main reason is you want to profit."

"As I laid out earlier in the week, if the violated owners can prove the property stolen by the pirates is theirs, the produce must be paid to them according to His Majesty's treaties, allowing a usual salvage to those who rescued them from the pirates. If no claimer appears, the same comes to the King, but no doubt his Majesty will think fit to reward the officers of his ships and others concerned in so considerable a service as the destruction of pirates."

"That is just another example of your overreach and precisely why you are always butting heads with us. Under your approach, the onus is on the wronged shipowners to make the case for ownership to the Virginian authorities, not for you the governor to try to seek out the original owners. You just want to keep the money and control of the restitution process for yourself."

"My foremost goal is protection of the colony."

"No, your foremost priority is to distract the Council and House of Burgesses from your own failing administration. That's why anti-piracy has become a singular obsession for you, your closest associates, and a few hirelings."

"How dare ye talk to me like that. I am a gentleman, but even a gentleman has limits to his patience."

"The only reason you have yet to be locked up for exceeding your authority in this regard is because this obsession of yours reflects the most fervent wishes of the Board of Trade and the Admiralty, both of whom you are so eager to flatter."

"And you have become so blinded by the prospect of removing me from my post, you are no longer fit for public office. Your intransigence knows no bounds."

"You have to accept the fact that most of the civilian residents of this colony and our Carolina friends to the south are not as committed to eradicating the sea rovers as you are."

"Thanks to the *Boston News-Letter*, that is changing. Now even your stubborn provincial townspeople and yeomen are changing their views."

"Those articles are mostly propaganda. They exaggerate the actual attacks on British shipping to ensure that the pirates are cast in an evil light. They stopped being factual accounts of the sea robberies more than six months ago."

"Are you saying that newspaper-inspired anti-pirate attitudes are on the rise and we are being led to the trough by tellers of tall tales?"

"No, but the accuracy of the supposedly factual details can no longer be trusted."

"Well, the newspapers may not be able to be trusted, but Captain Ellis Brand of the HMS *Lyme* protecting our waters most certainly can be."

"Is that who you're getting your information from?"

"That is none of your business. All you need to know is that as governor, I have control over the Admiralty."

165

"In Virginia's coastal waters—and nowhere else."

"That is up for me to decide."

"No, sir, it is not—and once again, this is yet another example of you overestimating your authority. You think I have been tough on you this morning—just wait until we're in session this afternoon. I believe you're going to have a lot of explaining to do, Mr. Lieutenant Governor."

"As are ye, Mr. Ludwell, when I make clear the extent of your seditious comments on my nice green lawn."

Ludwell grinned defiantly. "Your days are numbered."

Spotswood returned the challenge with a challenging expression of his own. "No, it is the pirates' days that are numbered, Mr. Ludwell. Especially that black-bearded hooligan Edward Thache I keep hearing about. It is high time he and his crew paid a little visit to our Execution Dock. Then they'll find out what happens to those who defy the Crown."

CHAPTER 36

NASSAU

MAY 5, 1718

"SO, WHAT'S THE GOOD WORD, EDWARD? Have you made your plans regarding your future?"

Thache took a gulp of his ale, sighed with satisfaction, and set down the pewter tankard on the table. He and his fellow pirate captain friend Paulsgrave Williams were seated beneath a sailcloth awning in Nassau's leading open-air alehouse overlooking the sparkling harbor: the Blue Parrot. They had debated their futures at length over prodigious bottles of rum during an unusually raucous evening celebration, even by Nassau standards, shortly after he had shipped into port yesterday afternoon; but at that point he still hadn't decided upon a plan. But today he knew. Despite his brutal hangover, he had made up his mind regarding his future and it involved leaving the Caribbean behind. Perhaps for good.

"As a matter of fact, I have made my decision."

The middle-aged silversmith from a wealthy Rhode Island family—who had left behind a wife and two young children to go to sea with Samuel Bellamy—grinned devilishly. "And what would that be, Mr. Blackbeard the Pyrate?"

Thache chuckled at the jovial sarcasm. "The commodore is heading north."

"Oh, commodore are we now? Blackbeard the commodore. I like it very much. Now what point of the compass would our esteemed commodore and his flotilla be heading? Would said commodore be in search of a fair maiden named Margaret of Marcus Hook by chance?"

"That is definitely high on the priority list. That is, if she'll still have me."

"That's what a romantic like me likes to hear. You're going to lose that fine lass if you don't get your arse up there and ask her to marry ye."

"I know that."

"So you're sailing north to see your sweetheart. You do remember what happened to our mutual friend Black Sam when he sailed north to see his dearly beloved, one Maria 'Goody' Hallett."

"Believe me, the coincidence has not been lost on me. I can only hope that I have better luck than our Sam."

Williams raised his tankard. "To Black Sam—God bless our beloved Robin Hood of the high seas. He was one of a kind."

Thache raised his ale. "Indeed he was. To Black Sam!"

Williams echoed him and they tossed back their ale and quickly ordered two more from the young and attractive mullato bar maid. Thache couldn't help but notice that the female population had not only grown in the past two years, but grown far more youthful and attractive. There were a particularly high number of West Indian, Negro, and mulatto women on the island that had managed to secure work as bar keeps and maids, seamstresses, bookkeepers, and laundresses, though sporting women and spouses still made up the largest percentage of female roles.

"You're not really sailing north just to see your beloved Margaret?"

"No, I'm not."

"So, you'll be taking plenty of plunder and are not planning on taking the King's pardon?"

"No, I plan to take plenty of plunder and *then* accept the King's pardon."

"Oh, you devil you. And where will you be doing your plundering and to which governor do you plan to request the King's most gracious pardon?"

"The crew voted to take one last crack at the Florida wrecks and then sail up the coast for the Carolinas and Delaware Capes. Once we're north, a portion of us are planning on obtaining pardons from Governor Eden of North Carolina. My Bath County lads say he's a man we can trust, and North Carolina has been so hard hit by Indians wars, Virginia's restrictive tobacco legislation, and internal political bickering that she is in dire need of revenue. That's where we come in. But first we need to take a dozen valuable prizes or so to make sure we can make a hefty contribution to the North Carolina office of customs. It will be a clean slate and new beginning mutually beneficial to both parties."

"But King George's royal proclamation only allows for the pardoning of piracies committed before January 5 of this year. You have been quite busy since that time, have you not?"

"But Governor Eden doesn't know that."

"I have heard of this Eden. Some of the men in the other companies have said the same thing about him, that he is the best choice to ask for a pardon. Just bring plenty of gold dust, coin, and supplies and you should have little trouble winning him over, or so it is said."

"Aye verily, but I have also actually met him."

"You know his governorship? Why aren't you the high and mighty one."

"Says the scion of one of the richest families of Rhode Island. But seriously, I had dinner at the home of customs inspector Tobias Knight and I met the governor there. Knight invited the captain of my ship at the time and me to a fine meal of ham and pudding. That was four years ago when I was sailing as mate out of Philadelphia and had just delivered a ship of armaments for the North Carolina militia. They were in a terrible fight with the Tuscarora at the time. I saw them several months later on a voyage to deliver more powder and weapons, farming implements, cocoa, and rice."

"So you know these North Carolina men? They'll look favorably upon you?"

"I don't know about that. But they were grateful for us bringing muskets, sabers, and powder for their stores, as well as the items we delivered to their colony during my second visit. They will remember me."

"Having some familiarity with a man is one thing. But being able to sail up to his docks and deliver pouches filled with gold dust, casks of sugar, and bags of flour and cocoa will no doubt be far more persuasive."

"I would say both make a difference."

"You said you were going to take prizes on your way north to Bath Town. Are you planning on visiting Charles Town per chance?"

"As a matter of fact, my plan is to blockade its port."

"Blockade? You're going to blockade Charles Town?"

He held his finger to his mouth. "Shush, not so loud. I haven't told my crew yet of my intentions."

"You haven't?"

"No, and I don't intend to until we get underway. I'll tell you why all the secrecy in a moment, but needless to say blockading Charles Town can be done. Bonnet himself did it a year ago."

"The disgraced lubber blockaded the South Carolina capital?"

"Aye, he's the one that gave me the idea. You see, all commercial vessels entering the harbor are forced to travel over a shoal and through a narrow channel. Bonnet was able to blockade the port in the *Revenge*, but he had to confine himself to a hit-and-run operation. He fled the scene before the city's residents came after him in their own sloops. But with my powerful fleet, I would have nothing to fear from the little armed sloops of Charles Town's merchants."

"What about the Royal Navy?"

"They have no permanent presence in the Carolinas, and even if a frigate happened to be in the harbor, it couldn't stand up to the firepower of my *Queen Anne's Revenge* and four consort sloops."

"By the devil's teeth, you'll bring the entire colony to its knees. Why you could even hold the town itself for ransom."

Thache leaned in towards his friend. "I'm doing it for different reasons than you think, Paul. Aye, it's about profit and sticking it to the Crown—but there's also another important reason to blockade the city. For me, it's the main reason."

"What is it?"

"My crew is in bad need of medical supplies."

"Medical supplies? What, you have an outbreak on your hands?"

"It's the pox."

"An outbreak of syphilis, is it?"

He nodded solemnly. "Since the last time I saw ye, I have nearly fifty men that have come down with it, or have had it worsen to where it has become a real problem. If I don't get them medical help, they're going to die. Several are already mad as hatters—and getting worse every day. Some suffer only from rashes, fevers, sore throats, and bad headaches, but others be far worse. Some are disorientated and confused, others weak and irritable, still others are violently angry all the time. It's driving me out of my mind and I've got to get them help. We had some mercury treatment devices—the doctors call them urethral syringes—from the *La Concorde's* doctors and other prizes we've taken, but our supplies have run out. We need more devices and more of the mercury."

"I must needs say I had no idea it was so bad. I've always had a handful of crew members suffering the affliction during a given voyage, but most men keep it to themselves and find a way to manage."

"Aye, the problem for me is my crew is too damned big. Plus I think we've got an epidemic. That's why I plan to blockade Charles Town—so I can get my crew medicine."

"Where do you think your men picked it up?"

SAMUEL MARQUIS

"They've always been getting it. It's just gotten worse in the past three months. I think some must have caught it in Nassau when we were here last summer, but most I believe got it in French Hispaniola when we were there in the winter. The pickings were slim and the men had to take what they could get. Not the cleanest wenches, I must say. Them Spanishers must have diseased them."

Williams took a jolt from his tankard and assumed a thoughtful pose. "A siege of Charles Town for medicine. My, my, the things we do for our crews. And you haven't told any of your men this?"

"Not yet. But they won't have any problem with the blockade. In fact, they'll be lively ho. But what they don't know is the main reason for doing it is to secure medicine. I don't want the crew to know how bad it has become. They know we've been on the lookout for more of the syringes and mercury, and more doctors to help us out in this area. But they don't know how bad things are getting. My French doctors tell me that if I don't do something about this, we could have a serious epidemic on our hands."

"Well, you're doing right by your men. That's the main thing."

He nodded and they settled into silence, quietly sipping their room-temperature ales. After a moment, Thache lit his clay pipe and began puffing on it, thinking about the uncertain journey that lay ahead for him and his men. After he had sailed into Nassau Harbor yesterday afternoon and divided the communal plunder, three hundred crew members had made official their decision to leave the company, which had thankfully lightened his burden. The arduous strain of managing seven hundred wild and rebellious sea rovers had taken a definite toll on him during the past several months, but four hundred pirates spread amongst four or five ships was still a challenge. Of those who were moving on, some had decided to join Williams and his crew, who were planning on heading soon for West African shores to prey on European slave ships. Others wanted to enjoy their earnings and wait out as long as they could by holding off on signing on with another ship until just prior to the arrival in mid-summer of Governor Woodes Rogers. Others planned to wait until his arrival and then take the King's pardon. Still others were Jacobite stalwarts who wished to stay behind with Charles Vane to await reinforcements from the Stuart court-in-exile and perhaps fight it out against Rogers and the Royal Navy.

Blackbeard had a different plan. He saw the writing on the wall: the time of active piracy was coming to a close. It had been a good run, but the Crown and its bulldog enforcer the Admiralty had reached a turning point and were now taking an aggressive role in combating robbery at sea. King George's pardon was creating divisiveness in the pirates' ranks by inducing many of the best captains and officers to surrender and scattering crews to the wind. On a personal level, Thache was impressed with Charles Vane's commitment to hold down the pirate base on New Providence at all costs. But he was too wily a strategist to join a hopeless cause, for the few hundred pirates in Nassau had little hope of repelling the formidable military force Rogers would soon have at his disposal.

Unlike Vane, Blackbeard had no intention of going out in a blaze of glory. He would rather be one of the few who got away with it all, which was why he was counting on one final orgy of plundering before obtaining a pardon for himself and his key crew members from Charles Eden. North Carolina's governor had little choice but to try to improve the commercial position of his poor, out-of-the-way colony. Under the protection of Eden, Thache would retire. Then, when the coast was clear and there was no doubt that he was fully pardoned, he would return to Philadelphia to be with his beloved Margaret. But first, he needed to capture a dozen or so big prizes. Then he would have the financial security he needed to start a new life as an honest, law-abiding citizen.

The truth was it was no longer safe to be a pirate. Why even his old sailing companion Hornigold and the pretentious Jennings were supposedly planning on surrendering as soon as they had the chance. When Woodes Rogers arrived in mid-summer, he would promptly reestablish the British government and formally demand the mass surrender of the pirates and, at that point, not a single island in the Bahamas would remain safe for use as a pirate base or secure haven. Blackbeard knew he had to find a way to obtain his own pardon from someone who wouldn't hold hard and fast to the January 5 date. Then he had to lay low and make sure the Crown wouldn't somehow change its mind and reverse its decision.

"Arrgh," he heard Williams say. "Look who be coming our way."

Thache looked up to see Charles Vane. "He's still on the warpath, is he?"

"You're damn right. He's trying to recruit holdouts to stay behind and fight. Woodes Rogers is going to crush him and it's not going to be pretty."

The vulgar, dangerously violent, but always entertaining former privateer stumbled up to them waving a half-drunken bottle of rum. "All right, here we go—now I'm getting to the cream of the crop. What say you gentlemen about joining my fight and sending King George's pawn to his Maker as soon as his governorship sets foot on our merry little island. We can win this war and retain our freedom, you know. We can do it, by thunder. So are you with me?"

Thache looked at Williams and they both smiled. "I'm sorry, Charles, but I'm afraid we can't join your crusade. We're both going on the account soon and will not be standing by waiting for the new governor's arrival. But we will drink a toast with you."

"All right, mates. What do we drink to then?" asked Vane in a slurred voice.

Thache allowed his smile to widen. "You know perfectly well what, Charles. It's your favorite toast."

"Aye, to the damnation of that nefarious scupperlout, King George!" he roared, holding his bottle up and swishing the amber fluid in the sunlight.

Three dozen barefoot pirates were up and on their feet. "To the damnation of King George!" they shrieked in unison and then they tossed back their ales and spirits.

When the noise quieted down, Thache looked at Williams and gave a weary smile. "It was good while it lasted, Paul. But all good things must come to an end. I wish ye the best of luck in Africa."

"And I wish ye the best of luck in the Carolinas. May you retire in comfort as a true gentleman of fortune. And for God's sake, marry your beloved Margaret and start a family. If you don't, you know you'll regret it."

"I know, Paul. In fact, I've known for some time."

CHAPTER 37

CHARLES TOWN BAR, SOUTH CAROLINA

MAY 22-23, 1718

NORTH OF FOLLY BEACH, the massive *Queen Anne's Revenge* looked majestic yet menacing. Her bristling six-pound cannons, arranged in a single row of gun ports, and muzzle-loading swivel guns peered out at unsuspecting Charles Town like thirty-eight black iron eyes. In her powerful wake trailed the *Revenge, Adventure,* and a Spanish tender they had taken off the Florida coast. At the moment, it was the most powerful pirate fleet in the world, and Edward Thache was feeling confident of success in his mission—a mission that he had yet to let his crew in on.

When Blackbeard reached the Charles Town bar, he seized the harbor pilot boat before it could sail to town to raise the alarm. Then, along an invisible arc nine miles south of town, the four vessels spread out across the approaches to the bar and waited, spiderlike, for ships to fall into their web. Behind the marshy point, Charles Town's ample harbor stretched back until it reached the headland where the Ashley and Cooper rivers converged. There, where the deep bay offered protection from hurricanes and marauding French or Spanish, lay the capital of the proprietary colony of South Carolina, a bustling city of some five thousand people. Founded in 1670, the small hamlet named in honor of King Charles II was swiftly turned into the only English walled city in North America. Boasting one of the best deepwater harbors in the colonies, it was perpetually filled with merchant vessels transporting goods in and out of the city via the bustling ports of Boston, Philadelphia, Port Royal, Bristol, and London. Two shipping channels linked the harbor with the open ocean. The smaller channel hugged Sullivan's Island, and the larger main channel ran just off the beach of Morris Island.

Blackbeard and his pirate flotilla sat off the bar between the two channels and patiently waited. He knew that Governor Johnson and the South Carolina militia were in no condition to resist his presence here. Though not in as desperate a condition as her proprietary neighbor to the north, the colony had been suffering from severe inflation and anti-proprietary factionalism from various planters and traders in addition to only recently recovering from a crippling Indian war of its own. At the entrance to Charles Town harbor, he would bring the entire colony of South Carolina to its knees and vowed that he would not leave until he had what he wanted: a simple chest of medicines. They would take considerable plunder too, of course, but the main thing they needed was of a medical nature. Since they had left Nassau without having any luck obtaining any mercury, urethral syringes, and other important items in combating his ship's syphilis epidemic, the doctors had been urgently clear about that. The medical situation was desperate.

Within two days, he and his pirate gang had captured five vessels: the one-hundred-eighty-ton *Crowley* captained by Robert Clark and fifty-ton ship *Ruby* of Charles Town captained by Jonathan Craigh, both outbound to London; the sixty-ton *William* of Weymouth, England, captained by Naping Kieves and the eighty-ton *Arthemia* captained by Jonathan Darnford, inbound from England; and a small eight-ton sloop, the *William*, headed home to Philadelphia. The first vessel captured, the *Crowley*, proved the most valuable in Thache's eyes. It wasn't the twelve-hundred barrels of pitch, tar, and rice stuffed into her holds that caught his attention—these were of little value to him—but rather the large number of paying passengers in her cabins. Among them were several of Charles Town's most distinguished citizens, whom he knew would command a handsome ransom in exchange for the critical medicine that his crew desperately needed.

As the ships were looted of provisions, the frightened passengers were rowed over to the *Queen Anne's Revenge*, where they were thoroughly interrogated: who were they, what was their vessel carrying, what other ships anchored in Charles Town, and what valuable possessions did they have on their person or tucked away in their luggage. The most prominent among the prisoners turned out to be Samuel Wragg. A member of the South Carolina's governing council who owned twenty-four-thousand acres in the colony, Wragg was returning to England with his four-year-old son, William. After politely interviewing the captives, Thache knew that they were worth more to him than all the cargo in the *Crowley's* hold. He decided to call a general council to decide their fate.

"Mr. Howard," he called out to his quartermaster upon the North Carolinian's return from the *Crowley*. "We have taken five vessels and it is now time to hold a council in accordance with the articles. In preparation, I want you to take the more than eighty captives and place them safely in the *Crowley's* hold."

"In the hold?"

"Aye, in total darkness. I want to make sure our already terrified guests remain properly motivated to ensure we achieve our aims."

"Aye, Captain."

"Wragg and the other passengers have heard plenty of tales of bloodthirsty pirates and they seem particularly fearful of me personally. It seems the name Blackbeard has taken something of a hold here in the colonies since last fall. I want you to herd them into the hold aggressively, but make sure not to bring any harm to anyone. Put everyone in together like a herd of cattle: rich with poor, sailors, servants, and slaves with passengers, men with women and children. There is to be no favored treatment according to class or state of servitude. In fact, I want Wragg and the other men of wealth to feel deeply uncomfortable at being treated no differently than anyone else."

"Aye, Captain. So it appears you are going to be making a point?"

"You shall soon see what trick I have up my sleeve. Now quick to it and sharp's the word."

ψψψ

Stede Bonnet studied Thache closely as the pirate commodore waited for the last of the crew members to assemble at the edge of the quarterdeck for his address. Blackbeard wore his trademark tricorn hat, faded crimson jacket with gold lace, waistcoat, muslin blouse, tarred-dungarees, ankle-high black cow-leather seaman's shoes equipped with heel plates, three brace of pistols hanging in holsters from a sling around his shoulders, and a cutlass in a scabbard hanging from his belt. To Bonnet, the man positively glowed with soft-spoken power and authority, but there was also an undercurrent of worry about him.

From snippets of overheard conversation and the general talk among the men, Bonnet knew, at least partly, the cause of his consternation. With the pirates' Bahamian base soon to be eliminated and an increased vigilance on the part of the Crown to bring an end to piracy, Edward Thache was in a state of crisis over his future. Bonnet and many of the other pirates in the company felt the same oppressive burden hanging over them, so he was sympathetic. But he was still surprised to see worry on the face of the unflappable Blackbeard. Deeply uncertain over his future, the man was human after all.

Despite the sympathy he felt for him, Bonnet knew that he was in far worse shape than his mentor and that his life as a pirate was a disaster. He had been in a state of depression for weeks, continuing to declare to all who would listen that he wanted to give up piracy. But there was just one problem: he was so ashamed to see the face of any Englishman he knew from his former life on Barbados that he believed he had no alternative but to spend the remainder of his days living incognito in Spain or Portugal. Though Thache tried to encourage him by telling him to take it one day at a time and that things would work out, Bonnet took little solace from his mollifying words. In fact, a part of him despised Blackbeard for encouraging him when he was such a failure as a sea captain and didn't deserve his support. As Bonnet's self-loathing increased, he often found himself trying to blame Blackbeard for his problems. Deep down, he privately hated the man for being everything that he was not.

"Gentlemen, I have a proposition for you," said Thache to open the meeting. "It involves the prisoners we have locked away in the hold of the *Crowley*. No harm is going to come to them. Their worth lies in the value Governor Johnson and his fellow Carolinians put upon their safe return to the city. In short, I plan to use these people as ransom. In fact, it is to acquire something very important.

"Most of ye have been aware of the health situation of our fleet for some time now with regard to the pox. Having been at sea nearly continuously for more than a year, it is no secret that intimate encounters in remote places of questionable hygiene have condemned us to an epidemic of the disease. The time has come that we must do something about it. Unfortunately, the medicines and devices we need to remedy the company's ill effects have not been available to us for some time. We were able to secure some medical supplies from Jonathan Bernard's sloops when we were near Belize, but we ran out and weren't able to find any supplies in Nassau. However, we believe they will have what we need here in Charles Town. So my plan is to get it for us."

"So your intention is to use the prisoners in the *Crowley* as ransom for medicine?" asked Israel Hands.

"Aye. I propose we make use of Samuel Wragg and the other leading citizens of Charles Town we have captured in exchange for the list of medicines and apparatus our doctors have drawn up. The doctors indicate the situation is urgent and we cannot lose a moment longer. Some of the men with the affliction are getting worse by the day. They need our help and they need it now."

"So that's what we're doing in Charles Town—we're here to get medicine to treat the damned pox?" grumbled a crew member. "That's why we be here?"

Bonnet saw the frustration on Thache's face. "No, that's not why we're here," responded Thache tartly. "We're here to take plunder just like always. But this time, part of that plunder includes important medical supplies to be used for the welfare of those who have been afflicted. So what do you say, men?"

Bonnet stepped forward. "So your plan is to send a boat into Charles Town to see the governor and demand the medicine in return for the captives?"

"Aye, that is what I propose."

"And if the town refuses, are you willing to threaten to bring harm to the captives, but also to sail into Charles Town, sink all the ships there, and perhaps attack the town itself? Because without that imminent threat, I don't see how we can expect to have success."

"Point taken, Major Bonnet. I have every intention of making sure the threat is believable, but do not plan on torturing or killing anyone to do so."

"Aye, we can't be harming ship passengers," said William Howard. "But the threat will have to be real enough to make the governor squirm."

"Who will we send in the boat to deliver the ransom demand?" asked Caesar.

"Whoever it is," said John Martin, who had rejoined the company in Nassau after serving as Hornigold's quartermaster, "there should be at least one of the passengers with them so the townspeople can verify that their citizens are safe."

"Such a person will also be able to convey how critical it is to swiftly comply," said Bonnet. "By sending one of the captive gentlemen in with whomever from the company is selected to deliver the demand, we will impress upon Governor Johnson just how serious the situation is."

There was a rumble of agreement. Bonnet was pleased to have contributed to the proceedings. He had been so marginalized during the past month that saying something valuable and contributing in any way was a godsend to him.

"Agreed," said Thache. "So is everyone on board with the plan?"

More murmurs of concurrence.

"Good, that settles it then. Mr. Howard, take some men with you and fetch Mr. Wragg and a handful of the most prominent citizens. We need to get that boat into Charles Town. There is no time to waste."

"Aye, Captain."

He took Caesar and several other men with him, rowed over to the *Crowley*, snatched Wragg and the others, and rowed back to the flagship. Thache and most of the crew were still waiting on the quarterdeck. Thache quickly explained the situation to Wragg and then asked him who he thought should be selected from the group of prisoners to sail into Charles Town, act as an intermediary, and help acquire the medical supplies.

"I believe it should be me," said Wragg.

"No, that's not going to work," objected Thache. "You are too valuable to us. It's going to have to be someone else. Your son is also out of the question, for he is too young to make the proper impression."

Always the canny strategist, thought Bonnet with a ghost of a smile on his lips. *He doesn't want to lose possession of his most valuable bargaining chip because if his bluff is called, he has no intention of actually harming young William Wragg and the other captives.*

"Well then, who should we pick to deliver the ransom?" asked Bonnet. "Are there any volunteers?"

"I'll do it," said a voice.

"And just who might you be?" inquired William Howard skeptically.

"The name is Marks—Jonathan Marks. I'm a landholder in Charles Town and know the governor. He'll listen to me."

"All right, Mr. Marks," said Thache. "And just what is going to be your message to the governor?"

"I will be very direct with him. He is to be given orders to secure a medicine chest with the full list of supplies listed on the sheet your men carry with them. I am to warn him that if he refuses, the pirates will murder all their prisoners, send up their heads to the Governor, and set the ships they've taken on fire. That's it, that's what you want, right?"

Blackbeard nodded. "Aye, that will do just fine. And if the governors not there, who will ye speak with?"

"The justice of the peace or head of the militia. Don't worry, we'll find the right people who can get us the medicine."

"Who will we send from the company?" asked Caesar.

"I vote for Captain Richards," said Thache. "Who he wants to take with him be up to him, but I want Richards. Agreed?"

A quick vote was taken and Richards, one of Blackbeard's most reliable lieutenants, was duly elected. Bonnet realized that he would have liked to have gone, but he knew too many South Carolinians and would be embarrassed in their presence for abandoning his family and life of privilege for a career as a not-very-successful pirate. The Bonnet family had strong connections to Charles Town and the South Carolina planter society, which was very similar to that of Barbados.

"I want to make one last point," said Thache in closing. "This needs to be done in two days' time."

"But does that give them enough time?" wondered Wragg. "What if something should go wrong?"

"Two days, Mr. Wragg, and not a day longer." He then looked hard at Marks. "Further, I want to make clear that if Richards or Marks fail to return in two days, we will sail over the bar and burn all the ships in the harbor. To save the lives of the hostages, Governor Johnson will need to have that chest aboard the *Queen Anne's Revenge* by sundown of the twenty-fifth. I expect full compliance."

"I understand," said Marks gravely. "If we don't return with the medicine in two days, ye plan to make good on your threats. I will make sure the governor understands."

"Get them an outfitted longboat, Mr. Howard, and be smart about it," said Thache. "There is not a moment to lose."

No, there isn't, thought Bonnet. *Two days—they only have two days. My God, they'll be lucky to make it.*

CHAPTER 38

CHARLES TOWN BAR, SOUTH CAROLINA

MAY 29, 1718

FIVE DAYS AFTER THE ORIGINAL DEADLINE HAD PASSED, Caesar discretely watched Blackbeard pacing the quarterdeck, balling his hands into fists and cursing under his breath as he stared off at Charles Town. He had been keeping an eye on the captain for five straight days now and could not remember seeing him this angry before. His eyes were dark as lumps of coal and he was constantly in a foul mood, stomping back and forth across the wooden deck like a caged lion. Two deadlines had come and gone and still there was no sign of Richards, Marks, or the medicine chest. Like a dark storm cloud, an air of tension with the threat of violence hung over the *Queen Anne's Revenge* and her growing flotilla of eight ships anchored around her off the sandbar.

Caesar was afraid the captain would lose his usual self-control and execute Mr. Wragg or one of the other captives if the medicine chest didn't arrive soon. The man seemed to be dangerously close to the edge, and Caesar couldn't recall seeing him so darkly ill-tempered before, though the captain was known on occasion to have his tempestuous or melancholy moods. They had been happening with increased frequency in more recent months, as the size of the pirate flotilla had grown so large as to become unmanageable, an unruly faction had emerged that routinely caused trouble, and Major Bonnet had continued to be at odds with his crew over his decision-making.

From a group of fisherman, Thache had been informed of the disaster that had befallen Richards and the other emissaries shortly after they had set off from the flagship for Charles Town. Early on during their journey, a sudden squall had capsized their boat. The three men managed to swim to safety on an uninhabited island and awaited rescue for much of the day, well aware that the clock was ticking. The next afternoon, hungry and bedraggled, they realized they would have to rescue themselves. They found a large wooden hatch cover on the shore, but it wasn't buoyant enough to support all of them. Lacking other options, they clung to the hatch and swam hard towards Charles Town, still miles away. Paddling throughout the night, they made little progress but were rescued by a group of passing fishermen, who brought them to their camp. Marks, realizing the captives' time was already up, paid the fishermen to sail to Blackbeard and inform him what had happened. Meanwhile, he hired a second boat to take the three of them to Charles Town.

When the fishermen had found the pirates two days ago to report the emissaries' condition, Blackbeard was in a rage. But once they related Richards's and Marks's mishap and requested, on Marks's behalf, for two additional days, the pirate commander consented. But then when the two more days came and went with still no sign of Richards and his group, he became apoplectic. Pacing the deck, he threatened Wragg and the others, promising that they should not live through the day if the emissaries did not soon return. Though Caesar could tell it was all for show and Thache was only trying to scare them, it seemed to him that something had turned inside him, and he wondered if perhaps he might actually follow through with his threats. He didn't like the look in his eyes—like a wild dog.

But after thinking about it, he realized what was really angering the pirate commander. He was so used to getting his way with prizes and controlling his own destiny that he was coming unraveled when he couldn't manage events to his satisfaction. Caesar understood that that's why he was acting so out of character. Thache was not well-equipped to handle the stress of not being in command of a situation. For years now, he had been master of the sea, acting as a king beholden to no one and taking prizes at will, and now his fate was in the hands of the governor of South Carolina and the citizens of Charles Town. Caesar realized that this was indeed something of an Achilles Heel for the captain. He couldn't stand not being in control and having his fate dictated by others. It seemed to have caused something to snap inside him and turn him into something far different than the normally calm, composed, and charismatic leader he was.

Suddenly, Caesar heard orders being barked out. It was Blackbeard shouting to the other ships through his speaking trumpet.

"Prepare to sail! Prepare to sail! We're going into Charles Town!"

The word was quickly passed from sloop to sloop and a cheer of huzzahs went up. To the crew aboard the *Queen Anne's Revenge*, Thache then bellowed, "We're going to rob her and blow her to kingdom come, by thunder, if we don't have our chest of medicines by the time I drop anchor! Now shake up your timbers and make sail!"

Caesar snapped to and darted quickly for the quarterdeck as more than three hundred men on the four vessels of the flotilla and the five captured prizes began climbing the rigging and preparing for departure.

"Get her under way swiftly, Mr. Gibbons!" Thache shouted to his new sailing master now that Israel Hands had taken over as captain of the *Adventure*. "All hands make sail!"

"Aye, Captain!"

Twenty minutes later, the flotilla had weighed anchor and was making steady progress towards the harbor with a strong onshore breeze at their backs. With the aid of the pilot, they followed the shallower South Channel that ran close to Cummins Point before turning into the harbor itself. There it split into smaller and even shallower channels. Out front sailed the *Adventure*, *Revenge*, and the small Spanish sloop, with the square-rigged *Queen Anne's Revenge* taking up the fourth position and the recent prizes captained by various of Thache's officers forming the rear of the menacing pirate flotilla.

The harbor resembled a large rectangular box some five miles long and one and a half miles across. Charles Town itself sat at one end of the harbor, while the other faced the open Atlantic. The main anchorage was where the Ashley and Cooper Rivers converged, and between this safe haven and the open sea lay a series of deepwater channels separated by ever-shifting sandbanks. Caesar saw a dozen or so ships of various sizes and types clustered around the wharves and mooring buoys in the Cooper River.

Soon the flotilla closed in on the walled city. As they approached, he could see panic seize hold of the citizens at the battlements and beyond. He couldn't help but feel sorry for them. The people of Charles Town were terror stricken as the nine ships came into full view of the city. Militia scrambled to Granville Bastion and the Half Moon Battery to man the cannons as the pirate fleet trained its guns on the city's walls. Merchant ships that had been trapped in the harbor for nearly a week cut their anchor lines and made a break for the open ocean. The carriages of the city's wealthy citizens, overflowing with possessions, clattered down the cobblestone streets, trying to make their escape. By the time the *Adventure* and *Revenge* set anchor, Caesar saw women, children, and old people running about the streets like mad things, while boys no older than fourteen or fifteen were being hastily handed flintlock rifles and pistols to defend the city from the invaders. Armed militia rode around on horseback, shepherding people to safety and trying to help them make an orderly exit, but pandemonium had seized hold of the city and people were running, riding, and stumbling in all directions.

My God, he wondered, *are we really going to attack these people?* He was reminded of the tales Thache, Howard, and Martin had told him of Captain Morgan sacking Portobello on the Spanish Main. What was taking place before his very eyes was like something out of an old pirate book from the century before, and he couldn't believe he was a part of it. He looked at Richard Greensail and could see that he didn't quite believe it either.

"Make ready the guns, Mr. Cunningham!" commanded Blackbeard. "All hands, stand by for action!"

The *Queen Anne Revenge's* cannons rolled out, one by one, and three hundred pirate throats lifted into the air in terror as one. Caesar checked his pistol charges and said a quick prayer. Though as a boy he had once drawn his spiritual power from the African animal gods passed down from his ancestors, he now believed in a Christian God—and he found that he especially believed in Him when he was about to go into action. He counted down the seconds in his head. He had never attacked a city before, and wondered how the fighting might be different from a boarding party. Somehow hand-to-hand fighting street-by-street seemed a dangerous operation, which was why he believed pirates attacked on land so rarely. They were sea marauders, not land soldiers, and were not properly trained for combat on *terra firma.*

He now saw South Carolinians fleeing the nine triangular bastions that protruded from the perimeter wall on the landward side. He supposed the purpose of the bastions was to ensure that any attacker attempting to breech the walls would come under flanking fire from the triangular-shaped bulwarks, allowing the defenders to sweep the ground in front of the walls with musket fire and grape shot. But with the men abandoning the positions in panic, there was no way the town could offer resistance.

Maybe they will surrender without a fight.

"Are you ready, Mr. Cunningham, to give them our welcome?"

"Aye, Captain, ready when you are!"

179

"Wait!" someone cried.

Caesar's and Richard Greensail's heads jerked in the direction of the voice. It was William Howard and he was pointing down into the languid, murky-brown river.

"What is it, man?" snapped Thache, his voice bristling with pent-up irritation.

"It's Marks, Captain! I see him in a longboat!" He pointed. "See him there?"

"Aye, mine eyes see him. But where in bloody hell is Mr. Richards?"

Scanning the river, Caesar quickly spotted Marks in the longboat coming from Rhett's Wharf. He was perched in the bow frantically waving a white scarf while two black oarsmen conveyed him towards the *Queen Anne's Revenge*. But Blackbeard was right: there was no sign of Richards or the seaman that had accompanied him into Charles Town.

"Hold your fire! Hold your fire!" commanded Blackbeard.

As the longboat rowed up to the pirate man-of-war, he again ordered his gunners to hold their fire. When the Negro oarsmen brought the shallow-draught vessel alongside, Marks was hoisted aboard along with a heavy wooden chest.

"Mr. Marks, you are late, sir!" roared Thache. "But I can see at least you have brought my supplies. And yet, rot my bones where be Captain Richards?"

"Right over there on the quay, Captain," said Richard Greensail, pointing to the two pirates stumbling along the waterfront with a crowd of townspeople trailing cautiously behind them.

"Aye, it's them all right," said Marks. "They went off and got drunk and I have had the whole town out looking for them. They were located just before you arrived to town from the bar, but I wasn't about to take a chance and allow you to attack the city. So I rowed out to you."

Thache frowned, but after a moment his face relaxed. "Very good, Mr. Marks. In that case, congratulations are in order."

"Are you going to let the hostages go now?"

"As a matter of fact, I am. But not until our surgeon has inspected these medical supplies and made sure we have everything we need. Doctor, if you would be so kind."

"*Oui, Capitaine.*"

While the French doctor proceeded to inspect the contents of the medicine chest, Marks informed Blackbeard of Governor Johnson's offer of a pardon to him and his men if he wished to lay down his arms. The pirate captain swiftly rejected the overture but soon released all the captives—once all the male prisoners had been stripped of their clothing—along with the captured vessels. Meanwhile, the drunken Richards and crew member who had accompanied him to town were rowed out to the flagship, where they were given an earful from Thache for their dereliction of duty. Once the first of the prisoners were sent ashore, the flotilla set sail again for the open sea, this time taking the deeper channel that ran near Sullivan's Island.

From there, the four ships turned north along the inner shelf and headed parallel to the coast in the direction of the Cape Fear River. They quickly detained two more South Carolina-bound vessels, the sixty-ton *William* of Boston loaded with lumber and corn; and the forty-five-ton brigantine *Princess* of Bristol, carrying a cargo of eighty-six African slaves from Angola. Plundering both vessels,

Blackbeard added fourteen black African slaves to the *Queen Anne's Revenge*. This brought his total slave count up to fifty, since many of the one hundred fifty-seven slaves originally taken from the French *La Concorde* had been allowed to become pirates or were given away to merchant captains. Those handed over to merchantmen to become working crew members were given in return for skilled seamen pressed into service or for good behavior for not having resisted the pirates.

When the final tally was in, the pirates had laid siege to a city and paralyzed a colony for more than a week for a chest of medicine, basic provisions including barrels of rice and corn, four thousand pieces of eight, silver and gold coins amounting to fifteen hundred pounds sterling, fourteen slaves, and the clothes off the backs of their gentlemen captives. To Caesar, it was a good haul from nearly a dozen ships and obtaining the chest of medicines had been critical, but what they had seized still had to be split more than three-hundred ways.

More than three hundred ways, he thought, as he and Richard Greensail stared at the receding coastline and royal blue sea they were leaving behind. *More than three hundred ways.*

It was then he had his first inkling of Blackbeard's game. And he knew it was going to be dangerous and messy.

CHAPTER 39

ATLANTIC OCEAN EAST OF CAPE FEAR RIVER, NORTH CAROLINA

JUNE 1, 1718

THACHE STARED OUT at the crowd of seamen that had packed into the great cabin of the *Queen Anne's Revenge*. A moment earlier they had been ensconced in conversation, but now, as he cleared his throat behind his captain's desk in preparation for his speech, the crowd deferentially hushed. There were thirty men in all: they were the same crew members with whom he had been laying the secret groundwork for a life after piracy for the past six months. Many of them—like William Howard, Caesar, John Martin, Joseph Curtice, Joseph Brooks Jr. and Sr., Thomas Miller, Nathaniel Jackson, Stephen Daniel, and John Philips—were Bath County pirates. Others were simply men who could be trusted, like Israel Hands, captain of the *Adventure*; Edward Salter, a cooper who had been forced from his sloop near Puerto Rico to join the pirate flotilla and became a reliable crew member; bosun Garret Gibbons and seaman John Giles; and Caesar's friend Richard Greensail and several other free black crew members that Thache believed could be counted upon, including Richard Stiles, James Blake, James White, and Thomas Gates who had lived and fought as equals alongside him for many months now and would do so again. These were Blackbeard's trusted men, those loyal to him that he was counting on to perform one of the greatest maritime deceptions of all time. They stood looking up at him with palpable anticipation, though he and his inner circle had talked in general terms about this very course of action for some time now and had an idea of what to expect.

"The time has come to make our move, gentlemen," he said to begin the clandestine meeting in which all the hatches were closed tight. "Instead of a blessing, our large size has turned into an impediment, and it is time that we make a change and look to our futures. To accomplish our goals, the first step is to break up the companies. That is the first order of business. There is simply no way around it if we are to survive in the new order of Woodes Rogers and the other colonial governors hostile to our interests."

Here he paused to ensure the men took a moment to reflect and understood the gravity of the situation. The crew was watching him closely and he couldn't help but feel traitorous. But he reminded himself that he was only being deceitful towards a portion of his crew, and that he was only doing so after he had secured the medical supplies that would be a godsend to every crew member afflicted with the pox. All the same, he couldn't help but feel guilty.

"The plan is to rid ourselves of our flagship and three-quarters of the total crew without harming a soul—and, in the process, achieve a liberation of sorts for everyone in this room, as well as for other conspirators we believe will come over to our side but aren't privy to the details. The first step is to deal with the *Queen*

Anne's Revenge. She be too conspicuous a target and her draught too deep for hiding amongst the shallow tidal channels of Pamlico Sound or Chesapeake Bay. So we must abandon her and make it look like a navigational accident.

"Now I know we all feel guilty, as we should, but there is an important reason we are doing this. The era of piracy is over. That's it, mates, it is done and over. The Crown's hands-off policy of benign neglect is no more and the Admiralty is coming after us hard now. You've all seen how the newspapers have turned against us— they no longer portray us as roguish heroes, but as murderous cutthroats and the enemies of human decency. We've had a good run, lads, surely we have, but we are finished and none of us wants to go out doing a death dance at the end of a rope like poor old Captain Kidd. We have all enjoyed successful stints at sea and it is now time to pursue a quiet life, or at least lay low until the worst has passed. As for me, I am planning on applying to Governor Eden for the royal pardon, and I hope that many of you will do the same. But no man in this room shall tell another what to do and each man must act of his own accord."

"Just how are ye planning on getting rid of a four-hundred-ton ship and two hundred fifty seamen?" asked Israel Hands. "You can't just make them disappear."

"We're going to run the *Queen Anne's Revenge* and *Adventure* aground at Old Topsail Inlet outside Fish Town—as I said, making it look like an accident. Then we're going to transfer the plunder to the Spanish sloop for ourselves, and send Major Bonnet off in the *Revenge* to seek pardons from Governor Eden in Bath Town."

"How are we going to make it look like an accident?" asked Garret Gibbons. "We may be able to fool most of the men, but I doubt we can fool everybody."

"The ships will cross the fifteen-foot-deep outer sandbar one by one—the *Queen Anne, Adventure, Revenge,* and Spanish sloop—and then proceed up the curving channel to the anchorage at Fish Town. The flagship will have no problem navigating over the outer bar, but as she approaches the entrance to the tidal channel under full sail, I'm going to order you, Mr. Gibbons, as helmsman to maintain a course that will take her straight onto the shoals. The big ship will shudder to a halt, rip open like the belly of a pig, and the bow anchor lines will snap and the anchor will plunge into the water. I'll send Mr. Howard up the channel in a boat to tell Mr. Hands to come down with the *Adventure*, supposedly to help get the *Queen Anne* off the shoal before the tide goes out. Mr. Hands will sail the *Adventure* straight into the shoal not far from the flagship. This will tear enormous holes in her hull. By the time the *Revenge* and the Spanish sloop reach the scene, the *Queen Anne* will be listing and her holds will be filled with water. We'll then pretend to make a valiant effort to drag the flagship off the shoal with the anchor winch, but the effort will be for naught for the ship will be doomed and all eyes will see it. We will then transfer all salvageable men and cargo to the *Revenge* and the Spanish sloop and head for Fish Town to regroup."

"What of ye townspeople?" asked Caesar. "What if one of the fisherman or someone else sees us and realizes what we're doing?"

Thache nodded to indicate it was a good question. "We have nothing to fear from the handful of families living there. Most of them have no problem with sea rovers such as we. And even if they understood what we were up to, they have no practical way to send overland for help."

"What about Bonnet?" asked Edward Salter the cooper. "How does he fit into the scheme?"

"When we regroup in Fish Town, I'm going to give him back the *Revenge* and tell him that he must sail to Bath Town. Once there, he will secure pardons for himself and his men from Governor Eden."

"What of ye men that will be left ashore?" asked Salter. "What will become of them?"

"Nothing," said Blackbeard. "They will be free to seek pardons from the governor and do as they like. But they will no longer be part of our company. I would venture that most of the men would disperse across the mainland. Some will quit a-pirating for good, others will jump back in the game. But they will be hunted down because our time is over, men. I'm sorry, but it just is."

More questions followed. Some were requests for more detail, others reflected guilt and were efforts to rationalize their involvement. Several of the men wanted to ensure that none of their double-crossed shipmates would be physically harmed or killed during the grounding and subsequent seizure of the communal treasure. Like Thache, many felt guilty for what they were about to do, but most understood that double-crossing more than two hundred fifty of their cohorts was an ugly necessity if they wanted to begin a new life in modest comfort.

"Once the ships have been wrecked, we'll flee the scene with the company's communal chest of plunder," said William Howard, who had long been in on the plot and assisted Thache in putting it together. "And that includes the slaves from *La Concorde* and the fourteen Angolans we recently seized from the *Princess* of Bristol."

"Aye, Mr. Howard is correct. The valuable treasure packed away in our hold belongs to every man here in accordance with his fair share under the articles. This is your payday, gentlemen. What I am offering you is a division of our fortunes by forty—instead of three hundred and thirty. Some might call it treachery, others downright cruel. But I have another word for it: I call it being practical. I call it getting a fair share in a world that has suddenly become all too complicated. The sand is shifting beneath our feet and the world we have come to know these past two years is gone. So I say we take what is rightfully ours one last time as gentlemen of fortune and then let the chips fall where they may."

"I still think they're going to know we double-crossed them," said Caesar. "They're going to realize it, and we're going to have to live with it and look over our shoulders for the rest of our lives."

"Aye," said Thache solemnly. "But the way I look at it is that's a chance we're going to have to take." He turned to his quartermaster. "Let's put it to a vote, Mr. Howard. I want this to be unanimous because once we move forward, there can be no discord amongst us. And there can be no turning back."

Howard nodded. "Aye, we need to vote. All those in favor say aye."

To Thache's surprise, the vote was unanimous in favor of the plan.

CHAPTER 40

OLD TOPSAIL INLET
FISH TOWN, NORTH CAROLINA

JUNE 2, 1718

AS THE PIRATE FLOTILLA ENTERED OLD TOPSAIL INLET, the *Queen Anne's Revenge* was in the first position, carrying more sail than Thache knew was prudent. But of course that was the whole point. The grounding and its immediate aftermath had to look real before the eyes of the squadron's four separate crews— and he wanted the sheer force of the impact to be terrifying to eyewitnesses. Making it look like an accident was critical, but he knew it wouldn't be easy.

Suddenly, a thousand different worries bombarded his mind and he wondered if he should still go through with it. Was he really going to allow his flagship and the *Adventure* to be driven into a sandbar and destroyed just so he and his inner circle could break up the company and retire in comfort? Or was there still a chance he could call it off and not foist this treachery upon his mostly loyal crew?

Feeling the world hanging in the balance, he looked at Garret Gibbons, who was manning the helm today per the plan. The young bosun was waiting for his go-ahead signal, but Thache had yet to issue it. He was deeply torn, especially now that he was actually about to go through with it. Once he gave the nod and Gibbons yanked the wheel hard to starboard, there was no turning back and the plan had to be followed to the letter. And yet…and yet a part of him still didn't want to commit.

Damnit, Edward—you must make a decision!

The *Queen Anne's Revenge* barreled towards the offshore bar, like a comet streaking across the sky. He estimated that she was moving at a clip of just under ten knots. He looked at Gibbons, who was waiting intently for his signal. The young man's muscles were taut, his concentration nursed to the highest level. Thache then looked shoreward, peering through his spyglass. Three miles away to the northwest, he could see the quiet village of Fish Town, and off his bow he saw barrier islands covered with sand dunes and sea grass. Most prominent among them was a distinctive sand hill a league distant from the village known as Bogue Banks. A handful of whalers and fishing vessels were anchored in the harbor and Thache could see people gathered on the beach and along the edge of the shanty town, watching him and his men maneuvering towards the narrow channel.

Old Topsail Inlet snaked its way northward through the sandbars, passing between the two sand-blown spits of land that separated the inland waterway of the back sound from the Atlantic. From his experience in these coastal waters sailing out of Philadelphia, he knew the main channel was between three fathoms and seven fathoms deep and about three hundred yards wide. A half-mile beyond the point the channel opened out into the back sound, allowing ships to enter the equally narrow coastal channel running east and west from Fish Town or anchor off the town proper.

Damnit man, I cannot wait any longer!

He looked at his helmsman. "Hard to starboard, Mr. Gibbons, and right into those shoals!" he said in a brisk whisper, commanding the helmsman to a course that took her straight onto the outer bar.

"Aye, Captain," and he spun the wheel of the pirate flagship crazily to the north as the consort of pirate ships in her wake prepared to follow the *Queen Anne's Revenge* through the narrow passage into the safety of the anchorage.

Suddenly, Thache felt the sails go slack as the flagship heeled violently, running hard aground on the submerged sand bar. The vessel shuddered to a stop, the force of the collision so violent that seamen were thrown off their feet and the lines snapped on one of the ship's bow anchors, which splashed into the water. Dozens of planks were severely bent and sprung loose, and the mainmast was instantly shattered. Howard, Gibbons, and Caesar—the only three with him on the quarterdeck—were forced to grab onto the railing so as not to tumble to the deck. As the ship heaved and groaned like a wounded elephant, he couldn't help but feel as if he had killed his beloved flagship dead.

But there was no time now for guilt. Instead, it was time to flawlessly execute the second phase of the plan. In theory, the wooden-hulled sailing ship, though she had been dealt a mortal blow, could still be saved—if he moved quickly. He had to be a convincing actor.

"Mr. Howard, if you would please take Caesar and a handful of men in one of the longboats to the *Adventure* and tell Mr. Hands to come get me off this blasted shoal before the tide goes out! Be quick about it man, or I'll bend a marlinspike around your loaf!"

"Aye, Captain!" and he and Caesar were off.

At that moment, Stede Bonnet—who was not in on the plan—came staggering out of the great cabin with a gash on his head. Thache realized he must have been thrown onto the floor or smashed into a wall from the impact. "What the bloody hell is going on? Are we under attack?" he cried.

"No, we've run aground on a damned bar. I've just sent Mr. Howard to get help from the *Adventure*."

"Good lord, are we going to be able to make it off?"

"With a little luck, we should be able to. But we have to act quickly."

Soon the *Adventure* came upon his larboard. He called out to Israel Hands at the helm, talking loudly through his speaking trumpet so that eyewitnesses would hear him. "Throw over lines to haul the beached ship off the sand! That way we'll drag her off the sandbar!"

"Aye, Captain!"

Thache looked around at the faces to see if the men were buying it. The lubberly Bonnet obviously was. Surveying the others, he didn't see any suspicious looks and suspected that the ruse was working. At least his actions made sense. He would have the *Adventure* pretend to drag his flagship off the sandbar with the goal of beaching her somewhere suitable at low tide, which would allow her crew to repair the damage to the hull. Once she was safely floating again, the men could work on any other damage to her masts and rigging. It would be a slow, laborious business, but it could be done. He just had to make sure the crewmen not in on the plan continued to be fooled.

The *Adventure* pressed towards him, Israel Hands rising to the occasion. Hailing Hands, he asked him to pass a tow rope and haul the pirate flagship off the submerged sandbar. Because the bar lay on the starboard side of the channel, Thache had the *Adventure* pass close alongside the port side of the larger flagship and secure the vessel with a cable. But the maneuver only managed to pull the *Queen Anne's Revenge* further onto the sandbar, damaging her keel and lower hull beyond repair. After readjusting the cable, Hands pretended to make a second attempt to save the vessel, but this time he sailed the *Adventure* straight into a shoal a pistol shot from the flagship. He, too, had managed to run his ship ashore and make it appear like an accident. The *Adventure's* planks sprung apart under the force of the impact, tearing enormous holes in her hull.

Both pirate ships were, for the moment, stranded wrecks. As the water poured into their immobile hulls, they settled in the shallow water. Thache continued to act out his part. Knowing Bonnet was watching him, he gave exaggerated expressions of mortification and ran about the boat giving orders and cursing his misfortune. He could tell the Barbadian was buying the clever deception hook, line, and sinker, and he exchanged conspiratorial glances with Gibbons to that effect. They both couldn't believe their eyes: the plan was working to perfection.

Now there was yelling and gesturing on board each of the vessels. By the time the *Revenge* and the Spanish sloop reached the scene, the *Queen Anne's Revenge* had begun listing to port, her holds filling with water. To make it seem as though he was doing everything possible to save his flagship, Thache commanded a group of pirates to row one of the vessel's anchors four hundred yards into the channel, set it, and then attempt to drag the ship off the shoal with their anchor winch, but the effort failed.

As the waves drove the massive flagship further onto her side and the *Adventure* was battered by the surf, it became clear that nothing could now save the two pirate ships. Thache ordered Howard to move all provisions and treasure onto the *Revenge* and the Spanish sloop, neither of which had run aground and were still afloat in the middle of Topsail Inlet. The water was pouring into both the *Queen Anne's Revenge* and *Adventure* so fast now that they would soon both have to be abandoned.

Ten minutes later, Thache heard the keel of the mighty pirate-of-war crack and felt a tremor beneath his feet. Almost tumbling to the deck, he was able to recover his balance and quickly chased down his quartermaster amidships.

"Master Howard, you need to double-time it and transfer the remainder of the cargo now, man! We've not but a few minutes until she's lost to the sea!"

"Aye, Captain! We'll see that she be done!"

He returned to Bonnet on the quarterdeck. "Captain Bonnet, if you would please come with me to your quarters, there's something I would like to discuss with you."

Bonnet was staring out over the railing at the immobilized *Adventure*. "My God, we've lost them both?" he gasped, unable to believe his eyes.

"I'm afraid so," said Thache soberly. "Now if you'll please step inside your cabin so we can talk in private, I'd like to lay out plans for the future."

"Yes, of course."

They made their way along the awkwardly tilted deck to the plushly furnished great cabin packed with Bonnet's books and fine clothing. "I'm giving you back command of the *Revenge*," Thache declared without preamble. "You'll be in charge again as soon as we pack up and make our way to shore."

Just as Blackbeard had expected, the gentleman pirate's face lit up and he suddenly looked like a new man. "I'm in command of the *Revenge*?"

"Aye, we are partners and sail as consorts once again. And as our first act reunited, I intend to seek the royal pardon from Governor Eden, and I suggest you do the same."

"But are we eligible for the King's most gracious pardon? It was my understanding that the offer only applied to those who had committed no crimes after January 5 of this year. So doesn't that mean that we would be hanged for our actions in the Gulf of Honduras and off the Charles Town bar?"

"Technically, you're correct. King George's act of grace extends only to those acts of piracy committed before January 5. Our attacks on the *Protestant Caesar* and the *Adventure* in the Bay of Honduras, as well as our actions at Charles Town, would under a strict reading fall outside the terms of the pardon. But the reality of the situation is that proprietary and colonial governors retain the legal ability to waive this clause and to extend immunity up to the moment a pirate surrenders."

"So Eden has the right to waive the timing clause?"

"Aye, and that's what opens the door for us to obtain privateering commissions on behalf of the Danes in St. Thomas." In fact, Thache was counting on it. The King of Denmark—one of Britain's minor allies in the War of Spanish Succession—was still at war with Spain and the Governor on St. Thomas, Denmark's' principal Caribbean colony, was granting commissions to captains and their crews willing to restrict their pirating to Spanish prizes. Thache and many of the men in his inner circle were planning on seeking the Danish commissions so they could wipe the slate clean.

"So your goal is for us to take advantage of King George's recent offer of pardon and then sail to St. Thomas to obtain privateering commissions. Will Governor Eden really go along with this?"

"A simple gift of some portion of our accrued plunder should enable the governor to put aside his scruples and issue the appropriate pardons."

"So I am to set a course from Topsail Inlet to the governor's home on the Pamlico River to obtain pardons for me and my men."

"Yes, and in the meantime I will stay here at Topsail Inlet and supervise the salvage of the *Queen Anne's Revenge* and *Adventure*. I'll make sure we have gotten everything off the ships for the company."

"But aren't you going to take the King's pardon?"

"I'll follow in two or three days' time, but I have to finish up here first. Once we have the pardons in hand, we can set a course for St. Thomas under a new privateering partnership on behalf of the Danish governor."

"What ship shall I sail to Bath?"

"We'll secure a sloop for you in Fish Town, or you'll take the longboat. The draught of the *Revenge* is too deep and I'll be busy refitting her here."

"And what gifts am I to bear for Governor Eden?"

"Drums of sugar and molasses, and perhaps a few special private gifts."

They heard shouting voices on the deck. Thache looked out the window to see men moving the wrecked ship's cargo to the *Revenge* and Spanish sloop.

"And you're confident Governor Eden is a man we can do business with?"

"I believe so. I've met him and his secretary, Tobias Knight, on two prior occasions. Their colony is poor and they need all the commerce they can get. We are going to have to put our trust in them."

It was a lie, he knew, but Bonnet didn't seem to suspect anything was amiss. The truth was he had little desire to offer himself up to the governor of North Carolina until he knew how flexible Eden might be. He needed someone to act as a guinea pig, and the perfect candidate was standing in front of him.

"With the *Queen Anne's Revenge* a wreck," he said to Bonnet, "we have little chance of holding our own against a determined attack by the Royal Navy in retaliation for Charles Town. The pardons will nullify their authority over us."

"But why do I have to go to Bath? Why can't you go?"

"Because I have to stay behind to make the two ships ready for sail, and you must prove to your crew that you are worthy of their loyalty. You will get the *Revenge* back just as I have said once I've completed the salvage work."

"And what makes you think my men will now follow me?"

"They will follow you once they know you are going to secure pardons for them and a letter of marque from the Danish governor in St. Thomas. War is likely to break out between Britain and Spain any day now so you may not even need to go to St. Thomas, but that is where it stands now. Your seamen will be loyal to you if they know you are looking out for their welfare."

Suddenly, the ship shuddered violently and heeled even further on its side. The two men stumbled but did not fall and stepped from the cabin.

"We have to get off this ship," said Blackbeard, gazing out at the scene of chaos. But first I have to make sure we've recovered as much as we can."

The *Queen Anne's Revenge* was being pounded by the waves now as she lay canted at a precarious angle along the shallow sandy bottom. Her back was broken, her hull staved, her decks awash with every incoming wave. The pirates were retrieving the last remaining items of value or usefulness from the reeling brigantine, including clothing, tar and pitch, hammocks, sailcloth, rigging, cordage, tackle, tools, and cooking utensils. They had already recovered all the livestock, medicine and surgical equipment, casks of food, gunpowder, lead shot, small cannon, navigational instruments, charts, spyglasses, and gold, silver, and jewels. What they would leave behind would be only the unwanted detritus of their past two years on the account: a couple dozen heavy cannon, spare anchors, tons of ballast stone, bronze bells, excess pewter plates, empty ceramic and glass bottles, cannon balls, barrel staves and hoops, and the captain's soiled "seat of ease."

With the sailors, the slaves, and the most important provisions stowed away on the *Revenge* and Spanish sloop, the two grounded vessels were abandoned and the two remaining ships made their way into Fish Town harbor. There, Thache addressed the full crew, laid out a plan of action, and swiftly followed through with it while there was still daylight. The first step was to transfer all the plunder onto the Spanish sloop. When this was done, Thache had Bonnet gather the bulk of his old crew and embark with them to Bath Town in a sloop supplied by the local Fish Town fishing and whaling community, whom the Barbadian pirate paid in gold dust. The remainder of his crew were ordered to set the *Revenge* to rights and prepare her for a voyage to the West Indies to coincide with Bonnet's return from Bath. Thache selected forty of his men to crew the small sloop, using her to transfer stores and men from ship to shore. Thirty of these pirates were his chosen men, the force he elected to keep with him while he abandoned the rest; the ten others were crew members he and his inner circle believed they could trust and would be able to count on moving forward, though they were not privy to the conspiracy.

By midafternoon, Thache was presiding over the outfitting of the two remaining ships while Bonnet and forty of his men were sailing northward through the inland waterways leading toward Pamlico Sound to secure the governor's pardon. Their holds were filled with barrels of sugar and molasses to offer as a customs payment. However, this was only the first stage of Blackbeard's plan, and he wasted no time laying the groundwork for the great betrayal that would follow. With the plunder on board the small Spanish sloop and whatever stores could be crammed aboard her, he was ready to make his move.

No sooner had Bonnet left than Thache and his conspirators drew their weapons and placed their two hundred fifty remaining shipmates under house arrest. Most of them were given a prodigious quantity of rum and left to their own devices on the beach, while sixteen particularly troublesome freebooters—men who had made Thache's life miserable during their winter voyage into the Spanish Main— and David Herriot, the *Adventure's* former captain, were marooned on Bogue Banks, a sandy uninhabited island three miles from the mainland. Blackbeard and his remaining contingent—forty white men and sixty blacks, ten of whom were pirates to go along with fifty African slaves to be traded or sold as property— clambered aboard the Spanish sloop and departed, taking the company's rich communal plunder with them.

When Stede Bonnet returned with his pardon three days later, the *Revenge* was waiting for him in Fish Town, but the treasure and Spanish sloop were gone. He soon rescued the Bogue Banks castaways and vowed to avenge himself on his onetime teacher Blackbeard. But he would never find him and they had seen one another for the last time.

With the deception carried to fruition, Blackbeard sailed first northward to Ocracoke Island on the Outer Banks to take on water at the Old Watering Hole, taking the outer passage around the barrier islands rather than the shallow inner sound, and then west across Pamlico Sound to Bath to obtain his own pardon. As Bonnet was sailing back to Fish Town, his heavily bearded nemesis had been just on the other side of the barrier islands, headed in the opposite direction. About the time Bonnet discovered his treachery, Blackbeard and his much-reduced retinue of forty seamen was making his way up a wide tidal creek leading to North Carolina's unassuming capital. He was no longer in command of a powerful pirate flotilla, but rather a single seventy-ton sloop armed with only a half dozen four-pound cannon, two three pounders, and a pair of swivel guns.

For Edward Thache of Spanish Town, it was like going back in time to his early, simpler days as a merchantman-privateer, and it made him think of warm summer afternoons in the arms of his beloved Margaret of Marcus Hook. But what he felt most of all was guilt.

After all, despite the fact that what he had just done was necessary to ensure the survival of himself and his key men under the Crown's new anti-piracy order, it was pure treachery. And the brethren of the coast he had left behind—men with whom he had once sailed, fought, drank, taken rich prizes, and shared laughter—would curse his name for the rest of their lives.

PART 5

RETIREMENT OF A KIND

CHAPTER 41

GOVERNOR'S PALACE
WILLIAMSBURG, VIRGINIA

JUNE 24, 1718

SEATED AT HIS MASSIVE MAHOGANY DESK, Spotswood looked over the letter he had just finished preparing for the Board of Trade. He wore a pair of reading glasses with silk ribbons fastened to the lenses and looped with separate ribbons around his ears. In the fourteen-page missive, which was shorter than most of his long-winded letters, he had done what he so often did: he highlighted all of his brilliant accomplishments during his tenure in office, with particular emphasis upon his recent triumphs, while at the same time providing a detailed indictment of his many enemies.

In this particular letter, he reserved his greatest criticism for his primary nemesis, Philip Ludwell, and the seven other men on the Governor's Council who were firmly opposed to him—whom he derisively referred to as the "Eight." They had openly refused his olive branch by electing not to attend his May 28 party celebrating the fifty-eighth birthday of King George I—and he was still smarting over the rebuke. Instead, Ludwell had thrown his own gala that night at the House of Burgesses, an event of inspired debauchery attended by not only him and his fellow dissenters but a large number of townspeople gleefully rebellious to the Crown. Spotswood considered it a slap in his face and an overt act of sneering contempt for Mother England.

Wearing his reading glasses, he perused the brief description of the event he was providing the Board of Trade then handed the letter across the desk to his friend and éminence grise, Robert Beverley, for his thoughts. The letter read:

"An invitation to my house after this reconciliation was slighted by them, and an entertainment with all the freedom and civility I could give, has not prevailed with one of the Eight to make me ye common compliment of a visit, nay, when in order to the solemnizing His Majesty's birthday [May 28, 1718], I gave a public entertainment at my house, all gentlemen that would come were admitted; these eight counselors would neither come to my house or go to the play which was acted on that occasion, but got together all the turbulent and disaffected Burgesses, had an entertainment of their own in the Burgesses' House and invited all ye mob to a bonfire, where they were plentifully supplied with liquors to drink the same healths without, as their M'rs did within, which were chiefly those of the Council and their associated Burgesses, without taking any notice of the Governor, than if there had been none upon the place."

When Beverley was finished reading the paragraph, he looked up at Spotswood, who was finishing powdering his wig behind his desk. "You've got to let this go, Alexander, or you'll drive yourself crazy," he said to his friend. "I know it won't be easy, but you must do it. You can't go on like this."

"But how can I patch things up when they continue to slander and provoke me? I ask you, have you ever known of any governor of Virginia to keep up, by his constant way of living, the honor and dignity of his majesty's government so greatly as I have done?"

"I know you've done a lot. I'm just wondering if a softer touch might—"

"And have you ever before in this colony seen our sovereign's birthday celebrated with so much magnificence as in my time and at my expense?"

"No, I have not, but that is not the point. These men—both in the Council and in the House of Burgesses—are bitterly opposed to you. They will not quit until they have seen you dragged kicking and screaming from your Palace."

"It is not a palace."

"To them it is. Look, eight of the twelve members of your very own Council are against you on every issue that confronts the legislature. The Ludwell-Blair faction will not go away. In fact, they are getting stronger every day."

"So I must roll over like a dog and capitulate, is that it? Even when they scorn me by ignoring an open invitation to my party?"

"It was a celebration of the King's birthday. They are as opposed to the King— or at least this particular German-speaking king—as they are you. They made it a point by sticking it to you both."

"That is treason."

"Maybe in Britain, but we are in America."

"America?" he sniffed, wrinkling his noise distastefully. "I am growing increasingly tired of hearing that seditious term bandied about."

"Yes well, you'd better get used to it. As Ludwell and his gang have made clear, these so-called 'Americans' are growing in power every day. Ludwell, Blair, and their followers are part of this nascent cadre of independent-minded rebels— and so is this Blackbeard who recently held Charles Town hostage."

"You're talking about this Edward Thache the common pirate?"

"Like Ludwell, Blackbeard and his sea rogues see themselves as patriots fighting the excesses of the Crown. They see themselves as Robin Hood figures."

"Robin Hood and his Merry Men? Surely, you jest."

"No, my brother Harry spoke to one of the captured ship captains. He spent hours aboard Thache's vessel. He said that Blackbeard's men spoke of their allegiance to Black Sam Bellamy, whose seamen were hung in Boston. They claim that they are all brethren of the coast and Robin Hood's men fighting the tyranny of the Crown, and it was because of this that they would burn all ships they took from Boston since it was her people that sent Bellamy's men to the gallows."

"Good heavens, where do they come with these falsehoods? They are but murderous thieves and brigands, the enemies of all civilization."

"That's not how they see themselves. They see themselves as Ludwell and his gang see themselves: as American patriots fighting the Crown and the world's mercantile system, which they view as unfair. They are out for their own profit first and foremost, but they are also in open rebellion with the status quo."

"Well, at least you and I can agree on one thing: they need to be stopped."

"My brother Harry says that Thache has been spotted on the Outer Banks and in Pamlico Sound. He wrecked his forty-gun flagship, the *Queen Anne's Revenge*, on a sandbar in Old Topsail Inlet and is reported to now sail a much smaller Spanish sloop with only eight guns."

"Are you saying that this scourge Blackbeard has taken up residence in our weak proprietary sister colony to the south?"

"I don't know what he's up to. Perhaps he plans on retiring from piracy altogether. He wouldn't be the first reformed pirate. As we both know, Providence, Rhode Island, Philadelphia, New York, and Boston are full of them. They now have wives, families, and servants—and, Bible and sword, they even pay taxes!"

"That's a myth. Once a pirate, always a pirate. Their rate of recidivism must be the highest of any profession."

"I don't know about that. My brother says that many reform."

"Come now, Robert, we both know that pirates are untrustworthy, as are these so-called 'Americans' who secretly support them and buy their ill-gotten goods. The proprietors' governments of the Bahamas and Carolinas certainly cannot be trusted to offer legitimate pardon to men of such low principle. They must be continually watched, restrained from carrying arms, and kept from associating in too great numbers, lest they should seize upon some vessel and betake themselves again to their old trade as soon as their money is spent."

"I don't know about that. I think many pirates believe in God and want to be reformed in accordance with Christian principles."

"I'm afraid we'll have to agree to disagree on that score. Now what do you think Blackbeard is doing in North Carolina?"

"As I said, I don't know. But he does seem to be establishing connections in the colony. For what purpose I don't know. Harry says that he likely sailed there before when he was in the merchant service and knows Pamlico Sound."

"I don't trust the scoundrel. No doubt he has designs on forming a new pirate nest in the Carolinas. Woodes Rogers will arrive in Nassau any day now and the rogues know they will be booted out of the Bahamas. Their days are numbered."

"Perhaps he is doing nothing of the kind and is planning on seeking a pardon from Governor Eden and retiring from piracy for good?"

"But the King's pardon does not cover acts of piracy committed after January 5 of this year, and Blackbeard is known to have taken part in the blockade of Charles Town and several other piracies. No, Robert, he is a marked man—and soon to be a dead one."

"Perhaps. But as you well know, proprietary and colonial governors both retain the legal right to waive the timing clause and to extend immunity up to the moment a pirate surrenders. That is the reality."

"Please don't lecture me on the law, Robert. I firmly believe this rogue should be hunted down and exterminated. It would be a fine day indeed to see his bearded head hanging from the bowsprit of one of the Admiralty's vessels."

"Why you sound almost as if you have it out for the fellow. Is he taking too much of the limelight, or is he perhaps just the diversion you need to get Ludwell and his pit bulls off your back?"

Spotswood knew it was a bit of both, but he wasn't going to admit that to his friend. The truth was he was jealous of all the attention Thache was getting in the newspapers and on colonial wharves and piers, but what fascinated him most about the pirate was his potential political value. The successful capture or killing of the infamous Blackbeard would distract his enemies, at least temporarily, from his perceived failings as governor. Furthermore, it would restore some of his fallen prestige and a sense of harmony with his legislature, or at least encourage mutual toleration. Right now, his ongoing battle with the Ludwell-Blair faction was a stalemate, with neither side able to win the argument without perhaps a Pyrrhic victory that would leave both sides decimated. Unless he managed to divert the attention of his Council and the House of Burgesses away from their internal power struggles with him, then his governorship would eventually be undermined by his adversaries. That was why—he understood right there and then—the ignominious cutthroat Blackbeard might very well prove to be a blessing for him.

"I can see from your expression how badly you want him, Alexander. Tell me what scheme are you cooking up in that head of yours?"

"It's nothing. I was just thinking."

"I know you better than that. Don't tell me you're planning on going after Thache in North Carolina? You know perfectly well that would be quite illegal."

"As governor, I command all land militia and naval forces of the colony."

"Yes, but that does not include making war against pirates in the territory of a neighboring colony."

"The Admiralty's ships retain the right to chase pirates anywhere at sea."

"You're parsing words like a lawyer. You know what I mean and must be careful about not angering our sister colonies. It is their right to operate in ways they see fit to maintain their own sovereignty."

"Why you sound like a lawyer yourself, Robert. In fact, a lawyer for pirates."

"I'm just warning you to tread carefully. And the truth is, Thache could be anywhere. He may have left Carolina waters."

"He may have left, or he may be sailing into Bath Town as we speak to secure the King's pardon. But don't you worry about me, Robert. Whatever course of action I choose, I will do everything by the book."

"I know you better than that. Just remember, you are answerable to our masters in London. Any conflict with your fellow colonial governors, or the colonists you rule, could reflect badly on you back home. Are you willing to put your career in jeopardy for the defense of the Crown?"

He pondered a moment, assuming a philosophical pose with his elbow on his desk and fist beneath his chin. "In the end, it's about who controls the power, isn't it? The real power is held by the elected local representatives, whether the House of Burgesses in Virginia or the Assembly in most other colonies. However, because I am Virginia's Vice-Admiralty representative, I have no legal requirement to answer to them in this matter. Should I decide to take it up, that is."

"Oh, Alexander, I can see you are up to no good. Well then, since I can't talk you out of it, will you at least take a bit of advice from an old friend?"

"Yes, of course."

"Follow the letter of the law—and let that be your guide."

"Aye, I will, Robert. I will indeed," he said, but he had no intention of doing any such thing, unless it promoted his own self-interests.

CHAPTER 42

BATH TOWN
PROPRIETARY COLONY OF NORTH CAROLINA

JUNE 24, 1718

FROM THE QUARTERDECK OF THE *ADVENTURE*—the name Thache had christened the Spanish sloop—the pirate leader stared out at the slate-green waters of Town Creek. Instead of being the commodore of a seven-hundred-man, five-vessel pirate fleet, he was the captain now of only forty men and an eighty-ton sloop. But she was a beauty. Stretching sixty-five feet in length on deck and twenty feet in her beam, she boasted sleek lines and an enormous bowsprit and main boom that nearly doubled her length to more than one hundred twenty-five feet. Thache took a deep breath of air. It was a torrid summer day, but the cool breezes running up and down the Pamlico River and her myriad tributaries made him feel comfortable. The wide creek was lined with tall, straight-trunked old growth pines, cypress, and juniper and ten- to fifteen-foot high bluffs.

Off his starboard beam, he could soon make out the familiar peninsula upon which the town of Bath Town had been built. He had been to the capital and principal port town of North Carolina twice before during his stint in the merchant service after the end of the war, but he didn't know the town or its inhabitants well. Although Bath was the colony's administrative center, oldest town, and official port of entry, the village itself was a modest affair. It contained three long streets, a pair of ordinaries, two dozen houses, a grist mill, a small shipyard, and a small wooden fort set along Town Creek. Another inlet known as Adams Creek joined Town Creek just below the village, so the stubby peninsula the settlement lay upon was bounded by the two inlets. The town's waterfront faced west, onto Town Creek, and a sandy lane named Front Street formed its main street, running parallel to the harbor itself.

The settlement was first founded in 1705 and named after the English aristocrat John Granville, the earl of Bath, who was one of Carolina's lords proprietors. It was now home to around a hundred people, including indentured servants and slaves. Governor Eden, Tobias Knight, and other North Carolina worthies had built homes in the area, and a handful of merchants had set up temporary stores on the edge of town to store large quantities of goods. The two ordinaries in town served the needs of the land travelers and sailors who passed through the port. Many of the original settlers were Huguenot and French Protestant emigres who had fled their native country to avoid persecution.

Growth and progress were slow and the town had failed to become the booming regional epicenter hoped for by North Carolinian authorities. Still, the town was growing. Its mill had been built in 1707, and its shipyard added later that year to construct the coastal vessels Bath needed to flourish as North Carolina's principal trading center. Tobacco, furs, and naval stores were all shipped through the port; however, since Pamlico Sound and the Outer Banks were too shallow for most large merchant vessels, most of these larger craft shipped their goods to Charles Town and other larger cities further up or down the coast.

Despite its progress, the town was fortunate to survive and had been on the brink of rack and ruin since its inception. During the past decade alone, Bath had barely managed to survive disease, bloody political disputes, a devastating Indian war, drought, and famine. And now, for the first time in its history, the quiet hamlet had pirates on its hands.

Looking out at the town, Blackbeard was confident he had found the right place for him and his men to set themselves up for retirement, or at least lay low for a while. With a small population, little commerce, and the ever-present threat of Indian attacks, North Carolina was nearly bankrupt and both the colony and its capital of Bath desperately needed an influx of hard currency, critical supplies, and sturdy men to defend against prowling native warriors. In Thache's view, Eden would have little choice but to accept his gifts in exchange for his endorsements of their royal pardons. With pardons in hand, the sleepy harbor would be a perfect pirate refuge for him and his men for at least the short term, which would give him time to decide his future. Right now, he was filled with uncertainty and he needed time to think things through. With Nassau no longer an option as a pirate stronghold, he needed one or more new bases of operation, or at least a refuge or two where he would be supported by local traders and a sympathetic colonial population resistant to an overbearing British Crown and wouldn't be actively hunted down. He was hoping that between the island of Ocracoke on the Outer Banks where he had anchored two days ago and Bath Town, he would have a pair of nice, quiet, out-of-way places for himself and his remaining men.

What made Bath perfect was that it had just enough trade to allow the selling of his pirated goods, but not enough for the merchants to form an anti-piracy lobby. As the colony's primary port, the town was subject to the scrutiny of Tobias Knight as collector of customs, but Thache was confident he could offer sufficient gold dust that the official wouldn't ask too many questions. But what gave him further reassurance that he could deal successfully with Eden and Knight was that he already had a connection to them from his merchant days and through his relationship to William Howard, the son of a prominent North Carolina landholder and well known in Bath, and the other Bath County pirates, whom Eden and Knight had sent to the Florida wrecks two years earlier.

The *Adventure* turned-up smartly before the wind off Tobias Knight's landing—a place familiar to him from his previous visits and where all arriving vessels were required to report to His Majesty's customs for the colony of North Carolina. Sails were lowered and the crew dropped anchor into the muddy bottom of the tannin-colored river. At Knight's stately house above the landing, a dozen people turned out to greet them, including several slaves. Thache saw a strapping, confident-looking Governor Eden and a sickly-looking Tobias Knight among them. They must have been conducting their political affairs in Knight's home, or perhaps someone had informed the governor that a large sloop was sailing upriver and he had headed over to Tobias Knight's house to greet the newcomers.

In any case, Thache realized, the situation was perfect, for he already had his audience with the two most important political figures of North Carolina. He tipped his tricorn hat to them and they returned the gesture, which he took as a good sign. Five minutes later, he was rowed ashore in a longboat along with a half-dozen of his men and several gifts. Stepping onto the dock, he and his men were led by a black slave to the house.

Arriving at the foot of the steps, he bowed courteously. "Edward Thache, Captain of the *Adventure* at you service," he said officially.

The gaunt-faced Tobias Knight looked at Eden and then back at him. "And what would be your business here today, Captain Thache?"

He gave his most disarming smile. "Why we are here to meet with the government in order to apply for His Majesty's most gracious pardon."

Now it was Governor Eden who responded. "We have been expecting you, Captain," he said deferentially. "Please, you and your men step into Esquire Knight's customs office so that we may hold a conference. Your friend Captain Bonnet of Barbados was here not but a few days ago to obtain the King's pardon, which was officially granted to him and his men, so we are aware of your situation. Come inside and have a drink and we shall talk awhile. I am sure you have had quite a journey."

"Aye, that we have, Governor. That we have."

With all proper formality, Knight then ushered him and his crew, including William Howard, John Martin, Caesar, Nathaniel Jackson, and Joseph Brooks Jr. and Sr. into a parlor where they sat at a small black walnut table surrounded by yellow-colored chairs and a wooden bench brought in by the servants. When they had settled into their seats, Governor Eden looked intently at the tall, dark-skinned pirate with the long black, neatly braided beard, faded crimson jacket, and six bandoliered pistols. When their eyes met, Thache saw what he had hoped to see. The forty-five-year old, bewigged English noblemen appeared not to be at all a pompous colonial official, but rather a reasonable man who would consider very carefully what the pirate was about to tell him. He knew Eden basically had no choice. As the governor of an impoverished colony, he had the thankless job of transforming his pestilent backwater populated by aggrieved Indians and penniless settlers into a strong, affluent colony in which hard-working men and their families would want to settle.

"I remember the first time I met you years ago," said Eden with a fatherly look in his eyes. "I said to myself then that one day you would be a man of some distinction."

"Is that so? Perhaps I have received more distinction than is healthy for a man in these perilous times, Governor," said Blackbeard with a wry grin.

"Yes, I see what you mean." He took a deep breath. "Well, as I've said, we've been expecting you and are glad you've made it."

"Your families are looking forward to seeing you, men," added Tobias Knight. "I must confess that, during these past two years since you sailed for the Spanish wrecks, I wasn't sure if I would ever see you all in Bath again."

"We weren't sure we would make it back either," said William Howard. "But it's good to finally be home."

"He's right, sir, it seems rather like a dream," agreed John Martin.

199

"Yes, well it's good to see you all." He looked at his former slave Caesar. "Caesar, my lad, welcome home."

"Thank you. It is good to be here."

"Just so you know, Esquire Knight, Caesar is a free man now," said Thache quickly so there would be no misunderstanding. "He's been sailing with me and gets an equal vote and share of all plunder, and I will not abide by his being a slave again. But we have fifty slaves with us as cargo aboard our ship and they will, of course, be made available to you two gentlemen, to shall we say, pay the necessary duties on behalf of His Majesty's customs. It is my understanding that Bath County could use productive laborers and defenders against Indian attacks, and that such men would indeed be quite welcome in these parts. They have been well fed and taken care of, and not one of them has been shackled in my hold. They have been free to move about the ship for much of the day when we're at sail. But they are pure African and speak not a word of English."

Eden exchanged a glance with Knight. "You have been informed correctly, Captain Thache," said the governor. "We very much could use such a labor force in our homes, in our woods, and in our fields."

"Good, then I would say we are off to a good start in these negotiations."

As one of Tobias Knight's slaves poured out glasses of wine, the black man and Caesar made eye contact and smiled at one another. Thache would later learn that the twenty-six-year-old was a close friend of Caesar's named Pompey and the two of them had come to Bath together as slaves from Charles Town years earlier.

Knight looked around the room at the other Bath County pirates. "I know your families will be most pleased to see you, gentlemen."

"And we look forward to seeing them as well," said William Howard. "Once we get down to business here and reach a favorable agreement."

"I see no reason that we cannot reach an accord," said Eden. "No reason at all. But we must first hear the details of your recent seafaring activities as well as your journey here. Acquiring the King's grace is a formal legal process, so we must make sure to dot all the i's and cross all the t's. As I'm sure you understand."

"But as the governor said," put in Tobias Knight quickly with an air of seasoned diplomacy, "we see no reason that a satisfactory accord cannot be reached."

"Then I believe a toast is in order, gentlemen," said Thache. "A toast to mutual understanding and to a bountiful future." He withdrew a big leather purse from his jacket pocket filled with gold dust, and laid it in the middle of the table. "And we want to cordially thank you up front for lending us your expert counsel with regard to our duty payment and the King's most gracious pardon. You see, gentlemen, our pirating days are done and over."

"Done and over?" said Eden, eyebrow raised. "Why that is music to our ears, Captain Thache. Music to our ears."

"Aye, we're done with the account, and I mean for evermore. And to tell you the truth, Governor, it feels quite liberating."

CHAPTER 43

CAPITOL, WILLIAMSBURG

JULY 10, 1718

THE STATE COACH glinted in the sunlight as it clattered down Duke of Gloucester Street towards the Capitol. Lieutenant Governor Alexander Spotswood looked out the carriage's open window at his red-coated outriders stirring dust spouts in the loamy sand of Williamsburg's main thoroughfare. Mid-July in Virginia brought oppressive heat and humidity—fine tobacco weather but a sickly season for the colonial inhabitants—but this morning it was refreshingly cool and the Assembly would be in session for another week before recessing from the summer heat. Harnesses jingled, wheels creaked, and hooves clomped as the carriage navigated its way down the swale-pitted dirt road along with the other traffic passing by on the crowded street. It was a busy summer day and Spotswood couldn't wait to get started with his formal proclamation against piracy, despite the hostility he expected to receive at the hands of his adversaries in Virginia's colonial government.

His gleaming coach with six matched horses drew up at the Capitol. Out stepped the lieutenant governor in his lengthy periwig, velvet coat, silk stockings, and silver-buckled shoes. As he strode into the portico a dress sword swung at his side. One wing of the H-shaped building comprised the Hall of Burgesses, with committee rooms above it; the other wing housed the dignified General Courtroom and above it the finely appointed Council Chamber. With his attendants behind him, the governor marched up the curved staircase to the Council Chamber, where he would announce his proclamation. In the crowded room, the members of his Governor's Council and House of Burgesses waiting to hear his address grudgingly rose at his entrance out of respect for tradition rather than for any affection for him. The governor saluted them, sat for a moment at his designated chair near the podium, and then stood up to speak.

Taking a deep breath, he stared out at his mostly unfriendly audience. His two foremost enemies, Ludwell and Blair, sat in the first row, glowering at him like pit bulls. While Spotswood and Ludwell had been at each other's throats for more than three straight years now, the relationship between the governor and Blair, while admittedly strained over the years, had only recently escalated to the point of bitter enmity. He had lately drawn the particular ire of the head of the colonial church and president of William and Mary College over whether the Crown or Church reserved the right to appoint ministers to the Virginia parishes. Spotswood firmly believed that the right was reserved by the Crown, that church and state were one body and could only have but one head, and that as the King's representative in the colony the governor should assign clergymen to their churches. The reverend, who believed in colonial self-determination, wanted the appointment of ministers to be in the hands of local churches in Virginia, while Spotswood, the army and empire man, sought to maintain autocratic British power and did not want to give up further ground to colonial freedom.

At the back of the room, he spotted several more of his enemies: Carter, Smith, Grymes, and Corbin, all scowling and as unwelcoming as a pack of wolves. With consternation, he realized that the best he could hope for was that his opponents wouldn't disrupt the proceedings. He prayed that they didn't have some clever trick up their sleeves to undermine or embarrass him. Lately, many of the Assembly sessions had deteriorated to shouting matches between his supporters and detractors, with him sometimes having to play referee and sometimes having to shout down Ludwell and his cronies.

"Gentlemen," he began in the formal imperious tone of the Crown's chief representative in Virginia, "once again, the safety and honor of the colony are at stake. We have survived the Indian troubles and have called upon the militia to defend our frontiers. But now we have a new threat in our midst. Pirates are once again threatening our coastal waters in large numbers. You've all heard about this so-called Blackbeard, the former Royal Navy officer known as Edward Thache, who blockaded Charles Town and then wrecked his ship in Old Topsail Inlet. The rogue is a murderer, a lout, and a thief and we don't want his kind living among us here in the good colony of Virginia. And there are more like him sailing north into our harbors every day. With the forthcoming arrival of the Royal Navy and swearing in of Woodes Rogers as governor on New Providence any day now, the pirates of the Bahamas have dispersed like sea birds before a storm. From the Admiralty, we have learned that many of these rogues are heading in our direction in hopes of obtaining the King's most gracious pardon. They are sneaking into the ports of Charles Town and Bath Town in the Carolinas, Philadelphia, and even here in Virginia, hoping to put their past crimes at sea behind them and go undetected. These pirates constitute a threat to our commerce and our very way of life, which is why I have issued today's proclamation. Beginning on this date, July 10, 1718, all former pirates, immediately upon their arrival in Virginia, are to make themselves known to some justice of the peace or officer of the militia, to deliver up their arms, and not to travel or associate in a greater number than a company of three. This is what I believe we need in order to ensure that these villainous brutes do not try to recreate a pirate republic here in the colonies. That is why I have gathered you all here today, to make clear my formal policy in this regard, which goes into effect immediately. I shall now read ye the full proclamation which shall be posted throughout His Majesty's colony."

He proceeded to read it aloud, noting as the words left his lips that most of his audience now appeared either bored, indifferent, or openly hostile. He couldn't believe his eyes. Sometimes, it appeared to Spotswood as if he was the only man in Virginia concerned with maintaining the integrity of the Crown and protecting the colony from danger. With eight of twelve of his own Council members and the majority of the fifty-one burgesses firmly opposed to him, most of the men in the room were his avowed enemies. He faced a hostile room and a hostile government and he could see no end in sight. But as he looked out at the faces of his adversaries, he vowed that he would never capitulate to such traitors to British hegemony. *Never!*

When he had read the proclamation in its entirety, Ludwell stood up and looked sharply at him. "Yes, we all know about this Blackbeard supposedly prowling around the Carolinas. But what happens in North or South Carolina is of no business to us here. I don't see any present threat to Virginia from these pirates, and I don't believe anyone else here does but you, Lieutenant Governor. The way most of us reckon it, we have more to fear from you threatening our colonial institutions than we do from this Blackbeard the pirate and the swarms of corsairs you contend are invading our coast. So why do we need a proclamation exactly?"

"Hear, hear!" came shouts of agreement from the other members of his opposition, at least two dozen voices strong, all of them loud and threatening.

"Are you contending these outlaws do not constitute a threat?" posed Spotswood rhetorically.

"Absolutely. And I'm not the only one saying it."

"Hear, hear!" came the confirmation from the gallery.

"Why these rogues are more than just an annoyance to this colony. They are prime recruits for any pirate captain willing to raise a fresh crew on the Atlantic seaboard, and a socially and politically divisive group that might entice law-abiding seamen to follow their example."

"But some of them are men who have dutifully received their pardons and want to quit a-pirating for good and go on to lead upstanding Christian lives," pointed out Reverend James Blair, who had stood up and looked like an implacable tree trunk with his broad-shouldered chest beneath his holy black vestments. "You want to lump together men who have been pardoned with those who remain defiantly piratical, but they are not one and the same."

"It is true I don't make such fine distinctions. That's because I don't trust the vipers. Their kind would sell their own mothers for a hundred pieces of eight."

The reverend shook his lion-like head. "The heart of men is not such a simple thing when atonement for one's sins is under consideration. Perhaps you did not know that Woodes Rogers, who is about to become governor of the Bahamas, was once a pirate."

"He was not a pirate—he was a privateer!"

"Come now, Alexander, everyone knows that one man's pirate is but another man's privateer. The point being is it depends wholly on who is putting forth the definition and where their vested interests lay. But most importantly, even outlaws can become respectable and law-abiding. That's what the Heavenly Father tells us."

"Aye, I agree," said Ludwell. "Why look at you, Lieutenant Governor. From a lowly soldier shot by a cannon ball to the tyrannical ruler of a colony for an absentee royal governor. Now that's respectability all right!"

This time the council members and burgesses roared with disdainful laughter. From his podium, Spotswood scowled. But he reminded himself that he must control his temper and not allow himself to lash back personally. Of course it was not easy. He truly hated these men: Ludwell, Blair, Carter, Grymes, Smith, Corbin—the list went on and on and on. *Damn them—damn them to hell!*

He pounded his fist onto the lectern, unable to control his temper. "These pirates are skunks and villains of the first order, and the very idea of them renouncing their piracy and going on to live productive lives is a sham. Why, gentlemen, I do believe your hypocrisy knows no bounds when it comes to the subject of pirates."

"How dare you speak to us like that?" growled Reverend Blair.

"And how dare you preach to me the virtues of a reformed pirate. There is no such thing, and that is why these men will be hounded until they leave my blasted colony!"

"It is not *your* colony—and neither does it belong to the earl of Orkney or the King of England!" protested Ludwell, his face enflamed with genuine passion. "It belongs to us that lives here and works this land. It belongs to we Americans!"

"And just who are these *Americans*, a rabble with pitchforks in one hand and a twist of tobacco in the other? No, sir, there is no such thing as Americans, and to talk of such a thing is sedition."

"Our blood may be British, but we are first and foremost Americans!" shouted Ludwell, raising up his arms to his fellow insurgents in the audience to rise up along with him.

"We are Americans! We are Americans!" roared the patriotic crowd.

Crossing his arms, Spotswood stood there fuming. The gulf between himself and these people was wide and growing wider every day, he realized. Clearly, they no longer saw themselves as loyal supporters of the Realm and sovereigns of Britain. They saw themselves as something new and different, so different in fact that they weren't even willing to condemn vile barbarians like Edward Thache, who would only be too happy to plunder their ships, rape their women, and seize their houses. He found even being associated with such men deeply disconcerting. These so-called Americans were nothing but an unruly and unsophisticated mob of profiteers, whiners, ruffians, cheats, and thieves. No wonder they seemed to favor villainous predators of the high seas over honest, law-abiding men like himself.

Now Ludwell stepped into the aisle. "We don't have a problem with freebooters in these parts, Lieutenant Governor. They bring in trade goods at fair prices, they bring coin and gold dust into our ordinaries, and, unlike you, they know how to spin a good yarn. And furthermore, as the good reverend has so adeptly pointed out, one man's pirate is another man's privateer. With war expected to come again any day now between Spain and England, that is no joking matter. We will need Edward Thache and any and every qualified sea captain just like him if it comes to war, I assure ye."

"We all know how the Crown operates," said Blair. "The Crown, in quick succession, issues proclamations that first commission privateers, then outlaw them, then pardon them, then revoke the pardon and order their hanging, then gives privateering commissions anew to those left alive before beginning the whole process all over again."

"The piracy proclamation is in effect," said Spotswood emphatically. "As of today, all former pirates who set foot on Virginia soil are to register with the authorities, regardless of whether they have been pardoned or not. The proclamation also forbids these men from associating with one another in groups of three or more. Failure of a man identified as a pirate to comply will result in his arrest as a vagrant seaman, confiscation of his money and property, and his possible impressment in the Royal Navy or incarceration. That is the letter of the law, gentlemen, and I will expect it to be strictly obeyed."

"You're a bloody tyrant, Spotswood!" shouted Ludwell. "We'll not quit until we see you removed from this continent altogether!"

"Yes, you're made it abundantly clear where you stand, gentlemen," he said, leering at his crowd of detractors. "But let me make it perfectly clear where I stand. With men like you in power, I take the authority, interest, and reputation of His Majesty's governor in this domain to be now reduced to a desperate gasp. In fact, if King George cannot reverse this terrible trend, then the inveteracy of you Ludwell, hypocrisy of you Blair, haughtiness of you Carter, brutishness of you Smith, conceitedness of you Grymes, and scurrility of you Corbin, with about a score of your base disloyalists and ungrateful Creolians for your adherents, must for the future rule this province. As for me, I would rather live in a state of anarchy than hand over the reins of this colony to the likes of you traitors to the Crown. And with that, gentlemen, I bid you good day."

He stormed out of the room before they could get a word in edgewise, having made up his mind about one more thing. When it came to Blackbeard and piracy in general, he would never again let the Council or burgesses in on his plans. From now on, he would trust no one and work behind a veil of secrecy.

And he would not quit until he had won.

CHAPTER 44

DELAWARE CAPES

JULY 14, 1718

STARING OUT OVER THE *REVENGE'S* LARBOARD RAILING, Stede Bonnet felt an overwhelming sense of despair. He had been a pirate for a year and a half and had even less to show for it than when he had first set sail from Barbados. His once-brand-new sloop was leaky and in bad need of careening. His crew of forty men was an unruly mob more loyal to their new charismatic quartermaster, the recently elected Robert Tucker, than to him. And by taking more than a half dozen prizes in the past two weeks since sailing north from Old Topsail Inlet, he had already violated the pardon from Governor Eden, who had granted him a clean legal record. Now regrettably, he was once again a wanted man.

The governor had been more than happy to issue him and his men endorsements of King George I's most gracious pardon in exchange for a generous gift of several barrels of sugar and molasses, a bag filled with silver pieces of eight, and a trifle of gold dust, and he had also issued Bonnet a commission to sail with the *Revenge* to St. Thomas to seek a letter of marque from the island's governor. But now none of that would be possible because Bonnet and his new crew—who were, in effect, led by the outspoken Tucker—had already taken several prizes and were once again being sought by the authorities as pirates. Now his pardon offered him no protection whatsoever.

But his situation was even worse than that. As a pirate captain, he was an abysmal failure and still commanded little respect from his men. His poor decisions had not only cost the lives of countless of his crew members in battle, but now he had lost all the company's treasure to a well-planned deception by Blackbeard that he should have seen coming. All in all, he had a ruinous reputation in both respectable and outlaw circles, and he could not bear the humiliation of returning to either his old life among the plantations of Barbados or living among his pirate peers in the Bahamas. But he was just as miserable aboard the *Revenge*. The well-liked Tucker had taken effective command of his ship just like Blackbeard previously, undermining his authority and making him captain in name only.

After Blackbeard had double-crossed him at Topsail Inlet, vanishing with the Spanish prize sloop and most of the company's treasure, Bonnet had spent much of June refitting the *Revenge*, gathering up his crew, distributing their pardons, and then trying to hunt Blackbeard down. When he had first returned to the inlet, he had found the *Queen Anne's Revenge* and the *Adventure* still lying battered and broken in the surf, but the Spanish sloop was gone, the *Revenge's* cargo and provisions had been removed to the vessel, a number of crewmen had been marooned on an island, and Blackbeard had long since sailed away. Bonnet's pulse had raced as he was gripped with the realization that the grounding of the massive flagship and Herriot's *Adventure* had been a ruse. It had all been part of an elaborate plan by Blackbeard to break up his huge company of pirates and keep all the hard-earned plunder for himself and a select coterie of his most trusted men.

When he heard a rumor that Blackbeard was at Ocracoke Inlet, fifty miles up the North Carolina coast, he sailed there in the *Revenge*, only to find a pair of deserted barrier islands. Incensed over being double-crossed, he had hoped he could surprise and overpower his betrayer and possibly recover some of the plunder, but by then the wily Blackbeard had already left Ocracoke for Bath Town.

Low on supplies, Bonnet pointed the *Revenge* north to the scene of his early successes: the cruising ground near the busy shipping lanes off the Virginia capes. Before leaving Old Topsail Inlet, the pirates had elected Tucker as their quartermaster. He was a mariner from Jamaica whom Blackbeard had seized from a merchant sloop some weeks earlier. Like many captives, he found that he liked the free-spirited, higher-paying life of a freebooter over the abuse and substandard pay of the merchant service, and he had quickly become a popular member of the crew. But he had little respect for Bonnet. When the crew discovered that the *Revenge* had but ten or eleven barrels of food aboard—Blackbeard having stolen the rest— Tucker resolved that they should simply seize more from the next merchant vessel they encountered. Not wanting his pardon to be invalidated, Bonnet was opposed to this plan and threatened to resign and leave the *Revenge*, but the majority of the crew didn't care whether he stayed with the company or not and they threw their votes firmly behind Tucker.

To conceal his identity and distance himself from his previous depredations, Bonnet instituted a number of changes to make it appear as if he was not the captain of a pirate vessel but rather a merchantman. First, he insisted that he be called Captain Edwards or Captain Thomas, a ruse that rarely fooled their captives. Second, he changed the name of the *Revenge* to the *Royal James* in homage to James Stuart, whom he and most of his crew considered the rightful heir to the British throne. But this, too, fooled no one. Finally, he insisted that the pirates give their captives "payment" for the goods they stole, so that they might later claim that they were traders, not pirates. South of Cape Henry in early July, they stopped a small coastal vessel, taking a dozen barrels of pork and four hundred pounds of bread and exchanging eight or ten casks of rice and an old anchor cable. At this point, he still clung to the notion that he could go legitimate and obtain a privateering commission from the Danes on St. John. But after a week or two, most of the pirates refused to participate in his ineffective subterfuge. Soon thereafter, the pirates were off the Capes of Virginia capturing and ransacking every vessel they could lay their hands on.

Off Alexander Spotswood's Virginia coast, Bonnet reaped a rich harvest, taking several prizes in a week. From a sixty-ton sloop, he pilfered two hogsheads of rum, a hogshead of molasses, and two slaves. Two ships bound for Scotland laden with tobacco were relieved of part of their cargo. From a sloop headed to Bermuda he acquired twenty barrels of pork and some bacon, giving in return two barrels of rice and a hogshead of molasses. Another Glasgow-bound vessel yielded only combs, pins, and needles and in turn received a barrel of pork and two barrels of bread. Off Assateague Island, Bonnet stopped a North Carolina schooner from which calfskins were taken for gun covers. Discontinuing his pattern of releasing his prizes, he kept the schooner as a tender for supplies.

Contrary to the images of bloodthirsty cutthroats and barbarians being promulgated in the *Boston News-Letter* and printed leaflets promoted by representatives of the Crown, none of these encounters involved violence or injury. Blackbeard had taught him well. Bonnet may not have mastered the art of seamanship, but he had become quite adept at obtaining the surrender of his victims with piratical bravado and bluster.

But he was still a wreck of a man. Though he felt brief flourishes of excitement whenever they took a prize, regained some lost confidence with every vessel taken, and reveled along with his crew in the success of the company, he was still for the most part an outcast on his own ship. He was lonely and miserable and immersed himself deeply in his books when he wasn't required to be on deck and play the glorified role of captain.

Though years had passed since his son's death, he still couldn't get young Allamby's face out of his mind. He often remembered back to the burial at St. Michael's churchyard on Barbados. He would never forget the sight of the tiny coffin being placed into the ground and covered up with soil. The smallness of the wooden casket and headstone seemed to underscore how pointedly unfair the whole thing was. Sons were not meant to die before their fathers, and certainly not his favorite child. He had been an adorable, ruddy-cheeked baby, a gift of God, and Bonnet would never forget him. Somehow, a part of him had died that very day his son had been taken from the world, and he had never recovered.

And now he was stuck on a ship with men he didn't give a lick about, an outlaw on the run being hunted by the Admiralty, a man who had been given a reprieve only to give it up and seal his own death warrant. As he continued to gaze out from the larboard railing at the rolling sea and wind-chopped waves, he felt the whole crushing force of it all pushing against his chest. He felt doomed, utterly doomed. All he was doing was hanging on by a slender thread while his men got drunk on rum punch and pretended to be merry. But there was nothing to be merry about in this cursed world, not for Major Stede Bonnet of Barbados.

For without the King's reprieve he knew he was ruined. And his account with the devil would be settled sooner rather than later.

CHAPTER 45

BATH TOWN

JULY 14, 1718

"I BELIEVE YE WILL FIND YOUR PAPERS IN ORDER, CAPTAIN," said Governor Charles Eden, nodding towards the two neat piles of paperwork on the corner of his desk. "When do you plan to set sail for St. Thomas?"

Without responding, Thache took the pile of signed pardons and began looking them over. He needed a moment to gather his thoughts before answering, wanting to make sure he didn't outright lie to the governor or say more than he should. They were sitting along with Tobias Knight in the wood-paneled office of the governor's townhouse at 22-23 Bay Street. Tied to the hitching post outside the two-story, wood-framed house were Eden's and Knight's handsome roans, their tails swishing and swatting at the swarms of ravenous deer flies feeding on their horseflesh. It was an oppressively hot midsummer's day, but a refreshing breeze trickled in from the cool waters of Town Creek to provide some respite through the open windows.

In their three weeks of forging a bond of friendship, Thache and the governor had come to an understanding. Eden would issue pardons to the pirate captain's men and in return he and his colony would receive an influx of gold dust, hard currency, and much-needed slaves and provisions. It was also tacitly understood that the governor would refrain from asking too many questions about where the "treasure" came from. In addition, the colony's Vice-Admiralty Court, upon which sat both Eden and Knight, would recognize Thache as the legal owner of the Spanish sloop captured by him north of Havana, Cuba, in April 1718 and now named the *Adventure*. Protected by Eden and Knight, Thache and his men would live free from fear of arrest and the pirate captain would have at his disposal an eighty-ton sloop that he legally owned and could use for legitimate commerce.

Blackbeard and twenty-five other men, including six free black pirates, were planning on remaining with the *Adventure*, which would divide its time between Bath and Ocracoke Island. Many of the original Bath County men, as well as a few others, were planning giving up a life at sea altogether, settling down in Bath, and going on to build homes, raise families, and lead honest lives. The remainder was planning on leaving North Carolina for Virginia, Pennsylvania, or New York.

Thus far during his stay in Bath, Blackbeard had diverted himself by going ashore amongst the planters, where he shared bottles of rum and regaled them with seafaring tales, which they couldn't seem to get enough of. Though Thache found that he and his men were well received from Eden, Knight, and the other townspeople, there was still an undercurrent of tension between the two sides. He couldn't tell whether they enjoyed spending time with him out of genuine affection or fear. But there was no doubt they enjoyed listening to his stories. His only slightly embellished tales of roguish high adventure on the high seas had garnered great interest in several private Bath homes and its two ordinaries.

"My men look forward to sailing south and applying for privateering letters of marque from the Danish governor on the island," responded Thache to the governor's question, "and we thank you for your letter of support. But we still have quite a bit of outfitting to do. I expect to weigh anchor by late-August."

"Late-August? So you will be guests of our colony for another month then?"

"Aye, that would be my best estimate, given our current situation. Of course, going forward we won't be staying in Bath full time, but rather splitting our time between your fine town and Ocracoke Island, where we will refit the *Adventure* in preparation for making sail for St. Thomas. Is the governor implying that it would be best if we leave Bath sooner?"

"No, not at all," said Eden, taking a delicate sip of brandy. "You and your men have shown exemplary behavior during your three week stay here in Bath. There was just the incident last Saturday night. It was but a minor disorder."

He frowned. "I regret to say I wasn't informed," he said, trying to conceal his irritation. The last thing he wanted was for his men to blow the whole plan.

"As the governor said, it was a trifle," said Tobias Knight.

"What happened, if I may so inquire?"

"There was a loud, profane disagreement over a woman that escalated into a drunken brawl at one of the ordinaries, but it was over as quickly as it began."

Eden nodded. "As long as there are no further incidents we don't foresee a problem. A quick word with your crew about the incident should be enough."

"Aye, I will do just that. I offer you my apologies on behalf of me crew. They can get overly excited and forget their manners, especially when on land."

"Again, it's nothing to worry yourself about. Once you have a word with them, I'm sure that will be the end of it," said Eden.

Thache was fortunate his crew had been on its best behavior the past three weeks and there had been but the one incident during their stay. The town was so small that with their arrival the population had doubled, and it was a wonder they hadn't gotten into worse mischief. It helped that he and most of his crew were sleeping aboard the *Adventure*, or there probably would have been more incidents. They had chosen to forsake the muggy rooms of Bath's ordinaries for the pleasant evening breezes and peaceful rocking of their sixty-five-foot Spanish sloop.

The governor took another sip of brandy. "There is one thing we did want to discuss with you before your departure, Captain."

Thache detected a trace of tension in his voice, but forced himself to give his most relaxed expression. "And what would that be, Governor?"

Eden nodded towards the stack of pardons. "Though we all know that the pen is truly mightier than the sword, I would advise you not to put too much faith in these pieces of parchment signed by me proclaiming that you and your men have received His Majesty's complete forgiveness."

"Why is that, Governor?"

"Because by now the whole country knows that you and your men led the blockade of Charles Town in May and are, therefore, technically outside of the bounds of the terms of His Majesty's forgiveness. Don't be alarmed—I just want you to understand why Esquire Knight and I here have been willing to give you the benefit of the doubt in these dangerous times. The *Boston News-Letter* recently published an article on the affair off the Charles Town bar. It is said that you held some of the citizens for a ransom of medicine on behalf of your crew. So we know you and your men were there, and as you know, the King's pardon only covers acts of piracy committed before January 5 of this year."

Thache gulped. What could he possibly say to that? He was caught red-handed and certainly couldn't deny it. That would be disrespectful to the governor and to Knight, who was studying him closely. Though the customs collector was thin as a rail, carried a sickly yellow hue, and was suffering from the fever, the gleam in his eyes revealed great mental acuity and a strong constitution.

"Once again, there is no reason to worry, Edward," said the governor. "We are not here to persecute you. We wouldn't have issued pardons if we didn't believe that you and your crew, or at least a substantial portion thereof, are serious about giving up your piratical ways. But we want you to know that we have taken grave risk on your behalf—and we have done so not because of the substantial sum of gold dust you have added to our coffers. We have a strong motivation for protecting you and we think it is important for you to know what that motivation is, in the hopes that ye will be careful going forward and give our relationship the proper discretion and respect it deserves."

"I understand that you gentlemen have gone out on a limb for me, so to speak, and I will do my best to honor our arrangement."

"Good, that's what we like to hear," said the hollow-cheeked Knight after taking a sip of his own brandy. "Now there are three very good reasons why we have been willing to turn a blind eye to your past transgressions and offer you and your men pardons. The first is many of your crewmen are native sons of Bath County, and the governor and I, well, we protect our own. We are the ones who sent them down to the Florida wrecks in the first place, so we must reap what we sow, so to speak. The second is that our economy here in North Carolina is, as you know, in shambles and you and your men have brought in much-needed coin of the realm, gold dust, and African slave labor for our plantations. We have been hard hit by restrictive trade laws, Indian wars, drought, sickness, and political and religious strife; and we suffer compared to our neighbors to the north and south through our lack of navigable deepwater ports and access to a workforce of slaves. The substantial amount of silver and gold you have generously given to the governor and myself has enabled us to take a certain risk on your behalf. But even more important is the money you and your men have delivered into the region along with the slaves and countless provisions you have brought. With the fifty Africans you have delivered safely to Bath, you have helped offset some of our financial difficulties, both through your personal gifts and spending and your men's land purchases in the region using the slaves as collateral."

Here Governor Eden jumped in to further emphasize the point, "Anyone who can bring viable commerce to our beleaguered colony as you have, Captain, has to be taken seriously. It is as simple as that."

Thache was sympathetic to their situation and realized just how fortunate he was to have surrendered to them instead of Governor Johnson of South Carolina, who had offered him the King's pardon, or some other British bureaucrat. These men were merely doing the best they could for themselves and their colony under difficult circumstances, which gave them added virtue in his eyes.

"And what is your third reason for treating me with such equanimity, gentlemen?" he asked.

"We've met you before on two occasions."

"Aye, I remember."

"Though we did not get to know you well, we both liked what we saw of you when you were a young mate sailing out of Philadelphia."

He grinned through his dark-black, heavily braided beard. "It was only three or four years ago. I'm not that much older now."

"Oh, but you have seen so much more of the world since then, Edward, and have grown considerably," said Eden. "But we saw what you would become even back then. We saw a natural leader who was familiar with our water ways and perhaps one day could help us bring commerce to Bath Town. Because of your two prior visits, we had some familiarity with you that has raised our comfort level, so to speak, to issue pardons to you and your men. I'm not sure we would have done it if we didn't know you personally, even if only on a cursory level."

"I appreciate your honesty, gentlemen."

"And we appreciate yours, Edward," said Knight. "So how did you decide to come forward and surrender? What made you think you could trust *us*?"

"Why William Howard, John Martin, and the other Bath County men, of course. They've always spoken well of you. That and the fact that I had met you two before. Like you, I felt a certain amount of trust in being familiar with you. You were not faceless bureaucrats that I would have to charm and offer a rich lode of fine silks, jewels, and gold. Ye were men who could be trusted to do what was best for your colony and returning Bath County sons."

"Yes well, I am glad it has worked out for the best," said the governor, and they fell into silence.

Lighting his white clay pipe, Thache thought of what had been accomplished thus far here in Bath and what remained to be done before he set sail for Philadelphia to see his beloved Margaret and then headed south for St. Thomas. He was refraining from telling the governor and Knight his precise plans because he didn't want them to think he might return to his plundering ways and revoke the pardons. Upon his arrival, his first action had been to address the allocation of plunder to the crew in accordance with the articles. Under Blackbeard, the captain received two shares; the quartermaster one and three-quarter shares; and the navigator, master gunner, carpenter, sailmaker, and bosun one-and-one-quarter shares. Common sailors like Caesar received one share per man. The second and more critical item had been to determine what portion of the plunder would be allocated to Eden and Knight to obtain the necessary pardons and sanctuary in Bath for his crew members. To accomplish these objectives, a portion of the fifty slaves were divided amongst the pirates in shares based on a man's role aboard the ship in the same manner they parceled out the silver, gold dust, and other prized possessions taken at sea. The crew members then used the slaves to make land purchases in and around Bath, or gain hard currency. In the end, a new much-needed labor force was transferred from the *Adventure* into Eden's reeling proprietary colony. And, as Thache knew from

Caesar and Howard, the Africans taken from *La Concorde* gained a better life than they would have if they had remained in the Caribbean. Though still slaves, they would be treated far better in the fledgling North Carolina settlement by men like Tobias Knight than they would be in the sweltering sugarcane fields of Guadeloupe, Martinique, or Saint Domingue, where death from tropical diseases was astronomically high.

The governor was gifted Thache's designated six slaves, Knight two slaves, and the officers and crew members one to four depending on their rank of authority aboard the *Adventure*. William Howard was awarded four slaves, two of whom he had sold and two he had taken with him to visit his father's three-hundred-twenty-acre plantation overlooking the Pamlico River ten miles east of Bath. For the rest of Blackbeard's inner circle, many of whom were the sons of Pamlico plantation owners, their shares of the *Adventure's* human treasure were transferred to their families and plantations. The slaves joined the households of the Marrins, Jacksons, Millers, Curtices, Daniels, and other families of Bath County. As Thache had correctly surmised based on what Caesar, Howard, and the other Bath County men had told him, an African labor force was the one "treasure" that was most desired on the plantations of the Pamlico River and worth more than a chest of gold, silver, and jewels. Of course, the arrival of a ship full of slaves at the mouth of Town Creek in the summer of 1718 was no accident—Edward Thache and his Bath County pirates had planned on it for six months, since they had first taken *La Concorde* and learned of the King's pardon.

"When do you plan to make your way back down to Ocracoke?" asked the governor, pulling him from his thoughts.

"I believe we will set sail tomorrow."

"With pardons in hand," said Tobias Knight.

"Aye," said Thache, blowing out a puff of bluish gray smoke. "I can't thank you enough for what you've done, gentlemen. I know not all of my men will honor these most gracious pardons, but most I believe will. And it is for those men that this act of forgiveness means everything."

"Thank you, Captain. We are pleased to have done your men a good service—and equally pleased with the gifts of commerce you have brought into our colony. You have already improved our financial standing for the year."

"Before you leave, I would like to host a send-off dinner for you along with Tobias and me tonight," said the governor. "Would that suit ye, Captain?"

"It would indeed, sir. What time shall I call upon your governorship?"

"Seven. We shall dine on a shoulder of mutton, dripping pudding, and boiled potatoes with parsley."

"My mouth is watering already, Governor. You can be assured I will be right on time."

The governor stood up, signaling the meeting was over. "I look forward to it, Edward. Perhaps you could regale us with a story or two of your adventures in the Caribbean. For example, the taking of a memorable French or Spanish prize."

"I would be delighted, Governor, truly delighted. Especially since now those roguish days be behind me."

CHAPTER 46

GOVERNOR'S PALACE
WILLIAMSBURG

AUGUST 1, 1718

"THANK YOU FOR COMING, CAPTAIN BRAND. It is good to see you again." Spotswood stood up from his high-backed chair, circled his spacious desk, and extended his hand to the commander of the Royal Navy frigate HMS *Lyme*. A married man with a young wife, two sons, and a large estate in Ipswich, Suffolk, Captain Ellis Brand stood immaculately groomed and ramrod-straight in his blue naval uniform. Assigned in February 1717 to command the twenty-gun sixth-rate, his orders were to protect merchant shipping from pirates on the approaches to the Chesapeake Bay and along the Virginia coast. For the past year and a half, the *Lyme* had taken part in the occasional voyage escorting ships from the mouth of the Chesapeake to as far north as New York, but for the most part had remained at anchor in the James River. While the presence of the warship in the James and occasional escort duty were enough to protect the colony from attack, Brand still smarted over the fact he had yet to launch a punitive expedition against the pirates running rampant along the Atlantic seaboard.

The two men took their seats and made small talk for a moment before beginning their scheduled meeting. The senior naval officer had previously escorted Spotswood from Virginia to Philadelphia in October 1717, which marked the beginning of their relationship, and they had maintained friendly yet sporadic contact ever since. Although the lieutenant governor carried the imposing title of Admiral of Virginia, the honorary rank came with no fleet and no actual authority and, therefore, Spotswood had only the most tenuous control over the British Navy in Virginia's coastal waters. Because it was merely a legal title, Brand and his naval officers didn't answer to him but rather directly to the Admiralty in London. Spotswood's chain of command was through the British Board of Trade in White Hall to King George I on the throne. But he and Brand had a solid working relationship, and Spotswood had found that he was like most naval officers stationed in the colonies. He knew where his duty lay and when there was no proper admiral to answer to, he had no problem obeying the orders of the colonial governor of Virginia even though he wasn't technically required to do so.

"So, what can you tell me about this Edward Thache, alias Blackbeard, who appears to be building up a new pirate base in North Carolina?" asked Spotswood to begin the meeting in earnest.

"We are watching his movements carefully," answered Brand. "My paid informants, and a recent interrogation of one of Thache's former pirates here in Virginia, has revealed that he deliberately broke up his company of over three-hundred men at Old Topsail Inlet by wrecking his flagship, the *Queen Anne's Revenge*. Now apparently these three hundred men—a mix of white, black, Indian, and mulatto—have been dispersed amongst two or three different ships. Many are making their way north on foot or by sail into Virginia, Pennsylvania, Rhode Island, and New York. "

"How many men are still with Thache?"

"Less than thirty, I am told. Our informants say he is dividing his time betwixt Bath Town and Ocracoke Island on the Outer Banks."

"Who are your informants?"

"I'm afraid I am not at liberty to divulge their names. But I can tell you that I have hired several mariners who regularly conduct trading trips in and out of the Pamlico and Albemarle Sounds to gather intelligence on the pirates' whereabouts. They keep me informed on mooring, plundering, and smuggling activities as well as how they fence their stolen goods amongst the people of North Carolina who support them."

"I am pleased you have a network of informants. It will enable you to keep an eye on this most notorious criminal."

"Are you considering a punitive expedition against Blackbeard, Governor?"

That was precisely what Spotswood had in mind if Thache continued to remain in North Carolina and pose a potential threat to Virginia, but he would not disclose that to Brand until he was sure the captain could prove useful to him and he felt he could take him into his complete confidence. Although he desperately wanted to be the governor who captured the legendary Blackbeard the pirate, North Carolina was beyond his jurisdiction and he had no legal authority to invade the proprietary colony to the south. Brand would know this. Which meant that until Spotswood had firm proof of Thache's crimes prior to the King's pardon date of January 5, he would have to work in secrecy, keeping his intentions even from his own Council, especially since he knew many of the members favored pirates. He would let Captain Ellis Brand in on his plan eventually, if Blackbeard persisted in making the Carolinas his home and the Royal Navy captain wanted to take a crack at him, but right now all he needed was to gather details of the pirate's precise movements and strength without alerting either Blackbeard or his colonial supporters and friends.

"No, I am not considering a punitive expedition against Thache, at least not yet. But if he continues to remain in North Carolina, I may have no choice but to send in an expedition to capture him. I cannot allow him to be a threat to this colony."

"Well, thus far he doesn't appear to be a threat to anyone. The word is he's been lounging about Ocracoke Island near the Old Watering Hole."

"So he has taken no new prizes?"

"None that I've heard of. He's been trading with some of the locals, but that appears to be the extent of his dealings, at least of late. But he is still a wanted outlaw who has committed depredations at sea that are outside the King's January 5 deadline. He blockaded Charles Town and took several prizes in late May and early June so he is guilty in the eyes of the law. In my view, he is not eligible for the King's pardon and should be hung from the neck until dead."

Spotswood did his best to conceal his delight at Brand's unsolicited bellicose opinion towards the celebrated pirate. *I'm beginning to think you are my man, Captain Brand, and will serve my needs quite nicely.*

"The only problem is that it is my understanding that Thache and his men have received special pardons recently from Governor Eden in Bath. Were you aware of this, Governor?"

Spotswood felt his entire body slump. "No, I was not," he said quickly in reply, trying to conceal his disappointment. "This is the first I have heard of it."

"Apparently, he and his men have received His Majesty's most gracious pardon, and the colony's Vice-Admiralty Court has recognized Thache as the legal owner of the sloop under his command. Her name is the *Adventure*."

"How did he manage to do that?"

"I don't know, but he is an exceedingly clever fellow. I'm afraid he's going to be quite difficult to catch."

"What makes you say that?"

"He's reported to be quite a good seaman."

"Yes, like you Captain Brand, apparently he was trained by the Royal Navy."

"He served on the HMS *Windsor* under Commander Whetstone. The Admiralty is not too keen about the connection, I must say. Which means, Governor, that you might want to keep this news to yourself."

"My lips are sealed. Based on what we've discussed here today, it appears quite evident that this Edward Thache should be put out of action. He is a threat to all the southern colonies. Where is he right now?"

"Presently, I'm not sure. He was last seen at Ocracoke outfitting the *Adventure*. But he appears to be dividing his time between Bath and Ocracoke."

"Just for the sake of argument, would you be able to launch an attack upon him, if you had Admiralty approval and were so inclined, and perhaps take him at his base in Ocracoke or at Bath Town?"

"No, I'm afraid not. Bath can be reached either by water or by land, but Ocracoke, fifty miles away, is a small island surrounded by shifting shoals that restrict access to all but the lightest sailing vessels. His Majesty's two warships here in the Virginia, the *Lyme* commanded by me and the *Pearl* commanded by Captain Gordon, are both much bigger than Thatch's Spanish sloop. They cannot operate in such shallow waters. So both Bath and Ocracoke would be out of the question for our warships stationed here in Virginia. No, to get Blackbeard, one would have to use smaller, shallow-draught vessels of fifty tons or less."

"I understand, Captain, and commend you on your analysis of the situation. That was very helpful. And so that we are up front with one another, all of this talk is mere speculation. At present, I have no intention of sending a warship to pursue Thache in North Carolina waters. But we do have to keep our options open and be ready should an opportunity present itself. Do you catch my meaning, Captain?"

"I do indeed, Governor. And I can say without equivocation that I would be willing to do all I could to find this notorious Blackbeard and his villainous pirates. If it is possible for me to destroy them, I would endeavor my best to do just that. I have said as much to London so this is nothing new. I have not engaged the pirates since I first arrived here in the colonies a year and a half ago, so it goes without saying that I am most anxious to do battle with them and show them what His Majesty's Navy is made of."

"That is good to hear, Captain. You and I will have to remain in touch then. I have a feeling that when the time comes, we will be able to help one another."

"Consider me your obedient servant, Governor. I am all yours."

Of course you are, Captain Ellis Brand. Of course you are.

Standing up from his chair, he gave a warm smile, the two men shook hands, and he saw the captain to the top of the stairs and bid him *adieu.* By the time he had settled back into his seat, a definite plan had taken root in his mind: he was going to destroy Blackbeard and his band of pirates. The vile rogue and his barefooted cutthroats represented the perfect external threat he had been looking for, the perfect political distraction, and Brand was the perfect accomplice to help him seal the pirates' fate. The use of military force to kill or capture Thache would divert public attention away from his own unpopular policies and perceived improprieties as colonial governor and onto the man he believed was serving as Thache's corrupt supporter, Governor Eden. But Spotswood knew he had to be successful; there was no margin for error. With a victory over the pirates and Blackbeard either apprehended or eliminated, he would simultaneously demonstrate his supreme value as the King's representative in the colonies and Eden's inability to keep his own house in order.

Spotswood had long fantasized about folding the North Carolina colony into his political domain of Virginia. Such a bold move, he believed, would increase his political power, keep his many enemies at bay, and earn him an even greater fortune through land acquisition. A victory over Blackbeard and his band of rogues would improve the prospects of a bloodless Virginian conquest and annexation, or at least mark the end of North Carolina as a proprietary colony. Whichever way one looked at it, he stood to gain from a war against Blackbeard and his fellow pirates and had little to lose—unless, of course, it all went terribly wrong. Unfortunately, failure meant he would play straight into the hands of his opponents, and the clamor for his removal from the Ludwell-Blair faction would be impossible for his cold and distant superiors in the smoky, wood-paneled government offices of London to ignore.

Well, he would just have to take that chance. He could feel victory within his grasp: he would hunt down and destroy Blackbeard the pirate and all would be well in Virginia. All he needed was some time to concoct the perfect plan and pull together his team of trusted co-conspirators.

CHAPTER 47

PHILADELPHIA

AUGUST 11, 1718

WITH MARGARET OF MARCUS HOOK ON HIS ARM, Thache stared out at the wide Delaware River, where a forest of masts from dozens of brigantines, snows, pinks, sloops, barges, fishing boats, and periaugers stood against the backdrop of a pastel-colored summer sky. He was a law-abiding man once again, with official government documents in his pocket to prove it. Governor Eden had granted him undisputed ownership of the *Adventure* and signed customs papers clearing him to take the Spanish sloop to St. Thomas, where he would be able to obtain a letter of marque from the Danish governor authorizing him and his men to sail the Caribbean as officially licensed privateers.

It was a sublime summer day. He and Margaret had just finished sharing a tankard of ale with several of his crew members at George Guest's Blue Anchor Tavern at the corner of Dock and Front Streets, and were now strolling casually arm-in-arm along the wharves to the northeast. The Blue Anchor was Thache's favorite tippling establishment in the Quaker capital. It was said that even the colony's founder, William Penn, had enjoyed his first taste of brew at the notable tavern during his second visit to Philadelphia years ago.

"That was fun," said Margaret, the gentle breeze coming off the river making her flowing blonde hair dance just a little. "Your crew members know how to make a girl laugh. But they certainly drink a lot."

"Aye, ye should see them when they're not holding back due to polite company. It's like sharks in a feeding frenzy."

"So they were on their best behavior because of me?"

"I had a little talk with them beforehand. It seems to have restrained them more than I expected."

"Did all of your crew come ashore today?"

"No, half are still on the *Adventure*. We take shifts in town. We need to keep a low profile in case His Majesty's most gracious pardons don't offer us as much protection as we'd hoped for. We live in precarious times."

"What, are you telling me that the pieces of parchment affixed with Governor Eden's signature and wax seal guaranteeing you and your crew are reformed gentlemen of fortune won't properly protect you?"

"One has to be careful is all. That's why I have to go to St. Thomas and secure an official privateering commission. Once I have that, I truly will be scot free and can retire in comfort."

She came to a halt, hands on her wide child-bearing hips. "But I thought you said you were going to stay here with me."

"I am planning to be with you, just not until after my privateering commission ends. I've got to have a clean slate, my love. You must understand that. A royal pardon is one thing, but an official commission is quite another. It will put me in good stead with the law from here on out, and I won't have to watch my back wherever I go. Then, once I know that my past is behind me, we can be married and raise a wonderful family. It is all within our grasp."

"But you lied to me."

"I didn't lie to you. I just didn't tell you about my plans with the Danish governor in St. Thomas. Governor Eden has already written me a letter of introduction and declared the *Adventure* to be legally mine, so this is a big opportunity for me. If I want to quit a-pirating and go on to live an upstanding life with you and raise a family, I have to take advantage of this. I cannot let the opportunity slip past."

"You're just going to become a pirate again. I know you. You're never going to be able to quit."

He took her by the arm, pulled her towards him, and kissed her on the lips. "Avast—stop this talk at once. I love you and want to be with you, but I have to make arrangements first. These arrangements will protect not just me, but you and our children as well. A privateering commission will enable me to retire on my own terms without me having to look over my shoulder for the rest of my life. I have to do this, Margaret. Not just for me, but for us. And for our children."

"How can you talk of children? We're not even married yet."

"But I love you and want to be your husband. You know that—we have talked about it often enough. I just need some time to get my life back on track as a legally sanctioned sea captain. Only an official commission from a credible colonial governor will expunge my criminal past."

"But you're going to be gone so long again. What will it be this time? Six months? A year? Two years?"

"I don't know," he replied, feeling suddenly on the defensive.

"I can't wait two years, Edward. It's too long."

"All right, one year then. I promise to return in one year, no matter what."

"I don't know if I can wait a year either. My feeling is I've waited long enough."

"What are ye saying?"

"I'm saying that I'm not sure I can wait that long. I'm tired of waiting around for you, Edward. I'm sorry, but it's the truth."

"What...what has brought all this out? Have I done something to displease you? Have I treated you badly? Is it my crew? Did they do or say something to upset you or see things in a new light?"

"No, of course not. I've been around rowdy seamen before. I just don't want to stand by and wait for you any longer. I'm not getting any younger, and if you won't come out and ask my hand in marriage, perhaps I should find someone else who will."

"But I love you."

"And I love you more than I have another on God's green earth, but it's not enough anymore. I need to have a future. I need stability in my life. I need to know you will be there for me when I need you. I can't count on you, Edward. You sail where the wind and the prospect of rich, fat prizes take you."

He felt exasperated. "I shouldn't have brought you to the Blue Anchor. My damned crew members getting all drunk and disorderly has turned you against me."

"Your crew was fine—I just don't want to wait for you to sail home to me for the next year or two. It's too long. I want to raise a family, preferably with you. But I'll not wait forever, Edward Thache."

They walked past a pair of Quakers. Thache tipped his tricorn hat at them, but the two ruddy-cheeked men did not return the favor and looked at him suspiciously. He wondered if they recognized him. After all, he was conspicuously tall, with the parchment-like skin of a sailor and an extravagant, bushy black beard that was a rarity in the colonies since few men in the age of enlightenment wore facial hair of any kind, and certainly not unusually long and rebellious-looking beards tied up in West-Indian-style braids. He had bundled and tucked the braids of his beard to make it look more trimmed, but he still stood out.

"Let's keep moving," he said, and they started walking again. When the Quakers were out of earshot, he asked her, "Is this all because you feel like you're growing older? Is that what this is about? You're still plenty young to have children and raise a family. Why you're only twenty-four."

"I'll be twenty-six this September, Edward. Have you been gone so long that you have forgotten how to count?"

"I'm sorry, I forgot. But twenty-six is still plenty young."

"Likely more than half my life is over. That's not young."

"All right, now you're just being ornery. We need to go back to your place in Marcus Hook, make love, and then afterwards I'll try to talk some sense into you. I'm not leaving you. I love you and you know that."

"Then prove it and stay here with me. You've got Governor Eden's pardon. I'm sure that will protect you more than you are letting on. It's a signed royal pardon."

"Aye, but I had violations after January the fifth of this year, which means that I am technically not eligible."

"Then why did Eden sign it?"

"He gave me and my men the benefit of the doubt. Many of them hail from Bath County and were originally sent by Eden and his number two man Tobias Knight to the Florida wrecks in search of riches, so he feels some responsibility in looking out for them. I have also met the governor and Esquire Knight previously when I worked here in Philadelphia as a merchant seaman and apparently made a positive impression upon them. That's why they were willing to help out me and my shipmates."

"Well then, I would say the governor's signed and sealed piece of parchment adequately protects you and you have nothing to worry about."

"It's not that simple. I need the Danish commission to erase my career as a pirate and guarantee me full protection going forward."

There were tears in her deep-blue Swedish eyes now, and he couldn't help but feel guilty. "I don't understand why we can't just get married and put all this piracy behind us," she said. "But at the same time, I wonder how you can ever be a father to my children when you have done the terrible things you've done."

"What things? I've never laid a hand on any captain or deck hand of any prize I've taken. My men have roughed up a merchantman or two to get them to reveal where they've hidden their silver and gold, there's no doubt about that, but I can't control them. I am only in charge from the time we decide to give chase to the completion of the boarding action and interview of the captain and his men. The rest of the time I wield the same power as anyone else and have but a single vote just like an ordinary seaman."

"I've read what you've done to some of the captains whose ships you've plundered. I read the *Boston News-Letter*, you know. Why I've got the clippings right here in my purse."

He reached out and grabbed her arm, bringing her to a halt. "You carry newspaper clippings of my exploits?"

"Dastardly deeds is more like it. Here let me read one of them to you." From her shoulder purse, she withdrew several yellowed newspaper clippings. "This is from last October. *'We are informed that a pirate sloop of 12 guns, 150 men, Captain Thache Commander, took one Captain Codd from Liverpool, two snows outward bound, Soford for Ireland, and Budger for Oporto, and Peters from Madera, George from London, Farmer for New York, a sloop from Madera for Virginia, all of which met with most barbarous inhumane treatment from them.'"*

"That is an exaggeration. We didn't harm anybody. The newspaper is lying."

"Lying are they? Then what about this?" She pulled out another strip of printed newspaper and began reading. *"'Arrived Linsey from Antigua, Codd from Liverpool and Dublin with 150 passengers, many whereof are servants. He was taken about 12 days since off our Capes by a pirate sloop called the Revenge, of 12 Guns 150 Men, Commanded by one Thache, who formerly sail'd Mate out of this Port. They have arms to fire five rounds before loading again. They threw all Codds Cargo overboard, excepting some small matters they fancied. One merchant had a thousand pounds cargo on board, of which the greatest part went overboard, he begg'd for cloth to make him but one suit of clothes, which they refus'd to grant him. The pirate took two snows outward bound, Spofford loaden with staves for Ireland and Budger of Bristol in the Sea Nymph loaden with wheat for Oporto, which they threw overboard, and made a pirate of the said snow; and put all the prisoners on board of Spofford, out of which they threw overboard about a thousand staves, and they very barbarously used Mr. Richardson, merchant of the Sea Nymph.'"* If that's not cruel and unusual punishment then I don't know what is."

"It didn't happen like that. The men were wild and rebellious, but no harm came to any captain or crew member."

"Are you saying the *Boston News-Letter*, the most reliable paper in all the land, is lying?"

"Aye, that's exactly what I'm saying. This brutal treatment of victims is only mentioned to make me look bad. The Crown is doing it so that the public will turn against me and other pirates when they are actually predisposed towards rooting for us. It's all propaganda."

"Is it now? Shall I read another?"

"I don't know, can you?"

She pulled out another clipping, her lips pursed taut with censure. *"Boston*

News-Letter, Monday July 7, a mere month ago. *'South Carolina, June 6. Captain Thache in a ship of 40 guns and two sloops and about 300 men, came here to our bar and took two outward bound ships from England.'* It then goes on to describe your abominations hurled upon one Samuel Wragg, his four-year-old son, and the other victims before concluding, *'We hear that they are bound to the northward and swear revenge upon New England men & vessels.'* That doesn't sound to me like the actions of a friendly sea captain."

"It's still all propaganda. These newspapers have created the great Blackbeard, can't you see? They have made me out to be this fearsome and ruthless villain so that they can turn people against me. That is precisely what the *Boston News-Letter* is trying to accomplish, probably under the orders of the Board of Trade or the bloody King himself. With their pardons they dangle a carrot, and with their newspaper articles they bludgeon us over the head to sway public opinion. This is the way they have chosen to destroy me and all the other freebooters of the Atlantic."

"You're still a brute who terrorizes poor innocent people. I used to think that what you did was sort of romantic and that you were a Robin Hood of the high seas. But when I read newspaper articles like these, I realize that ye are a cruel man."

"Damnit, I am not cruel. I take from those who can afford to give up some of their wealth and I fight back against an oppressive Crown that doesn't give a damn about the ordinary man."

"Oh yes, your cause is all high and mighty, isn't it? You're an American patriot, fighting against a tyrant king on behalf of the oppressed citizens of the New World. Fighting for this vision you have of a free colonial class of people who defy the king and strive for independence. But what is this America? Only you and other seamen seem to know what it means. Since the last time I saw you, I have asked people about this 'America' and these 'Americans' you profess to represent, and no one except sailors and a few half-crazed radicals know what I'm even talking about."

"One day, we will be free, all of us here in the New World. That is what America is—and that is what I have been fighting for all these years."

"No, Edward, what drives you is the prospect of riches. You are no different than other men driven by greed."

"Aye, I'm as greedy as the next man. But in all honesty, that is not the main reason I do it anymore. I plunder as a form of defiance to the Crown and to show my solidarity with the common man and the colonies. One day, we will be the sovereigns of this land and live in a democracy where the very idea of a king is foreign. Mark my words, one day it will be so, and that is the day when we will be able to walk proudly down the street not as English subjects, but as Americans."

"Captain, Captain!" he suddenly heard a voice cry.

He turned to see Caesar dashing towards him from the corner of High and Front Streets. Having left him and the other men in the Blue Anchor a mere hour earlier, Thache was surprised to see him and wondered what the emergency was. The black crewman ran up to him, gasping for breath. It was obvious that he had been running around the city for some time trying to find him.

"What is it, Caesar? What is happening?" he asked him.

"The King's men were just at the Blue Anchor," he pronounced. "Governor Keith knows you are in town and has issued a warrant for your arrest."

"The governor of Pennsylvania has ordered me to be arrested?"

"Aye. We were lucky to be warned and Mr. Hands, Mr. Gibbons, and the rest of the crew are heading back to the *Adventure*."

"Were all the crew members ashore notified of the governor's warrant?"

"Everyone but Curtice. He was next door with a sporting lass, and we left word with the barkeep to warn him. We had to skedaddle out the back door right quick and weren't able to tell him in person. The King's men were on us so fast we had to make a run for it."

"Who warned you?"

"A man named Crane, a Swede. He said he knows ye."

"Aye, I know Crane. Runs the upper ferry on Schuylkill and has brought supplies to me at State Island. He's a good man."

"But why would Governor Keith want you?" asked Margaret. "Is it for crimes committed before or after you accepted the royal pardon?"

"I don't know," he said. "But I have no intention of testing the validity of Governor Eden's pardon while I'm stuck in a jail in this Quaker colony."

"Governor Keith reported that you have been seen on the city's streets. You are well known here because you used to ship out of the port. He has told not only the militia and police about your presence here, but other law authorities. That's what Crane said. He got there only a few minutes before the King's men arrived."

"What else did Crane say?"

"Only that the governor thought the threat you posed was serious enough that if you weren't swiftly caught, he would fit out two sloops and hire men to go after you."

"Go after me?"

"He said they would patrol the waters off the Delaware Capes in the hopes of intercepting you and Charles Vane."

"Vane? Vane is here?"

"No, but he has been prowling around Charles Town and is reported to be heading north."

"Who is Governor Keith planning on commissioning to come after me?"

"Captain Raymond and Captain Taylor? Do you know them?"

"I know of Taylor. He used to be a privateer."

"You need to go," said Margaret. "This is serious."

"But I can't leave you like this—there's too much unsettled."

He took her in his arms. Caesar, realizing they needed a moment of privacy, tactfully stepped towards the railing several feet away and stared out at the river.

"You have no choice, Edward," she said to him. "You have to go now. You are a pirate, and they're never going to let you be until you are captured or killed."

"But I love you and want to marry you."

"You need to leave Philadelphia while you still have a chance, sail immediately south, and obtain your privateering commission from the governor of St. Thomas."

"But…but will you wait for me? I could be gone for at least a year."

"I'll wait for you. But I won't wait longer than one year. That's where, this time, I'm going to draw the line. Because I love you more than I have loved another soul in this world, I will wait for you for one year. But not a day longer."

He felt all muddled inside and yearning. "I'll be here by next summer. You just wait and see."

"You'd better be, or I will be yours no more. And that's a promise," she said sternly, but there were tears of love and pain in her eyes, tears that made him feel a wrenching guilt inside.

Why the hell can't you just marry her and lead a normal life? he wondered. *What is wrong with you? You're going to blow this whole affair and lose her altogether, you scupperlout!*

Suddenly, she lurched forward, took him in his arms, and kissed him on the lips. He felt a warm feeling envelope him, but also a crushing sadness. She leaned in close to him, willingly and desperately despite the tears flowing freely from her eyes, and he felt himself spinning in a wonderful yet terrifying way, as if he was navigating a vessel through a violent storm. After a moment, they pulled apart for air.

"I love you, Edward Thache. And that love will burn as brightly as a winter hearth for one year. After that, I don't know. I know that, deep down, you are a good man. You want to mend your ways and be a good husband and father. But I cannot wait forever. I have been waiting too long already."

"I won't let you down, I promise. I shall return."

She kissed him again. She tasted like apple butter and he felt as if he was under some sort of magic spell as they clutched each other tightly. When she gently pulled away, his body tingled all over. With tears in her eyes, she smiled up at him, and he felt the power of her emotions.

"I'm going to be there for you," he said. "Ye just wait and see—I shall return."

"I'm counting on it, my love. Now you can hail a launch from the landing at Vine Street near the Penny-pot house. It is less frequented than the quay at the Blue Anchor with fewer prying eyes and hopefully none of the King's men."

"Right smart idea that be." He took her in his arms again and squeezed her tight. "I love you, Margaret. I'm not going to let you down."

"I know you won't, my love," she said, the tears pouring from her eyes. "I know you won't."

"Then what is it? Why do you cry so?"

"Because I don't want you to die," she said.

"But I'm not going to die. I'm going to make it. We...we're going to make it. We're going to marry and have children and live a wonderful life together."

"Yes, my love, we will. Now go, before the King's men come to arrest you," she said. And she was still crying.

CHAPTER 48

DELAWARE RIVER

AUGUST 11, 1718

THEY WERE ABLE TO HIRE A LAUNCH at the Vine Street landing near the Penny-pot house, thereby avoiding the more closely watched quay at the Blue Anchor. As they rowed towards the *Adventure*, anchored in the dusky shadows of the Delaware, Caesar felt badly that Thache had been forced to rush away under such desperate circumstances and leave his beloved Margaret behind. The young black man had never been in love with a woman before—as an overworked male slave growing up in South and North Carolina he had rarely had the opportunity to mingle with the opposite sex—but he knew what a traumatic experience it was to be ripped away suddenly from someone you loved. The final scene between Thache and his Swedish woman reminded him of when he had been torn from his family in West Africa and shipped as a slave to Charles Town. Both events had come about swiftly and unexpectedly and, like Thache, he had been powerless to fight off fate. Governor Keith had put out a warrant for the notorious Blackbeard's arrest, and in the blink of an eye the man had turned from a pardoned pirate into a wanted criminal who had to leave the love of his life behind. It seemed pointedly unfair and Caesar felt a powerful empathy for the man. He understood his pain.

When they reached the *Adventure*, Thache instantly commanded his new quartermaster, Thomas Miller, who had replaced William Howard, to stand by to make sail. All of the crew had returned to the sloop except Joseph Curtice, and the captain intended to set a course for the Atlantic within the hour, hoping that would give the seaman sufficient time to finish his carnal pleasures and catch a launch to the *Adventure*. None of them had any intention of testing the protective capabilities of Governor Eden's pardon while waiting in a rat-infested Philadelphia jail cell. Within the hour, Curtice came on board and the *Adventure* weighed anchor and began to make her way down the Delaware towards the open ocean.

Just as they remained incognito when they had sailed upriver into port, they made sure that the *Adventure* looked like just another trading vessel plying the waters of the Delaware. They flew no Jolly Roger in the rigging, there were no name-boards on her bows, and the sloop's bosun Garret Gibbons made sure all the gun ports were closed taut and the rail guns and chasers stowed below deck. Caesar had to admit the charade was working: he could barely tell the difference between their Spanish sloop and the various snows, pinks, sloops, and fishing vessels jibing to and fro en route to Delaware Bay.

Two miles downriver, he stared back at the City of Brotherly Love receding in the distance. He had found the cosmopolitan Quaker city awe-inspiring, especially compared to dusty, tavern-less Bath Town and his first home on the continent of Charles Town. The Swedish and Quaker meeting houses, churches, and homes were noticeably larger and more handsomely and sturdily built than their Carolina counterparts. Fashioned of brick, sandstone, and granite with steeply sloped roofs of cedar shakes or metamorphosed slate, the architecture of the city and its surrounding villages carried a grandeur that surpassed anything Caesar had seen before. But most of all, he had enjoyed the freedom of strolling about High Street and sharing a tankard of ale at the Blue Anchor without anyone questioning him about what he was doing in the city or treating him like a slave.

That he was a seaman had never been in doubt by anyone that had set eyes on him in the city, even the Quakers who had gazed upon his coal-tar face and barrel chest with the two brace of pistols strapped about him with animal fear in their eyes. He was a free man, a worldly sailor and gentleman of fortune who walked with his head held high and his pistols loaded, not a lowly servant to white masters. One day he would live as a seaman in a burgeoning city like this, and he would never allow himself to go back to being a slave—never. Thache had given him his chance at freedom and he would not return to his lowly chattel world of before.

When they sailed past Marcus Hook seventeen miles downriver of the city, Caesar saw a slump in Thache's shoulders and the pirate commander turned somberly silent on the quarterdeck. From William Howard and the other crew members, Caesar knew that Margaret lived in a sawn plank house off Discord Lane and that was where Thache spent most of his time with her when he was in port. With her full head of flowing blonde hair, hourglass figure, and unusually high cheekbones, she was an uncommonly beautiful woman. The men called her Blackbeard's 'mistress,' but from their parting conversation tonight along the city's wharves a stone's throw from the Blue Anchor, Caesar knew that she meant a lot more to the captain than that. The two were planning to marry and settle down, and it was clear that they had talked about it on many occasions. Governor Keith's arrest order appeared to have made a sudden mess of their plans and thrown them both into disarray. Caesar could tell the two were terribly in love, and he vowed that one day he would find a woman and love her as much as Thache loved his Margaret. He imagined Thache smoking his clay pipe beside a stone hearth, or laying with his love in her bed chamber. A love like theirs was a love worth having, and one day he would have a love like that, a love with joy and hurt, romance and sadness.

They soon reached the busy port of New Castle, and then, a few miles south at the bend in the river the *Adventure's* course altered to south by west. By the time they plied the waters north of the Bombay Hook, near the point where the Delaware River spills into the bay, Caesar could feel an air of tension and danger aboard the sloop as the men began to coalesce around the quarterdeck. Something was going on with the crew, and Caesar realized he hadn't seen it coming. A moment later he found out what it was as Israel Hands called a council to discuss where they would go from here. But Caesar could tell from the sailing master's body language that he was agitated about something and was going to challenge the captain's authority. The two men hadn't been seeing eye to eye of late, but clearly the relationship had deteriorated even more than Caesar had thought.

"All right, speak your mind, Mr. Hands," said Thache impatiently, who despite the fact that he appeared about to be challenged left no doubt as to who was in ultimately in command of the ship.

"We've taken a vote among the men, Captain."

"A vote you say? Was it conducted amongst *all* the men?"

Hands glanced at Caesar, Garret Gibbons, and Thomas Miller. "Not all the men, but most of them. The others can cast their votes once I've said what I have to say."

"Aye, then get on with it, man. What is it that you want to address?"

"We're not ready to strike south for St. Thomas."

"Is that so?"

"Aye, and neither is the *Adventure*. She's in no condition to make it to the West Indies. It has been several months since she has been careened and she needs a good scraping, re-planking, and re-caulking. Her rigging is worn and tired and her sails need to be patched or replaced."

"I agree, Mr. Hands, that extensive refitting is in order. So what do you propose?"

"We need a new ship so that we can careen her. We had not planned on using our own money to maintain the *Adventure* and we need a new sloop to do the job properly. We also need new sailcloth, rigging, anchors, spare masts, and timber. Plus we're low on oakum and tar."

"So just so I understand, are you saying that you are willing to violate the King's most gracious pardon, signed and sealed by Governor Eden, the proprietary governor of North Carolina, to bring said vessel up to snuff? Is that what you're saying, Mr. Hands?"

Master gunner Philip Morton stepped forward. "We need supplies and we need to careen the *Adventure*. We can't do them both without taking a prize or two. It just can't be done, Captain."

"But we all took the oath. We agreed to give up the account and that our cruise to Philadelphia was not a pirating venture."

"Indeed it wasn't," pointed out Hands. "We haven't taken a single prize since the day before Old Topsail Inlet where we double-crossed our mates."

Thache's brown eyes flashed darkly. "We took a vote and all agreed to that plan of action, as regrettable as it may have been. This is not the time to second-guess yourself like a guilty schoolboy. What's done is done and we are, all of us here, the wealthier for it and with the King's pardon in hand. The company had gotten too damned big and unwieldly and there weren't enough spoils for all of us. It wasn't sustainable."

"No one disagrees with that, but we double-crossed some good men and left sixteen marooned on an island. Personally, I've come to regret what we did. There might have been another option open to us."

"I agree with Hr. Hands," echoed Morton.

"Me too, Captain," said the ever-loyal Garret Gibbons. "What we did was wrong."

"No, what we did was necessary," argued Thache, looking as though he would brook no opposition. But Hands and his supporters—at least a dozen men, Caesar estimated—appeared equally stubborn. In that moment, Caesar wished he had seen this coming. But obviously Hands had excluded him and a handful of others loyal to the captain from the first council meeting, most likely because Hands wanted to maintain the element of surprise and catch the unsuspecting captain and his loyalists off guard. In the case of a mutiny, it was best not to make your intentions known to too many people, and Caesar realized that Israel Hands had simply taken a page from Blackbeard's own book.

"It doesn't matter," said Hands, his sunburnished face taut and thin lips pursed tightly together. "We have the votes in this matter, and shall now hold a majority-rule council vote in accordance with the articles. The only remaining question is who is going to captain this bloody ship?"

He glared defiantly at Thache, as insolently as a cocksure game rooster. Caesar couldn't help but gulp when he saw the captain's eyes narrow beneath heated brow before him. He had never seen anyone openly challenge the notorious Blackbeard before in front of the whole crew, and he couldn't believe that the pirate captain had fallen so far from grace that he was being contested by the likes of his chief navigator. Obviously, Hands was still bitter about having to run aground Herriot's *Adventure* at Old Topsail Inlet and thereby losing his captaincy, and he was now jockeying to reclaim his lost position by ousting Thache. It was a huge gamble, but Caesar could tell it could go either way.

Still glowering imperiously, Hands said, "All those in favor of my proposal to no longer cower like defeated puppies, to return to the open sea, and to actively take rich prizes of any nationality, raise your hands and signal assent with your voice. Quartermaster Miller here will make a proper accounting of the vote."

To Caesar's surprise, fourteen of the twenty-one men aboard voted to return to the account. Clearly, Hands and his men were a force to be reckoned with and didn't feel the least bit influenced by their captain. Caesar looked at Thache, whose mind he could see was racing. For the first time in Caesar's two-year career together with the pirate captain, Thache's vote was overruled. It was a hard defeat for a proud and heretofore unchallenged leader, and Caesar couldn't help but feel the man seemed discombobulated.

Lordy Lord, he thought, *events are swirling out of control. First, he has to leave his woman behind, and now his crew is close to mutiny.*

In a gloating voice, Hands announced, "The vote is to return to our piratical ways. Now the question is, who shall lead us as captain?"

Quartermaster Thomas Miller stepped forward. "There ain't no captain of this ship but Captain Thache," he said, and the sentiment was quickly echoed by Caesar, master gunner Philip Morton, bosun Garret Gibbons, seamen Joseph Brooks and Joseph Curtice as well as the other five African crewman on board in addition to Caesar: his good friend Richard Greensail as well as Richard Stiles, James Blake, James White, and Thomas Gates.

"We're going to have to vote on it," said Hands. "Now where do you stand men? Who do you want as your captain?"

Caesar felt certain that the vote would turn out in favor of Hands and was surprised when the count was twenty-four for keeping Thache as captain and only three in favor of Hands, one of whom was Hands himself. Thache abstained from voting altogether.

"It's decided then," said Miller. "The captain stays but we sail in pursuit of plunder." He looked at Thache. "Where to, Captain?"

Caesar watched as the great Blackbeard took a moment to gather himself and recover his lost pride. Again, he felt for the man, and he was glad that Hands had at least been dealt a harsh blow in the voting for captaincy. "Set a course east-by-southeast for the deep blue and Bermuda," he said after a moment. "If I can't talk common sense into you numbskulls, I can at least make sure that the next prize we take isn't bloody British. I understand, gentlemen, that we need a prize and sacrificial ship. But we want to be careful about where we go a-hunting for it so we can avoid future entanglements with the government. A French vessel, or possibly two, will fit the bill nicely, I say."

Miller nodded. "So we set a course for Bermuda."

"Aye, the eastern side is where French ships are known to pass on their way home from their plantations on Martinique. With any luck, we will be able to take a prize or two and get ourselves a new tender and consort ship without attracting undue attention. But just so you know, in all likelihood we'll probably get caught and our pardons will be worthless. You might want to keep that unfavorable prospect in mind, gentlemen."

"That's a chance we're going to have to take," said Hands.

"How long will it take us to get there?" Caesar asked the sailing master.

"The run to Bermuda is more than a thousand miles. It will take a week with a favorable wind, longer if she be against us."

"Well then, crowd that canvas and make all sail, Mr. Hands!" said Thache loudly. "We've no time to lose!"

"Aye, so be it! More sail, you scallywags! Lively ho now!" thundered Hands.

With the debate settled, the crew jumped into the task of sailing the vessel with renewed vigor. Caesar felt as if a full mutiny had been narrowly averted, though the vote to keep Thache on as captain hadn't even been close. All the same, he couldn't deny a new feeling in the air, a feeling that they were no longer merely doing battle with the British Crown and its powerful navy, but were struggling to fight off a cancer from within. Since the deception at Old Topsail Inlet and subsequent obtainment of the King's pardon, something had changed. But now the situation had gotten worse. They had been pirates again for a single day and already they were turning against one another. To Caesar, it did not bode well for the future of the already-reduced company.

Not well at all.

CHAPTER 49

EAST OF BERMUDA

AUGUST 23, 1718

WHEN LOOKOUT RICHARD GREENSAIL spotted the pair of sails, Thache turned away from the speeding school of luminescent dorado he had been watching and pointed his spyglass eastward. After leaving the American mainland behind ten days earlier, they were now within a day's sail of Bermuda, which he knew was the final waypoint for vessels of all nationalities before making landfall in Europe. The sun was sinking low in the sky, but the visibility was still at least a dozen miles. After locating the two new interlopers, Thache sent the eagle-eyed Caesar aloft with a telescope to ascertain their type and country of origin. The black pirate was able to quickly verify that, although they flew no nation's colors, they appeared to be double-masted French merchantmen and the one to leeward was sailing light. Upon hearing the news, the crew gave a lusty cheer.

Calling Caesar back down to the quarterdeck, Thache quickly computed an intercepting path and commanded Israel Hands to crowd on sail and give immediate chase. The Jamaican-rigged *Adventure* raced towards the two French vessels from the northwest on a perpendicular intersecting course, sending flying fish scattering before its bow. Having scoured the shipping lanes for the past three days along with his crew, Blackbeard was excited to finally have a crack at a pair of prizes. During his Royal Navy career, he had particularly enjoyed taking the vessels of Britain's most important enemy after Spain, and he would be more than happy to plunder a pair of French Martiniquemen. There was just one problem: if he attacked, Governor Eden's pardon might as well be ripped up, for it would no longer offer him or his crew any protection whatsoever.

Just as the sky grew dark, the *Adventure* drew close enough that he was able to confirm that both vessels were indeed French. In fact, unbeknownst to the captain, the lead ship was a French merchant ship named *Rose Emelye* that had spent the spring following the winds and currents across the Atlantic from Nantes to tropical Martinique, and much of the summer unloading French cargo and taking on bags of cocoa and barrels of freshly refined sugar. Now the *Rose* was following the Gulf Stream home in the company of another French merchant ship, the *La Toison d'Or*, sailing just a stone's throw to leeward. The ships appeared to be slowly working their way northward on a great circle course bound for home, sailing close to the outer fringes of the Sargasso Sea and as far as possible from the depredations of Caribbean freebooters.

Like a stalking lion, the *Adventure* drew closer to the two French sloops. Studying them closely in the dying light, he wanted to be sure he could take them with his smaller-than-usual pirate sloop, armed with only eight cannons. The Frenchmen had not altered their course and had not shown their heels, so he suspected they weren't quite sure what to make of him. But by now they must be curious what the small sloop on the horizon, with Spanish lines better suited to shuttling cargo between Caribbean islands than to crossing an ocean, was doing way out here. The current ocean passage was usually traveled only by European-bound vessels departing from the Windward Islands that had no reason to call upon American ports. The French captains had to be perplexed as to what the *Adventure* was doing out in the open ocean, and why was it on an intercept course with their much larger oceangoing merchant ships. Well soon, very soon, he thought, they would have their answer.

But he had to be careful. The French vessels were larger and more heavily armed than the *Adventure*, and for a moment he was filled with doubt regarding his chances of success should they decide to put up a fight. Tonight's attack, if carried out, would be his first attempt on a prize since he had shed the greater part of his company at Old Topsail Inlet, and his first engagement as captain of the *Adventure*. Together, the two ships were out of his class. But he had the advantage of speed and maneuverability, and his crew were seasoned pirates instead of underpaid merchant seamen with little motivation to fight for their oppressive masters.

Soon Thache overtook the vessels and pulled alongside within cannon range. It was then he made his decision.

"Prepare your guns to fire, Mr. Morton!"

"Aye, Captain! Roll out the guns!"

"Mr. Miller, you may prepare your boarding party!"

Three cannon muzzles rolled out of gun ports on the sloop's sides and two dozen armed men crowded the decks, brandishing their weapons and yelling to intimidate the enemy as the Death's Head was thrown up the rigging.

But to Thache's surprise, the French didn't stand down. They just kept sailing to the northeast on their designated course as if nothing was happening.

Them Frogs be proud bastards, he thought. *What is their game? Do they really think they can resist and eventually overpower me?*

Now he heard shouting coming from the *Rose Emelye*. The captain was ordering his crew to prepare for action and instructing his master gunner to make the vessel's four cannons ready. He then reached for his speaking trumpet.

"Ahoy there!" he cried out to the *Adventure* in execrable English. "Whoever you are, you must remove yourselves, or we will fire!"

Thache looked around for his own trumpet, but couldn't locate it. But Caesar quickly found it and handed it to him. He spoke into it.

"You and your consort, strike your colors and lower your topsails so that we may prepare to board!"

"We will do nothing of the kind, *mon Capitaine*! I warn you again to stand down or we will open fire."

"No, you are not in control, my French friend! Surrender yourselves now and no harm will come to ye! But if you resist at all, you shall receive no quarter from me or my men! It is your choice and I would remind you to choose wisely!"

"*Non monsieur*, you must remove yourselves at once—or *we* will open fire!"

Thache just shook his head. "Curse and damn the scupperlout, we'll trounce the devilment out of him," he grumbled, and then he turned towards his helmsman.

"Mr. Gibbons, hard-a-lee, if you would please. We're going to this take this stubborn Frenchman by surprise and seize his consort."

"Captain?"

"You heard me, Mr. Gibbons! Hard-a-lee!"

"Aye, Captain! Hard-a-lee, hard-a-lee!"

As Gibbons pushed the tiller hard to the lee side to turn the *Adventure* into the wind, the crewmen released ropes and the sails briefly flapped. And then, like a well-trained horse turning on a penny, the sloop suddenly swung hard about and shot by the French ship in the opposite direction, sweeping in on the unarmed *Toison d'Or*.

Suddenly, Thache heard a whistling sound and, a moment later, an explosion ripped through the *Adventure*. He couldn't believe his eyes: the French captain had opened up with a broadside and the impact rocked every timber of the sloop. He saw Joseph Brooks and two other men slumped across the deck, lying battered and bloodied at one of the blown-apart gun stations. They weren't dead, but were definitely wounded as the smell of gunpowder filled the air and splinters of wood littered the deck.

"Give them a taste of shot, Mr. Morton!" cried Thache. Then to his quartermaster. "Mr. Miller, you and your men prepare to board the second vessel!"

As Morton opened up with his cannons, the *Adventure* closed on the *Toison d'Or*. A moment later, steel grappling hooks were tossed across and the wooden hulls collided with a heavy groan. Upon impact, the iron hooks found purchase in the wooden bulwark amidships and were pulled taut. With the vessels now lashed together, the pirates swarmed over the gunwales and onto the ship's deck. Surprisingly, the French offered no resistance and the pirates were able to seize the captain and all of his crew members without a single shot fired or loss of life on either side. To discourage further broadsides or small-arms fire from the other vessel, they kept several prisoners as human shields. In less than five minutes, they had secured the ship, removed all the French prisoners, and now set upon the *Rose Emelye* and her stubborn Nantes captain as not one attacker but two.

"A round of bar and chain shot, Mr. Morton! And a volley of musket fire, Mr. Miller!"

"Aye, Captain!"

Once again, the cannons discharged. Just before, the Frenchmen aboard the *Rose Emelye* wisely ducked belowdecks and made themselves small to avoid death and injury. A round of musket balls followed, flying over the captain's head and quickly mangling sails, masts, and rigging. A moment later, the captain turned the ship into the wind, drifted to a halt, and surrendered his command. A raucous cheer went up from the pirates.

Blackbeard just shook his head. He had captured two vessels more than twice the size of his own—but all he felt inside was anger. Three of his men were badly wounded and would need a surgeon. Damn the French for doing what Frenchmen weren't supposed to do: fight back. He couldn't believe the captain had seriously considered putting up all-out resistance. He thought about having the bastard flogged in front of his men for his effrontery, but then decided against it. His three gunners, though hurt, would survive their wounds and he couldn't help but admire the Frenchmen for their tenacity. But he would give the captain an earful and make him understand that what he had done might very well have cost him and his men their lives; and he would take the *Rose Emelye* as his new consort and pick the two French vessels clean of anything and everything of even the remotest value to put an exclamation point on the victory. With triumph in the air and fresh plunder in the hold, the pirate company would be happy again, and having a second vessel on hand would be of great help in careening the *Adventure*.

He ordered all three vessels to be rafted together. Thomas Miller boarded the prizes with his boarding party and inspected the holds and spaces belowdecks. While this was going on, Blackbeard interviewed Jan Goupil, the commander of the *Rose Emelye*, and the other French captain—and made sure Goupil knew how he and his men felt about the resistance offered. Miller quickly confirmed that the *Toison d'Or* was indeed "sailing light" with little cargo in her holds, while the *Rose Emelye* was transporting a modest consignment of sugar, cocoa, cotton, and indigo dye. But the ship had other plunder the pirates desperately wanted: rigging, sails, anchors, spare masts, oakum, pitch and tar, and timber for repairs. The ship also had food and water and even a few French delicacies like casks of confectionaries. Thache had to admit that the pair of prizes were just what the pirates had been looking for in preparation for sailing south to St. Thomas, provided they could fence the seized goods in Bath Town.

The men transferred the French crew of the burdened vessel to the empty *Toison d'Or* and sent them on their way. Now Thache and his men needed to take their prize back to Ocracoke. Here they would be able to work discreetly and peacefully to careen and outfit the *Adventure*. Here they had colonial friends to keep a weather-eye out for enemies, and they would be able to get a sympathetic doctor to quietly attend to the wounds of Joseph Brooks and the other two wounded pirates. And here they would feel at home and still under the protection of Governor Eden and Tobias Knight. But no one could learn of the seizure of the *Rose Emelye* or they would have to claim her as salvage, for they had committed an act of sea robbery for which His Majesty's pardon would not exonerate them. In the minds of his crew members, taking the Martiniqueman was necessary for their survival—or at least necessary to keep the *Adventure* afloat—but he knew the Crown would not see it that way. Then again, as long as no one learned the fate of the *Rose Emelye*, it was possible that the King's authorities might be none the wiser and the violation of the pardon wouldn't amount to any trouble. But they had to go somewhere safe, and if the French prize was somehow discovered, he would have to find a way to smooth things over with Eden and Knight.

They set sail for Ocracoke. The remaining days of August passed without incident as the *Adventure* and *Rose Emelye* followed the warm waters of the Gulf Stream back to the Outer Banks. On the second of September, the two ships sailed into Ocracoke Inlet and followed the right-hand channel up toward the Old Slough and Old Watering Hole. But Thache and his crew did not enjoy the privacy the pirate captain had hoped for. Over the next fortnight, they were watched by a British loyalist who was not a friend and didn't think much of gentlemen of fortune, a man who was quietly serving as an informant to Captain Ellis Brand.

And it would change their lives dramatically.

CHAPTER 50

BATH TOWN

SEPTEMBER 14, 1718

ONE STROKE PAST MIDNIGHT, Thache spotted the landing at Tobias Knight's house on Town Creek. With the careening of the *Adventure* completed using the captured *Rose Emelye*, the cannon remounted, and the crew busy with sail repair, tarring-down the new standing rigging, and transferring the French cargo to the tents on Ocracoke Island, he had decided to take a little trip, up country, to Bath Town. He had announced to Israel Hands and the other officers that he would travel alone with just four black pirates: Richard Stiles, Thomas Gates, James Blake, and James White. They would take the periauger and would only be gone for two or three days. Blackbeard's goal was to deliver gifts to the government in the hopes that Eden would again grant the *Adventure's* captain and crew entry into the colony—and to seek legal advice from Tobias Knight on what to do with the captured French prize.

They left Ocracoke Inlet in the periauger at dawn, sailing across the compact, choppy waves of Pamlico Sound for the mainland. It was a surreal moment for Thache. In two and a half years at sea, he had never had fewer men in his pirate company than he did now. A mere three months earlier, he had seven hundred men under his command, and now he had just four black men traveling with him as brothers-in-arms and a longboat stocked with gifts: casks of sweetmeats, a bag of cocoa, loaf sugar, and several boxes, the contents of which were known only by him. During the forty-seven-mile voyage across the sound and up the Pamlico River, he served as helmsman, pilot, navigator, and sailing master of the thirty-foot-long open periauger, while the four black pirates operated the sails and, when necessary, pulled at the oars to speed the vessel along.

Without a lookout up in the rigging as with the *Adventure*, Blackbeard relied on his local knowledge and a small, handheld pocket compass set to a course of 310 degrees north by northwest. Once they reached Pamlico River, the sea breeze weakened and then died away altogether a few more miles inland. Out came the sweeps again and the African pirates went to work, reaching Knight's landing just after midnight. The two-hundred-forty-acre plantation occupied a beautiful part of Bath County, but it was isolated from the town and far from help during Indian uprisings. It was also situated out on the river so that midnight visitors could come and go and no one in town at the north end of Town Creek would be aware of their presence.

Once they had tied off the periauger at the dock, Thache saw Pompey, Tobias Knight's slave that had grown up with Caesar, appear out of the gloom, carrying a yellow lantern. With Pompey's help, the exhausted pirates began to unload some casks and boxes as another slave, a man named Tom, walked out to the landing to greet them. After talking with them for a moment about their journey, he returned to the house to alert Knight. A minute later, the door of the house creaked open, a shaft of wavering yellow light spread over the barren ground at the foot of the steps, and the North Carolina council secretary, collector of customs, and interim chief justice appeared. Tom quickly returned to the periauger and led Thache up to the house where Knight was waiting, while Pompey remained with the four black crew members, who sat down on the dock. Eventually, they would be brought food, water, and blankets so they could comfortably rest.

"Captain Thache, my friend, what are ye doing here?" asked Knight as Blackbeard came walking up. "I thought you were going to sail for St. Thomas."

"I apologize, Esquire Knight, but a problem has come up and I found it necessary to seek out your most wise counsel."

Knight stared off at the periauger and the four black crew members faintly illuminated by the dock lantern. "Where is your sloop, Captain?"

"Back at Ocracoke. She is freshly careened and will soon be ready to make sail for the West Indies."

"Come inside and we will share a refreshment and talk. But please be quiet. My wife, Katherine, is asleep in her bed chamber on the second floor, and our guest Mr. Chamberlayne is staying in the lodging room on the upper story. No doubt they have been roused out of bed due to the commotion of your arrival, but if we could speak quietly from here on out, that would be greatly appreciated."

He led him into a parlor where his young female house slave, Phillis, was waiting and proceeded to pour out two stiff brandies. With drinks in hand, they took their seats at a small black walnut table surrounded by six yellow-colored chairs. Once they had settled in, the two men pulled out their long-stem white clay pipes, packed them with rich Carolina tobacco, and began smoking. Shadows danced about the painted white walls as the candles on the table flickered and the two men quietly puffed on their pipes. One was old and sickly, the other young and virulent—but what united the two men was their open-minded appreciation of the useful role of piratical-based commerce in the Americas and their wariness towards the excessive powers of the British Crown in distant London. After a moment, Knight looked intently at the heavily bearded pirate captain and, with a look of weary concern, said, "Now how can I help ye, Edward my friend?"

Exhausted from being in a boat for the past eighteen hours and suppressing the urge to yawn, Thache took a moment to gather his thoughts. Though he and Knight had developed a rapport in July, they were not yet bosom friends and he still felt he had to tread somewhat cautiously with the man.

"I have a serious problem on my hands, and I do not know what the best solution is to deal with it. Against my wishes, my crew—with me acting as captain—has committed an act of piracy and taken a French prize. Our actions most certainly will not be excused by King George's most gracious pardon. I want to know if there is a way we can legitimize the French prize such that we might still be able to be protected under the King's pardon."

"So that's what this be about? Well then, you must start from the beginning and recount your movements since you last visited us here in Bath in July. Where did you go?"

"To Philadelphia."

"You sailed to the City of Brotherly Love when you were supposed to set a compass for the West Indies? Why did you sail to Philadelphia?"

"So that I could see my Margaret and we could sign on some additional crew members for the voyage south."

"Margaret, is she your wife?"

"No, but I'd like her to be one day. Once I've obtained a privateering commission in St. Thomas and cleaned the slate once and for all."

"Did you obtain any new crew members in the city?"

"No, we had to leave too quickly. Governor Keith had issued a warrant for my arrest. That's when everything went to hell."

"What do you mean?"

"My crew nearly held a mutiny. They demanded we look for a prize, far out in the ocean where no one would know about it, in order to repair and resupply the *Adventure*. East of Bermuda we found her."

"So that's when you took the French vessel? What cargo was she carrying?"

"She was a small brigantine loaded with cocoa, sugar, and a few French delicacies. I have brought with me several gifts for you, including casks of sweetmeats."

"We can talk about appropriate payment for my expert counsel later in the evening. For now, I want to make sure I have all the facts. Tell me about the action at sea. How was it accomplished?"

He quickly described the incident with the French, beginning with the spying of the two sails on the horizon, and ending with the send-off of the vanquished crew of both vessels in the empty *Toison d'Or* and keeping the *Rose Emelye* as a prize. When he was finished, the lawyerly Knight probed him with more questions, which Thache answered before posing a question of his own.

"Would it be possible for me and my men to claim that we found the French ship abandoned at sea? In other words, could I proclaim the *Rose Emelye* as a derelict?"

Knight stood up and began pacing the room, thinking. Bookishly bespectacled, gaunt in his baggy bedclothes, and reeking of musty air and illness from his ongoing losing battle with the fever, the North Carolina official provided a striking contrast to the tall, robust, and healthy Blackbeard, dressed in calf-length boots, tarred-dungarees, and muslin blouse and wearing a long, braided beard that carried the salubrious scent of the sea.

"Yes, you could claim that you found the French ship at sea without a soul on board her. In legal terms, this would make the vessel 'unmanned and abandoned on the high seas.' By Admiralty law, this would make you the salvor in her possession, giving you the legal right to both the vessel and cargo."

"The French would no doubt see it differently."

"Yes, but if the second French ship continued on its way to Europe, it could be months or even years before an inquiry would find its way back to North Carolina. Furthermore, if no one knew the prize was brought to Ocracoke, the French would never be able to trace its whereabouts."

"So what you're saying is, if no suspicions are raised, then I could successfully claim I found the *Rose Emelye* abandoned at sea. I could claim that the vessel's

French crew may have been washed overboard in a storm."

"It will be tricky but it should work. Governor Eden is the official senior representative of the British Admiralty in North Carolina. He could request that I form a Court of Vice-Admiralty to formally hear your claim to the rights of salvage. Once that is completed, he would call another meeting of the court to determine ownership and conclude that the ship and its cargo belong to you."

"But I would have to prove my story."

"Ye will need several witnesses on hand in addition to yourself to tell the story of what happened and sign affidavits. Provided the French are out of the picture entirely and unable to make a claim, the governor will have no option but to grant you salvage rights over the French ship. It goes without saying that the stories of you and your crew members should be consistent with one another. You don't want any surprises."

"So if everything went according to plan, the court would, after serious consideration of all the facts in the case, adjudicate the prize."

"Yes, but remember that the physical ship would then be in evidence. Its rightful French owners, if they were ever located and made aware of your salvage case, could cause problems. That's why after the court has rendered its decision in your favor, you should claim that the ship is leaky and in danger of foundering in the inlet."

"Making it a hazard to navigation."

"Precisely. The governor would then issue you legal instructions to tow the brigantine to a place out of the channel and burn it to the waterline."

"Thereby destroying the evidence of piracy."

"Yes."

Again, Thache was so exhausted from his journey that he had to suppress a yawn. But his physical exhaustion couldn't conceal the fact that he was quite pleased with the discussion thus far. He had expected Knight to be helpful and sympathetic, but not *this* helpful and sympathetic. The man was, quite clearly, a brilliant legal mind, and Thache had no doubt he would make a most formidable advocate or opponent in a courtroom.

"And how are ye and the governor to be properly compensated for your expert legal advice in this matter and to offset your court costs?"

"By law the Court of the Vice-Admiralty typically claims a fraction of the cargo, usually a fifth, to offset administrative costs. In this case, the tariff would be paid to the governor as the representative of the government. A percentage of the cargo payable in the casks of sugar ye took from the *Rose Emelye* would suffice."

"What about you? I would like to make sure that you are properly compensated for your expert services."

"Officially, His Majesty's Customs does not require a payment. But as this is a case of salvage, a voluntary payment to me in the form of sugar would certainly not be refused for my expert counsel."

"I can deliver sixty barrels of sugar and cocoa to Governor Eden's plantation house, and a further twenty barrels here to your home on your behalf."

"That sounds like a most reasonable payment for the services rendered by the court. But as you and I well know, even though the governor and I would fully be within our legal rights to handle the matter in this way, the perception of the citizens of North Carolina, specifically our political enemies among the wealthy planters and traders, would be that we both personally profited from your piratical activities and were now the unlawful owners of stolen property. I would also further presume that the rest of your French cargo would be sold in Bath Town, and the profits divided amongst you and your crew. After all, gentlemen of fortune have need of money as much as the next man."

"Aye, we would like to receive money for the remainder of our cargo. We need to purchase additional provisions for our journey south."

"Yes, of course."

"So what is the next step?"

"You should return posthaste to Ocracoke and make your final preparations to set sail for the West Indies. Then you should return to Bath in ten days' time and report your finding of the derelict ship to Governor Eden. He will then convene the Court of Vice-Admiralty to formally hear your claim to the rights of salvage and then award you the ship and its cargo. But to pull this off, it is imperative to maintain absolute secrecy and not let anyone know what we have planned here tonight. I cannot stress this enough."

"I will make sure to keep my men quiet."

"You must have the complete cooperation and confidence of your crew. Otherwise, the plan will fail and we may all be convicted and hanged for piracy. But most importantly, no one can know that you and I met here tonight. If this meeting is discovered, there is nothing that can be done for any of us."

"I'll make sure to keep lay low here and in Ocracoke. I understand what is at stake."

They continued to work out the details of their strategy until 04:20 hours, when they had both reached the point of physical exhaustion. Knight then briefly examined the casks of sweetmeats and the valuable gifts of Spanish pieces of eight, encrusted jewelry, silver candlesticks, and gold dust in the heavy boxes Thache had brought along with him and not told anyone else about. The two men then said their goodbyes. At the last minute, Knight returned one of the kegs of sweetmeats so that the captain and his men would have sufficient food for their long voyage back to Ocracoke. As a weary and yawning Blackbeard walked towards the sloping path leading down to the landing and his African crew secured the cask of sweetmeats, the older man expelled a sickly cough and called out to him from the steps of the house.

"Don't worry yourself, Edward. As long as you and your men maintain absolute secrecy and cause no more mischief, everything will be fine."

The pirate captain tipped his tricorn to him and bid him good night. "We shall keep quiet as mice and all will be well," he said.

But inside, he was deeply worried about his future and that of his men. Taking the *Rose Emelye* had been a bad decision that he knew would cost them dearly.

CHAPTER 51

TOWN CREEK

SEPTEMBER 14, 1718

THREE TIMES HIS HEAD ROLLED FORWARD and he nodded off for a few minutes as they headed downriver. When he awoke the third time just before dawn, he spotted the pale gleam of a lantern rocking gently from the mast of another periauger moored near Chester's Landing. They were several miles from Knight's home along the northern shore, and he ordered his oarsmen to row in the direction of the light. He was hoping to go ashore at Chester's house and rest for a while since he was unable to stay awake. By this time, he had not slept for more than twenty-four hours since leaving Ocracoke the day before, and he hoped to catch three or four hours rest and resume sailing for Pamlico Sound by around eight o'clock in the morning when he was fresh. His men, too, would get a chance to rest.

But as they rowed near the other periauger, he abruptly changed his mind about landing at Chester's house and ordered his oarsmen to come up alongside the other boat. "Come up close now, lads, and we'll get ourselves a dram and then be on our way. We'll not stop to rest at Chester's."

They rowed towards the vessel. In the lantern light, Thache saw that it contained a young white man in colonial dress, a young boy who looked to be the man's son, and an Indian.

"Good evening, gentlemen," he said affably. "I'm sorry if I have surprised you, but I wonder if you might have a dram of brandy or other spirits aboard that you could offer a weary traveler."

"I have a barrel of brandy, but it is too dark for me to draw from it for strangers I do not know," the tall white man responded insolently. "Who are ye and from whence have you come?"

"I should ask you who you might be, considering you have an Indian in your company and this precinct has been under threat of Indian attack for some time now."

"I am William Bell and this is my son."

"Mr. Bell, I am pleased to make your acquaintance."

But his polite tone didn't seem to have the desired effect: the man was looking at him skeptically, probably on account of his long plaited beard, an uncommon thing in these parts. "I know the local sheriff and my father is a wealthy landholder from Hyde Precinct with holdings here in Bath, so you had better not engage in skullduggery. Who are you, sir, that floats up and down this river in the dark of night with four Negro oarsmen? I saw you earlier heading towards town and wondered what your business was here. Now I would appreciate it if you would tell me."

"It is no affair of yours, of that I am certain. Now are you going to give me a dram of brandy from that barrel of yours or not?"

"I would say that the answer is no, seeing that you appear to be a scoundrel."

Thache couldn't believe the insolence of the man. All he was asking for was some brandy for his long journey and now he was being subjected to an inquisition. In his already exhausted and fragile state, he felt a sudden burst of rage at William Bell's rudeness.

Acting on impulse, he jumped aboard the man's periauger.

"What are you doing, you scoundrel? You can't come aboard my vessel!"

"Like hell I can't! Now hand over that brandy, you scupperlout!"

"I told you, it's too dark for me to draw from my barrel!"

"Ye should be kindlier to strangers on the river, you cowardly whelp." He then called out to his men. "Mr. Stiles, my cutlass if you please. I need to teach this insolent man a lesson in proper manners in front of his son."

The black crewman handed the long, curved, steel-bladed instrument of war and piratical intimidation to him. Thache took it and waved it angrily at William Bell, while his four black oarsmen, the Indian, and Bell's son just stood there in shock, unable to believe their eyes.

"Now, Mr. Bell, place your arms behind your back so I can bind your hands."

"No, sir, I shall do nothing of the sort. I demand to know who you are and from whence you came?"

"I come from hell where I will carry you presently if you don't do as I say."

"You're a smuggler or a thief and I don't barter with smugglers or thieves."

"Perhaps I am a thief. If that is the case, where have you hidden your money?"

"I will not tell you a bloody thing, you scoundrel!"

Thache tried to control his anger, but was unable to. This William Bell—imperious son of a prominent Hyde and Bath landowner—irked him beyond all reason. "I swear damnation will seize you and I will kill you if you do not cooperate."

"Who are you and what is your business in Bath Town?"

"As I said, that's none of your business." He then shoved him, hard enough to pitch him onto the floor of the periauger, but to his surprise Bell didn't fall down. Instead, he gave the pirate captain a firm elbow to the ribs followed by a hard shove in return, nearly knocking him out of the boat. But Thache was able to recover his balance and, with the flat side of his cutlass, he struck Bell several blows across his arms and shoulders, frightening him and his companions with the dull implement rather than doing any damage. On the last blow, he was stunned to see that his blade broke on the impact and fell onto the soggy wooden planks of Bell's periauger.

"Well don't just stand there, Mr. Stiles!" he snapped to his senior oarsman. "You and your men, come to my aid, damn you!"

Stiles immediately jumped aboard the longboat along with Thomas Gates, James Blake, and James White. The four black sailors quickly restrained William Bell and the dumbstruck Indian and boy.

"Now what else have you got on board?" asked Thache, still beside himself with anger.

Bell resisted.

"Tell me, damn you!"

"All right, just don't harm me or my son! I have pistols and other valuables locked in that chest there!" He motioned meekly towards the chest stowed in the stern of the boat.

Thache motioned his men. "Break it open," he commanded.

"Please!" pleaded Bell. "You don't need to do that! I'll open it!"

"Be sharp about it then."

Finally realizing what he was up against, William Bell withdrew a key, quickly unlocked the chest, and pulled out the contents along with the other valuables stored on board the periauger. From the chest and the cargo of the boat, Thache and his men swiftly plundered nearly seventy pounds in North Carolina scrip, sixty yards of crepe fabric, a box of tobacco pipes, a half barrel of brandy, and a fine silver drinking cup. When they were finished, they towed William Bell's periauger out into the middle of the river and dumped his sails and oars overboard to allow themselves plenty of time to make their getaway before Bell could report the robbery to the authorities.

"Whoever ye be, you are a most villainous creature," snarled Bell as Thache and his seamen made their boat ready again to head downriver. "I'm going to go straight to Governor Eden in Bath and report this assault. A detailed report will be filed and the precinct's marshal will be alerted. And he will hunt you down and you will go to jail. Then, sir, I will know your name."

"Maybe, but you could have avoided all this misery if you had simply given a tired man a dram of brandy. I may be a thief as you say, but you, William Bell, are an insolent fool without proper manners. And for that, I blame your father and mother for not teaching you the ways of the world. Furthermore, I pity your poor son to be stuck with you as a father. Now, sir, I bid you good night."

And with that, he sailed off with his four oarsmen towards the rising red orb of the sun and Ocracoke Island, knowing that he had made his situation immeasurably worse by putting into jeopardy Tobias Knight's plan to keep their meeting a secret.

What a foolish thing you have done, Edward, he scolded himself. *What a foolish thing you have done indeed.*

CHAPTER 52

RALEIGH TAVERN
WILLIAMSBURG

SEPTEMBER 15, 1718

AS SPOTSWOOD was escorted by the maître'd into the Raleigh Tavern's half-filled Apollo Room, he found himself impressed by the establishment's simple elegance. Painted in gilt above the mantel at the entrance was the motto *"Hilaritas Sapientiae et Bonae Vitae Proles"*—"Jollity, the Offspring of Wisdom and Good Living." The dining room boasted hand-crafted oak tables, chairs, and sideboards sporting tassels, fringes, and trimmed in silk and gilded leaf; ornate wooden carvings; maroon velvet flocked wallpaper; and various polished brass antiquities lovingly imported from England. The walls were covered with handsome English oak paneling and ornately carved wooden Shakespearian caricatures. Baronial brass chandeliers hung down from the ceiling like a giant latticework of ice crystals. A spectacular limestone fireplace and mantelpiece, a grand piano, and several potted plants indigenous to Virginia rounded out the room.

Established only the year before, the tavern was named after its founder, Sir Walter Raleigh, and used for a variety of colonial functions. It was the site of slave auctions, was used to sell theater tickets and merchandise, and increasingly played host to balls, wedding parties, and other social events. The maître'd led him to his table, where his guest, Captain Ellis Brand of the HMS *Lyme*, was waiting for him. Smartly dressed in his naval uniform, his lengthy sword stuffed into its leather scabbard, Brand rose from his curved, velvet-backed seat with a smile and extended a hand.

"I apologize for my tardiness, Captain," said Spotswood, who took pride in his punctuality and attention to detail. "To my chagrin, I became embroiled in a fruitless argument with one of my unruly councilmen, a certain Mr. Ludwell. Trust me, I would much rather have been here."

"It's all right, Governor. I only arrived a few minutes before you."

"Good, that makes me feel better." He took his seat, briefly looked over the handheld chalkboard menu at the table, and then launched into the purpose of their meeting. "So, I understand you have important news for me."

"Aye, I do. Have you heard the name William Howard?"

Spotswood searched his brain. "No, I can't say I have. Should I know him?"

"He's a pirate of some infamy who has sailed on and off for the past two years with Blackbeard, serving as his quartermaster."

"What has this William Howard done to draw your attention?"

"For the past two and a half weeks, he's been hanging about the taverns and ordinaries of Norfolk and Kiquotan, as well as the fledgling settlements along the Nansemond River. He's been getting sloppy drunk night after night and enjoying the life of a retired gentleman of fortune. My sources tell me that he has a loose tongue and likes to boast of his adventures on the high seas under the notorious Blackbeard, particularly when he's deep into his cups. He's admitted to having plundered several vessels off our coasts last fall, as well as to the blockade of Charles Town and seizure of two more ships south of the Cape Fear River this past May."

"So what you're telling me is he's clearly violated His Majesty's most gracious pardon since he's taken part in piratical actions after January 5 of this year."

"Precisely," said Brand, glancing at the small chalkboard menu. "William Howard poses a clear and present danger to this colony."

"Are you suggesting that I have him arrested?"

"I leave that up to you, Governor. But know this: he's violated the terms of the pardon and failed to register with the local authorities, which as a former pirate he is required to do by your July 10 proclamation. But at the same time, it appears he's received a royal pardon from North Carolina's governor. He produced a piece of parchment verifying it in Kiquotan."

They paused for a moment as a waiter appeared at their table and asked them what they wanted for dinner. Spotswood opted for codfish dumplings smothered in oyster sauce, served with scraped horse-radish, sweet corn, cabbage, and Apple Tansey, while Brand went for halibut and oyster stew, egg soufflé, and small fried mackerel with sliced lemon and coarse salt. For drinks, they each ordered tankards of Boston ale. The waiter indicated his approval of their choices and shuffled off.

"The important thing is that he has not only been on a drinking binge for the past two weeks, but he has gotten into trouble for being drunk and disorderly on several occasions."

"Is there any indication that he intends to return to his evil ways and is actually recruiting seamen to join him?"

"As a matter of fact, there is. It is said that he has been trying to debauch sailors at every establishment within which he hath set foot. He regales them with stories of the *Queen Anne's Revenge* that was wrecked at Old Topsail Inlet and another ship called the *Revenge*. It is said that he desires to form a company of pirates and run away with some vessel, and so to pirate again."

"It would appear that Mr. Howard does not intend to remain retired for very long. Is he with anyone else?"

"Just two slaves, whom he has admitted he took as prizes from captured ships."

"Really? Now that is interesting. As to his money, does he seem to have acquired quite a bit from his piratical activities?"

"Aye, it would seem so. He's throwing around a lot of coin and gold dust. As quartermaster, he would have earned almost as much as Thache."

"Well then, based on what you've told me, I see no choice but to have him arrested and his possessions seized on the basis of his disorderly conduct and debauching the minds of local sailors. I'll get the justice of the peace to make out a warrant for his arrest this afternoon and the sheriff and his constables can make the arrest tomorrow."

The waiter delivered their tankards of ale. They paused a moment to guzzle their drinks and belch loudly before resuming the conversation.

"What do you ultimately hope to garner from his imprisonment?" asked Brand.

"I believe you know the answer to that, Captain. We want to send a message."

"A message?"

"A message that pirates are unwelcome here in Virginia. Which is why, once Quartermaster Howard is arrested, I am going to indict him for numerous acts of piracy and try him without a jury before a Vice-Admiralty Court right here in Williamsburg. And when we are finished with him, he will be found guilty and sentenced to hang from the neck until dead."

"The testimony against Mr. Howard will be most pertinent and useful for his captain, Edward Thache, I would imagine as well."

"Yes, I can see you are on the sharp end of this situation, Captain Brand."

"That's why I am here, Governor. Consider me your most obedient servant in this matter. I want to get these murderous brigands—they make a mockery of everything civilization stands for."

"I agree. The Admiralty calls them the villains of all nations and I believe the definition is quite apt. But unfortunately, the pirates themselves and their many colonial supporters don't see them that way. They see them as patriots, as rebels against Great Britain with the ultimate aim of achieving independence. But, in the end, they will be known only as greedy scoundrels who belonged to no country."

"Victors write the history, Governor, and in the present situation the victors will be you and I."

"Mr. Howard's biggest mistake has been believing that Governor Eden's pardon will protect him."

"That is why he has been so braggartly about his piratical activities of the past year."

"Quite, quite. His loose tongue will be his—and Blackbeard's—undoing. This is my opportunity to hold a show trial and make an example of Howard that will send a signal to all former pirates in the American colonies. He will be duly arrested as a vagrant seaman, his slaves and money will be confiscated, he will be tried and found guilty of piracy, and he will be executed. Then we will do the same with the mighty Blackbeard for all the devilment he has brought the Crown. Once he hangs, few of these so-called gentlemen of fortune will dare tread in our territorial waters and we will be rid of the miscreants once and for all."

"That sounds like a bold plan, Governor. Please don't hesitate to call upon me if I can be of further service in the apprehension or imprisonment of either of these rogues."

"Don't worry, I shall be calling on you soon enough. On that you have my word, Captain," said Spotswood with a knowing smile.

Five minutes later, he smiled again as the waiter brought his codfish dumplings smothered in oyster sauce, his Apple Tansey, and Brand's aromatic seafood stew.

CHAPTER 53

CAPE FEAR RIVER, NORTH CAROLINA

SEPTEMBER 27, 1718

"THE TWO VESSELS are heavily armed sloops with sixteen guns total and more than a hundred men. They laid in anchor during the night guarding the river entrance and fly the King's colors," said Ignatius Pell, bosun of Stede Bonnet's *Royal James*, which he had renamed from the *Revenge* in honor of James III living in exile.

Bonnet looked at him a moment, then at his pugnacious and charismatic quartermaster Robert Tucker, not wanting to believe the disconcerting news. With only one vessel, ten guns, and a crew of forty-five men, he was outclassed, outgunned, and outmanned. The pirates had observed the two motionless masts less than a mile downriver and believed them to be wayward merchant vessels that would make easy prizes; but now that Pell and his men had returned from their reconnaissance in their three canoes, Bonnet knew better. The vessels were well-armed British sloops-of-war, and instead of being grounded on the outer bar, they were anchored for the night and ominously waiting for the pirates at the mouth of the Cape Fear River. He knew his only chance was to slip past or fight them off on the morning's rising tide.

"Very well then," said Bonnet. "Mr. Pell and Mr. Tucker, make preparations to clear the decks, ready the guns, and do battle in the inevitable fight that we have coming at dawn. If these interlopers think we will surrender without fierce resistance, they are dead wrong."

"Aye Captain, we'll be ready," said Pell.

In preparation for battle, they transferred all arms and prisoners to the *Royal James* and abandoned the other two ships in the pirate flotilla, the *Francis* and *Fortune*. After capturing more than a dozen prizes between the Virginia Capes and New Jersey in July and August, Bonnet had finally convinced his unruly crew to take a break from plundering to careen the hull of the *Royal James* in the seclusion of the Cape Fear River. The careening operation had begun in mid-August and was taking longer than expected due to the leakiness of the vessel, which had required extensive new planking from a stripped boat. With the abundance of plundered provisions now aboard the *Royal James*, the pirates had decided to remain in the safety of Cape Fear until the end of the height of hurricane season at the beginning of October. Then they would take safe passage south to St. Thomas and begin their new lives as legally-sanctioned privateers.

Unfortunately, with the spotting of the King's vessels at the mouth of the river, the first of October had proven a few days too long to linger at Cape Fear. Unbeknownst to Bonnet and his crew, Governor Johnson of South Carolina had finally responded to the public clamor to take action against piracy and had hired veteran sailor and soldier Colonel William Rhett to mount an expedition to North Carolina to capture or kill the pirates continuing to pose a threat to his beleaguered city. The cantankerous Rhett had previously proved his valor in defending his colony against the outside threats posed by northward-probing France and Spain during Queen Anne's War. Intelligence from Rhett's sources revealed that a pirate ship was careening with two prizes near the mouth of the Cape Fear River.

To engage the pirates, Rhett had at his disposal the sloop *Henry* with eight cannons, commanded by Captain John Masters, which would serve as his flagship, and the *Sea Nymph* with eight cannons, captained by Fayrer Hall. He set sail from Rhett's Wharf in Charles Town in mid-September with a combined force of one hundred thirty men on the two sloops-of-war—and now he had found his quarry. There was just one problem: he believed he had in his gunsights not Stede Bonnet but Charles Vane, who had recently been terrorizing Charles Town.

The pirates spent a sleepless night making preparations for the coming fight. The opposing sides could hear the sounds of each other's feverish clearing, prepping, and stacking resonating over the surface of the river. But it was Bonnet who seized the early initiative by setting sail first. He got the *Royal James* under way in the predawn darkness, and as the sun rose they were already heading into the main channel, straight for the two enemy sloops. He liked his chances. Though he had only forty-five men under his command and was outnumbered, his men were armed to the teeth with multiple pistols for each man and the *Royal James's* ten guns were primed, double-shotted, and absolutely lethal. The sailors on both sides had slept by their posts, their guns loaded and ready, but it was Bonnet who got the early jump, taking advantage of the ebbing tide and making a run for the open ocean. His plan was to race past the two sloops with guns blazing, forcing his way past the pirate hunters and to the sea. He knew his only hope was to avoid being boarded and engage in a running fight until the *Royal James* could clear the mouth of the Cape Fear River.

Peering through his spyglass from the quarterdeck, he saw that the two unknown sloops flying British colors—which he would only later learn were the *Henry* and *Sea Nymph* under the command of Charles Town's hero and defender Colonel William Rhett—were heading towards him, hoping to board. He gave the order to raise the Jolly Roger and give battle. Minutes later, as the vessels jockeyed for position and the early morning sun crept over the surface of the Atlantic, it quickly became apparent that the closer of the two vessels—the *Henry*—would intercept him and his men and they would not be able to make it safely to the open sea. The King's men had effectively blocked his escape route. He had hoped to surprise the enemy in a running engagement, but his opponent had foiled the plan and appeared to be preparing to sail his sloops upriver towards the *Royal James*, where he would pin her between his ships and then board her.

"Mr. Ross, prepare your port guns to fire!" Bonnet shouted to his master gunner, George Ross.

"Aye, Captain!"

Next he gave an order to his quartermaster. "Mr. Tucker, prepare to defend against boarding!"

All he received in return was an insubordinate grunt, but he knew the order would be carried out. He and Tucker seldom saw eye to eye, but they were least in conflict when taking a prize or in the heat of battle.

As the lead boat, the *Henry*, bore down on them, the *Royal James* was forced to maneuver precariously close to the river's western shore. Waiting in reserve behind the *Henry*, the *Sea Nymph* sailed further downriver in case the pirates were able to slip past the *Henry*.

"Port cannons, open fire!" commanded Bonnet to Ross.

It was then, in the blink of an eye, that everything went to hell. Bonnet was looking defiantly across at the enemy captain wearing a feathered tricorn hat and auburn military uniform when he and a dozen of his men were suddenly and violently thrown forward onto the deck.

"Son of a sea hag, we've run aground!" cried Tucker.

"To quarters! To quarters!" cried Bonnet. "We're going to have to make a fight of it!"

"Wait a minute—look over there!" said Ignatius Pell, pointing. "They've run aground too!"

Bonnet scanned the sea. Unable to take in sail so quickly, the enemy sloops had shot past him and indeed run aground, but not in the position their British commodore would have chosen. The *Henry* had drawn within two hundred feet of the *Royal James* before she, too, grounded on the same shoal. Further downstream and on the outer edge of musket range, the *Sea Nymph* joined the other two vessels and ran hard aground. At least now, thought Bonnet, it would be impossible for his attackers to fire broadsides at him from two directions.

"Open fire with pistols and muskets! Fire at will!" commanded Bonnet once he realized their situation.

The *Royal James* and *Henry* immediately began to exchange small arms fire. Bonnet knew that none of the three sloops would be able to move until the flood tide lifted them clear; then the first vessel to break free of the bottom would be able to slip across the bows of her wallowing opponent and rake her with a full broadside. He could only keep his fingers crossed.

For several minutes, the two sides fired upon one another with no advantage to Bonnet or Rhett. And then luck fell in favor of the gentleman pirate. The three vessels listed dangerously on their sides due to the grounding, but in the falling tide Bonnet and his men soon gained the advantage over their adversaries. Sailing downstream, the *Royal James* had grounded on the starboard side of the channel, and heeled over to starboard. The other two sloops heeled to port, but they faced upstream. This meant that while the hull of the *Royal James* acted as a bulwark protecting the men behind it, the sloping decks of the *Henry* and the *Sea Nymph* lay fully exposed to the enemy. With the *Royal James's* deck inclined away from the *Henry*, the pirates were able to take cover behind the railing, while the deck of the *Henry* was fully exposed to the *Royal James*, and the pirates poured deadly shot into the King's men. As both sides began peppering their opponents with small-arms fire, it was Rhett and his men who received the worst of the exchange. However, the cannons proved useless to both sides. The cannons of the *Royal James* and *Henry* were neutralized as neither Bonnet or Rhett could bring their guns to bear from their tilted decks. The *Henry's* gunners were unable to position their cannons high enough, and the pirates could not range their cannons low enough to accurately and effectively blast the enemy.

Throughout the battle, Bonnet restlessly paced the deck, bravely exhorting his men and threatening to shoot anyone who tried to quit. In between the musket volleys, ugly taunts were exchanged by both sides. The Jacobite pirates lodged insults against King George, and in return, the crew of the *Henry* mocked James III, referring to him as the "Pretender." Those who dared to poke their heads above the cover of bulwarks were mowed down. Despite his current advantage, Bonnet was only too aware that the battle's victor would be the first vessel able to refloat. The pirate ship continued to list to port as the tide continued to fall, providing cover for the freebooters to shoot from behind the starboard rail. Meanwhile, Rhett's *Henry* continued to list towards the *Royal James*, exposing the colonel's squadron on deck to lethal gunfire from the pirates.

During the engagement, Bonnet noticed a seaman named Thomas Nichols across the deck, cowering and refusing to fight. Having only recently joined the *Royal James*, Nichols had found the pirate life not to his liking and had refused to sign the articles, which had angered Bonnet and the other crew members.

With a pistol in one hand and cutlass raised in the other, Bonnet called out to him: "Fight, godamn ye, or I'll blow your fucking brains out!"

"But I...I can't."

"I said engage the enemy, Mr. Nichols, or I will shoot you down like a mangy dog! Now man your station with your mates!"

"But I don't want to be here!"

With blood boiling in his veins, Bonnet carefully made his way over to Nichols, bullets ricocheting and pinging all around him. Stepping up to him, he raised his pistol and pointed it at the terrified seaman's head.

"No, please don't kill me! I just can't do it! I'm not cut out for pirating!"

"Fight, I tell you, or I'll fly your bloody head as my banner!"

He covered his face with his hands. "No, no, please!"

Bonnet waved his pistol menacingly at him. "You have let your shipmates down and for that you must pay the ultimate price!"

"No, please, I beg your mercy!"

Bonnet leveled his pistol at his face. But as he started to squeeze the trigger, a shot rang out. Turning in the direction of the shot, he saw the musketeer standing next to him get struck in the head by a bullet. In the next instant, Bonnet was covered in a spray of blood, bone, and tissue. The seaman, a favorite of the gentleman pirate's, toppled over dead onto the deck. As Bonnet wiped away the blood and brain matter from his face, he came under a galling fire from the *Henry* and retreated back to the quarterdeck, while Nichols scurried to safety down into the hold.

The battle was waged with spurts of violence followed by lulls for nearly six hours as both ships anxiously waited for the next high tide. During the contest, the pirates flew the red flag of defiance, and at one point tied a strand of line around its center, making a "wiff," and hoisted it back up, calling for the pirate hunters to come board them. A wiff in a flag was the common signal for a pilot to come aboard, and thus the pirates were humorously daring the pirate hunters to make a suicidal attempt to board them. But Rhett and his pirate hunters were undaunted, shouting "Huzzah!" in resolute reply and letting the pirates know that "it would soon be their turn." The British were right. When the tide finally turned, the fortunes did too, and it was the

Henry that floated free first. A great cheer rose up from the men on board as the battered sloop eased off the river bottom, sailed out of range, and the British sailors began to make quick repairs to the ship's rigging.

"Damn them for villains!" snarled Bonnet. "Mr. Pell, get us off this sand bar! We should have been the ones to break free first!"

"There's nothing that can be done," replied the sailing master. "We've already tried to pull her off with the longboats!"

"Damnit man, we're sitting ducks! If we can't get off this bar, then we shall have to fight to the last man!"

Bonnet couldn't believe his bad luck yet again. He had inflicted heavy casualties on his immobilized enemy for nearly six hours, but the rising tide had lifted his enemy free first. Still grounded and facing the *Henry's* cannon, he knew his situation had gone from bad to downright bleak. But he would rather fight to the death than surrender and suffer the humiliation of being tried and hung as a pirate. No, there would be no macabre dance of death for him!

"Great scot, she's coming for us!" cried Tucker.

"She be hellbound on our prow!" echoed master gunner George Ross.

Bonnet and the rest of the crew stood there with mouths agape as Colonel William Rhett and his *Henry* sailed towards the pirates to board their vessel and finish them off. The *Sea Nymph* was soon also free, and both sloops-of-war began to bear down on the still grounded *Royal James*.

"We're outgunned and have no choice but to surrender," said Pell. "We've killed and wounded quite a bundle, but there's just too damned many of them."

Bonnet shook his head in disgust. "We are not going to submit, damn you!" He turned to his master gunner. "Mr. Ross, prepare to light a fuse to ignite the ship's powder magazine. I would rather send each and every one of us to the river bottom than submit to King George!"

"You can't blow us up!" protested Pell. "We might very well be acquitted in a courtroom! After all, we have been granted the King's pardon!"

"Avast, Mr. Pell, or I'll shoot you down myself!" He drew out his two pistols and pointed them at him. "Listen to me, you men!" he yelled to the thirty or more men presently on deck. "I will shoot any man that stands against me! Do you understand me? I will shoot them down like a scurvy dog!"

But he was met with protest not only by Pell, but more than two dozen seamen, who began pointing their guns at him and shouting him down. With the blood pumping through his veins, Bonnet yelled back at them that they were cowards and that he would rather blow himself and his crew to kingdom come than surrender to the enemy. Back and forth the two sides argued as Rhett's men once again opened fire with muskets and pistols from the *Henry* and repositioned their cannons to accurately fire. Bonnet and his men, deeply embroiled in argument, were forced to duck down to avoid being hit.

"Now that they've broken free," pointed out Tucker, "they can open up on us with partridge, case, and burrel shot—or hit us with a broadside or two. I agree with the majority that the game is up. We've seen enough bloodshed for one day and must take our chances in a courtroom rather than face certain death. They be too many and we're outgunned to boot. So I say we surrender with honor!"

"There's no honor in surrendering, you bastard!" protested Bonnet. "They're just going to hang us all as pirates if we surrender! All you're doing is delaying the hangman!"

"Well then, so be it!" said Ignatius Pell to a rumble of concurrence from the bulk of the crew. "It's obviously what the men want. You know the rules, Captain: one man, one bloody vote!"

Before Bonnet could utter a further word of protest, one of the crew members—no doubt exhausted by the six-hour battle—ran a white flag of truce up the mainmast.

Bonnet shook his head in disgust, but knew he was powerless to persuade the crew to stand behind him. His authority had long ceased to carry any weight.

"Very well then. If this is the way you want it." Feeling bitterly defeated, he reached for his speaking trumpet and called out to the approaching *Henry*.

"Stay where you are and stop firing!" he called out to the vessel. "I'm sending a flag of truce aboard you!"

Five minutes later, he, Pell, Tucker, and a handful of his senior crew members had rowed over to the *Henry*. They were received by four dozen armed men led by a middle-aged, scruffy-faced adventurer wearing a brown-dyed wool military jacket and black leather seaman's boots.

"I am Colonel William Rhett," he said, with what Bonnet could see was some irritation. "Am I to understand that you are asking me to surrender when you are still grounded and have no avenue of escape?"

Bonnet stepped forward and bowed formally. "No, sir, I am submitting before you. My name is Captain Stede Bonnet of Barbados." He withdrew his cutlass and handed it over with both hands. "I hereby surrender myself and the crew of my sloop, the *Royal James*, to you in good faith that we will be treated fairly."

Rhett frowned as he took the sword. "Stede Bonnet of Barbados? Why I thought you were Charles Vane. In fact, we all did."

He motioned towards his crew, who gazed upon Bonnet with puzzlement, which made him feel embarrassed. After a moment, smiles came to the faces of the colonel's men and they roared with laughter, as if they had just heard a good joke. Pell and Tucker chuckled along with them, which angered Bonnet further. He vowed to get the last laugh on them one day for their gross insubordination and the disrespect they had shown him these past several months at sea. To do that, he knew he had to find a way to escape from his captors before he was put on trial. It was his only chance to go on and live another day and obtain his revenge on all those who had laughed at him behind his back and directly to his face.

When the laughter subsided, Rhett bowed graciously. "I accept the surrender of you, Captain Bonnet, your ship, and your crew. And since you have fought and surrendered honorably, I promise to plead for mercy for you and your men, even though the battle has cost me dearly."

"Where will you take us?"

"To Charles Town—where you and your men will receive a fair trial."

Stede Bonnet felt his whole body shudder. He stared off at the shimmering Atlantic just beyond the approaching *Sea Nymph*. He had been so close. He had only needed to sail another quarter mile to make it to the safety of the open ocean, where likely nothing would have stood between him and a Danish privateer's commission in St. Thomas. He shook his head in despair. So close—and now all he had to look forward to was a rat-infested cell and the gallows. The governor of South Carolina and Charles Town's merchant class, plantation owners, and other members of the landed aristocracy loyal to the Crown would bring picnic lunches, jeer, and cheer along with barefoot commoners in rags when he and his men were hung from the gallows at White Point. The thought of such a humiliating, un-Christian end made him tremble in his shoes.

Looking back at the *Royal James*, still leaning awkwardly to port, he wanted to cry. The fight that would become known as the *Battle of the Sand Bars* was over and so was his life.

Following the battle, Rhett remained in the Cape Fear River for three more days while the wounded were tended to and repairs were made to the damaged vessels. The *Henry*, *Sea Nymph* and *Royal James*, as well as the pirate prizes *Francis* and *Fortune* and their crews taken captive by Bonnet, set sail together southbound on September 30, arriving in Charles Town on October 3 to the relief of Governor Johnson. The King's men suffered eighteen total killed and twelve wounded in the engagement, with fourteen killed and ten wounded on the *Henry* totaling one-third of her crew, and four killed and two wounded on the *Sea Nymph*, which had been out of range most of the time. Among the pirates, nine men were killed and five were wounded. Rhett took thirty-six prisoners to Charles Town.

Shackled in the *Henry's* hold during the uncomfortable journey, Bonnet cursed his bad luck and wished he could turn back the clock to the time before he chose to become a pirate. What a mess he had made of his life. It seemed unthinkable that he had thrown it all away just to escape from his tyrannical wife, to overcome his melancholy over his son's death, and to experience a taste of adventure on the high seas. But his year-and-a-half long stint as a gentleman of fortune had borne no similarity to the romantic vision that had filled his mind before he had set sail from Bridgetown. He was nothing but a common outlaw, a brigand, and a mediocre seaman. But what pained him most of all was that that if his beloved Allamby had still been alive, the boy would be embarrassed and revolted by the actions of his father.

Embarrassed and revolted in the extreme.

CHAPTER 54

OCRACOKE ISLAND
OUTER BANKS, NORTH CAROLINA

OCTOBER 2, 1718

"NOW THAT, LAD, IS DAMNED FINE COOKING!" exclaimed Blackbeard. "What do you call it?"

Caesar smiled at the captain, delighted that his epicurean creation had caught his fancy. He really wasn't much of a cook; he just knew how to prepare a handful of dishes from his years lending a hand in Colonel Robert Daniel's and Tobias Knight's kitchens during his younger years as a slave. They stood on the west-facing shore of Ocracoke Island, staring out at the vast expanse of Pamlico Sound with a dozen other pirates, a mere stone's throw from the Old Watering Hole long used by the indigenous Indian tribes of the Outer Banks and sea rovers alike. Anchored a hundred yards offshore in the tidal slough was the freshly careened *Adventure*, and spread the length of the crescent-shaped beach was the pirates' base camp and their supplies: sailcloth awnings and tarpaulin ground-cloths; open cook fires bearing an assortment of seafoods and fresh meats; stacks of firewood and driftwood piled here and there; small kegs for stools circled around games of dice or cards; ceramic jugs of wine, rum, and brandy; and stacks of cutlasses, blunderbusses, and muskets, ready for action. The air along the gently lapping shore was infused with the fragrant smells of the sea, wood smoke, pipe tobacco, and Caesar's freshly prepared dinner.

"I call it turtle hash," he said, after taking a bite from his own plate. "I have to admit, it's one of my best."

Thache smiled wryly. "Turtle hash, eh? That's a new one. What are the ingredients, if I may so bold as to inquire from his master chef?"

"Loggerhead turtle, wild onions, potatoes, clam juice, cayenne pepper and red pepper, and a little bit of salt pork."

"It's delicious, I'll say that. What do you say men?"

"It's bloody marvelous!" gushed Garret Gibbons. "Perfect cure for my hangover!"

"Aye, one of the savoriest dishes I've ever had the pleasure to devour, drunk or sober," said the company's quartermaster, Thomas Miller.

"I'm afraid you missed your calling Caesar," said master gunner Philip Morton. "With cooking like this, you could run your own eatery in New York or Boston instead of being a Godforsaken pirate."

"It's not too late. I do have the King's pardon and am a free man of only twenty-three. I have my whole life before me."

"A pirate's life is a short and merry one, but not for old Caesar here!" cried Gibbons. "Why he's going to live to be a hundred, he is!"

They all laughed ribaldly with pelicans and gulls wheeling overhead against a backdrop of blue sky. Thache winked at Caesar as if to say, "Well done, mate!"

"Now you're all probably wondering what the key is to making turtle hash," said Caesar, explaining his culinary craft. "The key is to parboil the loggerhead for a half hour to make it tender. Then you cut the meat off the bone and cook it with onion, potatoes, and salt pork. Near the end, you throw in the cayenne pepper, red pepper, and clam juice with sea salt. And there you have it—turtle hash. The first time I ever tasted it was in Charles Town. But I was a slave then, so I have to say this tastes much better now."

There was a round of good cheer. "I've never tasted anything so good," said Thache. "It's a damned sight better than the worm-infested dried beef, salt pork, and moldy biscuits we keep in the sealed casks below decks, wouldn't you say, lads?"

There were murmurs and nods of agreement all around and then the group returned to eating from their pewter plates with their fine silverware pillaged from a half dozen merchant ships. They had been on Ocracoke for more than a week now, after returning from the Vice-Admiralty Court held in Bath Town on September 24. Tobias Knight's and Thache's master plan had been successful and Governor Eden had lawfully recognized the captain's claim that the French ship was abandoned at sea and was rightfully his to bring into the colony—provided the customary tariffs be paid to the government. Sixty casks of sugar were to be delivered to the governor on behalf of the colony and another twenty casks were to be allotted to Knight as collector of customs. During the court proceeding, Thache also received approval from the governor to beach the French vessel *Rose Emelye* in shallow water nearshore and burn her to her waterline, so that the leaky vessel would not pose a risk to North Carolina shipping. The hearing had been held the week before and now the *Adventure's* company had returned to Ocracoke to begin the transfer of cargo across the sound to Bath. And they were also making preparations to put the torch to the mast-less French ship, although it had not been decided where to send the vessel to her watery grave, or when.

The pirates finished their sumptuous meal. Garret Gibbons then produced a Jew harp and began to play. Soon thereafter, after a round of vigorous belching, they pulled out their red and white clay tobacco pipes and began to sing. The familiar strains of *A-Roving* took to the woodsmoke- and turtle-hash-scented air, followed by *Drunken Sailor* and *Coast of High Barbary*. An hour before dusk, the sky turned from cobalt to salmon pink and a voice called out from the topmast of the *Adventure* anchored offshore.

"Sail! A sail!"

Turning to the south, Caesar spotted a mast several miles in the distance, clearly standing in to the inlet. Unlike the usual small trading vessels bound for Bath Town, this vessel was well armed. An alarm sounded on the ship into the speaking trumpet and Thache ordered everyone on shore to return to the ship at once with their weapons. Once on board, he gave the "All hands to quarters!" command and instructed Israel Hands, Garret Gibbons, Thomas Miller, and Philip Morton to leave their anchor at the mooring, make sail swiftly, and prepare to engage the new interloper since they were unsure if she was friend or foe.

Upon an ebbing tide, the *Adventure* made quick time out of Ocracoke Inlet and jibed towards the approaching vessel, which Caesar could now tell was a brigantine. He tried to recollect if he had seen the ship before, but it was unfamiliar to him. But to his surprise, whoever was in command of the vessel seemed to recognize the *Adventure* because suddenly a Jolly Roger unfurled off the brigantine's backstay and began snapping in the brisk northwesterly breeze.

"Let's show her our colors, mates! Hoist the black flag!" shouted Thache right away in reply, and Caesar saw a gleam in his eyes. Whoever this new interloper was, he was a fellow brethren of the coast and likely posed no threat.

"Who be it, Captain? Do you know?" asked Caesar, acting as his steward on the quarterdeck.

Thache peered through his spyglass. "I'm not sure. It could be Williams, Hornigold, or La Buse. Or maybe someone else. The ship is not one I've laid eyes on before, I know that. But she be one of us, mates."

"What do you want us to do, Captain?" asked Morton.

"Roll back your guns and stand down. The brigantine is heaving to under our cannon."

"Aye, Captain."

Looking at Caesar, Thache scratched at one of the plaits holding together his long black beard. "I'm still wondering who she belongs to. Has anyone seen her before?"

There were nays all around.

"Wait a second! Now just hold onto your trousers! I think it's Charles Vane!" declared Israel Hands, peering through his own glass.

"How do you know?" asked Caesar.

"Because that wild Jacobite from Jamaica is standing on the quarterdeck with the one man in the world who never fails to wear calico."

"By thunder, you're right," cried Thache. "It is Vane, and standing next to him is Calico Jack Rackham himself."

Caesar smiled. He liked Charles Vane's young quartermaster. The members of the Flying Gang in Nassau had dubbed him "Calico Jack" because of the colorful patch work clothing he frequently wore and that seemed to capture the attention of the ladies of New Providence. Caesar could make out the man's multicolored Indian prints clearly even from a distance.

"Aye, that be Calico Jack all right—or I be a lubberly Dutchman," said Philip Morton.

Before Vane's vessel and the *Adventure* came within hailing distance. Vane's crew fired an honorary six-gun salute as was customary during friendly encounters amongst pirate companies. Thache had Morton return a rousing blast from two of his cannon and shouts of huzzah resounded the length of the deck. As the two ships neared, Caesar studied Vane's brigantine. Equipped with twelve guns and manned by some ninety seamen, it was a formidable pirate ship-of-war.

The two vessels sailed through the inlet and anchored next to one another within pistol shot of the Old Watering Hole. Fifteen minutes later, Vane rowed over from his Spanish brig *Ranger* and came aboard the *Adventure* for a visit with several of his officers. He and Thache shook hands and embraced as Vane's men hauled a keg of rum up onto the larboard railing. Then the visiting pirate captain turned to address the crowd.

"Greetings, men," he began. "We are going to have one hell of a party, but first I am sorry to bring bad news. Nassau has fallen to Woodes Rogers, who with a large force has taken over as governor of the Bahamas. The islands no longer belong to us. Since his tenure began in July, he has convinced a great many of our brethren to accept His Majesty's royal grace. But he has done even worse than that. He has hired on Hornigold, Jennings, Cockram, and others to hunt we pirates down like dogs. Aye, I kid you not, they have turned on us and are pirate hunters. Why we were almost taken by Hornigold just a couple of fortnights ago at Green Turtle Cay."

The heads hung low for a moment before the men from both vessels erupted in a string of curses against the King and his pirate hunters. The angry epithets rose up in the dusky night and were carried off on the sea breeze skating across Pamlico Sound. After letting the men vent a moment, Vane continued with his news update.

"I have also just learned that Stede Bonnet, whom you lads previously sailed in consort with, was captured along with forty-five of his men in the Cape Fear River just a few days ago. Apparently, one Colonel Rhett sailed into the mouth of the river, engaged him in battle, and their boats were grounded. Bonnet went out fighting and took many casualties, but he and his men were taken to Charles Town. Governor Johnson of South Carolina is behind the whole thing, as he's the one who commissioned Rhett. Apparently, the bastards thought they were coming after me."

"Well, you're no Stede Bonnet, Charles," said Thache. "We all know that."

"And thankfully so, but he was a proud Jacobite and for that we must still say a prayer for him, and especially for his men who deserved a far better captain than he. The man just seemed to have a knack for meeting the wrong people at the wrong time—and that includes you, Edward, you old scallywag."

The men all laughed, and Vane's officers began passing around the keg of rum. Though Caesar had never had a problem with Charles Vane and considered him a charismatic and entertaining figure, he had heard the unpleasant stories of his cruelty towards his captives as a pirate commander. Unlike his friend Blackbeard—who was falsely built up by the *Boston News-Letter* and British leaflets to be a notorious villain and predator—Vane was the real thing. Caesar had heard many stories and they had been verified by many sources. He was reported to have on several occasions severely beaten and abused captured merchant ship captains and their crew members to very near the point of death. It was also said that he liked to burn the eyes of his victims with matches, hang them upside down, and slash them with knives to get them to disclose where they had hidden their valuables. Caesar knew probably not all the stories were true, but there was a pattern of violence he found disturbing and he would make sure not to cross Charles Vane in any way during his stay here at Ocracoke.

"All right, that's enough talk of sniveling English vermin and the meddling rascals of the Crown," declared Vane. "It's time to get this party started!"

"Oh, is it to be a banyan then?" said Thache with a big smile on his face.

"Aye, a full week of drunken debauchery and the telling of sea tales, one or two of which might even be true."

"A week, is it? Then I hope you have brought plenty of rum."

"It just so happens I have," said Vane gleefully. "So let us drink a toast, gentlemen, to the eternal damnation of King George!"

"Good lord, Charles, is that the only toast you can make?" chided Thache.

"I'm afraid so. So join me, lads: To the damnation of that insufferable fool and bloated carcass of a man who doesn't speak a lick of English, King George! But also to that scupperlout Woodes Rogers!"

The pirates gave a rowdy cheer. "To the damnation of King George and Woodes Rogers!" they cried again and again, raising their Monmouth sailor's caps, tricorns, and wide-brimmed Spanish hats snipped on the sides giddily in the air.

Caesar smiled. They were in for one hell of a banyan.

PART 6

A CONSPIRACY
OF MURDER

CHAPTER 55

GOVERNOR'S PALACE
WILLIAMSBURG

OCTOBER 7, 1718

"WE CAN HELP ONE ANOTHER, GOVERNOR. We both want the same thing and I believe we can help each other get what we want."

Spotswood raised an eyebrow at Edward Moseley, prominent North Carolina landholder and lawyer as well as former speaker of the House of Burgesses and surveyor general. "And what is it, Mr. Moseley, that we both desire?"

"We would both like to see Governor Eden run out of the colonies and an end to this piracy that has befouled our waters. I, Governor, can help us accomplish both."

Here Moseley—who was said by his peers and rivals to have a tongue as smooth as the Commissary—paused to let his oratory resonate. Spotswood took measure of the man. They were seated in the governor's office with early fall sunlight spilling through the diaphanous curtains at the window overlooking the Palace Green. Though he and the paunchy, thirty-six-year-old Moseley were not intimate friends, the North Carolina landowner had close ties to the Virginia government and he and Spotswood had had political dealings with one another regarding the colonial tobacco trade on several prior occasions. The owner of nearly one hundred slaves, Moseley lived in Chowan Precinct, which had a good road leading northward into Virginia's Nansemond County and the ferries that crossed the James River to Williamsburg. As Governor Eden's chief rival in North Carolina, Moseley had been aligned with the Popular Party, a political faction that opposed Tobias Knight, Colonel Thomas Pollack, and other leading gentry of the province who supported the current Eden administration, known as the Proprietors Party. Any opportunity to highlight Eden's liabilities as governor would be capitalized upon by Moseley, whom Spotswood knew had greedy designs on the chief office for himself.

The governor took a ship of his sherry and leaned back in his high-backed leather chair with a relaxed expression on his ruddy face. It was good for once to be in the presence of a supportive political ally rather than being hounded by his scores of enemies. "Please tell me what ye have in mind, Edward."

"Yes, of course," replied Moseley. "But before I do that, I wanted to make you aware of the current situation. I have some useful intelligence for you."

"I am all ears."

"As you are aware, the pirate Edward Thache who goes by the alias Blackbeard has set up a new base of operations on Ocracoke Island and the town of Bath in my colony to the south. He has done so with the approval of Governor Eden and Eden's second-in-command, customs inspector Tobias Knight. Both have benefited financially from Blackbeard taking up residence in North Carolina."

"Ye have proof of this?"

"As a matter of fact, I do. A Vice-Admiralty Court was held in Bath Town a fortnight ago and attended in person by an informant loyal to me. In that hearing, Thache and three of his men serving as eyewitnesses claimed that he recently found a French ship abandoned at sea off the coast of Bermuda. The pirate claimed it was rightfully his to bring into the colony and Governor Eden agreed, provided he pay the appropriate tariff to the government."

"What was the tariff?"

"Sixty casks of sugar were to be delivered to Eden on behalf of the colony, while Knight as collector of customs was allocated twenty casks."

"Are you suggesting that the French ship was not derelict?"

"It is my understanding that it was piratically taken."

"What makes you say that?"

"Because three of Blackbeard's men were injured and required the attention of a surgeon upon their return to Ocracoke. The injuries were brought to light during the testimony. A passenger named Isaac Freeman, who had been passenger aboard a brigantine captured recently near Ocracoke by another pirate named Richard Worley, is the one who related the story. He says Thache brought in the French ship to Ocracoke in September and was busy unrigging and plundering her. He said that no man was allowed to go on board except a doctor to treat his wounded men."

"So you're saying that the French crew resisted the taking of their ship? That's how Blackbeard's men were wounded?"

"That's exactly what I'm saying. Thache maintained that the injuries took place when one of the ship's poorly restrained gun carriages broke free in a heavy sea, pinning his men against the bulwark."

"But you don't believe that."

"Not for a minute. We're talking about pirates here. Vermin. Though the officers of the court, Knight and Eden, seemed satisfied with their petitioner's response, they are driven by greed. Their foremost priority is to line their pockets with silver and gold and encourage trade with pirates to increase commerce in the province."

"What else was said during the proceeding?"

"Thache also claimed that the French ship's hull was leaky. He falsely maintained she was in danger of sinking and blocking the only navigable channel passing betwixt the sound and the sea. He asked the court what he might do with the worthless vessel."

"How did Eden rule?"

"He suggested the pirate captain beach the ship someplace on shore and burn her to her waterline. It was at that point that my informant asked the pirates how a leaky derelict found off Bermuda was able to be sailed by so few men—and fewer to operate the pumps—some seven hundred miles without incident, but which was now in danger of foundering at anchor?"

"How did Thache respond?"

"He had no answer."

Spotswood smiled with stinging amusement. *Of course, he didn't. He's a bloody liar and thief—and I'm going to capture or kill him.*

"Where is Blackbeard now?" he then asked.

"He and his crew have returned to Ocracoke. They are preparing to begin the transfer of cargo across the sound to Bath and to fire the mast-less French ship."

Spotswood shook his head with disgust at the disgraceful behavior of the governor and his chief justice. In his eyes, North Carolina's highest officials had entered into an illicit agreement with a lowly pirate in the name of financial profit. The seizure of the French vessel was a clear case of piracy, and instead of having Thache arrested, Eden and Knight had connived in their crimes and were soon about to be amply rewarded for their illicit conspiracy.

"Thache has also terrorized the citizens of Bath Town, and his crew members have been arrested for public drunkenness and lewd behavior."

"Citizens have been terrorized? What citizens?"

"A friend of mine named William Bell was robbed by Thache on the river three weeks ago. It happened early in the morning before dawn's full light. The pirate took most of his belongings and terrified the wits out of an Indian and Bell's young son who were with him. He is a menace to the good citizens of the colony."

"Is that the only incident ye are aware of?"

"Yes, but I am sure there are others. These brigands think nothing of stealing anything that doesn't belong to them."

Spotswood nodded and they fell into silence. The governor could tell that Moseley was determined to prove Eden's and Knight's collusion with the pirates, and it was obvious that he would go to extreme lengths to do so. Like Captain Brand of the HMS *Lyme*, he appeared to be a valuable ally in his crusade against piracy and, even more importantly, in the apprehension or destruction of Blackbeard. The pirate captain and his men didn't know it yet, but they were no more than pawns on the colonial chessboard and a means to destroy Eden. Spotswood had long been intent on extending his control and influence over Virginia's southern border, which he never considered to be far enough south, and he had little respect for the poor, struggling proprietary colony of North Carolina. And now Edward Moseley and a man he didn't know named William Bell provided him with what appeared to be an open invitation to invade his neighbor to the south and push out Eden once and for all. The proximity of the pirates in the colony of North Carolina conveniently served Spotswood's political needs. Now instead of battling with his own House of Burgesses and Council, who had been agitating the Lords of Trade in London for his removal from office, he could be the savior of North Carolina and Virginia both by eliminating Blackbeard and proving his collusion with Eden and his customs inspector.

After taking a delicate sip of his sherry, Moseley broke the silence. "It is my understanding that ye have arrested Thache's former quartermaster, William Howard, and he be under interrogation."

"How did you hear that?"

"Word travels fast not only in Virginia but North Carolina as well, especially when it involves notable individuals."

"There's nothing notable about William Howard. He is a villain of the first order who has feloniously taken silver and gold, Negro slaves, and other goods and merchandise belonging to the subjects of our Lord the King."

"Yes, and he is also the son of a prominent North Carolina landowner. Philip Howard owns a three-hundred-acre tract outside Bath Town. Obviously, his son is no babe in the woods. I understand he has retained the services of John Holloway."

Spotswood's face tightened into a frown. Holloway, one of the most respected and experienced lawyers in all the Virginia colony, had been a thorn in his side for the past two weeks in his representation of Thache's former quartermaster. He wished he could be rid of the pesky man, who had infuriated him to the point where he regarded him not so much as a lawyer, but as a patron and advocate of lowly pirates.

"Yes, that is correct. He has retained as counsel John Holloway. But we had to arrest Howard. For three weeks straight he was drunk, disorderly, and bragging about his nefarious exploits to all who would listen in every tavern from here to the James River. And he was actively trying to recruit a new crew for a forthcoming piratical voyage. So we arrested him. He had some fifty pounds of currency and was accompanied by two black slaves. The money and the slaves were duly confiscated, and Howard was arrested as a vagrant seaman."

"A vagrant seaman?"

"His insolence became so intolerable, without applying himself to any lawful business here in Virginia, that the justices of the peace thought fit to send him on board one of the King's ships as a vagrant seaman."

"So where is he now?"

"Chained belowdecks on board HMS *Pearl* anchored in the James River."

"The *Pearl* commanded by Captain George Gordon?"

"That is correct. The *Lyme* is commanded by Captain Brand. But before Howard was dragged kicking and screaming on board, he somehow managed to secure the services of Holloway with a few ounces of hidden gold dust. Whereupon the lawyer caused not only the justice who signed the warrant but Captain Gordon and his subordinate Lieutenant Robert Maynard to be arrested for wrongful imprisonment. Holloway is seeking five-hundred pounds damages in the civil action he has instituted against the justice of the peace and two naval officers in the common-law court of Virginia. That pirate-loving lawyer has created a mess and made a mockery of our criminal justice system."

"Holloway is a clever one. He seems to have turned the tables rather quickly."

Spotswood frowned again, feeling his anger coming on, as he took in a trifle of sherry. He hated to admit it, but he was up against a formidable opponent. Howard's legal advisor was of the highest caliber, a well-respected lawyer and property owner from a distinguished family with deep ties in the colony. An attorney of the Marshalsea Court of London before emigrating to Virginia, he was indeed one of the most eminent legal minds in all of Virginia. And yet, despite Holloway's clever lawyerly maneuvering, Spotswood was slowly building a case against William Howard and Blackbeard both. The problem was he was on shaky legal ground. Technically, he had no legal power to try men for piracy, a legal loophole that he had been informed would soon be closed by fresh legislation sent from London. But the new orders from the Crown had not arrived yet, which meant that he had no right to arrest Howard without trial and confiscate his goods. But despite the lack of legal precedent and guidance from the King, he was moving forward with a case and was planning on charging Howard for piracy, since the former quartermaster's own testimony revealed that he had violated the terms of the royal pardon.

"It would seem that William Howard knows how to fight back," said Moseley. "Are you planning on trying him for piracy?"

"That is the plan, yes. The rascal certainly deserves it. He ought by the judgement and sentence of the court suffer such pains, penalties, and forfeitures as by the laws of Great Britain are inflicted upon pirates and robbers on the high seas."

"I see. And by holding a show trial and making an example of Howard, your goal is to send a signal to all present and former pirates in the American colonies that there is no safe haven for them here. But what about the reformed pirates?"

"There is no such thing in my book. Sea rovers who take up the pardon will inevitably return to their old profession like dogs to the vomit. In Howard's case, we have direct evidence that he was trying to recruit a fresh company of rogues and commence a new piratical voyage of pillaging and plunder."

"So you're using Howard to get to Blackbeard, and Blackbeard to get to Eden."

He nodded in the affirmative. "During the trial, Howard will tell us everything we need to know about Blackbeard's previous sea robberies as well as his current whereabouts, crew strength, and fighting capability. But his most valuable evidence will be in proving that Thache and his crew have violated the terms of His Majesty's most gracious pardon."

"So are you planning on invading North Carolina to apprehend Blackbeard?"

Spotswood held up a hand. "You are jumping the gun here, Edward. No one has said a word about invading anything, and you would best be served to put such thoughts out of your mind. At least until we have a clearer picture of Thache's and Eden's dealings in Bath Town and all our ducks, so to speak, are lined up in a row. Do you understand?"

"You've made your mind quite clear to me. Honestly, I just want to help."

"No, you want much, much more than that, Edward. Now it's time for you to be specific. What do you want to get out of this?"

"Special privileges for the export of my tobacco through Virginia's ports. That would be a good start."

"You're aware that such things are normally prohibited by my policies."

"Yes, but there are always exceptions for the King's representatives in the colonies, especially when the distance between London and Williamsburg is three thousand miles and it takes a full two months for the Crown's directives to reach our shores."

"And what specifically can you offer me in return."

"I will deliver Blackbeard's head on a platter to you. Me and my loyalists will continue to act as spies on your behalf. We will keep an eye on the dealings between the pirate captain, Governor Eden, Tobias Knight, and local Bath traders, especially those willing to turn a blind eye to piratically taken goods and provisions. Thache is scheduled to deliver the casks of sugar and other supposed tariff goods, and he likely has substantial items to sell on the black market to the local traders. My men will be there to, shall we say, keep an eye on things and note if there are any further disturbances in Bath on the part of the pirates. And once all your ducks are lined up in a row and you decide that you do want to arrest Blackbeard or Eden, me and my men will be able to act as guides through the territory, which we know like the back of our hands."

Spotswood smiled, barely able to conceal his excitement. Moseley was the perfect collaborator, the perfect accomplice in his ambitious plan to destroy Blackbeard and Eden. With him on board, he would be able to win a grand victory for himself in the eyes of his superiors in London and thwart his stubborn colonist detractors. It was all coming together clearly now. Together, they were going to win this epic struggle to combat piracy and push aside the unethical Charles Eden once and for all. As the feeling of exultation navigated through his body, he glanced at the miniature golden horseshoe on his desk inscribed *Sic Juvat Transcendere Montes*—Thus It Is A Pleasure To Cross The Mountains. The souvenir had been given to each of the members of the immortal order of the *Knights of the Golden Horseshoe*. He remembered how potent and alive he had felt during his expedition to the Blue Ridge Mountains in the fall of 1716, and he felt like that now, as if anything was possible and all his hopes and dreams would come true.

He held up his glass of sherry in a toast. "I believe this could the beginning of a wonderful relationship, Edward. I say let's drink to success."

Moseley held up his glass in return. "To success," they toasted in unison.

To which Spotswood then added, "And to absolute secrecy, because that, Edward, is what will ultimately win us the day."

CHAPTER 56

OCRACOKE ISLAND

OCTOBER 8, 1718

THE TWO JAMAICAN PRIVATEER-TURNED-PIRATE FRIENDS—Edward Thache and Charles Vane—stared out from the *Adventure* at the ongoing banyan taking place on the sandy beach near Ocracoke's Old Watering Hole. Amid the cool fall breezes of Pamlico Sound, the combined one hundred fifteen crew members of the *Adventure* and *Ranger* had been drinking, feasting, swapping tales of swashbuckling adventures, singing, and playing music with a tightly stringed, wooden cittern and a pair of Jew harps for almost a week. But now it was time for Vane and his crew to leave: they were set to depart tomorrow at first light for Eleuthera.

"I will be sad to see you go, Charles," said Thache with genuine feeling as they watched the revelers on shore with the sun setting over the sound and the sky a dusky pink. The familiar strains of *Seven Drunken Nights* rose up into the salty air. The song told the story of a gullible drunkard returning night after night to see new evidence of his wife's lover, only to be taken in by increasingly implausible explanations. "It has been one hell of a party."

"Aye, it has indeed, my friend," responded Vane, his sun-crinkled face catching the last rays of sunlight. "And the good news is the rum hasn't even run out."

"Aye, that is good news," agreed Thache before taking a gulp from his glass of brandy and assuming a thoughtful pose. "But these are perilous times, Charles. It is not easy to know which way to go."

"I understand why you've taken the King's pardon. You want to tie up all the loose ends so you can retire from a-pirating, marry Margaret, and go on to live a normal life. But that's not the way for me. I enjoy the pirate's life too much to quit."

"His Majesty's Navy will hunt you down sooner or later and you know it. You should get out while you still can."

"I know I should. But just think, if we could recruit two more captains and their crews, like Paulsgrave Williams or La Buse, we could take the Bermudas and turn it into our own Madagascar. We could do it, Edward my friend, we could really do it."

"You know it will never work. Big pirate companies just become too unwieldy. That's why I ran the *Queen Anne's Revenge* aground and split up my force. And even if we could secure a new base, King George will send in the navy to run us out as Woodes Rogers has done in the Bahamas."

"So you believe the game is up? I never took the great Blackbeard for a bloody fucking defeatist?"

"I'm not a defeatist—I'm a realist. Our time is finished. But even if it isn't, my men and I have opted to accept the King's mercy. For many of these men, it represents a new start, a fresh beginning. You and I never planned to become pirates. It happened by bloody accident. So when a chance like this comes along, we'd be fools not to take advantage of it."

"And what if I told you that there are rumors that the King may soon declare war on Spain and make privateers of us all."

"I've heard the rumors too. If it actually happens, I say bully for all of us gentlemen of fortune. But for the time being, I'll take my chances with the governor of St. Thomas."

"So you're definitely sailing south to obtain a privateering commission?"

"That's been the plan for me and my crew all along. But first, before I leave I have to make everything right with Governor Eden."

"What are you talking about? He's already pardoned you."

"Aye, but I still have to fulfill my obligations to the governor's Court of Vice-Admiralty by delivering eighty casks of sugar to Bath Town. It will take four or five days and take two trips."

Vane took a huge gulp of rum, gargled it in his mouth, drank it down, and gave a resounding belch. "These pardons are a slippery slope, Edward. They just don't seem to be a long-term guarantee."

"Well, they're supposed to be. That's what Governor Eden assured me."

"Aye, but once the authorities discover that you've committed depredations after the January 5 grace period, do you honestly believe that they will honor it still?"

"I don't know. I suppose I will have to take my chances."

They fell into silence and again watched their crews reveling ashore in front of a backdrop of live oaks, red cedars, bayberry, and yaupon holly. The forest fringing the sandy beach concealed the Old Watering Hole used by Indian tribes for centuries before it was taken over by sea rovers. It was the last night of the banyan—the traditional British Royal Navy term for a period of shore-leave rest and relaxation that, by the late seventeenth century, had been adopted by the pirates to refer to any open-air gathering on the seashore. Thache stared out at the merrymakers sitting and talking around the open cook fires upon which whole bluefish and choice cuts of meats were being roasted and buckets of clams were being boiled; kicking back in makeshift driftwood chairs; passing around kegs and jugs of wine, rum, and brandy; and showing off their pistols, cutlasses, and muskets. Throughout the week, the men had been eating well. They eagerly hunted and roasted wild game, fished, and gathered fresh clams, oysters, and other shellfish, or purchased it from local traders rather than eat the ship's stores of worm-infested beef and moldy hard tack. Surprisingly, sprinkled among the odiferous pirates were a handful of women. Charles Vane had managed to strike a deal with two of the local trading vessels to have a few North Carolina women brought ashore to share in the celebration.

Throughout the week of the banyan, Thache and Vane had held many conversations, both drunk and sober, on the current state of affairs in the pirate world. Thache brought his Jamaican friend up to date on everything that had happened since the *Queen Anne's Revenge* departed from Nassau before their blockade of Charles Town in June; how he intentionally scuttled his unmanageable

French slaver at Old Topsail Inlet and duped Bonnet into leaving to seek the governor's pardon without his share of the company's plunder. He also told of his hastened visit to Philadelphia to visit his true love Margaret, whom he aimed to marry once he had secured his commission in St. Thomas, and the capture and return of the *Rose Emelye* with a consignment of sugar, cocoa, cotton, indigo dye, and casks of confectionaries. The hard-bitten Jacobite Vane filled in his counterpart on the recent events at Nassau: the arrival of Governor Woodes Rogers and the shameless betrayal of Thache's old sailing partner, Benjamin Hornigold, and Vane's former captain, Henry Jennings. Both Thache and Vane found it not only infuriating but deeply disheartening that their former brethren of the coast were now groveling before the Crown like lapdogs and had become traitorous pirate hunters. The pirate world was shrinking every day and it was only a matter of time before the Admiralty closed in and put an end to piracy on the high seas once and for all.

At the edge of the group on the beach, he saw his sailing master Israel Hands talking to Vane's second-in-command, Calico Jack Rackham, and gave a frown. It was the fifth time he had seen them talking alone together with no one else around, and he couldn't help but feel they were plotting. Since the incident at Old Topsail Inlet, Hands had grown more and more disobedient with every passing day, to the point where the two men had almost come to blows. Hands had made it clear the reason for his displeasure: he was angry at his demotion. In the blink of an eye, he had gone from captain of a consort sloop and commander of his own ship to a subordinate role as sailing master of the *Adventure*. In two of their recent arguments, Hands had insisted that he rightfully deserved to be quartermaster, but that job was entrusted by the crew to Thomas Miller. Thache had suspected before the treachery at Old Topsail Inlet that Hands might cause problems following the breakup of the pirate companies and had, therefore, considered not even including him in the secret plans to wreck the *Queen Anne's Revenge*. But in the end, he had included him in on the conspiracy, valuing his skills as a navigator and overall seaman. Looking at Hands and Calico Jack talking, he wondered if the two men might be venting their frustration at their respective captains.

"How are things betwixt you and Calico Jack?" he asked Vane.

"Why do you ask?"

"Because Mr. Hands and Mr. Rackham are alone talking to each other again."

"Aye, they do seem to have a lot to talk about. You think they're a-plotting, do ye?"

"Mr. Hands is disgruntled over losing his captaincy. He and I have been butting heads of late, and just before your arrival I came very close to boxing his ears off and drawing my sword."

"A calm and composed man like you, Edward, losing your cool. I must confess I am surprised."

"So have you had any differences with Calico Jack?"

"I've had differences with a lot of my crew members. They claim I be cruel and violent."

"They're right, you are cruel and violent, especially when you're well into your cups."

"What, you've heard them talking?"

"I've overheard some things and so has Caesar. He keeps his eyes and ears open for me with regard to the crew."

"What does my crew say about me?"

"That you have begun to exhibit moody, volatile, and sometimes even outright barbaric behavior."

"Is that so?"

"Aye, 'tis just so and you need to avast and likewise belay—and I mean starting first thing tomorrow when you set sail. Otherwise, you're going to lose your crew. It could be Calico Jack, or it could be someone else."

"What else do they say about me?"

"That you've tortured some of your victims with burning matches and performed other forms of savagery. They also say that you're too obsessed with the failed Jacobite cause."

"But it's not a losing cause."

"It is for the time being. And you shouldn't be torturing anyone. Remember what Black Sam said, we are Robin's Hood's men, not common thieves and ruffians."

"What are you talking about? You have tortured merchant captains."

"No, I haven't. I've allowed my men to rough up a French captain or two who were reluctant to part with their valuables. And I've let them poke and prod a pair of Boston men who deserved a good whipping for what happened to Bellamy's crew, but no one else. Not one of them was hurt at all."

"That's not what the newspapers say? I've read the *Boston News-Letter*, Edward."

"Aye, and they lie and exaggerate about me every time to spin a terrifying tale to sell their papers and increase their readership. They have manufactured the great Blackbeard legend, calling me a 'sea monster,' 'devil incarnate,' 'predator,' 'scandal of human nature,' 'enemy of mankind,' and 'robber, opposer, and violator of all laws, humane and divine.' But it's all balderdash. I haven't done one tenth of the things they claim I've done, and haven't imposed a single one of the base cruelties they say I am guilty of to the captured prisoners taken aboard my ships. It's all part of the Crown's effort to make me out to be a murderous thug instead of a simple sea captain, which is all I ever wanted to be, by thunder."

"I'm sorry, that just sounds a little holier-than-thou to me, my bearded friend."

"It's the God's honest truth. I just don't believe that we need to be scoundrels and abuse those we take plunder from. But I will gladly burn the ship of any Boston man."

"Aye verily. We should hoist a cup to Bellamy."

"To Black Sam," said Thache.

"To Black Sam," echoed Vane, and they tossed back their spirits and stared off at the banyan on the beach. The men were now singing the pirate song *Henry Martin*, having finally tired of crooning the bawdy *Seven Drunken Nights*. Thache looked at Vane and they smiled at one another and began to sing the words they both knew by heart.

There were three brothers in merry Scotland
In merry Scotland there were three

And they did cast lots which of them should go
Should go, should go
And turn robber all on the salt sea

The lot it fell first upon Henry Martin
The youngest of all the three
That he should turn robber all on the salt sea
Salt sea, the salt sea
For to maintain his two brothers and he

They had not been sailing but a long winter's night
And a part of a short winter's day
When he espied a stout lofty ship
Lofty ship, lofty ship
Come bibbing down on him straight way

"Hello, hello," cried Henry Martin
What makes you sail so nigh?
I'm a rich merchant ship bound for fair London Town
London Town, London Town
Would you please for to let me pass by?

"Oh no, oh no," cried Henry Martin
This thing it never could be
For I have turned robber all on the salt sea
Salt sea, the salt sea.
For to maintain my two brothers and me

Come lower your tops'l and brail up your mizz'n
And bring your ship under my lee
Or I will give you a full cannon ball
Cannon ball, cannon ball
And all your dear bodies drown in the salt sea

Oh no, we won't lower our lofty topsail
Nor bring our ship under your lee
And you shan't take from us our rich merchant goods
Merchant goods, merchant goods
Nor point our bold guns to the sea

Then broadside and broadside and at it they went
For fully two hours or three
Till Henry Martin gave to them deathshot
The deathshot, the deathshot
And straight to the bottom went she

When they finished the final verse, Vane said, "When I go from this world of pirating, I will not go quietly and miserably like that lubberly Bonnet. I will not let them take me alive."

"What do you plan to do?"

"I will blow my brigantine's powder magazine and send my enemies, myself, and my crew to Davy Jones rather than suffer the indignity of being hanged by that German pig King George."

Thache stroked the long stiff braids of his beard, pondering what going out with a bang would entail. He knew he didn't want to see the end of a rope and agreed that Bonnet had been a fool for allowing himself to be backed into a corner by Colonel Rhett and the King's men. But what Bonnet's capture signified for the future was what was most distressing. Clearly the numbers of safe havens for pirates were diminishing, and Thache knew he had to get out now while he could by securing his privateering commission in St. Thomas once he settled his affairs here in North Carolina and finished the outfitting of the *Adventure*.

"You would really blow yourself and your crew up rather than be taken alive?" he asked Vane.

"Aye, and you would be well advised to do the same unless you want to do the dance of death, foul your britches, and have people spit upon you and throw stones and rotten vegetables at you. There's no honor in an ending such as that."

"No, there's not," agreed Thache, and he told himself that if he ever found himself cornered like Bonnet, he would follow Vane's advice by igniting his powder magazine and blowing himself and his enemies to kingdom come.

CHAPTER 57

GOVERNOR'S PALACE
WILLIAMSBURG

OCTOBER 28, 1718

"GENTLEMEN, I MUST ASK YOU TO SWEAR AN OATH OF SECRECY. No one is to know what we discuss here today, as there be too many favorers of pirates in these parts."

When Captain Ellis Brand and Edward Moseley promptly agreed and took their oaths, Spotswood gave an inward sigh of satisfaction. His plan to rid the Americas of Blackbeard, once and for all, was coming together slowly but assuredly; all he had to do was continue to gather evidence of wrongdoing and build his legal case against William Howard and soon everything would fall into place. Brand and his subordinate, Captain George Gordon of the HMS *Pearl*, had been sharing intelligence with him on Thache's movements for months, and they had more than proven their worth and that of their spy network in the Pamlico Sound and Bath County areas. The well-connected Moseley, possessor of one of the most extensive holdings of private property in North Carolina, also had extensive spy resources at his disposal in the form of shallow-water pilots, traders, seamen, and merchants keeping a careful eye on the pirate captain's movements.

"I apologize for the cloak and dagger, gentlemen, but as we all know, three may keep a secret only as long as two of them are dead," said Spotswood with the vows of secrecy complete. "Now what information do ye have for me?"

Captain Brand cleared his throat to speak. "It has been brought to my attention from local pilots and informants on inbound sloops that the notorious pirate Charles Vane, who recently raided Charles Town, and a large number of his pirates have gathered with Blackbeard along the northern shores of Ocracoke Inlet. It appears the corsair and his nearly one hundred men have since moved on, but it is possible they could return."

Spotswood nodded. It was an ominous turn·of events. The first thing he needed to do was move faster with his anti-piracy efforts and take bolder action to protect the profitable southern plantations. In his view, it was obvious that Blackbeard was fortifying Ocracoke and making it a general rendezvous point for the sea robbers. Somehow, the pirate nest had to be dispersed—or eradicated.

"You're sure that Vane has left?" he asked Brand.

"That's what the traders say."

"All the same, it is clear the pirates have built up a stronghold in the area."

"I would most vigorously agree."

Powerful landholder and merchant Edward Moseley then made his opinion on the matter known. "All Blackbeard needs now is a half dozen more pirate ships and he can build an impregnable bastion on the Outer Banks. Governor Eden's certainly not prepared to stop him, and is unlikely to lift a finger even if he could."

"I quite agree," said Spotswood acerbically. "He and Tobias Knight are in bed with the man, and because of that, we will soon have a new armed pirate fortress at Ocracoke to rival Madagascar or Nassau."

"Unless they can be stopped," said Captain Brand. "The Lords have ordered me to do my utmost to destroy these vipers and I intend to do just that."

Spotswood nodded. "Which means that the Admiralty has, in turn, given me the authority to take whatever measures I wish to remove men like Thache and William Howard as threats to the colonies. I plan to bring the quartermaster of the *Queen Anne's Revenge* to trial shortly and that legal case will provide irrefutable evidence of these men's piratical activities both before and after the January 5 amnesty date. And when it's done, even the capable John Holloway won't be able to save Howard from the hangman and a cold iron gibbet along the James."

"Whether Vane or other pirates band with Thache on Ocracoke," said Brand, "it is clear that Blackbeard has established a formidable redoubt and will openly encourage them to take up residence there, whether they have taken the King's pardon or not. This gives him a remote pirate headquarters from which to operate, while still being close enough to Bath to sell his plunder to local merchants and unscrupulous ship owners."

"I concur, gentlemen. Furthermore, I assume that we can all agree that this is what makes Blackbeard doubly dangerous."

"How so?" asked Moseley.

"It raises the very real possibility that Ocracoke will not only soon become a bustling pirate haven, but will attract the very pirates who have refused the pardon or have agreed to it falsely and have no intention of honoring its terms. The Outer Banks lay close to the Virginia Capes, and so pirates based there could lie off the Virginia coast, plundering at will. If threatened, they could easily evade any larger pursuers in the shallow waters of Pamlico Sound."

"Which means they must be routed out of their viper's nest," said Brand.

"Yes, but first we need to continue to gather intelligence and build up our case. Mr. Moseley, what new information do you have for us in that regard?"

"I believe Blackbeard visited with Governor Eden or Tobias Knight, and possibly both, the night that he robbed William Bell."

"Do you have proof?"

"Unfortunately not. But I believe the reason Thache sailed his periauger all the way from Ocracoke to Bath Town was to gain the counsel of one or both men regarding the disposition of the seized French vessel he claimed was derelict."

"I would wager that that's precisely what the notorious Blackbeard the pirate was doing in Bath. But if you have no direct proof, it will be difficult—"

"There may be no proof of a midnight meeting, but we now have proof of payments from Thache to the governor and Knight in the form of eighty casks of sugar and cocoa. Sixty for Eden and twenty for Knight, to be precise. They were delivered during two separate trips, and in fact the pirates are still in Bath. So we now have direct evidence pointing to a profitable business arrangement between the pirate and the two officials."

"Ye be referring to the payment due to the Admiralty Court of one-fifth the salvage?"

"Yes."

"But the local Admiralty representative is allowed to claim a fifth of the cargo for himself to offset administrative costs."

"Yes, but Tobias Knight isn't formally entitled to anything as customs collector. I think it's nothing but a bribe. And Eden and Knight weren't the only ones to benefit. More than five dozen barrels were reportedly fenced in Bath and the profits divided among Blackbeard's crew. Knight has apparently allocated him a warehouse outside town for the express purpose of selling his stolen goods."

"What about depredations committed by the pirates? Has there been anything since the robbery of William Bell?"

"Unfortunately, none that I am aware of," said Moseley, clearly wishing Thache had committed more crimes so the case against him would be stronger.

"Are you sure? Nothing at all?"

Moseley shook his head. Spotswood looked at Brand, but he, too, had no evidence of any further criminal actions on the part of the notorious Blackbeard. "However," pointed out the naval captain, "that does not mean that Thache has treated everyone except William Bell in the territory civilly. There are several mariners who regularly conduct trading trips in and out of the Pamlico and Albemarle Sounds and gather intelligence on the pirates' activities, moorings, and rumored ravages of North Carolina's population. They have informed me that Blackbeard and his brigands frequently trade with the colony's inhabitants but the prices for the items purchased—primarily food, alcohol and tobacco—are almost always determined by the buyers. I am told that this was the practice employed by the rogues of the Bahamas before Governor Woodes Rogers arrival, wherein they maintained a symbiotic if one-sided relationship with their neighbors."

"So what you're saying is that, for the most part, Blackbeard and his men have been trying their best to remain within the law after receiving their pardons—the lapse with William Bell notwithstanding."

"That is correct. But some of the Carolina traders no doubt feel they have not gotten a fair deal when selling their goods to the pirates and appear to be complaining to anyone who will listen."

"Count me among them, gentlemen," said Moseley. "I am all for ending the pirates' unfair trading practices."

Spotswood couldn't help but smile. "I believe Captain Brand and myself are well aware of that, Edward."

They shared a laugh. Moseley then said, "Just because we have not heard of further depredations doesn't mean that more haven't taken place. These pirates are monsters and a death knell to free trade in the colonies. Why the very idea of a pardon is a sham for these miscreants. And Blackbeard has flouted the terms imposed by the King by blockading Charles Town and beating up William Bell."

"Don't worry, Edward. He's not going to get away with it. Captain Brand and I here are quite determined to hold Thache to account for his actions."

"But you have no authority in the Carolinas and neither does Captain Brand."

Spotswood felt a little twitch of irritation. It was true, neither he nor Brand had the full legal authority to invade another colony and arrest anyone, even a pirate. And yet, had not South Carolina Governor Johnson already taken matters into his own hands by sending out Colonel Rhett's anti-piracy patrol that cornered Stede Bonnet in the Cape Fear River? And had not Pennsylvania Governor Keith fitted out two sloops recently for anti-piracy patrol duties in Delaware Bay? If Eden had neither the protection of the Royal Navy nor the resources to create his own anti-piracy flotilla, why couldn't Spotswood, as leader of a colony that did have a powerful naval presence due to the rich tobacco trade by Micajah Perry and other Virginia tobacco merchants, help make up for his neighbor's weakness. If Eden lacked the power to deal with pirates within his own dominion, why couldn't Spotswood do the job for him, just as Governor Johnson had done?

After a moment, he realized the answer to his own question. It was true that if he sent in a naval expedition to capture or kill Thache, he would grossly exceed the powers granted to him when he took the job. After all, he was only allowed to intervene in the affairs of other colonies "in case of distress of any other of our plantations," and only then "upon the application of the respective governors thereof to you." Governor Eden had made no such request, which meant that he would clearly be meddling in the affairs of another colony and doing so using military force. So he had little wiggle room from a purely legal standpoint.

But looked at from a more practical standpoint, Governor Johnson had already set the precedent by launching an attack into a neighboring colony, and was at this very moment proceeding full speed ahead with a show trial of Stede Bonnet and his forty-five crew members in Charles Town. If Johnson could claim he had no direct guidance from London, and thereby had to take action first and seek approval for his actions later, couldn't Spotswood do the same? And what if it could be firmly established that Thache and his crew had not been eligible for His Majesty's pardon, wouldn't that be enough to justify intervention? And with William Howard's incriminating testimony from his depositions and trial part of the official documentation, wouldn't convictions for Thache and his remaining crew be guaranteed?

But he did not yet want to let Brand or Moseley in on the full breadth and scope of his legally and ethically questionable scheme. He needed more time to build his case and for Blackbeard and Eden to make a costly mistake that would make an invasion of North Carolina legally uncontestable.

"I believe it is premature, at this point in time, to speculate on how Thache, Eden, and their piratical associates can best be apprehended," said Spotswood, not wanting to show his full hand just yet. "Instead, we should continue to focus our efforts on gathering intelligence so when the day to take bold action draws near, we are fully prepared to triumph over our enemies."

"Hear, hear," agreed Captain Brand. "We'll catch these rogues soon enough."

"Yes, we will," said Spotswood with a reptilian smile. "And hopefully, sooner than we all think."

CHAPTER 58

TOWN CREEK, BATH TOWN

OCTOBER 28, 1718

HEARING A TENTATIVE KNOCK ON HIS CABIN DOOR, Thache put down his musty, leather-bound copy of Exquemelin's *History of the Buccaneers of America* and called out to his visitor, "Tacks and braces, come in!"

The door opened and Caesar appeared, his glossy clean-shaven pate glinting in the candlelight. Sitting at his desk, Thache could tell at once that the young man was troubled with something and likely had bad news. Days earlier, the *Adventure* had dropped anchor into the muddy river bottom off Tobias Knight's landing and promptly delivered the second shipment of sugar and cocoa to Governor Eden and Knight. This fulfilled the pirates' 80-cask payment on behalf of the Crown and His Majesty's customs for the colony of North Carolina in lieu of Admiralty court and administration fees. Now the crew were spending a few more days of comfortable leisure in town, though they slept on the river aboard the ship.

He waved his guest to the chair before his desk. "What brings you here, Caesar my friend?" he inquired innocently.

Taking his seat, the African paused a moment to gather his thoughts before speaking. "I have some troubling news to report, Captain."

He poured him a glass of rum and handed it to him across his messy captain's desk, covered with charts, mariner's instruments, books, and the like. "Troubling news, you say?"

"Aye, Captain. 'Tis being whispered that Master Hands is seeking to lead a mutiny of ye ship."

"Go on."

"He's been quietly spreading the word that he's lost faith in you and believes he can do a better job as captain."

Though the news wasn't surprising given their recent arguments and nearly coming to blows on two separate occasions, Thache was still surprised to hear that Israel Hands was planning on taking over his ship. "Has Mr. Hands spoken as to the cause of his dissatisfaction?"

"He doesn't believe your heart is in it anymore and that he can do better. But he also doesn't like that we've been dilly-dallying these past two months. He believes we should be headed south to secure our privateering commissions."

"Lord knows if we had not taken the French prize, we would not be here in Bath mollifying the governor and would already be headed for southern climes. In any case, thank you for informing me of this development, Caesar. You are a good and loyal seaman, and on the blood of Henry Morgan I wish I had three dozen more like you to sail with me to St. Thomas."

"Thank you, sir. Some of the men, like Mr. Gibbons, are saying that Mr. Hands was riled up by Jack Rackham during the recent banyan. They're saying that Calico Jack is the one who's been planting these thoughts in his head."

"Do you believe them?"

"Aye, 'cause I heard them talking. They drank to the damnation of you and Charles Vane as much as they did bloody King George. They want you two out of their way so's they can take over the *Adventure* and *Ranger*."

"How many men do you think would go along with the mutiny?"

"No more than a handful. As you know, many among the crew don't like Mr. Hands. That's why Thomas Miller was voted quartermaster and Mr. Hands only sailing master after the incident at Old Topsail."

"What do ye think I should do about this planned mutiny?"

"I don't know. I'm not a captain."

"But what would you do if you were? Would you punish Master Hands?"

"I suppose I would have to with his being a traitor and all."

"Did Mr. Hands say anything else that I should be aware of?"

"Only that if he did mutiny, he would, out of respect, do it while we were anchored here in Bath Town. He claimed it was because several of your closest allies like Gibbons, Brooks, Miller, and myself have close ties here. This way we would be marooned nearby to our friends and families."

"Well, that's certainly thoughtful of Mr. Hands." He tossed back a half glass of rum then refilled his glass and threw back another two shots of the fiery liquor. He could feel his growing anger fueled by the alcohol.

"Again, Caesar, thank you for bringing this to my attention. Now I'd like you to fetch Master Hands for me. I'd like to have a word with him."

"What?"

"You heard me. I want you fetch Mr. Hands. I want you to bring him to me so that he and I can have a little chat."

"A little chat?"

"Aye, it is time that Mr. Hands and I resolve our differences once and for all. The truth is our relationship has been festering for some time now."

"I was aware of that, Captain, and I'm sorry for it. There was a time when you two were very close."

"Aye verily, there was. But with the Crown's new anti-piracy measures, everything is changing. The sand's shifting beneath our feet and the tide is going out."

"Aye, Captain. I'll fetch Mr. Hands now."

When Caesar left the cabin, Thache withdrew two of his pistols from his bandolier, carefully removed the lead shot and cartridge, and loaded each pistol with simple gunpowder cartridges and no shot or mini ball. He placed one pistol on his lap so that it would not be visible to a man sitting in the chair opposite his desk. The other he placed back into the lowest leather holster of the bandolier, even with his lower stomach. He then placed the lit candle in the center of his desk. Then he waited. Minutes later, Caesar returned with the sailing master, who was mildly drunk. His ruddy face was filled with wariness and distrust.

"Thank you, Caesar. Leave us please."

"Aye, Captain," and he was gone.

Despite the air of tension in the cabin, Thache poured Hands a glass of rum, filling it nearly to the brim, and the two of them clinked glasses like gentlemen and tossed back four fingers each of the amber fluid. Thache then poured out another for each of them and launched into what he wanted to say.

"It has been brought to my attention by several members of the crew that you plan to take over my ship and serve as her captain. That, Master Hands, is what is known as a mutiny and I don't believe I will allow it."

Hands sneered with disdain. "You won't allow it? Why you don't have any bloody say in it. It's the crew that will cast their votes."

"And you believe you will carry the day if it comes to a vote?"

"You don't command the men's respect any more. You're too indecisive."

"Indecisive, is it?"

"You're torn betwixt heading back to the City of Brotherly Love to be with that strumpet of yours or striking for the West Indies to become a privateer. You just don't know what you want any more."

Thache felt himself cringe at the word *strumpet*, but tried not to let his displeasure show on his face. "And you know what you want and what is best for the men, is that it?"

"Aye, you can scupper, sink, or burn me if I can't do a better job than you, these days. That pardon poisoned your mind, turned you away from who you truly are. You're a pirate and will always be a pirate, but your mind hasn't wrapped itself around that yet. You're all confused on account of your strumpet back in Philadelphia."

"She's not a strumpet. Her name is Margaret."

"I don't care what her name is. She's nothing but a wet hole and body to keep your bed warm at night. So don't be making her out to be no queen."

He clenched the pistol with his right hand below the walnut desk, barely able to control his anger. The pistol was trained directly on Hands's right kneecap. One pull from the trigger and he would be maimed for life—but mercifully not killed—from the powder charge.

"What's wrong with you, Israel. Why are you so angry at me?"

"You know why I'm angry. I've told you a half dozen times now."

His voice carried the quiet desperation of a spurned ambitious man who had not fulfilled the lofty goals he had set for himself, and Thache couldn't help but feel pity for him. *By God, by shooting him in the kneecap I'll be doing the sod a favor.* At that moment, he heard a burst of laughter from the men on deck over the sound of the gentle slap-slap-slap of the river's flow against the *Adventure's* wooden hull. Suddenly, a hundred different worries stampeded through his mind as he realized the grave risk he was about to take.

Should I go through with it? What if it doesn't work or I get caught? In the aftermath, will the men side with me or Hands? My God, what would Margaret think?

"So, what you're saying, Israel, is that you're still angry over having lost command of the *Adventure* and being demoted after the confusion at the Old Topsail? Does that about sum it up?"

"That was a bad affair. There were friends of mine you double-crossed."

"Aye, I can see why you'd be angry over that."

"And then you lied to us when you sailed to Bath Town in the periauger."

"What are you talking about?"

"Those diverse goods you said you bought in the country were stolen goods."

"Stolen goods?"

"Don't play dumb with me. You lied to me and the other crew members about how you came by the box of pipes, the yards of fabric, the barrel of brandy, and the silver cup. Why did you feel it necessary to lie to your shipmates?"

"Let's just say I had me reasons."

"What were they?"

"I wanted to conceal the fact that I stole the items from an impertinent trader up the river. I didn't want to be the one who had violated the King's pardon."

"That's it?"

"I weighed the fact that the robbery was a criminal offense subject to the laws of the proprietary colony and not the Admiralty laws of the high seas, and I crossed my fingers I would not be discovered. I made a simple mistake."

"You should have trusted us. We're your crew members who signed the articles."

"Aye, you signed the articles as did I. But that doesn't mean I'm going to let you take a ship that is rightfully mine. I own it and Governor Eden has declared as much. So you can mutiny all you want, but you won't be taking my ship."

"Your behavior has become erratic. You need to stand down."

"No, it is the world that has become unpredictable, what with Woodes Rogers, Ben Hornigold, Henry Jennings, and the HMS *Scarborough* and other ships of the Royal Navy hellbound on our trail. That's what they're trying to do with these pardons and making pirates pirate hunters—they're trying to remove us from the high seas and wipe us off the map once and for all."

"It would be best for everyone if you just stand down. There can only be one captain, and it can't be you, not anymore."

Another burst of riotous laughter filtered in from the aft deck. The sound cut through the sound of a seaman softly singing a favorite ballad. Thache quietly pulled back the hammer of his pistol. His mouth felt as dry as a kiln. Taking a deep breath, he steeled himself.

You have to do this. Just get it over with.

Hands tossed back his glass of rum, dribbling some down his chin, grabbed the bottle, and greedily poured himself another full glass. Thache glanced towards the cabin window. The wooden blind was pulled shut, but there was a narrow gap along the edges, enough to allow someone to peek inside the room from the deck if they so desired.

You're running out of time! You've got to do it now! Your only chance at a future is to be rid of him. But what will Margaret think?

"Why are you looking at me like that?" asked Israel Hands.

"Like what?"

"Like a wild dog. What are you doing beneath the desk? Are you hiding something?"

Despite his heart thundering in his chest, he told himself to remain calm. "I'm not doing anything."

"Yes, you are. You have something that you're hiding."

"No, I don't."

"Yes, you do. Don't lie to me. That's all you've been doing the past four months is lying to us. Well, I can tell you the rest of the crew and I are sick of it."

You must distract him, Edward. "You know there are rumors ashore of an Indian uprising in the country. What do you think of that, Master Hands?"

"Indians…what does that have to do—?"

"The Tuscarora War ended just three years ago, and Indian attacks are fresh on Governor Eden's and everyone else's mind."

"What the hell is wrong with you? I don't care a lick about bloody Indians."

Shoot him—you've got to shoot him before he stands up!

His heart quickened as he raised the nose of the pistol so it was directly on Hands's right kneecap beneath his captain's desk. Inside, he felt a palpable sense of danger. His aim had to be dead and true so that the sailing master wouldn't be able to recover and get off a shot with either of his pistols.

"I don't believe you would make a good captain, Master Hands."

"And why is that?"

"I don't believe you be ruthless enough. A captain has to be willing to take drastic action for the betterment of the entire crew, not merely his favorites."

"What's wrong with you? Do you have the pox like some of the other crew members? You haven't been yourself since Charles Town."

Breathing in a controlled rhythm, he tightened his right hand around the grip and visualized the line the powder charge would take in its travel path to Hands's right kneecap. All he really wanted to do was frighten the sailing master enough that he would quit the company without taking more than a couple of his loyalists with him. That was why Thache was poised to fire his pistol beneath the desk loaded with only a gunpowder cartridge, and no shot.

"You have violated my trust. For that, you will have to be punished."

"What the hell are you talking about?"

"Curse your prating insolence, sir. You are about to become a cripple."

His finger curled around the trigger. There was no wobble or quiver; his hand was steady as a surgeon's. But inside he still felt guilty for what he was about to do. *Margaret will understand,* he told himself to steel himself against his self-doubt. *I have no choice. Margaret will understand and soon I will be in her loving arms again.*

"Goodbye, Mr. Hands. I'm afraid this is where we part company and our stories become separate. Despite your quarrelsome nature, I wish you a good life."

"Be this a jest? What are you up to? I'll have no more of this tomfoolery."

"I know ye won't. And neither will I."

Thache calmly leaned forward in his chair and blew the candle out, a whisper of wind riffling his thick black beard. Then, with the utmost deliberation, he removed the other pistol so that he now clutched a loaded weapon bearing a powder charge in each hand beneath the table.

"What are you—?"

But Hands's words were cut off as Thache squeezed each trigger, one right after the other.

Boom! Boom!

The two gunshots that exploded from inside the cabin were followed by a shriek of pain mingled with astonishment from the *Adventure's* former captain and current sailing master. In the next instant, Israel Hands had fallen from his chair to the floor and was crying out in agony. Thache calmly rose from his chair and inspected the wound. It was as he had planned. Hands' knee was badly maimed and he would be crippled for life. But because Thache had used only a powder charge instead of small caliber "bird shot" or a mini ball at point-blank range, he had not delivered such a fearsome wound that his adversary's leg was severed from his body and he would bleed to death. He had punished him severely for attempting to subvert his authority, but he had deliberately spared his life.

He took a heavy cloth rag, pressed it against the wound, and took his right hand and pressed it firmly against his injured right kneecap. Hands moaned and squirmed in agony.

"Avast, Mr. Hands. Stop your crying and wriggling and keep pressure on that wound, or you'll die."

"Look at what you've done to me, you bastard! I'll never walk again!"

"Aye, but you will, Mr. Hands—in due course yet with a limp. Just remember, whatever has happened to you, you did it to yourself. Never forget that."

"I'll blast you to Davy Jones one day, I will! You're going to have to look over your shoulder the rest of your natural days, you savage cur!"

"Save your breath and look to your wound. Your vengeance can wait."

He rose from his feet and started for the door, bumping the lantern hanging near the entrance. He then stepped from the room, his tall, lean, sinewy frame silhouetted by the swaying yellow lantern-light coming from within the cabin. The sounds of Israel Hands's screams of agony rose above the sound of the water lapping against the hull of the boat. A dozen seamen quickly assembled before him with stunned expressions on their faces. Caesar, Garret Gibbons, and Joseph Brooks Jr. and Sr. were the first to arrive on the scene and stood up front.

Looking into the accusatory eyes of his men, he couldn't help but feel guilty for what he had just done. But he also knew it was the right thing to do. Hands had poisoned his ship with all his mutinous talk and there was no choice but to cut him loose from the remaining company. The man had backed him into a corner and had now paid the price.

"Caesar and Mr. Gibbons," he commanded, "prepare a boat at once and go fetch the local surgeon. His name is Dr. Patrick Maule and he lives at the corner of Bay and Craven Streets."

"W-What happened?" stammered Caesar, trying to peer inside the cabin where the moaning and screaming was coming from.

"I'm afraid Master Hands has had an accident. Now please fetch the doctor."

CHAPTER 59

CAPITOL, WILLIAMSBURG

OCTOBER 29, 1718

FROM HIS ESTEEMED SEAT in his Governor's Council Chamber, Alexander Spotswood looked around the table at the eight councilors in attendance. With eight of the twelve members still firmly opposed to him, he had not had any tangible success at reconciliation and was still under siege. The problem, as he saw it, was that they were too independent-minded, like impetuous adolescents grappling to break free from their parents. All the men in the room considered themselves loyal British subjects, but many had never even set foot on British soil and they saw themselves as distinct from the ruling classes of London, merchants of Bristol, and yeomen of York—and Spotswood was growing tired of them.

If his friend and mentor Robert Beverley was to be believed, they considered themselves "Americans" of the Royal Colony of Virginia first and foremost—and Englishmen second. Like Beverley, some even liked to go so far as to call themselves "Indians" to further distinguish themselves from the Old World back in England and demonstrate their closer affinity to their more free-spirited and less orthodox indigenous counterparts in the New World. But Spotswood was George I's representative in Virginia, the instrument of the King's rule in a distant colony, and it was his job to unquestioningly fulfill the prerogatives of the Crown and look out for the interests of Great Britain, protectors of its loyal colonial subjects. To that end, he could not allow these intransigent provincials, these petulant children, to prevail or limit his authority in any way.

"Today's order of business, gentlemen," he began in his customary high-pitched, authoritarian tone, "is in regard to the trial of the notorious pirate William Howard. He is second-in-command to Blackbeard and quartermaster of the *Queen's Anne's Revenge*. As you are aware, Mr. Howard came into this colony in late August with two Negroes which he owned and were piratically taken, one from a French ship and the other from an English brigantine. I caused them to be seized pursuant to His Majesty's instructions, upon which, encouraged by the favorable reception he received in our colony from supporters of pirates, he commenced a suit against the officer who made the seizure. His insolence became so intolerable, without applying himself to any lawful business, that the justices of the peace where he resided thought fit to send him on board the HMS *Pearl* as a vagrant seaman. Hereupon, he caused not only the justice who signed the warrant but Captain Gordon and Lieutenant Robert Maynard of the man-of-war to be arrested, each in an action of five-hundred-pounds damages. Captain Brand of the HMS *Lyme* firmly believes that Howard, whom he regards as one of the most mischievous and vilest villains that has infested the Atlantic coast, should be criminally tried. I wholeheartedly agree and hereby propose that Howard not be given a jury trial pursuant to the Statute of Henry VIII, c. 15, but rather be tried without a jury under Statute 11 and

12 William III, c. 7.29. That is our order of business for today, gentlemen, to decide how to instigate criminal proceedings against the felonious Mr. Howard."

Glances were exchanged and a note of disapproval rumbled through the chamber. Philip Ludwell and Reverend James Blair, seated to Spotswood's immediate left, scowled at him, as if what he was proposing was preposterous.

"Do I detect a note of objection amongst you gentlemen?" he inquired stiffly.

Ludwell leaned forward in his seat. "It is my understanding that Mr. Howard has retained the services of John Holloway, one of the chief lawyers of the colony, as his legal counsel."

"Yes, that is correct. Howard was assisted by influential friends of low character ashore who apparently alerted the lawyer. Mr. Holloway is a man of equally questionable morals in my view. He is, after all, a constant patron and advocate of pirates."

Reverend Blair scoffed. "You have just unjustifiably imputed the character and reputation of Mr. Howard's counsel. Mr. Holloway—an attorney of the Marshalsea Court of London before emigrating to Virginia—is one of the most eminent lawyers in all of Virginia and does not deserve such unwarranted censure."

"What the good reverend is trying to say is that most of us in this room don't share your enthusiasm for crucifying sea rovers, Lieutenant Governor," said Ludwell. "Particularly when we know this crusade of yours is all a ploy to distract from your inadequacies as the King's representative to this colony."

Spotswood forced himself to maintain his composure. "William Howard, Blackbeard, and the other pirates infesting this colony and our neighbors to the south represent a threat to Virginia's commerce, and their very presence encourages others to piracy."

"That may be true," allowed Ludwell, "but that is not the real reason for your decision to move against these pirates. Like politicians before and since, you have launched a crusade against an enemy that is more imaginary than real to divert public attention from your own improprieties at home. And you are ignoring one simple fact: pirates are good for business. They bring money and cheap goods into the colony, and it is for this reason that most of us provincials, as you are so fond of calling us, have no problem with them. We, sir, do not mind English pirates, so long as they prey on vessels of other nations or just take provisions as needed."

"But Blackbeard, Howard, and their confederates prey upon the vessels of all nations and have had a negative impact on English trade here in the colonies."

"The governor speaks the truth," said Cole Diggs, one of the governor's minority of supporters. "During the war, privateers helped our businesses. But in the last two years, there have been far too many British victims of English pirates, and many of those on the Virginia coast where we conduct our business."

"I agree with Mr. Ludwell," said John Grymes, Ludwell's nephew, who had for several years now been one of the governor's most active opponents in the House of Burgesses. "I think this whole obsession with pirates is to distract us, the burgesses, and the people of this colony from your own failing administration."

"It is true," added Reverend Blair before Spotswood could get a word of protest in. "Anti-piracy has become a singular obsession for you, your closest associates, and a few hirelings. Why this obsession, Alexander? Is it truly just a ploy to distract us all from your other questionable actions?"

He reminded himself once again to keep his temper in check. The more pugnacious council members like Ludwell, Blair, and Grymes often attempted to stir him up during meetings and make him lose his composure, but over the years he had learned more and more not to rise to their baiting and to at least maintain a veneer of professional courtesy.

"With all due respect, gentlemen, this is not my obsession. The eradication of piracy is the most fervent wish of the Board of Trade and the Admiralty."

"Both of whom you will go to extremes to flatter," sniped Ludwell. "The civilian residents of this colony are more like-minded to those in neighboring North Carolina and other America colonies. The Board of Trade and Admiralty may want piracy terminated, but most provincials do not."

"I agree with my esteemed uncle," echoed Grymes, who was quickly echoed with "Hear, hear!" by Carter, Smith, and Corbin, who also seldom saw eye to eye with the governor. "Furthermore," he went on, "you have no actual legal authority to try anyone for piracy. And you most certainly don't have the legal right to arrest someone without trial and confiscate his goods."

"Well, at least I know where you and your uncle stand, John. You favor the rights of pirates over the denizens of this colony. No, sir, I will not be a party to that kind of madness. By my authority as the chief official of this colony, I am hereby charging William Howard with piracy. The only question is whether he will be tried by a jury or before a Court of Vice-Admiralty without a jury. So, which is it to be, gentlemen. We've wasted enough time quibbling like schoolboys and debating matters of no consequence. Now it's time for the council to make an important decision."

"If William Howard is to be tried at all," said Ludwell, "I say he should be given a jury trial pursuant to the Statute of Henry VIII, c. 15."

"I second that motion," said Blair.

Murmurs of agreement sounded from several other council members.

"Now just wait a minute," said Spotswood, opening his law book with several marked pages. "I believe that with a careful reading of the Act of the 11th and 12th of King William—the *Act for the Effectual Suppressing of Pirates*—you will agree that a trial before a Court of Vice-Admiralty is more appropriate."

He passed the open, leatherbound law book to Cole Diggs, whom he knew would support him. After taking a moment to read the relevant sections, Diggs said, "Yes, I quite agree. Mr. Howard should be tried without a jury under the Statute 11 and 12 William III, c. 7.29."

"Here, let me and the others see that," said Ludwell. He took the British case book and set it at the edge of the table so that he and the rest of the council members could read the articles. "All right," he said after a full two minutes had passed. "It would appear the law is on your side, Lieutenant Governor. But I would remind you that in a trial of pirates previously held in Virginia on May 13, 1700, both grand and petit juries were used. And it is my understanding that in the ongoing trial of Stede Bonnet and his crew being conducted in Charles Town, the pirates are being judged by their peers. It is a matter of judicial fairness."

"I don't particularly care about fairness for pirates," said Spotswood.

"Yes, you've made that abundantly clear," said the reverend. "But I would humbly remind you that most Admiralty courts in America and most colonial-friendly British officials resist trying their pirate friends."

"Yes well, I am no friend of the pirates, nor of these rebellious colonials you refer to as *Americans*."

Ludwell scoffed. "Why we are all here Americans, Lieutenant Governor. Everybody but you that is. For us, the colonies come first—not the King. I would have thought you would have learned that lesson by now."

"That kind of talk is treason against the Crown—and you know it, Philip Ludwell. Please do not try my patience any further with such treasonous talk, even if you are doing it solely to shock me."

"My apologies if I have upset his governorship. But make no mistake, that is the thinking of most everyone in this colony. So you had better learn that accommodation is the better part of valor."

"I would not in this lifetime perform any such accommodation unless I thought it appropriate and met the needs of the Crown. But for now, let's take it one step at a time and get down to the details of Mr. Howard's trial. Shall we?"

Several of the councilors voiced their approval and, for the next two hours, the nine men thrashed out the legal groundwork for the coming trial of Blackbeard's quartermaster. The piracy law passed by William III specified that a governor could hold a pirate trial without using a jury only in a time of crisis, so Spotswood's first task was to convince the councilors that Edward Thache and his remaining and former crew members in Virginia and North Carolina constituted a pirate "crisis" that threatened the colony. They then went over the piracy charges. The indictment against Howard cited several attacks made by Thache in 1717, then claimed the attacks continued after January 5—thereby making the quartermaster and his captain legally ineligible for the King's pardon. At Spotswood's urging, the councilors were eventually willing to ignore the fact that Governor Eden had extended the pardon to Thache and his crew, making the pirate commodore a legal claimant beyond Virginia's southern border.

The charges focused on the Spanish sloop captured off Havana, which he had renamed *Adventure* and now legally owned thanks to Eden, as well as several other attacks after the January 5 cutoff date, including the capture of the slaver off the Charles Town bar. This was important because one of the two slaves accompanying William Howard when he was captured was first seized by the pirates on board that slave ship. The slave, therefore, provided proof that Howard took part in the attack. When they were finished listing all the charges, Reverend Blair asked what the next step was in preparation for trial.

"Mr. Howard will be moved to the public jail in Williamsburg, and a trial date will be set," answered Spotswood.

"Who will serve on the Vice-Admiralty Court?" asked Ludwell.

"Captain Brand of the HMS *Lyme*, his colleague Captain Gordon of the *Pearl*, and John Holloway, I should imagine. They're the ones who have sat on the court for the past year."

Ludwell scoffed. "You think that Brand and Gordon will serve in the trial if Holloway sits on the court? After all, the crafty lawyer just indicted them for wrongful imprisonment. I should think they would be smarting over the incident."

Spotswood realized his adversary was onto something; Brand and Gordon, two prideful by-the-book men, would most likely be unwilling to work together with the lawyer after what he had done to them. But he needed these esteemed and uncontestable representatives of the Admiralty in his show trial to ensure that the outcome would be ratified by the British government.

"If Captains Brand and Gordon are unwilling to participate with Esquire Holloway, then I will have to ask the lawyer to recuse himself."

"Is that so?" said Ludwell. "You know in that case Howard will no doubt swing from the gallows. It won't be a bloody trial—it will be an execution."

"To prevent any disturbance on the bench that might ensue upon their publicly excepting against Mr. Holloway, I will send him a civil message to desire him not to expose himself by appearing on the trial. He will have no option but to accede and I will secure replacement counsel for him."

"Yes, and William Howard will be left to fight for his life in court without the support of a lawyer. You know the man comes from a good North Carolina landholding family. And let's not forget that he was pardoned by Governor Eden."

"Yes, but Mr. Howard is in violation of the terms of the pardon. He has to answer for his transgressions in a court of law."

"A rigged court, I say."

"No one said life is fair, Mr. Ludwell. Especially no one who has had to live in these lawless colonies and come under attack by these marauders of the high seas. Now I believe we have concluded our session, gentlemen, and it is in God's hands now. If William Howard is tried and convicted as a pirate, then it was God's will that it should be so. If not, then he will be found innocent of all charges."

Ludwell shook his head. "I'm just wondering who in this particular case *God* is, Alexander. A part of me can't help but think it is you, the Lord of Virginia."

Spotswood gave a supercilious smile. "The Lord of Virginia. Why thank you, Philip—I must say I rather like the title."

CHAPTER 60

VICE-ADMIRALTY COURT, CHARLES TOWN

NOVEMBER 12, 1718

AS VICE-ADMIRALTY JUDGE NICHOLAS TROTT—South Carolina's chief justice—prepared to deliver the court's final verdict, Stede Bonnet felt his leg shaking. His future looked bleak. The presiding judge and his panel of ten assistant justices had, during the past two weeks of a highly-public trial, found twenty-nine of the major's thirty-three seamen guilty of piracy. Twenty-four of them had already been marched down to White Point, the southern tip of the city facing the Ashley River, and hanged in front of a large jeering crowd, leaving only Bonnet and five of his crew members to still face justice. Looking into Trott's stern visage, Bonnet lamented that his courtroom defense had fallen on deaf ears. It would be the rope for him for certain. He shuddered at the thought of a public hanging and having his unconsecrated mortal remains dumped into an unmarked grave between the low- and high-tide lines of White's Point, where his soul would roam restlessly for all eternity. It was too grim a fate to contemplate and one he had not anticipated when he had abandoned his family and first set sail from Barbados to go a-pirating.

"Major Stede Bonnet," began Trott, "you stand here convicted of two indictments of piracy—one by verdict of the jury, the other by your own confession. Although you were indicted but for two facts, you know that at your trial it was fully proved, even by an unwilling witness, that you piratically took and rifled through no less than thirteen vessels since you sailed from North Carolina. So that you might have been indicted and convicted of eleven more acts of piracy, since you took the benefit of the King's Act of Grace, and pretended to leave that wicked course of life…"

As Trott droned on with yet another one of his lengthy harangues on sin, repentance, and divine justice, the gentleman pirate couldn't help but feel that he had wasted his entire life. His fateful decision to become a pirate had turned out to be a disaster for not only himself and his family, but for the twenty-nine men who had already been hung or were about to be shortly. He wished he could turn back the clock and start anew, but that was an impossible fantasy.

"You know that the crimes you have committed are *evil* in themselves," Trott railed on, "and contrary to the light and law of nature, as well as the law of God, by which you are commanded that you should not steal, Exodus 20:15. And the apostle St. Paul expressly affirms that thieves shall not inherit the kingdom of God, I Corinthians 6:10."

Here the judge paused and glared at the accused, and Bonnet couldn't help but feel a sinking feeling in his stomach and a spinning sensation in his head. Suddenly, his handsome lace-trimmed clothes, velvet jacket, buckled black shoes, and periwig felt terribly constricting. God, could he use a jolt of rum or brandy right now to settle his jangled nerves. He felt Trott's eyes burning right through him, and he couldn't help but draw a mental image of Cotton Mather, the fiery New England preacher who, it was reported in the pirate community, had sanctimoniously browbeaten Black Sam Bellamy's captured men to repent their sins and ask God's forgiveness for their wicked, dissolute ways. The condemned men locked in a Boston jail cell had been unable to shut up the loquacious Puritan, who held Atlantic pirates and the witches of Salem in equal disdain.

But in Bonnet's view, the overbearing Trott was even worse. The unfortunate pirates hauled before the bar in the chief justice's court had received little sympathy during the proceedings. It was obvious he detested pirates, considering them "enemies of God and humanity" who had endangered his city for far too long. For two weeks straight, he had delivered interminable orations and tedious religious discourses that reviewed the law on piracy since ancient times, drew moral homilies from the Bible, and characterized Bonnet and his crew as "brutes and beasts of prey." He reminded the jury that South Carolina had long suffered from "the evil of piracy," stressing how many of its finest men had gone to Cape Fear to rid the colony of pirates and paid with their lives "by the hands of those inhuman and murdering criminals," and that "the blood of those murdered persons will cry for vengeance and justice against these offenders." Convinced that Bonnet had slipped from religious doctrine, he urged him to seek repentance to save his soul and pay with his life by suffering "in the lake which burneth with fire and brimstone." In this censorious atmosphere, it came as no surprise to Bonnet that the jury had returned a verdict of guilty for most of his crew and sentenced them to hang.

"But to theft you have added a greater sin, which is murder. How many you may have killed of those that refitted you in the committing of your former piracies, I know not. But this we all know. That besides the wounded, you killed no less than eighteen persons out of those that went by lawful authority to suppress you, and to put a stop to those rapines that you daily acted..."

He had a sudden urge to jump up from his courtroom seat and run away. But there was no escape, not a second time. In early October, when Colonel Rhett had delivered him and his crew to Charles Town as prisoners, Bonnet had been treated courteously, but he had taken advantage of that courtesy. He and two of his men that had been placed under arrest at the marshal's home rather than the prison had escaped. Not wanting to stand trial and be handed the death penalty, they had set out northward in a small open boat. They had little food or water, the weather suddenly turned stormy, and the pair was forced to turn back to Sullivan's Island. Here Rhett captured Bonnet again, and this time the attitude of the authorities towards the pirate captain turned harsh. He had forfeited the sympathy many South Carolinians had previously held for him as a "gentleman," and the escape attempt had only confirmed that he couldn't be trusted.

And now, he sat in Trott's courtroom being charged with thirteen piracies and the murder of eighteen men in the battle at Cape Fear. His own men had testified to the ships he had taken and his crimes, a jury had found him guilty, and he was likely about to be sentenced to hang right along with them. It was a monumental stroke of misfortune in a piratical career filled with endless bad luck, and he couldn't believe what a horrible pirate he had been. It was then that Trott leaned forward from his judge's chair, wagged a bony finger at him, and proceeded to again shame the gentleman pirate for his corruption and remind him of his need for repentance.

"You, Major Bonnet, being a gentleman that have had the advantage of a liberal education, and being generally esteemed a man of letters, I believe it will be needless for me to explain to you the nature of repentance and faith in Christ, they being so fully and so often mentioned in the Scriptures, that you cannot but know them. But that considering the course of your life and actions, I have just reason to fear that the principles of religion that had been instilled into you by your education, have been at least corrupted, if not entirely defaced, by the skepticism and infidelity of this wicked age; and that what time you allowed for study was rather applied to the polite literature, and the vain philosophy of the times, than a serious search after the law and will of God, as revealed to us in the Holy Scriptures..."

Glancing around the room, he saw the assistant justices and several people in the crowd scowling at him, admonishing him for his wickedness, but there were also several women who looked at him tenderly and a pair of younger women who were openly crying. He politely nodded his head to them, wanting them to know that he appreciated their support. But these women were not going to keep him from the gallows.

And yet, a part of him didn't even want to live any longer. The truth was he had been deeply unhappy for most of his year and a half as a pirate, and during that time the adventure, excitement, and danger had never measured up to his imagination or expectations from reading Exquemelin, Dampier, and Rogers. The only time he had felt alive was when he and his crew took a prize or fought in battle—but even the three pitched battles he had fought had proved supremely costly to him and his men. As a man once favored with wealth, the company of the best society on Barbados, and the veneration of his friends, he now felt an overwhelming numbness at his own insignificance. What a waste his life had been.

Now Trott wrapped up his speech with a harsh rhetorical flourish that made Bonnet feel as if he would most certainly go to hell.

"And therefore having now discharged my duty to you as a Christian, by giving you the best counsel I can with respect to the salvation of your soul, I must now do my office as a judge."

Here he paused and a hushed silence fell over the courtroom. Bonnet couldn't help but feel embarrassed and angry at the humiliating dressing down and morality lesson he had received from the bombastic judge. And yet, a part of him wondered if it might be possible to avoid the hangman's noose. Perhaps Judge Trott's stern lecture was a warning and the sanctimonious martinet was going to allow him to go free. For a fleeting instant, he allowed himself the fantasy that he would be pardoned, as Governor Eden had done.

But then he heard the chilling words as the judge pronounced the age-old ritual sentence.

"The sentence that the law hath appointed to pass upon you for your offenses, and which the court doth therefore award, is that you, the said Stede Bonnet, shall go from hence to the place from whence you came, and from thence to the place of execution, where you shall be hanged by the neck till you are dead. And the God of infinite mercy be merciful to your soul."

The courtroom gave an audible gasp and several young women began to cry. Though he had expected and prepared himself mentally for such an outcome, he was still taken aback. He felt his whole body stiffen as the doomed reality of his situation struck him like a hammer blow.

Tomorrow or soon thereafter, he would wear the hangman's hempen halter, swing from the gallows on White Point, and be buried unceremoniously between the low- and high-water marks, accompanied by the last few pitiful members of his crew. It would be a dreadful, unchristianly way to meet his Maker and little Allamby up in heaven would be ashamed.

Utterly ashamed.

CHAPTER 61

CAPITOL AND GOVERNOR'S PALACE WILLIAMSBURG

NOVEMBER 12, 1718

AS WILLIAM HOWARD was removed from the courtroom in chains, Spotswood smiled inwardly. The judge had just passed sentence and Thache's former quartermaster was to be hung from the neck until dead for his acts of piracy, which meant that Spotswood's plan was coming off to perfection. Now that Howard's testimony was transcribed into the court records, the governor had a clear picture of what Blackbeard was up to, where he spent his time, and how he was definitely not eligible for His Majesty's most gracious pardon and had merely bought the protection of the senior-most officials in North Carolina. Now it was time to act on his newly acquired intelligence and aggressively hunt down the pirate.

He now had the confidence that he could—if not legally then at least semi-officially—enter his neighboring colony, apprehend Thache and his gang of misfits, and haul them in shackles to Virginia to be put on trial. Though not a legal action in the strict sense, he knew without question that Thache and his crew were not eligible for the King's pardon due to piracies committed after the January 5 grace period, and he had the precedent of Governor Johnson in the apprehension and trial of Stede Bonnet and his recently condemned crew. With Howard's incriminating testimony now a part of the official records, convictions for Blackbeard and his remaining crew members dividing their time between Ocracoke and Bath Town would be virtually guaranteed.

With the attorney general of Virginia and two naval dignitaries sitting as judges, there had never been any doubt as to the outcome of the trial. John Clayton, the colony's attorney general whom Spotswood had chosen to replace John Holloway, and Captains Ellis Brand and George Gordon, the commanders of the two British men-of-war stationed in Chesapeake Bay, had performed their roles to perfection by simultaneously sealing Howard's fate and paving the way for an invasion of North Carolina in pursuit of the notorious Blackbeard. And now, with the courtroom proceedings complete and the verdict of death by hanging rendered, he could now meet with the Royal Navy officers without raising suspicions, as both were in Williamsburg on routine business to serve as officers of the court.

While William Howard was being unceremoniously shoved back into Williamsburg's tidy brick gaol, Spotswood escorted Brand and Gordon the four blocks from the resplendent H-shaped Capitol, through the market square, and down the Palace Green to the Governor's Palace. Once seated in one of the second floor's opulent meeting rooms, Spotswood pulled out a large map of continental North Carolina and its Outer Banks. He then laid out his plan before the two naval officers to invade the neighboring colony to the south and capture both the pirate and his treasure. The gentlemanly Brand and Gordon looked immaculate in their blue dress uniforms, periwigs, silk stockings, and silver-buckled shoes, their sheathed dress swords dangling from their sides with the proper hint of bellicosity.

"What I envision, gentlemen, is a two-pronged assault to apprehend Blackbeard—or kill him, if he is foolish enough to offer resistance. Because we are unsure whether he and his crew are presently in Bath Town or on the island of Ocracoke, we will need to launch a surprise attack at both locations. To accomplish this, I propose that one contingent takes an overland route to Bath, while the other contingent sails to Ocracoke to confront the pirates and ensure that they do not escape into the Atlantic, should they be there instead." Spotswood then indicated the two routes—one by land, the other by sea—by tracing his index finger along the map on the conference table. "The Bath contingent will be supported by Mr. Moseley and his gentlemen friends of North Carolina. They are intimately familiar with the territory to the south. Now this plan is only preliminary and the actual details will have to be worked out here today and in the coming days. But we must not delay or else the pirates might be alerted to our intentions by their loyalists here in Virginia and in the Carolinas.

"The plan must also be executed under a cloak of secrecy, so we cannot tell anyone of our intentions except those who must, by necessity, be in the know and are firmly loyal to the operation. I have not informed my governing Council or the House of Burgesses of my intentions, nor am I planning to, and I am certainly not going to air the matter with Governor Eden. The pirates are simply too popular and their many favorers in these parts, including several men on my own Council, might send intelligence to Thache. So what do you say, gentlemen? Are you willing to throw in with the Royal Governor of the Colony of Virginia and rid our colonies, once and for all, of these villains that infest our peaceful waters?"

Brand, the senior officer and Gordon's direct superior, spoke up without equivocation. "It would be an honor, Governor, to take the fight to this nest of vipers. In fact, I sayeth it's high time. So count me and my men in. I promise we won't let you down and will do the colonies of Virginia and North Carolina and His Majesty King George honor. I also agree that a two-pronged attack to flesh out the pirates is the best approach given the present situation."

"I wholeheartedly agree and am fully on board as well, Governor," said Captain Gordon. "We have wanted to take a crack at these rogues for quite some time and I know our men look forward to the opportunity."

Spotswood gave his most ebullient smile. "That's what I like to hear, gentlemen. Now let's get to the details. I presume, Captain Brand, that as the senior naval officer in these waters ye would be in overall command of the operation?"

"That is correct, Governor. I will also lead one of the contingents."

"And who shall lead the other?"

"It will be Captain Gordon here"—he motioned to his Royal Navy colleague to his right—"or perhaps his subordinate Lieutenant Maynard, depending on potential threats along the coast as the date of embarkation approaches."

"I would like you to set out by the end of the week."

Brand made eye contact with Gordon. "I don't see that as a problem. But what *is* going to be a problem is a matter that you and I have discussed previously."

"And what is that, Captain?"

"The fact that the *Lyme* and the *Pearl* are both far too large to negotiate the dangerous shoalwaters of North Carolina's rivers and sounds inside of the barrier islands. I've consulted the charts for Pamlico Sound and can tell you without equivocation that both vessels will be useless in the coming campaign against Blackbeard and his pirates. The *Lyme* is a good deal smaller and substantially lighter than the *Pearl*, displacing three hundred eighty-four tons, but she still draws ten and a half feet of water. And the *Pearl*...well, she's out of the question. She's nearly ninety-eight feet long, displaces over five hundred thirty tons, and draws thirteen and a half feet of water from the waterline to the bottom of her keel. The draught of both vessels is too great to pass over the coastal sandbars that link together the islands of the Outer Banks."

"Then I will charter, at my own expense, a pair of nimble sloops of much shallower draught that will meet your specifications—once you have again consulted your charts, of course. The rented vessels will be placed at your disposal."

The two officers looked at one another again, this time with raised brows. "You're willing to outfit a pair of sloops at your own expense to catch Blackbeard and his crew?" asked Brand.

You don't know the half of it, he thought. *I would give my left arm to see this sea robber and his motley crew swing from the gallows. I despise the man and everything he represents.* "Put it this way, gentlemen. I will do whatever it takes to see that the job is properly done. If we don't put a stop to Blackbeard and his gang of miscreants now, then we will only have ourselves to blame when the Outer Banks are turned into an armed pirate fortress, a new Madagascar or Nassau."

"Very well, Captain Gordon and I agree to man, arm, and supply the sloops procured by yourself and place them under our command. I take it that meets with your approval, Captain."

"Yes, absolutely," said Gordon.

"I can also offer you and your men an extra incentive," said Spotswood. "Since this will be a dangerous mission into enemy territory, so to speak, I believe you and your crews should be given appropriate compensation."

Brand gave a chivalrous smile. "You'll get no argument from Captain Gordon and myself on that score," he said. "What are ye prepared to offer?"

"In addition to the possibility of claiming some of Blackbeard's treasure, I am prepared to offer you a special bounty for the capture or killing of the pirate and his crew members."

"A special bounty?"

"Yes, as an added incentive to the crews of the two sloops, I will see to it that the Colony of Virginia pays a bounty for the pirates, dead or alive. Consider it a variation on the established naval policy of paying out money for captured vessels. I have a draft copy of what I propose right here." He reached into his foldover leather satchel, withdrew a piece of foolscap, and handed it to Brand. "I have prepared this *Act to Encourage the Apprehending and Destroying of Pirates*. I will submit the proclamation tomorrow and have it ratified by the legislature. It refers to information elicited at the recent trial of Howard, emphasizing that the pirates threaten revenge on the shipping of this colony for the death sentence of the quartermaster and that it is for these reasons the governor and Council think it absolutely necessary that some speedy and effectual measures be taken for breaking the knot of robbers prowling our local waters. As you can see, the reward amounts you and your men would receive for your services are listed in the draft proclamation."

The naval captain read the proposed proclamation aloud. *"'For Edward Thache, commonly called Captain Thache, or Blackbeard, one hundred pounds. For every other commander of a pirate ship, sloop, or vessel, forty pounds; for every lieutenant, master or quartermaster, bosun, or carpenter, twenty pounds; for every other inferior officer, fifteen pounds, and for every private man taken on board such ship. sloop, or vessel, ten pounds.'"*

"I'm liking this plan more and more as we speak," said Brand, a gleam of avarice in his eyes.

"Aye, it's good to know that if we catch the pirates, we will be properly rewarded for our efforts," agreed Captain Gordon.

Spotswood concurred with a vigorous nod. "Yes well, if it all goes according to plan, the endeavor will prove not only patriotic but profitable for all of us as well as the Crown."

"And if it doesn't go according to plan?" asked Gordon.

"I don't want to even contemplate that prospect, gentlemen. As you well know, there is no margin for error here. Together, we will either be saviors or laughingstocks in the eyes of our countrymen and history. I, gentlemen, do not intend for us to be the latter."

The room went tensely silent. "Don't worry, Governor," said Brand after several anxious seconds had passed. "We won't let you down."

"No, gentlemen, you must not let the *Crown* down."

And with that he sent them on their way to make their preparations.

CHAPTER 62

GOVERNOR'S PALACE
WILLIAMSBURG

NOVEMBER 12, 1718

THREE MINUTES LATER, he stood at the window watching the two naval officers walking across the Palace Green, their dress swords swinging at their sides. His plan was falling perfectly into place. But contrary to what he had said to Brand and Gordon, he knew there would be plenty of obstacles ahead. For his plan was not merely to destroy Blackbeard; he had to also topple his political nemesis Governor Eden along with Tobias Knight.

He knew perfectly well that, despite the veneer of legitimacy afforded him by the trial of William Howard and by Governor Johnson's actions, his plan was still patently illegal. After all, neither he nor his newly recruited naval officers had the authority to invade another colony. And as he had noted to Brand and Moseley, Blackbeard was, legally speaking, a citizen who had broken no laws and was in good standing. He had been pardoned by Governor Eden for his previous piracies, had applied for and received legal approval to salvage the French vessel captured near Bermuda from that same governor, and he had yet to be indicted for any crime. Spotswood knew he was essentially seeking to kidnap the resident of one colony and transport him to another to face legal action. But he was not bothered by the overt illegality of his scheme. He had already made up in his mind a month ago that he was going to go after Thache without reservation, by taking action first and seeking approval from the Board of Trade and lords proprietors later. He wanted the notorious Blackbeard—and Governor Eden too—so badly that he could taste it.

The most important thing he had going for him was precedent, though it was not precedent of a legal nature. Other colonial governors had taken aggressive action against pirates without being granted specific authority from the Board of Trade or Admiralty to do so—and they had not been accused of wrongdoing. Indeed, the most recent example had taken place in North Carolina itself. South Carolina's governor had taken matters into his own hands by sending out Colonel Rhett's anti-piracy patrol from Charles Town that had cornered and captured Stede Bonnet and his crew in the Cape Fear River. Then there was Governor Keith of Pennsylvania. The threat posed by the Atlantic rogues was considered serious enough that he had fitted out two sloops, commanded by Captains Raymond and Taylor, to patrol the waters off the Delaware Capes, in the hope of intercepting either Vane, Bonnet, or Blackbeard. And finally there was Woodes Rogers. With the backing of powerful British warships, he was currently extirpating New Providence and every other island of the Bahamas of the nest of vermin, thereby destroying the pirates' base once and for all. In extremis, Spotswood knew he could always maintain that he was only following the example of these three colonial governors.

True, he was taking advantage of Governor Eden and his weak colony, but he didn't care. If Eden lacked the teeth to arrest or eliminate sea bandits within his own borders, then Spotswood would do the job for him. He had no respect or patience for the governor or his fledgling proprietary dominion. He viewed such colonies run by titled men of wealth in London as inferior to Crown colonies run on behalf of the monarchy, like Virginia, and he hoped his actions would expose the ineffectiveness and moral turpitude of the Carolinian proprietary system. But what truly nettled him most of all was that his counterpart to the south didn't merely seem to tolerate the pirates, he appeared to actively support them in their endeavors and even socialize with them.

Spotswood could never see himself receiving a share of the plunder from a pirate, and he couldn't understand how Eden, a wealthy British loyalist from a prestigious family, could debase himself by associating with pirates. He himself would never consider striking a deal with such outlaws, pardoned or not, and he certainly would never provide a pirate with a safe haven close to his colony's main township. After all, pirates were the morally corrupt villains of all nations, men who belonged to no country and, therefore, had no real rights under the law. Proprietary governments could not be trusted to offer legitimate pardon to these rogues, who must be continually watched lest they return to their wicked ways as soon as their money was spent.

He knew his plan to invade North Carolina using the threat of violence went far beyond the official authority vested in him when he first assumed office on behalf of the earl of Orkney. But he was on a mission to destroy two men—Blackbeard and Eden—and in his mind legal niceties did not apply to cutthroats and their supporters. More importantly, if things went according to plan, his political stock would rise and he would be given a clean slate with his Council and the House of Burgesses. The law clearly stated that he could only intervene in the affairs of another colony in case of distress to its plantations and only through the written approval of the governor of the affected colony. Eden, of course, had made no such request, but Spotswood didn't care. He was willing to take the gamble based on the precedents set by Governors Johnson, Keith, and Woodes Rogers and based upon what he viewed as Eden's complicity and corruption with Blackbeard.

He knew that he would not only be meddling in the affairs of another colony, but would be doing so using military force, which Eden and the lords proprietor would view as tantamount to invasion. But again, he did not care because all he cared about was the end, not the means with which he arrived there. The news of Colonel Rhett and his men hunting down previously pardoned but recidivist pirates across the South Carolina border into their northern neighbor and engaging them in a bloody and decisive battle consumed his imagination. The truth was he was bitterly disappointed he had not been the first governor to authorize such a heroic and righteous punitive expedition against the pirates.

Ludwell was right about his motives. He was using an outside threat and the prospect of military force to distract the Virginia people and his political opponents from his much-criticized policies and to personally profit. He also knew that by inserting himself into North Carolina's affairs, he was taking grave risk. Only if Blackbeard and his pirates were caught or killed could he achieve victory. While his actions would no doubt be condemned by Eden and some of his superiors in London, with success even his detractors would have to concede that he had eliminated the nearby pirate threat and that Eden couldn't keep his own house in order. That, in turn, would enhance the possibility of a Virginian takeover, which was Spotswood's foremost priority. Since taking his oath as governor, he had been eager to extend his control and influence over Virginia's southern border, which he had never considered to be far enough south. In fact, he had long secretly harbored plans to annex North Carolina and fold it into Virginia—an event that would dramatically increase his power and make him an even richer man under the Crown.

Ultimately, Spotswood knew he had little to lose and much to gain from his scheme against Blackbeard and his fellow pirates—unless it somehow all went to hell. Failure meant he would play straight into the hands of his adversaries in the Governor's Council and House of Burgesses, and the calls for his removal would be impossible for Governor George Hamilton, the earl of Orkney, and the Board of Trade to ignore.

His Achilles' heel was the whole legal question. Taking steps to apprehend Blackbeard was one thing, but what would happen when Brand and his naval force actually caught the pirate? Most likely, the rogue would be arrested on North Carolina soil or on the high seas, and then transported back to Williamsburg in chains to stand trial. All Spotswood needed was another colonial rabble-rouser like William Howard's lawyer John Holloway for his whole anti-piracy crusade to be exposed for what it really was: a distraction, and a highly illegal one at that, to disguise his own culture of corruption and profiteering nurtured during his eight years of oversight of the colony on behalf of the *in-absentia* Hamilton. Without the permission of His Majesty allowing him to conduct pirate trials within the jurisdiction of Virginia, he was vulnerable to attack from his political enemies at home and Byrd in London for overstepping his charter. His one advantage was that he was Virginia's Vice-Admiralty representative, which would allow him to control the legal process. Unlike in normal court cases, there was no requirement for proceedings heard under British naval law to be put to trial by jury. As the Admiralty's representative, Spotswood could, therefore, manipulate the trial to his advantage by selecting the venue and panel that would sit on the Vice-Admiralty Court, which would allow him to stage-manage the proceedings as he had when he had stacked the case against William Howard.

But he could worry about the legal consequences of his actions further down the road. The first step was to engage Blackbeard and capture or kill the rogue along with his crew. For Captain Ellis Brand and the British Royal Navy, it would be an expedition fraught with peril. But the prospect of success was intoxicating. Spotswood was only too aware of what the heroes of Charles Town, Governor Johnson and Colonel William Rhett, had accomplished by engaging and capturing Bonnet two months earlier. Such a coup had been accomplished once—and it could be done again. But more importantly, the government of North Carolina had lodged no backlash of protest against Johnson for invading his neighboring colony in September.

And yet, Spotswood couldn't help but feel that, even if the plan was successful and Thache and his crew were vanquished, he would come under heavy fire from many quarters for his decision to invade North Carolina. That's why to justify his interceding in its affairs, he had to prove that his aggressive actions were necessary to protect the Crown's interests. That meant proving that Eden was a criminal who had knowingly received stolen goods from the pirates as payment in return for ignoring their illicit activities. But Spotswood was not prepared to challenge Eden to his face, or to accuse him of impropriety without unimpeachable proof. That was the problem: he knew that such proof would be hard to come by. In fact, he could only hope that by the time Blackbeard and his crew were captured or killed, hard evidence would emerge demonstrating collusion between the pirate and Eden, as his fellow conspirator Edward Moseley, who was equally desperate to bring down Eden, had told him there would be. What he and Moseley were banking on was that there would be incriminating documents linking the Eden administration to Blackbeard. At the same time, Spotswood knew that once he interceded in the affairs of Eden and his neighboring colony, he would lay himself open to countercharges of irresponsibly overstepping his legal mandate as the governor of Virginia.

All the same, the game was afoot and there was no turning back now. He was not a man to be trifled with and his mind was made up. He would eliminate the nest of vipers at Bath Town or Ocracoke, or in the Pamlico Sound in between, thereby ending the threat posed by Blackbeard once and for all. And in the process, he would expose Governor Eden and his North Carolina minions as complicit in piracy, demonstrating that they were an embarrassment and disloyal to the Crown. And when it was all over and done and the smoke had cleared, he would emerge victorious and be a part of history.

Just like the noble English knights of old.

CHAPTER 63

KIQUOTAN ROADS, VIRGINIA

NOVEMBER 17, 1718

AT 15:02 HOURS, First Lieutenant Robert Maynard, first officer of the warship HMS *Pearl*, swept his glass over the languid, murky tidewaters of the James River. With his survey complete, he gave orders to raise anchor and get his designated flagship *Jane* and its consort sloop *Ranger* under way. The two shallow-draught civilian vessels had been hired out by Governor Spotswood to hunt down Blackbeard. At Maynard's command, seamen's voices were raised, lines yanked free, and sails hoisted. The cream-colored sheets of canvas flapped in the squally Virginia breeze as the two trading vessels now refitted for war took to the wind like spry colts and navigated downriver towards Chesapeake Bay. For colors, the vessels flew the British Royal Naval ensign, a field of red with the Union Jack in the upper left corner, at the stern; a commission pendant on the single mast; and a Union flag on the bowsprit's jackstaff.

The lieutenant stood on the quarterdeck of the *Jane*, his first-mate and other key officers at his side. He wore a blue coat with brass buttons, gleaming in the late afternoon sunlight, and a modicum of gold braid trimming his sleeves. The oldest officer on station in the American colonies at the age of thirty-four, the Royal Navy veteran was anxious to distinguish himself in action against the notorious pirate and thereby gain himself his coveted captaincy. But he was also anxious for the chance to seize pirate treasure and the reward of one hundred pounds being offered by the governor for the pirate's head, as well as the various lesser sums for Blackbeard's subordinate officers and crew members. The capture of Edward Thache and his freebooters offered him a chance to make his own mark upon history and garner some much-needed income to supplement the meager pay granted him by his parsimonious king.

He had received his official orders only this morning from his superior officer, Captain Brand, who was in overall command of the two-pronged attack into North Carolina territory: a march overland to capture the pirates in Bath Town, and a seaborne attack on Blackbeard's sloop off Ocracoke. Brand would command the main force of the expedition, which would march cross-country from the James River to Bath with the strength of the column augmented along the way by Colonel Edward Moseley and the North Carolina militia. Brand and his manservant would cross the boundary line between the two colonies of Virginia and North Carolina near Windsor, at which point Spotswood's legal authority ceased to exist. Brand would be relying on speed, surprise, and a small force of only himself and his servant to counter any move by the North Carolina authorities or the pirates to prevent him from carrying out his job. At Queen Anne Creek, he would link up with Moseley, his brothers-in-law Colonel Maurice Moore and Captain Jeremiah Vail, and their contingent of militia. From there, Brand's expeditionary force would strike for

Governor Eden's residence in Bath, growing in strength along the way with fresh forces gathered up by the North Carolinians.

Meanwhile, Maynard would lead the second contingent, an armed naval force consisting of the Spotswood-chartered *Jane* and *Ranger* in a seagoing expedition to Ocracoke Island. The Royal Navy provided the crews: thirty-five sailors from Captain Gordon's *Pearl* and twenty-five from Brand's *Lyme*. Maynard was in overall command of the two sloops and all the seamen headed for the Old Watering Hole along the protected interior of the barrier island. It was here Thache was reported to have set up a pirate base camp. Maynard's force would capture any pirates left behind on Blackbeard's base at Ocracoke before crossing the fifty miles of Pamlico Sound to the mouth of the Pamlico River. Once in place, Maynard could blockade the town from the sea while his commanding officer swept into Bath from the landward side. Captain Gordon drew the short straw and remained behind on the James River with the *Lyme* and *Pearl* men-of-war, commanding the floating reserve of two warships with half-strength crews.

The larger *Ranger* and more compact *Jane* sailed east down the river, the *Ranger* a hundred yards abreast of the flagship's larboard beam. Both sloops were fast, light, clean, stiff, and weatherly, and as Maynard stared out over the railing at the *Ranger*, he was confident that both boats would do the job set out for them. The only thing that worried him was that neither vessel was equipped with heavy cannon or even swivel guns. It was anticipated that the additional weight would make them less maneuverable in the shallow waters of Roanoke Inlet, Pamlico Sound, Town Creek, and Ocracoke Inlet. He and Midshipman Edmund Hyde of the *Lyme*, who captained his consort *Ranger*, had an ample supply of pistols, muskets, cutlasses, daggers, boarding axes, *grenadoes*, and boarding pikes to go along with their months' worth of provisions. But with no cannon and only sixty men, Maynard knew that if his sloops were the ones to encounter Blackbeard, they would have to surprise him at anchor. Otherwise, they would be even more vulnerable to attack than the pirates they were being sent to fight.

Feeling the wind on his face, he was glad to be at sea again, and even happier to be leading an expedition of such importance. From Brand's intelligence reports, he knew that Thache had a greatly reduced crew, but that didn't mean the man wouldn't put up a vigorous fight. In fact, Maynard was expecting it and actually looked forward to the opportunity to cross swords with the rogue if it came to a pitched battle. His only hope was that, if they did get into a scrap, the pirate captain wouldn't be able to unleash his eight guns against him. He and his crew would stand no chance against the pirates' broadsides.

Maynard was a cautious officer. Intelligent and professional, he was intent on succeeding in the mission for which he was assigned, and he had no desire to be a first lieutenant forever. And his orders were clear. They called for him to navigate his way through Roanoke Inlet, sail the length of Pamlico Sound to Brant Island Shoals, strike east for Ocracoke's southeast tip, and capture any pirates he could find on the island. If Blackbeard was not there, he would then cross the fifty miles of Pamlico Sound, proceed up Pamlico River, and head for Bath Town. Once in place he would blockade the river, hopefully trapping Blackbeard's *Adventure* in Town Creek. He and his men would act as a floating reserve for Captain Brand's force, which would sweep in from the landward side. If everything went according to plan the pirates would be caught in a trap. Naturally, their inclination would be to fight, and Maynard had to be ready to thwart any attempt by the pirates to escape by sea. However, as no one knew exactly where Blackbeard was, Maynard had to rely on his initiative, and stand ready to do battle with the pirates wherever they might be. When fighting a dangerous and wily former British Navy officer like Blackbeard, he knew nothing could be taken for granted.

But he and his men were ready. The sixty men in his invasion force were well armed. He had two local pilots familiar with the waters of Pamlico Sound, one aboard each sloop, to guide him, including Master Pilot William Butler who was said to have no equal when it came to navigating the treacherous shoaling waters of North Carolina. And his men were more than willing to fight—indeed, they seemed to relish the opportunity. They had been inspecting and cleaning their pistols and muskets, checking their powder, sharpening their swords, and practicing their fighting skills for much of the day.

In seven years of naval warfare fighting the French, he had put himself in harm's way time and again, especially in the sea battle off Dunkirk in 1708. But somehow he could feel that this bout with the notorious Blackbeard the pirate would be much bigger than any engagement he had fought before. He could feel in his bones a great contest, a battle for the ages. As he imagined it in his mind, he and his heavily bearded, cutlass-wielding adversary would be right in the middle of it all, two lead actors in a sword duel on a brightly lit stage.

And then together, they would forever be linked by history.

CHAPTER 64

OCRACOKE ISLAND
OUTER BANKS, NORTH CAROLINA

NOVEMBER 21, 1718

SITTING PEACEFULLY NEXT TO THE OLD WATERING HOLE, Edward Thache read over the secret letter from Tobias Knight a second time.

My friend,

If this finds you yet in harbor I would have you make the best of your way up as soon as possible your affairs will let you. I have something more to say to you than at present I can write; the bearer will tell you the end of our Indian War, and Garret can tell you in part what I have to say to you, so refer you in some measure to him.

I really think these three men are heartily sorry at their difference with you and will be very willing to ask your pardon; if I may advise, be friends again, it's better than falling out among your selves.

I expect the Governor this night or tomorrow, who I believe would be likewise glad to see you before you go, I have not time to add save my hearty respects to you, and am your real friend.

And Servant.

T. KNIGHT

When he was finished reading, a half dozen grackles flew in from the west. They touched down upon the gnarled limbs of a canopy of live oaks that spread out like the arms of an octopus. He studied the crow-like avians for a minute as they chucked and chattered, their yellow eyes poking out devilishly in the hauntingly beautiful forest of the barrier island. Then he read the letter a third time before looking up and staring thoughtfully again at the ominous, black-headed birds.

Most of the crew was aboard the *Adventure*, sitting about drinking, playing games of chance, and entertaining the local trader Samuel Odell and his shipmates, while the remainder, including Thache, Caesar, Garret Gibbons, Richard Stiles, James White, and Joseph Brooks had come ashore to collect water and dig for clams. The clams would supplement the goose and duck supper the captain was intending to host that night in gratitude to Odell and his crew, who were being feted for recently pulling the grounded *Adventure* off Brant Island Shoals. It was to be a farewell feast before the company set sail for St. Thomas.

Having already spoken at length to his bosun Garret Gibbons, the bearer of the letter, Thache knew what Knight was telling him. The letter was not a warning, but rather an announcement of good news and potential reconciliation. By referring to the end of the Indian War, Knight was alluding to the fact that the much-feared conflagration in Bath County had turned out to be nothing more than false alarm. The potential threat of a new Indian war was the impetus that had hastened the

Adventure's departure from Bath shortly after the incident with Israel Hands three weeks earlier. With regard to what Tobias Knight wasn't able to disclose in his letter and that he had instructed Gibbons to further elaborate on, Knight was telling him that an extension of the King's pardon was on its way from England. It was not a message the secretary of the Governor's Council and customs inspector for North Carolina could convey in writing, hence his sentence: "I have something more to say to you than at present I can write."

Based upon his conversation with Knight, Gibbons wasn't able to elaborate further upon the nature of the extension except to say that the time period covered by the pardon had likely been extended beyond the date of January 5. This was important because it meant that Thache and his crew would no longer be in violation of the King's pardon with the taking of the French vessel *Rose Emelye* in August. If true, this was a huge change in his fortunes and would mean that he didn't need to sail to St. Thomas to seek a privateering commission from the Danish governor in that West Indies port. Instead, he could return to his beloved Margaret in Philadelphia and go on to live the life with her that he had always dreamed of without having to look over his shoulder as a hunted man.

If he sailed to Bath, Knight had made it clear the governor would like to see him, no doubt to communicate in person the details of the new pardon. As Gibbons had relayed it to him, even before the first pardon had expired, King George's Privy Council at St. James's Palace in London had apparently begun to consider the possibility that an extension might be necessary if they were going to be able to recruit an effective privateering force to raid Spain's treasure fleets sailing from Central and South America. Word had recently reached the colony that the King was expected to declare war on Spain this year, though no firm date for the recommencement of hostilities had been set. In anticipation of the coming conflict, the Privy Council was extending His Majesty's *Proclamation of Indemnity*, but the precise dates for its limitations had yet to be made officially known. A ship bearing the new pardons was expected by early- to mid-December, and colonial governors were expected to follow the letter of the law accordingly.

The second part of the letter was the more troubling and enigmatic. The "three men" that had some "difference" with him, whom Knight believed wanted to reconcile with him, were none other than Colonel Edward Moseley and his brothers-in-law, Colonel Maurice Moore and Captain Jeremiah Vail. During his multiple stays in Bath Town, the three merchant-landowners had tried to strike an exclusive arrangement with him to sell his piratically taken goods to them. But Thache had refused. While he and his smuggled sugar, cocoa, indigo, and other provisions had been welcomed by Bath County colonists and Pamlico Sound traders, Moseley, Moore, and Vail were well known for their high prices and predatory business practices and wanted him to sell them his pirated goods at ridiculously cheap prices. During his last meeting with them, he had again refused to work with them and they had gotten into a heated argument. Threats had been made by the three wealthy North Carolina businessmen and he had stormed out of the tavern. Now, they apparently wanted to reconcile. In the absence of an agreement with these gentlemen, he had become unwanted competition. They were obviously afraid that he would undersell them and hurt their business since he could deal directly with consumers. Now that he had been granted the King's pardon, the three powerful North Carolinians likely feared that he would continue to remain a major competitor—not in Nassau or Jamaica but in their own back yard.

But somehow he didn't believe that Moore and his brothers-in-law were as willing to reconcile as Knight suggested. All they really seemed to care about was that his cheaper goods posed serious competition. Without some business arrangement with him for access to those cheaper goods, they could not hope to profit. So it made sense for them to try and reconcile. But somehow he didn't think they would do that and would try to undermine him. He wasn't sure how they would accomplish such a feat, but he had a feeling, deep down, that that was precisely what they were doing. At the very least, they were not to be trusted in any smuggling or trading arrangement with his last supply of goods and provisions remaining on Ocracoke.

Suddenly, he heard a stirring in the woods. He nearly jumped up from the gnarly bough of live oak he was sitting on. He looked up to see Caesar.

"Caesar, by thunder ye scared the devil out of me, man!"

"I'm sorry, Captain, I didn't mean to. I just came by to see how you were doing."

Thache stuffed Tobias Knight's secret letter into the pocket of his captain's jacket. He would keep the news from Caesar and the other crew members until the new pardon was made official. "I'm sorry, lad, I didn't mean to yell at you." He smiled. "You took me totally by surprise. Why you're as sneaky as an Indian."

"Aye, that's because I've had to fight them. When I was with Master Knight, I had a scrap or two with the Tuscarora. Now those red men be true fighters. They can split an apple in two with a bow and arrow, they can."

"No doubt. The letter I was just reading bears good news from Esquire Knight. The much-feared Indian war is a sham. The Indians are still at peace."

"That is good news. I am glad to hear that Mr. Knight is safe. Are you…I mean, were you planning on coming back to the beach?"

"Aye, I just came in here to relieve myself and get a drink of water from the well. I seem to have sat down and lost myself in thought. I must be getting old because I lost track of time."

"You just needed some time alone to think, Captain. It has been a tough time these past few months—no doubt you have much on your mind. In fact, that's why the men were worried about you."

"Worried about me?"

"They just wanted to make sure you were all right. We've dug up six buckets of clams and are ready to return to the ship."

"Well done, lad. It's going to be quite a feast. I am sure Mr. Odell and his companions are in for a treat. But you don't need to worry about me, or about the crew. There are merry times ahead for us all. Merry times indeed."

"That is good to hear, Captain. The men will like hearing that."

Standing up from the fallen live oak branch he was sitting on, he slapped Caesar good-naturedly on the back as a peal of laughter rose up from the beach a hundred feet to the west. "Let's get on back then. I'm getting hungry just thinking about those fresh clams."

302

"Aye, Captain, so am I."

ψψψ

They walked along the narrow, sandy trail that sliced through the forest of hydra-like oak and red cedar until they reached the beach looking out onto Pamlico Sound. Along the beach lay tattered and patched sailcloth, temporarily erected as canvas tents and fluttering limply in the light breeze. Spread out along the sand, black needlerush, and cordgrass were empty bottles, broken ceramic jugs, piles of various animal bones, wide circles of ash from cook-fires, and other flotsam from the great banyan with Charles Vane held six weeks earlier. Neatly tucked away along the edge of the tree line were eleven casks of cocoa, two dozen hogsheads of sugar, several barrels of indigo, five bales of cotton, and the other articles remaining to be traded before setting out for the West Indies.

The wind was down and there was a chill in the air that made Caesar shiver. Weeks earlier the weather had turned and now periodic nor'easters had begun to blow, bringing cold winds and squally rains, one after the other. Like the other eighteen men of the company still remaining here on Ocracoke, he was anxious to begin their journey south. Most of the men were in agreement that winter at sea was for navy and merchant swabs, not for gentlemen of fortune like themselves. Furthermore, though the *Adventure* was freshly careened and ready to set sail, most of their money was gone, they had no suitable winter clothing, and provisions, rum, and morale were running low. But Caesar and the other crew members were unwilling to press the captain on the issue, as he had said they would be leaving any day now. Several of the other crew members were whispering amongst themselves that he had become sullen and irritable, especially since the two-masted French Martiniqueman had been brought in from Bermuda three months earlier.

Staring out at the mercury-colored sound, it seemed unfathomable to Caesar that nineteen pirates, thirteen whites and six blacks, were all that was left of the formidable 700-mate, four-ship, 60-plus-gun flotilla that a mere six months earlier had rivaled the strength of any pirate fleet in history. But what pained him most of all was that even after the clever and necessary downsizing of the pirate crew at Old Topsail Inlet, the infighting, petty squabbles, and betrayals had continued. The captain was believed to have deliberately shot Israel Hands with a powder charge, and he and two other crew members, accused of disloyalty by Blackbeard, had just been left behind at Bath Town. Still, the loyalty of Caesar and the other eighteen who remained on board the *Adventure* was beyond measure. All they needed, thought Caesar, was an official letter of marque and all would be well again. Furthermore, they would be protected from the Woodes Rogers's and Governor Johnson's of the world.

"Captain, I want to thank you," said Caesar as Garrett Gibbons and the other clam diggers started over towards them.

Thache looked at him quizzically. "Thank me for what, lad?"

"For setting me free and giving me the chance to serve with you as a seaman. You changed my life and I can never repay you. I know things have not been easy for you these past few months with the breakup of the crew and everything else that's happened, but I wanted you to know that I be grateful. I also want to thank you for sharing your books with me."

"Well, truth be told, I stole a few of them from Major Bonnet." He gave a mischievous wink, which made Caesar smile. "Like the prizes we take, he had more than he needed and could afford to give a few up."

"You are a devil indeed, Captain."

"So the newspapers say. In fact, if the *Boston News-Letter* is to be believed, I am a monster that enjoys sadistically torturing and murdering my fellow man. Why after reading but one of the recent articles, I almost feel guilty for my having never tortured or killed a bloody soul. Not a single one."

"The British have to make you out to be a murderous cutthroat. That way they can turn the American people against you."

"Aye, it's called propaganda, and the newspapers are doing a damned fine job of it. If I did half the things they say I did, I would be far more dangerous than Lucifer, I tell you that."

Bosun Garret Gibbons and the other men came walking up with their buckets of freshly-dug clams. Dusk was nearly upon them, with paint brush strokes of pink and gold as the sun trickled through the wisps of gossamer clouds hanging over Pamlico Sound to the west. From the water and the Old Slough to the south, Caesar could hear the noisy comings and goings of waterfowl: geese, brants, ducks, seagulls, great egrets, ibis, and pelicans.

Suddenly, Gibbons was pointing. "Two sail—two sail!" he cried.

Instantly turning his eyes to the southwest, Caesar spotted the masts of a pair of trading sloops along the western horizon, approaching the swash at the sound-side entrance of Ship Channel.

Thache pulled out his brass eyeglass. "They be coming from the Royal Shoal. Local traders, I suppose, but I know not who they might be. Maybe Master Odell will know."

"We just sailed that way ourselves, so they may be Chowan or Currituck traders from up Albemarle way," said Gibbons.

"One looks larger than the other," observed Caesar.

"Aye, and they do not look familiar," said Thache.

"They can't be Royal Navy," said Joseph Brooks, which drew a nod of agreement from the captain. "Those vessels ain't no more than eighty tons."

"I can't see any colors, but they've got to be Carolina men from up around Albemarle," said Caesar. "They wouldn't do us harm, would they, Captain?"

"Nay, I don't think so. We can send a boat over in the morning to see if they have anything worth trading for in preparation for our journey south. We have nothing to fear from Carolina men, lads. Nothing to fear at all."

CHAPTER 65

OCRACOKE ISLAND

NOVEMBER 22, 1718

AT 08:57 HOURS, Lieutenant Robert Maynard of the Royal Navy instructed the officers of his flagship *Jane* and Midshipman Edmund Hyde, captain of the *Ranger*, to weigh anchor and commence their approach towards the two sloops anchored off Ocracoke Island. He knew that the larger of the sloops—the one with Spanish lines bristling with eight deck guns and a bow chaser mounted in the forecastle—was Blackbeard's *Adventure*. But he was unfamiliar with the other vessel, which looked to belong to a local trader. The two sloops lay at anchor off the southern edge of the flat triangular spur of the barrier island. On the far side of the spur lay the landing place the pirates used when they wanted to go ashore, or to refill their water casks from the island's spring, known as the Old Watering Hole.

With a longboat out front to take depth readings in the shallow waters of Pamlico Sound, the *Ranger* in the number two position, and Maynard's flagship *Jane* taking up the rear, the three-vessel naval flotilla slowly navigated its way from the anchorage on the east side of Beacon Island southeast through Ship Channel towards Ocracoke Inlet. The longboat's five-man crew was equipped with a sounding line, which they would use to take soundings as the procession of ships sailed southeast along the main channel and then turned into the left-hand tidal channel, or slough, that led to Thache's anchorage and the watering hole. Maynard had no intention of allowing his civilian-rigged sloops to run aground on the constantly shifting sandbars and shoals of Ship Channel or the northwest-southeast trending slough where the *Adventure* and the trading vessel were anchored.

The sound was calm, the sky overcast. The lumpy seas of the past few days had given way to tranquil ones, and there was only the lightest of breezes to propel them on their route. With only a modest wind, both of His Majesty's vessels were forced to lay out the sweeps, using the large oars to augment the sails and thereby limit the time that they would be under fire from the pirates' guns.

As they neared Ocracoke Inlet, Maynard realized that he had lost the element of surprise. Peering through his spyglass, he saw the glint of the morning sun's reflection off a similar glass from the pirate sloop. Someone was spying on him in return. His plan had been to lure the pirates into thinking that the *Jane* and *Ranger* were simple trading vessels so he could get close enough to cut them off before they attempted to escape through the inlet to the open sea. But already the rogues were tracking his movements and stirring about the *Adventure's* deck like busy bees, unfurling sails and making their cannon ready to fire a warning shot and, if necessary, engage the enemy.

"They're rolling out their guns! Crowd that canvas and have those oarsmen bustle to it!" he shouted to his first-mate and second in command of the flotilla, Lieutenant Baker, and his helmsman, the Scotsman Abraham Demelt. Standing next to the three officers was Maynard's North Carolinian master pilot, William Butler, who was intimately familiar with the treacherous local waters.

"Aye, Lieutenant!" Baker scrambled across the deck and repeated the order to the oarsmen, who were already sweating heavily from exertion.

Bloody hell, we're not moving fast enough, thought Maynard, worried that they would be sitting ducks once they came under Thache's guns. He estimated that time would be shortly after they turned hard to port and struck north along the nearshore tidal slough that led to the Old Watering Hole. A hundred yards offshore of the watering hole was where Thache was waiting for them, guns a-ready. If heavy casualties were to be avoided it was essential not to reveal his identity until he had closed to within musket range, or roughly two hundred yards. By then it would be too late for Blackbeard to make his escape or to cripple the *Jane* or *Ranger* with heavy cannon fire. He had to keep the pirate guessing he was a simple trader for as long as possible, for the vessels under his command had no guns and his men had weapons suitable only for a boarding action: muskets, pistols, cutlasses, pikes, *grenadoes*, and boarding axes.

Soon they neared the point where the slough met Ship Channel at a ninety degree angle. Maynard gave the order over the speaking trumpet to the flotilla to strike north and replace the oarsmen of each vessel with eight fresh crew members as well as add two more men to each party. They needed to increase their speed in the feeble breeze and enable both vessels to close the deadly gap in front of the *Adventure's* guns in as short a time as possible. The fresh bodies and two extra crewmen per vessel were swiftly deployed to augment the power of the sails.

Again peering through his spyglass, he could now make out each of the *Adventure's* nine guns. As best as he could tell, Blackbeard was armed with eight three- to four-pounders and a smaller bow chaser, all the brass cannon glinting in the sunlight menacingly like projecting spearpoints. The pirate was also equipped with swivel guns on his quarterdeck. The light anti-personnel weapons were typically loaded with scrap metal and musket balls and had a range of sixty yards. If fired in the last moments before a boarding action, they were particularly lethal. Studying the pirates' bristling armament through his spyglass, he wished he had sacrificed a little draught and speed by mounting swivel guns of his own on the *Jane* and *Ranger*. But it was too late now. If he so desired, Thache could inflict lethal damage with his carriage-mounted guns and swivel guns, ending the assault before the attackers were within musket shot of the pirates.

"Larboard your helm and ease into that slough!" Maynard shouted through his speaking trumpet to Hyde in the *Ranger* and to the crew manning the longboat up ahead. "We don't want to be running aground now!"

The flotilla made the turn and followed the slough north with the incoming tide, picking its way carefully amidst the shoals and sandbars towards Thache's anchorage. The *Ranger* in the lead was two points on the starboard bow of the *Jane*, both vessels heading parallel to the marshy shoreline in the direction of the Old Watering Hole. Long, thin, and inhabited only by seasonal fisherman and herders, Ocracoke Island was covered in sand dunes, marram grass, gnarly live oaks and cedar trees, and scrub, with some reed beds on its inner side facing Pamlico Sound. With the wind down, sounds carried well over the water. Maynard could hear honking waterfowl over the sound of the water against the hull as the invaders knifed through the slough towards his adversary.

As the *Jane* closed the distance to around a thousand yards with the longboat and *Ranger* out front, he looked again through his powerful British Navy spyglass. As there was an incoming tide, the bow of the *Adventure* was pointing south, directly towards him. Slowly, as the *Jane* closed the distance between them, he could make out more and more of the details of the wanted brigand—the notorious Blackbeard the pirate—among the members of his outlaw crew. He stood out on account of his towering height, his crimson captain's jacket, and his long black beard that appeared to be tied up in plaits. For a moment, Maynard's breath was taken away. The man was leaner and sinewier than the naval lieutenant had expected, and he had a powerful air of command about him. He also appeared appropriately menacing with what looked like six pistols bandoliered about his midriff and a huge cutlass sheathed in his belt.

Maynard committed the towering figure to memory and sized him up. So this was his opponent: a tall, spare man with a commanding aura about him no doubt largely gained from his years as an officer in the British Royal Navy and as a privateer. Even from a distance, there was a look of indefatigable determination about the man and it was this feature that intrigued Maynard most of all. All in all an able foe, he decided, a brave and daring man who would not capitulate easily.

At that precise instant, he heard the explosion of a cannon. He had been so focused on Blackbeard the legendary swashbuckler that he hadn't been paying attention to what the rest of his crew was doing, and now it appeared as if Thache had fired off one of his guns as a warning shot. Given the direction his sloop was facing, it could not have been easy, but Maynard quickly realized it was the bow chaser. The cannon ball whistled over the heads of the longboat crew and splashed into the water, producing a great gusher as if from the spout of a whale.

"Pipe to quarters!" he shouted to his bosun. Then to Lieutenant Baker and the other officers and crew: "To your stations and take cover! The next one won't be a warning!"

"Aye, Lieutenant! To stations! To stations!"

Maynard peered through his spyglass again at Blackbeard and the *Adventure*. If they continued to close on the pirate, the next shot would likely be in range and on target.

"Pull that longboat! Get them out of there now!" he yelled to his bosun.

"Aye, Lieutenant!"

Another explosion thundered across the stillness of Pamlico Sound, sending the squawking water fowl near the Old Slough in all directions. The bellicose noise was swiftly followed by a whistling sound like a demon unleashed from hell. Maynard saw the splash of water a mere twenty feet off the *Ranger's* larboard quarter. A great gasp of shock mingled with dread rose up from the men aboard both vessels as well as the longboat.

"They have our range! Get that damned boat and those men out of the water now!" he shouted again.

He looked at his silver mariner's pocket watch, wanting to know the time, as his heart rate picked up in his chest from the excitement of being fired upon, even if it was only a pair of warning shots. It was 09:52 hours. Over the next three minutes, the longboat sounding crew was pulled back on board while the small craft was tied off and towed astern of the *Jane*. While the *Ranger* continued to close in on the *Adventure*, Maynard debated showing his colors.

No, make the great Blackbeard wait a little longer, he told himself. *Already you have him confused as to who we are. You need to buy some more time before we come under fire from his powerful guns.*

The *Ranger* and *Jane* continued to sail towards Thache's well-armed sloop. The trading sloop remained anchored to the northwest and Maynard would not bother with it. As they drew closer to the quarry, he could feel his heart thundering in his chest. His body was on high alert with the rush he had felt in anticipation of battle on so many occasions during Queen Anne's War, but not in recent years in his fruitless anti-piracy patrols in which he had never actually confronted any sea rover. He remembered back a decade earlier to the sea battle off Dunkirk, recalling the intoxicating combination of mortal fear and excitement coursing through his veins when he was in his mid-twenties. He couldn't help but feel as if his whole life had led up to this moment in history, a life and death struggle off Ocracoke Island in the Year of Our Lord 1718. He could smell history in the air. Since he was a little boy, he had wanted to fight in a great bloody battle against an able foe and vanquish him. Right here and now was his chance against the notorious Blackbeard, scourge of the Atlantic and Lord of the Outer Banks.

He looked to the heavens, his legs trembling ever so slightly as he stood on the quarterdeck in supplication before the Almighty. *Five more minutes, oh Lord. That's all I ask of ye. Five minutes delay before the devil opens up with his guns. Then we will show our colors and the bloody battle will begin.*

And when it's all over and done, may ye Lord have showered his divine mercy upon me and my brave men.

CHAPTER 66

OCRACOKE

NOVEMBER 22, 1718

PEERING THROUGH HIS SPYGLASS, Blackbeard searched in vain for signs of a flag on the two vessels but saw none as the enemy closed the distance to a thousand yards. His head throbbed from last night's drunken festivities on behalf of trader Samuel Odell and his crew, but his body was now on high alert. It was normal for warships to unfurl their colors before they opened fire, but in his fights with the French and Spanish during the war he and his opponents had often concealed their identities until the last second, and any trick that helped to delay the enemy opening fire was considered fair game. But still these new interlopers were behaving strangely. In many cases, captains flew false colors to keep their enemy guessing, but why were these two vessels not presenting their flags unless they were not the simple trading sloops they pretended to be. After all, they carried no guns and seemed to be crewed by ordinary seamen.

"Who are these infernal bastards prowling around our waters?" he wondered aloud, turning his eyeglass from one boat to the other.

"I don't know, Captain," responded Thomas Miller, quartermaster of the *Adventure*. "But they're not standing down and I don't like the looks of them."

"Neither do I, Captain," said Caesar. "They are sneaky devils and surely deserve a taste of our lead and iron."

Thache nodded, feeling his blood rising. Whoever these new interlopers were, they were not following the standard script and standing down. He wondered who the hell they could possibly be—these two well-manned sloops hailing from Carolina waters with no carriage guns to speak of, sailing slowly towards him like stalking crocodiles. The world all around him seemed strangely surreal, like a dream unfolding inexorably before him that he was powerless to stop. He had no idea who these brash newcomers were or from whence they had come except somewhere to the north. Morton had fired the traditional two shots across the bow, and now he and his badly hungover crew were waiting to see what would happen next. He wished they hadn't gotten so bloody drunk last night.

"They be nine hundred yards and closing. They'll be in musket range any moment now," warned master gunner Philip Morton from his forward position at the bow chaser. "What do you want me to do, Captain?"

"Avast and stand by, Mr. Morton. We have the advantage of guns and they will pay dearly if they try to board us." To his bosun. "Mr. Gibbons, if you would kindly hoist the Jolly Roger and let them know who we be. I will not be skulking about in anonymity for the likes of these rude gentlemen. Show them our colors and be quick about it, man!"

A cheer went up from the mixed crew of white and black men as the order was carried out. But the wind was so slight that the black flag with the pierced heart drooped like a soggy piece of bread.

Blast, that is not a good omen, he cursed. *It appears we will soon be in for the fight of our lives, and all we have is this damned droopy black flag?*

The two sloops made a formidable enemy, he could now tell, as he began counting the number of men on the two decks. Whoever the bastards were, they clearly had more men than him and the odds would be heavily against him if not for the advantage of his guns. He could still evade them by coming about and escaping to the north through the inlets and channels he knew so well, but that was not his nature. A voice inside him told him to sail right at them and fight it out. He quickly decided that that's what he would do.

There was just one problem. It was already too late to pull the cumbersome anchor, even though the *Adventure* lay in less than thirty feet of water. He would have to cut it. The anchor was firmly embedded in the sand-covered bottom, with around seventy feet of cable laid out. To man the capstan and winch in the thick rope anchor cable would simply take too long—his crew would still be manning the capstan when the sloops reached them.

As he started to give the order to sever the cable, something unexpected happened. The sloop in the second position, the bigger of the two, shuddered to an abrupt halt.

"Look, they've run aground on a bar!" cried Caesar.

"Aye, they be in trouble now!" observed Garret Gibbons.

Though the two sides were still beyond trumpet-speaking distance, the pirate crew gave a rousing jeer and two of the crew members pulled down their trousers and exposed their arses in a taunt. Blackbeard smiled. So far things were going his way. But his optimism didn't last long as the smaller sloop out front continued in its course directly towards him, and the crew of the second vessel began heaving her ballast overboard to lighten her load and reduce her draught. Thache was then surprised yet again. Though the smaller boat in the lead drew less water, she, too, ran aground. Her crew quickly began tossing her fresh water casks overboard to re-float the sloop, apparently recognizing that it was better to be thirsty than dead. Thache wondered if the commander of the flotilla had neglected to secure a pilot for navigation, or if the pilot simply didn't know what the hell he was doing. He watched as the crews of both vessels worked mightily to get their vessels afloat by throwing objects overboard and using the oar crews.

When the larger sloop broke free, he gave the order to move out to engage the enemy. "Mr. Gibbons, cut the cable! Hoist sail and let's away!"

"Aye, Captain!" answered the bosun. Then to Joseph Brooks and two other crew members standing by at the windlass. "Don't stay to take up anchor! Cut the cable!"

They did as instructed as the deck of the *Adventure* sprang to life. Bosun Garret Gibbons and his team began to hastily haul on the jib's halyard and others scurried up from below with armloads of cutlasses, flintlock pistols, *grenadoes*, black powder cartridges for the cannon, and three pair of grappling irons. Master gunner Philip Morton and his crew loaded the starboard guns with cartridges and swan shotpieces of old iron, spick nails, and other lethal odds and ends. In the flurry of battle preparations, Thache instructed Samuel Odell from the trading vessel to go below into the hold and pretend to be a prisoner in case they were boarded. The trader had gone too deep into his cups last night to row back to his vessel and had slept aboard the *Adventure.*

Four and a half minutes later—with the anchor cable severed, the mainsail and jib raised in the light wind, and both crew and cannon armed for battle—the pirate sloop shoved off. A marker buoy was left behind so they could later recover the anchor and what remained of the cable. Once the oncoming sloops had been dealt with, Thache would then be able to come back and recover the anchor. Now on the move, the *Adventure* swung parallel to the coastline and began heading on a compass angle ten degrees off the bow of the smaller, grounded sloop. With any luck, his adversaries might run aground again on one of the sandbars that ran parallel to the shore. To the west, Samuel Odell's trading sloop remained at anchor and would not take part in the battle. For a moment, Thache considered augmenting his sail with his sweeps, but he lacked sufficient manpower to man the oars, cannon, and rigging at the same time and the wind seemed to be picking up a tad. He would just have to count on the jib to do a fair job of it.

All in all, it was a risky endeavor, but he had the advantage of firepower with his carriage and swivel guns and he felt more than up to the task despite their wicked hangovers. Mounted on the *Adventure's* quarterdeck, the light anti-personnel swivels were quick to load and easy to aim and fire using either scrap metal or small cannon balls. All Morton and his gun crew had to do was point the swivel guns at the enemy using an iron tiller, clap a piece of burning slow-match into the touch-hole of the powder chamber, and blast away at the two enemy sloops once they had closed to within sixty yards. The effects would be devastating, particularly if fired just before a boarding action. However, at the *Adventure's* current distance of slightly over two hundred yards from the lead sloop, still out of effective musket range, they were merely a clamorous way of warning the boat crew off.

Suddenly, the pair of enemy vessels raised their colors. Thache saw one Royal Naval ensign hoisted up followed quickly by another, the two crimson flags with the Union Jack in the upper left corner riffling only slightly in the modest breeze. They had refrained from presenting their Union flags at the masthead to keep him guessing and delay him from opening fire upon them until they had closed to three-quarters' musket range—one hundred fifty yards.

Clever bastards, he thought. *They waited right until the very end. You will soon have a taste of my lead and iron for your skullduggery.*

"They be Royal Navy, lads! Let's show them what we're made of!"

Now the larger sloop out front broke free and both vessels were heading towards him, their decks crowded with men. Peering through his glass, he could now make out the commander of the flotilla, a tall, side-whiskered officer in a ruffled white shirt and blue naval jacket of lieutenant grade standing next to the wheel on the larger sloop. Even from a distance he could see the fierce resolve on his face beneath his feathered tricorn hat.

"By the blood of Henry Morgan, we are in for a scrap, lads! That there is a first lieutenant in the British Royal Navy and it appears he is well coiffed for the occasion!" he shouted with a pugilist's grin. "Mr. Morton, make ready your guns to fire! We shall cut them asunder with swan shot and eat their gizzards for supper!"

The crew gave a rowdy cheer. Not one among them was sober or in tip-top fighting shape but their blood was up, giving them the perfect antidote for their hangovers, and they were more than ready to fight. With the wind picking up, the *Adventure* sailed south against the incoming tide. After threading his way around a sandbar that ran parallel to the shore, Thache was positioned to take an inner passage along the island side of the two vessels, passing to windward along their port beam. He quickly closed the distance between himself and the smaller British sloop. Having pulled herself free of the sandbar, the vessel's captain bravely attempted to intercept the pirate sloop by altering her course to leeward. But it was a mistake that Thache knew would cost her captain and crew dearly.

"Mr. Morton, you may unleash with vengeance and fury when ready! Give them a taste of our hospitality!"

As the two vessels closed the distance between them to half a pistol shot—twenty-five yards—the *Adventure* fired a deadly broadside of swan and partridge shot and larger metal fragments. Flames blasted from the muzzles of the pirate cannons and, a split second later, the burst of spreading shot tore across the *Ranger's* foredeck, eviscerating and maiming sailors and demolishing her foresails.

The Battle of Ocracoke Island had begun.

With the excitement of battle throbbing inside him, Thache realized the die was cast and there was no turning back. By taking up arms against and killing sailors of King George's Navy, he and his crew had committed an act of treason for which no governor's pardon or letter of marque and reprisal would ever protect them. Their fate was sealed. Regardless of the outcome here today, they would die at gunpoint, sword point, or by dangling from the hangman's noose—for in delivering their broadside against the enemy, he and his fellow gentlemen of fortune aboard the sloop *Adventure* had signed their own death warrants.

There would be no amnesty and it would be a bloody fight to the death.

CHAPTER 67

OCRACOKE

NOVEMBER 22, 1718

LIEUTENANT ROBERT MAYNARD would always remember the moment just before it happened. One minute the two ships were slowly approaching one another, the *Ranger* to the lee of the pirate sloop, and the next the *Adventure's* cannons exploded with flame and dealt a lethal broadside that shook the *Ranger* like an earth tremor.

"Take cover!" he screamed to his consort vessel just before the first gunburst, but he was too far away even with a speaking trumpet and his warning was in vain.

The hailstorm of iron and lead raked across the decks of the *Ranger* like Death's horrible scythe, killing the ship's commander, Midshipman Hyde, and Maynard's third in command, Allen Arlington, the *Lyme's* coxswain. When the smoke cleared, Maynard was stunned to see that no officer remained to command the vessel and more than a dozen men appeared to be either killed or wounded. The deck was practically cleared of seamen, like an army of toy soldiers knocked down by a sudden gust of wind. There, on the *Ranger's* blood-soaked deck, the wounded men writhed and convulsed as the sloop slowed to a virtual stop.

He raised his fist defiantly in the air. *Damn you, Blackbeard! I'll get you yet by thunder! This is not over—the battle has just begun!*

He looked at his men. To his dismay, even the veterans among them appeared deflated. They could hear the screams of death and anguish from their fellow sailors aboard the stricken *Ranger*, and the sounds made them wonder what in the hell they had gotten themselves into. Going straight at a pirate vessel armed with nine guns and commanded by the fiercest pirate commodore of them all was not merely reckless, it was insane. And yet, it was now grimly apparent to one and all that they had no choice but to slug it out. They were no longer fighting for King and Country, but for their *very lives*. And they would not have the support of the *Ranger* as she had been put out of action, at least temporarily. They were now on their own against a well-armed ship filled with bloodthirsty pirates.

"Brace up, men! We're still in this fight!" he yelled, trying to rally them. "You know what you have to do! We cannot escape the pirates' hands even if we had a mind to! Right here and now, it is either fight like a lion or be killed like a lamb!"

The crew gave a rallying cheer, but it wasn't as loud or convincing as Maynard would have liked. All the same, his men knew how desperate the situation was and would neither give nor expect quarter when the time came.

He looked back at the *Adventure*. The broadside appeared to have been so effective that Thache slipped past the *Ranger* uncontested. Or so Maynard had first thought, before realizing that amid the confusion, some of the sailors had managed to get off a volley of small arms fire as the *Adventure* swept past. With the concentrated musket firing, they were able to sever the *Adventure's* fore-halyards, sending her jib—her sole means of propulsion—crashing to the foredeck in a tangled mess of canvas and snarls of tarred rope. The end result was that the critical line holding up the pirates' foresails caused the *Adventure* to abruptly lose speed. And in the confusion, whoever was steering the pirate sloop allowed her to slip onto a nearby shoal.

A determined gleam came to his eye. *That's it! There's my chance!*

If he came up alongside the enemy, he could attempt a boarding before she could bring her guns to bear. His greatest strength was his numbers so to have any chance of success he needed to get close to his quarry, board her, and allow his weight of numbers to win the day. But the clever Blackbeard, despite losing control of his vessel for a brief moment, took only a minute to get off the bar with his men throwing objects overboard on the still-rising tide.

Maynard cursed his bad luck. But then things went from bad to worse. Having dispatched the *Ranger*, Blackbeard's pirate ship was to windward and coming straight for the *Jane* just as decisively as Maynard was heading for the pirates with a third of his crew straining at the oars.

As the smoke drifted off, he could see his opponent clearly now on the quarterdeck. Thache stood out from his gang of motley seamen, presenting a towering, eye-catching figure with his black tricorn hat, crimson jacket, bandolier of pistols strapped about his waist, and his thick, plaited black beard like something out of an Exquemelin adventure tale. But what struck Maynard most of all was his complete calm in the midst of battle. There was nothing frantic or desperate about him. He had clearly commanded in battle before, whether it was from his boarding actions in the Royal Navy serving under Admiral Whetstone, his later bouts as a privateer and pirate, or both.

At fifty yards and closing, the pirate commander called out to him with his speaking trumpet. "Damn you for villains, who are you? And from whence have you come? Leave us alone and we shall meddle not with you!"

Through his own speaking trumpet, Maynard roared back, "You can see by our colors we are no pirates, and it is you we want, sir! And it is you we shall have, dead or alive, else it will cost us our lives!"

"Damnation to you and King George then, you cowardly puppies! We will give no quarter, nor take none in return!"

"Nor shall we, sir!" he roared back before turning to his men and issuing a command. "Fire at will! Fire at will!"

A dozen muskets opened fire, pouring into the pirate vessel, as the oarsmen manning the sweeps put their backs into it and continued to close the distance between the *Jane* and the enemy to twenty-five yards. At the same time, the pirate commander ordered his crew to strafe the deck of the *Jane* with swivel-guns and small arms fire.

The result was a terrible fate similar to the *Ranger*. Maynard and his pirate hunters were massed on deck, with no protection from gunwales or barricades, and the lethal mix of swan shot, spick nails, and pieces of old iron tore through the *Jane's* crew like a hurricane. There were a series of loud BOOMs and puffs of smoke all along the deck of the *Adventure*, and Maynard was shocked by the instant carnage. He saw a wet pink cloud of blood and tissue fly out the back of a seaman standing

314

near the bow of the ship. He saw his bosun twitch and his arms fly out helplessly, as if he were groping through the darkness, and then fall to the deck grievously wounded. He saw blood spray over another crew member from a seaman near the starboard rail torn apart by buckshot-sized swan shot; it looked like crimson paint spattered across an empty white canvas. He saw another seaman take a hit to the kneecap and swiftly lose the unwinnable battle with gravity as his legs buckled like a stringless marionette and he slumped to the deck. Finally, he saw another of his crewmen go down hard, blood gushing from his torn pant leg from lead shot mixed with old iron scraps and nails.

Despite what his eyes told him, he couldn't believe what was happening. The violence was almost too horrifying to be real. The world seemed to move in slow motion, as if he was caught up in a terrible nightmare. And then the realness of it all came crashing home as he heard the shrieks and moans of the wounded slice through the horrible incubus, summoning him back to reality.

Another blast came from the pirates' swivel guns. He dove for cover on the quarterdeck, falling awkwardly with his sword in its sheath. The *Jane* gave a convulsive shudder from the swan shot and then the two sides exchanged musket fire. The air quickly became choked with a thick cloud of blue-gray smoke from the gunpowder blasts of cannon and small arms fire, and with little or no wind, the heavy pall added to the confusion of the fight. In less than a minute, the deck of His Majesty's sloop had become strewn with dead and wounded sailors. Scanning the bloody, smoke-filled deck, he estimated that eight of his men had been killed and perhaps as many as a dozen wounded, which meant that between the two naval vessels under his command he had already sustained close to fifty percent casualties.

Hearing the screams of agony and looking through the haze of smoke at the scene of devastation, he realized that he was lucky to have avoided being hit. To stern, he heard the voice of his helmsman, the big Scotsman Abraham Demelt.

"Are you all right, Lieutenant?"

He quickly checked to see if he was hurt. No blood, but his left wrist was numb from falling awkwardly upon his sword on the quarterdeck. "I'm fine, I think. How about you?"

"I'm covered in blood. But it's not mine."

Someone screamed, "Make ready to fight! They're going to board us!"

Good Lord, we're all going to die, he thought, still struggling to process the grisly close-quarters sea action he had just witnessed. *You must do something.*

And then it came to him.

There was no doubt that, having delivered a devastating blast of swan shot and taking down at least half of his men, Thache would now try to board the *Jane*. To counter the move, Maynard would, under the cover of the gunpowder smoke, order a dozen or so uninjured men to hide in the *Jane's* hold and await his signal to attack. Another similar broadside would be crippling, and would leave him with too few men to continue the fight. He had already had the hatch covers removed and a second ladder fitted for the companionway for just such an eventuality, but in the heat of battle he had forgotten. Now he would implement what he had prepared for and turn the tide of battle in his favor. Once he and Thache came alongside one another, the hidden men could race up the ladders and take the pirates by surprise.

He looked through the haze at the approaching *Adventure*. The two boats would be abreast of one another any second now. He quickly assembled his first mate, helmsman, and pilot.

"Lieutenant Baker!" he shouted. "I want you to take the remaining unwounded men below decks, lay in wait until the pirates board us, and then take them by surprise in an all-out attack! I will lie low with Mr. Demelt and Mr. Butler here, signal you when the pirates come over the side, and join you in the fight! We are going to lure them into a trap and turn the tables on them!"

"Aye, Lieutenant! So, you'll give me the signal then?"

"Aye, as I said I will remain here with Mr. Demelt and Mr. Butler, who will stand beside the whipstaff!" he said, referring to the steering tiller that operated the ship's rudder. "I will whisper orders to you both during the pirates' approach, letting you know where they are and when you and your men are to rush up the ladders and take the pirates by surprise!"

"It shall be done, Lieutenant! Godspeed!" and he was off to gather up the men.

A moment later, as the last of Lieutenant Baker's men were hiding belowdecks and the two converging vessels closed upon one another, the smoke began to clear. Maynard, Demelt, and Butler stood at the helm, guiding the *Jane* and waiting to see if Thache would take the bait and attempt to board her. Watching with a combination of dread and excitement as the gap between the two vessels closed, he whispered down to Lieutenant Baker and his men to hold steady. A moment later, Blackbeard's grappling hooks hit their target and dug in like the claws of an eagle and then, in a slow-motion but violent ballet, the *Jane* and the *Adventure* collided with one another. Several hand-made *grenadoes*—powder- and shot-filled case bottles ignited by fuses—broke across the deck and exploded among the wounded, maimed, and dead, eliciting howls and shrieks of agony from the living, one or two of whom went silent from the blasts.

Then, with a new smoke cloud hovering above the *Jane*, there was a terrible, excruciating silence.

It was then Maynard felt a bead of sweat trickle down his cheek. *God of sweet merciful heaven, I do hope this works,* he prayed, as he gazed through the smoky haze at the towering, bearded figure cloaked in red hovering off his bow, clutching a pistol in one hand and a gleaming steel cutlass in the other.

CHAPTER 68

OCRACOKE

NOVEMBER 22, 1718

AS THE TWO VESSELS CLOSED THE DISTANCE between them to forty yards, Thache surveyed the crippled enemy through the smoke-filled haze and confidently barked out orders to his officers and crew.

"Come alongside her, Mr. Gibbons! Prepare to board, men!"

Though he couldn't see precisely how many had been killed in the broadside, the shotgun-like blast of swan and partridge shot had been extremely deadly at such close range and he had witnessed more than a dozen men knocked to the deck. Now as the smoke lifted, he could see that the deck was indeed covered with a large number of bodies. There also appeared to be a clump of officers and crew members still huddled around the wheel at the stern of the ship. In preparation for boarding, he would have his men toss in a few of their improvised hand grenades they had made by stuffing gunpowder, musket balls, and bits of old iron into empty rum bottles. That should finish them off. But if it didn't and somehow he was driven back and the enemy prevailed, he would most certainly not allow his men to be taken captive and be subjected to the same miserable fate as Stede Bonnet and his crew. With that in mind, it was time to implement his backup plan.

He pulled Caesar to the side. "In less than two minutes, I am going to lead a boarding party onto that enemy sloop," he said in a solemn but urgent voice. "I am hereby entrusting you with an important mission because it is you—above all others, Caesar—that I trust to successfully carry it out."

"Aye, Captain, what do you want me to do?"

"I want you to stay aboard the *Adventure* and—"

"What? But I am in the boarding party!"

"Just listen, lad. What I am entrusting you with is *the* most important task of all. Be that plain enough?"

"All right, what do you want me to do?"

"I want you to blow our powder stores below decks in the event we are captured."

"You want me to blow up the ship?"

"We have talked about just such an eventuality many times before, and the whole crew has always been in agreement that it is better to die as free men upon our own swords than to hang from the King's rope. There shall be no hangman's hempen halter for me and my men, and I want you to make sure of it if things should go badly and we are somehow whipped in the next few minutes. I don't expect it to be so but I want to be prepared."

"Aye, Captain, we have long talked about this possibility, but I dare say I never thought the day would come. But I shall do my duty as a loyal crew member. It is you who set me free, and it is you to whom I owe these past two and a half years of freedom as a seaman and not a slave."

"Don't do it for me—do it for the company, Caesar. As I said, I trust you the most to carry this out if our defeat looks imminent."

"It pleases me that you put your trust in me. Where do you want me to hide out?"

"If you stand on deck at the companionway, you can see which way the battle goes. That's where I want you to stand. Then, if somehow when we board the enemy should prevail, you are to quickly proceed belowdecks and blow us all to kingdom come."

"I have matches and will take care of it."

He patted him on the back. "I know you will. That is why I have chosen you, Caesar. You are my best all-around seamen and a free man—and I want you forever to be a free man."

"Thanks to you I am. Whatever happens, you are my captain forever and I shall never forget you."

"And I shall never forget you, lad. You have served me well and made this old salt proud. Good luck to you and a fair wind. Now go!"

When Caesar dashed off, Thache turned back towards the enemy vessel. The two ships were closing fast. He looked at his men: it would be a boarding party of ten men including himself. They were armed with pistols, cutlasses, *grenadoes*, boarding axes, and half-pikes, and if the hand-to-hand fighting became particularly violent they all had at least one knife and could wield their belaying pins as improvised clubs in a desperate pinch.

"Prepare to board! Grenadiers light your fuses!"

The vessels were nearly upon one another now. With the smoke dissipating, he scanned the deck. It would be a fight with no holds barred, fought in a confined space with nowhere to run or hide. He estimated the deck of the British sloop between the main hatch and the bow to be no more than twenty feet long, and tapered from fifteen feet wide amidships to just a single wooden stempost beneath the bowsprit. The deck itself also contained the capstan, a small covered hatch, and what appeared to be at least a dozen fallen figures. As the smoke continued to thin out in the light breeze, he could see that several of the enemy were not dead, but incapacitated and writhing on the deck from their crippling wounds. What he found surprising was that the lieutenant in the blue uniform seemed to be shrugging off his casualties and continuing to have his helmsman close on him and the *Adventure*. Did the naval officer perhaps have some trick up his sleeve?

"Yellow has never been a pirates' color, men! Give no quarter and expect none in return! Either we win or we die!"

The men waved their guns and blades of forged, curved steel and roared like lions. "Aye! Aye!"

"Hands, grapnels at the ready! Prepare to board!"

His heart thundered in his chest as the gap between the vessels closed to twenty feet, ten feet, five feet, then—impact! Just before the two vessels contacted one another, iron grappling hooks flew through the air, clanked across the bulwarks of the enemy vessel, and were pulled taut. With the bows of the two sloops now touching, the grappling hooks firmly lashed the two sloops together, making sure it would be a fight to the finish.

The pirates threw several hand-lit *grenadoes* onto the deck. Thache heard screams as the powder- and shot-filled bottles blew up, spewing out lethal balls and shards of iron casing in all directions and penetrating human flesh and bone. Then, with the smoke from the *grenadoes* still swirling over the open deck, the ship went surprisingly silent except for the low moans of the wounded. Thache looked at his heavily armed men: they stood along the bow, their bodies arched with eagerness and ready to spring into action. There were no longer signs of a hangover on any of the faces.

He carefully scanned the deck of the enemy vessel. Through the smoky haze, he saw only three or four men: the naval officer in the blue jacket, his helmsman, and one or two others in seaman's dress. Clustered like sheep at the helm at the stern of the craft, they looked to be an insignificant group, pesky flies to be swatted away. On the deck before them lay a dozen or so badly wounded men amid the detritus of the broadside and *grenado* attacks. Smoke continued to swirl over the decks, from the *grenadoes* and from musket and pistol fire as the pirates who remained on the *Adventure* took aim and popped off rounds at the small knot of British sailors to stern. Gazing out at what appeared to be a vanquished enemy, to Blackbeard victory looked certain.

"Boarders away! They appear to have all been knocked in the head but three or four of them!"

"Let's jump on board and cut them to pieces!" exhorted Thomas Miller.

Again, the pirates roared with confidence, like lions. Thache waved his arm forward and the boarding party of ten men including himself jumped onto the bulwarks and started for the forecastle, howling and firing at anything that moved. As he dashed forward at the head of the boarding party, Thache looked to the stern of the ship, but the Royal Navy men hiding at the helm had disappeared. *Damn, where have they skulked away to? Have they taken refuge belowdecks?* He and his men quickly swarmed the smoke-filled deck amidships, maneuvering around the dead and wounded. Those who begged for quarter were graciously given it, despite Thache's bold claim to the contrary. He saw sprawled corpses and mangled limbs. He saw disgorged blood coagulating in pools and forming into small meandering rivulets that drained out the scuppers and into the turquoise waters of Pamlico Sound, tincturing the sea with blood around the vessel. Looking around at the carnage, he cursed.

By the devil's teeth, I didn't want this damned fight. So many lives lost and all for nothing.

"Something's not right, Captain," whispered Philip Morton as the smoke drifted off. "Not but a few minutes ago, I had thirty-odd men on this deck in the sights of me cannon. But where have they all gone?"

Indeed, Thache had felt something was amiss, too, as he had begun to tally the total number of dead and wounded in his head and the numbers didn't add up to the numbers he had observed on deck through his spyglass. The boarding had been unopposed and all too easy, as if the British had wanted them to come aboard and had a surprise waiting for them, perhaps a hidden swivel gun filled with swan shot or a bucketful of *grenadoe*s of their own.

And then—a mere thirty seconds after he had boarded the ship—his worst fears were confirmed.

He saw the officer in the blue jacket jump up from the quarterdeck and yell a command to his men belowdecks.

"Aloft to repel the boarders! For King and Country, strike them down!"

Suddenly, a dozen of the King's men clambered up from a pair of ladders built into the sloop's hold, armed with pistols, muskets, and cutlasses and screaming battle cries at the tops of their lungs. The men pouring out of the companionway took his men up front by total surprise, and the deck swiftly turned to a confused tangle of bodies fighting hand to hand. Blackbeard instantly saw what was happening and yelled out commands to rally his astonished men.

"Stand fast and give it to them, lads! Show them your lead and steel!" he cried, exhorting his crew not to back down despite their sudden change in fortune.

Wheeling towards the advancing squadron, the pirates opened fire, but they were a split-second too late and were quickly dispatched or dispersed across the deck. The three boarders up front were shot down at point-blank range, turning the advantage instantly to the British. Thache couldn't believe his eyes: what had seemed to be a sure victory had, in a fraction of an instant, turned into a life or death struggle in hand-to-hand combat. Even worse, he was in the blink of an eye outnumbered two to one by the enemy. There was no way out of the fight: it would be a battle for survival where surrender was not an option and he was greatly outnumbered. Especially given that his crew aboard the *Adventure* was preoccupied with the other naval vessel, which had regained its sails and was working its way towards the pirate ship.

He looked at the British lieutenant. Now he could see his opponent up close. The officer clutched a pistol in his hand and was striding towards him with a determined expression on his face as he shouted out encouragement to his men. He was older than Thache, in his mid- to late-thirties with thick side-whiskers that ran down both cheeks and terminated just before the jawline.

You clever son of a rum puncheon! You've outfoxed me, you have! But I'll cleave your skull asunder before this battle is through!

A British seaman with a bloody chin fired his pistol at him, but missed. He shot the man in the stomach with one of his six pistols. The man fell to the deck with a grunt. Thache tossed aside his smoking gun and grabbed another loaded pistol from his leather bandolier holster. Each flintlock pistol was good for only a single shot and he had but five loaded firearms left so he had to make every shot count.

"Brave up now, lads! Let's show these British bastards what we're made of! Shoot them down and pin them to the mainmast with your cutlasses!"

The lieutenant came towards him, pistol pointed at his chest. They opened fire upon one another at five paces.

But Thache's bullet missed his target and he was hit. It was only a grazing wound at his midriff, but it still burnt like hell. He glared flints at his adversary.

"Lieutenant Maynard at your service! As I have told you, Blackbeard, it is you I have come for and no other!"

"Damn you for a villain, sir! When my sword is through with you, I promise to see your entrails dangle from my foreyard!"

He withdrew his cutlass from its leather scabbard and threw his second, now-useless pistol at the officer, striking him in the gut. Maynard emitted a grunt as he was hit and heaved his own pistol at Thache. But the throw was high and the pirate captain simply ducked and stepped towards him, sword in hand. Maynard withdrew his own blade and the two adversaries closed on one another quickly as the hand-to-hand battle swirled around them on the deck, like a violent ballet.

He swung his large cutlass with ferocity at the naval lieutenant, who at the last second was able to dart to his left to avoid a murderous blow.

Maynard then made a thrust, the point of his sword poking into Thache's cartridge box, made of leather and lined with thin wood, and bending it to the hilt. In response, the pirate broke the sword's guard and made a quick slash at the officer's sword hand, hoping to disable him and end the fight right there. The slash found the target, but it was only a glancing blow at the top of Maynard's right hand between the thumb and forefinger. But it was enough to disable him momentarily, and the officer now looked fearful and struggled to pull out his second flintlock pistol lodged in the naval sash about his waist. Meanwhile, all around the two combatants, men fought, skidded, and fell upon the blood-slicked deck amidst the bang and smoke of pistols, the clashing of swords, and the shrieks of the wounded.

Thache closed in on Maynard with his gleaming cutlass high in the air and ready to slash down in a cruel arc. But at the last second the officer recovered his composure, pulled out his pistol, and opened fire. The bullet caught Thache in the upper shoulder, luckily missing his heart and lungs, but the force of the shot drove him backwards into one of his own men and he almost went down. He took a step forward towards the now-fumbling Maynard, who was struggling to throw away his spent pistol and raise his cutlass.

It was then the pirate was shot a third time by a young Royal Navy seaman with a tarred queue, this time in the left arm. It was another non-lethal wound, but he knew his three injuries together would soon wear him down. He charged Maynard, intent on striking him dead quickly to sap the spirit of his men and win the day. But his opponent proved a skilled and well-trained swordsman and he was unable to quickly dispatch him. Their forged-steel cutlasses clanged against one another as they pirouetted about the ship, grappling for advantage and struggling to strike the death blow, the Royal Navy officer and the notorious pirate captain whose name was now well known in the New World and on the grimy streets of London, thrusting and parrying in a hand-to-hand battle for the ages.

But as they fought, Blackbeard could tell that already—in the mere two minutes that had passed since he and his men had boarded—the battle was slipping away from him. His men were falling all around him and there was no one to replace them. Out of the corner of his eye, he saw Garret Gibbons go down, his shirt and jacket smoldering from a point-blank-range pistol shot. He saw Philip Morton get run through with a cutlass, groan heavily, collapse onto the deck, and go still. Then he himself was driven backwards by a gunshot, his fourth, followed quickly by a burning sensation along his ribcage.

My God, I've been hit again? Damn if I can take any more!

He staggered for a moment, feeling the collective pain of all his wounds as the deck around him erupted in a confused melee. Bodies flew past in a blur. Bursts of flintlock pistol fire echoed across Pamlico Sound as the blood from the scuppers turned the shimmering aquamarine waters a diluted red. Primitive-sounding screams and grunts added to the orchestra of violence as the two sides—one a motley crew of pirates, the other a highly disciplined military unit—battled in close quarters.

Despite his four bullet wounds, Blackbeard attacked Maynard with fury, knocking him to the deck with the flat end of his cutlass. He followed up by punching him in the face with the crossguard, drawing blood from the lieutenant's left nostril. As he raised his arm to deliver a blow with the sharp edge of his sword, he was knocked hard from behind by one of his own men. It was Thomas Miller, who had been shot in the face and driven backwards into him.

What the blazes, now my bloody quartermaster has fallen? This is a disaster.

He and Maynard went at it again, thrusting and slashing but doing little damage. But Thache could feel the traumatic blood loss kicking in and knew he wouldn't be able to last much longer. The twenty-foot-long, fifteen-foot-wide space between the main hatch and the bow was now completely slick with blood and littered with bodies. With their superior numbers, firepower, and training, and having benefitted from the element of surprise, the British were winning the battle and driving the *Adventure's* crew back. As the pirates retreated back towards the bow, their casualties mounted and Blackbeard found himself isolated, allowing Maynard's men to move around behind him.

But the British naval officer, too, was bleeding and vulnerable, and Blackbeard moved in to administer the coup de grâce. He struck a powerful blow, snapping off Maynard's sword blade near its hilt. A blow of such terrific force would ordinarily have knocked the weapon from his hands, but Maynard still gripped the sword tightly as if his very life depended on it. Hurling the broken hilt at his adversary, he stepped back to cock his pistol. At the same instant, Blackbeard moved in for the finishing blow with his cutlass. But just as he swung his cutlass aloft, he saw a flash of shiny steel in his peripheral vision—one of the King's men suddenly materializing to his right. A huge red-haired seaman stepped forward and delivered a terrible wound to his neck and throat and Thache's cutlass, raised for the finishing blow, swerved as it came down and merely grazed the knuckles of Maynard, cutting them only slightly. Thache stumbled but did not fall as blood sprayed from the horrible wound, spattering the blood-drenched deck.

Emboldened, a half-dozen of the King's men that had been standing back timidly in fear closed in around him to finish him off. But he continued to fight furiously, swinging the weapon in a wild windmill attack that no one in front of him could repel with a blade. In response, several of the British seamen swung in behind him to stab him in the back with their swords.

But still the towering figure refused to go down. As a fifth bullet struck him and he was slashed a seventeenth time by a British sword, he remained standing, swinging his heavy cutlass in proud defiance, like a wounded and cornered wild animal. As he fought for his life, the American was fueled by one thing and one thing only: an image of his beloved Margaret of Marcus Hook. He pictured holding his Swedish beauty in his arms next to a warm winter hearth along the banks of the

Delaware. They were joking and laughing, playing the silly name games that lovers play, and she was softly singing in his ear and delivering sweet, moist kisses that made him quiver and tingle with joy for the tender things in this world, the better angels of man's unseemly nature. Love, he knew, was the only thing worth living for. His beloved Margaret was the one sweet angel that had always reached right down and grabbed him and made him magnificently alive and yet all muddled and yearning and dizzy in the head at the same time. Like a fool, he had had the love of his life in his hands and he had let her slip away. His fine Swedish beauty.

I am sorry, Margaret my love. I am sorry that I have made a mess of everything and will not return to you.

Alas, I hope you can forgive me.

CHAPTER 69

OCRACOKE

NOVEMBER 22, 1718

FROM THE QUARTERDECK OF THE *ADVENTURE*, Caesar watched as the tide of battle turned and his pirate brethren were driven back. Blackbeard had rallied his men, but it was all for naught as they were swiftly dispatched around him until he was the only one left, fighting for his life. He was standing his ground and battling with great fury, but even through the smoky haze Caesar could see that he was badly wounded and running out of strength, and that the battle was lost.

He knew now what he had to do: blow the powder magazine and thereby deny the hangman.

And yet…and yet he couldn't bring himself to do it, not yet. He could not take his eyes off the battle and wanted to see what fate would befall his captain, who was grappling with the officer in the blue jacket. The smoke was beginning to clear again and he could hear the metallic clang of their swords as they fought on the aft deck. It looked as though the pirate captain had the upper hand, but as he stepped forward to deliver the death blow, he was intercepted from the rear by a British seaman with a bright shock of auburn hair, who proceeded to deliver a terrific wound to his neck with his broadsword. The pirate's cutlass blow failed to land on the officer in blue and blood spurted from his gashed neck. He then staggered on the deck, his legs wobbly though he continued to shout out defiantly and slash away to fend off his attackers, who were now emboldened and stepping towards him to finish him off. His grievous wound, coupled with the many other bullet and sword wounds he had sustained, had weakened him and made him vulnerable in the eyes of his enemies. Seeing that he was approaching his end and that the heavily armed British seamen were moving in for the kill, tears came to Caesar's eyes.

He held his breath in dreadful anticipation.

The enemy seamen, who had kept clear of Blackbeard until now, closed in from behind like a pack of hyenas to stab the great pirate with their cutlasses. The British, wary of combating him face to face from the front, delivered thrusts and slashes to his back and sides as he continued to fight with the naval officer. And then, as he was cocking a pistol for a shot, the beefy seaman with the red hair swept in again and gave him a second stroke, this time cutting off his head and laying it flat on his shoulder. Blackbeard toppled over, not quite headless, and Caesar turned away in horror, tears streaming uncontrollably down his face.

"Noooo!" he cried. "Noooo!"

Unable to believe his eyes, he felt a part of him die right there and then along with his captain. He felt a powerful sense of loss: an era had come to a sudden and bitter end. Yet in his heart, he knew that his beloved Blackbeard could not have chosen a better way to die. He had fallen in the heat of battle, fighting like a wounded lion, and that was worth something.

In fact, it meant everything.

Suddenly, he heard whizzing sounds, a burst of heavy gunfire on the starboard quarter. The larger sloop that they had attacked first had come free and was advancing towards the *Adventure*, her decks swarming with the King's men. He realized he had been so preoccupied by the fight aboard the smaller British sloop that he had forgotten about the larger enemy vessel to the north. If the battle wasn't completely lost before, it was now. With no one to sail the *Adventure* and now two enemy ship's to contend with, it was time now to execute Blackbeard's wishes and blow the three vessels to kingdom come.

He started for the companionway as his friend Richard Greensail and fellow seamen John Carnes, Richard Stiles, Thomas, Gates, James Blake, James White, and the remaining holdouts left to defend the *Adventure* opened fire on the British sloop sweeping in from the north. With Thache and his boarding party defeated, the enemy from this larger British vessel were now moving to board the pirate vessel as well. In the confusion of battle, someone had cut the lines joining the *Adventure* and the smaller enemy sloop, and they had momentarily become separated and drifted apart. But now the grappling hooks again locked the two sloops together and they were touching at their bows. Any second, the *Adventure* would be boarded by thirty of the King's men from both enemy ships.

That would be the time to blow up all three vessels.

He quickly climbed down the stairs and began making his way to the powder room in the stern of the ship. He had a leather pouch filled with powder and a box of stick matches so it would take no time to turn the room into an inferno. Then it would be only a matter of seconds before the powder kegs blew. Though nervous at the prospect of committing suicide, he was intent on fulfilling his promise to his captain that had granted him his freedom. That way, he and his fellow gentlemen of fortune could go out on their own terms and avoid the hangman's noose. He had heard Thache talking about such a final exit strategy with Charles Vane, Sam Bellamy, and other pirate commanders on several occasions. During their drinking binges, he had also heard his comrades in arms swear oaths that they would blow themselves up rather than be captured and hanged like dogs. He had often wondered if, when the moment actually arrived, such men would have the courage to light the match, or if they would hold out hope that a heartfelt confession, or a claim to have been kept as a prisoner, or the arrival of a new royal pardon, might yet spare them the noose. He had long doubted if even one in ten of his brethren of the coast who made such boasts would go through with it.

But he would not let his captain down. He had been assigned a critical mission and he intended to follow through with it. It was his duty as a free seaman.

He pushed open the door to the powder room. Thankfully, it was empty. He stepped forward to the powder kegs in the corner, removed the cork from the bunghole of the already opened keg, and poured out a trail of powder from his pouch from the middle of the room to the open powder keg to ignite it and set off the entire store. He then said a little prayer. He could tell that the battle on deck was already winding down. The gunfire had stopped altogether, and he could hear heavy feet on the wooden planks and gruff voices barking out commands. The *Adventure* had been taken by the two naval sloops and the King's men now controlled the ship.

It was time to fulfill the captain's order.

Lighting a match, he leaned down to put the match to the trail of powder, but as he did so he turned the match in his hand and it went out.

Damn.

He lit another. It was then, with the lit match in his hand, that he heard a voice. "What the bloody hell are you doing, Caesar?"

Turning towards the sound, he saw the trader Samuel Odell and the pirate James Robins, who had recently returned from Bath Town with Garret Gibbons. Apparently not wanting to take arms against the King's men, they had hidden behind a clump of powder barrels in the *Adventure's* hold.

"What does it look like I'm doing?" he replied, certain that he was doing the right thing in obeying his captain. "I'm going to blow the ship. The battle is lost and we will all be hung if we surrender."

"Now just hold on, Caesar," said James Robins, holding up both hands. "You and I are mates, and there is no reason to be rash. None of us here in this powder room will be hung as long as we don't bear arms against the King."

Caesar hadn't thought of that, but what difference did it make? His captain had given him an order and he must carry it out. He held the lit match just above the powder trail and the two men gave a little twitch. "The captain has ordered me to set fire to the powder stores and blow up the ship. It is what I must do since we have failed to defeat our attackers and will all be captured. I cannot disobey a direct order from the captain."

"But you can't blow us all up, man!" protested Samuel Odell. "I'm no pirate and none of us has taken up arms. Have you actually lifted a hand against the King's men, Caesar?"

"No, but that doesn't matter. They will hang us all anyway."

"No, they won't," said Robins, moving to his left. "Now just stop and listen."

But Caesar was done listening. His match was almost burnt out and he knew they were going to try and stop him. He started to touch the match to the powder.

"No, Caesar, no!" cried Robins, and he and Odell jumped forward to restrain him.

But they were too late. The lit match set fire to the powder trail on the floor leading to the keg. But he had to keep them from stomping out the flame before it ignited the powder kegs. He started to withdraw his knife to fight them off, but the young and solidly built Robins tackled him to the floor and clamped down his arms against the hard wood as Samuel Odell attempted to stamp out the fire with his heavy shoes.

"Damn you!" protested Caesar, fighting to push the heavyset Robins off. "Now we'll all be hung like dogs!"

"No we won't!" replied Robins. "We just have to play our cards right and say we didn't take part in the fight!"

"They'll never believe us!"

"Aye, they will! Now just stay down, damn you, and let them capture us here down in the hold! We'll pretend to be prisoners!"

"You fool, they won't believe that either! Now let me up so I can follow through with the captain's order!"

"No way in hell, lad!" said Samuel Odell, who had put out the fire and was now helping Robins to restrain the black man.

At that instant, a pair of British seamen bearing muskets and an officer armed with a cutlass burst into the room.

"Don't shoot! Don't shoot!" cried Samuel Odell, holding up his hands. "We are prisoners aboard this ship!"

"Is that so? We'll see about!" snarled the officer menacingly. "On deck with your hands behind your heads! Now be quick about it—it seems you are our prisoners now!"

The armed seamen jabbed their muskets at them and they rose up as commanded and went on deck. All three sloops were lashed together. Caesar and the survivors aboard the pirate vessel were duly hauled back on board the blood-soaked deck of the smaller British sloop, which Caesar could see was named *Jane*. There they were kept under guard, and left to patch their wounds as best they could.

Looking around the blood-stained deck, he couldn't believe how much carnage had taken place in so short a time. The entire battle had lasted no more than fifteen minutes from the initial broadside directed against the larger British sloop through to the surrender of the last of the *Adventure's* crew. He estimated that there were ten dead pirates and another six or seven wounded, while the British, though they had won the battle, appeared to have suffered more grievous losses of ten to twelve dead and around twenty-five wounded. To Caesar, the fighting seemed to have lasted an eternity though in actuality it had taken no longer than the time it takes for a hungry man to eat his supper.

The silence was acute as the stunned, deafened, and disoriented survivors regained their strength, hearing, and sanity. In the aftermath of battle, Caesar couldn't help but feel deeply dispirited. Looking around at the faces of the survivors on both sides, many of whom were badly wounded, he could tell that many felt the same. Victors and vanquished alike had seen many close friends killed or wounded. Those that had survived were wondering how they had escaped with their lives. For Caesar, his good friend Richard Greensail was alive, but Garret Gibbons, his bosun buddy, had not made it.

Feeling a numbness in his weary bones, he watched as the officer in the blue uniform ordered the British wounded, but not his fellow pirates, to be looked after. While this was being done, the lieutenant had his mangled hand dressed. Caesar thought he was lucky to be alive; if not for the red-haired man who had partially cut off Thache's head, he would have been killed by the pirate. But Caesar had to admit he had fought bravely, and he had been clever to conceal the bulk of his forces belowdecks until Blackbeard had boarded. While the British wounded were being attended to and the pirates neglected, the officer and one of his men tallied up the cost of the action. Their count of the dead and wounded jibed with what Caesar had estimated from closely examining the decks of the combined ships.

After a few minutes, he stood up to look at his captain. The great Blackbeard's tall, spare, blood-soaked corpse lay sprawled across the deck, his nearly severed and heavily bearded head staring grotesquely at his British vanquishers. But there was a hint of a smile on his lips, or maybe it wasn't a smile at all but simply a frozen grimace that now looked like a smile. But in it Caesar could see a hint of rebellion and mischief, as if the great pirate commander had somehow managed to have the last laugh. A weary smile and look of pride creased Caesar's face. Suddenly, the world around him on Pamlico Sound seemed serene and filled with beauty—and he did not fear death.

"What the hell are you smiling at?" asked Thomas Gates, one of the other five free black African pirates. "We have lost and will now be hung like dogs."

"No, we haven't lost. We have won. Look at the captain's face—the bastard is smiling because he knows we have won."

"What are you talking about?" sniffed Gates. "He's dead."

"Aye, he may be gone from this world," said Caesar with a knowing smile. "But he and everyone who fought under him this day shall live on for all eternity. For we are—and shall forever be—Blackbeard's pirates."

CHAPTER 70

COURT OF GUARD AND WHITE POINT
CHARLES TOWN, SOUTH CAROLINA

DECEMBER 10, 1718

STEDE BONNET'S appointed execution day of December 10 dawned clear and sunny, but the fair weather did little to ease his mortal fear. Over the past week, as the time for his public hanging had drawn nearer, he was in such a state of terror that he could neither sleep nor eat. The prospect of a piratical "dance of death" at the end of a rope unnerved him. But now that the appointed day had come all hope was lost. His appeals to Governor Johnson for mercy had fallen on deaf ears, and there would be no more delays, no more stays, no more chances at escape, no timely rescue from a mob of pirate-friendly American colonists dashing in to spare him from the gallows. Bonnet had played his last card, and his time had run out and judgment day come.

Outside the Court of Guard where he was imprisoned, he could hear a steadily increasing rumble of voices. A crowd was gathering. A pirate hanging was not only grand theater but a public holiday, and all of Charles Town's citizens and even settlers from the outlying townships and plantations were turning out to watch the spectacle. Some came from as far as twenty miles away to make a picnic day of it. He could also hear the yelling and shouting of the street hawkers selling food and drink. But the most dreaded sound of all was yet to come: the slow creaking of the hanging cart. He knew what it sounded like, for he had heard the macabre sound every time one of his twenty-nine crew members had been hauled away to White Point to be hung.

Feeling butterflies in his stomach, he stood up on his tiptoes and peered through the window of the watch house on Half Moon Battery. In the distance, he could see the calm morning waters of the harbor and the open sea beyond. Just over the walls of the Half Moon Battery lay trackless miles of sea where he had spent the last year and a half of his life as a freebooter. He remembered it only as a bad dream. In the foreground, he saw the citizens of Charles Town chatting and milling about amid the street vendors who would profit from his hanging. For the hundredth time, he cursed his misfortune, closed his eyes, and held his head in his hands.

It was then he heard the dreaded sound of the creaking wheels. It was the hanging cart.

A crescendo of shouts rose from the crowd on the streets: "Seize him! Bring out the murderer!"

"No, no!" he whispered desperately, his legs now trembling beneath him. He heard the scrape of the jailer's boots on the stone floor approaching his cell. Two burly men who reeked of foul body odor and drink swiftly bound his hands together and proceeded to escort him from his cell. But his feet were frozen to the cold floor and wouldn't budge. They grabbed him roughly and carried him along, his toes barely touching the ground. To the murmurs and jeers of the crowd, he was removed from the Court of Guard and hoisted into a horse-drawn cart. Down the length of Broad Street, he could see the throngs of people lining the street all the way to Charles Town's western gate. With his hands bound tightly in front of him, he was paraded up Broad Street past the throngs of people who had turned out to see his execution. He thought the conveyance would take him straight to the gallows, but instead the horse drawing the cart turned in the opposite direction.

The route proved to be a circuitous one, turning down several Charles Town streets so the assembled crowd could see him pass. Young boys in rags followed the cart, thrusting morbidly curious faces up at him. Some spectators jeered and spat upon him, but there were many colonists who cheered him on. For a brief instant, Bonnet felt emboldened by these Americans who regarded pirates not as villains and ruffians but as cultural heroes, romantic figures, contributors to colonial trade at fair prices, and challengers to imperial British rule. He had seen many such people in the courtroom during his trial and heard their whispers of encouragement outside his prison cell, for there were many who did not want him to hang. But overall, they were a minority to those who supported the Crown. A moment later, the city's gate was opened and the crowd followed the cart over the Vanderhorst Creek bridge and along the outer wall towards the marshy area of White Point. After crossing the bridge over the tidal creek, Bonnet caught his first glimpse of the noose hanging from the crossbeam of the wooden gallows.

Whatever composure and fortitude he had displayed during his trial now abandoned him. Gone were the silken shirts and cravats of the gentleman "man of letters" and the blown kisses from the ladies in the courtroom. He knew that he now appeared as a dingy, worn-out, quaking figure in a pitiful hanging cart. A mixture of words of support and mostly leering insults came from the crowd. A well-heeled gentleman stepped forward next to the moving cart with an engraved silver flask and gave him a jolt of rum to help dull his senses.

Arriving at the place of execution, the cart was positioned directly beneath the square-framed gallows. His public hanging was timed to coincide with the low tide. In accordance with Admiralty law, pirates were buried in shallow, unmarked graves in the mud just above the low-water mark. He could see his own shallow grave dug into the mud flat, knowing it lay next to the twenty-nine men from his crew and nineteen others recently hung for piracy during the course of the previous few weeks. Banished to the in-between world that was neither land or sea, he knew his spirit would find no peace as the tides washed over his grave for all eternity. No headstone or marker could be placed on his grave, so no mourners could ever visit or lay flowers in tribute.

Once the cart was positioned beneath the wooden frame, the noose was left to dangle next to him but was not yet placed around his neck. A naval representative stood at the foot of the gallows carrying a silver oar—the symbol of the British Admiralty. As the preacher began his prayer for the dying and harangue against the evils of piracy, a little girl ran up to the cart and thrust a bouquet of wild posies into his manacled hands. Her mother yanked her back and scolded her, but the gesture gave Bonnet a momentary feeling of happiness, making him remember back to the best moments he had shared with his own children that he had left behind on Barbados.

The preacher resumed his stern lecture, admonishing both Bonnet and the crowd concerning the dangers of piracy to the established order under British rule in the Americas. He droned on for more than five minutes with his execution sermon, a meditation on terror with God presented as "the king of terrors" and hence the source of all social discipline, and pirates relinquished to the status of fierce and forbidding villains and blood-lusting monsters bent on destroying the social order. Stede Bonnet and men like him, he declared, were the bane of not only ministers, royal officials, and the merchant and ruling classes, but to all of mankind. As pirates sought to commit crimes against mercantile property and disrupt the social order, they needed to be eradicated like rats. It was, therefore, the civic duty of every citizen here in South Carolina, indeed throughout the New World, to protect property, to punish those who resisted its law, to take vengeance against those they considered their enemies, and to instill fear in sailors who might wish to become pirates. This they should do in the name of God Almighty.

At the end of his tirade, the preacher asked Bonnet if he had anything to say, giving the condemned the opportunity to address the crowd. The gathered throng became quiet, eagerly awaiting his last words. The hope from the preacher was that the gentleman pirate who had left behind a world of opulent wealth to go on the account would stand penitently before the crowd, warn those gathered to watch the execution on the evils of piracy, instruct them to obey their parents and superiors and not to curse, drink, whore, or profane the Lord's day, and acknowledge the justice of the proceedings against him. But Bonnet did not ask for forgiveness, did not praise the authorities, did not affirm the values of Christianity, as he was supposed to do. Nor did he publicly rebel and rail against the injustice of it all to his captors. Instead, when the preacher was finished, the usually eloquent Bonnet was unable to form any words at all. Mouth dry as a kiln, he opened his lips to speak, but no words came out.

The crowd waited. They, too, were expecting the usual Christianly repentance or word of warning to the men in the crowd on the folly of becoming a pirate. Or possibly a few unrepentant remarks to ignite controversy. But it was not to be. An excruciating silence hung over the somber tidal flat, and Bonnet's entire body trembled as if with ague. He opened his mouth a second time, but again no words came. Now the people let out a roar of contempt and disappointment. To hear a condemned man's last words before he died was one of the most thrilling parts of a hanging, but all the plantation-owner-turned-pirate would do was sit in the cart, shaking, unable to speak a word. Street urchins shouted insults and hurled pieces of discarded food at him, hoping to get some response. None came.

A gesture from the Admiralty official was all that was necessary for him to be pushed from the cart into space, but still he could not bring himself to utter a word. Feeling an overpowering sense of regret, he stared up numbly at the heavy noose silhouetted against a periwinkle South Carolina sky.

The Admiralty officer gave the signal for the noose to be placed around his neck and the hanging to commence. Now, finally, he found his voice.

"Dear Lord, what have I done? What have I done?"

With words finally uttered, he drew a mental image of the small headstone that marked the grave of his son Allamby in St. Michael's churchyard on Barbados. The life-shattering loss of his firstborn son was the event that had precipitated his running away from his life on the British island to become a pirate, which, in turn, had led him to today's terrible death on the gallows of White Point. Then he thought of Blackbeard. Word had reached Charles Town several days ago of the epic sea battle at Ocracoke two and a half weeks earlier between the pirate commodore and the British Royal Navy, and when Bonnet had first heard the news he had wished that was the way he could go, with his pistols belching fire and cutlass swinging. But there was no escaping his prison cell. A part of him was still angry at Blackbeard for his deception at Old Topsail Inlet when the pirate captain had deliberately grounded the *Queen Anne's Revenge* and broken up the companies. But he knew he could not blame the man for his own terrible fate.

Thache had been treacherous, true, but he had also gone out of his way to teach him how to sail, use the astrolab, and lead a boarding party—in short, how to be a sea captain—and the man had graciously allowed him to use his personal cabin. Time and again, the wily pirate leader had put up with his eccentricities and his ignominious defeats in battle. It was only when Blackbeard's own crew had pushed for Bonnet's removal as captain that the pirate commander had reluctantly agreed to replace him with first-mate Richards. No, he couldn't blame Blackbeard for his troubles, though he still smarted over having been duped at Old Topsail. But even then, Blackbeard was the one who had instructed him to obtain pardons for himself and his men from Governor Eden. Bonnet knew that if he had simply followed Blackbeard's order and sailed south to St. Thomas and secured his privateering commission from the colonial governor, he wouldn't be standing here before the gallows today. No, he could not hold Blackbeard accountable for his misery, for it was not Blackbeard's actions that had set into motion the events that brought him to today's noose—they were of his own making and that of his insistent crew.

With the noose tightened around his neck by the hangman, he blurted out, "Dear Lord, what have I done?" one last time before he heard the crack of a whip on the horse's rump. The cart jolted out from under him and Stede Bonnet the gentleman pirate stepped into eternity. The fall from the cart was not enough to break his neck though, so with a searing collar of pain around his throat, he felt himself hanging in mid-air and suffocating as he twitched and struggled.

As he writhed in torment, there were seconds when the past streamed through Bonnet's brain. He thought of strolls on the beach with his children, horse rides through verdant tropical fields, sharing a cool rum punch on the veranda of his fine plantation home, and to the good times with his family before he had become a broken man from Allamby's death and his wife's domineering cruelty. After several minutes with still no sign of death, a pair of Blackbeard's pirates who had taken the King's pardon rushed forward and pulled hard on his legs to expedite the process and end his misery. His last earthly thought as he was in the midst of his death throes was of Allamby. His former life in Carlisle Bay as a Barbadian planter seemed like a lifetime ago, but he could see the boy's proud visage as if it were clear as day.

I love you my son. I love you and I am so sorry. Then he made the same apology to his other children—Edward, Stede Jr., and baby Mary—but not to his wife. He would never apologize to her for it was Mary more than anyone else that had driven him to escape his plantation on Barbados for a life of piracy.

Even after his death convulsions ceased, his manacled hands clutched the tiny bouquet of wildflowers. Then the fingers relaxed and the handful of posies fell to the ground. The little girl who had given them to him escaped her mother's grasp, dashed in quickly to scoop up the bouquet, and melted back into the crowd with tears in her eyes.

The "Gentleman Pirate" was no more. His body would be left hanging on the White Point mudflat between the low- and high-tide water line for four days as a warning to other pirates.

A warning of British terror to the rebellious Americans.

CHAPTER 71

GOVERNOR'S PALACE
WILLIAMSBURG, VIRGINIA

JANUARY 10, 1719

"MAY I PRESENT TO YOU, GOVERNOR, the head of Blackbeard the pirate."

Alexander Spotswood gave a gentlemanly bow of approval to the dashing Lieutenant Maynard, and his senior commander, Captain George Gordon of the HMS *Pearl*, before turning his attention to the severed head of the notorious pirate he had fantasized about destroying for the past six months. As if presenting a grand show room, Maynard held up the rotting, thickly bearded head for the governor and his guest Robert Beverley to see. Though it was a grisly sight and instantly permeated his opulent office with a foul odor of decay, Spotswood couldn't help but feel triumphant. He had won after all, had emerged victorious and defeated the villainous robber of the high seas that had been hogging the spotlight; and, in the process, he had removed the barbarous and inhumane wretch and his band of cutthroats once and for all as a threat to Virginia's commerce. The mission into North Carolina had been a success, by thunder, and he had won!

"Well done, Lieutenant Maynard—well done indeed!" he declared ebulliently.

The British naval officer, long since recovered from his cutlass wounds, bowed chivalrously. "Thank you, Governor. It is an honor to have served you on this punitive expedition."

Spotswood glanced at Robert Beverley to gauge his reaction to the trophy, but he wrinkled his nose in disapproval. The governor wished his political associate, friend, and mentor would share in his jubilation, but the sight of the decomposing appendage appeared to have made him queasy. Sensing his discomfort, Maynard placed the trophy back in its protective, scented container. Throughout most of the journey to Williamsburg, the lieutenant had kept the head wrapped and stored in the airtight container, which had limited the decomposition and reduced the horrible odor to some extent. Though Spotswood found the trophy revolting, he was quite happy to see the gruesome figure of his arch-enemy's bloody, rotting head. He had once been an army officer and had seen his share of gore, and he was too thrilled by the success of the mission and his victory over his long-time adversary to care much about the rancid smell.

After the battle at Ocracoke, a mop-up operation with Captain Brand in Bath, and delays due to foul winter weather, Lieutenant Maynard had arrived six days earlier to Kiquotan Roads. With him, he had fifteen suspected pirates from Ocracoke and Bath shackled in his hold and Thache's head slung from the bowsprit of the captured *Adventure* to present to the colony of Virginia. With the pirate captain's grisly head swinging to-and-fro, Maynard formally saluted Captain Gordon and His Majesty's *Pearl* with a nine-gun salute, receiving the like number in return, and then sailed up the James River to the landing at the road to Williamsburg. From there, the fifteen suspected pirates and their captain's rotting head were delivered to Virginia's capital city—the prisoners going to the gaol and the head to the Governor's Palace along with Maynard and Gordon.

Spotswood said, "Captain Brand has reported to me about your amazing battle. But I must confess I would enjoy hearing about it in your own words."

Maynard proceeded to do just that, with what the governor suspected was only minor embellishment.

"And your casualties?"

"Twelve dead, twenty-two badly wounded, and five lightly wounded, including myself."

Now Spotswood looked to the senior commander, making sure that Gordon felt included despite the fact that he had been stationed on the James River throughout the fight and had not taken part in it. "Captain Gordon, can you tell me the total number of pirate dead and number of prisoners you have brought from North Carolina for trial?"

"The pirates suffered ten killed in action," replied Gordon, looking to Maynard for confirmation as he spoke. "Nine survivors were taken as prisoners at Ocracoke, six black men and three white, and six were arrested and taken into custody in Bath."

"That is correct," confirmed Maynard. "Several of them have, of course, loudly proclaimed their innocence. But I should think that only a handful fall into that category. One of them, Samuel Odell, claims to be a trader who merely visited the ship for some sort of celebration the night before the attack."

"Proclaims his innocence when he consorts with pirates, does he?" sniffed Spotswood. "Well, we'll just have to see about that when we take the depositions from the pirates in preparation for trial. We shall have to closely examine specifically who took up arms against you and your men, shan't we? I should think that would decide the prisoners' fates. In any case, I must commend you, gentlemen, on a job well done," he added, making sure to thank them both this time, even though only Maynard had engaged the pirates in battle. "You two have done this colony a great service."

"Thank you, Governor," said Gordon and Maynard together.

He looked again at the senior officer. "And what, Captain Gordon, is the total haul seized from the pirates. What I mean to say is what will you and Lieutenant Maynard be delivering to me as His Majesty's representative here in Virginia on behalf of the King? I am, of course, referring to all piratically-taken gold dust, goods, coin, objects, and other materials recovered from the pirate sloop *Adventure* and from Governor Eden and Tobias Knight in Bath Town. Can you please give me an accurate accounting, sir?"

"Yes, I can. On Ocracoke Island, we recovered ten casks of sugar and one hundred forty bags of cocoa. They were stored beneath a tarred-canvas sail erected as a tent on the shore near the Old Watering Hole. With respect to Governor Eden and Mr. Knight, we seized sixty hogsheads of sugar from the governor's storehouse in town and another twenty located at Knight's out on the plantation by the river. Plus we have the *Adventure* itself, a fine Spanish sloop. Governor Eden also handed over six slaves he acquired from the pirates. We estimate the total value of Thache's plunder to be approximately two thousand five hundred pounds, including the vessel."

"That's all that was recovered? There was no treasure to speak of?"

Gordon looked at Maynard. "There may be some other odds and ends, but I don't think they're worth very much," said the lieutenant. "In any event, the complete inventory of recovered supplies are aboard Thache's sloop, awaiting shipment to Williamsburg."

Spotswood was skeptical there wasn't more, but wasn't about to challenge them on it. He had expected the great Blackbeard to have a vast treasure of silver and gold. "So be it," he said laconically.

Lieutenant Maynard then surprised both the governor and his senior commander Gordon with his next words. "When do you think we can expect to receive our reward, Governor?" he asked.

Spotswood's eyebrows went up. "Reward?"

"The reward you promised us for killing and capturing Blackbeard and his crew."

"Oh yes, the reward."

"My men are counting on it, sir. They suffered terribly in the fight. I lost more than half my men as casualties and you promised that we would be promptly paid."

"They are not *your* men, Lieutenant," pointed out Captain Gordon. "They serve under Captain Brand and I, as we are the captains of the *Lyme* and *Pearl*."

"Yes, I know, but I'm the one that led them in combat and the men are looking to me to make sure they receive their just dues. More than thirty fell during the battle, and many of those that survived will never be the same. It was a bloody battle, sir. The men deserve their just compensation."

"Lieutenant, you are out of order, sir," bristled Gordon. "It is not your place to question the governor—or your superior officers. The responsibility of ensuring proper compensation falls to myself and Captain Brand."

Spotswood held up a hand. "It's all right, Captain," he said to mollify the situation. "I understand Lieutenant Maynard's concern." He looked at the junior officer, who he could tell was a man of courage and honor and was only looking out for the men he had led into battle. "I can promise you that the said rewards will be punctually and justly paid, in current money of Virginia, according to directions of the signed Act."

"It was one hundred pounds for Blackbeard, twenty pounds for his officers, and ten pounds for every seaman, sir," Maynard reminded him.

"The governor does not need to be lectured on the amounts, Lieutenant," seethed Gordon, clearly disappointed in his subordinate for tactlessly bringing up the terms of payment for the bounty on Blackbeard and his crew. Hoping to avoid further embarrassment, he then quickly changed the subject. "How do you anticipate the trial will proceed, Governor? Of course, Captain Brand, Lieutenant Maynard, and myself are prepared to testify on behalf of the Admiralty."

"Yes, we will need your testimony, gentlemen," said Spotswood, quickly smoothing over the awkward moment. "Over the next few months, we will take depositions and firm up our case. Then we will try the pirates and hang the guilty parties based upon who is willing to cooperate and who took up arms against the King's men."

"May I ask what is your view on the King's new pardon?" asked Gordon. "The pardon that spared William Howard, Thache's quartermaster, from the hangman's noose."

Spotswood couldn't help but grimace with irritation at the question. Since the King's latest proclamation had arrived by ship from St. James's Palace in London just a few weeks before—and, shockingly, the night before Howard was to be executed—the governor had been deeply worried. The King's new pardon graciously extended the dates for which pirates would be eligible to surrender and receive the Crown's mercy and clemency, which made his invasion into the sovereign colony of North Carolina completely illegal. While the King's proclamation of the previous year had specified the date of January 5, 1718, as the date after which acts of piracy would no longer be eligible to be forgiven, the subsequent pardon that arrived on his desk in mid-December listed no such date. He had memorized the key passage in the proclamation so he could be certain of what the King and Privy Council intended: "Every such pirate...shall have our gracious pardon of and for such his or their piracy or piracies, by him or them committed before such time as they shall have received notice of this our royal proclamation." The King's intentions were perfectly clear. The new proclamation was worded to encourage more men to surrender and return to honest, productive lives. There was no specific calendar date after which acts of piracies would no longer be eligible to be forgiven—only those piracies committed after the pirates received notice of the royal proclamation would be ineligible. In other words, every piracy committed before a pirate heard about the new pardon would be forgiven.

"Have the prisoners been made aware of the new proclamation?" he asked the two naval officers.

Gordon looked at Maynard. "They were not informed by me or Captain Brand," said the lieutenant. "But I only learned of the second pardon recently."

Gordon nodded. "The men arrested at Ocracoke and Bath Town will have to formally receive notice of the new proclamation now that they are incarcerated here in Williamsburg. And every piracy they committed prior to their being notified will have to set aside by you, right Governor?"

Spotswood shook his head. Despite the obvious intentions of the King and the letter of the law, the lieutenant governor had no intention of letting any of the pirates off the hook. He was certainly not about to allow them to get off on a technicality just because the King needed privateers when war was resumed with Spain. He would bend the letter of the law as far as he could—and break it outright—if he thought he could get away with it. The new pardon was an obstacle, but he would find a way around it. At the very least, all those who had taken up arms against Maynard and his seamen would swing from the gallows just like Stede Bonnet in Charles Town.

He would, or course, forge ahead with the process of extracting statements from the pirates, or at least from those who were willing to cooperate or could be bullied into cooperating. He already knew a great deal about Thache's piratical activities up to the grounding of the *Queen Anne's Revenge*, but from depositions of the fifteen newly captured prisoners he hoped to learn many more details. Specifically, he wanted to know more about the capture of the French ship and its cargo, Blackbeard's suspected visit to Tobias Knight's house, and his documented assault on prominent North Carolina citizen William Bell on the river.

In his estimation, the investigation would proceed swiftly. His prosecutors would prepare for a thorough but speedy trial before the Court of Vice-Admiralty, with himself acting as head, for deciding the guilt or innocence of Blackbeard's captured crew members. But this was merely for show. He was not about to rely upon the testimony of lowly pirates for evidence to determine who would or would not be convicted of crimes at sea. He didn't need a trial to decide the outcome for his mind was already made up: some of the men would be found guilty while others would be found innocent—with guilt or innocence decided purely on the basis of who had taken up arms against the King, which he hoped would be all or most of Blackbeard's crew. The pre-trial depositions would not be about collecting damaging evidence against Blackbeard and his band of misfits. The depositions would be about fishing for incriminatory evidence against the two top officials of North Carolina whom he believed had been in bed with Thache: Charles Eden and Tobias Knight. They were and always had been the ultimate targets of his witch hunt, and William Howard and Blackbeard both had always been nothing but stepping stones to undermine or destroy them.

He needed to prove to the people of North Carolina and Virginia, and to the authorities in England, that the government officials in the colony were corrupt and that they were deriving a profit from the piratical acts of the notorious Blackbeard. This would enable him to increase his own position with his Council and the House of Burgesses and gain control over North Carolina. At the very least, he should be able to secure a tighter grip on colonial power. He could do this either by extending the boundaries of Virginia some distance southward, or by forcing the Crown to end the reign of the lords proprietors and make North and South Carolina into proper royal colonies instead of unregulated, private commercial enterprises where pirates were given refuge and free to plunder. It was a bold plan but he was confident he could pull it off, though he dare not tell the two naval officers about his scheme. For in his view, they were mere pawns on the colonial chessboard just like the notorious Blackbeard.

"I have not yet considered all the particulars of the trial, gentlemen," Spotswood lied in answer to Captain Gordon's question. "The only thing that I can say at this time is justice will be served and I look forward to working closely with you, gentlemen, to secure the outcome that we all desire. As I have said, you have done this colony a great service. My esteemed colleague Mr. Beverley, who like you has given inestimable service to Virginia through his writings and years of political service, and I thank you from the bottom of our hearts."

"Hear, hear," said Beverley. "Well done, gentlemen. Well done indeed."

"Huzzah—I heartily second that," said Spotswood with a fatherly smile. "And as a small token of our gratitude, we have waiting for you downstairs two casks of wine and brandy, a collection of sweetbreads, and a honey-roasted ham."

He stood up and bowed to signal that the meeting was over.

The two naval officers stood up from their silk-embroidered chairs and saluted.

"Thank you, Governor," said Gordon.

"Yes, thank you, Governor," echoed Maynard.

Spotswood smiled his most ingratiating smile. "No, the thanks belong to you, gentlemen. And I promise you, Lieutenant Maynard, you and your brave men will be promptly paid."

"We have complete faith in His Majesty's royal governor," said Gordon. "And what, pray tell, should we do with Blackbeard's head?"

"Oh, please leave it with me."

"If I might ask," inquired Maynard, "what does the governor plan on doing with the trophy?"

"I'm glad you asked. I plan to suspend it from a pole on the west side of the Hampton River as an admonition to would-be pirates to reconsider their chosen profession. What do you think? Will that meet with your approval, gentlemen?"

"Yes, that should do nicely," said Maynard. "I will say one thing for the pirate commodore. He fought bravely to the bitter end. Despite no less than five gunshot wounds and a score of nasty sword cuts, he kept on fighting. I must confess that, in the heat of battle, I was worried that he was immortal and could not be smote down."

"Come now, Lieutenant, we don't want to make a myth of the man," groaned Spotswood. "He is but a common robber and thief, a barbarous wretch and murderous villain to all humanity. Six months from now no one will even remember his name."

"I wouldn't be so sure about that," said Robert Beverley. "I wouldn't be so sure about that at all."

"Neither would I," agreed Maynard. "And I should know. After all, I'm the one who fought a sword duel with the man and barely escaped with my life to tell the tale. And I say, despite his being a lowly pirate, he fought like a lion and his valor will be talked about for a very long time."

"Yes well, we'll just see about that. We'll be in touch, gentlemen," snorted Spotswood, and he gave an impatient frown and sent the two Royal Navy officers on their way.

CHAPTER 72

PUBLIC GAOL
WILLIAMSBURG, VIRGINIA

MARCH 10, 1718

SITTING ON THE FLOOR of his dirty, stench-ridden, frigid holding cell, Caesar wondered when he would be tried and hung. After two straight months of incarceration and fourteen weeks of being held against his will as a prisoner, he just wanted to get it over with. At this point, the life that he and his condemned sea mates were living was worse than being a slave.

He would gladly trade his cold and disgusting prison cell in Virginia for a return to a life of slavery at Tobias Knight's home in Bath Town. At least then he could sing songs, swap stories, and make merriment with his old friend Pompey. At least then he would be well fed, clothed, housed, and cared for by Dr. Maule, whom he had visited several times at his house at the corner of Bay and Craven Streets when he had the fever or some other such illness. At least then he might be able to feel a woman's kiss or caress on a cool summer evening along the river. Despite being a slave owner, Knight had always treated him and the other slaves well, all things considered, and he would return home to the Pamlico River country of his youth in a heartbeat if by some chance he was released.

He glanced around his ten-foot by ten-foot cell that he shared with five other black inmates captured following the battle at Ocracoke. Since their incarceration, he and Richard Greensail, James Blake, Thomas Gates, James White, and Richard Stiles had been kept in a separate holding cell from the other white prisoners, who had already gone through the legal process and no longer occupied the two adjacent cells. The six African prisoners were shackled with leg and wrist irons, and tethered together by lengths of chain. A doctor had been on hand to inspect them when they had first arrived at the jail, but that was two months ago and since that time they had been crammed together with no medical aid in their freezing, cramped chamber, with little in the way of light or comfort save dirty straw and rats for company. They had remained fettered throughout their incarceration, even though the likelihood of escape was virtually nonexistent. They were kept alive, but just barely, living on a diet of salt beef and cornmeal.

The only thing that kept them going was that they were well informed on the goings-on in the outside world. From the son of the tavern owner who brought their meals and one of their jailers, they were given regular updates on the status of the public pirate trial and what was turning to be a major clash between the governments of North Carolina and Virginia over the invasion of the proprietary colony by Governor Spotswood. From the tavern owner's son—whose father, like many colonists, had proved to be quite friendly to pirates since it helped augment his income—Caesar had learned that only one of the white pirates, John Carnes, had been executed. He had been hung at the mouth of the Hampton River. Nine others had either been pardoned or acquitted, including Israel Hands, who it was said had given testimony against Thache and the other crew members.

According to the tavern owner's son and the jailer, the Admiralty court had reached a decision on the guilt or innocence of the crew members based on specific criteria. Those that had been pardoned were those who were arrested in Bath Town and who were not aboard the *Adventure* during the engagement, and thus were eligible for the King's newest pardon that arrived in mid-December. The two acquitted—Samuel Odell and James Robins who had remained below decks, pretended to be prisoners, and restrained Caesar from blowing up the ship—had been released from custody because neither bore arms against the King's sailors, and their lives were spared. The remaining white pirate that was hung, John Carnes, was executed because, even though he was not part of the boarding party that had tried to take the *Jane*, he had defended the deck of the *Adventure* when it was boarded on the other side by sailors from the *Ranger*. He was not eligible for His Majesty's forgiveness because he had openly fought Maynard's men, possibly wounding or killing some of them. For that offense—considered high treason against the Crown—King George offered no amnesty, and he was hung.

According to the jailer, Caesar and the other remaining pirates, all black men, were to be tried in the next day or two. Apparently, the governor had needed to wait until the harsh winter weather abated to hold a meeting with his scattered Council to decide whether the Africans would be tried as slaves or free men. But it didn't matter to Caesar. He knew that he and his fellow condemned Africans would be hung. After all, they were black men in a white man's world. It didn't matter if they had given evidence that would help the Admiralty's case, as he knew four of his jailmates had done. James Blake, Thomas Gates, James White, and Richard Stiles had all been bullied by Spotswood's lawyers into giving testimony against Thache and the other crew members in their depositions. To gain the mercy of the court, they had recounted their sailing adventure across Pamlico Sound to Bath in September of last year to visit Tobias Knight and the subsequent robbery on the river of a man named William Bell. They had not wanted to testify against the pirate captain who had given them their freedom or their fellow crew members, but Spotswood had guaranteed that they would be given favorable treatment by the court for their testimony on behalf of the Crown, like Israel Hands.

Caesar didn't believe that for a minute, and he had stubbornly refused to answer any questions posed by Spotswood's lawyers during his incarceration. During their futile attempts to question him, he could tell that they were up to something. From the very nature of their queries, it was obvious that they were less interested in the crimes of Thache and his crew than they were in Governor Eden and Tobias Knight. Spotswood and his legal team seemed determined to obtain incriminating evidence to prove their collusion with the pirates, and they were obviously willing to go to extreme lengths to get the information they sought. As best as Caesar could tell, they wanted to lay bare the corrupt relationship between Eden, Knight and Blackbeard's gang of pirates during the *Adventure's* various visits to Bath. After two interrogation sessions, Caesar realized that he and his fellow pirates were nothing but a means to an end for Spotswood. He suspected that the pompous ass had designs on forcing Eden out of office and taking the Carolina government for his own.

At that moment, he heard a footfall outside the cell in the prison corridor followed by the jingle of a set of keys and the sound of the jail door opening. Two well-fed armed white guards stepped into the cell.

"Caesar, you come with us," one of them said.

So this is it—I'm to be tried and hung today, he thought. He wasn't sad or angry, only surprised that it had taken so long. Part of him was grateful, for his cell had been so freezing cold the past two months that he would almost rather die than endure the unbearable cold any longer. He and his cell mates would have frozen to death if not for piling up loose straw around themselves to conserve body heat during the frigid winter.

The guards unlocked his chains. He said a quick goodbye to his friend Richard Greensail, who, like him, had not testified against his captain or the other crew members to save his own neck. He could not bring himself to say any parting words to the others, whom he regarded as traitors for giving testimony on behalf of the Crown, as Israel Hands had done. With his hands shackled in front of him, he was led from the prison cell down a pair of dank corridors until they reached a meeting room of some sort. Seated at the table in the center of the room was none other than Alexander Spotswood along with one of his lawyers that had questioned Caesar on the two prior occasions. The governor wore a freshly powdered wig, fine white silk tunic, pale blue hose, and a stiffly quilted blue velvet doublet. On his head he wore a pair of reading glasses with silk ribbons fastened to the lenses and looped with separate ribbons around his ears.

Caesar felt his stomach twisted in knots. He made eye contact with the governor, who merely scowled at him and returned to his paperwork on the table in front of him. He then looked at the young lawyer who had tried unsuccessfully to take his depositions, but found his face unreadable.

As the heavy steel door closed behind him, he gave a little start. There was a jarring note of finality to it: with despair he realized that his fate was sealed and they were here to tell him that unless he cooperated he would be hung. But he would never cooperate. He took in the grim face of the guard who had remained behind posted at the door. Then he took another breath of air to calm his nerves and looked out the window. Dark billowy clouds had settled over the Virginia capital, dampening the already dull sunlight with an unwelcome hint of doom and gloom.

Spotswood broke the excruciating silence: "Sit down, Caesar." It was an order, not a request.

He did as instructed. He knew he was in deep trouble, probably for refusing to talk, but at the same time he couldn't help wondering if there was a glimmer of hope and he wouldn't be hung. That was doubtful, he decided. His gaze met Spotswood's and the periwigged lieutenant governor looked him in the eye with a supercilious expression on his face.

"You, Caesar the Negro slave, are a person of a very notorious character for your piracies. By any fair and just God, you should be hung from the neck until dead and buried below the high-water mark for your villainous deeds. Wouldn't you agree?"

He gave a little gulp, feeling suddenly dry and constricted in his throat. How could he possibly answer such a loaded question? Did the bastard want him to confess so that they could hang him and be done with him altogether? He said nothing.

"Very well. If you have nothing to say on the matter, there are two other items that have been brought to my attention. Items which you failed to disclose in your depositions. Though it must be said that you did not yield much of anything in either session with my secretary here." He nodded to his young aide, the lawyer seated next to him.

Again, Caesar said nothing, waiting for the governor to inform him what he had failed to reveal.

"It appears that you are the property of Tobias Knight, the council secretary, collector of customs, and interim chief justice of North Carolina. Is this correct?"

"I once belonged to him, but I am now a free man."

Spotswood looked at his aide and rolled his eyes sarcastically. "'I am a free man,' he says. 'I am a free man.'" Now his dark eyes flickered menacingly, like a hectoring judge. "No, my felonious Negro, you are not free—you are a slave." He pulled out two sheets of foolscap. "This document, signed and sealed by Mr. Knight, and the accompanying bill of sale make it quite clear that you are his legal property. You were purchased in 1713 at the age of eighteen by Mr. Knight from the Robert Daniel family of Bath Town. The price was twenty pounds and it appears that your current owner wants you back. He has indicated such in his letter." He pushed the documents across to him. "Would you like to review them? I understand you can read."

"Aye, and as well as you, I imagine." He took the documents and examined them closely. He didn't understand every word, but he wasn't about to let Spotswood know that. In reading the documents, he realized that Knight was requesting that he be returned to him to spare him from the hangman. The letter was written in a formal manner and requested the release of "my legally-purchased servile property, the twenty-three-year-old Negro known as Caesar" from custody in Virginia and his "prompt return to Bath Town to his rightful owner."

When he looked up, Spotswood was peering down his nose at him. "How did you learn to read? It is forbidden for most slaves."

"Tobias Knight's wife taught me. Mostly the Bible. But it was Captain Thache that opened up a whole new world to me with the books on his ship."

"So the pair of you are educated book readers—ahoy, how enlightened our thieving rogues. Now regarding the other matter which you failed to disclose to my secretary here. It has been brought to my attention that you attempted to blow up the *Adventure* and the two naval vessels by setting fire to the powder stores belowdecks. Is this true?"

Caesar took a breath, sat back in his chair, and licked his lips, trying to buy himself time. He had wondered why Spotswood's men hadn't brought it up before. He had surmised that Samuel Odell and James Robins, the two men that had stopped him from igniting the powder stores, must not have mentioned it in the trial, most likely because it might have implicated them as well. So they had kept quiet about the incident to protect their own skin. But now somehow the governor had found out about it.

"Who told you this? Did someone bring it up in court?"

"That is not important. The question is whether or not it is true?"

Weighing his answer carefully, he decided that it was better to lie and claim, like Samuel Odell and James Robins, that he was hiding out in the hold of the ship to avoid the fighting. He couldn't claim that he was not a pirate aboard the ship, but he could truthfully maintain that he had not taken up arms against the King's men since the trader Odell and Robins had prevented him from blowing up the *Adventure*. Was it possible that that would be enough for him to gain his freedom?

"No, I did not try and blow up the ship. That is a lie."

"Are you sure? The word around the docks is that a Negro tried to blow up the ship. I think it was you."

"Well then, you would be wrong. It was not I."

"Then who was it?"

"I do not know."

"It appears, Mr. Educated Negro Caesar, that you are aware that such an offense is considered high treason against the Crown. That is why you proclaim your innocence, isn't it?"

"No," he said crisply. "I only know that there was no explosion. How can there be a crime if nothing was blown up?"

"Malicious intent is punishable as a crime too, Caesar. But I wouldn't expect a mere Negro to be aware of such legal niceties." He suddenly sat upright in his chair. "Very well, you are hereby pardoned and free to go."

He wasn't sure he had heard correctly. "What…what did you just say?"

Spotswood snapped his leatherbound book shut and removed his reading glasses. "I said you are free to go, provided you are willing to pay the fee due the attorney-general. I am, of course, referring to the fee he receives for making out pardons for condemned men, even a Negro such as yourself."

"But I have no money. Your men took it from me."

"As luck would have it—even though, as I have said, you a person of a very notorious character for your piracies—you shall have the money that was on your person when you were captured restored to you."

He wasn't sure he believed his ears. "You're telling me my money is being returned to me?"

The governor made a snooty face, as if he had caught a whiff of something malodorous. "Even though you have been condemned, there is no proof of your monies on your person to have been piratically taken."

"I see. And why am I being pardoned again?"

"Let's just say you have benefitted from King George's most gracious proclamation that arrived in mid-December. It is the same that spared your former quartermaster, the villainous William Howard, from the gallows. Now, without further ado, I must make you aware of the terms of your pardon."

"Terms?"

"You are to leave the colony of Virginia posthaste and return to your rightful owner, Mr. Tobias Knight, of Bath Town by the end of March. Any violation of the terms of your pardon and you will be punished to the full extent of the law. My secretary here has your pass, which is good through to the end of March. Which means that you have three weeks, Caesar, with which to convey yourself southward to the home of your proper owner. I would advise you to get started as soon as possible. But first, is there anything you would like to tell me and my secretary about Mr. Knight that might illuminate his interactions with your captain, Edward Thache, the notorious pirate known as Blackbeard? I believe it is in your best interest to unburden yourself and come clean now that you are set to go free."

"To go free as a slave, you mean."

"Yes well, you are a Negro. I did not devise your station in life—that is God's doing."

Caesar saw what the lieutenant governor was up to and was not fooled. He knew the man was fishing for information that would implicate Tobias Knight. That was the whole reason for the trial: it was all a fishing expedition to uncover dirt on Governor Eden and Knight, not to prosecute Blackbeard and his pirates.

"No, I know nothing of their *interactions*. Except to say that the twenty casks of sugar delivered to Mr. Knight was payment for services rendered."

"Services rendered?"

"In his role as customs inspector and officer of North Carolina's Vice-Admiralty court. That be all I know."

Spotswood sneered. "Oh, that's not how it was, my Negro friend. It was a bribe, pure and simple."

"I disagree. Now if there are no further questions, I should be going."

Spotswood signaled the guard. "Unshackle and release him." He looked back at him. "Truth be told, I shall be more than happy to be rid of the likes of you and your remaining criminal associates."

"What will happen to them?" he asked as the guard unlocked the shackles around his wrists.

"What will happen to Mr. Gates, Mr. Greenleaf, Mr. Blake, Mr. White, and Mr. Stiles? The truth is, I don't know. My Council is scheduled to arrive tomorrow to decide whether they are to be tried as slaves or as...*gentlemen of fortune*, as you and your ilk are so fond of calling yourselves."

He rubbed his unshackled wrists to get the blood flowing again and ease his pain. "And if it is decided that they are to be tried as pirates?"

"Then they will hang, for the depositions clearly show that they took up arms against Lieutenant Maynard and his men. You should consider yourself lucky that you are not being subjected to a similar fate. Now I have one more question, and before you are allowed to leave I am going to insist that you answer it. What was *he* like?"

"What was he like? You mean Blackbeard?"

"Yes."

He could see the deep curiosity in Spotswood's eyes, a curiosity that crossed the line into desperation. It was obvious that he was secretly obsessed with the man, like the hunter who greatly admires a massive grizzly bear or whale but all the same sets out to kill the creature. "He set me free and was a great sea captain. A man could serve under no better."

Spotswood gave a dubious snort. "Come now, he was murderous brute, one of the most bloodthirsty and ruthless corsairs to ever live. In fact, he has been scrupulously described in the newspapers as 'grotesquely conspicuous a villain as can be found in the annals of crime.' I saw his severed head and can only imagine that in life he must have provided a picture sufficiently repulsive without calling in his dusky face and savage eyes with a supernatural glare."

"You didn't know the man. He was nothing like that."

Spotswood edged closer in his chair, like a titillated schoolboy at the sight of an alluring young woman. "Then, truly, what was he like?"

"He was my hero. But he was also just an ordinary man who was in love with a woman. That's why he gave up piracy and waited so long to go south to St. Thomas. He was torn and wanted to return to her. He could not bring himself to go, but he had to deal with the crew."

The governor waved his hand dismissively. "I don't believe that for a minute. You're telling me that monster, with all his savage and pernicious designs, was in love with *a woman*?"

"Margaret of Marcus Hook, a young Swedish lass with fair hair. He loved her like no other and wanted to be with her for the rest of his natural days."

"Blackbeard the lover. Humbug, I don't believe it. Why that murderous, throat-slitting rogue wasn't capable of loving or being loved by anyone."

"Aye, but he was. And it was because of her that he had turned his back on piracy. He didn't want to take the French Martiniqueman—Israel Hands and the rest of the crew almost mutinied and made him do it. He was ready to put it all behind him. He was prepared to live the rest of his life as an honest man, he was."

"I don't believe that. Though born into wealth and privilege, the man was a villainous thief and bloodthirsty cutthroat to the core."

"No, Governor, you are wrong. And it is because you are wrong that you have done him a terrible injustice. You murdered him, plain and simple—and because of the King's and Governor Eden's pardons, you had no right to do it."

Spotswood's face crimsoned with embarrassment. "How dare you talk to me like that! Why you're nothing but a Negro slave!"

"And you are not half the man he is, or rather was. He was a great sea captain, as fine as ever sailed the seas, and *you* murdered him. That's all he ever wanted to be was a great seaman—and by thunder, he was that, sir!"

"Why I should have you shackled and put back in your cell for your intransigence! But you are not even a man—you are property!"

"No, Governor, I am a free man. I will always be free because of him. I will always be free because I sailed with the great Blackbeard. Mark my words, three hundred years from now, no one will remember you. But *everyone* will know of the legendary Blackbeard."

"Guard, get him out of my sight before I have him drawn and quartered! Return to him his effects, point him south, and give him a swift kick in the rump! And that's an order!"

"Let's go! On your feet!"

The guard grabbed him gruffly and shoved him towards the door. When they reached it, Caesar turned around to get one last word in. He knew he should just keep his mouth shut and get going, but his blood was up and he wanted to put the pompous governor in his place.

"You, sir, are no Blackbeard," he said. "He was a great man and that is something that you will *never* be."

Spotswood was up out of his chair and screaming, the veins in his neck bulging. "He was nothing, I tell you! Nothing!"

"No, he is and always will be an American hero," Caesar said calmly. "Unlike your name, his will ring out for all eternity."

And with that, he walked out of the room with his head held high, collected his money and belongings, and started south, knowing that he would forever be a free man whether he returned to Tobias Knight or not. After all, he had sailed with the legendary Blackbeard and had lived through the adventures of ten lifetimes as a free man.

He would forever feel the free spirit of the open sea and the pirate commander who had liberated him inside him.

AFTERWORD

Blackbeard: The Birth of America was conceived and written by the author as a work of historical fiction. Although the novel takes place during the Golden Age of Piracy and incorporates actual historical figures, events, and locales, the novel is ultimately a work of the imagination and entertainment and should be read as nothing more. Though I have strived for historical accuracy and there is not a single character in the book that is not based on an actual historical figure (with the exception of Major Stede Bonnet's original quartermaster when he set sail from Barbados in the spring of 1717, whom I have named Ishmael Hanks since I could not find any reliable reference to his actual quartermaster), the names, characters, places, government entities, armed forces, religious and political groups, and incidents, as portrayed in the novel, are products of the author's imagination and are not to be construed as one-hundred-percent accurate depictions. Also, the reader should know that the name of Thache's first sloop that he officially captained (as documented in the deposition of the captured Henry Timberlake, captain of the *Lamb*, on December 17, 1716) has escaped history. I refer to the unknown sloop as *Margaret* in the novel in honor of Thache's historically documented love Margaret of Marcus Hook.

With regard to the historical events of the novel, I have tried to place the actual historical figures in a given scene and have used, to the extent possible, their actual words based on transcripts, documents, and other quoted materials. Most of the scenes in the book are based on known events with specific historical figures present, but a minority are based on events that are generally accepted to have taken place but have unfortunately not been documented by history. In both cases, the interpretations of character and motivation are mine and mine alone. Thus, the book's characters are ultimately a part of my overall imaginative landscape and are, therefore, the fictitious creations of the author, reflecting my personal research interests and biases. Below I present the ultimate fate and legacy of the three primary historical figures and point-of-view characters of the book: Edward Thache, Alexander Spotswood, and Caesar, with secondary POV characters Stede Bonnet and Lieutenant Robert Maynard worked into the discussions of Blackbeard and Spotswood.

EDWARD THACHE (BLACKBEARD)

The image of Edward Thache as a cruel and ruthless villain was largely created by propagandist newspaper accounts in London and America, the British Board of Trade, colonial governors like Alexander Spotswood, and Captain Charles Johnson's (Nathanial Mist's) *A General History of the Robberies and Murders of the Most Notorious Pirates*, first published in 1724 six years after Blackbeard's death. As Blackbeard historian Arne Bialuschewski states about the latter: "This book has been plundered by generations of historians, despite the fact that it is riddled with errors, exaggerations, and misunderstandings." Unlike my ancestor Captain William Kidd (I am his ninth great-grandson on the Marquis side of my family), whom famous pirate writer-illustrator Howard Pyle said should be "relegated to the dull ranks of simply respectable people," Blackbeard has attained a mythical status. In doing so, he has represented many different things to many different people over the past three hundred years. To some he is a hero, to others a villain, to still others an antihero or something else in between the two extremes.

He has been called as "grotesquely conspicuous a villain as can be found in the annals of crime" and a thief who perpetrated "the most abominable wickedness imaginable," "carried out acts of mindless destruction," and "committed more private murders than he could number on the fingers of both hands" despite the fact that he never killed a single person until Maynard's attack at Ocracoke on November 22, 1718. To his legion of supporters, he has been called everything from a "canny strategist, a master of improvisation, a showman, a natural leader and an extraordinary risk taker" to "the boldest and most notorious of the sea rovers in the New World in the early 1700's" to "the bravest and most daring corsair of them all." One historian recently proclaimed, "Meaner or more evil characters existed, but none were as flamboyant, theatrical, and bold as Thache." Former Navy Seal and pirate scholar Benerson Little, author of *The Golden Age of Piracy: The Truth Behind Pirate Myths*, states that if "Blackbeard was not the greatest of pirates" he was "at least a great one." He believes "Blackbeard's greatest triumph was his image" which "indeed was a fierce one"—but only enough to terrify "merchant seamen, lubberly shore-based merchants, and armchair adventurers" and not the "English naval seamen who killed him in action." So, in the judgement of history was Blackbeard a hero or villain, and just how "great" was he? Was he a nefarious brute who stuffed lit matches in his beard and gave up his sixteen-year-old Bath Town wife to his crew to be raped? Or was he a brilliant marine tactician like Horatio Nelson, or a dashing swashbuckler like Errol Flynn? Or was he perhaps just an ordinary man in love with a woman named Margaret of Marcus Hook, a man who aspired to be nothing more than to ply his trade as a sea captain but was overtaken by the events of his day?

As this book has set out to illustrate based on the latest research on the man, the myth, the legend—he was, to some extent, an amalgamation of all these stereotypes. Ultimately, he was a complex and mysterious figure, and most certainly no caricature like *Treasure Island's* Long John Silver or Captain Jack Sparrow of *Pirates of the Caribbean* fame. He was brilliant, bold, daring, successful, generous to his family, and beloved by his crew, yes, but he could also be ruthless, treacherous, and violent towards those who threatened him (such as Israel Hands) or didn't fit into his plans (such as Stede Bonnet and the members of his crew he abandoned at Old Topsail Inlet). And let's not forget he was a pirate. As Benerson Little states: "it's hard not to be violent in a violent trade, and we should not forget that even the threat of force is a form of violence." Furthermore, there is no doubt that in the last six months of Blackbeard's life he was lonely, disillusioned, deeply torn concerning his chosen path in life and what to do about his future, and he no longer commanded the weight he once had with his greatly reduced crew. Most of all, he was a man of contrasts, which I believe arose from the internal conflict he felt inside. On the one hand, he was a man of legitimacy as the son of a wealthy plantation-owner from Jamaica and as a Royal Navy officer and privateer on behalf of the British Crown. On the other, he was a non-holds-barred outlaw taking the vessels of all nations, a Robin-Hood-like figure and American patriot fighting against British domination and the Atlantic mercantile system that favored the 1% of his day. As Kevin Duffus, author of *The Last Days of Black Beard the Pirate*, has said, "He was a paradox in a paradoxical age."

But again in the words of Duffus, "Who, truly, was Blackbeard, and from whence did he come?" This work of historical fiction has attempted to answer that question based upon a detailed synthesis of available historical records and the research findings from Blackbeard experts David Moore of the Queen Anne's Revenge project, Bialuschewski, Duffus, and Little referenced above, and Colin Woodard, Angus Konstam, Baylus Brooks, David Cordingly, Marcus Rediker, and others cited in the references following this "Afterword." The last two decades have yielded a treasure trove of information that has radically altered the Blackbeard narrative, based upon deed, marriage, and death records, court transcripts, and first- and second-hand accounts in British, French, Jamaican, and North and South American archives. This information has been incorporated in detail into this historical work.

We now know, for instance, with a reasonable degree of certainty, that Edward Thache was born not far from Bristol, England, to an upper-middle-class, landowning family around 1687, but that he moved to Jamaica at a young age. According to maritime historian Baylus Brooks, author of *Blackbeard Reconsidered: Mist's Piracy, Thache's Genealogy* and *Quest for Blackbeard: The True Story of Edward Thache and His World*, genealogical research has demonstrated that "Edward Thache of Gloucestershire and/or Bristol, possible grandson of Anglican minister Thomas Thache of Sapperton, was…Blackbeard the pirate" and that he and "his family lived in Spanish Town, St. Catherine's Parish, Jamaica" by around 1690. Additional records from British archives compiled by Brooks reveal that Thache served in the British Royal Navy, likely as an officer or similar elevated position befitting his social standing, aboard the HMS *Windsor* commanded by Rear Admiral William Whetstone, a relative of Stede Bonnet. Thache's father Edward was buried in Spanish Town, Jamaica, on November 16, 1706, and a deed of his father's inheritance to his step-mother Lucretia, dated December 10, 1706, shows that he served on the *Windsor* at that time. He was listed in the ship's pay book as joining that vessel on April 12, 1706, on the southern coast of England, and, according to Brooks, he likely served on the vessel past June 30, 1708, the date the pay book ends. Benerson Little believes that the Brooks hypothesis that Blackbeard "was born in Jamaica of a well-off family, was formally educated, and had served aboard the HMS *Windsor*" has merit, but the theory has only been recently put forward and remains to be formally accepted by the majority of Blackbeard scholars.

The link to Jamaica has long been put forward by historians, beginning with Johnson (Mist), who claimed in the first edition of *A General History* (published in May 1724) that Thache was "born in Jamaica" and in the second edition (December 1724) that he was "a Bristol man born, but had sailed some time out of Jamaica in privateers, in the late French war." However, there is not a single primary document that describes any of Edward Thache's service as an officer or privateer during Queen Anne's War (1702-1713), or as a possible merchant ship officer or privateer following the war. However, reliable secondary sources have Thache sailing as a first-mate merchantman out of the ports of Jamaica and Philadelphia following the war before he became a pirate.

Many previous scholars have stated that Thache was born into and nurtured in a world of at least modest privilege with ample educational opportunities. In his 1974 biography *Blackbeard the Pirate*, author and law professor Robert E. Lee maintained that Thache was "born into an intelligent, respectable, well-to-do family" and was "an educated man" on account of his ability to read and write (he corresponded with merchants and Tobias Knight), his nautical skills (to captain a ship he would have required rigorous training in mathematics and navigation), and his social grace (he was as at ease with governors and other high-ranking officials as he was common seamen). Supporting evidence is provided by his records at sea prior to his becoming a pirate, indicating that he held greater status than his male peers and had accumulated wealth. According to Brooks, he had a larger sea chest and payed more for stowing it than his peers, and he "joined *Windsor* of his own free will as a skilled merchant and was not pressed or forced to join as often happened with common sailors, many of whom never had experience at sea. He was specially noted as 'Barbados Merchant,' indicating that he had served on this vessel and was probably trained in mathematics; he could navigate." During the Golden Age of Piracy, captaining a large vessel such as a sloop or brigantine was a skill typically possessed only by those with some degree of wealth who had received a liberal education. As Brooks states, "the only people capable of navigating ships were the educated, usually wealthy men who could afford the necessary training in mathematics...such as Henry Jennings from Bermuda, Edward Thache of Spanish Town, [and] Richard Tookerman of South Carolina."

As many researchers have suggested, Blackbeard likely began his piratical career in late 1715 or early 1716 in response to an epic event that was the decisive factor that launched the Golden Age of Piracy. On July 30, 1715, a hurricane destroyed ten Spanish vessels headed to Spain through the Florida Straits. The sinking of the massive treasure fleet aroused the entire Atlantic community, and even the squeaky clean Alexander Spotswood wanted in on the action. As Brooks states, "'Fishing' wrecks was a common activity all along the American coast, including the American West Indies." There is a strong likelihood that Thache participated in, or led as captain, one of the small salvage parties from colonial America that appeared off the coast of Florida during the winter of 1716, to collect the "14,000,000 pesos in silver, and significant quantities of gold" that had been spilled out of the Spanish treasure galleons wrecked in the hurricane the previous summer. Spanish authorities estimated that near the end of January 1716, nearly a dozen English vessels were anchored over the wrecks, and many of these treasure hunters were young men who had heard about the Spanish gold from published accounts in the *Boston News-Letter*. As Duffus makes clear, they were simply looking for adventure and the chance to collect a vast and easy fortune by scavenging Florida's beaches and shallow waters, and then returning home to a hero's welcome. According to Brooks, Edward Thache joined either Jamaican privateer Henry Jennings or his rival Benjamin Hornigold to fish these ten wrecks, and he did so with a barely legal commission "signed by the governor of Jamaica" that was "disputed by both Spain and the Crown until that governor was finally removed." Brooks further states that by the spring of 1717, "Thache and other ex-privateers, expelled by new Crown authorities from Port Royal, had been observed on New Providence, an island in a neglected proprietary colony called the Bahamas, owned by six of the eight Lords Proprietors of Carolina." So began Thache's transition from legitimate privateer-seaman to prowling sea rover, and it was only a matter of time before he became the fearsome Blackbeard the pirate, taking British, French, and Spanish prizes with equal enthusiasm and alacrity.

Three important questions have nagged Blackbeard scholars for three hundred years: when did Thache attain his own command, what was the name of his first vessel he captained, and what was the relationship between him and Benjamin Hornigold during his early days of piracy? Based upon new research by Brooks, *Blackbeard: The Birth of America* takes a stand on these critical questions by breaking from Johnson-Mist and the traditional narrative. In the book, I have Thache captaining, as a legally-sanctioned privateer, a vessel called the *Margaret* (a fictional name in tribute to his Swedish lover from Marcus Hook) in which he owns a substantial interest. This is the vessel that I have him sailing in to the Florida wrecks as part of the Henry Jennings expedition in late December 1715. My basis for this is I agree with Brooks that Thache was "likely independent, working for himself, and financed by his family" considering his experience in the British Royal Navy and his social station as a Jamaican upper-middle-class gentleman. Brooks further states that, "There were many Jamaican ships involved with the wrecks and not all of them have been identified" and Thache was likely commissioned by Governor Hamilton since he "certainly had the experience and his family's financial and logistical support."

Regarding the Hornigold as "teacher" and Thache as "pupil" narrative that has permeated virtually every study of Blackbeard, the relationship between the two men in the novel is based largely upon the new Brooks paradigm, which argues that in 1716 and 1717 the two sailed in consort on occasion as equal partners in piratical ventures. Previous historians have claimed that Thatch was Hornigold's pirate "pupil," but the only source for this is *A General History*. Johnson (Mist) wrote that despite Thache's "uncommon boldness and personal courage, he was never raised to any command, till he went a-pyrating, which I think was at the latter end of the year 1716, when Capt. Benjamin Hornigold put him into a sloop that he had made prize of, and with whom he continued in consortship." According to the deposition of Henry Timberlake, Thache and Hornigold had equally matched sloops of ninety tons each in December 1716 when Hornigold in the *Delight* and Thache in command of an unnamed sloop seized Timberlake's *Lamb* as a prize near Hispaniola. This is the first known reference to a vessel captained by the future Blackbeard, and he is revealed by Timberlake as sailing under his own independent command as an equal consort with Hornigold, not under him as his first-mate or other high-ranking pirate officer. As Brooks states, "Thache never needed a teacher. He was the most experienced mariner of recorded pirates" and the traditional Hornigold as "master" and Thache as "pupil" narrative is based upon "Johnson-Mist's story of Hornigold and Thache" which "utilized this as a literary device for his tale of Blackbeard." This author agrees and has written of the Thache and Hornigold relationship as one of equals and occasional consorts.

With respect to the provenance of Thache's 8-gun sloop that he used to plunder Timberlake's *Lamb*, Allen Bernard, the quartermaster of Jennings's *Barsheba*, testified that he saw Hornigold in his vessel sailing with a French sloop as a consort around April 8, 1716 off the bar near Bahia Honda. According to Brooks, Hornigold's vessel was the *Benjamin* and the French sloop was the *Mary of Rochelle*, which "may have been the unnamed 8-gun vessel captained by Edward Thache with 90 crew, mentioned by Henry Timberlake in the taking of his vessel *Lamb*" six months later in December 1716. In the absence of contradictory information, in the novel I have Thache giving up his Jamaican privateering vessel *Margaret* (a fictional vessel) to the captured French captain and taking over the *Mary of Rochelle* and then later renaming her the *Margaret* for his true love.

That Thache had an intimate relationship with a beautiful Swedish woman named Margaret of Marcus Hook and had a close connection to the city of Philadelphia where she lived has been well-established by Duffus and other researchers, although the sources are secondary. The house where she lived and where the two cavorted is reportedly a 16-by-20-foot, sawn plank house on Discord Lane, located on the western shores of the Delaware River fifteen miles below the city of Brotherly Love, as described in the book. The details of their relationship are not known, but would have taken place in the time frame of 1713-1715 following the end of the war when he "sailed as mate out of Philadelphia" and in the fall of 1717 and summer of 1718 when he was known to have been in Philadelphia. These are the times when I have the two lovers together in the novel.

The unusual relationship between Thache and Stede Bonnet has always intrigued Blackbeard scholars—and been a source of puzzlement. Bonnet will forever be remembered as the most incompetent freebooter in the Golden Age of Piracy, perhaps all time, and his bumbling pirate career has to rank as one of the worst midlife crises in history. In the spring of 1717, the retired British militia major and owner of a profitable sugar plantation on Barbados abandoned his wife, children, estate, and fortune, built and outfitted a sloop at his own expense, and turned to piracy on the high seas. Though his crew and fellow freebooters judged him to be an inept captain, Bonnet's adventures earned him the nickname the "Gentleman Pirate," and today his legend figures prominently in the annals of pirate history. But why did a man who seemed to have everything give it all up for a life of crime? More importantly, why did Blackbeard treat him with kid gloves until the day he deceived him at Old Topsail Inlet? It is a mystery that has perplexed Blackbeard aficionados for three hundred years.

With the recent revelation that Thache was raised on a Jamaican plantation to a prominent family, it should come as no surprise that Blackbeard tolerated Bonnet's idiosyncrasies due to their similar upper-middle-class backgrounds and the fact they may have been acquaintances prior to their September 1717 meeting in Nassau. Blackbeard not only welcomed the clumsy Bonnet, he even allowed "him to remain on board and heal from his wounds while enjoying his library" and sleeping in the "commodious and coveted great cabin in the aft portion of his sloop." Thache was willing to accommodate, train, and shoulder the Barbadian planter's day-to-day shipboard duties because in return he became captain of a vessel superior to his and he and Bonnet, as the scions of wealthy Caribbean plantation owners, had a shared upbringing and could relate to one another. They also may also have known one another as Thache was posted in Barbados during his British Royal Navy career aboard Admiral Whetstone's flagship HMS *Windsor*, and Bonnet was the grandson of the admiral's first cousin.

Duffus maintains that "if Black Beard had been completely unfamiliar with Bonnet and became acquainted with him for the first time in the late-summer of 1717 at Nassau, he would have had little motivation for accommodating Bonnet's ineptitude and eccentricities, even if he were 'borrowing' the Barbadian's own sloop for a piratical cruise." This author agrees. As Brooks ponders rhetorically, "why did the 'vicious' and 'wicked' pirate not just take the vessel from the less experienced man?" The explanation for Blackbeard's uncharacteristic patience for Bonnet is that the backgrounds of both Thache and Bonnet have more in common than history has previously suggested and they were likely acquaintances prior to their first recorded meeting in the fall of 1717, as presented in the novel.

With regard to Blackbeard's purported cruelty, violent disposition, and murderous nature, there is not one iota of evidence to support the Thache-as-Edward-Low narrative. Unlike Low, who tortured and killed his victims in ways that would make Hannibal Lecter squirm, Thache typically showed his victims respect and let them down easily after taking their ships as prizes, giving them vessels in trade, food and provisions, and even receipts for merchandise. In an age when violence was commonplace, he did no more harm to captured ship captains than to detain them for a brief period of time. As Bialuschewski states: "I haven't seen one single piece of evidence that Blackbeard ever used violence against anyone." Colin Woodard, author of *The Republic of Pirates: Being the True Account and Surprising Story of the Caribbean Pirates and the Man Who Brought Them Down*, concludes plainly, "Blackbeard was remarkably judicious in his use of force. In the dozens of eyewitness accounts of his victims, there is not a single instance in which he killed anyone prior to his final, fatal battle with the Royal Navy." In his book *Blackbeard: America's Most Notorious Pirate*, maritime historian Angus Konstam points out that, "While Blackbeard fought at least one close-quarters boarding action off Ocracoke in November 1718, there is no evidence that he ever had to cross swords with anyone else during his career. This didn't mean that he was unwilling to test his mettle in combat, but rather that he was highly successful at what he did. Put simply, he managed to overpower his victims without having to resort to fighting. He was gifted in all the other skills a pirate captain needed, and therefore knew where to find his prey, how to approach them, and above all, how to intimidate them into submission." Peter Leeson, author of *The Invisible Hook: The Hidden Economics of Pirates* agrees: "[U]ntil Blackbeard's final battle…the world's most notorious and fearsome pirate hadn't so much as killed a single man. Apparently he didn't need to."

There are many other ridiculous Blackbeard myths that this book has refuted, or not included to preserve sanity. With regard to Blackbeard's marriage to sixteen-year-old Mary Ormond of Bath Town and his pimping his new bride out to his crew to be gang-raped, his supposed sickly condition due to syphilis, and his stuffing slow-burning fuses in his tangled beard to intimidate his victims, there is no evidence to support these ludicrous assertions. For starters, there's no written documentation he even had a wife—ever. Legend has it that during his brief sojourns to Bath Town during his six-month semi-retirement in the summer and fall of 1718 (i.e., when he was splitting his time between Bath, Ocracoke, Philadelphia, and the open Atlantic to take the *Rose Emelye*), he had the time to marry Ormond, the sixteen-year-old daughter of a local planter, supposedly his fourteenth wife. Due to severe time constraints, that scenario is highly unlikely and it is for this reason his supposed marriage to Ormond does not appear in the novel. With regard to the pernicious syphilis charge which for some inexplicable reason many Blackbeard scholars cling to, a single urethral syringe with residual traces of mercury (commonly used to treat syphilis during the early 18th century) recovered from the *Queen's Anne's Revenge* does not make Blackbeard a ranting, raving Stage II syphilis victim. All it means is that one or more members of his crew likely had the disease and the captain tried to ensure that the doctors on board treated the condition for those afflicted. His holding Charles Town under siege was to procure medical supplies for the affliction—but that was for his crew not him. Otherwise, more than one of his crew members would have known if their captain was sick with syphilis and you can bet it would be documented. One common manifestation of the disease is rough, reddish-brown spots on the bottoms of your feet and on the palms of your hands, which would not go unnoticed, especially by Israel Hands and others he had had a falling out with. And if he had syphilis he would most certainly not have gone to Philadelphia in August of 1718 to see his beloved Margaret of Marcus Hook. Furthermore, other symptoms of the disease include fatigue, muscle aches, and joint pain. At Ocracoke, Maynard and his Royal Navy fighters reportedly shot Blackbeard five times at close range and stabbed him more than twenty times with their swords before he faltered, and even then he did not stop fighting until he had been decapitated. Granted he was fighting for his very life, but that still does not sound like a seriously debilitated man with syphilis—it sounds more like the Incredible Hulk. Then there are the mythical sparkling fuses in his beard that in pictures make him look like a Rastafarian on PCP, an invention of Captain Johnson (Mist) and no one else. The always-astute Duffus has neatly put this one to rest: "Common sense also tells us that the 'lighted matches under his hat' in times of a pursuit or battle would simply be impractical. Had Black Beard stood among dozens of men upon the deck of his pirate ship as they were attempting to intimidate their prey into surrendering, his smoking face would not have been readily discernible, especially from hundreds of yards away on board a pitching, rolling ship. As his men would be preparing for a boarding action, their captain, most likely, would have been trying to keep his hair and hat from catching fire. He would have looked ridiculous."

Another important question of Blackbeard scholars is the political leanings of Blackbeard and how this may have influenced him to become a pirate. Most historians agree that he was a lukewarm Jacobite who identified more with the American colonial "common man" than his oppressive British rulers, was opposed to the Hanoverian-elector King George I who spoke no English, and supported James III, Prince of Wales, who lived in exile in France and in Rome following the failed Jacobite Rising of 1715. But what ultimately drove him to become the commodore of a five-vessel flotilla with seven hundred men under his command, the largest pirate fleet ever to sail in the Americas? What drove a well-to-do sea captain from a good, upstanding Jamaica plantation family to go all in on piracy and, in the process, make a grandiose political statement. Johnson-Mist and tradition have it that he became a pirate purely for the money, but more recent and detailed research suggests that while this may have served as the initial motivation for his entry into a life of crime, it is not what ultimately sustained him or drove him by the middle of 1716 and thereafter. By this time, a closer reading of the man reveals that something much larger and patriotic was at work in molding the legendary Blackbeard, and it was the reason he named the captured *La Concorde Queen Anne's Revenge*. Unlike his friend Charles Vane, it was not ardent Jacobitism that drove the well-bred, heretofore-loyal-to-the-Crown, British-born Edward Thache to declare total war on the British Empire and the accumulated wealth of all nations—it was the Pirates-As-Robin-Hood's-Men philosophy of his good friend Samuel Bellamy that was truly transformational. It was a philosophy cast in stark, easy-to-understand terms of good vs. evil, Colonial America vs. Britain and Global Big Money. Virtually overnight, it turned him from a privateer who was content with taking only Spanish or French prizes to a hardcore revolutionary bent on destroying the commerce of the country of his birth. Yes, pirates were after monetary rewards and plunder first and foremost and their democratic governance arose from their criminality (see Leeson's excellent *The Invisible Hook: The Hidden Economics of Pirates*), but Thache and Bellamy were politically motivated as well and the pirates-as-social-justice-equalizers theme of Marcus Rediker and the pirates-as-early-American-patriots-and-resisters-of-British-oppression model of Brooks have strong explanatory power.

In their short time spent together on at least two extended occasions in 1716, the young yet enormously charismatic Bellamy literally changed Edward Thache's life. Black Sam had no qualms about seizing the property of all nations and desired to openly wage war against the British Crown that had treated him so miserably as a Royal Navy seaman, as well as the wealthy merchant class that did the Crown's bidding. Envisioning himself and his men as Robin Hoods of the sea, the influential Bellamy sparked something in Thache that turned him into Blackbeard the pirate and made him understand that what they were doing was a political revolution much bigger than simple robbery, disruption of commerce, and transfer of accumulated wealth upon the high seas. When in 1717, Thache learned that Bellamy's men were to be hung or had been hung in Boston, he went ballistic at the King's impertinence and destruction of Robin Hood's men. In retaliation, he seized or threw overboard all merchandise or belongings and burned the vessels to the waterline if they were from Massachusetts where the British trial was held. There were no exceptions. While pirates in general felt a sense of solidarity, proclaimed themselves as "people without a nation," and hoisted the black flag and their tankards of ale to drink damnation to King George, Thache and his men were not embarking on an anti-national crusade as a gang of proletarian outlaws solely to redistribute wealth—they wanted to stick it to Great Britain to limit its domineering influence over New World interests. In short, they—like Washington, Jefferson, Franklin, and their revolutionary brethren a half century later—wanted to cut the giant down to size and for American interests to be left alone.

As Woodard states, pirates like Blackbeard were "folk heroes." While the British authorities characterized him and other freebooters as "devils and demons, enemies of all mankind," he declares, "many colonial citizens supported them. People saw pirates as Robin Hood figures, socking it to the man on their behalf." He further maintains that there were many ordinary people during the Golden Age of Piracy that supported Thache and other pirates because they were "upset about the growing gap between rich and poor, and the growing authoritarian power of the British empire." *Blackbeard: The Birth of America* explores the Blackbeard-as-proto-American-Revolutionary theme advanced by Woodard and Baylus Brooks in detail because I believe it best explains Thache's devotion to Bellamy and the Robin-Hood's-Men paradigm of the Golden Age of Piracy.

Countering the fledgling colonists—who were, unknowingly, a mere sixty years from victory in what would become known as the American Revolution—was the powerful British Board of Trade. As historians Bialuschewski and Brooks make clear, the Board wanted to quell smuggling and piracy to preserve commerce and fund British expansion and dominance over the New World—and pirates like Blackbeard, Hornigold, Bellamy, Paulsgrave Williams, and Vane resisted what they viewed as an incursion into the Americas, forming their own Republic of Pirates on New Providence, Bahamas. The British Crown knew that the pirate revolution was not just about redistributing accumulated wealth, but was political in nature and firmly against the new Hanoverian king who spoke no English. Which is what made men like Thache so dangerous. They also knew popular American sentiment remained with the pirates, and in order to eradicate them, public perception across the Empire had to be altered. Therefore, the British began to demonize and punish those who practiced America's favorite economic practice. That is what marked the end for Blackbeard and the Golden Age of Piracy. Once pro-British colonial newspapers like the *Boston News-Letter* and various pamphlets began presenting biased accounts of pirate attacks, providing readers in the New World with embellished accounts of vicious behavior and horrific details of pirate life, Blackbeard was living on borrowed time. All it took was a single highly motivated and relentless colonial governor named Alexander Spotswood to put an end to him and his motley crew once and for all.

But what Spotswood hadn't counted on was that in his efforts to destroy Blackbeard, he more than anyone else secured the man's place in the pantheon of great American antiheroes, and as history's most illustrious pirate and one of its most colorful characters. In the end, few people remember or care about Alexander Spotswood—but virtually *everyone* knows the name Blackbeard. To this day, three hundred years after his death, he is the only pirate who remains a household name. And the truth is, he has earned it. The privateer-turned-gentleman-of-fortune who did not kill a single soul until the day he was illegally trapped, murdered, and beheaded; who graciously bequeathed his family inheritance to his step-mother and half-siblings; who desperately loved a Swedish woman named Margaret; who freed a black African slave named Caesar and made him a seaman drawing equal shares aboard his ships; and who viewed himself and his motley crew as Robin Hood's

Men and patriots combatting British oppression deserves his immortality.

Even more than my ancestor Captain Kidd.

Why?

Because Blackbeard—the real man explored in this book *and* the legend—was and will forever be the quintessential sea rover of the Golden Age of Piracy.

ALEXANDER SPOTSWOOD

On February 14, 1719, Spotswood wrote a letter to Lord Cartwright, a proprietor of North Carolina, in which he attempted to explain his justification for invading his lordship's colony. It was one of the British lieutenant governor's usual interminable fussy letters, and in it he falsely boasted to have rescued "the trade of North Carolina from the insults of pirates upon the earnest solicitations of the inhabitants there" and he hoped his actions would "not be unacceptable to your lordships." He admitted that he had not informed either the proprietors or Eden about his invasion plan, but chose not to mention that this was because he believed Eden to be conspiring with Blackbeard. Instead, he claimed to have done Eden a service by excluding him, for had he been "let into that secret" the pirates might have attacked him if Maynard's operation had failed. Besides, as Spotswood indelicately put it, Eden and his friends "could contribute nothing to the success of the design." Spotswood further wrote that the "prisoners have been brought hither and tried, and it plainly appears that the ship they brought into Carolina was after the date of His Majesty's pardon." According to Duffus, what Spotswood was trying to convey was not the guilt or innocence of Thache's men for bringing in the French merchant ship *Rose Emelye*, but that Lord Cartwright's senior representative in North Carolina, Governor Eden, had been collaborating with and harboring unrepentant pirates, and that he had no business finding on behalf of Blackbeard that the French ship was legal salvage.

The death of Blackbeard and subsequent trial of his crew in which one white man and five black pirates were found guilty and hung and the rest were pardoned or acquitted marked the beginning of a legal dispute between Spotswood and Eden that would consume their lives until Eden's death in March 1722. According to Blackbeard biographer Robert E. Lee, Eden and the citizens of North Carolina resented not only Spotswood's invasion of their proprietary colony, but the heavy-handed manner in which he had conducted it. They justifiably felt that their powerful neighbor had taken advantage of North Carolina's weakness and that Spotswood had acted without authority. In response, Eden challenged his legal right to invade the colony, which is what forced him to have to explain himself before Lord Cartwright and his London superiors. The episode served only to rekindle the ill feelings that already existed between the two colonies and both sides hardened their positions until the question of jurisdiction was lost in a tangled web of legal arguments. Ultimately, it became clear to the Board of Trade and governments of both colonies that Spotswood had overreached and disobeyed both his superiors and the rule of law, but that Eden had lacked the power to do anything about it. Consequently, Spotswood was not punished for exceeding his authority by the Board of Trade or the King, but unlike Governor Johnson of South Carolina he was given no praise from London for his anti-piracy measures.

For a short time, Spotswood rejoiced in the success of the attack against Blackbeard. But the political difficulties it created contributed to the growing clamor mounting against him, and his illegal invasion of his southern neighbor did little to silence his many critics. While the governor was busy with his war against Blackbeard and his pirates, and later Governor Eden and Tobias Knight, his three political arch-enemies—Philip Ludwell the Younger, William Byrd in London, and Reverend James Blair—continued to lodge formal and behind-the-scenes complaints against him to the British government, repeatedly demanding his removal from office.

Spotswood's well-documented bombast, dismissiveness towards colonials of all stripes, and steadfast support of the Crown at the expanse of the increasingly independent-minded colonists whose interests he was supposed to represent has not endeared him to history. As Duffus states, "The former army officer must have been an exceedingly pompous and tiresome bore, which becomes evident by reading just one or two of his diffuse, long-winded letters to his superiors back in England. With a slight paunch, receding hairline and supercilious expression, Spotswood took enormous pleasure in his lordly station, even though he was merely a deputy governor for the absentee Earl of Orkney, George Hamilton." One of his more disgraceful actions was to deny payment of the promised reward money to Lieutenant Maynard and the other Royal Navy seamen who had battled Thache at Ocracoke until four years after the battle—even though Spotswood had, by binding decree, promised prompt payment upon the capture of the pirate and his crew (as presented in the novel). After four years of delay, many of those who had fought valiantly and spilled blood upon the decks of the *Jane* and *Ranger* had died or retired from the service, and so never received a penny.

Spotswood had a habit of overplaying his hand and then using his powerful position to brush aside dissent, but eventually his old tricks caught up with him. He learned too late that he had several masters to please, each with a different set of interests: English merchants, imperial bureaucrats, and the Virginia planter elite. It took four years of lobbying by his political enemies following the death of Blackbeard, but the open ill feeling continually gnawed at Spotswood's position until on April 3, 1722 he was toppled from government due to "an accumulation of grievances." Experienced Scottish soldier and diplomat Hugh Drysdale was duly named as his successor. However, by that time Spotswood had made so much money from questionable land deals that his governorship had become immaterial. He would remain the wealthiest man in Virginia until his death in 1740. In 1724, at the age of forty-eight, Spotswood returned to England to secure title to his lands in Virginia and to determine the taxes on the vast grants. That same year, he married for the first time in his life to Anne Butler Brayne of St. Margaret's Parish, Westminster, with whom he had two sons and two daughters.

When war with Spain broke out in 1739, Spotswood resumed his military career. He was appointed a brigadier general in the British army and second in command to Major General Charles Cathcart. At long last, Spotswood had fulfilled his dream of military advancement. But he never saw battle: after suffering a short illness, he died on June 7, 1740, in Annapolis, Maryland, where he had traveled to organize troops and consult with colonial governors. His burial site is unknown.

Although he had successfully taken on the most feared pirate captain of the day, Spotswood's bold operation against Blackbeard was overshadowed by years of political infighting. However his twelve years as governor had a lasting impact on Virginia, as noted by the Privy Council, which recorded that he had done "more than any other person towards peopling the country." But with regard to Blackbeard, the judgement of history has been more severe: he knowingly launched an illegal expedition in violation of the King's and governor of North Carolina's pardons to destroy the freebooter (who was likely retired from piracy) and his crew at Ocracoke, all in an effort to gather evidence to be used to undermine Eden and Tobias Knight and thereby further his own career and financial gain. In the end, the reputations of Eden and Knight were only mildly tarnished by Spotswood's aggressive maneuvers and history has shown them to be guilty only of being mildly cozy with Blackbeard, who brought much-needed capital and commerce into their struggling proprietary colony.

In the eyes of history, it is Spotswood that is far more criminal, immoral, and unethical than Blackbeard, Eden, or Knight. Not only did he knowingly and illicitly violate the sovereignty of a neighboring colony, he conspired with and was closely associated with the ethically suspect Edward Moseley, Colonel Maurice Moore, and Captain Vail. In December 1718, the Moseley gang broke into the house of Secretary John Lovick in an attempt to examine Council records for incriminating evidence against Eden and Knight. When Spotswood's North Carolina conspirators Moseley and Moore were tried the following year, the event was a sensation and Moseley was fined and barred from public office for three years. Spotswood did his best to distance himself from Moseley and Moore, but his critics knew better. In the end, he is remembered as a slave-owning British elitist, stodgy bureaucrat, hypocrite, and profiteer who used the governor's office to lord over "the people" in the name of the Crown, promote his own self-interests at the public expense, and destroy his political enemies or those, like Blackbeard, that he disapproved of.

He will always be Inspector Javert to Blackbeard's Jean Valjean from Victor Hugo's *Les Misérables*.

CAESAR

The background and exploits of the black African slave named Caesar remain shrouded in mystery to this day. Newly discovered research by Blackbeard scholar Kevin Duffus has unraveled part of the mystery of Caesar, who is believed to have served as a free seaman under Edward Thache throughout much of his piratical career. Contrary to popular mythology, the Caesar who sailed with Blackbeard was not the legendary "Black Caesar" whose Wikipedia page claims, amusingly, that he was "a prominent African tribal war chieftain" widely known for his "huge size, immense strength, and keen intelligence" who "evaded capture from many different slave traders" to become a pirate who sailed under Blackbeard. That Black Caesar apparently also had an island named "Caesar's Rock" in his honor near Key Largo that is the "present-day site of his original headquarters" and upon which he had a harem of "at least 100 women seized from passing ships, as well as a prison camp which he kept prisoners in stone huts hoping to ransom them." Whoever the Black

Caesar of popular legend and Wikipedia fame was, he did not sail with Blackbeard and probably never existed at all.

According to Duffus, the real-life Caesar was likely brought to Bath as a slave from Charles Town by Colonel Robert Daniel in 1705. At this time, Caesar would have been ten years old. For the next ten years, he served as a slave at the Daniels plantation along with more than twenty other slaves, including a male three years older than him named Pompey, who was likely his friend. Caesar and Pompey were subsequently acquired together by Tobias Knight when Knight purchased the Daniel plantation in 1716, though Duffus concedes that they may have been purchased earlier, between 1710 and 1715, when many records were lost or improperly preserved due to the war with the Tuscarora Indians. Once acquired by Knight, Caesar is believed to have taken part in an expedition sponsored by Governor Eden and the proprietary colony of North Carolina to the Florida wrecks, with the end result that his piratical career began in much the same way as that of Thache, Hornigold, Jennings, Vane, and countless others during the Golden Age of Piracy. As Duffus states, "In 1716, with Tobias Knight's help and connections, Eden likely approved sending forth the Bath County treasure salvors, who included...William Howard, John Martin, et al, bound for the Spanish treasure fleet wrecks off the Florida coast. Caesar was Tobias Knight's investment in the salvage company; he may well have been one of the divers."

Thus, Caesar is believed to have sailed with Thache and the Bath County men—who would later become the Bath County pirates like William Howard and John Martin—"from the very beginning of their piratical adventures." Historically, Caesar's claim to fame stems from two things. First, he was a black pirate who served under Thache as a free man for several years and was described by Alexander Spotswood as a "person of a very notorious character for his piracies." Second, Caesar somehow inspired sufficient confidence that Blackbeard entrusted him and him alone with the critical task of igniting the *Adventure's* stores of black powder to destroy the ship and all the men aboard if the pirates were subdued during the battle at Ocracoke. He did this to prevent the crew's capture and the indignity of being hanged. As we know, Caesar failed to accomplish his mission because he was restrained by two men hiding out in the hold of the sloop, who are believed to have been trader Samuel Odell and pirate James Robins.

The true identity of Caesar and the relationship between Caesar and Thache has always intrigued historians. Why would the black African be willing to commit suicide at his captain's request? The answer is he most certainly wouldn't have made the ultimately unsuccessful attempt if he was merely Blackbeard's slave and not a full crew member. As historian David Moore of the Queen Anne's Revenge project and pirate author Lindley S. Butler have concluded, Blackbeard would never have entrusted such an important assignment to someone who was not a full voting crew member drawing his equal share of the plunder. Nor would Blackbeard have entrusted such a difficult assignment to someone he didn't have absolute faith would competently carry out the mission. As Caesar made a concerted attempt to follow through with Blackbeard's command, this indicates that Caesar and Blackbeard were close and trusted one another. Within the narrative of the Battle of Ocracoke in *A General History*, Captain Charles Johnson (Mist) refers to "a negro whom

(Blackbeard) had bred up" as the crew member assigned to destroying the *Adventure* and its men, intimating a long-term, personal relationship between the two men. According to Duffus, this anecdote was corroborated in the letters of Alexander Spotswood, though neither Johnson nor Spotswood identified the "negro" by name, further supporting a close professional association if not active friendship. Peter Leeson states that Caesar was "close to Blackbeard personally" and that he had risen to a position "of importance, and even authority" within the crew, which was why he "was given the important task of blowing up the pirates' ship should authorities overtake his crew." Pirate scholar Mark Hanna points out in his book *Pirate Nests and the Rise of the British Empire, 1570-1740* that after 1716 "a remarkable number of black crew members appeared on pirate vessels, including one of Blackbeard's officers." The black "officer" Hanna is referring to is, of course, Thache's compadre Caesar.

Unlike black pirates Richard Stiles, Thomas Gates, James Blake, and James White, Caesar never gave any testimony against his beloved captain, Eden, or Knight in return for leniency, which he no doubt would have done if he was a slave relegated to performing the menial work aboard the *Queen Anne's Revenge* and *Adventure*. As Robert E. Lee says, "Caesar, who had long been a member of Blackbeard's crew and was a favorite of all the pirates, could not be persuaded to turn against his Brethren of the Coast." Of the seven prisoners that received pardons, Caesar was the only whose money was returned to him and who could pay the attorney-general the common fee due for making out the pardons, which Spotswood claimed was because "there was no proof of its being piratically taken." Caesar was ultimately pardoned because, although he had tried to blow up the ships, he had been stopped before he could accomplish his mission and he, therefore, had not taken up arms against the King's men.

Following his pardon and release from Williamsburg prison in early March, or earlier, Caesar returned to Tobias Knight's plantation on Town Creek in Bath. He was twenty-four years old. Knight's inventory on September 15, 1719, shortly after his death lists Caesar's age and his value as sixty pounds sterling. There's no record of him after that known to this author and history does not tell us what he did after sailing as a free man for two and a half years under Thache. With his mentor Blackbeard dead, his life as a pirate was over and returning as a slave to his familiar home on Tobias Knight's plantation and to his likely friend Pompey were obviously more appealing than striking out somewhere else in colonial America on his own. Especially after he had witnessed the killing of ten of his pirate brethren and spent several brutal months as the British Crown's prisoner.

SOURCES AND ACKNOWLEDGEMENTS

"Pirates believed in equality in more ways than just votes, shares, and disability compensation. In fact, one can argue that pirate democracy was a grand form of rebellion, one that stood defiantly against the reigning social order—against the rule of kings and nobility. Indeed, pirates were in many ways far more democratic and egalitarian than their contemporaries."
—Benerson Little, 2016, *The Golden Age of Piracy: The Truth Behind Pirate Myths*

To develop the story line, characters, and scenes for *Blackbeard: The Birth of America*, I consulted over a hundred archival materials, non-fiction books, magazine and newspaper articles, blogs, Web sites, and numerous individuals, and I visited most every real-world location in person. These principal locations included London, Bath, Ocracoke, Beaufort, Bermuda, the Bahamas, the U.S. and British Virgin Islands, and other locations in the Caribbean. All in all, there are too many resources and locations to name here. However, I would be remiss if I didn't give credit to the key historical references upon which this novel is based, as well as the critical individuals who dramatically improved the quality of the manuscript from its initial to its final stage. Any technical mistakes in the historical facts underpinning the novel, typographical errors, or examples of overreach due to artistic license, however, are the fault of me and me alone.

In addition to primary reference materials from British, French, West Indies, and American archives, many of which are included in Joel H. Baer's 2007 four-volume compendium of primary documents entitled *British Piracy in the Golden Age: History and Interpretation 1660-1730*, and the *Calendar of State Papers, Colonial North America and West Indies* series, I relied heavily upon sixteen secondary sources dealing specifically with Blackbeard and the Golden Age of Piracy. These references were invaluable and included the following: *Blackbeard off Philadelphia: Documents Pertaining to the Campaign against the Pirates in 1717 and 1718* (2010) and *Blackbeard: The Creation of a Legend* (2012) by Arne Bialuschewski; *Blackbeard the Pirate: Historical Background and the Beaufort Inlet Shipwrecks* (1997) and *A General History of Blackbeard the Pirate, the Queen Anne's Revenge, and the Adventure* (1997) by David D. Moore; *The Last Days of Black Beard the Pirate* (2014) and *Rush to Judgement—An Analysis of a New Interpretation of the Pirate Blackbeard's Origins* (2016) by Kevin Duffus; *The Republic of Pirates: Being the True Account and Surprising Story of the Caribbean Pirates and the Man Who Brought Them Down* (2007) and *The Last Days of Blackbeard: An Exclusive Account of the Final Raid and Political Maneuvers of History's Most Notorious Pirate* (2014) by Colin Woodard; *Blackbeard Reconsidered: Mist's Piracy, Thache's Genealogy* (2015) and *Quest for Blackbeard: The True Story of Edward Thache and His World* (2016) by Baylus C. Brooks; *Blackbeard: America's Most Notorious Pirate* (2006) and *Blackbeard's Last Fight: Pirate Hunting in North Carolina 1718* (2013) by Angus Konstam; *The*

Golden Age of Piracy: The Truth Behind Pirate Myths (2016) by Benerson Little; *Pirate Nests and the Rise of the British Empire, 1570-1740* (2015) and *A Lot of What Is Known about Pirates Is Not True, and a Lot of What Is True Is Not Known* (2017) by Mark G. Hanna; and *The Firsts of Blackbeard: Exploring Edward Thatch's Early Days as a Pirate* (2015, blog) by David Fictum.

My conceptual model of Edward Thache the innocent little boy, British Royal Navy officer, peacetime merchantman-privateer, lover, and eventual pirate is based upon a synthesis of primary documents and the most plausible interpretations by the modern-era Blackbeard experts listed above and others, who include maritime historians, documentarians, journalists, authors, lawyers, former Navy Seals, and researchers—all equally important perches from which to critically examine the life of Blackbeard. I have gone to great lengths to avoid using Captain Charles Johnson's (Nathanial Mist's) *A General History of the Robberies and Murders of the Most Notorious Pirates*, completed six years after Blackbeard's death, except as a backup to a primary source or if the idea advanced is plausible and has been accepted by one or more credible modern-day scholars. With regard to the character and motivations of Blackbeard, I knew I would be treading in dangerous waters as to his family origins and career as a pirate, so I relied most heavily on those texts by respected researchers that seemed to provide a balanced and well-rounded perspective, or that at least presented convincing arguments with ample supporting documentation. Readers knowledgeable about Blackbeard will no doubt recognize that the sixteen references listed above paint a detailed and sometimes contradictory picture of a most complex human being, one who at times merits our awe or admiration and at other times our firm disapproval and criticism. I earnestly hope that *Blackbeard: The Birth of America* provides a full and complex portrait of the man; after all, Edward Thache was a complicated and conflicted human being in one of the most intriguing and romantic eras in history: the Golden Age of Piracy and the stirrings of America as an independent nation founded on enduring democratic principles.

In writing the novel, there were many excellent historical books and articles in addition to those listed above from which I drew facts and inspiration to flesh out the Golden Age of Piracy and the other key point of view characters: Alexander Spotswood, Caesar, Stede Bonnet, and Lieutenant Robert Maynard. The interested reader is referred to the following additional sources. The list is especially useful for those who would like to know more about the Golden Age of Piracy and the historical figures in the book.

<u>Golden Age of Piracy</u>: *Proprietaries, Privateers, and Pirates: America's Forgotten Golden Age* (2016) by Baylus C. Brooks; *Under the Black Flag: The Romance and the Reality of Life Among the Pirates* (1995), *Pirates: Terror on the High Seas from the Caribbean to the South China Sea* (1996, Ed.), and *Pirate Hunter of the Caribbean: The Adventurous Life of Captain Woodes Rogers* (2012) by David Cordingly; *Between the Devil and the Deep Blue Sea: Merchant Seamen, Pirates and the Anglo-American Maritime World, 1700–1750* (1989), *Villains of All Nations: Atlantic Pirates in the Golden Age* (2004), and *Outlaws of the Atlantic: Sailors, Pirates, and Motley Crews in the Age of Sail* (2015) by Marcus Rediker; *Daniel Defoe, Nathaniel Mist, and the General History of the Pyrates* (2004),

Between Newfoundland and the Malacca Strait: A Survey of the Golden Age of Piracy,1695–1725 (2004), *Black People under the Black Flag: Piracy and the Slave Trade on the West Coast of Africa, 1718–1723* (2008), and *Pirates, Markets and Imperial Authority: Economic Aspects of Maritime Depredations in the Atlantic World, 1716–1726* (2008) by Arne Bialuschewski; *Hostis Humani Generi: Piracy, Terrorism and a New International Law* (2006), *The Pirates' Pact: The Secret Alliances Between History's Most Notorious Buccaneers and Colonial America* (2008), and *The Politics of Piracy: Crime and Civil Disobedience in Colonial America* (2014) by Douglas R. Burgess, Jr.; *The Sea Rover's Practice: Pirate Tactics and Techniques, 1630-1730* (2005) and *How History's Greatest Pirates Pillaged, Plundered, and Got Away With It: The Stories, Techniques, and Tactics of the Most Feared Sea Rovers from 1500-1800* (2011) by Benerson Little; *A History of Pirates: Blood and Thunder on the High Seas* (2004) by Nigel Cawthorne; *A General History of the Robberies and Murders of the Most Notorious Pirates* (May and December 1724 Editions) by Captain Charles Johnson (Nathaniel Mist); *Pirates of the British Isles* (2005) by Joel Baer; *Pirates: Terror on the High Seas* (2001), *The Pirate Ships, 1660-1730* (2003), *Pirates: The Complete History from 1300 BC to the Present Day* (2008), and *The World Atlas of Pirates* (2009) by Angus Konstam; *The Pirate Wars* (2006) by Peter Earle; *Flying the Black Flag: Revolt, Revolution and the Social Organization of Piracy in the 'Golden Age'* (2007) by Chris Land; *Pirates, Merchants, Settlers, and Slaves: Colonial America and the Indo-Atlantic World* (2015) by Kevin P. McDonald; *The Invisible Hook: The Law and Economics of Pirate Tolerance* (2009) and *The Invisible Hook: The Hidden Economics of Pirates* (2009) by Peter T. Leeson; *The Buccaneers of America* (1678, English translation 1969) by Alexander Exquemelin; *Black Jacks: African American Seamen in the Age of Sail* (1997) by Jeffrey W. Bolster; *Black Men under the Black Flag* (2001) by Kenneth J. Kinkor, in *Bandits at Sea: A Pirates Reader*, C.R. Pennell (Ed.); *Pirates: Scourge of the Seas* (2006) by John Reeve Carpenter; *The Many-Headed Hydra: Sailors, Slaves, Commoners and the Hidden History of the Revolutionary Atlantic* (2000) by Peter Linebaugh and Marcus Rediker; *The Pirate Primer: Mastering the Language of Swashbucklers and Rogues* (2007) by George Choundas; and *The Real Pirates of the Caribbean* (2014) by Colin Woodard.

Edward Thache and Stede Bonnet: *Blackbeard the Pirate: A Reappraisal of his Life and Times* (1974) by Robert E. Lee; *Blackbeard and the Meaning of Pirate Captaincy* (2002) by Michael T. Smith; *Blackbeard: The Real Pirate of the Caribbean* (2006) by Dan Parry; *Blackbeard's Capture of the Nantaise Slave Ship La Concorde: A Brief Analysis of the Documentary Evidence* (2001) by David D. Moore and Mike Daniel; *In Search of Blackbeard: Historical and Archaeological Research at Shipwreck Site 003BUI* (2001) by Richard Lawrence and Mark Wilde-Ramsin; *Boston News-letter, 1704-1726*, Boston, Massachusetts; *Calendar of State Papers, Colonial Series, America and the West Indies, Preserved in the Public Record Office.* Edited by Cecil Headlam. London: Cassell & Co. Ltd., 1930-1933; *Pirates, Privateers and Rebel Raiders of the Carolina Coast* (2000) and *Blackbeard's Terror* (2011) by Lindley F. Butler; *Legends of Black Beard and His Ties to Bath Town: A Study of Historical Events Using Genealogical Methodology*

(2002) by Jane Stubbs Bailey, Allen Hart Norris, and John Oden III; *Blackbeard and Other Pirates of the Atlantic Coast* (1993) by Nancy Roberts; *The Pirates of Colonial North Carolina* (1963) by Hugh F. Rankin; *The Tryals of Major Stede Bonnet and Other Pirates* (1719) by the South Carolina Court of Vice-Admiralty; *Blackbeard and the Queen Anne's Revenge* (2009) by Wendy Welsh; *Pirates: A History* (2008) by Tim Travers; *The Gentleman Pirate: How Stede Bonnet went from Wealthy Landowner to Villain on the Sea* (2007) by Amy Crawford; *Stede Bonnet: Charleston's Gentleman Pirate* (2012) by Christopher Byrd Downey; *The Notorious Blackbeard Was Most Probably Also A Health-Conscious Pirate* (2016) by Dattatreya Mandal; *A Fury from Hell—or Was He?* (2000) by Constance Bond; *Shiver Me Timbers—Blackbeard not an Englishman?* (2009) by Jerry Allegood; *Pirates of the Carolinas* (2005) by Terrance Zepke; *Blackbeard, the Corsair of the Carolinas* (1889) by Stephen B. Weeks; and *Historian: Blackbeard's "Friend" Was Likely His Slave* (2015) by Jeff Hampton.

Alexander Spotswood, Charles Eden, and Colonial America: *Alexander Spotswood: A Portrait of a Governor* (1967) by Walter Havighurst; *Alexander Spotswood: Governor of Colonial Virginia* (1932) by Leonidas Dodson; *Official Letters of Alexander Spotswood, Vol. II* (1885) by the Virginia Historical Society (R.A. Brock, Ed.); *From Colonies to Nation: The Emergence of American Nationalism, 1750-1800* (2006) by Alexander Ziegler; *The Carolina Pirates and Colonial Commerce, 1670-1740* (1894) by Shirley Carter Hughson; *Calendar of State Papers, Colonial Series, Am. and West Indies, Vols. XXIX-XXXII; Colonial Records of North Carolina, Vols. I-X. Edited by W.L. Saunders* (1958); *A History of the Bahamas* (1962) by Michael Craton; *A History of Colonial Bath* (1955) by Herbert R. Paschal; *Annals of Philadelphia and Pennsylvania, Vol. II* (1857) by John F. Watson; *The Journal of John Fontaine: An Irish Huguenot Son in Spain and Virginia, 1710 and 1719* (1972) by Edward Alexander (Ed.); *The Story of the Bahamas* (1975) by Paul Albury; *How the Nation Was Won: America's Untold Story 1630-1754* (1987) by Graham H. Lowry; *Charleston and the Golden Age of Piracy* (2013) by Christopher Byrd Downey; *Research Guide to the Life and Career of the Former Lieutenant Governor and Colonel Alexander Spotswood* (2015) by Devin Leigh; *Alexander Spotswood (1676–1740), 2017* Encyclopedia Virginia, contributed by Randall Shrock; *Charles Eden* (1986), NCPedia by Jaquelin Drane Nash; *Charles Eden (1673-1722)* (2017) by North Carolina History Project; *Alexander Spotswood's Struggle with his Council* (1967) by Joan Schools; *Marlborough's America* (2013) by Stephen Saunders Webb; *Beaufort County, North Carolina Deed Book I, 1696-1729, Records of Bath County, North Carolina* (2003) by Allen Hart Norris; *Historic Bath N.C. Historic Sites* (2018) by North Carolina Office of Archives & History; *Minutes of the North Carolina Governor's Council, including a deposition, a remonstrance, and correspondence concerning Tobias Knight's business with Edward Teach* (1719), Colonial and State Records of North Carolina. Documenting the American South, University of North Carolina at Chapel Hill; *Tobias Knight* (2018), Golden Age of Piracy website (informative and mostly accurate website).

I would also personally like to thank the following for their support and assistance. First and foremost, I would like to thank my wife Christine, an exceptional and highly professional book editor, who painstakingly reviewed and copy-edited the novel. Any mistakes that remain are my fault, of course.

Second, I would like to thank my former literary agent, Cherry Weiner of the Cherry Weiner Literary Agency, for thoroughly reviewing, vetting, and copy-editing the manuscript, and for making countless improvements to the finished novel.

Third, I would like to thank Stephen King's former editor, Patrick LoBrutto, for thoroughly copy-editing the various drafts of the novel and providing detailed reviews.

I would also like to thank Austin and Anne Marquis, Governor Roy Romer, Ambassador Marc Grossman, Betsy and Steve Hall, Rik Hall, Christian Fuenfhausen, Bill Eberhart, Fred Taylor, Mo Shafroth, Tim and Carey Romer, Peter and Lorrie Frautschi, Deirdre Grant Mercurio, Joe Tallman, John Welch, Link Nicoll, Toni Conte Augusta Francis, Brigid Donnelly Hughes, Peter Brooke, Caroline Fenton Dewey, John and Ellen Aisenbrey, Margot Patterson, Cathy and Jon Jenkins, Danny Bilello and Elena Diaz-Bilello, Charlie and Kay Fial, Vincent Bilello, Elizabeth Gardner, Robin McGehee, and the other book reviewers and professional contributors large and small who have given generously of their time over the years, as well as to those who have given me loyal support as I have ventured on this incredible odyssey of historical fiction writing.

Lastly, I want to thank anyone and everyone who bought this book and my loyal fans and supporters who helped promote this work. You know who you are and I salute you.

ABOUT THE AUTHOR
AND
FORTHCOMING TITLES

Samuel Marquis is a bestselling, award-winning historical fiction author. He works by day as a VP–Principal Hydrogeologist with an environmental firm in Boulder, Colorado, and by night as a spinner of historical suspense yarns. He holds a Master of Science degree in Geology, is a Registered Professional Geologist in eleven states, and is a recognized expert in groundwater contaminant hydrogeology, having served as an expert witness in several class action litigation cases. He also has a deep and abiding interest in military history and intelligence, specifically related to the Golden Age of Piracy, Plains Indian Wars, World War II, and the current War on Terror.

The ninth great-grandson of legendary privateer Captain William Kidd, he is the bestselling, award-winning author of historical pirate fiction, a World War Two Series, and the Nick Lassiter-Skyler International Espionage Series. His novels have been #1 *Denver Post* bestsellers, received multiple national book awards (Foreword Reviews Book of the Year, American Book Fest Best Book, USA Best Book, Beverly Hills, Next Generation Indie, Colorado Book Awards), and garnered glowing reviews from #1 bestseller James Patterson, Kirkus, and Foreword Reviews (5 Stars). *Bodyguard of Deception*, Book 1 of his WWII Series, was a winner of the Foreword Reviews Indie Book of the Year and an award-winning finalist of the USA Best Book Awards. *Altar of Resistance*, Book 2 of the WWII Series, was an award-winning finalist of the American Book Fest Best Book and Beverly Hills Book Awards. Critics and book reviewers have compared *Bodyguard of Deception* and *Altar of Resistance* to the epic historical novels of Tom Clancy, John le Carré, Ken Follett, Herman Wouk, Daniel Silva, and Alan Furst.

Ambassador Marc Grossman, former U.S. Under Secretary of State, proclaimed, "In his novels *Blind Thrust* and *Cluster of Lies*, Samuel Marquis vividly combines the excitement of the best modern techno-thrillers." Former Colorado Governor Roy Romer said, "*Blind Thrust* kept me up until 1 a.m. two nights in a row. I could not put it down." Kirkus Reviews proclaimed *The Coalition* an "entertaining thriller" and declared that "Marquis has written a tight plot with genuine suspense." James Patterson said *The Coalition* had "a lot of good action and suspense" and compared the novel to *The Day After Tomorrow*, the classic thriller by Allan Folsom.

Below is the list of novels that Samuel Marquis has published or will be publishing in the near future, along with the release dates of both previously published and forthcoming titles.

Historical Pirate Fiction
Blackbeard: The Birth of America – February 2018

The World War Two Series

Bodyguard of Deception – March 2016 – Winner Foreword Reviews' Book of the Year Awards (HM) and Award-Winning Finalist USA Best Book Awards

Altar of Resistance – January 2017 – Award-Winning Finalist American Book Fest Best Book Awards and Beverly Hills Book Awards

Spies of the Midnight Sun – June 2018

The Nick Lassiter – Skyler International Espionage Series

The Devil's Brigade (formerly The Slush Pile Brigade) – September 2015, Reissue April 2017 – The #1 Denver Post Bestseller and Award-Winning Finalist Beverly Hills Book Awards

The Coalition – January 2016, Reissue April 2017 – Winner Beverly Hills Book Awards and Award-Winning Finalist USA Best Book Awards and Colorado Book Awards

The Fourth Pularchek – June 2017 – Award-Winning Finalist American Book Fest Best Book Awards and Beverly Hills Book Awards

The Joe Higheagle Environmental Sleuth Series

Blind Thrust – October 2015 – The #1 Denver Post Bestseller; Winner Foreword Reviews' Book of the Year (HM) and Next Generation Indie Book Awards; Award-Winning Finalist USA Best Book Awards, Beverly Hills Book Awards, and Next Generation Indie Book Awards

Cluster of Lies – September 2016 – Winner Beverly Hills Book Awards and Award-Winning Finalist USA Best Book Awards and Foreword Reviews Book Awards

Thank You for Your Support!

To Order Samuel Marquis Books and Contact Samuel:

Visit Samuel Marquis's website, join his mailing list, learn about his forthcoming suspense novels and book events, and order his books at www.samuelmarquisbooks.com. Please send all fan mail (including criticism) to samuelmarquisbooks@gmail.com.

CPSIA information can be obtained
at www.ICGtesting.com
Printed in the USA
FSOW02n1134010218
43876FS